THE
LORD
OF
POWER

WANTED GIRL

L.J.S MAGWAZA

To order additional copies of this book, contact:
Xlibris
800-056-3182
www.Xlibrispublishing.co.uk
Orders@Xlibrispublishing.co.uk
784351

THE
LORD
OF
POWER

CONTENTS

CHAPTER 1

A Bad Morning

Let us begin at a particular period in time, on a day that happened quite some time ago, long enough to be called history.

It was an early morning, before the light of day had even sprung. On a day that poured down heavily, watering the earth naturally. The weather had been like this for quite a while with the absence of dear fearful lightning and the loud hammering of thunder.

A peaceful rain we all love to enjoy spending our time with inside, mostly in the comforts of our own homes, sleeping in, keeping ourselves warm whilst performing enjoyable indoor activities which may include reading a book or just watching TV.

Yes, this is the morning that we all have the privilege of having from time to time, something we always cherish when given.

This morning as you can already tell will be quite the opposite, something you may not have ever experienced in the slightest.

This drenching morning takes place in a very small town of wooden houses, a village you might call it, and judging by its time and period, it works as an appropriate name.

The ground on which you walked was gravel, which had been watered on like a garden and turned into mud. The side of the road had even created its own little streams similar to the gutters we see today.

It was a silent morning, with only the sound of rain that could be heard, with a few manmade objects in the mix, such as the sign boards that swayed in the breeze, creaking and squeaking their rusted metal parts.

Amongst all this silence, there was one who wandered about in this rain, a little girl of about seven years of age. She looked lost in this place, it all seemed a new world to her. It was certain she did not belong anywhere and her current state in terms of visual appeal, was a little disturbing. Something one should not have to see when they come across a young, little girl.

She had long black hair that had been straightened by the rain, wearing only a small black, torn dress that reached down just past her thighs. There were no shoes to cover her feet and the rest of her body, bared small cuts and bruises, most present on her elbows and knees. Her wrists and ankles were cuffed, but the chains broken in the centre, leaving them hanging by her side and drag across the mud behind her. It was clear from the tint of red beneath the shackles that she had been wearing these for quite some time.

The young girl had just recently arrived, shaking from the cold rain, grabbing her arms in an attempt to feel warmer. Taking small steps as the water passed through her toes.

No one else was present at this time, no one around to offer some help.

As she walked down the road, looking around at all the locked doors and closed curtains, she wondered about the events that transpired in these households, how everyone else felt on this bitter morning and as the young girl she was, wished with all her heart, to at least be away from this weather.

As she continued down the road she came across an alley to her left with some garbage and dustbins laid to the one side. The area was closed off, with a few steps leading up to a door on the other end. A place like this had a reduced amount of cold wind which meant a little more warmth for her.

She stepped into the small alleyway and felt a significant difference in the weather with the absence of the wind. She continued down the path and came to a halt by the dustbins and garbage, and for a moment, just stared at them, lost in an endless storm cloud of thoughts, about to make a decision. Her gaze now placed onto her abdomen for another moment, then back at the dustbins.

She was hungry.

Her choice had been made though, she continued on passed them and took a seat on the small steps leading up to the door. She gave her arms a quick rub, trying to keep as much of the cold out as she shivered. Her eyes turned to the heavens, only seeing a portion of this clouded sky and watched the rain pour.

For a while she sat there, just letting the time pass. The morning had a little more light to show now, but the rain had not yet decided to calm down for the better. One thing that did, however, lighten up her mood in this unhappy time was the presence of another life in this alley.

An adult grey cat that seemed to be in the same situation as her, stranded outside and soaked from the ever pouring rain. She was happy at the fact that this feline did not fear her and take off like a lot of other stray cats, though, it did give her a little bit of a stare before the trust part started to settle in.

The cat had giving the garbage a sniff before looking for some shelter. It came up to the little girl, shaking as well from the cold.

"Hello," she greeted the cat, giving it a smile.

For a moment there, the cat stopped and glared up at her, most probably surprised that she had spoken, but then made its way beneath the wooden steps, away from the rain.

The little girl continued on with her mission to keep warm since she was still receiving the rain.

The cat stuck its head out from between the steps and began to meow continuously.

She turned to it and lower her hand to its level. The cat gave her fingers a sniff before it meowed again.

"Sorry," the little girl apologized, "I'm hungry too."

The cat settled down again after a while.

Some time had passed, the girl had not moved from her place on the steps, really tired and unable to fall asleep.

From outside her little hideout in the alley, the footsteps of a group of people splashed in the near distance. She jumped, immediately alerted by the sounds, giving her tiny heart a race as she stared down into the opening, waiting for whomever it was that was nearby to just walk passed and leave her unnoticed.

The wait made her very anxious and where she had seated herself was now quite comfortable, she did not want to move from the spot.

Right now she was in plain sight and the more she thought about it, the riskier it became, she came to the conclusion that this was not worth it so she stood up from the steps and ran over to the dustbins where she crouched behind and hid from view. Her curiosity became present and decided to take a peek just to see who it was.

She waited a few moments.

The people that finally came to pass were just a group of guards, dressed in steel plate armor, bearing pikes and shields.

It was only about four of them, most probably doing their morning patrols around the village.

She let out a long sigh of relief and leaned against the wall as her sight drifted off towards the cat, which stared right back at her, eyes wide open.

Feeling sorry for the feline, she made it her motivation to gain the gut and do something about it, but not yet, right now she had to wait a few more moments before trusting that the coast was clear.

After the footsteps were beyond hearing, it was time for her to step out from hiding and make her way to the entrance of the alley. Standing at the one corner, she leaned forward and scanned the area for any persons.

It was clear.

The next thing she had to do was search for anyone's residence that was not too far from her current position.

Stepping out into the open, she made her way to a house nearby and started up the porch whilst the chains from her ankles rattled across the wooden floor, she made her way up to the door.

Nervous about her first encounter, she raised her hand, gave it a soft knock and waited.

With no response at the door, she decided to make it a tad bit louder. She knocked again and waited.

After a few moments of waiting, she heard the footsteps of the owner come closer to the door. It was her moment of truth, something that made her nerves go insane.

The person to answer the door was some grumpy looking man, with some heavy bags under his eyes and messy hair. He had the look of someone who had just awoken from hibernation.

He had only opened the door wide enough for his head to show. The man, at first, expected someone of a similar height to be at the door, looking ahead of himself, but did catch on a moment later.

The little girl put on her smile to seem more welcoming before saying anything, "Morning Mister," she greeted, "Do you have any fo-,"

The man angrily interrupted her, "You woke me up!" He shouted, slamming the door shut.

Her smile faded as she heard the man lock the door from the other side.

She remained there for a while, lost in disbelief and shocked at how terrible the events turned out, and so quickly. Her heart had sunk away to the bottom, unable to move.

It took a few moments to take it in before she was able to move on again. In some way she saw this as her own fault and thought of the valid reason for why he would not hear her out. She did wake him up from his peaceful, warm slumber after all, she imagined that no one would be, at all, happy if they were disturbed at a time like this.

After placing a reason on top of this cake, she was able to take a deep breath and turn away from the door, thinking… maybe, just maybe, there was someone nearby who would help her.

From the grumpy man's porch, she scanned the area for another door she could go knocking on before stepping out into the rain again.

Climbing up the steps to the next porch, she took a deep breath, nervous even more now, with a pinch of fear of the outcome added into the mix, thanks to her first encounter.

This time she picked a place that was a little different from the first, she was a hundred percent sure that the people living here were now awake, the inside smelt of a morning breakfast. Perhaps this kind of encounter might be much better since she would not now be a disturbance to someone's slumber.

She took in another whip of air and placed a smile on her face before knocking on the door.

Waiting a few moments, the door was answered by a woman wearing an apron over her clothing.

"Oh…," she uttered, looking down at the little girl, "Hello," she greeted, feeling a little uneasy.

"Sorry to disturb you," the little girl started, "Do you have any food to spare?"

The woman had a worried look on her face, a look the little girl had mistaken for being pitiful.

"Oh, I'm so sorry… no," she replied, closing the door behind her.

The little girl stood still and quiet as a mouse, this time without the look of shock, she felt a little more understanding, since the woman did not get angry at her. She was more polite than the man she had started with and in the little girl's silence, she was able to catch a few murmurs from the people on the other side.

"Who was it?" A male voice asked.

The woman replied, "Oh, some stranger, I think the guards might be looking for her, she had chains around her ankles and wrists… don't worry, I locked the door."

The girl then grew a little nosy, wanting to know whether the woman was lying to her or not so she quietly walked over to the window, preventing as much noise as she could.

She peered through the window and immediately regretted it.

What she saw made her feel even worse.

The woman was seated at a wooden table with her husband, enjoying some of the breakfast that she had smelt, but the feeling only came after, when her eyes wandered off to a separate table across the room. On it, she could see a large basket of bread, containing about six loaves.

Her stomach began to speak to her again, so she looked away and stepped from the window to avoid being caught.

She began to think to herself, that maybe they really needed it and that was why she could not spare any… so maybe, she was not lying.

Then the thought of what the woman had just said sunk in, about the chains that she dragged around, they could be sending the wrong message and installing some level of fear into whomever sees them.

She looked down at herself, then at the shackles around her wrists and thought that maybe she did lie, only to make her go away because of the way she looked.

Still standing on the porch, away from the rain, she grabbed the shackle around her left arm and attempted to pull it off.

It did not work.

She tried harder.

The only thing she managed to gain from these attempts was a lot of pain.

"Ow," she whispered, letting go of it.

At this point she had already felt like giving up and going back to the cat. One more chance was all she was giving it for now, though, now she was worried about another outcome that she was now aware of. The bonds she dragged and her appearance, it could drive people off, just as the woman had pointed out. There was still a little positivity in her though, that maybe there was someone who would not mind either-or and decided to help her if they can.

Off the porch she stepped and back into the rain in search for another place to try out.

The little girl knocked on the door three times and waited for a response.

While she waited for this next encounter she repeated her procedure and this time held her hands behind her back to try conceal the shackles, as for her ankles, that could not be helped.

The door was answered by a younger man this time.

"Hello," she greeted.

The young man looked at her for a moment, "Young girl, what are you doing out here?" he asked, just before noticing the shackles around her ankles, "Why are you in chains, you will need to go to the guards about this," he said stepping outside onto the porch.

She was happy that the man was concerned about her wellbeing, but the situation quickly turned sour as soon as he redirected her to the guards.

"Please don't!" She pleaded.

It was a little too late, the young man had leaned over the railing and cried out for the guards. He turned back to the girl, "Why not, you need help... guards!" He shouted again.

The little girl started to panic and decided it was best to leave before anyone else showed up. She stepped out into the rain in quite a hurry, without carefully watching her step and slipped. She fell into the mud from one of the last steps and splashed soil all over her body. Ignoring the pain she got up to her feet immediately and made a run for it.

"Where are you going1?" The man shouted.

She did not reply or turn back, she kept running as best as she could whilst trying her hardest to ignore the pain of all the little rocks that she stepped on.

She continued on till she reached another alleyway. Standing at the entrance, she did a quick check for any persons that may be occupying the place.

It was clear.

But it was too late.

"There she is!" a cry came from the near distance which startled her.

She turned to the source and saw them.

A group of soldiers that wore a completely different attire as compared to your normal town's guard.

These were agents, wearing no amount of armour accept for the silver steal gauntlets bearing the symbol of a bird. The rest of their attire consisted of a red and black hooded trench coat, tied together across their chests with a belt around their waists, wearing black pants and dark brown leather boots.

This group of agents really did put the scare on her as she turned tail and ran away from them, tired and unable to see all too properly from the rain dropping onto her face.

The agents began their pursuit and gained on her easily.

She ran past the first house she had knocked on and neared the alleyway she had spent most of her time in.

"Stop her!" One of the agents shouted.

In front of the girl, out came another group of agents and some guards in the mix to block her way forward. With no place for her to continue, she turned left and went for the alley she had come from, but one of the agents blocked her way through.

The agent towered over her with a large smile on her face.

The little girl was frightened, unable to move as she stared right back into the eyes of this woman, whom thought that it would be right for her to shove the girl with a lot of force, throwing her back into the mud.

The agent took a step forward towards her and the little girl moved away, "Please leave me alone!" She screamed.

From behind her came a silent sinister laugh. An agent that walked up to her and lowered himself to about her level, "We finally found you, clever little rat," he stood up again.

This commotion was enough to bring out all the residents in the surrounding area to witness as these events unfolded. Most of them kept to their porches away from the rain, all remaining silent.

The child, shaken from fear, struggled to her feet with all these people standing around staring down at her. She looked up at the agent that had just spoken to her, "What-."

She was interrupted by a backhand slap across the face which threw her off balance and again, sending her into the dirt.

The civilians were shocked at what they were seeing, most only replying with gasps but with no intention of aiding the child at all.

She held her palm over the now red, shaded cheek, moments away from crying, "What do you want from me?" She uttered.

The agent replied, "Your life."

The little girl was not understanding this at all, why they hated her so much. As she looked at the other civilians, noticing the woman that had turned her down amongst others, wondering, why no one wanted to help her, why they just watched. The thought alone made her heart weigh a ton.

She turned back to the agent that had just assaulted her, "Why… what did I do?"

"Well… you were born," he smiled.

The agent turned to the rest of the crowd and witnessing citizens, "To everyone witnessing this!" he shouted, "We have ourselves another cursed child, and believed to be the last!"

The child did not like being in the dirt so she climbed to her feet once again.

The civilians seemed to endorse the claim the man made.

"Down with all of them!" A man shouted from one of the porches.

Some of the other civilians cheered it on.

The child was lost in confusion, her jaw dropped from the sheer shock, that all these people were supporting this agent and his actions.

As she watched the people now put smiles on their faces and speak horrible words to her, she could feel a tear run down passed her cheek amongst all the other rain water. At this moment she began to realize that everybody hated her, nobody cared about her, even though she was about to be killed for a reason she did not know or understand.

One thing she had hoped for from all of this, was to at least see someone come forward, someone who cared, but no one did. The only person she recognized was the woman that rejected her, she stepped inside, went back into the house.

From all the hate she was receiving from the people around her, the little girl remembered the one life that did not reject her. She turned to it, still sheltering beneath the steps, also confused by all the commotion.

The agent turned back to the child, "See… nobody cares for your life, they would much prefer that you were dead," he leaned forward, "How does that make you feel?"

The little girl could not comprehend with the feelings her heart was carrying right now, she just stared right back at him.

Just before she could gather the strength to say something to the man, something hit her across the face, putting her to the floor again. She shook her head and looked for whatever it was that hit her while the others laughed in the background.

It was a loaf of bread.

She turned back, only to see it was the same women that had walked back into her house.

"There's your spare food!" She shouted over the crowd.

"I still don't understand!" The girl cried.

"And you will never," the agent replied, pulling out his sword, "We, the Dead Crow will fulfill its promise to the world."

The little girl could not take her eyes off the silver blade as the agent raised it above his head and swung it.

CHAPTER 2

Jake Mauntell

Now we jump to the present, where we will be meeting some new people.

We start this one on a morning as well, a Saturday morning. This one had the clearest of blue skies, all lit up by the bright sun, making it a day one would choose not to spend in the comfort of their own homes. These great for engaging in outdoor activities like our new friends here.

This morning takes place in a small town, in a quiet and peaceful neighbourhood, at the local park, a really large place when you took into account the grass field that seemed to go endless, the small forests and isolated trees, and near to the centre of the whole area, a large crystal lake where you will find the three boys we are to meet. All of them, quite bored out of their mind, busy skipping stones over the still waters, disrupting its peace by creating an endless array of ripples which destroyed the perfect mirror reflection of the sky and nearby trees.

First we meet the one who is engaging in this activity the most, a tall boy with short brown hair, wearing your everyday casual clothing, a boy going by the name, James Lamaine.

The second boy, whom gave it his all, but still found it hard to get the designated amount of skips James was accomplishing, was also quite tall, about an inch shorter than James next to him, with longer blonde hair and a few dots on his face, Daniel Rikone.

The third boy, whom did not engage at all in this activity, who preferred to seat himself on the grass and just chuck the rocks as far as he could was shorter than the others and a little chubbier, with dark brown hair and a lot more freckles on his face. This was Mark Mewell.

There were off course a lot of others who chose to spend their day at the park. Some choosing to just go on walks or reading their books whilst sitting on the given benches. You also had a group of boys playing a game of soccer not too far away from the lake.

"Wow, great day at the park guys," Mark groaned, pulling out some grass in front of him.

Daniel turned to him and shook his head, "We need the fresh air and peace... trust me, it makes you concentrate a lot better," he threw another stone into the lake.

Mark chuckled in response, "There is nothing, not even your concentration boosting method, or whatever you call it, that will make me pick up a book for that test," he looked over at James, "I mean, look at James, he is not clearing his mind at all."

"Yeah, you're right," he agreed, skipping another stone, "I am really trying to skip ten times, but always seems to stop around eight if I'm lucky."

Mark sighed, "Why does this subject have to be compulsory, I was never going to pick it... why is it so important that we all learn about history anyway, it's the most boring stuff I've ever heard and I think it has the largest text book out of all the subjects."

James failed to skip a stone, "Maybe they just want to rub in the fact that they banned the use of all and any kind of magic."

"They say it was for good reasons," Daniel added.

"Yes, they will give us as many good reasons and stories that we will eat till we stop questioning anything," he replied, "They have not mentioned anything else, the people we must acknowledge, the laws passed, blah blah blaaah."

"I'm with James on this one, they could have told us in one simple sentence and for those interested in the whole story, they can pick the subject," Mark said.

Daniel was surprised, "I'm not picking sides here," he glanced at them both, "I'm just saying... look at the hundred year shift."

James decided to just throw the rock into the water as hard as he could in an attempt to make a large splash, "That's another thing I don't understand, we had the shift yes, but we still have to spend every single long holiday out camping and learning how to survive in the wilds for no known reason at all... I just don't see the relevance."

Mark lay back on his elbows, "Yup, I mean, it would be more fun if the camping was done during school... but that's impossible," he tried to add some positivity to the conversation, "At least we get the end of the year off."

Daniel attempted again, "Well... let's not get all negative now, the next camp is only in a few weeks."

After some time, their little activity had gotten a little too boring for Mark. He turned to the soccer match and watched it for a brief time, thinking about what to do next. Watching it, made him feel a little more energetic and grew the urge to join in on the match. He looked at the other two and stood up, "Guys, let's leave the lake alone, the soccer match is calling our names."

Now that was something they all could agree upon. Something much better which involved a lot more movement than their current activity.

Some time had passed since their decision to join the soccer match. It was close to midday now and hot as ever when they decided it was time for them to leave the park and head on back.

There were not too many learners from their own grade at this time. Most had remained indoors due to the test that was being written on the Monday, another weekend stolen away.

If you were to think about it for just a few moments, this 'day off' thing on Saturday and Sunday did not exist, that feeling remained with me amongst many days whilst in high school. The math teacher would tell us that if we wanted to pass the subject, just doing it at school, during the lessons was definitely not enough, he would suggest we go over all our math every day and have it embedded in our minds... hardest thing to even think about, just about impossible to implement, for me, since my mind was all over the place and much preferred it that way.

Our new acquaintances here had started to feel a little guilty for not caring too much about this history test. Playing soccer with the others, learners that had not touch a single book in weeks had made them think about it a little, obviously, only after getting tired from the match.

Right now, heading back on foot, they saw fit to put themselves into the shoes of those who did, somehow, manage to put in every tiny bit of their time into reading these text books and generating colourful notes out of them.

"Where should we start with this test man?" Mark asked.

Daniel chuckled, "I read over the stuff yesterday and it was a little too much, I think that from now, probability might be the only way to go."

Down the streets they walked, surrounded by a neighbourhood of houses and a forest amount of trees. From their perspective it was only a few, trees placed at random spots just before the pavements, but once you get an elevated view of the whole neighbourhood, you see a forest, which is surprising a lot of the time.

"Yeah, reading over what our instincts tell us seems to be our only chance," James agreed.

"I want it over and done with, but I don't want it to start either," Mark complained, "I just want to relax and enjoy this Saturday."

It is what we all say just before procrastination. Tell ourselves we got a whole Sunday ahead of us, another day we could use to try cram everything into our minds.

"I see where it's going," James said.

Passing by another residence, they came across a young girl of their age, throwing out the trash. She recognized them, "You three," she came up to them.

They stopped on the sidewalk and wait for her to say her piece.

"Yes, it is us," James said.

"How are you doing?"

"Oh, good, just came from the park, did a little sport," James replied.

"Hmm," she nodded slowly, "You do know there's a test on Monday, right?"

"Yes," Daniel replied, "History."

"And you studied?" She asked raising her brows in concern.

James and Mark did not know how to reply to that question, but Daniel spoke, "Yes we did, quite a bit actually, we were just taking a breather."

She nodded, "I'm glad you know there's a test…"

Mark frowned at that little statement she made.

"… I'm busy now, so good luck for Monday."

"Thanks, you too," James replied, making sure to take that luck.

She went off into the house and they continued on down the street.

"We just lied to ourselves there," Daniel pointed out.

Mark shrugged, "If we had told the truth, we were never going to receive that 'good luck' we just got there, and that's something we need right now, not some 'you are going to fail' story."

Yes, a lot of lies take flight when it comes to school studies and that next test. There is no friendship when it comes to it, everyone wants to do better than the other and this is a competition that is famous among the smart ones, but also quite popular amongst the failures, all so they can say 'I don't know how I got this mark'.

Failing with your friends is very scarce, and this comes from another quote teachers like to use, 'When you fail, you fail alone'.

The rest of their way back was spent trying to figure out some kind of solution to this impossible equation. They were all heading back to James's residence.

A place similar to most of the other houses in this neighbourhood. A double story house, fitted with a backyard surrounded by a lot of trees and small bushes. The front having a drive into a garage with a small lawn occupying the rest of the space.

James lead the way from here and was the one to open the door and be the first to step in.

They stepped into a kitchen, where they found his mom busy at the counter chopping up some vegetables.

The lounge was in view of the entrance, fitted with black couches and a small glass coffee table, bearing a small vase of flowers, and a large TV on a stand up against the wall. Beside the stand were two tall vases with artificial plants in them and on the other end of the room, facing the entrance, was a sliding door leading to the backyard. The floors were tiled in white and the counters made from granite.

The walls were a crème white colour with some paintings hung up to fill up the empty spaces.

His mom was quite tall and had long, brunette hair.

"Oh, you back," she turned to them, "How was the park?"

"It was great, had fun," he sounded unenthusiastic, "We just need to check a few things quick."

Mark and Daniel greeted her and followed James upstairs to his room.

James's room was not big, having one large window to the one side of the room, curtains pulled back for light. Right beneath the window, placed up against the wall was his single bed with a wooden frame and a blue duvet cover over it. Next to his bed was a large wooden desk, which had some books stacked to the one side with a bit of stationery, and a large section taken up by his PC.

Against the wall at the foot of his bed was his wardrobe.

"Okay," James sighed, "Let's see what the topics are and go over them," he walked over to his school bag, leaning against his desk.

Mark went over to his chair and seated himself whilst James searched and Daniel made himself comfortable on his bed.

Mark started spinning in circles on the chair, "At least we will have done something today."

James pulled out the text book on history. He opened it up at a placeholder he had put there before and pulled it out before placing the textbook on his desk.

"Okay," he checked the contents of the paper, "The banning of Magic, then there's the hundred year shift and finally the M.G Government."

Mark picked up the textbook and started paging through it, "What page is the banning?" He asked.

"172," he replied.

Upon finding the page, he cringed, looking at the different topics listed under the heading, "Ew, that's a lot."

"And it's the least out of all the topics, and the most interesting out of the three," Daniel added.

"What's the first topic?" James asked.

"The origin of magical objects," he read.

James started to pace a little, "That one does sound like it needs a lot of attention."

"I would guess the war and rebellion," Daniel suggested.

Mark agreed.

"Okay, we know the war was started because of the creation of dark magic outside the five subjects and idle magic."

Mark nodded, "And his name?"

"Reeve Joducas," Daniel replied.

James snapped his finger and pointed at them, "And this was started round about the sixteenth century."

They continued to question each other on the topic.

A short while after, down stairs, James's mom, busy searching for something in the fridge, heard a knock coming from the door. She closed it and went to answer it.

"Hello… how may I help you?" She asked

It was someone she did not recognize.

Standing in front of her was an old man with short grey hair, wearing a black suit in the shiniest pair of shoes.

"Sorry to disturb you ma'am," he started, "Are you Jane Olivia Lamaine?"

Jane put on a concerned look, wondering how this stranger knew her name, "Yes…,"

"My name is Jake Mauntell and I work for the DCA and G.M Government."

"Oh," she turned surprised, "What can I do for you?"

"May I please speak to your son, James Lamaine and his friends?"

She wondered again, this time of how he knew they were all here, but she could not turn down such an authority figure, "Off course… come in," she made way for him to enter.

Jake proceeded and was given a seat at a single couch by Jane.

"I'll call them down," she said heading upstairs.

She pushed open the door and stepped in, "James, there's someone here to see you three," she said, looking a little worried.

James closed shut his history book, "Who is it?" He whispered.

Jane shrugged, "Some old man named Jake… he's from the G.M Government"

They all exchanged concerned glances, confused as to why someone of such status would be seeking an audience with them.

Jane pointed at them, "I hope you three haven't done anything illegal now," she whispered, "This man is wearing a black suit."

They were not too sure about anything illegal.

For a few moments, they all ran a scan through their memory database, finding nothing that could be potentially unlawful. Did they do it unconsciously?

"Well?" She whispered aloud.

They all began to shake their heads slowly, pretty sure nothing illegal or troublesome had occurred recently.

"I don't think we've done anything," James replied, already starting to feel a little nervous about the situation, he could feel his heart slowly start to lose control.

"Well, don't be keeping the man waiting!"

Everyone started rushing while Jane made her way downstairs.

All three of them followed closely behind, unable to stop thinking about the next few moments and how they were going to play out.

He came into view as they took each step down and so did the old man to them, sitting there very patiently and ready to lay down judgement.

Jane put on a friendly smile, "Sorry to keep you waiting.

The old man gave a slight nod in return.

"Here they are, I'll be here in the kitchen if you need anything."

"Thank you."

Intimidated, is what the boys felt at this moment as the old man watched their every move. They seated themselves on the biggest couch facing the TV.

The man sat forward and rubbed his hands together as soon as they were comfortable.

That gesture sign alone was enough to enable a prediction that this is not news anyone would want to hear.

Jane did not ignore this meet at all, she kept an ear open.

The man began with the greetings, "Afternoon, young boys."

"Afternoon," they replied as if in a grade one class, foreign to the language.

"My name is Jake Mauntell, I am a member of the DCA and G.M Government.

The government was something they were familiar with but the DCA did not ring much of a bell to them.

"Am I right in saying you are James, Mark and Daniel?" He asked pointing at them individually.

They nodded in return.

"Now, I understand that you three have been questioning your history studies, mostly about the laws and policies to do with the banning of magic."

None of them knew how to answer that, it was true that they were having such conversations and have had thoughts of using said banned magic, but there was no way any of that would happen, if they could, for a fact. To them, these were just normal conversation that were, admittedly, somewhat ambitious, something only to remain as just a part of their imagination.

One thing that did stump them though was the question of how in this world he knew at all about any of such conversations, that mostly occur behind closed doors. Was it something this government was doing or something to do with this DCA he said he was a part of.

"What I am here to do is ensure that none of these casual conversations you are having do become something serious and drive you to commit something unlawful."

They nodded in return.

Was this really happening? James was not catching on at all, how could this be the reason for his arrival here. If it were true, then almost every kid would be receiving a visit from these people. How is this drawing the attention of government officials, a few conversations. *Had someone perhaps tried to commit such crimes and if so, how?*

"Am I right in saying that you do not have any motives?"

"Yes," Daniel replied.

The other two just nodded, speaking was an ability they did not seem to have anymore.

Jake sighed, "Now, it's quite clear you three are believers in this magic and wish for its return, so I am going to have to do something about it."

James sat there, producing sweat as if he were in a marathon, thinking of every possible outcome that was to behead them next. This was now the part where judgement was to be brought. It was hard to even read this man, speaking so very calm and well-mannered like a professional, wearing no emotion on his face.

"Now…," he began, "You are not the only ones that have been noticed," he reached into his hidden blazer pocket.

Jane had stopped, or most probably forgotten what she was doing, standing in the kitchen, listening and watching.

Out of all things James had predicted would be pulled out of this man's pocket, some including a paper that would speak about their apparent crimes, a business card for some odd reason, a pen or a warning sheet. None of these were even remotely close to what actually came out.

Their eyes could not detach from the objects, reflective and transparent they were as well.

Jake had pulled out three diamond necklaces, the size of gold nuggets.

What remained undecided in their heads was the way they were supposed to react to this situation, something they did not expect to see.

A man shows up, claiming to be from the government and speaks to them about the wrongs they did, now decides to pull out diamond necklaces from his pocket. This was beyond their intuition or imagination.

Moment after moment felt was way too unpredictable for James, so he tried not to see the next bit that was going to play out.

Jake placed these diamond on the coffee table, "These are diamonds that I have been tasked to hand over to you," he explained, "Crafted by our Artificer."

Daniel frowned, "Why?" He had to ask.

"For safe keeping," he replied, "You are to keep them on your persons at all times, and as a secret from everybody else… it's just a little experiment that we've put together," he explained, "I'm sure you know it's a crime to harbor such gems, that belong to government?"

They nodded in return.

"It will only be for a few days," he added

Yup, predicting his motives was useless. Now they were a part of some kind of experiment.

This would have been an easy enough job, if they were allowed to just keep them at home, but having to keep them on themselves at all times, this was going to be of some challenge to them, and again wondering why, why such an experiment?

"Go on, take your pick," he instructed.

They felt forced, but did as they were told and each of them picked a diamond, one by one, untangling the chains.

"Now please put them on."

They all complied.

As soon as James had his one put on, something strange happened to his whole body. He began to feel sick and very weak, as if all the muscles in his body had suddenly stopped responding. His heads fell forward with his chin resting upon his chest, feeling a little dizzy. He shook his head trying to clear it. This made the dizziness go away and immediately remove the feelings of sickness and weakness.

Jake just sat there and stared at them.

James came to think about this feeling. He had never worn a diamond necklace in his life but was pretty sure no such feeling came with them.

They all remained quiet about the strange feelings they were experiencing and just brushed it off as soon as they felt better again.

Jake took a deep breath, "Well then, that means we're done here," he said standing up from his couch, "Thank you for your cooperation and I believe that you will be successful in your task."

He headed for the front door, "Mrs. Lamaine," he gave her a nod, "Thank you for allowing me to speak to them."

He opened the door and stepped out, closing it behind him.

There was a moment of silence after he stepped out, Jane waited for his footsteps to disappear before hurrying over to them, "I wonder what that was all about," she said grabbing ahold of the necklace James wore.

James shrugged, "I have no idea, but he did say we weren't the only ones with these."

She frowned at them, "So you have not done anything that would upset them, anything illegal right?"

"Off course not mom," James replied.

She let go of the diamond, "You'd better do what he says, it may be that they have eyes everywhere."

"Yup, it seems," Mark agreed, "I want these few days to be over already."

Jane went back to the kitchen, able to continue with what she was doing now, "You can go back to your studies, I only called you down for that man."

Up in his room they were able to speak more freely. They did not start with their studying just yet, still clouded by the events that had just taken place, still finding this situation way too random.

"That was the weirdest encounter I have ever had in my entire life," Mark said throwing himself onto the chair.

"No doubt about that," Daniel agreed.

James picked up the textbook and began to page through it, "Did you guys feel anything weird?"

"I felt weird throughout that whole conversation," Mark replied.

"No, I meant when you put on the diamonds."

"Oh yes," Daniel blurted out, "I felt all sick and weak for some odd reason, but it went away."

"Yeah yeah, it was only for a few seconds or something," Mark confirmed, he did not really care about that. He looked at his diamond, "The first time I get one and I don't want it."

"Do you think they are magic?" James asked.

Mark chuckled, "Yup, sure," he spoke sarcastically, "The very people who ban the use of magic are the ones that start giving it out... makes sense."

"I agree with Mark, it can't be," Daniel said, "Beside, I don't think we should be asking questions about it whilst we got that history test on Monday, it's more important right now."

"Okay okay," James said as he began his search for the page they were on.

The study session became a bore almost immediately after they had begun. There was just way too much to look at and no fixed point at which to start. They were foreign to the concept of summarizing their work or making notes of all the important bits, a method that could help out all year round, if you are not careless enough to dumped them along with your knowledge right after the test.

So after figuring out that this was the worst idea, when in actual fact it was just their brains trying to find better ways to spend this time, they slowly drifted away from the subject of studying and engaged in more interesting conversations and the textbook James held became an object to fidget with.

Their minds had just made a mention of the Sunday they still had and it became fine after that.

Later that evening, with his friends long departed, he found a more fun way to spend this Saturday night away from the textbook. On these days, he would much prefer to play or watch something on his PC or just read a book, something fictional. But today had something different, he just spent it reflecting on how strange the day was, trying to figure out the relevance of such an 'experiment'.

Laying back on his bed, he took the diamond off and held it above his head, he stared into it as if trying to find something inside, but there was nothing, it was all clear. Keeping in mind the bizarre theory that this thing might be some kind of magical object.

He began to sway it, allowing his eyes to follow it as if he was to be hypnotized by its swinging motion. Then he put it on again, expecting to be attacked by the wired feeling, but nothing happened this time.

After that little test, he decided it was best to call it a day, so that he may have more time the next to study for the test.

He could not keep the diamond on so he placed it into one of his drawers on the desk.

CHAPTER 3

A Strange Week

Sunday blew past in just a few minutes. It was a day that seemed somewhat useless in the amount of time it provided.

It was now Monday, very early in the morning. The day most of the world disfavoured and never wished to face unless something really exiting was happening, but that is very scarce. This one was not, it was a lot worse than a lot of the Mondays you get at school, having it filled with the responsibility of writing a test.

It was, however, filled with a lot of happiness for the prepared, ready to tackle it and be done as soon as possible.

The phone on his desk began to ring, it was set for 5:30.

His eyes opened up quickly and picked up his phone, facing its bright light into his eyes in an attempt to switch it off and placed it back on his desk once accomplished.

Though today was not the best of days, he was not going to start it off in his usual sluggish routine. His mind was already filled with the thought of this test, chasing away his drowsiness as he stared up at the ceiling.

A dim amount of light had already started seeping through the curtains, providing some lighting in his dark room.

Since even the slightest thought of the test had diminished all the sleep that would have dwelled in him, he saw himself arriving at school quite early today, which was his plan anyway.

After eating and having a quick shower, first thing he did was open the dictionary of a textbook and place it on his desk on one of the many pages he had to study. While he dressed, he would read over all that he could and try keep it in his mind by repeating it a few times.

His uniform was your typical, consisting of black shoes, long grey socks, long grey pants, a black belt, white T-shirt, red tie and a navy blue blazer with the schools badge on the left pocket.

When he was ready, before he could continue on with his studying, he remembered the diamond Jake Mauntell had given him. He stared at the drawer for a moment, wanting so bad to leave it behind and forget about it until Jake returned, but since his warning, he feared more that he would be caught off guard without it and since he had proven himself as someone who had been watching without their notion, there was no other choice.

He pulled it out of the drawer and held it up in front with both his hands, about to put it on, he remembered the rule against wearing jewelry on school premises and the fact that Jake had strongly recommended that this be kept a secret. He thought of a better way of carrying it around and just shoved it into his hidden blazer pocket.

With that bit of distraction out of the way, he picked up his text book and started pacing back and forth, reading over whatever he could.

Whilst the studying was ongoing, one thing James forgot was the time, and when he had realized, it was when his mom called, telling him his friends were just outside waiting for him.

"I'll be down in a sec!" He shouted back, shoving his textbook into his bag.

He wore it and hurried to the door.

The strangest thing happened, which had a really painful aftermath.

James found himself running into the door, at a blur of speed, knocking his forehead into it with a loud thud, sending him falling back onto the floor with both hands pressing against the pain.

"Ow!" He whispered aloud, "What!" He said shaking his head.

Jane heard the loud thud, "James...are you alright?"

"Yes," he replied struggling to his feet.

He went for the door again, and this time went slowly. Down the stairs he climbed, with one hand grabbing the railing whilst the other tried to compress the pain.

Jane noticed and gave him a strange look, "What happened?"

"Nothing, just hit my head a little, I'll be fine," He replied.

He said his goodbyes and exited the house.

Daniel and Mark were waiting for him on the side of the road. Daniel was busy asking Mark a few questions about the test, working on each other's knowledge and memory. This was not as effective because every time he would ask, it was him again who would give out the answer.

James stopped meddling with his forehead before making himself present to them with a clap, "What are you guys doing?" He asked.

Mark turned to him, "Oh, morning, did you forget about school or something?"

James shook his head and greeted them with a handshake.

"We going over the notes," Daniel replied.

"You mean the textbook right?"

"I guess, no one did make any."

Mark started up the street, "Come on, we'll go over the textbook on our way there."

The weather today did not reflect on the way they felt. It was clear blue skies with no clouds to be spotted and a soft breeze.

"The day to day lecture we get on this subject may get us a few marks," Mark said.

"Yes, if you remember such," James replied, "I don't think the brain stores information when it's bored."

Daniel disagreed, "Maybe it does... I mean, it's got nothing else better to do," he chuckled.

"Hmm," Mark gave a second of thought, "The brain... useless it is, it abandons you right when its exams," he said, noticing the small bump on James's forehead, he gave it a poke out of curiosity.

James flinched.

"What happened there?"

"Is it visible?" He asked giving it a few taps.

"Under the right light, yeah," he replied.

Daniel also noticed it, "I hope that was not an attempt at trying to get your brain to work," he giggled.

James shook his head, "What, no, it was something stranger."

They waited anxiously for him to give them an answer.

"I ran into the door."

His reply was very poor, which resulted in their laughter.

"I'm serious guys," he calmed them, "I was in a hurry and as I was about to leave my room, I found myself hitting the door at a blur, it happened so fast."

They became silent after his, somewhat, supernatural explanation.

"Did anything strange happen to you guys?"

Daniel started to take him a little more seriously, "This was after you put on the diamond right?

James had not really seen any correlation between the two, but now that he thought about it, it began to make more sense so he nodded in response.

"Something weird happened to me a well," he started.

"Go on."

Daniel took a deep breath and began his explanation, "When I was done dressing, I put it on, well, in my pocket and left the room while reading my textbook. I obviously knew where the stairs were so there was no need to focus on that... so after I started my way down stairs, which was what I thought I was doing at least, when in actual fact I was continuing on straight, in midair," he explained, "The only time I realized I was walking in midair was when my head hit against the wall just above the stairs, and that was when I fell down... thankful they were carpeted and came out unhurt... did feel a lot of pain though."

Mark gave him a funny look, "So you were walking in midair?"

Daniel nodded.

He chuckled in return, "It seems yours will be the craziest."

"Well, what's yours then?" He frowned.

Marks reply was also very poor, "I couldn't leave my room."

James's imagination made him chuckled, "Did you expand in size or something?"

Daniel laughed.

"No!" he replied, finding no humour in it, "There was some kind of invisible wall that kept me from leaving."

"That's a better explanation," James pointed out.

"Whatever, I wasn't done explaining myself."

"This is serious, what do you think that man gave us?" Daniel asked.

Both of them shrugged in return.

"We must just keep them on us at all times, that's all I know," James said.

Mark shook his head, "And again we are sidetracked by a mile."

Daniel frowned, "What do you mean?"

Mark reached over and snatched the textbook from Daniel's grasp, "We supposed to be studying."

It was only a few minutes after their realization that they arrived to their destination, Waterbridge high school. Not very different from your average school, classes everywhere, large sports fields, a hall and so on. The emblem was in the shape of a red and blue shield with a wooden bridge from one side to the other over a river of water beneath it.

At the gate was a security guard and a teacher on duty that stood there checking for anything out of place in the students' dress codes.

There were many learners already, which meant that they were not as early as they wanted to be, meaning their morning study time had been reduced immensely. This would call for another way to buy back their time, the method of studying during lessons, a tactic that required a great deal of stealth and no small amount of courage.

Although this morning provided some bit of group studying, it was nowhere near enough for our party, so operation: study during other lessons, was their plan.

Being in the tenth grade, they were not in the same class most of the time but did share the same history class given it was divided into three since it was a compulsory subject.

Today they had a double lesson and cutting in between it was their break, which meant the test was to be written during the second by vote of the students.

Their history teacher, Mrs. Hatter was quite tall and old, not enough though, to have a maze on her face or the winter hair. And as you might expect, she was not very famous amongst the students, not many of the old staff care for such fame, only there to do their job and in a very strict manner.

The democratic vote she offered to the students had actually come as a surprise to them, or just put there as a way to throw them off. The test papers had not yet arrived so writing after break was inevitable.

Most of the students had thought they would be given the opportunity to study during this lesson but that would have been like defying the laws of physics with this teacher.

Instead, Mrs. Hatter decided to teach and continue on with the lessons, which was expected but something that would confuse some minds. She was teaching about other things right now, things that dealt with other worlds.

"Now, ancient history tells us that there are worlds, larger worlds that surpass our land, Maramel," she explained, "Scientists say, that according to deciphered text, written by those at the beginning of the third cycle, the other worlds were separated by the gods... but now, this starts to become a little more fictional since there is no proof at all of the existence of these other worlds. Though written in tomes and scrolls, we are still yet to figure out whether these were just stories or actually true."

This was throwing some people off course. James was having trouble keeping what little information he had stored in his head. The stuff he was listening to right now was actually quite interesting.

It was almost the end of this first lesson when the intercom for the class beeped.

"Mrs. Hatter, are you there?" A lady asked.

"Yes ma'am," she replied.

"Please come down to the office," she requested.

"Okay, I'll be there in a minute."

The intercom switched off.

Mrs. Hatter walked over to her desk and took he handbag and cellphone, "You may leave as soon as the bell rings," she said, "And don't be late, I want to start immediately, exam rules apply," she exited the class.

As soon as she was out of sight, the talking started. Many of the students took this opportunity to start studying for the test whilst others continued on about the past weekend.

Daniel, whom was sitting to the far left of the class had opted to be one of the learners who studied, he sat there in his silence, reading about something in his textbook. The amount of writing laid out in front of him was not motivating even though they were only a break away from writing. Next to him was a girl that was clearly prepared for the apocalypse, everything noted down and summarized properly, with highlighted headings and sections of importance, he had to.

"Jeanette, can I read over some of your notes?' He asked politely

"Sure," she agreed, handing over a few to him.

"Thanks."

These were so much easier to understand and read, everything was ordered and short, unlike the textbook which added a whole lot of unnecessary information. He wonder to himself, while he read, why he was never able to bring himself to do such a task, it was clear to him that it was more helpful, but he just never could.

The time with these notes was cut short as soon as the bell rang and she requested them back.

Everyone left most of their things there and went out for break.

Daniel on the other hand had begun to face some really strange complications. Complications that did not allow him to leave his desk. He became worried about his current state.

Both his feet were some centimetres off the ground, which was something impossible since he was not applying any force on the desk. His legs felt light, only drawing up to the conclusion that he was having his midair experience again.

At first he tried to solve this problem by pushing them back to the ground. This succeeded only as long as his hands were applying the force.

His new plan was to wait it out, hopefully it would stop.

"It's break Daniel," Jeanette reminded him.

Daniel nodded in return, acting as normal as he could, "I'll be out in a minute."

She gave him a concerned look, then turned down to her notes, "You can have some for break if you need," she offered.

Daniel accepted, "Thanks, you a lifesaver," he said taking them whilst keeping his legs on ground level with this other hand.

She went on out of the classroom to break.

Daniel placed them face down on the desk.

He was not alone yet, Mark had noticed his love for the chair and questioned why he was not leaving it. He made his way over to him, "What are you still doing here, it's break?"

Daniel did not want to deal with him at the moment, "Yeah, yeah I know, I'll be there in a minute, I just need to check something quick."

"Okay," he replied making his way out of the class as the last person, carrying his textbook with.

The class room fell silent, with only the distant murmurs. The effects of whatever was happing to him were not wearing off, they were getting worse. It was now his arms that had decided to stop listening to gravity.

"What the hell his happening," he murmured to himself, lowing them to grab ahold of the desk.

It did not stop there, the next to defy the laws was the rest of his body and this time, there was nothing he could do to keep himself from rising.

The only thing that played along in his favour was the position of this class, it was on the second floor which decreased the amount of prowlers significantly.

After a few moments had passed, he found himself in midair, trying every way possible not to continue on floating even higher. The only thing working now was his hands, they had grabbed his desk, keeping him in place.

This idea was only temporary, since the force pulling him up ever so slowly seemed to have a much greater pull than the gravity holding down the table, that, or this table was extremely light because he was now pulling it up with him which was not going to end well the longer he held on to it.

His decision to let go made a really loud noise. After its release, he was pulled up to the ceiling swiftly and was no stuck up there.

For a moment he just stared back at his desk, really jumbled by this inconvenience. His gaze then turned to the windows, where he then realized that his recognition was a risk up here so he decided to use his hands to drag himself, using the ceiling as his new ground. He pulled himself to the front of the class, hovering above Mrs. Hatter's desk.

Now that the moving part was over with, he was now faced with the challenge of figuring out how he was going to make it back down, but that time had not come yet as a favour had now come to pass.

A teacher had walked into the class, a young one, bearing a stack of papers in her left arm, presumably the tests and a phone in her other.

To Daniel's fortune, her line of sight had be cut greatly, since her focus was on the phone. Though in luck, his heart did not slow down, beating hard against his chest. The thought of being caught was way too scary, it would get him into a lot of trouble with this Jake character.

She placed the stack of papers onto the desk and seated herself on Mrs. Hatter's armchair. Placing her phone aside, she began to go through some of the papers, paging through them just to see if they were all set without any mistakes.

The fact that this was just a coincidence that Daniel happened to be right above her whilst she was going over the test made it an innocent crime to him, so he watch with very little guilt.

Being on the ceiling, he felt it should have been impossible to see the small writing printed on the paper, but it was quite clear to him, the only problem was that this teacher seemed to be in quite a hurry, she was paging through everything so swiftly.

After a minute or two, she felt the tests were ready for the students so she got up from the chair and walked out of the classroom, still busy on her phone.

The silence came back again followed by a long sigh of relief, the feeling of being caught slipped away and the problem of getting down came back again.

While up there, he had tried a few things, swimming downwards being one of them, but all these types of attempts failed. He did not want to be found up here like this, he had to figure out a way down and the sooner he did, the better.

His mind went back to the moment he heard James and Mark's story, giving it some thought, he figured out the similarity in all their tales, including his. It was worth trying, he unzipped is hidden pocket and pulled it out.

Holding it in his hand he waited, hoping for the effects to wear off, but nothing happened, he remained up against the ceiling.

Then it came to him, what if holding it in his hand was the same as wearing it, the effects were present even though it was not resting around his neck.

It was time to put this to the test, he loosened his grip and let go of the diamond.

The diamond fell to the floor along with him, landing with a loud thud.

"Ow," he murmured to himself getting up to his feet.

Dusting his uniform, he noticed the diamond lying there next to his shoes. He just looked at it, afraid to pick it up, so unsure it was going to cause him further trouble, but this thought was useless, he was unable to leave it there anyway. The only thing he could hope for now, as he lowered his hand to it, was that it would not be activating again.

He picked it up and waited for the levitation to start again. A few seconds passed and nothing, it seemed to be showing him a bit of mercy. He turned towards the exit when a thought came to mind that halted him. His gaze made its way back the desk where the test papers were currently at.

The choice of viewing these papers now would be a lot more haunting since it was not an innocent crime anymore. He had to decided quickly, frozen in a moment in time.

The one side of his mind had just told him no, to just leave it all to a mystery whilst the other side was a lot more convincing, making the crime seem a lot less wicked. This side of his mind spoke of his friends benefiting as well as himself, telling him that this was an opportunity that he should seize whilst whispering on about this being the only time this crime would be committed, that he wouldn't do it again… just this once. It had come with a lot more offers.

So, wasting no time, he decided to start paging through it quickly, very aware of his surroundings, memorizing some of the things he saw and closed it.

The crime was committed and there was no going back. He took a deep breath and put away his diamond. It was time to leave so he made his way to the door and peered both ways for any signs of life and stepped out into the corridor from where he made his way to his friends with the news.

After break came fast and it was time for people to head back to class. It was time for history. Daniel having shared his knowledge with his friends whom were now extremely happy, not even asking of how he gained the information, they just put their trust in him since this was the only hope they had.

In class, everyone was tasked with removing everything on their tables, keeping only their pens and other necessary stationery with them.

Mrs. Hatter picked up the stack of papers and stood in front of the class, "Everyone, please silence yourselves," she instructed.

The whole class died out and Mrs. Hatter immediately began handing out the tests.

Daniel paused for a moment, really thinking about the occurrence of another episode and how he would not be able to contain it. Mrs. Hatter was still busy handing out in the first row, so he unzipped his pocket and pulled it out.

Jeanette grew curious of what he was doing and kept an eye.

Daniel just smiled back and quickly shoved the diamond into a small pouch on the one side of his bag, away from sight and at a place where it would not bother him anymore.

Jeanette leaned over and whispered, "What was that?"

"Oh, just a piece of paper," he replied, "I don't want to be a suspect."

She nodded in return.

After the handouts were complete, Mrs. Hatter walked up to the front, "You may begin, you have until the end of the lesson."

Everyone picked up their pens and began to write.

At first, the test was very easy, especially for James and Mark since their savior Daniel had shown them the way. All was really well for them both, but only for the first few minutes, then it all spiraled out of control.

Let's start with Mark. For him, writing became impossible, he was unable to lay a single stroke of ink onto the blank lines anymore, no matter how hard he attempted, for what lay in front of him, just above his paper, was the invisible wall he had described earlier. This was the worst place for such a thing to materialize. From the beginning of the test, he was flowing and now come to a sudden stop, similar to the one question in math that steals all you brain power and motivation in the exams.

The wall did not want to go away and at the same time he could not attempt anything too drastic since drawing the attention of those around him was not on the list, especially Mrs. Hatter, who was patrolling.

She did come to notice his sluggish gestures and felt the need to say something, "There isn't enough time to be sitting around."

The girl sitting next to him noticed but ignored and continued with her paper.

Mark felt his tears gathering at this point, wondering to himself why this was happening.

Next we have James, who was also off to a great start, jotting down a lot of the good answers. His problem, however, did not leave his paper blank like Mark's, no, his one was making him write a little too quick. All he or anyone else could see on his paper was just a bunch of scribbles.

His attempts at writing really slow did not help at all, as soon as he put his pen down on the paper, his hand would take over, scribbling down a bunch of nonsense, line after line. He felt embarrassed by the level of clumsiness he was displaying on his test. Having all the knowledge and answers he could possibly get but all to be marked wrong, all because his writing could not even be deciphered.

Mrs. Hatter, passing by, saw this wreck, she did not even have a comment for it, only giving it the two seconds of attention it deserved before moving on up the row.

The girl sitting next to him looked over at his piece of paper and could not help but burst out laughing, whilst keeping her voice muted.

James felt so defeated, questioning whether this was some kind of KARMA for cheating or some kind of messed up luck. Whichever it was, this was way too much of a punishment, this was a fail. All he wrote depicted the accuracy of a five year old, maybe even younger.

The only benefit of his paper over Mark's was only that his one showed signs of life, that it had at least been worked on.

He never did stop working on his handwriting, even though all attempts failed right until the end.

Everyone handed in their tests after the lesson and headed on to their next classes, feeling so very disappointed, everything given to them on a silver platter, and even so, produced horrible marks.

It is a really painful feeling knowing that you have failed a test, it haunts you until you get your mark's back. The feeling of not knowing whether you passed or failed was a million times better and well... knowing you passed was just transcendence, which is the feeling Daniel had walking out of that class with, having taken the precautionary measures.

It was only until afterschool when they had seen each other again, their subject choices were completely different.

The very first topic of that afternoon was the test, which was brought up by Daniel himself, feeling so very lifted.

He could tell by their expressions that there was no rejoice, which begged the question why, so he chose an approach, "So... how was the test?"

"Shh," Mark silenced him, "Shh, we got better things to talk about."

Daniel put a smile on his face, "You weren't very happy after the lesson, word has it, you Mark, did not touch your paper and James... what's wrong with your handwriting?"

"What did I say about the test?" Mark became upset, "What's done is done, it's not as if anything is going to change if we talk about it," he became a little more broad, "Why do people always talk about the test afterwards, I don't see the point."

Daniel shrugged in return, "I guess it is to know if they were right, to put their minds at ease... besides, I'm only asking because I gave you what you needed Mark and still left most of the paper blank."

James on the other hand, was busy trying to understand this diamond and its phenomenon in silence, he decided it was best if he were to step in and spill out his part of the story, "I think it was because of these diamonds Jake gave to us, there is something wrong with them... first this morning and now at the expense of the test," he explained.

Daniel grew intrigued even though he as well knew it to be true, "What do you mean?" He asked.

"My scribbling was a result of this thing, every time I wrote something, it would happen too quick, I could not keep up, it was the same this morning when I went for the door."

"Yeah, same thing happened to me," Mark said, "There was an invisible wall over the paper blah blah blah, I failed the test and this time, it was not my fault," he sounded a little cheerful.

James noticed the one flaw, "What about you?" he asked, "You wrote the test with ease, it would seem you scored a good 90 percent for yours... no strange magic?"

Well... this was time for him to come clean, no doubt they would hate him despite his own troubles, "I took it off."

The first to react in shock was Mark, "Bastard!"

"You took it off!"

Daniel gestured for them to calm down, "Wait, I can explain what happened during break."

"You knew this was going to happen?" Mark asked, giving him no chance to explain, "And you did not even care to tell us about it?"

"Mark, I did not know... now will you please allow me to explain."

Both remained silent and waited to see if he was worth redemption.

Daniel's story was not cut short and brief as he was trying to slip in a detail or two in, to try and raise the level of understanding for them.

It was a wasted effort.

"All I heard was, 'Don't tell Mark and James to remove their diamonds, I'm sure something similar is going to happen to them' laugh laugh," Mark concluded.

Daniel sighed.

James looked at it differently, "You disobeyed a government official and that might not turn out well for you."

What James had just said did put him in some state of worry and as from that moment, he was thinking up excuses to keep stored in his little cabinet should the time come if they are needed.

Then he tried to deal with Mark, "Bro, I did not know that this was going to happen to you as well, if I had, I would have given you a heads up."

"You keep telling yourself that," he replied, "I'm guessing this is why teachers keep saying, 'If you fail, you fail alone', they know that stories of lies and betrayal are happening all the time... you could have at least warned us."

Daniel sighed again, having given up.

"It's been two days, how long is this old man going to take," James mumbled, "I'm not liking that he contributed to my failure."

James unlocked his door and stepped into the house. At this time, he was at home alone.

Today was a little different than all the other afternoons, there was another character in his household, sitting silently on the couch.

The old man Jake Mauntell again.

He sat there, imitating some secret agent in his black suit again.

Before James could wonder of the many reasons for his visit again, he stared down at his keys for a moment, thinking, if he had just unlocked the door himself to gain entry, how was it possible for him to be inside without anyone else around to welcome him in.

His train of though was interrupted.

"Afternoon James," he greeted.

James greeted back and closed the door behind him.

Before he could get any more uncomfortable Jake had a small job for him to do.

"Before you make yourself comfortable," he started, "Can you fetch your friends please... before they get too far, I want to have a word with you three."

James nodded in return, there was nothing else his frightened body could do right now except for obeying his orders. He dropped his bag on the floor and exited the house.

Some few minutes later, all three of them found themselves seated next to one another on the largest couch. All terrified by this unexpected visit and at the same time, feeling a little relieved.

James and Mark were in a similar position between all three, having followed the man's orders precisely to this day, only having to wonder why he was here today, one strong thought being the fact of having these diamonds removed from their possession so that they could return to their carefree lives. This was the only though that contributed to their feeling of relief.

Daniel was the only one who had a terrible imbalance between the two, being a grave more terrified than relieved since he had removed his diamond not too long ago and now this man was here again. He was imagining the consequences now.

"Afternoon," he greeted them all, "I am sure you are wondering about my visit... don't worry, it's not because I'm taking the diamonds away from you."

Don't worry? this was the exact statement that removed the only feeling they carried of relief. Things could only go sour from now on. Now they just waited for whatever reason it was that brought him here.

Jake began with his reasons, "I am here because I understand that you may have been facing some complications of late, am I right?"

"Yes," Mark replied, "They have been giving us trouble."

Jake sat back, "May you please describe to me the kind of trouble they are causing you... what it is they are doing?" He asked, "James, let's start with you."

It took some time but he got through to all of them individually.

"So from what I hear, what conclusions do you come to?" he asked, "What do you suppose they are doing to you?"

Ruining our lives James thought to himself, a reply that he really wanted to get off his chest, but it seemed a horrible one that could strike some static between them so he chose a more sensible reply, "Mine is making everything faster... I guess."

Jake turned to Daniel, next to him, and awaited for his reply.

After seeing Jake except the reply James gave, he had an idea of what kind of response was expected so he gave himself a second to put it all together, "I would guess mine allows me to levitate... ignore the laws of gravity," he replied, making it sound a little less magical.

"And you Mark?" He turned to him.

"Walls," he replied, "Mine makes invisible walls."

Jake glanced at each one of them with a frown, "Interesting."

James guessed that this was now a part of the 'experiment' Jake mentioned, seeing as he was also out of notion.

"Are these magic?" Mark asked.

Jake shook his head, "No, magic is a forbidden practice, this is something else, you must not speak of it to anyone."

"What is it then?" James asked.

Jake sighed, "That's not for me to say... because I do not know," he replied, "I'm just the one making the delivery."

James frowned, *Okay, so he does not know*, he thought to himself.

"But I do know they were created a few days ago," he added.

"Why would they just give these things to a bunch of kids?" Mark asked.

Jake shrugged, "I do not know, as I said, I am just the delivery boy in this scenario."

"And you going to take them back when time has exceeded?" Daniel asked.

"In time yes," he replied, "Right now I want you to keep them as you have done the last couple of days," he gave Daniel a sharp look, "Don't remove them from your persons."

Daniel could feel it. Somehow he knew about that slight mishap.

"These are strict rules that you must follow no matter what, even when facing problems that seek to unearth them," he explained, "It will soon be over... I can give you the expiration date if you want."

The all nodded, so eager to know of their deadline.

Jake sat forward, "You will have them till Saturday."

It was quite a stretch, judging from the amount of trouble they have caused them today, but it was, at least, just a few days away, having expected for him to say something over a month.

Jake had more to say, "On this Saturday, you are required to wait for me at the park, in the same place you were this past Saturday, near the lake where you were skipping stones."

Mark gave him a weird look.

Jake stood up from his seat, "In the meantime, find out anything else new about them, I'll be waiting for an output," he instructed, fixing up his suit, "I thank you for you cooperation," he said making his way to the door, "I'll see you then," he opened it and stepped out, closing it behind him.

All of them were left sitting there in silence for a few moments, broken by Mark clearing his throat.

Daniel took a deep breath, "Another weird conversation I got to live through and see to the end."

James slumped into his couch and sighed in relief, "At least we know more about these things and that we are just experiments."

"I wonder what for?" Daniel asked.

"Nope," Mark stood up, "I'm not going to be pulled into this wondering, we got our deadline and that's all that matters," he stretched his arms, "Besides, I'm more glad this test is out of the way, now I can relax."

Daniel stood up after him, "You're right on that one."

"See you tomorrow James," Mark said giving him a fist pump.

Daniel did the same, "See you buddy."

They showed their way out of his house.

James remained on the couch for quite some time and reflected on what had transpired the past few days.

The rest of the week was surprisingly good, all had went well for them. There weren't any crazy instances caused by the diamonds given to them, though, during that duration, they had spent most of their time in constant fear and alarm, afraid of the next activation, especially during school hours, a place crowded with students and teachers.

Knowing their deadlines was nice but it did not seem to make time accelerate, instead, it may have slowed to a definite stop, making every single day feel endless.

I suppose it's the way things work when it comes to patience and thought, when you are asked to do something you don't want to do for a week, you will find that week passes by in just a day and if you really want the final date to arrive as soon as possible, like in their instance, one week can take as long as a month. The wonders of why the brain would do such a thing, you end up suffering both ways.

Saturday was ruined for James, having heard his alarm go off at 5:30, the time he would normally wake up on a school morning. Hearing it was the worst experience, he did not want to be up this early on a Saturday.

But this one was his own fault, out of the many alarms that he had set, one of them was also scheduled for Saturday and Sunday. He made the changes immediately.

His attempt at falling back into a deep slumber fell short, now that his mind was again filled with the thoughts of today, it was impossible to clear them away.

The one thing that did not bide too well for him this week was his test. The interview received from the students in his class was not good either, coming up with some excuse to explain his revolting handwriting. At least he was not the only one, but the one receiving the most attention. It was all in the past and so was the fear of another episode on school grounds, he felt so relieved, he was going to hand the diamond in to Jake today. *I suppose we will never find out why we were actually given these in the first place*, he thought to himself, *What experiment were they conducting?*.

All these thoughts were going to linger on in his mind for as long as he remembered.

Since he was wide awake now, he saw it was best to just get himself cleaned up in the same way he would on a normal school day, only much slower, but instead keep in his pajamas for the time being whilst the new day prepared itself as well.

He powered up his PC, and while it started he walked over to his curtain and checked the skies for his own weather report.

It would seem the sun would be unable to show its brightness today. The clouds covered everything so perfectly, without any cracks or breaks, not allowing even the tiniest ray to pass through. It was most probably going to rain at a later stage of the day.

For the rest of this early morning, James spent it playing games, something to allow the hours to pass by without his notice.

He concentrated for a few hours before he saw it was about time to be heading out, checking the time on his phone, it was now just after the eleven o'clock mark. He took off his headphones and put them away. He went to check for the weather again and saw that it was raining, but not so bad, just a little more than a drizzle blowing in the wind, not something that would soak you in a few minutes.

After that, he dressed for the occasion, wearing takkies, jeans and a hoodie before heading downstairs to meet with his mom. She was sitting in front of the TV.

"Morning," she greeted, "I saw you playing your video games so I did not disturb you."

James greeted back, "Morning, I'm going out to the park."

"What for, it's raining?"

"You know that Jake guy who gave us the diamonds?"

She nodded in response.

"Today is the deadline, we giving them back, I don't want to keep him waiting," he explained, "The exact time was not mentioned, but I still have to go fetch Daniel and Mark, since they are not here yet."

"Okay, make sure to stay warm and say 'hi' to Mary and Denice for me."

"Bye," he said opening the door.

He stepped out into a much colder environment.

The drizzle was not so bad, he actually enjoyed this kind of weather over the clear skies. Both still did have their benefits, depending on the mood or plans.

He made his way to the pavement with both his hands stuffed into his hoodie pockets and headed down the street, looking around, house to house, for any signs of life that chose to be in this weather. There was no one around him, not even the creatures were out, the skies and grounds were empty.

He decided it was best to just watch the slow streams that travelled down the side of the road with him and into the sewers. Doing this gave him the feeling of picking up any random floatable object and just placing it into the stream, follow it to the end of its trail.

The road curved up and he continued. Placing his hand on his chest just to make sure the diamond was still there, because such things, do tend to find themselves misplaced right when they are needed.

A couple of minutes passed and finally came to a stop, in front of another house that looked similar to his, well, most are similar to begin with. Not exactly a copy and paste scenario but it came close enough.

He made his way up to the front door and gave it a loud knock.

The woman who came to answer the door was quite tall, with a fit figure. She had long dark brown hair, some freckles on her face and brown eyes.

She recognized him and greeted cheerfully, "Oh hello James."

"Morning Mrs. Mewell," he greeted back, "If it is still morning," he looked up into the sky.

She laughed, "Come in, come in, before you get soaked," she said stepping out of the way.

James wiped his feet on the door mat before getting in, to find Mark sitting in front of the TV. At least he looked dressed to be outside.

"My mom's says 'hi'," James delivered the message.

"How is she?" She asked.

"She's doing well," he replied.

If you are wondering, this is Mary.

"Would you like something warm to drink?" She offered.

James declined, "No, I'm fine thanks, here to pick up Mark, we have some business to attend to at the park," he turned to him.

"You finally made it," Mark greeted, "You are late," he said standing to his feet.

James frowned, "Are you saying I was supposed to fetch you?"

"You're here aren't you?"

James sighed, "I'm here because you did not show up, besides, it would have been more ethical, less up and down walking for me."

"You need the exercise."

James chuckled shaking his head.

Mark shook his head and made his way to the door, "Come on let's go, can't keep him waiting."

"Be back soon," Mary said as he stepped out.

Outside, Mark finally realized there was something missing, "Where's Daniel?"

James shook his head, "What... he did not enter the house... he must be feeling a little irresponsible today as well."

"So we are going that way first then?"

James nodded.

"Why didn't you start with Daniel?"

"Shh, let's go," he silenced him.

They headed onto the pavement again.

It was a while before they had made it to Daniel's house.

Mark knocked on the door and Denice was the one to answer it, Daniel's mom.

She was tall with long blonde hair and green eyes.

"Hello boys," she greeted, letting them in.

"Hello, Mrs. Rikone," James greeted.

"What brings you out on such a day?" She asked.

"We're looking for Daniel," Mark replied, "We got to go somewhere."

She closed the door behind them, "He did mention something about that earlier, he's getting ready," she made her way around the kitchen counter, "Daniel!" She shouted.

"Yes!" A faint voice replied.

"Your friends are here!"

"I'll be there in a sec!"

Whilst they waited for him to show up, James delivered his mom's message and just passed the time by speaking a little about life.

It was only after a few minutes when Daniel showed up, ready to go with a surprised look on his face.

"Hmm, thought I'd be the one to wake you two up."

"You a little late for that," Mark replied, "Don't want to keep the old man waiting."

"Old man," Denice grew a little concerned, "What old man?"

There was a moment of silence after Mark's little slipup as they tried to gather up an excuse.

"Umm... just an exaggerated expression," he replied, glancing over at the other two as they agreed with him as well, "I'll be back soon, just visiting the park."

She nodded slightly, unsure if they were telling the truth, "Okay, make sure to keep warm."

He nodded and followed his friends outside. From there they headed straight to the park.

The rain had become a little lighter on their way there, becoming nothing more than an annoyance in the wind.

By this time, they were on the pavement entering into the park's radius via a brick pathway.

Their surroundings were of a different kind of beauty under a clouded sky, with everything moist and brighter in colour without the sunlight to absorb it. The few benches they could see around them were soaked and unoccupied. Not even the trees could provide proper shelter from rain, after being drenched for such a long time.

The lake which they were headed to was quite a walk away, but visible to the eye from their current positions. This did not stop them from scanning the area around them for of the old man and his black suit.

"No sign of Jake yet," Daniel sighed, "Maybe we are early."

"If so I'm leaving," Mark replied, "I'm not waiting around to be soaked."

"We not even there yet people," James stepped in, "Can we just get there first."

"Easy for you to say," Mark said kicking away a twig.

James frowned, he did not, at all, understand what Mark was talking about, since they were all stuck in the same position. He did not dwell on that thought since the words could just be there to spark some kind of disagreement, but asked anyway, "In what way?"

Mark shrugged and hummed the words *I don't know*.

He was right, Mark was just saying random words.

When the park's lake was close enough for them, they stepped away from the path and crossed over into the greens until they made it to the water.

The rain drops were so small and light that they seemed almost invisible as they splashed into the water, unable to generate larger enough ripples to be seen grow out and even without the suns light, the water was still mirroring the sky and trees that grew near it.

James found himself lost in the beauty of the mirror whilst Mark quickly fell into the pit of impatience, constantly scanning the area for any other person that could be wondering around in the park. Daniel found himself some smooth stones nearby which he could use to start passing the time.

"Okay, we're here," Mark started, sounding a little panicked, pacing back and forth.

"Give it a few minutes man," Daniel said coming back, "You like a monkey on a leash."

"That's outside, in the cold rain, knowing it could be doing something better with its time elsewhere," he completed the sentence.

Daniel shook his head and skipped the first stone over the lake.

James was broken out of his trance when he began to notice the large ripples begin to warp the reflection. He turned to Daniel and held out his hand, "One please," he requested.

Daniel dropped one into hand, it was soiled with a bit of mud, which he rubbed of clean before giving it a shot.

Mark saw that his growing anger was not making the man appear so he decided to calm himself and stop with his pacing. He thought that maybe it would be best if he just joined James and Daniel.

The walk to them was put to a stop, which surfaced even more anger than before. It was because of the invisible wall, it appeared right in front of him, which he walked into face first, throwing him into a minor fit.

"Ow!" He shouted grabbing his nose, "What the hell!"

James turned to him giggling, "Did another one appear?"

He nodded, checking if his nose was bleeding, "I can't wait to get rid of this thing," he said taking a step forward with his palm out in front of him.

When he came into contact with the wall, he kept his palm on it and started walking off to one side.

Daniel looked at him with confusion, "What are you doing?"

"Finding my way around," he replied.

As he made his way, he came into contact with another one, which he walked into as well. He nodded to himself, "I think I'll just stay here," he announced, taking a step back.

It was about another five minutes of waiting before the first sighting of another human life was seen and it was Jake, making a rather unexpected entry, appearing from the forest, his attire, same as always, holding a transparent umbrella over his head with his right hand whilst the other settled in his pocket.

By now, the walls around Mark had disappeared and was now standing beside James and Daniel, "Finally," he whispered to them.

James nodded in agreement, also having succumbed to the impatience.

Jake made his way over to them and took his standing about two metres away from them.

"Good day boys," he greeted.

"Hi," Mark greeted back.

The others just nodded in return.

Mark proceeded to remove his diamond but Jake held up his hand, "Not yet."

Mark lowered his hands.

"I am going to ask you again, what do these diamonds do… Mark, you go first." He instructed.

Mark sighed, "Mine keeps creating these walls around me at random places… once, it did trap me, it created something similar to a barrier."

He gave him a slight nod and moved on, "Daniel?"

"Mine just makes me levitate and at times I can walk in midair as if there is a platform there."

"James?"

"Mine just makes me accelerate, in ways I can't keep up, but in one instance, I did find myself moving at a normal pace whilst everything around me slowed down."

"Interesting…"

Mark really wanted to get rid of the diamond, "Can we give them back now?"

"No," he replied, "I'm not removing them from your custody."

All their faces warped.

Jake could sense some sought of retaliation approaching so he decided to explain himself immediately, "There is something that you must know about these diamonds… and me," he started, "In actual fact, I do not work for the DCA or the government… these diamonds are not of their property either."

All of a sudden, they all started to feel more afraid of him, now he could be anything else but what he just confessed not to be. This could be some kind of criminal operation, caused by some syndicate. Things did really turn for the worse.

Jake continued with his explanation, "I did tell you that you weren't the only ones with these, in total, there are fourteen diamonds, each with their own differences, some owned by children like you…"

James did not understand what was happening, or was this all out of his prediction radius? He wondered why this old man was coming clean right now and explaining every detail to them, was this the part where he killed them, after gaining whatever information that he wanted? This though was a bit extreme but he had seen many instances of it before. For now it was too early to come up with any conclusions.

"... You are going to keep these diamonds with you... because you are going to need them," he smiled.

All the thoughts they had of a criminal syndicate seemed to diminish after the last line.

Jake took a deep breath and looked around at the scenery, he turned back to the boys again, "Alright then... I'll see you in the past," he said giving them a slight nod, turning away and heading off in the same direction from whence he came.

James, Mark and Daniel were left in the darkest of pits unable to understand Jake's last words, but their thoughts were cut short by a loud noise in the sky, like cracking glass.

Mark was put into an alerted state, "What the hell was that?" He looked around for the source.

The sound came about again, this time it seemed to be coming from everywhere.

"I don't know," James replied.

"I think we should leave," Daniel suggested, starting his way back, with the others following very close behind.

The next sound was different, it was a shatter followed by shards falling out of place.

This forced them all to stop as a sharp, piercing pain developed at an instant in their minds, a pain that had them grabbing their heads.

"What's happening?" James asked as he fell to his knees.

No replied came from the others. He closed his eyes tight, trying to suppress the pain.

A moment later, the shatters continued around them.

James opened his eyes and looked around for the source and found something more intriguing.

The rain drops had stopped falling.

They remained in a still position as if time itself had come to a stop, but then his eyesight blurred and his mind started spinning in circles.

"What-," he uttered as he tried to reach his friends, whom were already laying on the ground, still.

He felt weak as well and fell back with only the solid colour of the sky to see, but that was not it anymore.

Just above him, he could see a crack in the sky, shining brighter than the sun's light. It was as if light was trying to escape, but this was not exactly the case, as his blurred sight followed the cracks, he met up with an area that had been opened, where the glass had shattered.

Through that hole, he saw the complete opposite of what he had expected.

Total darkness.

It was the last thing he saw before his eyes forced themselves shut.

CHAPTER 4

Leaving the Present

Emptiness. The place we find ourselves in right now, a place where even the weight of light cannot be felt or its brightness seen to give us sense of direction. Trapped in a void of just darkness, an abyss that contains no amount of dreams or a sense of time.

Even with our eyes closed, we can see a little light, trapped inside, of the moment we just saw before closing them, and in our conscious minds, our third eye can see everything we have seen before, and as well imagine other possibilities that we may create, so in some theory or another, if we have seen light, even for a fraction, we will always be able to visualize it.

We now jump into the mind of James, as you know, he passed out. Unaware of himself or surroundings, he lay adrift in the dark abyss, unable to imagine the light, unable to wait for anything to happen. His mind trapped in a frozen state without any notion of its own existence.

An unknown pit which he shall now be pulled out of and travel to the unconscious realm, pass it until he finds himself conscious and off course, awakens.

Slowly, as if waking on his laziest school day, James opened his eyes, unable, at first to make out what he was seeing but knew in which direction he was facing.

He lay on his back.

His other senses gradually started to become aware of his surroundings. One in particular, that shook him was his nose, only realizing when his chest was closing up that he was not breathing. It forced him to fill his lungs with the unknown atmosphere, just to get his body feeling a little more stable, soon after was the smell and it was not pleased with the stuffiness of the air around him, it was all dry and dusty.

The rest of his body came to, and with some close thought to his position and the way he was facing, he would deduce that he was laying on a bed. The covers over him and the soft cushiony feeling on his back contributed to his realization.

When he finally decided to take heed of his sight. The ceiling he was staring up at was not of any familiarity at all. Built from now aged and decaying wooden planks without any source that could support light.

The room was giving away the fact it was during the day time at this moment. His vision was still cut off, only seeing the top corners and edges of the house as well as what took the shape some kind of wardrobe, it was time for him to make his first move.

The first to move was his neck, turning to his left, it felt stiff as if he were stuck in this position of many days. Not too much pain was felt, only some bit of relief from the minor stretch.

First he noticed there was a bedside table covered in dust as well as a candle stand with a small unlit candle placed on it.

Lowering his eyes, he saw the wardrobe and beneath that was the doorway out of this room.

His mind was a little hazy, unable to comprehend with his surroundings, all he was doing right now was observing, mind unable to process anything yet. He just did it without thought.

Next, he pushed away all the covers over him and sat up, placing his hand up against his forehead, trying hard to think. Turning to the right he was met with the bright light of the sun, at least what managed to pass through the thin, white, stained curtain. It forced him to look away and thereafter shake his head in an attempt to clear his mind.

It seemed that the items James has noticed were the only things present in this room with him, leaving a lot of floor space.

One thing that put his mind into a more confused state was the sight of his feet. He was wearing black shoes. The part that confused him was knowing that he was on a bed but wearing shoes at the same time. The thought did not make him feel good, it was not making any sense to him and considerably growing at his temper for an apparent reason so he decided to fix this and place them on the floor where it will no longer bother him.

Sitting on the left side of his bed, he stood up and gave his whole body the much needed stretch that it was craving and made his way around toward the curtains.

He opened up a small bit and peered out into the day.

The first thing he realized was that he was on the second floor of this unknown house, the next was mind blowing, in the sense of being unable to understand.

His view was met with a lot of medieval vibes. The road passing by was made of gravel, with wooden woven fences built at random places. He noticed a few other houses in the distance, built from wood. There was nothing more for him to see really, the place looked abandoned, mimicking the room he was currently in.

"What?" he whispered to himself, "Is this some kind of farm... how did I get here?"

It was at this point when James tried to remember anything that could have lead straight up to this moment. It was all very hazy, but he did fall upon the old man in his black suit, Jake Mauntell, as well as the words he last spoke to them.

"I'll see you in the past," he repeated them to himself. He frowned, trying hard to understand this, "What could that possibly mean?" he asked himself, *was this some kind of riddle or is it in a more literal sense.*

For this, he tried to use his surroundings for help. The room he was in was very old and worn out, which gave him explanations for both sides of his thoughts. One was that he was really in the past in some old house, which he doubted with most of his mind and the other suggested that he was in some old abandoned house far away in some forgotten farm. Now this was what he could find himself believing.

Dwelling longer in this room with his thoughts, he came to remember more, one for instance, he place his hand up against his chest and felt around for any bulge, and it was there, the diamond Jake had given him, resting under his clothing, which was the next thing he came to realize.

He was not wearing the clothing he last remembered, this attire was old fashioned. What accompanied his black shoes were a pair long grey pants and a white T-shirt with a black cotton pullover above it.

"Hmm," he said to himself, beginning to believe his past theory a little more.

Off course there was the option of being in an unconscious state, dreaming all this up, but that thought was kept to the one side, he had no time for it right now. All he wanted to do now was satisfy his unending curiosity which carried quite a hefty load of fear along with it, and the first step of realizing it was leaving this room he found himself in.

He stepped out the bedroom and made his way down the staircase. That was the plan, but before taking the first step down, the thought of not being alone here crept in and made him quite scared of the unknown now.

Standing up there, looking down, he felt it was best to make any persons that might be present, aware and cancel out the element of surprise, which he also did not want at all so he raised his hand and knocked on the wooden wall beside him quite loudly.

"Hello," he spoke.

He knocked on the wall loudly.

"Hello!" He shouted.

There was no response that followed after so it was safe to presume his solitude in this residence and proceeded downward the staircase in a quiet fashion. The silence was killed by the loud creaking of the stairs, lowering his level of stealth.

He made his was down casually and began the observation of his new surroundings.

The house was quite small in size, having a kitchen and dining table with a hearth leading up through a chimney.

The place was now home to the dust particles, invading upon every surface of the house, which was also left in bad condition. It was as though people had broken into the place and looted everything, turning it upside-down.

Across his position, he could see the doorway out of the place and into the open. The actual door lay on the floor, a red carpet into the house.

Being some investigator was not part of James's curriculum now. All the dust in the room was making his nose feel a little itchy, going outside for some proper air was the priority so he made his way around all the obstacles and stepped out, where he was met by a soft breeze of fresh air which he took in with a deep breath.

Funny enough, he began to feel a lot better, almost immediately. His mind regained its full potential and now it was time to wonder about and find out where he stood.

He made his way to the edge of the road, kicking away at the tall grass growing in this house's front yard.

First he looked to this right for any signs or people that could be wondering. Then he looked to the left and in the near distance, spotted a carriage, pulled by a single horse, driven by a man heading in this direction. He was loaded with some cargo placed in boxes. Behind this man's carriage, much further in distance was another carriage, this time pulled by two horses, but too far for him to see what was being transported.

He was surprised that such a dead looking neighborhood had received the attention of people, even if they were just passing by. Must have been some kind of important route leading from somewhere.

About a minute passed before the first carriage reached him. The man riding it, looked a little over his sixties, with long grey hairs, dressed in old robes.

James's first thought was to greet the man as to show some level of respect, but then the man gave him an unsettling, surprised frown, as if he had known him or just found him weird in some way. James just raised his hand in greeting, but again the man replied strangely.

All he did in response was turn away and signal for his horse to travel at a much faster pace.

James's jaw dropped in disbelief, wondering, why the reaction, "Disrespect," he murmured to himself.

He waited for the other carriage to near him and seemed quite relieved when he came to recognized the driver, being Jake himself and the large cargo in the back being Daniel and Mark.

They came up and stopped right in front of him.

"Good day, Mr. Lamaine," He greeted.

"Hi," he replied with some amount of confusion.

First of all, he was not in his black suit anymore. Now he just wore these long grey robes. This type of apparel did not suit him at all and had made him look very different.

Daniel and Mark, behind him in the carriage, were also covered in robes, only blue in colour and for some reason chose to wear their hoods.

"What are you waiting for?" Jake asked, "We need to get going."

James did not realize that he was just standing there staring right back at them, "Oh," he said crossing the road.

Mark threw a piece of clothing over to him, "Here, put this on."

James caught it in a nick of time, it was another one of the robes they were wearing, "Thanks, I guess."

"If you're happy in the clothing you're in now, you can give it back," Mark replied, "It's not compulsory."

James frowned at him, he was already putting it on.

After completion, he climbed on from the back and sat across from them.

"Ready to go?"

"Yes…," James replied, really feeling uneasy about how casual everyone was about this situation.

Jake started up the road again.

"So how are you guys doing," James started.

"Doing good, could be better I guess," Daniel replied.

"Not doing good," Mark replied, "Feeling really bad actually."

James raised a brow, "You mean after what happened yesterday?"

Mark chuckled "You mean a week ago."

"What?"

"It's true," Daniel supported, "Jake was telling us right now… that it has been a week and we have been sleeping in these abandoned houses the whole time."

"What about the hole in the sky?"

Daniel and Mark glanced at each other.

"What are you talking about?" Daniel asked.

"When we heard the glass shatter, it was the sky right above us... with a bright light and complete darkness?" He explained.

Daniel showed no sense of realization or remembrance.

"Didn't you see the cracked sky?"

Mark shook his head, "I never looked up at the sky, I fell flat on my face right before passing out."

"Same."

"Oh," he said turning to Jake, "Did you see it Jake, the weird cracks and breaks in the sky?"

"I left before anything you claimed to have happened, happened."

James realized he was a little sidetracked, asking all the wrong questions. It was now time for him to gain some degree of understanding.

"What is happening," he asked first, "Where are we?"

Mark faced Jake as well, "Okay, now I'm sure we are going to get ourselves some answers, we are all here now after all."

Jake sighed, "I suppose you deserve some piece of the cake," he began, "It is obvious really, you are in the past, just as I said in your present."

"Okay, that answers where, now why are we here?" James continued.

"I'm not sure," he replied, "I'm also in the dark in terms of why."

James could not believe this, there was no way he was telling the truth

"What, you just some delivery boy or something?" Mark asked.

"I only know what I am told and do as instructed," he replied.

Mark shook his head.

"If you are as in the dark as we are... how come you mentioned the fact that we would need the diamonds you gave to us?" Daniel pointed out.

"I knew at the time that you were going to be put here in the past, a place that you do not know of," he replied, ordering the horses to take a left turn.

"I still don't understand anything... you have told us nothing," Mark said, "You've just been avoiding or blocking every question."

James thought of a better way to go about this, "Okay, forget the questions we have asked you so far and explain everything from the very beginning."

Daniel and Mark sat in silence and awaited for the whole story to be given out to them on a silver platter.

"Okay," Jake agreed, "From the beginning... before arriving at your doorstep on that Saturday afternoon, I received the diamonds, which I told you only came into existence a few days before," He started, "I had received instruction to hand them over to you and so I posed as someone important to make it a lot easier to do so. At the time, I had no other notion but to deliver them to you and so I did... a few days pass and that's when the second visit happened, where I was supposed to check on you about their abilities, just to satisfy my own curiosity and off course deliver the message to you, about handing them back, by which I already knew that it was actually a scheduled time for when the time jump would happen and so we met on the park and... ended up here."

James was disappointed with this reply. All Jake spoke of now, was all that they had already knew, being present for 99% of the story, but it did, however, bring to light some questions that he did want answered.

As of right now, their carriage was making its way passed more fields of houses that had their own vegetable gardens and flowers planted to decorate. Some had their own cattle grown in small pens and free roam chickens.

Just ahead, there was a large collection of houses, the centre of this little town where all the shops would be and all the trading would take place.

Mark had given Jake's little story a little more thought since he had told it, "Wait... we already know that happened, we were there."

James proceeded to the next question, "I thought that time travelling was just a fantasy, nothing of such defiance has ever existed, even in a time when magic was around, it's impossible."

"And yet we are here," Daniel said.

"Did science make such a breakthrough?" He asked.

Jake shook his head, "No... and you're right, it's impossible to control time, not even magic is capable of doing such a thing to the universe."

"Then...?"

"Look... I'll tell you what I can, when I can," he replied, "Right now you are here in the past and we are going to Marridor."

"Marridor?" Daniel frowned.

"Yes, the city of magic," he replied.

There wasn't any point in arguing or questioning, the only thing they could do right now was enjoy their time here since it was clear there was no going back to the present.

Things had started to become a lot more lively when they reached the town, suddenly it was crowded with people going about their own business and working their businesses. The area was made up of many shops that provided a variety of goods and services.

Most of the people here wore peasant clothing. It sure did fit the standards at which these people were living, a small self-sustaining town.

Their road was met with a lot of people and a few carriages with goods to trade or deliver, being the only ones that seemed to be living cargo. The people had become a lot more interested in them, but not in a good way, giving them a few awkward stares before moving on. Jake on the other hand was a familiar sight to these people, receiving greetings from almost everyone that passed by. Greetings that had some sought of foundation or famous reputation attached to them.

"How do they know you Jake?" Mark asked.

"I am from this time," he replied.

That was some new bit of information that they had never knew.

It seems that some answers that they were not looking for but seemed helpful will just come out when they least expect them to. James now had a completely different outlook on this, now that he knew that Jake was originally from this time.

The market district was filled with quite a number of interesting things that only existed in this time. They had passed by a blacksmith shop, given the name : The Red Forge, with an old man hammering at an anvil just outside.

Another shop they spotted was called the General Goods Trading Store. The name said it all for this one, selling a variety of goods to the customer, hence its large size.

One in particular caught their eye. A shop they came to pass called : The Alchemist's House. The sign board had carvings of what took the image of potion flasks and bottles.

"Jake," Mark called, "What exactly do they sell in an alchemist shop?"

Jake noticed the place Mark was mentioning, "Oh, that's where they sell the many different types of ingredients that you can use to create all the potions and poisons you wish to make," He explained, "The shopkeeper is an alchemist herself and sells some already crafted items to those who are unable or are without recipes."

"So… it's magic stuff?"

"Yes, both magic and non-magic," he replied, "Though in areas poor and dormant of any magical activity like this, you won't find such potions, not as much as the mages of Marridor and every other major city."

"The city we're heading to?" James asked.

"Correct."

Marks curiosity was still attached to the potion lady, "Can we get a potion from the shop, maybe browse a little?"

"Off course not, we have no time for such curiosities… but before you awoke from your sleep, I did purchase a few," he said reaching into his baggy pocket and pulling one out.

The potion was in a small sphere shaped bottle with a cork sealing it and a transparent sticker on it containing the name and information of the potion. The solution was light grey in colour and seemed a thick liquid by visual context.

Jake handed it over to Mark.

"What does it do?"

Daniel took the solution from Mark and gave it his own examination, actually reading the contents.

"It's a mixture of a bunch of counteracting ingredients to help cure a lot natural poisons," he explained, "This solution was particularly pricey."

"Why is that?" James asked, picking it out of Daniel's hands.

Jake was a little surprised by the question, "Why? A cure for a huge number of natural poisons. It may be all you need when surviving out in the wilderness," he explained, pulling out another from his pocket, "I purchased one for each of you."

"Thank you," Daniel said taking the solutions from him.

"Unfortunately, this one is useless when it comes to magic infused potions or complicated concoctions, even something that has been tampered with... basically all poisons manmade."

Looking up into the clear sky, you would be able to tell that it was midday. The place they were in was also packed with stalls, people selling a variety of consumable goods.

It seemed a peaceful town, though accompanied by a few guards that enjoyed themselves as well, making conversation.

Nearby was an inn as well, going by the name : Woodmead, with a picture of a wooden tankard on the sign board.

"Hmm, an inn," Daniel nodded.

"Yes," Jake replied, "a stop for most travelers passing by and a good place to gather yourself some information... as well as a place to find work, for example, bounty hunting."

Mark came up with an interesting thought, "What day is it today?" he asked, "Might it be one that we were supposed to attend school?"

James shrugged in return, "Maybe."

"No," Jake said, "You are between terms actually and the next one is just about to start in the next few days... which is the precise reason for why we cannot dilly-dally."

"School?" James asked.

"Yes, you are going to a new school... and judging by what I've seen in your present, compared to the place I am taking you, it will be a lot more interesting, it won't be a boring all day classroom experience of just books that you are now used to, there are more practical's to be done."

"Hmm, so this is some sought of new life, new beginning type scenario?" Daniel asked, a little less excited.

Jake did not answer that question.

Passing out the village centre, they entered again into the fields of crops, isolated farmhouses and fenced cattle.

Jake seemed awfully insecure about their current position for some odd and unknown reason which left the others somewhat confused. His head kept turning from one side to the other as if he were looking for something in particular, or just possibly enjoying the scenery.

"Before I forget," he spoke, "You do have your diamonds right?

"Yup, I have mine," James replied.

Daniel and Mark first checked before giving out their confirmations.

"Though I don't see the purpose of these, other than having them block your way every other time," Mark said.

"Just learn how to use them," Jake replied, "I may be able to help you in due time, but they must remain a secret."

"This is still so confusing," James sat back, "Now you're telling us we can learn how to use them as if we were supposed to know that, we could have avoided a lot of trouble at school if you had just taught us."

Jake did not seem to be taking any interest in what James was saying and just moved on to another matter he wanted to get off his chest, "Oh and I just remembered," he said shoving his hand into the other pocket, "You must eat these sweets," he pulled out three sweets that were wrapped in thin pieces of paper.

"Sweets?" James took them and distributed, "What for?"

"They will help with any future headaches that may come to pass... due to the time jump."

Mark had already unwrapped his one, it had the letters XP engraved onto them. He brought it to his nose and gave it a little sniff. The smell was indescribable, it was strange, what nothing would smell like if it did have some sought of scent.

"Just don't spit them out," Jake instructed.

That line gave them all some very precautious thoughts. Now they were afraid to eat them, fearful of the unknown taste they would be bringing upon their tongues.

They glanced over at each other and decided consciously that they would place them in their mouths at the same time.

The sweet immediately began to dissolve in their mouths and distribute all the flavor everywhere.

As for the taste, you would thing that it was dipped in the sewers. It was just revolting.

"Wow, what do you think?" James asked, speaking with the sweet, just settling over his tongue.

"Of what?" Daniel frowned.

James chuckled, "Is it nice?"

"You have your own, figure it out," he shot back.

James and Mark were both surprise by the outbreak from Daniel.

"I was just asking," he said shaking his head.

He turned to Mark, who did not seem to be with them, carrying a really blank expression. It seemed the contents of the sweet were not bothering him at all.

Mark caught notice of James's stare, "What are you looking at?" He asked, giving him a disgusting look.

"I am looking at what is supposed to be a human," James replied, "Don't your taste buds work?"

"Oh… I suggest you take that back," he spoke calmly, with all his anger buried beneath.

One of the carriage wheels rode over a pretty large rock stuck to The ground, which sent them into a bit of a topple.

"Oh good grief," Daniel said looking over the side, searching for the rock responsible, "Don't they have any road maintenance in this time?"

"I want to leave this history lesson right now and go back to the present… it's unending," Mark shifted away from his pursuit for James.

James interrupted them both, "Stop complaining, you're being five year olds, please grow up."

Jake cleared his throat loudly, drawing their attention, "Eat up your sweets, swallow them if you must."

"Hmm," James shook his head, swallowing the sweet like a pill.

There was some silence for a few moments, but thereafter everyone began to feel a little normal again.

Daniel brought his hand up to his forehead, "What in this world was that?"

Mark shook his head, "Yeah, I could not control my anger there for a second."

"Is this some kind of magic trick Jake?" James enquired.

"It's the sweet," he sighed, "It's a side effect that takes place when you consume it, it alters your emotions to the point that even the slightest gesture can cause extreme anger."

James did not understand, "Why do that to a Panado?"

He shrugged in return, "Just be glad you did not have weapons with you," he chuckled.

Daniel did not find that humour to be the least bit funny.

CHAPTER 5

Lonestar Inn

It was now a full day since our acquaintances had awoken in this unknown timeline caused by their guide Jake, whom also claimed to be in the dark for most of the part.

Today they had travelled swiftly upon the carriage without any rest through yet another day filled with the warmth and light of the sun and full absence of any clouds.

Jake had lead them straight up through the main road, travelling up north across the empty plains, constantly drawing closer to the promised destination of Marridor.

Today, however, was not going to be as dreadful as the day before, containing little to no rest with only their robes to keep warm during the night. It was going to be a much better experience, and perhaps a tad bit more luxurious for their first experience here.

The place they were going to next, in the early afternoon was greater and more formal than the farming town they had come from. This town had a border around it, a wall of logs split in two vertically and sharpened at the top into pointy arrows and by the looks of it, much larger than the previous.

Their road lead straight up to the main entrance which was guarded by two soldiers dressed in chainmail armour with normar helmets.

Upon arrival at the gates, one of the guards stood in the way of the entrance and held up one of his hands, "Halt!" He shouted.

Jake slowed his horses to a stop.

James was intrigued by the type of armour these soldiers wore. Looking up at the entrance, on either side were two wooden poles with short, dark blue banners hanging from them, outlined with a thin white cloth and a symbol that seemed to be the towns emblem, was of a large silver bright pentagram star, with the top and bottom points stretched out more and around it, a circular woven pattern.

"What brings you to Lonestar stead?" The guard asked, making his way around the horses to Jake.

"We are just travelers, we are on our way to Marridor and will stay here for the night," he explained.

The guard walked around to the back and gave the passengers a sturdy look for a few moments before heading back to the front, by which he gave clearance for them to enter, "Enjoy your stay."

Jake smiled and nodded his head at the guard before allowing his horses to start walking again.

Behind the walls of the town Lonestar, not too much was going on. Quite a few houses were built with quite some distance apart with only a few people present. Some just remained seated on their benches placed on porches whilst others were busy carrying around baskets filled with goods. It was only the entrance so, the lack of liveliness was understandable.

There was no shortage of guards that patrolled the area or remained stationed at certain points, some of which wore a more fancy type of armour, steel plate.

It was some time before they came to the more populated area of the town, keeping on the same route of the main road, shops started popping up more as they went on.

Jake continued until he came up to a blacksmith's shop.

There were stairs leading up to a porch and sitting there, on a bench, leaning against the wall was a large, bald, old man with a short white beard, smoking away at a pipe, wearing stained clothing under a black apron which hugged his belly tight.

He remained on the spot and just stared at the carriage, eyeballing Daniel and Mark with a lot of distrust since they had been caught staring back at him and now unable to break it.

James turned around to examine the two story shop, he ignored the old man and looked up at the sign board which read Warrior's Hut.

"Please get off," Jake commanded.

Mark broke the stare and turned to him, "Huh?"

"Get off," he repeated.

Mark glanced over at the others with a shrug and followed his instruction by standing up from his place, stepping passed Daniel and James and jumping off the back onto the gravel road. Afterwards the others followed behind, still a little muddled by the request.

He turned back to them and explained himself, "You are to enter the shop and pick some weapons."

Daniel made his way closer to him, "What for?"

"For whatever purpose weapons have," he replied, "For the current moment, I don't have much money so I suggest you pick something simple. A short sword and some shoes that you can move in will suffice," he instructed, "I will be back in a while, I have to go find a place for the horses to remain," he signaled for them to continue up the road, leaving these three on their own in front of the shop with an old man staring them down, installing some sought of fear.

Mark looked down at his shoes. He moved his robe out of the way for a better look. They looked familiar to him, "Hmm, school shoes."

"This is kind of cool, in a way," Daniel whispered, "Without the reality part."

James nodded in return and became the first person to step on this man's residence. There was no turning back now, if he wanted to avoid an even more awkward situation. Daniel and Mark followed behind as sheep till they reach the porch where they froze near the man whilst he blew away smoke.

"Uhh…," James began, "Is the shop open?" He asked.

The old man blew out some smoke, "Yes we are open."

"May we enter?"

The old man frowned with confusion, "It's a shop, is it not?"

"Thank you sir," Daniel said reaching for the door.

The man giggle, "No need for such titles, refer to me as Weldin… Weldin the smith… has a nice ring to it," he coughed, "But surely you do not expect me to allow you youngsters into my shop whilst in those robes, we would not want you to be stealing anything now would we?"

James shook his head, "No."

"Place them on the barrels over there," he pointed at a couple against the wall.

They did as they were told, first pulling out their potions and placing them on the first before removing their robes and laying them on the other.

Now they were ready to go into the shop and begin browsing for the things Jake requested.

"My wife inside will help you with what you need," he said.

Daniel opened the door and allowed for them to step into the Warrior's Hut.

They all walked into a large hall filled with rows and rows of shelves, by which I mean two, with the others leaning up against the wall. All of them filled with a large variety of goods.

This first experience walking into a medieval shop for them was game changing. It was a tick on the literally impossible bucket list. Though such things can be found in the present and often give you the feeling of being part of such a time, it was not the same as being in the era as well.

Slowly, the thoughts that confused them about all the unanswered questions began to drift away into the deep storage vault as this now started to become a tourist visit.

As they started down their own aisles, they began to notice more about the shop.

Up against the walls between some of the shelves were weapon racks, carrying the more larger and heavier weapons like Warhammers, battleaxes and great swords amongst others, some crafted out of iron and the more decorated ones, containing leather wraps and carvings in the blades were made from steal.

In some places, at the ends of the shelves were tall placed woven and straw filled mannequins that wore completed sets of armour for both males and females.

Up front at the other end of the shop was a counter and standing behind it was an old lady with a shoulder length of blonde to white hair wearing a long dress. She noticed and greeted the boys, "Welcome to the Warrior's Hut, travelers are always welcome here, take a look around and see what suits you."

"Thank you ma'am," Daniel replied politely.

His attention was stolen away by the ranged weapons that he caught sight of, placed near the back of the shop. He examined closely the different types. Long bows, recurve bows and their simple and beautifully designed quivers already filled with arrows. The crossbow seemed to be his favourite, going so far as to aiming one and loading it with a bolt.

There were other types of ranged weapons amongst these that he took an interest in.

James and Mark had, as well, forgotten about the requests made by Jake and were now exploring the shop as well. Both were stolen by the melee weapons, the singlehanded ones that could also be used for dual-wielding, like your average broadsword, axe, tomahawks, maces, morning stars and others they could not name.

This played on for quite some time and Jake had still not found his way back to the shop.

James became a little more curious.

Near the old ladies counter was a wooden railing and a staircase leading down underground to some sought of basement. He walked over to the railing and looked over the edge only to see the steps lead down to a door. Predictable, but it did allow him to ask some questions.

"Um, what's down there?" He asked turning back to the lady.

"Oh, other trinkets and armours," she replied, "The more valuable ones that we have traded along the years amongst other things we wish to remain under the shop... you may head on down there with your friends if you wish young boy," she smiled.

James only heard the words that gave him clearance to enter the basement, which he took to heart greatly. He gathered up his friends and all headed to the staircase, whilst the old lady carried a constant smile on her face which grew to be kind of creepy the few moments they made eye contact with her.

They made their way down the narrow stairs till they came to a stop in front of the wooden door which began to make their imaginations start to kick in and send chills down their spines.

A sign hung from the door, held up by a string and nail. A thin white board with the words : Enter at own Risk, painted over in red.

The very first thought James had was of the old lady, her picture and innocent smile was all he could see for the moment and the next thing to pop into his head was the possible conclusion that she could be some kind of witch. Normally he would chose to debunk this kind of fictional idea but now that he was standing their thinking about it and throwing all the factors of impossible events that have just occurred... he started believing in what he was imagining.

After all, all it takes for a person to start questioning everything he once did not believe is for one thing unbelievable to happen.

Daniel had a more realistic play through to all of this, but it was a most unlikely event when brought to probability. He imagined these people may have known their little change in the timeline and perhaps were seeking to be first to capture and hand them over to the authorities. Something more possible but just as improbable to be the scenario in this case.

Mark's story was just as insane as James's, only, his conclusion was of being stewed up in some giant cauldron.

With his heart throbbing, James, who was in the lead, glanced over at them with some uncertainty.

Daniel frowned at him, looking a little confused by the holdup, "Well... open the door," he whispered without any show of fear.

"Why don't you?" He whispered back.

"What are you talking about, I'm standing right behind you guys."

That was a problem James and Mark were very happy to solve. They both made way for him to pass by leaning against the wall.

He glanced at them, going back and forth, "What are you guys doing?"

"Well... we're not in front of you anymore," Mark replied.

Daniel remained, fixed in his position, really sad that this was the outcome of this little 'guts' quarrel between them. He too did not want to be the first to step into his room.

"Hey," a voice came from behind them.

Frightened by the unexpected sound, they all turned towards it.

It was the old lady.

"What are you youngsters doing down there?" She asked.

None of them felt the need, or even wanted to reply. At least they did not have to in the end.

The old lady came to notice the sign hanging from the nail and giggled, "So the door sign has been what's keeping you from entering… just ignore it, there is nothing in there that can harm you in any way," she explained, "It's just there to scare off some folk who are up to no good, though, I do urge you to be careful down there, I don't want you to be breaking anything," she walked off with a few last murmurs to herself, "I should have taken it down this morning."

It was only after her reassurance that they were able to gather up their courage to open up the door. One thing was sure to them, the sign did do its job by scaring them.

James grabbed ahold of the silver rusted handle and pushed the door open, creating a loud creak.

They stepped into a dimly lit room and were met by a great decline of fresh air filled with the scent of dust. The only candles here were hanging by the small chandelier lighting up the room. The wall torches and table candles were all put out.

This basement was relatively small, about half the size of the shop's floor with only a few shelves, round tables and chairs to fill most of the empty spaces. All, however, were filled to them max with a more exotic variety of goods, as described by the old lady.

Though much dimmer than the ground floor, the beauty of all the weapons, trinkets and armours stood out immensely.

The weapons here were not only made out of your standard materials, such as iron or steal. Pricey minerals including gold and silver were amongst them, some of which having gems and crystals mended into the handles for extra value and beauty. They were not only made from the different materials, but were also crafted in different shapes, to serve for a more gruesome ending or to illuminate a more tribal meaning. A lot of this was shown by the bows and crossbows, having different kinds of war paints to illustrate meaning and region.

Quite a few of these weapons and trinkets they were coming across had a slight glow to them, giving the impression that these objects might be enchanted.

This was now the equivalent of being in some kind of magical fairytale. Nothing in here was a replica giving the feel of an antique shop.

They really wanted to pick their weapons from here now, something they would care about even more, thanks to their uniqueness and obvious value.

"This stuff looks really cool," Daniel complimented, whilst examining a small black dagger with runes carved into its blade and its smooth bumpy handle with silver rings around it, "Do you think Jake would allow us to pick from this place?"

Mark swift to reply, "Off course not, look at this stuff, it's treasure."

"Yeah," James agreed, "The old lady might not even want to sell this stuff."

They spent quite a bit of time in the basement before calling it quits, in fear of Jake having to wait for them for a time, impatiently.

"I suggest we head back up to the shop and start picking out the things we need before Jake arrives," Daniel said heading for the door, "We need to check shoe sizes as well."

Mark was already close to the door, examining some of the more valuable stuff, trinkets included. He put back a small golden sapphire ring into a chest before following after Daniel, "James let's go," he reminded him before disappearing.

"I'll be there in a sec," he murmured to himself, still checking out a small dagger.

The feeling of being alone down in this basement was to quick creep in when all other sources of sound from around him disappeared. Suddenly, he was not so interested in the silver, reflective, gem fitted dagger he was gawking at the past few minutes, trying to see his own reflection in the poorly lit room. He returned it to the shelf, placing it carefully to avoid any unnecessary noise.

Turning away from the shelf he headed for the door. His goal was cut short to only two steps before he came to a sudden halt which froze him in place.

Almost letting out a cry in terror, he gasped, swallowing his ability to generate sound.

The room temperature was reaching absolute zero as chills began to travel up and down his spine causing his body to shiver in both cold and fear.

In front of him was a chair which he could not take his eyes off, and seated on it was a little girl.

A girl that he guessed to be about six or seven years old, seated on the wooden chair facing him, dressed in a dirty, ragged, short black dress without any sleeves, which looked torn off. She had long black messy hair which fringed over her face as she stared down at the floor. Her whole body covered in small cuts, sores and bruises with patches of dusty soil here and there.

The little girls wrists and ankles were shackled in irons but unbounded by broken chains which now dangled freely as a nuisance.

It was as if she also felt the sudden drop in temperature, as she too was looking a little shaky.

The one thing James found most surprising about this unexpected encounter was the girls lack of visibility to him. She was a tad bit transparent, which, after realization, nearly threw James back into the unconscious realm.

He did not know what to do with this moment he found himself trapped in, the one side wanted this to be over as soon as possible whilst the other had begun to feel sympathy and curiosity for the figure he could not yet make out to be. Jumping back and forth between choices, whether this was just some kind of illusion of his imagination or whether this ghost was really there. Either or, he wanted out of this situation immediately.

But now something happened, that made him think and allow for his heart to sink like an anchor.

The little girl began to move, she rose her head slowly till she was able to look up at him, revealing her face. She was drenched in tears and had a sadness that was very contagious. She open her mouth and utter three words, "Please... help me."

James was unable to respond, even if he wanted to he could not because the little girl then faded away like smoke.

For a moment, he remained in the same spot, afraid to take another step whilst a countless number of questions bombarded his mind. Though within the next, his body was able to gain control of itself and allow him to calm his nerves a bit which made him sweat.

He did not wait around for the ghost to show up again, he headed straight for the door and closed it shut behind him before rejoining the living upstairs.

Daniel and Mark were still speaking to the old lady behind the counter, asking for Jake, whom had not yet made his arrival.

Mark was really starting to get impatient, he had seen his fair share of the shop and was good and ready to go.

Daniel on the other hand had a great solution to help kill time and it was actually a part of Jake's request, "Can you help us find the right shoes?" He asked the lady.

She was happy to help, "Well off course, what is it you're looking for?"

"Something comfortable that we can easily move in... for travelers," he described.

She nodded, "Yes follow me," she left the counter and went to the shoe section of the shop, with only Daniel to follow her.

Mark's attention was stolen away by the delayed appearance of James, he frowned at him with an added balance of confusion and worry, "What happened to you?" he asked changing to a giggle, "You're sweating, did you just see a ghost or something?"

James did not want to give an honest reply, knowing Mark, he would just make fun of him and that was not something he was willing to stomach right now, so it was best to just make up some excuse, he shook his head, "Nah, it was just hot down there, need some fresh air is all, I'll be fine."

"Hmm I felt rather cold down there," he shrugged, "Maybe it was just me, but anyway, we are picking our shoes right now, let's go."

After the lady had provided them with some good quality, brown leather boots, the very first half of the job was done and it was now time for them to each pick a short sword and the appropriate sheaths.

Since they were under a strict cheap budget which they did not know the limit to and the shoes the old lady recommended were of good quality according to her, their sword browsing was going to be very simple, nothing fancy, even something with a minor carving was out of the picture so they just opted for the regular steal broadsword and their belted sheaths.

When they were all done, it was time again to continue with their wait and this time it was in boredom. Right now it was either browse the product again or just sit on the barrels placed near the counter.

James was still concerned by the events that transpired in the basement. As of this moment, he was standing in front of a weapon's rack and just gazed into the abyss, reliving the same moment, over and over again, asking himself the same question, *What just happened?*.

Even in his confusion, he still found this to be highly distasteful, seeing a young little girl, even as a ghost, seeing the suffering she might have been through was not right in the slightest, shackled and covered in sores. The words she also spoke, were also fresh off the top of his mind, wondering in what way she needed help, or better yet, how he would be able to accomplish such a task, if say… he wanted to.

"James?" A whisper came from the distance.

"James?" The whisper turned up its volume.

The next thing he felt was a tug on his shoulder, which was the remedy that shook him back into reality, "James?" the voice spoke again, this time recognizing it and its bearer.

It was Daniel and he was bringing to his attention the arrival of Jake, that it was already time to start paying up at the ladies counter.

James did not have his things, he had left them in the custody of Mark whilst he drifted away with his thoughts. He followed Daniel back the front where Jake had already placed the boots and swords onto the lady's counter, searching his money pouch for the appropriate amount to pay her.

Jake placed on the table, a whole stack of about ten gold coins, which the lady took and place behind the counter, bringing out a few silver coins as change.

"Thank you for your purchase at Warrior's Hut," she said, "Please come by at-," she froze in her tracks, stolen away by a most pretty sight.

The priceless mineral that hung around James's neck, on display for everyone to see. Off course James did not realize this slip up until she mentioned it to him.

"That's a really beautiful diamond you got there."

Everyone else turned to James with the most horrific expressions and nothing to say to him.

James saw it and hid it under his shirt again, "Thank you," he said trying to keep everything as normal as could be

He did not recall giving the diamond any attention whatsoever, not since yesterday when he first arrived at this place. He tried to calm himself from the immense nervousness he was feeling and waited for everyone to continue as if nothing had happened.

The old lady thanked them again before picking their individual goods and following Jake out.

The time spent hanging around in the shop seemed to have flown by. The sun had already made its way to the other end of the world, slowly starting to shift itself from its bright yellow to a slight tint of orange.

The old man was nowhere to be found, the bench he had been sitting on since their arrival was unoccupied and now used by the boys to help change from their current footwear to their leather boots.

Their belts were strapped tightly before covering everything with their robes, which, surprisingly had not been touched since, as well as their potions that were left alone on the barrel under no one's care.

From the shop, if you were to look out and up into the sky, you would see a gathering of clouds, shifting ever so slowly towards the town from the east, so rain could be something to expect in the evening.

Jake took to the road as soon as the others were done clothing themselves.

The streets were now decreasing in activity, a lot of the stalls had now shutdown and owners disappeared. The town's guards were still active as ever, patrols and posts still held but with a lot less interaction between each other, maybe their shifts were about to come to an end.

"Come on now," Jake picked up his pace, "The inn is up this way."

Jake lead them to a large house with a wide porch. A small sign was posted in front of the steps leading to the entrance, hang from a pole. The sign had an image of a bright yellow star and a small hut beneath it.

"Lonestar Inn," Daniel read.

"Yes," Jake replied climbing the steps, "This is where we will be spending the night."

By entering this building, they were immediately met by a completely different atmosphere, filled with a majority of warm colours, mainly sourcing from the hearth built in the centre of the room.

All the cold shrunk away and the decreasing liveliness brought back by the cheerful people interacting here.

Surrounding the hearth were many wooden square tables positioned out neatly, each with four chairs around them and some smaller, containing two. Each table was fitted with a candle stand in the centre for some visibility. Other sources of light included the torches placed on the wall.

To the far right of the room was a counter with a lady standing behind it receiving orders from a younger girl of about thirteen years. She also played the role of the server, providing the customers with their food and drink.

Some entertainment was provided by a group of hired bards which sat near the centre, just in front of the hearth, playing away some melodies using a drum, flute and guitar.

It was not as packed as expected, a lot of the outer tables were empty, this was probably because the sun was still on this side of the world.

"Hmm, seems cozy," James whispered to the others.

Jake cleared his throat, "Ok, find yourselves a place to sit, I'm going to speak to the owner."

They all dispersed immediately, with only Daniel among them to take heed of what Jake had just instructed. He took to the outer edge of the room and started a quick visual examination of each desk, looking for the most suitable in terms of positioning for light and which looked most sanitary.

Mark was stolen away by the many different animal trophies that were placed on the walls, he just played a game of 'guess the animal'.

On the other end of the room, James had been attracted to a large notice board that stood on its own with a countless amount of papers stuck to it. His interest was on what laid on them and it seemed, by his deduction, that these were the different jobs that bounty hunters would take. There were wanted posters of a number of thieves and murderers as well as a certain number of missions for people who were up for searching for missing possessions or people. All he did was skim through most of them, but came across a note was placed in the centre of the board which stood apart from all the others. This note read :

For all rewards on the posters of this board,
Proof of completion of any of these jobs
PLEASE CONTACT : THE DEAD CROW

A symbol was also drawn beneath the writing of what James would now guess be a dead crow, but no information on how to contact them.

He was a little thrown off by the lack of contact details but more so by the name, "Strange," he mumbled to himself.

He could not decide if this was some kind of syndicate type of organization or the local police.

"Hey there boy," some man called.

James turned to him.

The man was aged, now probably over sixty, with a really bushed up white beard and unattended hair. His eyes a tint of dark red with clothing that immediately gave away his position in society, and to James, he guessed it was the lowest. His right hand was gripping a tankard which was half filled with ale. To conclude, he was a poor, drunk old man.

After noticing that James was now paying attention to him, he proceeded, "Get away from there, you're too young to be trying to hunt down a murderer or looking for someone else's diamond ring, go on, get out of here," he ordered.

James decided it was best to just listen to the old man, he was speaking some sense in his trance but also for the reason of staying out of trouble. He scanned the room and spotted Daniel, already seated at the chosen spot, he went on and joined him.

"What were you checking over there?" He asked.

"Oh, just a bunch of wanted posters, till some old man decided to chase me away?"

Daniel chuckled and started waving his hand over the candle.

James began to wonder about the time but could not see a clock anywhere, this pushed his thoughts furtherer into the meaning of time which brought upon a question he had to ask.

"What do you think happens to the present?" He asked.

"Daniel was brought back to this moment, "Hmm?"

"What do you think happens in the present?" he repeated, "Do you think our parents have discovered our absence or is the present frozen from the moment we left?"

Daniel shrugged in return, "No idea... both of them I suppose, I mean, it depends on the moment in which we return."

Mark came down to join them, "What are you talking about?"

"Just random theories about time," James replied.

Some minutes passed before the young girl came to their table.

"Hello," she greeted politely, "Is there anything you want, food or drink?"

James shook his head slowly, "No thanks," he replied.

She had long blonde hair and some bit of freckles on her nose, wearing a white apron over a long orange dress.

She bowed her head, "Okay, let me know if you need anything, my name is Bertha," she smiled, before noticing something on James, "That's a nice necklace," she complimented before walking off.

James saw it and immediately covered it with his hand. He placed it under his robe again, really heart stricken by this phenomenon.

"Woah," Daniel said checking for his, "I didn't even notice yours was out until she mentioned it."

"Are you mad!" Mark whispered aloud, "This is dangerous, people might try to take it from you."

"I put it away, you even saw me at the shop," he retaliated.

"Sure you did," Mark did not seem to believe him.

James was surprised by his tone, "You were looking right at me."

Mark sat back, "I know, I know," he confessed, "It did not stop you from trying to flash it at everyone though."

"What are you talking about?"

"I'm just saying hold your horses, we going to start school in a few days... just relax."

James was lost for words, nothing wanted to come out whilst Mark waited, slowly growing a smile on his face.

He just sighed in return.

"I don't think money helps much though," Daniel added, "We're in a different time... I wonder how the rules work here."

Jake was finally done with his little chat with the owner and now came to join with the others as the forth.

"Alright, we have the room we will be sleeping in and the food will arrive shortly."

"Thank you," Daniel said.

Jake cleared his throat, "Well... It would seem everything is going just fine, tomorrow we head straight for the school, should not take longer than two days on the carriage."

The rest remained silent, trying hard to figure out Jake's reasoning for this, it was way too planned out to be something he too was in the dark.

James took a deep breath and began with the questioning again, "Jake, are we the only ones here, you did not bring back our parents right?"

He shook his head, "No, not at all, it's only you three."

"Do you perhaps now know why we are here?" Mark asked, "I don't want to think of what's happening now in the present since our disappearance."

"No, I haven't the slightest idea why we are here," he replied, ignoring the second half of Mark's statement.

"Is there anything you can tell us?" Daniel asked a broader question.

Jake nodded, which did bring some life to them, "Your diamonds, I have an idea of what abilities they may hold within them, and I may just be able to teach you how to use them when we get the time."

This was not exactly what they were looking for but it was something, and something that would definitely draw them away from their current questions and allow themselves to immerse into the new place they now apparently call home.

He turned to Mark, who was sitting on his right, closest to the wall, facing the direction of the hearth, "Mark, you spoke of invisible walls and how they kept popping up in random places around you."

Mark gave him a slight nod in return.

"Now I believe the diamond you have chosen gives you the ability to create shields or barriers around you to protect you from foes."

"But it did not create a shield around me, it made me fail my history test," he frowned.

"Oh... sorry about your history test," he apologized, "I noticed it was a compulsory subject...,"

"Hmmhmm," he nodded in confirmation.

"The diamond was not in your control then, which is something I want to help you with."

Mark really loved the idea of using supernatural powers so he let the test slide and just shrugged in response, "Sounds good."

He gave him a nod and turned to James, who was seated across from him, "According to the descriptions you gave me, your ability involves the acceleration of your whole body, to move faster than anyone else at unknown speeds."

James was happy with his description, "Some kind of speedster," he nodded.

"Yes... I guess," he replied, acting as though he knew what he was talking about, "And last, you Daniel, your levitation stories could only mean your diamond allows you to fly, that's all I can say."

"It's understandable," he said.

"We'll try them out on the road tomorrow," he declared, "Now... is there anything you might want to know... about this time off course."

James raised his hand, his elbow still attached to the table.

"Yes..."

"I was looking at the notice board over there and came across a strange name, The Dead Crow... who are they?"

"Well... they're like the FBI or CIA of your time I guess, they are of greater status than the guards you see and are basically this time's symbol of justice," he explained, "They are not confined to one city, but all, I'm pretty sure we'll come across one sooner or later."

"Hmm, I did not expect 'symbol of justice' to be attached to such a name," Daniel added.

"The Dead Crow," Mark repeated, he shook his head, "Nope, wouldn't trust them, sounds like a group of assassins."

A few minutes had passed before their food was brought to them.

After they had consumed everything and satisfied their hunger, it was now time for them to be hitting the hay. They were directed to their rooms by another woman working at the inn.

They were given a large room of six single beds placed in a row up against the wall, each with a bedside table carrying a lit candle in the centre. The room only had one window on the other end covered with a thin white curtain which allowed for a tiny bit of light to pass through.

Everyone prepared, blew out their own candles and went to sleep.

Quite furtherer into the night, after all the noise had been diluted and everyone else in some deep slumber. James, whom slept farthest away from the door, lay there awake facing the table beside him. He had just come to his senses some time ago because of some dream he had and now all his symptoms were evading him with thoughts he did not want to deal with right now, for the simple fact of not knowing the answers to them, though, even this change in time was serving some inconvenience to him, he did, secretly, want to visit the past, I mean, who wouldn't want to time travel to the past and witness life as it was outside the text books and TV screens he was used to. If Daniel's theory was right on the money, then perhaps he should enjoy his time here in this history lesson before it was time to go back, see everything and its benefits here, especially the use of magic.

As he lay there under the sheets trying very hard to fall back into his dreams, something we all know to be quite impossible when downed by thoughts

In his moments of attempt, he heard something that sprung away his weariness and replaced it with a lot of fear and alertness, his heart had begun to sound like the drums of the hired bards, sending shockwaves all over his body as he lay there still as a corpse.

It was the door, pushing open ever so silently without the ringing of rusting joints, they were well taken care of.

His body temperature rose, causing him to start producing beads of sweat.

When the door was at a large enough degree for a person to slip through, a figure did so, as dark as a shadow on the wall, tip-toeing towards Mark, who lay dead closest to the door.

James did not know what to do at this point, still arguing within himself as to whether this was actually happening or not. He knew though, that he could not take the chance, doing something was the only way to alter the outcome of the next few moments, so he watched, so very hesitant to do anything about it as he drew closer.

He managed to throw away all emotion that held him in this paralyzed state for just a second.

Swallowing his spit, he threw the covers over him away and sat up, "Hello?" He greeted aloud.

The figure near Mark's head was stunned and decided to remove his stealth and hasten his current objective. The figure pulled something from Mark which also woke him up.

The shadow had some trouble as he tugged at the diamond around Mark's neck.

"Ow!" he screamed, getting up into a sitting position, waking up the others while doing so.

This allowed for the figure to take off Mark's diamond and head for the door.

James acted without any thought, pulling out his sword from the sheath, jumping out of bed and heading after him, "He took his diamond!"

Daniel and Jake stood up and followed out through the door, leaving Mark behind as he struggled, suffering from the pain of having the chain violently pulled at his neck.

James chased after the man through the darkness into the hall, dimly lit by the remaining light from the hearth.

This being the very first time in such a situation, his body was just moving, his heart racing and adrenaline reaching peak levels.

The shadow, now assuming it was a man, toppled chairs and tables as he made his way to the main entrance forcing James to slowdown and pay closer attention to the new obstacles since his feet were bear and would not dare to feel the pain of having one of his toes collide with them.

The man jumped through the doors which made James wonder why the door was unlocked at this time of night. He did not have the time now to question such things and jumped out as well into the unwelcoming night to keep his eyes on the target.

As he left the porch he was met with the singing signs that swayed back and forth as well as the ice cold droplets of the unexpected drizzle.

The man made his way around the corner and on to the main road

One thing James was not prepared for right now was the terrain, the ground which he walked upon was dirt that had now softened up from the water but still carried all the little stones in the mix. This was going to be a horrible setback on his part but he continued anyway feeling the sharp pain from the many stones stabbing at his feet.

He made it around the corner, trying his hardest to ignore the stings as he saw the man slowly start to blend into the darkness. Behind him, he could hear the others but knew they would suffer the troubles of this rough terrain as well.

James slowed down, knowing any further pursuit would only allow for more pain with no success.

In his moments of failure, he felt his head begin to feel a little light and his heart rate increase, he tried to calm himself but it only kept increasing until it began to vibrate. He felt helpless in this situation as he leaned against the outer walls of the inn, trying hard to keep his balance.

He blacked out.

In the next moment, he found himself at the mercy of his own body, unaware of what was happening or what he was doing. He found himself in a different place and in front of him, a figure began to appear, running toward him, from the dark.

James did not seem to flinch, wearing a blank face, even as the rain dropped close to his eyes.

The next thing he did was raise the sword up in front of him sluggishly, pointing it at the man as he drew nearer with no notion of this sword in front of him.

The man came to this realization in just a nick of time and was halted by shock, right in front of the tip of his blade, struck by disbelief, leaving him frozen in that spot.

James did not seem to be paying any attention to this man, still wearing the blank face, keeping his eyes to the ground. His next move was of his left hand, holding it out, expecting the man to comply and hand over the diamond to him.

"Wh-when did, how did-," the man stuttered with a shaking voice.

James's response scared the man even more and all he did was raise his eyes to his face, and right there, the man felt himself helpless, staring right back into his eyes, intimidated. He did what was expected of him and reached out, placing the diamond in his hand.

Just as he did, both Daniel and Jake appeared from behind.

At first, Jake took it upon himself to apprehend the man by pushing him aside and grabbing him by the chest. He did not resist at all, instead he glued his sights to Jake, and looked at him as if he were a ghost.

Jake turned to James and was also confused by his lack of movement and blank expression but glad to see that the diamond was in his hand.

Daniel made his way passed them both, up to James to investigate his current state.

Jake removed the hood from over this man's head. He was just some old fellow in his forties, "Who are you!" He interrogated.

The man's jaw just shook and glanced over at James again.

Jake gave him a violent shake, "Who are you?"

Daniel gave him a nudge on the shoulder, "James?"

No response came from him.

Both the man and Jake took notice and watched.

Daniel tried a little harder, "James!" He raised his voice, "James!"

At that last shout, James regained his conscious self, looking confused as to where he was, also panting, out of breath.

"What happened?" he asked, trying to assess his surroundings before realizing he had the diamond in his hand, "How did I-," he shook his head trying to clear his mind.

"Answer the question," Jake returned to the man.

"I-I'm just a poor old man, nothing more," he replied, stumbling over his words.

Jake did not want this man present anymore, before he finds out the diamonds are not just diamonds, "I don't want to see your face ever again," he said shoving the man hard, throwing him into the dirt, allowing him to make a run for it.

Daniel looked around and noticed the absence of guards that he thought were supposed to be out patrolling and looking out for criminals. He did, however, see the bright side to this, now they did not have to answer any questions about their diamonds.

"Let's head on back inside," Jake instructed starting in the direction.

James struggled to walk and had Daniel help him keep his balance, but something then caught his eye. Laying on the floor was a piece of paper, still dry, suggesting that it had just found its way there.

Daniel picked it up and unfolded it, "Jake," he called, "I found something."

Jake came back to him, "What is it?" He spoke grumpily.

It was an A5 piece of paper with a bird inked on it.

"Hey, I've seen that before," James said, "That's-," his mind searched for the right answer.

Jake took the paper and upon looking at it, he remained silent for a moment and looked around for the presence of the old man he had just let go.

He was nowhere to be seen.

"This is the symbol of the Dead Crow," he said.

Upon their return to the inn, their feet soiled by the mud, and mildly drenched from their long exposure to the drizzle, they found Mark busy setting up the tables and chairs with Bertha and her mother, the owner of the inn.

"Were you able to get it?" Mark asked putting his work to a stop.

Jake nodded in return.

"What happened to the thief?" Bertha's mom asked.

"He got away," Jake replied, "Does anyone else know about this?"

She shook her head, "We are the only people here, for some odd reason, nobody else rented out a room today besides you, not even the regulars," she explained walking over to the door and locking it.

"Strange," Jake said handing over the piece of paper to her, "But also understandable."

She was surprised, "The Dead Crow... you mean to say..."

Jake nodded, "Go warm yourselves up," he instructed Daniel and James.

Bertha's mom folded the piece of paper, "I don't understand... what do they want?"

"I don't know."

CHAPTER 6

A blind man?

The next morning started off really early for this group, still being the only ones to be staying at the inn. Starting so very early was no problem at all after the incident experienced. Sleep was one of the last things on their minds.

After their ill rest, they got themselves ready for the new day and it was off to a really silent start as well. No one was well enough to mention the Dead Crow. Jake being the one most worried about the group, bothering him about it was not a good idea right now.

Bertha and her mom, Mabel, were already up, preparing in advance for the first customers to pop in when the outside was a little more lit up.

James walked up to the only window in the room and peaked through the curtains. The sound of rain had muted but the clouds were still present, probably blocking away the sun, if it had already risen.

As he turned his gaze to the streets, he could now notice the presence of the guards, that had decided to stay away during the night.

He turned away from the window, "Hey-," he paused just as he realized he was the only one in the room.

He exited with haste, shutting the door behind him and joined with the rest in front.

The hearth in the centre was put out and Mark was busy helping Bertha refill it with more fresh firewood. Daniel and Jake were seated at a table close to the counter whilst Mabel moved up and down packing something together.

"You know, I've just noticed something," James said walking up to them, "There were no guards posted out yesterday… is that something they do around here or was it because of the rain?"

"I also noticed that yesterday, it was just us and that man," Daniel added.

"It was probably just a yesterday thing," Jake replied.

"He's right," Mabel agreed, "Normally the amount of guards posted is doubled in the night by the jarl just to ensure nothing bad happens."

"Yes, someone must have seen you with these diamonds and tipped off the Dead Crow about it."

"Wait," Mark dusted his hands, "You said the Dead Crow were the good people, all justice and stuff."

"I did not say that they are in the wrong," Jake replied, "The one who tipped them may have added an extra detail or two."

"Where will you be heading now?" Mabel asked wrapping up some food.

"Our road is still true, we are heading to the city of magic."

"Well, I hope your journey there is safe and this incident does not spread because the Dead Crow love that place," she said handing them the food.

"Thank you," Jake said picking up a batch, "And goodbye."

The others said their farewells as well and took whatever was left on the counter for them.

They stepped out into a cold morning breeze which forced them to hood themselves for extra warmth.

With Jake leading the way, they followed him onto the main road and headed up the same direction they had run, chasing the thief.

The streets were already prowling with people getting ready to open up their businesses and set up their stalls.

The walk to the other side of town was not so long, they were able to bear with it, walking against the cold wind. Jake lead them to some stables located at the edge of town where he had dropped off his horse and carriage.

Just outside the house, sat a man on the bench of his porch, dressed for the winter, he sat with his arms crossed and head bowed down, showing mostly his short afro.

Jake came to a stop in front of the man, "Good morning," he greeted cheerfully.

The man looked up at him and upon recognition, stood up from his bench and greeted back with as much enthusiasm, "Up so early, I reckon this is not much of a social visit, bringing the rest of your party here as well."

"I'm afraid not Sam, here to pick up my horses and be heading," he replied.

Sam made his way down the stairs carrying a ring of keys, "Why so keen on leaving this town?" He asked, "Was the experience unwelcoming?"

"Oh no no no, not at all," he replied, "We're just in a hurry, taking these young ones to school, a new term is about to begin."

"Well then, won't you please follow me, don't want to be the reason you are late," he chuckled.

Sam lead them around back to a large barn which he unlocked with his keys and allowed for Jake to bring out both horses. With his help steering the other out to another area close to a wooden fence where some of the carriages were placed, he attached the horses to Jake's.

Jake lead them out front to the main road where James and the others could get on and placed the food and water right beside them.

"Always good to see you Jake."

"Same to you Sam... same to you."

"You know... these brief visits make me wonder what it is you're up to."

"What can I say, I'm a busy man."

"You couldn't have said it better, farewell, and safe journeys," he said waving at the boys as well.

Jake started the carriage, "I'll see you when I see you."

Sam returned to his porch bench when they had moved on for some distance.

Making it passed the gate was easy, no questions were asked or any checks conducted for any leaving travelers.

As they headed on into the main road, James watched as the guards continue to socialize and consume their early breakfast, but just in front of the gate, standing right in the middle, was something that made his heart skip a beat and his eyes bulge out.

It was the little girl again, the same one from the old ladies basement.

She just stared up at him, carrying the same face as before.

James was paralyzed again, unable to take his eyes off her as the carriage rocked on the tiny stones that got in its way.

The little girl's face grew a faint smile, she raised her hand and gave James a slight wave before fading away with the wind.

Even though she had faded, James could not stop staring at that spot as he spiraled into a chamber of many thoughts, trying to figure out his own reasoning behind this.

This is the second time she has shown up, which could mean that this was actually real... and now she waved at him which kind of put James in a position of possible outcomes that may have already played out.

He remember the words she had spoken the day before, she had asked him for help. *Was this help supposed to have been carried out already?* And she was now saying her goodbyes because they were now leaving the town. He really did hope this was not the case, even though he had no idea what it was she wanted help with anyway, being a ghost and all.

Daniel, who was sitting across from him noticed and stared in the same direction he stared, only to see the town slowly start to shrink away as they moved forward, "You looking a little pale James, what are you seeing?"

James snapped out of his little daze, "Oh, nothing," he replied, "Just the cold."

Daniel decided to move on to something else, "Jake, how fast does news travel in this time?

"Why the question?"

"I mean, if these Dead Crow people continue to look for us, since they saw the diamonds..."

"Oh, quite quickly actually... at first I was betting on it being let go just because they thought we were small time thieves but since James pulled that little stunt, things may just get a little complicated."

James sighed, "I didn't know I was going to use it, the thing activated itself."

"We can't afford for such an incident to occur again... which is why we are going to start uncovering their abilities today," he announced.

The small town from which they left this morning had long since passed their line of sight. Now finding themselves surrounded by nature, which mostly consisted of a majority of grass. The landscape was mostly flat, with a few ups and downs in some areas.

Jake had kept to the main road heading in the north direction, very rarely passing by any turns that had sign boards showing people which directions to head off to.

The sky still remained covered at this time, but they guessed that it was about midday now. The only change in weather was the wind, blowing stronger that before.

After some time, Jake had decided to take the carriage of the main road, the horses pulling it through the tall grass, doing their best to avoid any giant rocks that may sabotage their ride.

The terrain was a lot bumpier than the actual road so the passengers had to keep ahold to the sides of the carriage for balance until it was time to jump off. This happened a short distance inland.

"Alright, this is where we get off," Jake said jumping from his seat into the plain.

He continued on away from the road

James, Mark and Daniel jumped out back of the carriage, relieved at the fact they were now able to stretch their legs from the hours of sitting.

Seeing a different view for once had put a smile on James's face, an area of great proportion containing nothing for miles.

They followed Jake for a few minutes till he came to a stop, he scanned the area in case of any human activity, just to be sure they weren't being watched by anyone.

"If this is the training place, we could have stopped an hour ago," Mark spoke, looking at his surroundings, "I see no difference."

"Well, we are an hour furtherer away from Lonestar," Daniel replied, "The furtherer the better."

"I was just saying."

All three of them came to a stop in front of Jake, standing in a row awaiting instruction. Waited for their first instructions from him as they just watched him continue to scan out the area.

Mark was the first to lose interest in his random gestures and found more by staring up into the covered sky, trying to figure out the direction in which the clouds were moving and at what speed, "It's going to be cloudy for the rest of the day... by the looks of it."

Daniel's attention drifted with the passing wind and began to find the activities of a butterfly more interesting than the current situation he was stuck in. He did not want to bother Jake with whatever he was doing.

James on the other hand had grown quite impatient, noticing Mark and Daniel's drift, just like Jake's, he felt he was not doing something, he became the very first to say anything, "What must we do?"

"Wait for instruction," he replied.

James frowned and said nothing after that.

After a minute that took hours, James had seated himself in a lazy position next to Mark who was also sitting busy getting hypnotized by the motion of the clouds whilst Daniel kept an eye on the butterfly he had taken interest to.

Jake finally stopped with what he was doing and turned his attention to them, "Okay, we can begin now."

Mark released himself from the dream and stood up.

James did the same and leaned closer to him, "I don't think it takes that long to check a perimeter of a grassland, do you?"

"Shh, he's an old man, we have to work at his pace," he whispered back, getting to his feet.

Daniel came back to the party, "Okay, we're ready."

Jake held his hands behind his back and started pacing, "Okay," he started, "This should be easy to get off the boat, first to give you a brief notion of your abilities, Mark you can generate shields, Daniel, your ability allows you to levitate or fly and James, you can move really, really fast."

James was hoping for a better definition.

Jake continued, "Now, the way these artifacts work is very simple, a bit too simple actually... through your minds, in thought, but your bodies may be slower to adapt to their abilities which is why you may suffer some minor setbacks as you begin to control them with your will, practice always makes for better results," he paused for a moment, "Now, by my intuition, this is going to play a little more differently than when they activated themselves and since you are beginners at this, you may need to perform some gestures to prepare you bodies for the diamond's activation."

James put his hand up as if he were in a class.

"Yes James."

"Why do they activate themselves?"

He gave it a moment before replying, "That much is unclear to me," he continued, "Okay, moving on, since they are irresponsive to your minds at the moment, here are some examples that can help you get started," he faced James, "Trying running on the spot for a few seconds till you feel something," he turned to Daniel, "You may need to jump very high before anything decides to happen and Mark, yours may require a little more brain power."

James giggled which made Mark a little angry, "Shut up."

"Anyway, Mark, just hold your hands out beside you and try to generate what you can... give yourselves some space and give it a try."

"I'm seeing ourselves look like idiots in third-person view," Daniel mumbled, taking a few steps away from the others.

Each of them began with a few warm up stretches and exercises while Jake stood there mentoring.

Daniel started with his jumps, at first they were relatively small, only because of how stupid and senseless this felt to him, nothing was happening, no different feeling whatsoever. James started off with a small jog on the spot which slowly progressed into a run that continued until he was almost out of breath, noticing no difference in the speed that he was running at.

Nothing transpired on the end of Mark either, he just stood there with his hands apart, waiting for something to materialize at the end of his palms.

"Well, that didn't work," James concluded.

"It won't activate right off the bat, just keep trying until you at least start to feel something."

"Like what?" Mark asked.

"That, I don't know, each diamond has its own properties," he replied, "Now again."

Before anyone could continue with their little training session, they heard a man's voice, "Good afternoon," it was a voice that sounded lively.

Jake froze in shock whilst the others turned towards the source.

The man just stood a few metres in front of them, tall, with long black hair reaching his shoulders with dyed red strips in no particular pattern, it was not too messy or straight either. On his face he wore a red-brown cloth over his eyes tied at the back of his head, hidden by his hair. He wore a black sleeveless trench coat that was outlined in red... as for his bare arms, he had them bandaged right up to his palms, bearing a tint of brown from dirt. He fitted on dark brown leather boots and wore black pants that looked to be red with paint on the bottom half.

He looked cool to the three boys, but they did not show it.

Jake got a little angry, "What is it you want?"

The man gave a slow sarcastic laugh in return, "You have no manners... where are they?"

James felt he should just greet the man, to be a little more respectful, but Jake had something to say, closing the opportunity.

"What do you want?" He asked for a second time.

The man looked surprised, even with half of his expressions covered, "Oooo, old man," he giggled, "I am respecting you, as my elder," he bowed, "You know what, it may seem we started on the wrong foot," he displayed his right foot, "Let's just start again, I don't detest this hostility I'm sensing here, I just want to meet the new."

James remained there, just watching as the man tried to be polite to them, whilst Jake over here came across a bit more aggressive, wanting nothing to do with him as if they knew each other, maybe with some ill history. It could be true, after all, Jake did mention that he was from this time.

The strange man decided to pick it up from the beginning again, "Good afternoon," he greeted with a smile.

Jake kept his mouth shut.

The man started to feel a little down.

"Afternoon," Daniel greeted back.

James and Mark followed after.

Their greetings brought upon a cheerful smile on his face, "Thank you, that was all I wanted in return, you make me feel happy, knowing there's a generation of good people still to come."

All three of them remained silent, made weird by the words he just said but at least quite happy that he was not at all hostile.

He turned his attention once again to the old man, "Jaaaake... I still have not received any form of acknowledgement from you."

Okay, James was right, in thought, on the fact that these two might know each other.

"You said you wanted to meet the new, you have exchanged greetings haven't you, now you can leave."

The man's jaw dropped in shock which slowly turned into a chuckle, "Okay," he started to pace, "You listened well, but that's not the only reason I am here, I want to ask you this question again," he stopped, "What on earth are you doing?" he asked, "Now I hope that this time you will provide me with a proper answer," he smiled and stood straight with his hands behind his back.

"I will tell you again, what I am doing is none of your concern, go do your job instead of sticking your nose in other people's business."

The man pulled a straight face as some strands of his hair brushed across his face. He smiled again, turning his attention to the boys again, "Young boys, apologies for this, but I do thank you for greeting me, It's nice to meet new people," he bowed his head, "Now... I see you lot have these strange artifacts, can you tell me about them?"

"Enough of this!" Jake shouted, taking a few steps forward, "You are not wanted here."

The man took a step back and apologized, "I'm sorry... it clearly seems my presence is ill," he smiled, "In this beautiful place, but fun while it lasted, it was nice meeting you lot, always a pleasure meeting new people."

To James, this man did not seem too bad at all. He just wanted was to greet them. The only strange thing he did notice though was his knowledge of these artifacts, having not seen them at all. Another thing he could not wrap is head around was the cloth over his eyes, *was he... a blind man?*

The man turned away from them and pointed at an emblem on his back, "Remember this symbol, I always show it to those who do not know me."

The symbol on his trench coat was of a large circular bomb with a big red smiley face on it with sharp teeth and crosses for eyes. The bombs ignition point had a spark on the end.

"I bid you farewell, may our paths cross again," he said throwing a small object onto the ground which exploded into a black smoke that rapidly engulfed him and blew away.

He was gone.

"That was strange, magic?" Mark nodded to himself, "He looked strange as well, I liked it."

Both Daniel and James agreed.

"Do you think he's blind?" Mark asked.

"A blind man?" Daniel repeated, a tad bit surprised.

"Yes, I mean, he has a cloth over his eyes."

James turned back to Jake, "What do you think or know?"

"I think we should leave and I know that it is someone you cannot trust," he replied grumpily, starting towards the carriage.

The others followed.

"Do you know him?" Daniel asked.

"Yes."

Mark stepped in with a question that seemed to be bothering him, "Is he blind or something?"

"You should have asked him that while he was here," he replied climbing onto the front seat, "Come on, let's go and don't ask any more questions about him."

They obeyed and stopped with the nose picking, climbed on back and left

CHAPTER 7

The City of Magic

Two days had passed since their encounter with the strange man out in the open fields and have traveled with haste since, keeping on the main road, posing as your average traveler.

Today was cloudless and they had now reached the outskirts of their destination, a forest that seemed to stretch out for miles in both directions and in the centre, on the main road, a path leading right through it.

They traveled down the path swiftly till they reached the other end where they could now see the high walls of the city.

Jake came to a stop next to a barn located on the inner edge of the forest. The barn was placed near a small wooden house where they all spotted a man seated just outside on a stool, fast asleep.

"Wow," Daniel looked ahead, "A whole city surrounded by a forest."

"And large walls," Mark added.

Jake jumped off his seat and walked over to the man in the stool. He gave him a shake on the shoulder and woke him up.

The man jerked up, "Huh, what's happening," he said shaking his head, getting to his feet as quickly as he could.

He was a short old fellow with a beard to his chest, wearing brown pants tucked in his boots and a white shirt.

The old man turned his sights to the carriage in front of him, and wondered why the passengers were still onboard. He then turned to the one who woke him up. The man was surprised, "Hey!" He greeted cheerfully, "Jake, it's good to see you... again."

"It's good to see you to, Burne," he greeted back.

"My my, you really do travel back and forth," he turned his sights to the carriage again, "It seems you have some boys this time."

James and the other got off their carriages to greet him.

"Yes, it's a new bunch, James, Mark and Daniel," he introduced.

They exchanged handshakes, "I'm Burne Baxter."

"Well, I'm afraid I can't make much of a conversation today, they start school soon," Jake explained.

"No need, I will just look after your carriage and horses till you return," he said.

"Thank you."

Now they stood in front of the gate, all in a straight line as if they were in the army. In that moment of silence that they were caught in. The boys were breathless at the sight of the massive gate that stood tall and strong in front of them like some sought of immovable object. It's sheer height brought to their attention that something was hidden behind it and the walls that seemed to stretch out for miles in both directions. It was the gates design itself that removed every bit of vocab from them. An indescribable beauty of different, carefully molded carvings of statues and probably the first bit of magic they have ever seen in the flesh. There were hovering balls of light that shone brightly in different colours, five to be exact, and quite faded in the sunlight. One green, one purple, another held the colour red and the last two, blue and yellow.

Each one of the orbs were transparent and inside containing a symbol.

The gate as a whole had a base colour of black and a bit of gold to allow some of the more interesting parts of it stand out and reflect beams of sunlight that could be spotted from beyond the forest surrounding the city. It was obvious the gate was for show, symbolizing the wealth of the city.

Jake didn't seem too interested in the gate, he'd been here before, he was the first to take a step forward and stood closest to the gate, "Hello!" he shouted at the gate as if it were a living thing.

The others just looked at him with concern, but there faces changed as soon as they heard a mechanical construct sound come from the gate as it slowly started to open up inward.

Jake waited for the gate to be fully opened before taking another step. The others did the same, following Jake's every move in this new landmark.

On the other side, stood what looked to be a city guard, dressed in shiny silver armor holding a pike about twice his height. Most of his face was hidden by the helmet he wore, but he didn't seem to be where the attention was, it was the man that stood next to him, dressed in old robes just as Jake did, and old… about the same age as Jake. Though… he at least wore a welcoming smile on his face.

"Welcome back Jake!" He greeted him with open arms.

"It's good to see you again," he greeted back.

As James, Mark and Daniel stood there in silence, watching, the thought came to them. *How do old people all know each other.* Even the guards just stood there and watched, probably waiting to do their jobs. But no, the two old men continued to exchange words.

"It's been three months since your last visit," The old man pointed out, "And I see you have brought three this time."

"Yes, yes, another bunch, interested in learning about magic," Jake replied turning his gaze to them, "Boys, this is Galvani," He introduced him.

They greeted in return, with a handshake.

This time? The words echoed in James's head. Jake has been here, not three months ago with another group of people joining the school. To his mind, he thought maybe it's another group from his present time. Probably bearing their own artifacts with a unique ability, that thought alone got him excited. But then he wondered, *how many times does this old man jump through time as if it were some kind of sport?* In school, though magic was forbidden, they were told a thing or two, but time travelling did not exist.

It was all very puzzling. A few kids from the present year are now walking about in some old century with magical Diamonds that are being hunted down by some justice organization with the word *Dead* in it and probably by that apparently blind man with a cloth over his face. None of it made sense and on top of it all, Jake, the source of it all, didn't even try to explain anything.

All these muddled up thoughts brought up a terrible memory of the near past. A thought that jump started his heart and made him feel a bit dizzy. The ghost he had now seen twice, in the previous town. A memory he was still compelled to keep within for he wasn't too sure if he was going crazy, but to be safe he scanned the area for anything.

His endless train of thought was brought to a stop by a small nudge on the shoulder by Mark, "Come on, it's time to go."

Galvani seemed to be their escort, walking side by side with Jake, Speaking as more than just acquaintances. As if brothers from a young age.

James and the rest just followed close behind, but not too close.

The guards had finally received their chance to seal the gate again.

They walked into a gravel road, that was bordered by fields of grass, and a bit further on both sides, you could see farmlands with a few farmers tending to their isolated farm houses with windmills, barns and carriages surrounded by cattle forever grazing on the endless fields of grass, as well as a few shady trees stationed at random places.

Just ahead you could see a cluster of wooden houses, near the main road. This was not at all the great gate entrance brought to mind.

"Well, this wasn't what I expected," Daniel said, "Big shiny glowing gate, hiding a bunch of cows and wooden house."

"Same here," Mark agreed.

One thing that did surprise them was the size of what seemed to be endless plains, on the left and the right, and ahead, beyond the little wooden village, they could see another wall, one a bit higher than the outer wall.

"I think that's where we're going," James said pointing at the wall, "Maybe that's where the goodies are."

"I'm kind of excited, magic school," Daniel said picking up his pace a bit and immediately slowing it again when he realized the others didn't correspond.

"Yeah," James agreed, "No more history lessons about what magic did or used to be, we going to be studying it and using it."

Mark didn't seem too thrilled about it, "Eh, we just going to be shooting fireballs or something," he dampened the mood, "And history, we cannot escape, all history has history."

As they travelled up the road and drew closer to anything different. Something reflected the light of the sun and shone brightly in the corner of Mark's eye. He spotted the object and judging by its reflective powers he presumed it valuable. It lay near the grass amongst the rocks and pebbles. The item had the effect of a light bulb.

Mark's sudden change in direction got the other two interested and both spotted the object as well.

He picked up the object. It wasn't a coin as anyone would presume. It was larger.

James looked over his shoulder, "What is it?"

"No idea."

The golden object was the size of his palm with a blue ribbon attached to it, it took the form of an amulet that contained something inside, probably even more valuable than its golden shell. The amulet had a symbol on the surface of what seemed to be the top. One they didn't recognize at all.

Mark brought it to his ear and gave it a shake but nothing generated any sound. He then looked for a place that would open it up.

He tried to unseal, using all his strength but it was no use, the amulet was sealed tighter than a clam.

"Do you think we should take it?" Daniel asked, "A souvenir,"

James gave the amulet a thought filled look, "I don't think so," he replied, "Remember, we are in a magic world, and better yet, a magic city."

"What's your point?" Mark asked, his eyes still glued to the beauty of the item.

"Could be a cursed object," He replied, "And that symbol looks very…unsettling, that dot looks like an eye."

Mark didn't want to part with it, now that it was in his hand.

"Hey!" Jake shouted from the distance.

Mark jumped at the unexpected call and accidentally dropped the amulet.

James and Daniel had already started jogging toward them. Mark kicked it closer to the grass, really disappointed he'd decided to leave it behind. What James had just said to him about the amulet was kind of making sense to him. And carrying around an evil amulet was not on his wish list.

"Don't be falling behind now," Jake said, "What caught your attention?"

Before Daniel could be some honest savior of the day, Mark spoke over him, "Some messed up looking creature," He put on the most unconvincing smile, "Never seen it before."

Daniel kept silent and let it play out. James went on a supported his lie.

Jake gave them an untrusting look, but it seemed he had better things to do, or speak about so he let it slide, "Okay," he turned and continued to walk with the old man.

"You young boys shouldn't touch or get too near something you don't know of," Galvani instructed, "Could be the cause of you death, and that's just sad."

They all agreed and promised not to do so.

James was yet met with another question, *how was it possible that Jake and Galvani missed something so shiny?* But then again, he and Daniel were on the same boat so it wasn't something he wanted to dwell on. Lying about it was probably the right thing to do, for a selfish person, but again, the truth would have brought upon more confusion anyway and Jake wasn't going to explain a word to them.

They were finally out of the sea of grass and now entering the little village. It died for a moment as soon as they were noticed. A lot of the people stopped with their business just to glare at the boys like some prisoners. Jake, on the other hand, didn't receive the silent treatment.

The town was actually larger than expected, accompanied not only by the people's residences, but small shops, smiths and an inn was even in the mix.

The people seemed a bit too interested in the boys, as if new comers were a gold coin dropped onto the floor for them.

Keeping away from any eye contact was almost impossible, with eyes from all round. They decided to either give a faint smile and nod, which often had a cold response, or just look at random objects that may seem a bit more interesting. The walk was more awkward than an unsuccessful chat with your crush, maybe not that much. Though at least some people didn't care about their presence and it was not as though the stalkers were up in their faces rubbing it in.

Midtown wasn't so bad, where most of the shops were located and where business was live. Everyone continued as normal, nobody cared, so they felt more blended here. It was quite crowded, with people bartering from stalls and making conversation.

It was at that moment, when the boys realized they hadn't consumed anything since breakfast and it was right about lunch now.

As it was just the beginning of their hunger, they felt it best to wait for a suitable destination before eating anything.

It wasn't long before they were passed the town and were now climbing up a road that lead to the next wall which wasn't too far a distance, about a hundred metres in length. The road was now made of grey cement bricks and decorated with small pot plants and flowers.

This second entrance had no gate and only a few guards posted at it and one robed, holding a staff. From where they currently were, you could see that buildings lay beyond. The beginning of the real city, away from villages and strange people. They made their way up a slightly slanted hill and to the entrance. The doorway stood thinner and much taller than the man gates.

As they passed through the entrance, the road turned a slight and started heading down hill. The path which they were on was the largest and passed through the centre of the city. It was way more crowded, they could hear the chatters of hundreds of people going about their day.

"From this point on, it's the great Market District," Jake declared as he started down into the crowds followed by Galvani.

As for the new comers, their attention jumped from place to place trying to take everything in. What stood out the most in this marvelous place was the people's attire, unique and magical from one person to the next, fitted with many fabrics and patterns sewed in different colours, most especially the women's clothing. They added to the magical aspect of a Magic City. Though the pointy hat business which they imagined they would see a lot of, was rare.

"The people who designed these clothes must be legend," James came out with a compliment.

"Yes, yes, this city is known for its apparel around most of Maramel, although, most people think it's just the work of a spell rather than the quality of craftsmanship," Jake replied.

This time, James and the others remained close to their escorts, it would be easy to lose your way in this district.

It was quite clear they were in the Market District of the city. On both sides of every street were small shops with exceptions of a few that looked to be large businesses, all selling both inside and out for advertising purposes. People stood outside some shops shouting out specials and inviting people to browse their wears, some traders preferred bartering their goods outside, selling small trinkets and everyday goods.

The place was packed with stores, yet each had something different to offer, most of which our new party didn't know of yet. Many that they could make out were the Jewelry stores, clothing shops and ones that supplied household goods. There was a medical bay around one of the corners but this was just one of the many streets that connect this district.

At least there were also quite a few things they could recognize from all the gaming and history they had learned at school, the potions and poisons of an alchemy shop they passed was of some familiarity.

The buildings were four stories high at most, stock piled with many windows and balconies. The height was slowly reducing in number as they were leading out of the main areas of the District.

James couldn't help but notice the similarity in this time and the present, the neglecting of the unfortunate people whom had next to nothing to their names, they hid in the alleyways that were dark and abandoned, mostly used to pile up trash. This city was indeed magical to everyone who arrives to be bewitched by its wonders, but if you take a closer look, you will notice similarities found everywhere, horrible ones.

"At least we're out of the most crowded chaos," Galvani spoke in relief.

The light of the sun was flickering as the scattered clouds passed under it. The wind had begun to tire and calm down a bit and the day was becoming a bit too warm for their robes. The city wasn't heavily guarded by the city soldiers, only a few were posted around every corner. Some patrolled in groups of about four.

James was hoping to see a few of them holding staves, "Do the guards make use of magic?"

Jake nodded, "Yes, but very few of them are needed as most people here don't really use magic," He explained, "You'll see them wearing a cloaked uniform and obviously with their staves."

Knowing what he was looking for made it easier for him to spot the prey. But could only find two, posted in the same place enjoying themselves, not worrying much about their surroundings. If people don't often use magic then their job must be really simple.

They travelled a while longer, down the main road from whence they came, till they reached a massive building to their right entitled with a large sign : Marridor Library.

The building looked the size of a warehouse from the front with high wooden Double-doors that had their own beauty in craftsmanship. The indoors were carpeted in blue.

"We're here," Jake announced, climbing the few steps and making his way in.

Mark was a bit interest in the doors at the entrance, but all excitement and interest drained away as soon as he sighted the first book, "Wait, we're in a library."

"That's a sharp eye you got there Mark," Galvani said.

Mark stared down into the distance, between two bookshelves and didn't see an end from where he stood. The wall on the other side was a bit far from the entrance, showing that it was more of a labyrinth of endless shelves.

A lot of the sounds of everyday seemed to mute away inside this palace of books.

Before Jake and Galvani could go on and do whatever they had planned in this library, they got rid of the boys, asking them nicely to explore the library.

"Well," James took a deep breath, "This should be more interesting than the average library."

"Yeah, I'm actually quite excited," Daniel agreed.

James and Daniel didn't seem to mind at all, they headed in their separate directions drifting to their own interests. Mark wanted to complaining about the request but then spotted a notice board to the far left side of the library.

Like the apparel of the people and the designs of the gates and doorways of this city, the books were treated no different. Each book had a specific design and vibe to it, each one was designed with value and time. Some of which having 3D covers and variations of texture.

James found himself admiring the book covers over the contents that lay within. He just picked a shelf and went down the row, also keeping an eye out for any topics or titles that may compel him to read a little bit about.

It was about thirty minutes into the exploration of these books when he had begun to grow a tad bit bored with his cover observation. He was now just paging through them, only noticing the really good illustrations. While he paged through one filled with weapons and shields, someone caught the corner of his eye. He turned away from the old pages and look down the aisle and there he saw her, a young teenage girl that looked into the pages of some book. He was compelled by her beauty, her long straight brunette hair, laying gently over her shoulders with a bit of a side fringe. She wore a purple sweater, navy blue jeans and black ankle boots.

James had this 'Dear in headlights' look and it would be kind of a weird stare if she caught him in the act, but he couldn't bring himself to ignore the bright light. She was paging through a book she had just picked up and now headed to the nearest table that was positioned between the aisles, before the beginning of the next set of shelves.

She looked up.

James never moved so fast before, changing his gaze and burying it in the book he forgot he was holding. His heart raced, hoping she didn't catch him, his hands even picked up a bit of a shake as he turned the pages.

She turned away and headed around the shelf and out of sight.

He decided to go in the same direction as she was going and probably say something to her. He abandoned the book he was holding and went down the aisle, stepping around the many ladders that were used to get to the books that stood beyond reach.

He made the turn and entered into a section of the library that had a lot of tables in one area, it looked to be the centre of the warehouse. The area was pretty crowded, with people going about reading and bringing books to more piles they had created, none of it distracted him from his current task. He began scanning the area, jumping from one person to the next. His scan resulted unsuccessful. He widened his gaze, looking at the farther tables and it also ended in vein. His heart sank as he turned around, seeking to return to his book, "Woah!" He jumped.

The girl was standing right behind him. For how long, he did not know.

"Hi," she greeted him with a smile.

James was confused, but more happy, "Hey," He greeted back, "How did –,"

Her eyes were a caramel and green colour, and her skin so fair, accompanied with a few freckles on her nose and cheeks.

"How did I get behind you?" She completed it

James gave a slight nod. Standing there, feeling as cold as winter.

"Why were you staring at me?" She asked him with a serious glare.

Okay, she did catch him after all. He couldn't answer her question honestly, an apology always does the trick, "Sorry," he uttered out.

"I'm just joking," She giggle, "And how I did that little trick there, Jake taught it too me."

Jake, him again, James thought to himself. *Is he some kind of icon or something to these people. Anyways*, he couldn't remain in his thoughts this time, not with this girl in front of him.

"You know Jake?" He blurted out

She nodded in return, "Everybody knows him for some odd reason," She said, "Anyways, I'm Mia," She held out her right hand.

James shook her hand, "I'm James," he introduced himself.

"Nice to meet you, James," she said with a lively smile.

Mia moved closer to him, with their hands still locked, it made him feel...a lot of different, indescribable emotions.

She whispered to him, "James hmm, what an interesting name, oh, and that's a nice looking diamond you got there," she said, letting go of his hand and walking off, going back to the aisles.

James realized a bit late that she had mentioned the diamond. He quickly checked to see if it had somehow magically reappeared above his robe again. It wasn't, luckily, which raised the question of how she was able to tell he had a diamond or was it another magic trick that Jake taught her?

This was quite confusing in the long run, despite the fact that he knows her, that just made him feel happy inside. But the mentioning of the diamond worried him a bit and decided to cast away the thought by continuing with his book browsing.

It was about an hour now and James had decided it best to go looking for Jake and Galvani up front where he last saw them.

Upon his arrival, he saw her again, Mia, she was making conversation with Jake.

He made his way over to them, "Hello Jake, Hi again Mia," He greeted.

"Ah, I see you have met already, I was just about to introduce you, Mark and Daniel," He looked around, "Where are they?"

Mia was surprised, "There's more?"

"Yes," He replied leaving, "Now where are those two," He muttered to himself.

James turned to Mia, "So you're from the present as well?"

"Yes," she replied, "One of the fourteen I suppose."

The puzzle pieces of this matter fit perfectly, she knew about the diamonds all along.

James lowered his voice and couldn't help but ask, "So what's your power?"

"What?" She sounded confused.

James gave her a concerned look, "The diamond, your diamond power,"

"Ohhhh," She realized, he face quickly turned disappointed, "I didn't get one."

"Wait what?" James was surprised, "Jake said there are more diamonds and people."

"Yeah, I heard the same thing, but when it came to receiving mine, he said it was lost or something and that he would find it, just before he lured me out and sent me to this time," she explained, "He just told me to join the school and take Alteration."

Hmm, that didn't sound suspicious or insanely odd at all, "Sorry to hear that, sounds a bit odd though."

She shrugged, "It is what it is, he seems a bit old to be jumping back and forth in time, I'm not surprised he lost them."

James nodded, "That's exactly what I think."

"So what's your power?" She asked, leaning against the counter.

"Oh, I guess you can I'm The Flash," He replied with confidence.

"Nice, super speed."

"Yup, pretty much," he replied, "But I don't know how to use it yet, it made me fail a history test," He shook his head, "but we cheated so I guess I got what I deserved."

Mia Laughed, "Off course then, if you cheated,"

"I still have no idea why we have powers or time jumps but I'm not complaining, just going with it," he said, "But the last time I used it I blanked out, we were trying to catch someone from a group called the Dead Crow, they tried to steal one of the diamonds, but I saved the day," He boasted, "Unintentionally, off course."

"Impressive," She complimented, "The only weird thing that has happened to me on the way here was the person we met, crazy guy that covered his eyes and wore bandages around his arms, also had red and black hair," she described, "He was strange."

"Oh, so you met the crazy blind dude?" James said surprised, "With the smiley face bomb on his back."

Jake came back with Mark and Daniel accompanied by Galvani, whom had also wondered off into the depths of the library. There was a quick introduction, to make Mark, Daniel and Mia aware of each other and headed to the entrance of the library.

It was starting to get a bit chilled again, as the sun began to leave them for the day, now hiding itself behind the buildings of the city. The streets were still packed to the brim with people, still going about the afternoon.

They headed further away from the main district, where most of the shops were, to a less crowded area of the place.

"So what powers did you get from your diamonds?" Mia asked anxiously.

"Please reframe from the word 'diamond' Mia," Jake instructed, "People love valuable things."

"Right... sorry," She apologized, still unhappy that he didn't give her a one, she turned to Mark and Daniel, "Anyway, what's your powers?"

Daniel was the first to reply, "Mine is supposedly supposed to make me fly, levitate, something along those lines," He wasn't too sure, since he had only levitated just a few feet from the ground.

Mark's reply was neither confused or exciting since he didn't really correspond with the ability he received, "I protect, make shields or something."

"They activate by accident," James explained, "We can't control them."

Daniel asked her the same question James did earlier, out of curiosity.

She replied with silence for a moment and turned to Jake who was ahead again, with Galvani, "A certain someone lost it."

"Wait, you lost it?" Mark began to laugh.

"No, Jake lost it," She specified.

James and Daniel didn't reply to that, only Mark, adding a bit more negativity to the plate, "That must suck," He replied.

Mia nodded and sighed, "Yeah, but he taught me a few spells that I've learnt to use."

"We know nothing about magic, if it makes you feel any better," James said trying to cheer her up.

She just hummed in return.

"We're going to a magic school, to learn about magic, we all going to know something about magic," Mark decided to add his bit into the mix.

Everyone ignored his remark and moved on from the topic.

"It's nice to meet people from the same time," Mia said, "The kids here are cool and all but as you may soon see, a little outdated, you may have to blend in a bit."

"Blend in?" Daniel asked himself, "Shouldn't be too hard."

Mark laughed, "We going to be talking to fossils."

"Yeah," Mia agreed, "Just use normal English with them, or you going to have to explain yourself quite a bit."

The one crucial thing that was absent from their presence now, was the life force of all humanity in our present time, which was the great creation of technology, an aspect of our lives that we are unable to live without. Where they resided now had no such thing. No computers, no televisions or our most prized possession, the phone.

Right now it had barely popped up in their heads, I suppose when you replace it with the fantasies of magic and powers we often wish we had, we can start to forget about its presence a bit.

School is a bore to most people in this time, but Mia was giving the exact opposite opinion about this one, having attended a few months already, she enjoyed the unique and magical aspect of it. The others were convinced, a little, they wanted the proof for themselves before getting their hopes too high.

"I assure you, you won't get bored," She continued, "Magic is a good substitute to technology, a tad bit better actually."

"Yeah, I'm kind of liking this new, err, old world so far," James said, "It's something new."

Mia picked up her pace, "Come on, let's catch up."

It was a little while longer before they reached a slightly different area. They had made it to the residential part of the city. A more modern cluster of houses built from brick and grey stone with wood in the necessary places, far different from the village that lay on the outskirts of the inner walls. This area was a bit more expensive.

The road started down the hill again when they had reached this sector.

"Today, you'll be staying at my place," Galvani announced, "And tomorrow u go to school."

It was not long before they reached his house. It was quite the same as every average house in this neighborhood.

Galvani walked up the front porch to the door and searched for the keys in his robe. Upon acquiring them, he opened the door and stepped in, "Come in," He welcomed them.

Everyone was required to wipe their feet on the doormat before entering his place. The interiors were a bit dim with only a few lit candles placed around the room. They entered into a large area, that had both the sitting room and the kitchen off to the one side. Most light came from the sitting area that was lit bright orange by the fire place against the wall that lead up to a chimney and from a small chandelier with a few lit candles. The couches were placed around a carpet with a small round wooden table in the centre and small wooden chairs that were place right in front of the fire and an even smaller square shaped table between them. On the other side of sitting room was a small working table riddled with paper and books and a cupboard beside it and windows letting in light.

The kitchen counter was built against the wall and the table was cleaned, set with cutlery and plates.

The room was warm as none of the windows were opened.

Galvani went into a different room, one of two doors near the kitchen.

Jake ordered James, Mark and Daniel to remove their robes and place them on a random box that was placed on the corner closest to the door.

Mia sunk herself into one of the sofas, it was obvious she had been here before.

She took notice of their attire and laughed, "I see why you wear the robes."

"We woke up wearing these, ok," Mark explained with force.

James examined hers and only realized now that her clothing was modern, something someone would wear in the present time., "Where did you get your clothing?" He asked, "I can tell it's not from this time."

"They're mine, from the present," She replied, "Jake brought them back as well, clothes are a bit expensive around here, these don't really make people go crazy, it's not all trends and stuff, casual clothing is just casual clothing," She explained, "We are only about 200 years back, just before the 100 year shift, according to history."

"Hmm," Mark said, "Hmm," he hummed again, with no words to say. He just wondered what they were to wear as casual clothes.

After having eaten for the night, Galvani there after gave Daniel and Mark pillows and sleeping sponges which they placed between the two couches on the carpet, after removing the table. Mia and James each slept on a couch. It was the best place to sleep for the night, with the fire just a few feet away from them still lit and warming the room.

At first, no one was able to sleep, they just had quiet conversations about random stuff. It slowly got them drifting into their own worlds one at a time.

The time was unclear, but later that night, James awoke from an unpleasant dream and because of the current temperature of the room, It was quite hot, but the room was a bit darker. The flames had gotten smaller by now.

Waking up set in motion new problems for him, one being finding a comfortable position to rest in hopes to regain his sleep again and hopefully be welcomed by a better dream.

It was not working at all. He saw everyone was still asleep and decided he should watch the fire for a while.

This was a horrible choice, that he regretted instantly, for what he saw almost gave him a heart attack. It skipped a beat but it continued on after that, really fast. He was frightened and shaken from the shock.

Next to the fire, on one of the small wooden chairs was a transparent figure, the same girl again, from the previous town.

She just sat there, swaying her head from side to side, humming a rhyme to herself. She was still in the same state that he first saw her.

James could not bring himself to look away or close his eyes. He was paralyzed.

A few moments passed and she suddenly stopped her song and little dance.

James could only watch.

The girl swiftly turned her head and looked at James.

From nowhere, James was able to muster the strength and courage to pull the blanket over his head.

The temperature escalated under the blanket, he started breathing unevenly with beads of sweat forming on his forehead. He could feel the thump of his heart beat all over his body, shivering as if he were outside in the cold. Countless thoughts interrogated him with events of horror and questions he didn't know, understand or want to answer. *Was this the ghostly fear people get when they've seen a spirit?* He was horrified, ready to pass out if he could and let the event carry out without his notice.

After a few moments, he began to tell himself it could all be just an hallucination, and with that belief growing in his mind he gained himself a bit of might, the power to lift the covers from over his head and investigate.

The investigation gave him a fright more deadly than the one he had just received.

The little girl was right in front of him, bent over with her face right up to his.

At first she had a curious look on her face, but then it quickly turned into a smile.

James had lost his ability to breath, but her smile, it was adorable.

She gave him a small wave of greeting.

He was still trapped in his fear, but for some reason it seemed greatly reduced, and replaced with quite a bit of confusion. It was now clear to him, that she was definitely not there to harm him in any way.

She stood up straight and walked over to the fire again, she sat on the chair and hummed her song again till she faded away.

James was left to tend to his horrible shock and heart injuries for the rest of the night.

CHAPTER 8

Time to Learn

A good night's rest is what we all need before the beginning of a new school day, but this wasn't the case for James. He was unable to get sleep after his little ghost friend visited him.

He lay most of the night staring up at the wooden textures of the ceiling and the flickering candle light from the small chandelier. Every few minutes or so he would take a quick glance at the small chair by the fire, hoping not to stop his heart again, but it seemed she was only here to greet him for some odd apparent reason and be off to where ever she came from.

No welcoming thoughts knocked at the doorstep of his mind after that, hence the urge not to sleep at all for the rest of the night.

In that long and lonely silence he heard the repetitive tick of the long arm of a clock, he didn't notice it when he'd arrived but there was one on Galvani's work desk. Too bad it wasn't standing upright for him to see, it lay facing up on the desk and getting out of his comfort zone was not an option, not while there was some possibility the ghost could be waiting somewhere unexpected, getting ready to scare the living out of him.

His eyes were red with a burning bitter pain that allowed tears to gather and try sooth them, his body had produced enough sweat to soak up the blanket.

But off course, this shocking experience didn't last long, it wasn't at all as traumatizing when he pictured the little girls adorable smile.

After this experience he had felt less compelled to keep it a secret, but as the victim of this trauma he could already see the outcome of spilling the beans, no one is going to understand, they will brand him insane, especially with Mark around, and being the only one who has seen her, he too began to question his sanity.

This is her third visit, and the only time she spoke was when she had asked for help. His next idea would be to try communicate with her whenever she decides to visit him again.

Just as James was about to realize his dream and fall to sleep out of severe weariness, it was all interrupted by two hands reaching for the ceiling and a loud yawn.

Before he could scream in terror, he quickly realized it was Mia, she was awake.

James's eyes bulged out, it was already morning, but early in the morning, really early.

He looked down at Mark and Daniel, they were dead, nothing was going to bring them to life.

"Morning," She greeted with another yawn.

"Hi," He replied.

Her expression turned to a confused frown, she noticed James sleepless state, his red eyes, "What's wrong?" she enquired, "Was it a bad dream or you didn't sleep at all?"

"None of them, I suppose," He evaded, turning his head to the chair.

"You're awake too early and your eyes are red."

"Why are you awake so early then?" He redirected the questioning.

She signed, "School sleep schedule has not changed since last term, it keeps waking me up around this time."

He saw fit to answer since she did, "Bad dream."

"What?"

"Had a bad dream," He repeated.

"Oohh," she replied, "Sweet."

James didn't understand why she just said that, but did not care nonetheless, he sighed, "I reckon it's a bad way to start school."

Mia turned to the ceiling, "Nah not really, today you just going to be welcomed, it's tomorrow where the bad dreams and sleepless nights must stop."

For his reasons, the sleepless nights may not stop, but he was able to come up with something that would get his mind off it and cheer up a bit, "Hey, Mia," he whispered.

She turned to him, "Yeah?"

"You said Jake taught you some magic right?"

She nodded, "Some from the school as well."

"Can you teach me something, a spell, anything?"

She shook her head, "No,"

James frowned.

Mia could see the next question so she answered it before it could be asked, "You need a staff to do magic."

"Well that sucks," he replied, "You have to carry around walking stick like some old man to do magic."

"It sucks for you," she giggled.

"Huh?"

"Watch this."

She reached out her left hand over both Daniel and Mark. A few seconds later, from the palm of her hand, a small bit of blue mist started to appear.

James was astonished, seeing magic for the first time in his life, "Wow."

The mist from her palm drifted down over both Mark and Daniel and settled. She removed he hand from above them, "Now just try act normal."

James couldn't contain his excitement and act normal, he waited had watched.

Moments passed and they both started to fidget under the their blankets, pulling them closer to themselves.

James couldn't help but start laughing quietly. Mia joined in.

They started to murmur, as it was clear to them it was cold.

The mist started to fade away as one of them began wake up, "What is wrong with this weather," Mark mumbled grumpily.

James and Mia were out of breath, still laughing silently.

Daniel opened his eye and sat up to see if the fire was still burning. There was a tad bit of flame, "Screw this," He threw his blanket aside.

He stood up without noticing James and Mia and went to go sit on one of the stools right in front of the fire. He rested his hands over the dying flames, "This weather is playing tricks," He muttered to himself.

"I agree," James replied.

Mark was happy to get up and go sit buy the fire, but he was the who noticed them both laughing. It was his cold body that he had to tend to first, before he began the questioning. He frowned at them both, "Why aren't you guys freezing to death, and laughing."

James shrugged, "I have no idea man," he lied, "We were surprised you felt cold at all, being all fidgety."

He turned to Mia and gave her a suspicious look.

She returned the look but couldn't hold it for long, she burst out laughing, "You got me," she confessed.

"Wait what?" Daniel looked up.

"We've been tricked," Mark explained, "She used some kind of witchcraft to freeze us to death."

Daniel shook his head in disappointment, "You mustn't, you shouldn't disturb someone while they sleep," he said sadly, "It's just something you don't do."

"I'm sorry," she apologized.

"Guys, it's school today, you're supposed to be up early anyway," James added.

"A little shake will have done the same job," Daniel replied, "No need for this freezing magic."

Mark became more interested in the spell she cast, now that he was warming up to the fire, "Anyway," He switched the topic, "Did you learn that magic in the school?"

"No, Jake taught it to me," She replied.

"What is it, ice magic or something?" Daniel asked

She sat up, "Yes," she replied, "But it doesn't fall under destruction magic according to Jake."

"Destruction!?" Mark raised his voice, "You used destruction magic on me."

"I just said, it doesn't fall under destruction magic, according to Jake," she repeated herself.

"Still," Daniel added, "Freezing people to death is pretty destructive."

"What are your sources to this claim then, hmm?" She asked, putting her feet on floor.

"Games and stuff," He replied.

Mia giggle, "Okay, so you still think that this is some kind of game?" She asked rhetorically, "This is history, all this once existed and we're in its existence," she tried to explain, "But Jake said that this type of magic I just used is different and not taught by the school, though it does look similar an ice destruction spell."

"Well that's pathetic," Mark said, "The school can't teach us how to create that ice misty thing you just did."

"Well, there is the ice destruction spell, but that's dangerous."

"What, and that's not dangerous?" Mark enquired seriously.

"Ugh, you'll see."

Their conversation was interrupted by the presence of Jake, entering from another room, "Ah, up and early," He said, "Eager to start school I see."

"Morning," Mia greeted.

About an hour and a half later, everyone was ready and had eaten breakfast, just simple porridge. They now sat around the table and had a conversation with Jake.

"So how is it going?" Jake asked, "You guys getting along well?"

James was quick to answer, "Yeah."

Mia nodded in agreement.

"Well," Mark said, giving in his input, "I don't know…it's difficult to say."

Daniel put his finger in the air, "I also can't decide, I mean, my morning was ruined."

They were being rather honest in opinion.

Jake was confused, "What's happening?"

Mark sighed, "Does trying to freeze someone to death while they sleeping give a 'get along' vibe?"

"Oh come on, it was just a joke," Mia stepped in.

"Ha, you have poor taste then," Mark replied, "I for one don't recall laughing."

"Okay," Mia put her hands up in front of her, "Let me be a bit more specific, it was a prank."

James was a bit too tired to say anything, if anything could be said, he just remained in the background yawning. Daniel on the other hand was just enjoying the show with his head resting on his hand.

"Do you know what a prank is?" Mark shot back, "Trying to kill someone is not in the Job description little miss."

And the name calling started.

Mia took a deep breath, "You had to go there didn't you!?"

Jake felt he had to step in before it became a little too aggressive, "Woah!" He silenced them, "It's clear, that you are not getting along."

Galvani was busy on the counter with the dishes, "Give them a few days, they'll be the best of friends," he laughed.

"I don't get what's his problem," Mia added.

"I don't get what's your problem," Mark repeated.

"Okay, that was obviously the wrong question to begin with," Jake said.

Galvani stopped with his current activity and sat at the table, "I think we can start with our discussion," he said to Jake, "They must go to school soon."

"Yes indeed," Jake replied.

Everyone was intrigued.

Even James woke up a little, "About what?"

"Probably the first real reason why you are here in the first place."

Everyone's attention doubled. Was this the big reveal they've been wanting to here since his visit in the present?

They all waited anxiously for him to speak up again.

"This is what I have," He started, "As your first task..." He silenced himself.

Task?, what happen to the reason part? They wondered. But they keep silent, it was about the only bit of information they would get.

"Your first Task is to figure out what your first task is," He smiled.

All four of them frowned in confusion and disappointment.

James shook his head, getting rid of some drowsiness, "What?"

"I-I just can't," Daniel said in defeat, "You just got our hopes up for nothing."

Jake had gone a bit too far with his clueless riddles and his lack of understanding. Even Galvani sat there confused with his reply, it was not meant for him so he did not try to get anything out of Jake.

"You're not explaining anything again Jake," Mia pointed out, "What you just said is not applicable in any way."

Jake shrugged, "It's all I know," He said, "Sorry, probably not a good start."

"'Probably'?!" Mia said raising her voice, "That's nothing to go with," she frowned.

Jake sighed and put his hands together, thinking of a way to make the situation better because he was telling the truth, he knew nothing else.

Daniel sat up straight and took a deep breath, "Can we just go to school," He suggested, "I think we going to be late."

In their perspective, Jake is the old wise man that is supposed to be their guide and explain everything that is happening and tell them what to do...in a more understandable and inculcate way. In their inexperienced eyes, he is some grand time traveler from the movies who was seeking assistance from a bunch of kids. It did not make sense to them.

Everyone was really happy with Daniel's suggestion.

Before anyone could stand, Jake had something to say, "Just please keep an eye open for anything that may be your task."

Galvani nodded in agreement but had a little to add, "Just focus on school for now."

"Yes, there is a lot of history that you need to learn," Jake said, "The real history."

Mia rolled her eyes, stood up from the table and went to the sitting room.

James was quite up now, the rise in excitement and the sudden drop to disappointment must have affected him and his drowsiness. His mind was trying to get everything together, it was making him really angry inside because it seemed that Jake was not taking any of this seriously. He was now asking himself if this old man knew what he was doing. The Dead Crow organization is hunting them for these diamonds yet they still knew nothing. They are stuck in the past, yet still know nothing. They are given a task, and yet still know nothing. Jake's way of doing things did not seem very effective, but sending them to school is a good way to start understanding the time period before the hundred year shift and keep them safe from the Dead Crow.

I was but minutes before they were greeted by the outside world, the scent of cold fresh air. The greatest feeling in the morning, wind brushing against your face and waking you up. It was chilly again. The clouds were back, hiding the colour of the sky and the light of the sun.

These residential streets were barely occupied, a lot of the people were already in the market district or heading there.

The weather caught Mia by surprise, "Woah, not what I expected," She mentioned as she pulled her sleeves over her hands.

"A little taste of your own medicine," Mark replied to the statement.

Everyone else was perfectly fine with the breeze, wearing the robes.

Jake fixed up his robe before heading down the steps off the porch. Galvani made sure to lock the door to his house before following behind him. Their heading was taking them even further from the Market District.

"How far is this school?" James asked following down the stairs.

"We've barely taken a few steps and you're already asking," Mia said jumping off the last step.

"I just want to know how far we going to walk," He replied.

"If you must know, it's there," She pointed at a massive cluster of buildings in the far distance, really far, "It's way, way bigger than it seems."

"Meaning, a long walk," Mark added picking up the pace.

"Yeah, pretty much."

Down the road they went, walking in the exact opposite direction as most of the people. This area was not as heavily guarded as the market, coming across a guard was kind of rare.

Mark and Daniel were ahead of everybody, even Jake and Galvani. There was no possibility of ever getting lost, it stood in plain sight, surrounded by nothing but the grass and scattered trees, and the high walls that border it, dividing the other districts.

Mia looked just ahead and noticed Mark kick away a rock, "Your friends really do hold a grudge don't they?" She asked James.

He shook his head, "Nah, you probably don't know how cold your blue mist is."

She giggle, "Blue mist?"

"Yeah," He frowned, "I'm sure that's an appropriate name for the blue mist that came out of your hand."

She nodded, "No one's named it, I guess that could be right," she looked at her palm.

James thought there for a second that she was about to summon the mist again. When I didn't happen he decide to enquire, "Can you do it again?"

She shook he head and put her hands into her small jean pockets, "I'm not able to use it in front of people," she explained, "Jake said I'm not allowed."

"Why is that?"

"Apparently, I am really different," She replied.

"Yes…," He said, hoping for her to explain why she is different.

She just smiled, "You'll see," she looked ahead, "let's catch up with the others.

They picked up their pace.

About half an hour later the downhill had started to go uphill and at the end of the path, they reached another gate, it had the same look and features as the main gate of the outer wall, only a bit smaller in size. It used the same mechanics and opened by itself when they got close enough.

This city was a big fan of high walls and fancy gates. Every section had to be separated.

"Jake?" James called, "What is this city scared of."

"What do you mean?"

"Uh, walls everywhere."

Jake looked at the wall, thinking, "I guess, they are scared of what might happen."

They walked into a courtyard, with pillared passages on either end. Everything was made of a light grey stone, the ground was fitted with stone slabs that created a path down the middle, small fountains of exotic statues stood on the grass by the small gardens on both sides and in the centre stood a manmade pond with a statue of a wizard that stood in it.

The yard was silent and empty, with only the fountains pouring water and the few birds that visited the area.

The newcomers were really impressed with the entrance to the school.

"Hmmm," Daniel said staring at the statue, "This must be a really expensive school."

"That, you must not worry about," Jake replied.

He really wanted to ask why, but he remembered all the other disappointing outcomes from all the other questions he had asked, so he just continued to admire his surroundings.

Mark looked into the waters of the well, "I wonder if wishes really do come true here."

James stood next to him and stared at the coins that covered the base of the well, "Maybe."

"Come on," Galvani ordered, "You already late."

They made their way to the other end of the courtyard and had to climb a few steps to reach the next door, which also stood tall. It had the words Marridor Magic carved into it.

"That's a grand entrance," Daniel admired.

"Yeah, this is nice," James agreed.

Mark had to say something negative, "Yeah, it's a bunch of statues, nothing magical."

Daniel gave him the sour look and shook his head in disbelief.

Jake went up to the door and pushed it open.

Now that small act was very surprising, this whole time, doors have be opening themselves, but know this one decided to be different.

Inside, they walked into reception. The room was circular in shape and had a staircase on each side leading to a door just above. The floors were carpeted in blue and just in front of them a counter stood, a table with dark skinned lady sitting behind it and above her a great golden chandelier hung, from a ceiling that looked to be very high above them.

The lady at the counter stood up as soon as she saw them and greeted politely, "Morning."

She wore very formal and definitely in the fashion that was being portrayed all over the Market District.

Jake greeted back and walked up to the table.

The others stood silent.

Behind the counter, James noticed another door. Probably a staff room he thought. The door above seemed to be the entrance.

A while later, the lady by the counter turned to James, Mark and Daniel, "So you're the new students."

They nodded and stepped forward.

"Nice to meet you," She smiled

They greeted her in return.

She took three sheets of paper with printed writing on them. She picked up a quill and dipped it in ink, "Now I'll need to know your names," she requested.

"James Lamaine," He replied first.

She inked onto the paper.

Daniel waited for her to be done, "Daniel Rikone."

"Mark Mewell."

"Thank you," She place the quill into the jar of ink, "Now... you are a bit late, but you're lucky Jake informed me of you beforehand."

They just nodded in return, with no notion of what she was talking about.

"I'll let you in now, just look for the new group, they shouldn't be too far," she instructed them.

Jake turned to the boys as soon as the lady was done with the instructions, "This is where we part ways," he smiled.

This was bit unexpected, but also understandable.

"If any of you need any kind of help, Galvani will be in town."

They said their farewells to each other. Jake and Galvani exited the room and closed the doors behind them.

It was strange, the silence that grew after, it was their very first time being separated from Jake since the change in timeline, and even though they were unaware of anything really, the moment after he left the room and closed the doors, they felt lost.

The lady took their attention, "Alright then, since the group is gone, you will need help," she looked at Mia, "Miss Milmoure."

"Yes, Mrs. Elditch," She replied.

"I ask you please escort these boys to the new group," She requested.

She nodded, "Yes ma'am."

"Good then, you may enter into the school," she said showing them the door above.

Mia lead the way up the stairs to the door.

Funny enough, this door was not decorated at all. This one was just your average wooden door. She grabbed the door knob and turned it.

On the other side of the door, all beauty was removed. They entered into a tower that had similar interiors to a light house, just the stairs and small windows all the way to the top.

James and Daniel stood at the middle of the tower and look up. The stairs spiraled up to a specific point far above them.

"Oh come on," Mark said, "Now we have to walk upstairs."

"This is the entrance tower," Mia said.

James turned to her as she started up the stairs, "How many entrances are there?"

"Quite a few," she replied, "but we need to hurry."

Everybody followed behind her and naturally, one of them stopped by the very first window he came across to gain some kind of view of the school. But it was a failed attempt, the windows were made of stained glass.

"I thought these windows were only meant for fancy places," James said disappointed.

He looked up and saw Mia was rushing her way to the top and hurried up after her.

A few moments brought them to the top which consisted of only an arched door frame. On the other side was a stretched out wooden platform, a path, with railings on both sides and a triangular shaped roof above it.

Mark laughed, "Now it's a bridge, we not getting to this school," he said, tired out from the stair hike he just experienced.

"Yes," Mia replied, "It comes with the best view, at least."

As soon as they stepped to the bridge a strong gust of wind hit them. It was much stronger up here and colder. The only one whom suffered mostly from the wind was Mia, so she did not at all endorse the idea of viewing the school from up here. But she couldn't complain about it and ruin their first sighting of the great school, Marridor Magic.

All three of them scurried over to the railing and leaned over to experience the 'best view' Mia just spoke about.

All their jaws dropped at the castle in front of them. With towers that reached up for the skies. Large buildings with high glass windows surrounded by stone walls, with very steep gable roofs.

"Woah, woah, woah, woah," James expressed himself, "Can't wait see this."

Mia stood rubbing her arms as the wind blew passed, carrying her hair while they admired the view.

Mark was actually really impressed for the first time since we met him, but it was quickly drained as soon as he decided to find out how far above from the ground they were. He pulled away from the railing immediately. He was panting.

"You hate heights?" Mia asked.

He nodded in return.

"Come on, we are late," Mia said making her way to the other side of the bridge.

Mark followed, remaining in the centre of the bridge, so as to blind himself from the ground beneath them.

James and Daniel joined a few moments later.

At the other end of the bridge, there was nothing, not stairs leading to ground level, it was a dead end with a railing in their way. On one of the corners stood an old wooden staff.

"Uhhhh," Mark said with a baffled expression, "I feel I should be saying something, but I'm not going to," he shook his head.

James walked over to the edge and took a look over the railing, "What's happening now?" He sighed.

Mia pushed him aside, "Move over," she picked up the staff.

Everyone else waited, curious as to what was about to happen next.

"Nepo Riats," she spoke.

James raised a brow in response to the words Mia Just spoke. He turned his gaze the Daniel and Mark. They just shrugged in return.

The railing that was in their way, slid to the side.

"Huh?" Daniel expressed with shock.

James took a step back because now, without the railing, it was a freefall to your death if you slipped or tripped over.

From the emptiness that lay beyond the edge of the bridge, a plank of wood flicked out from under.

Everyone besides Mia was startled by its sudden appearance.

From under the plank, another plank flicked out, and then another from the next. As the process continued, it start to take the shape of a pizza, then a semi-circle. It was some kind of wooden platform. It started to create a railing around the edges.

James, Mark and Daniel had put on some very interesting expressions as they watched the platform take shape. They watched without any words to say.

Mia placed the staff back where she found it and stepped onto the platform.

The others were not compelled to do so. The second half of the platform was missing.

A moment later, another flicked out from under the platform and from there it was creating a stair case in a spiral leading to the bottom as well as a railing at the same time.

Daniel nodded, "Impressive."

"The staircase is constructing itself," James mentioned.

Mia broke their train of thought, "Let's go," she started down the staircase.

The stairs were still constructing when they joined her.

"Was that a different language you just spoke there, or some incantation?" James asked looking over the edge, checking whether the stairs were done. They were still constructing.

"It's English," She replied.

"No it's not," Daniel replied immediately.

James had to repeat the words in his head first before realizing it himself, "I can't be."

"It's the words 'Open Stair' backwards," she explained, "It's just a password."

"That makes a bit more sense," Daniel said.

They were about half way down the staircase when it was done with construction and the wooden plank noises had stopped.

"For those of you who didn't listen in history or watch the news, this place is owned by the GM Government in the present, turned into a science lab and the only place that is allowed to use magic," Mia said.

"Hmm, I wonder why they still used magic though, it was the cause of all the horrible things we were taught in history," Daniel said.

"Its scientists," Mark said, "They can do whatever."

"Yeah, they just want to use it themselves, have the power," James added, "I think that's why History is a compulsory subject, so they can feed us these lies," he tapped the railing, "I mean, guns and bombs are just as dangerous."

"Well, this is our chance to see if anything is different," Mia concluded.

At the bottom of the stairway, they were met by another path of stone tablets that led up to the school. They couldn't see the entrance from where they stood currently.

They were surrounded by short lush green grass with a few trees clouded by leaves with stone benches near them.

James turned to and looked up at the bridge and noticed its structure, it did not look too stable, but then again, he didn't know much about architecture.

He looked at the stair case, waiting for it to disappear again. But it didn't.

Mia headed up the path, "The way in is just up ahead."

James took a few steps walking backwards, with his eyes glued to the staircase.

A few moments passed but nothing moved, "Fine," he said to himself, tuning around and jogging up the path to the others.

The school was even bigger, up close. They realized when they passed by one of the towers attached to the main school buildings. The walls were built from stone and gave off a rustic look and feel.

"Ah, last entrance," James announced, as they walked into view of the main door.

The entrance door was wide and tall with the words Marridor Magic on it with the emblem beneath, surrounded by a lot of other patterns. Above the door was a large silver renaissance clock.

It was about half past nine.

"I expected a little less silence, this far into the school grounds," Daniel said, listening to the second hand.

Around them was a corridor against the walls of the building, with wooden benches places against the wall.

"We are outside the school…basically," Mia replied, "There are more grounds and fields beyond here that are closer to the classrooms and dorms."

James was a bit more concerned about the door in front of him, "Why is it not opening?"

Mia walked up to the doors and placed each hand on one, with a hard push, she was able to open them both at the same time.

The doors opened smoothly.

"Okay, not a magic door," James said disappointed.

They stepped into a large hallway that resembled a throne room. The floors had smooth and reflective tiles placed in a black and white pattern. On the other end of the hallway another large arched door stood, the left and right walls were also fitted with doorways. Arched windows on either side letting light filter in well into the room. The ceiling was also arched with a large silver chandelier hanging down in the centre of the room unlit. From the ceiling, five banners also hung in a row down the middle. Each banner was a different colour and bore a different symbol.

There were quite a number of students that roamed this hallway already in their uniforms, which consisted of a black blazer and a dark purple tie, long grey pants for the boys and eggplant purple skirts for the girls. The girls either wore white socks or black stockings and everyone wore black shoes and white T-shirts.

An old woman stood, some distance away from them, and around her, a large group of about twenty children, all wearing their casual clothing. They seemed to be under instruction, James, Mark and Daniel were also in casual clothing.

"Follow me," Mia instructed.

James took notice of the Banners, "These flags have the same symbols, like the main gate," he pointed out.

"Yes, the five classes of magic," Mia replied, "you'll be choosing one tomorrow."

It became a stare frenzy that could make anyone feel a bit uneasy for the short time they walked from the main door to the crowd which they could begin to blend in with.

Mia went around to the front where the old woman was standing explaining something to the children.

"Morning Mrs. Mannikral," she interrupted.

Mrs. Mannikral turned to her, "Yes Miss Milmoure," she greeted with a welcoming smile. She quickly turned her gaze to the boys.

"This is James, Mark and Daniel," She introduced them, "They are also starting today, sorry we're a bit late," she apologized.

She looked at the boys with concern, "Late on the first day."

Daniel was the first to come out with an apology, "Sorry."

The crowd of new comers just stared as everything transpired.

"Oh, well, thank you Mia," she said, "Join the group," she spoke to the boys.

James, Mark and Daniel slowly made there was to the back of the group.

Mrs. Mannikral turned back to Mia and looked at her attire, "Best you get into uniform."

She nodded in return, "Yes ma'am," she made her way through the doorway on the left.

Mrs. Mannikral put her hand over her mouth clearing her throat, "Okay, where was I?"

She was an old member of the staff, about the age of 60 and quite tall. She wore very formal witch-like clothing that was mostly black in colour, patterned in a light grey. Her long grey hair was tied back into a bun with a white floral headpiece.

"Ah," she remember, "I was telling you about this evening, you will be standing in front of the hall and you will be distributed according to your age groups," he explained, "But first I am to take you to your dormitories so you can begin to look the part." She scanned the area a bit for some unknown reason, "Okay, please wait here, I won't be long," she turned around and headed away through the door.

At first, everyone was afraid to move, but when they though Mrs. Mannikral was far, they started to settle, speaking to each other, and exchanging names in most cases, in awkward ways as they were bundled up in a pile.

The people seemed to be more welcoming than predicted.

James was able to exchange and introduce himself just fine, one of the boys decided to make conversation with him, a young black boy with a fade afro.

"Hello," he greeted, holding out his hand for a handshake, "I'm William."

James shook his hand, "James," he replied with a smile.

"Nice to meet you," he started being formal.

"Likewise."

"So what age group do you fall under?" He enquired.

James didn't know anything about the age groups or how they were said so he just replied with his actual age, "16…I guess."

"Nice," William replied, "I fall under the same age group, I thought it was only us three," he turned to the crowd, looking for the other two learners.

James stood there, lost as a duck among geese for a few seconds, until William returned.

"Opal and Claude, this is James," He introduced, "He's our age."

They both exchanged handshakes with him.

Opal was a short girl with a lot of freckles on her face, with short dark brown hair and a fringe that touched her brows. She was a tad bit shy and kept her smile a bit faint. Claude was a tall boy, about the same height as James, just about an inch taller with very short blonde hair and a little chubby in size. He was more cheerful at heart and very happy to meet someone else.

"I guess that makes just the four of us," William declared, "We the oldest age group here."

James shook his head, "Nah, there are two others," he corrected him.

"Oh, I'm guessing the ones you arrived with?"

James nodded while he scanned the area. They both disappeared, "Just give me a sec."

He spotted Mark sitting on one of the slanted window sills with his arms crossed, he looked as if he didn't want to be here. James called him over.

Daniel was in the crowd meeting new people but James interrupted him and called him over as well.

James introduced them and from there, decided to stick with each other.

Everyone was enquiring about each other's age groups and joining together. Was it about something Mrs. Mannikral said or are people just more comfortable that way?

"Did Mrs.…," James didn't recall her surname, "The teacher that was here tell you to be in age groups?"

"Mrs. Mannikral?" Opal shook her head, "No, it's how we will be placed though."

James nodded slowly and acted as if he understood what she was saying.

"How did you three manage to be late on your first day?" Claude asked, "I mean, today we were supposed to be here half passed eight which is very late compared to the time we'll be waking in the morning of tomorrow."

Mark shrugged, "Very cold morning I guess," he replied.

"Fair enough," he said changing the subject, "So who was your very pretty escort?" He asked with a closed cheek-to-cheek smile.

"A girl we met yesterday," James replied.

"Is she in our age group?" Claude enquired.

"Claude," William shook his head giggling.

"What, I'm curious."

It was just a few minutes after when Mrs. Mannikral returned with two other staff members following her closely behind.

She stood some distance away from the group of learners that were still settling down and gathering them. She began to explain what was to happen next, "Sorry for the delay," She apologized, "Now, I will assign you to a teacher according to your age groups."

The children silenced themselves and awaited orders.

"Those aged twelve and thirteen, please stand this side with Ms. Bennting," she pointed at her. She wore more colourful attire and wore a boater over her brown hair.

The youngest children followed and gathered around her. They were the majority.

Mrs. Mannikral moved on to the next group, "Those aged fourteen and fifteen will join Mrs. Annister over there," she gave them a spot to gather.

Mrs. Annister looked to be in her fourties in dark green witch clothing and had her hair tied up.

"And ages sixteen and seventeen will remain here, with me."

No one was aged seventeen so it was only the six of them that remained.

"Hmmm, quite a few," she said, "Good, now will you please follow me."

Mrs. Mannikral lead them through the doorway on the left, walking really fast with good posture.

The school was riddled with corridors and stairs that served as a connection for all the buildings and towers that made up the place. A maze with many different floors, a place that would take a really long time to get used to or map out. For every corridor they turned, they would forget the previous few.

Every passage had a similar look to it. High walls with one or two chandeliers hanging from the ceiling and silver sculptured candle stands bolted to the walls on either side. Some had doors leading to other rooms, classes and storage. Some corridors had windows, all arched, being the source of light during the day time and some others were outside.

The class rooms were much larger than the ones James, Mark and Daniel were used to, and some of them very different from your standard set ups.

As the new students of the school, they received some cold stares from the other learners, save only a few who gave welcoming smiles and those that greeted Mrs. Mannikral when she passed by. She was busy giving them a little bit of a tour and background of the place while heading to their destination.

It was a while before they reached a stop, at the end of a hallway, at a door, quite large and arched dissimilar the rest and on it a sign that read : Dormitory, and beneath it the numbers 16 – 17.

Mrs. Mannikral turned to them, "This is going to be your dormitory from now on," she opened the door and stepped into the room.

They entered into a large scope with a ceiling high enough to have two floors under it with a decorated chandelier, with already lit candles. The room consisted of many home welcoming features like a hearth against the right side of the wall, surrounded by single and double couches. The rest of the room had five round tables and chairs. Against the walls, book shelves filled in the spaces. The walls had the same banners hanging off them and on the far end of the room was a high arched window. The whole floor was carpeted in a maroon.

It was more than any of them have ever seen, a silent jaw dropping moment for all.

Mrs. Mannikral was quick to move on, "This place will be your study," she explained, "Off course you can use the libraries, but this is mostly for after hours."

Libraries? James thought to himself, *how many libraries are there?*

"Okay," she said, "Now boys stay here while I show Miss..." she look at Opal.

"Opal Braden," she replied.

"Thank you," she said, "While I show Miss Braden to her dormitory."

She led her through the only other doorway in the room, it was a stair case.

Everyone dispersed in their own directions, curious about the place.

James took this opportunity to sit on a chair at one of the tables and lay his head, he took a deep breath, "Haven't had a sit since Galvani's place."

Mark took a seat on the couch, very close to the hearth, "I still think that freeze spell is affecting me," he said.

James shook his head and didn't reply.

Claude was curious about what Mark said and sat down across him, "What happened?"

Mark wasn't interested in telling the tale.

William examined the shelf closest to James's table and picked a random book from it, "So where you people from?" He asked curiously.

None of them remember the name of the town which they awoke in, they don't remember Jake ever mentioning it. Daniel was standing at the window, taking in the closed off view of the school.

"From down South," James replied.

"Down South where?" He enquired turning the pages of the book.

James was not up for this questioning at all, he just wanted to enjoy the few moments of peace Mrs. Mannikral gave them, "Some small village."

"Without a name?"

James just nodded in response which confused William.

Before he could bombard him with another question, Mrs. Mannikral stepped into the room alone.

"Boys, your turn," she headed up the staircase again.

Everyone rushed up after her.

The stairs turned in two directions at a point. Mrs. Mannikral led them up the right till they reached the top.

"This is your dormitory," she said.

The door had a sign on it, reading : BOYS.

Mrs. Mannikral opened the door and let them into a large rectangular room. Accompanied with eight beds, four against each wall facing inward, placed quite a bit apart with each one having a small wardrobe next to and a dressing table on the other side. There were small windows above each dressing table and a bigger one on the other end of the room with a clock on the wall. All the beds had bags either on or next to them.

"There are six more like this, three on this floor and three more above it," she explained, showing them the doorways on both sides of the room.

They all just nodded right after she finished saying something and kept silent.

"You lot will be upstairs," she led them through the doorway on the right and into another room identical to the previous one.

All five of them were placed into the first room they entered into, "The beds with the uniforms are yours, your names will be on a piece of paper on the uniform."

Again they all just responded with a nod.

Mark said something, "Okay."

"Now," she started, "You have this time to get into your uniform and unpack your luggage," she instructed, "When you done, don't go and get lost, it's best you stay in the dormitory, I'll come and escort you to the hall, later, in the evening."

James's eyes bulged, the evening was about eight hours from now. Just thinking about the amount of time they must spend without leaving made him very anxious.

"I'll take my leave," Mrs. Mannikral said.

They thanked her and she went down stairs.

William and Claude seemed to recognize their bags so they went straight to their beds. As for James, Mark and Daniel, they relied on the pieces of papers that were placed on their uniforms.

The luggage part was the most confusing. Each of them had a trunk similar to William's and Claude's but no notion of ever having them since waking up in this time. Jake must have prepared this for them beforehand.

Without putting too much thought into the how's and why's of the situation, they went on and opened them up.

James unclipped his and viewed the contents of his trunk. He was surprised with the first bit of clothes he saw. It was his clothing. This bit at least explained why Mia was also wearing those clothes.

They were also given school bags which had everything they needed.

He stood up and opened the wardrobe and inside was a shelf on top and beneath it, a section to hang clothes with wire coat hangers pushed over to one side.

Packing in some of the clothes into the wardrobe was everybody's first job. There was enough space beneath their single beds to kick the trunks under.

"I wonder how is it they know our sizes?" Claude asked buttoning up his shirt.

Daniel shrugged, "No idea, it's kind of scary."

Daniel's bed was across from Claude's, he hadn't started changing yet.

Claude had basically thrown everything into his wardrobe.

James, Mark and Daniel's first priorities were to conceal their diamonds before attempting to change.

About half an hour later, they were dressed and ready.

Their diamonds were placed into their hidden blazer pockets.

William looked at his badge, "We don't have a second badge like the other learners," he noticed.

Everyone else took notice of his discovery.

"Maybe we will still get them," Daniel said, "They not all the same."

James placed the paper with his name on the dressing table, to remember where it was he slept. It had a candle stand on it. He still felt a bit tired and less lively after missing most of his sleep. The clock said it was noon, still some time before Mrs. Mannikral arrives. Using this time to sleep was the only thing on his mind, so he decided to lay on his back and closed his eyes.

"Let's go to the study," Mark suggested.

It was a good idea to everybody but James.

"Yeah, I saw a chess set on one of the shelves," Daniel said, "We can kill some time."

Claude walked up to James and shook him, "Come on, we going down stairs."

William, Mark and Daniel had already left the room.

"I didn't get any sleep Claude," he replied with one eye open.

"Hmmhmm," he said, "It's a bad idea sleeping now."

"I don't know, It feels like the best idea for me."

Claude took a deep breath, "You are going to mess up your sleep schedule."

James thought about it for a bit and realized he was telling the truth, "Uggh, fine."

"See you," Claude said leaving the room.

Down stairs they met up with Opal who was sitting alone on the couch. James came down a few minutes after.

Daniel went straight to the shelf that had the chess set, "Who's game?" He asked bringing it to the nearest table.

Claude walked up to him, "Strategy is one of my specialties," he took a seat across from him and helped set it up.

"Oooh, pretty pieces," Daniel admired.

They were sculpted into people, not your standard Staunton design.

William went and sat with Opal and had their own conversation about whatever came to mind, James sat on one of the chairs at a table and stared at the clock, calculating the exact amount of time left before Mrs. Mannikral arrived.

Mark was drawn to the competition held between Daniel and Claude, "Two noobs having at each other," he stood watching over them with his arms crossed.

Claude frowned at him, "Noob?" He turned to Daniel, "What's a noob?"

"Oh, it's another word for beginner."

Claude chuckled, "Ill beat you after I beat him, how's that sound?"

Daniel nodded in disbelief, "Hmm, after you beat me you say," he place down his last piece, "Go."

Claude had the first move and the last against Daniel, but at least the match wasn't quick, Daniel was able to hold out with his strategies. Mark was the next to be place on the silver platter.

The match against him ended rather quick and unacceptable in his eyes, "Beginners luck I see," he said, "This calls for a rematch."

Claude shrugged, "Okay."

They reset and played again and this time it lasted a little longer, but only because he sat there thinking forever.

"One more time" he asked for another rematch.

Daniel shook his head, "No, it's my turn, sorry bro but you lost," he stood up from his chair.

Mark sighed and spoke calmly, "Daniel, shhhh, and sit down, I can beat this guy," he pointed at the chair he got up from, "Trust me."

"Hmhmm," Daniel didn't believe him, he turned to Claude, "Can you make it quick?"

"Depends."

"On?"

"How long it takes him to think this time," he laughed.

Daniel giggled.

"Haha...ha," Mark started getting real competitive, "I know your strategy," he gave a sinister smile.

A few moves later.

"I'm done," Mark stood to his feet.

"Oh, you finally accept defeat," he started to set it up.

Mark frowned, "What, No!" he went to stand behind Daniel's chair, "I just need a different perspective," He placed his hand on his chin.

Daniel took his place and the match between him and Claude began.

It was another intense battle, that required both of their greatest strategies.

"Yes!" Daniel hit the table with the palm of his hand, "One win."

"Nice one," Claude said getting up from his seat.

Mark stopped him, "Why you getting out of your seat?"

"I lost."

"I still have to verse you," he said.

Daniel signed, "That's not how it works Mark," he explained, "The loser swaps with the next player."

Mark sat in Claude's Place.

Later that afternoon, after the chess matches were over and there was not much to do that could possibly be of great interest, they all gather on the couches and just spoke to each other, in efforts to kill the forever growing anxiety and fear of being introduced to the rest of the school and off course to speed up time in hopes to get this over and done with so they could start getting settled with the other students.

It was a lot darker outside at this time, it was about six in the evening now.

"I wonder what kind of subjects there are?" Daniel asked, "They didn't give us a list or anything to choose from."

Opal shrugged, "I heard we are going to choose tomorrow."

"Ah, so tomorrow is basically another free day, nice," Mark added.

James looked up at the banners again, "What do you suppose these symbols are for?"

"No idea," William replied, "I only arrived to the city a few days ago."

"We all did," Claude said, "Otherwise we would have started last term."

"They look pretty cool though," Mark added.

James decided to ask the same question William did, "So where you guys from?" He asked sinking into the couch.

Claude was the first to go, "I'm from the East of this place, the city of Badalin."

James turned to William and waited for him to answer.

"I'm just North from here, Adornfell, it's not far."

"And I'm from Mitheral," Opal replied.

"Oooh, Mitheral," William said, "Now that's a city."

James, Mark and Daniel had no notion of the city names, they must have changed over the years.

There conversations were really dry at this time, they just wanted to leave now.

"I wonder why no one is coming into the dorms," Claude spoke, "I'm sure someone would have wondered in here by now."

"I'm thinking they're restricted," William suggested, "Us new students here and all."

"They are in the hall, they going to do the introduction thing and it's the first day of the term," Opal said.

A few moments passed and they heard the door open. Their dying souls were saved as the presence of Mrs. Mannikral filled the room.

They all stood up from the couch and gathered in front of her.

"Sorry to keep you waiting, I trust you're ready?"

After leaving us for more than seven hours to fend for ourselves, you still don't think we would be ready? James thought to himself.

"Yes ma'am," Opal replied.

The others just nodded in response.

"Okay, follow me," she instructed leaving the room.

As they left the room they had finally grown comfortable in, all there nerves returned, seeking to give them the worst feeling ever as they walk through the empty and hollow, echoing corridors.

The walk that seemed to take forever ended just as quick. Mrs. Mannikral led them through a small office and into the stage of the hall. Not at all what they thought, thinking they would have to walk from the entrance and pass by every student giving them a cold stare.

The hall was the size of a great cathedral and similar in design, with the high arched windows on both sides and behind them. The stage was set low with steps all round. On stage was a long table where the teachers sat behind and in front of them was an announcement stand which someone stood behind.

The whole hall was lit up by chandeliers as well as candle stands on the walls. More of the same banners were hung from the ceiling on each side of the hall.

The rest of the hall off stage was just filled with long tables placed vertically, about five a row, making four rows from the main entrance of the hall. On either side of each row were long wooden benches where the learners sat and by the looks of it, each row was a different age group, judging by the appearances of the students, with the youngest on the far left and oldest on the right.

In front of these students was plates filled with food and cups with beverages, and down the centre of each table, candles and small platters of other food, an endless variety.

James had never been in a boarding school before and this one as a start made him feel school may be a lot better. This place was very appealing to the eye, the age in a lot of the designs, and the use of old design movements that he had just started learning about in the present.

The one thing that was unsettling was the lack of chattering. None of the learners spoke, no whispers were heard. One thing that was a problem in the present was keeping children quiet, especially in the hall, but here they were doing a really good job.

On stage in front of the announcement stand, on the stairs stood the other learners.

Mrs. Mannikral whispered to them, "Go stand with the other children," she proceed to her chair.

The setting reminded James of a wedding, the people on the stage behind the long table were the hosts and the people in the hall, the guests.

All six of them followed her order and walked up to the other new learners, their new school shoes banging against the varnished wooden floors in the undying silence. They joined them on the steps and stared back into the endless eyes. It was a really nerve wrecking experience.

"Good evening!" the man behind the announcement stand spoke, "For the new learners, I am Principal Patchwalker."

The man was a little old, maybe about fifty, tall with long black hair combed down reaching his shoulders, kept in place with some kind of moisture. He had a pointy nose, his facial hair consisted of a goatee and mustache. He wore a black trench coat and shiny well-polished shoes. His voice was intriguing and very calm.

"Today is the beginning of a new school term and we are joined by new learners," he started, "A new term is for new beginnings, a fresh start in the process of learning, especially for those who did not do well in the previous," he sighed with a bit of disappointment, "but there is always room for improvement and hope that you develop in your more difficult fields... to our new students here," He continued, "let them feel welcome on their first few days and help them whenever they need assistance," he looked down at a piece of paper for a moment before continuing, "Now, tomorrow won't necessarily be a school day for some, a select few will be tasked with helping the new learners choose their subjects, further details will follow tomorrow."

Everyone listened quietly.

"Before I continue with the announcements I'll be allowing the new learners to join you in their age groups," he explained, "I'll read the names by age group, you will be seated, youngest on the far left row to the oldest learners on the right."

Mr. Patchwalker switched papers and read out their names, the rest of the hall applauded at the end of each age group that was read.

For the oldest group present on stage, the party of James, Mark, Daniel, Claude, Opal and William, were placed on the third row from the left, they weren't the oldest age in the school. They proceeded down the steps and to their row while the rest of the hall applauded.

Mia raised her hand to gain their attention and called them all over to where she was seated, which was quite far from the front. She had kept quite some space for them to sit, next to and across from her.

There was no time for any introductions yet, as soon as they were seated, Mr. Patchwalker ordered that they be quiet so that he could continue.

"Okay, now that we have settled down," he started, "Now to move on to a more serious matter," he looked at his piece of paper again, "I have received a notice that there's some talk of dangerous activities beyond the school walls, now, I am not allowed to mention it here yet but it puts all of you out of safety," he explained, "Therefore, by order of the Dead Crow, beginning today, no student will be allowed off the school grounds on any of the allowed weekends."

This came to a big surprise to everyone and broke the silence, bringing up chatters of complaints.

Mr. Patchwalker brought the silence back, "Quiet!" he shouted, "All parents have been informed and have agreed to only see you at the end of the term."

The whispers continued.

"Thank you, and enjoy your evening," he concluded making his way into the office which the new learners arrived through.

Everyone started to eat and the noise level shot through the roof.

Mia immediately began with the introductions, "These are my friends," She said, "Angelina and Clara, they arrived here when I did."

Angelina was a coloured, with long curly hair and hazel eyes and Clara a blonde girl with green eyes and fair skin.

Everyone introduced one another, even the other students nearby made them feel welcome.

The first day was long and boring but not bad at all.

"Thanks for saving us the spots," William said.

"No problem," Mia replied, she didn't really expect there would be others, there was just enough space.

Everyone started to eat.

James and Mark, put on their silver plates, more food than they could consume. Mark didn't balance his plate with an equal amount of carbohydrates and vegetables, it just consisted of meat.

"To be honest, I wasn't expecting this kind of principle in this kind of school," James said.

"You mean Patchwalker?" Mia asked.

James nodded.

Mia chuckled, "What were you expecting, an old wizard?"

James sniffed, acting like he was crying, "Yes."

Clara was confused, "Why is that?"

"Oh, no real reason."

"Hmm," Angelina said.

"Mr. Patchwalker is kind of new, from what I hear," Clara mentioned, "Picked by the owners of this school, the Maithindor family."

They pretended to know who she was talking about.

"What happened to the old principal?" William asked picking something new to eat.

Clara shrugged, "I'm new here too."

James became clouded by the thought of what the mission could be, it was giving him a headache just thinking about it, but then he quickly remembered that they had said that they should focus more on school for now and learn a bit of history. He decided to move away from the thought, "Well, this term started off a bit rocky, we not allowed to leave."

"Yeah, I guess," Angelina said, "there is nothing that can change that, I'm just curious about what is happening."

"Maybe it will be in the newspaper," Clara said.

"Maybe," Angelina replied.

About an hour later, they had been emptied out now, people were allowed to depart from it whenever they saw fit. Most students were already in their dormitories, tired and asleep. James was one of many that did not waste any time going to bed, and as a new person to these luxuries of food, he had consumed a bit too much.

Not far from them, in the girls dormitory, it was silent, everyone here too was asleep, everyone except Mia, she sat on her bed with her legs crossed thinking to herself about what Jake had told her before she arrived at the school.

She looked at her palms and made her hands into fists. Her gaze turned to the rest of the room, checking if anyone was awake.

She checked the time, it was almost 12am.

She covered her whole body with the blanket, still sitting with her legs crossed.

In her head, the same words repeated themselves, *You are very special and rare, you must tell no one about your ability as it would mean a lot of trouble.* She keep it a secret as if it were one of the diamond artifacts that the others received.

She continued to look at her palms, from the one to the other, wondering what it is that was so dangerous about her, dangerous even without one of the diamonds, what made her different?

The diamond bearers are easy to distinguish, they all possess a special ability, unknown, what for yet but you can tell why they must not share their secret.

She wanted to know what she really was, "What am I?" She whispered to herself.

Jake did not give her a heads up, was it because she would ask questions?

But even so, she was hell-bent on finding out her mystery.

She looked at one of her palms, and just above it, a small ball of light appeared, glowing dimly.

She closed her hand and made it disappear.

It was about time she went to sleep so she lay back on her pillow and drifted into her own deep slumber.

CHAPTER 9

First Lessons

The next morning was off to a terrible start, waking up so early in the morning is no one's strength, especially at the beginning of a new term, or after sleeping at a late time, but it's what they all had to deal with from now on, especially today. Getting themselves out of this resting place is the hardest, but once such an excruciating task is complete, at least for most of them, they were fine with continuing on with the day.

All this was not the same for the new students, James, Mark, Daniel, Claude, William and Opal. No new student was entirely dimmed about their first day in school, more so in this case.

Down at the study, it was almost empty. Most of the students had already left for class. The clock had just hit eight and the only people that remained were the new students, Mia and her two friends, Angelina and Clara with three other boys.

Mia introduced them to everyone else, their names were Stanley, Melvin and Wilbur.

James seated himself on the couch and lay back, wondering why the other six learners were here, "What are you guys doing here?" he asked, "You are supposed to be starting your school day."

Mia shook her head, "No, I'm sure I mentioned that we are here to help you, even Mr. Patchwalker said so."

James shook his head with a confused frown, "I don't recall such."

Daniel was meddling with the fireplace poker, moving around the wood and stirring the ashes, "Why did you tell us put away our bags?"

"You won't need them," Angelina replied, watching him play with the fire. She sat at one of the tables with her legs crossed.

James placed his hand on his chin, "You're helping us you say?"

Most of them nodded in return.

"Funny, how you three were selected… what are the chances?" He rose on brow, "Coincidence?"

Mia sighed, "We volunteered, okay," she was getting upset.

"Volunteered you say?" James asked, "When did this happen?"

"Just let it happen, James," she replied out of frustration.

Mark and William were engaging in a match, He wanted to beat someone, "You going to miss a whole day of school, aren't you worried?" William asked.

"Not me," Wilbur replied, he was sitting with them watching the chess game. His face riddled with freckles with red hair, "I'm not ready to sit in class yet."

Clara agreed, "They just going to be explaining a lot and breaking down what we going to do this term."

"I did it to skip class," Melvin said. He was quite fat with very chubby cheeks and short black hair.

"Same," Stanley added, a tall boy with brown hair wearing glasses.

"Wait, we not going to class?" Daniel asked hitting the fireplace poker against the fender, then putting it away. He dusted his hands even though they were nowhere near the ashes.

Wilbur shook his head, "We going up the towers, to the halls of magic," he replied, "But we just call them towers, because we use towers to get there."

Mark turned his attention away from the chess game, "What!?"

Mia stepped in, "It's where we will assess you on each field of magic," she explained, "It's close to an initiation, we test you, then you choose which field suits you best."

"Subject choices?" Daniel asked.

"Exactly," she agreed, "There are five you will choose from," she took a deep breath, "Destruction magic, Restoration, Conjuration, Illusion and Alteration magic."

"Ah, I get it now," James said.

"It's nice," Mark added, "Pick your own magic class to focus on."

"Sadly, your choice is only between those five, every other subject is compulsory," Mia said.

It was only then when James noticed the additional badges again, and with a closer look, he realized they were the exact symbols on the banners that hung everywhere, "And I'm guessing the colourful badges have something to do with it?"

"Yes," Angelina replied looking down at hers, beneath the school badge. Her one was the picture of a flying phoenix with stitches on it and was a bright orange colour in majority with a bit of red and white in the mix, beneath the badge was the words : RESTORATION, "My class is Restoration," she tapped it.

"I chose Alteration," Mia said looking at hers. It was an image of a tree with roots down the centre, having all the elements infused with it. It was mostly light green in colour.

Melvin showed his, "I picked destruction." His one was in the shape of a drawn snowflake with torched flames on the outer ends.

Wilbur also had the Destruction badge.

Stanley's badge was a dark blue colour. An eye with a black pupil and a black and white spiral from it. I had other optical lines on it with spikes on the edge of the badge. It was labeled : ILLUSION.

Clara had the final class, Conjuration, which consisted of what looked like five black portals in a large purple circle of flames.

"And that's all of them…" Mia said, surprised at the fact that all five badges were present."

"Well, the flags are everywhere so…" Daniel said.

"Banners," Mark corrected him, he turned back to the chess match.

He nodded in return, "Banners."

Angelina chuckled.

"All other subjects are compulsory," Mai added, "They include, alchemy, enchantment, history, English and PE."

"Great, six subjects," Mark said.

A few minutes passed by and with it the concern of whether their day was going to begin or not as the sun continued to rise. Daniel had decided to continue playing with the poker, Mark was now in a match with Stanley.

The door to the dormitory opened.

Everybody jumped.

In came another student.

At first they thought it was just another one of their roommates but he came in with some sheets of paper.

Another student followed in behind him, a girl this time.

"Good morning students," he greeted politely, "May you please gather around."

Everyone stopped with their current activities and walked up to them.

He was an older fellow to their eyes, from the oldest age group by the looks of it.

"My name is Edward Dolltry and the Head Boy of this school," He introduced himself.

"And I'm Josephine Silder, the head girl," she introduced herself cheerfully, "We welcome you to the school," She smiled. She was much shorter than Edward.

Somehow that smile was more than welcoming, it was really adorable and enchanting with a pair of dimples on her cheeks.

The new learners nodded in return, their eyes fixed on her.

Until Edward spoke, "As you may know, today is your choosing day for which ever field of magic you want to do," he explained, "Here I have a timetable that you will follow throughout the day."

"Volunteers please step forward," Josephine instructed.

Edward handed out a piece of paper to each of them and further explained, "Each sheet will pair you with one of the new students."

Josephine continued with the explanation, "As you may see at the bottom, the spells you will be allowing them to cast."

The volunteers replied, "Yes."

"Now, you are to start immediately and be done by this afternoon before the choosing ceremony, good luck new learners, hope you do well," said Edward.

"Enjoy your day," Josephine said as they both left the room.

"Head girl huh?" Claude nodded to himself.

Mark giggled.

"Let's get started," Angelina said looking at her paper, "I'm paired with Daniel," she went and stood next to him.

"William," Clara read out his name.

William went to her, "You can call me Will if you want."

"Okay, Will," she smiled.

Opal was paired with Wilbur.

James was with Mia.

Mark with Stanley

Claude was with Malvin.

They stood there in their pairs exchanging glances with each other.

"Uhh… is this the part when we walk out the dorm?" Mark asked.

"Yes," Mia replied, "let's go, I'll see you in the afternoon then," she headed for the door.

"Where do we go first?" James asked.

She stopped with her hand on the door knob and looked at her paper, "Let's see, Restoration," she replied, "That's pretty far," she opened the door.

James followed her out the room behind her.

"Okay, Mark," Stanley spoke, "We're going to Destruction."

"Yes," Mark said with excitement, "Time to destroy things."

"Daniel, it is Alteration for you," Angelina read her paper.

"Hmm, Don't really recall that field, but okay, let's go."

Opal and Claude were both headed to Conjuration and William was going with Clara to the field of Illusion.

"Come on," Mia made a turn at a corner and headed down another corridor, "The Restoration tower it this way."

The corridors and hallways were empty, save the one or two students that were probably on errands. The classes were all occupied and silent. It was only the voice of the teacher that they could hear as they passed by.

James was unable to make notice of anyone using magic in any of the classes they were passing by.

The majority of the classes were using their books, the one really interesting think James wanted to try out when he officially started with school was the ink and quill. Something he has never attempted before, a dead practice since the ink pen was invented.

They walked down a corridor with no classrooms, it was the only time James felt he was allowed to talk, "I haven't seen anyone use magic in any of the classes we've passed."

"Off course not," Mia replied, "Magic is only used in the five halls, it is only alchemy and enchantment that is used outside the halls."

"Geez, no need to speak as if I'm supposed know what you're talking about," he said, "Anyway, you know why?"

"Why what?"

"Magic is only allowed to be used in the halls."

She shrugged, "Maybe to stop students from causing trouble... I don't know."

They eventually made it to a hallway with a large arched-double door on the other end. The door had the same phoenix symbol carved into the wood with the word : RESTORATION above it in some fancy writing.

They made their way down the hallway to the other side and stood in front of the entrance.

James nodded as he examined the door, "Nice door," he complimented.

"Ye, pretty nice is it not," she said stepping forward. She pushed them both open.

On the other side of the door, they were met with a spiral staircase leading up to a point. It was similar to the Entrance tower, only much cleaner and bigger.

"Hm," James sounded unimpressed, "Another entrance tower, I'm guessing there's a bridge up top, no?"

Mia started up the stairs, "Yes this is an entrance tower and there's a small bridge leading to the hall of Restoration."

James followed behind her and stopped by one of the windows, it was not stained glass this time and he was able to see the outside. From where he was, he was able to see a giant building that stood pretty high from the ground.

James noticed the stairs continued to go up despite the destination being reached, "What's up there?", he leaned against the railing and looked up.

Mia also joined in and looked up, "Hmm, I don't know actually, haven't been too curious as to go up there, not even when I'm heading up the tower of Alteration," she said, her voice giving a bit of an echo in the empty hollow tower.

She turned back to the door and opened it, "Maybe it's like a watch tower or some place for the birds.

They entered into a small bridge that looked a lot more stable than the entrance one and a lot shorter, but was not closed off with windows either, so they felt the fresh breeze and the warmth of direct sunlight against their skin.

James had a comment about these bridges, "Safety isn't really a priority here is it?"

"What do you mean, there's a railing?" Mia replied looking over the edge.

"Aah, nothing is stopping me from throwing you over this bridge… nothing," he replied.

"You want them to put windows or something?"

She read his mind but didn't want to admit it, "Yeah, that's a pretty good idea," He agreed, "I mean if I was angry with someone and had the intent to kill, I mean, this would be the perfect place, There has to be some story of a learner who fell over or something."

Mia giggled, "No not really, not that I've heard of either," she replied, "This school is kind of new, and I think, people still cling to their humanity, you're the first I hear the speak about throwing someone overboard."

James ignored that, "Maybe it's just how they built it, the design and stuff," he shrugged.

Mia opened the door on the other side of the bridge, "Prepare to be impressed," she stepped in.

James stepped in after her, "Woah," he dragged it out as he took in everything at once, all that was a part of his mind, his imagination, was right in front of him.

They were in a massive room, about the size of the main hall, with high arched windows. The sunlight filled the hall as it was still just rising over the horizon.

The hall was divided in half, the first took the form of an infirmary, with people using their staves to help heal and mend together dummies. The other was a little bit calmer, it was separated into two rows of large blue rectangular carpets, each one inhabiting two individuals with staves creating transparent withering shields in front of each other and having the second person test it with their staff, they would take turns doing so. This hall was a little chaotic with the youngest of the age groups attending it and few teachers supervising.

James immediately remembered something from yesterday regarding Mia, "Staves?" he said, "Why do we have to use staves, you did magic without one?" He frowned.

Mia shoved him, "Shut up."

"What?"

"Don't speak about that at all, not one word about it," she got angry and put her finger to his face.

James raised his hands as if about to be arrested, "Okay, Okay, I won't speak about it," he lowered his hands.

Mia turned away and headed over to the wall, which consisted of weapon racks carrying staves lined up right next to each other.

"Why though?" he asked, "Why mustn't we speak about-," he didn't know how best to describe it with exposing it, "-the magic thing... I guess?"

She walked down looking at each staff as if each was a different piece of clothing. They all looked the same to James, he just wanted a reply.

"Jake just said so okay," Mia replied picking one from the weapon rack and handing it over to him.

"He just said so?" James repeated, holding his staff up.

Mia sighed, "You know he doesn't explain anything."

James grew I bit more curious about this mystery, "Is it some kind-,"

Mia interrupted him, "Look, do you want to do this or not?" She picked up a staff and glared at him.

James put on a fearful face and stared back, expecting to be hit. Her question was a bit confusing at first, but the situation came back into his mind, "Let's do it?" He said unsure of himself.

His expression made her smile and shake her head as she walked passed him.

She picked an empty carpet, closest to the entrance.

James jumped onto the carpet, excited, about to learn and cast his first magic spell, "So how is this done?" he took notice of the boy on the carpet next to him, he observed his stance and decided imitate it.

He turned to see Mia giving him a weird look, as if he was crazy.

James decided to quit with the stance and loosen his body, preparing for what's to come next.

Mia pulled out the piece of paper from her blazer pocket and read the part that listed the spells she should test. She shoved it back into her pocket, "Okay, you know Restoration right?"

"Off course," he replied with confidence, "Healing and protection."

Mia put on a worried look, "good enough," she shrugged, "Okay, the first spell that I will be testing you on is the basic shield spell, Protelius, it protects you from material objects, living is not counted here."

James was containing his excitement, nodding after Mia spoke, so happy to be talking about, and learning about this magic.

"Huh?" He realized, "What are you talking about material objects."

Mia took a stance and held her staff horizontally, pointing at James, "Let me show you," without saying a word, just a few inches from her staff, a shield started to appear, it grew in the shape of a circle and was about the height of her body when she was done, "Now tap it," she instructed.

James extended his arm with the staff and hit it.

The staff didn't pass through, instead it bounced off, "Cool," he complimented, "But you didn't speak the name of the spell."

She shrunk away the shield, "You don't have to, If you know the spell, you just have to think it," She explained, "Though it is suggested that you say it, as a beginner and if you know a lot of spells, your mind may think of another and give the wrong order," she stood straight, "Okay, now it's your turn."

James copied Mia's stance.

"Protelius," she repeated.

James cleared his throat and shook his head, preparing himself, he took a deep breath, "Protelius," he spoke clearly.

The same type of circle shield appeared, but his one grew rapidly, at an instant, it was the same as Mia's.

She was impressed, "Wow, that was quick," she said, "Took me quite a while to get that one," she frowned, "Not on my first try."

"But is it legit?" He asked, "Can it block material objects?"

She step forward and reached out with her staff and touched it, "Hmm, I was sure it would pass," she gave it a knock, the shield was good, "Impressive," she stepped back.

"Hmmmmmmm," James hummed with a smile, "I think we're discovering some talent here."

Mia rolled her eyes, "Yeah, you could make a great healer," she laughed.

James didn't understand the laughing part after her compliment, if it was a compliment, he doubted it now, "What's funny?"

"Sorry… Nurse," she laughed.

"Ohh, I see now," he realized.

"I'm just joking James," she said calming herself a bit, "Okay, next spell," she announced, "this one deals with blocking non-material things, can you guess, what I mean by 'non-material'?" She enquired.

James raised his brow, confused, "What could possibly be not material, people?" he asked himself, "No, people are material," His mind was searching through archives and archives of memory, trying to find something that could be non-materialistic or think up something from his imagination. He looked at the ceiling, then back at Mia, "Nope, nothing, got nothing," he replied.

"Magic," Mia replied.

"Huh?" James replied surprised.

"Mostly Destruction magic," she further explained, "Illusion, Conjuration and Alteration need something more…complicated."

"Okay, what's the spell?" he asked, eager to move on from the theory of magic and non-material objects.

"Protelius Migei," she spoke the spell, "It's the same, with just another word."

James repeated her, "Protelius Migei."

"Now, you going to have to do it without me demonstrating it," she said.

"Why?"

"I'm the only one here who is able to cast Destruction, between the two of us," she explained, "Nothing's changed."

James took the same stance, "Okay," he said preparing himself again, "Protelius Migei," he said.

Nothing happened.

"Wait what?' He said puzzled, "Protelius Migei," he repeated.

A shield started to grow slowly, "Ah, there we have it."

Just at that moment of happiness, it began its rapid growth again. Only this time, it didn't stop growing.

It was three times his size now, still growing, passing through the floor beneath him and spreading wider.

The boy on the carpet next to him quickly avoided the shield.

"What's happening?" James said, watching in fear.

The whole hall began to take notice of the ever growing shield, striking a bit of panic amongst the young ones, distancing themselves from it.

Mia was really shocked and surprised, frozen and staring.

"Mia!" James shouted, "What must I do, I can't stop it."

Mia snapped out of it, "Let go of the staff," she instructed.

James dropped the staff immediately and fell back onto the ground.

The shield shrunk away and disappeared.

Mia went over to help him up.

The rest of the hall was in complete silence, staring at James.

One of the teachers supervising walked over to the pair, with an upsetting expression on her face, "What's going here?" she asked, she noticed Mia's badge, "You not supposed to be here, you wear the badge of Alteration."

"Sorry ma'am," Mia apologized, "I'm-," she was interrupted by the teacher.

"And you, you don't have a badge."

James didn't know what to say in response.

"Yes ma'am, he's new, I testing him," She said pulling out the piece of paper.

James nodded.

She examined the piece of paper and handed it back to her, "Alright, but please stop causing a scene," she turned away from them, "Everyone please continue with your class!" She shouted.

All the students continued with their lessons and the chattering volume was increased again.

James sighed in relief, "What happened there?"

Mia shrugged, "I don't know," she replied picking up his staff, "How are you that powerful, you have never even touched a staff."

"Hmmmm," he wanted to continue with his 'talent' talk, but felt the situation was a bit more problematic, "I am clueless."

"With you, it's not the matter of whether or not you can cast it properly, it's whether or not you can control it."

He chuckled, "Let's not get ahead of ourselves here," he said, "We've only just started, let's just call it a mistake."

She handed his staff to him, "It can't be... but let's move on."

On the other side of the school, standing in front of another door was Mark and Stanley.

"Impressive, isn't it?" Stanley asked.

Mark gave it a closer look, "Hmm, it's a big door I'll give it that."

"I meant, what it looks like," Stanley explained, trying to make some kind of conversation.

Mark blinked a few times and looked at him, "It looks like a door."

Stanley shook his head, "Never mind," he stepped forward.

"What do you want me to say?" He chuckled.

Stanley pushed open the doors and stepped it.

The entrance tower was very much the same as the one Mia and James walked up.

Stanley started up the staircase.

Mark followed behind, "Oh, come on, I mean I have to walk upstairs as well for this," he complained.

Stanley sighed, "You really do complain a lot don't you?"

The hall of Destruction was equal in size to the one of Restoration, but had a completely different setting. The hall was filled, all round with upright mannequins and archery targets, organized properly to use up the space efficiently. This hall was not a safety hazard at all, keeping all learners and students very safe from any destruction magic as it was all harmful. For starters, each and every mannequin and archery target that stood, behind it was a large wooden board in case of any person missing the target. There was a line that could not be crossed by the students, one they had to stand behind.

Something caught Mark's interest. The targets did not burn to ash by the magic. Each target had some sought of regenerative ability that acted swiftly every time it was hit. The targets would regenerate to their original state, ready to be hit again.

"Okay," Mark spoke out, "This is impressive."

"Yeah, Destruction is kind of nice," Stanley admitted.

He took note of the mannequins, "I like how these mannequins heal back," he pointed out, "Restoration magic I presume," he turned to him acting smart.

Stanley shook his head and pushed up his glasses, "Nope, not at all," he made it clear that he was wrong, "It's an enchantment actually, placed into the mannequin, set to regenerate every time, till the cube wears out, then another is placed."

"Cube?" Mark repeated.

"You'll learn about it in Enchantment class tomorrow."

He shrugged, "Okay, teach me something then."

There were four teachers supervising and the students that were performing the Destruction arts were the seniors.

One of the teachers noticed them standing doing nothing, with smirks on their faces. He was tall and kind of scary wearing black robes and a dark blue tie with a staff in the one hand.

Mark and Stanley noticed him approach them, and they did nothing but stare at him as he drew closer.

He stopped right in front of them, frowning down with a piercing stare, "What's happening here... you lost?"

One of the students nearby chuckled.

"No, sir," Stanley replied respectfully.

Mark shook his head, unable to say a word.

"Explain."

"Um," Stanley began, "I volunteered to help, this new student, Mark, with his choice today."

"Ah, Okay," his expression changed, becoming more lively, "You're the first group today, please, take an empty spot," he instructed politely, before turning his attention back to the rest of the hall.

Mark sighed, "Okay, I suggest we do what he says."

"Good idea," he replied, heading to the weapon racks.

They found a reasonable place to start testing their magic, a place that was one empty mannequin away from the nearest Destruction student.

They both stood behind the line.

Stanley checked the piece of paper he was given and began to explain, "Okay, Destruction is an offensive form of magic, nothing to do with defense, just attack," he began, "There are three main types of spells in Destruction, -," He was interrupted.

"Let me guess," Mark said.

"Okay, guess away."

"Fire, Ice and Lightning," Mark smirked at him.

Stanley nodded slowly, "You're right, can I continue?"

"Off course."

"Yes, the three main types of spells for destruction are Fire, Ice and Lightning, they all branch out from each category to more dangerous spells, but even the most basic of these spells can be lethal."

Mark just nodded in return.

"Okay," he began, "To cast an ice spell, you use the word 'Izolts'," he explained, "That's the root word for the other advanced spells," he stood in front of the target, "Oh, and there's no need to speak the word, but because you're new to this, it's best you say it."

He aimed his staff at the mannequin and spoke the words, "Izolts", and from the staff a strong gust of blue wind blew out toward the target. The mannequin slowly turned to a blue shade as if it were getting some kind of frostbite.

Stanley put the magic to a stop, "Like that."

"Neat," Mark replied, "Let me give it a go."

Stanley stepped aside, "Be my guest."

The mannequin was returning to its original colour quite rapidly.

Mark aimed at the target and spoke the words, "Izolts," and the same thing happened.

"Nice," Stanley complimented.

Mark stopped the magic, "Okay, next spell, I've got the hang of that."

Stanley pushed up his glasses, "Next, we will be dealing with lightning, and the root word would be 'Blesk'," he explained.

"Huh, Blesk?" He said, "What language it this?"

Stanley shrugged, "No idea, but I read that these spells are just a bunch of languages and made up words put together, apparently, languages of another world," he said, "There is no specific language or language that is magic," he stood in front of the target, "Lightning can be very dangerous, I think it's the most dangerous out of the three, in my opinion," he aimed his staff, "Blesk," he said, and small bolt of blue, bright lightning shot out from the staff, hitting the mannequin instantly.

"Woah," Mark said surprised, blinking his eyes from the bright light.

The lightning left a black mark on the target.

Stanley stood aside, "Now it's your turn."

Mark was a little bit nervous, his heart racing, taking some deep breaths, "I hate lightning," he said.

Standing in front of the mannequin, he forgot the word used to summon it, "What's the word?"

"Blesk."

He noticed a girl closest to where they were, standing in front of her target, firing what appeared to be ice spikes at her target. What stood out was the fact that she was not aiming her staff at the target, the staff was upright, yet the spikes shot out straight into the mannequin.

"Stanley, how are they doing it without aiming?" he enquired.

Stanley turned to the girl, "Oh, that's taught later on, advanced stuff, not for beginners," he said, "never do it unless the teacher says you can, otherwise you going to be breaking some furniture or injuring someone badly."

"Looks pretty cool," he said turning his attention back to the target, he looked at the staff, then the mannequin, "Blesk," he said.

The jolt of lightning scared him, he closed his eyes and turned his head as soon as he saw the bright light.

A few moments later, he peeked through one eye, investigating.

No lightning to be seen.

He calmed himself, "That wasn't so bad," he said.

Stanley nodded in response, "I'd say you doing pretty well, now let's get to the last category so we can follow the timetable to our next subject," he said taking his place in front of the mannequin, "Fire, is the easiest of the three, so this shouldn't be a problem, the word you speak is 'Feur'," he said as a breath of flames breezed out of the staff, burning the mannequin.

He stopped and let Mark have his turn.

"Feur," he spoke.

Nothing happened.

Mark frowned, "Hmm," he repeated, "Feur."

Nothing happened.

"Easiest you say," he brought the staff to his face.

"Maybe, you didn't pronounce it properly."

"Maybe the staff's broken," he said aiming it at the target, "let me try again," he took a deep breath, "Feur."

The fire shot out like a flamethrower.

Mark nodded, impressed at his flame.

Just suddenly, the flame grew to a great significant size, as if it were a dragons doing.

Mark grew to fear the fire as it began to feel very hot. Even the students around him took notice and stopped with their practices.

"Mark, stop the magic," Stanley said taking a few steps back.

"I can't," He sounded terrified.

"Drop the staff," he instructed.

Mark did as he was told immediately and stepped back, away from it.

The flames extinguished.

The whole hall was silent, staring at the aftermath.

The mannequin was gone, burnt away to ashes, save the wood bit it that acted as the mannequin's skeleton, but even that was burnt to a crisp.

Everyone waited for something to happen, but nothing did. The mannequin didn't begin its regenerating routine. It just stood there with a small bit of smoke rising from it. Even the board of wood behind was scarred.

Mark was in a panic state, breathing hard with his heart pounding away at his chest.

Stanley was frozen in shock, just staring at him.

The same teacher from before and another came to investigate the scene.

"What's going on here?" the female teacher asked examining the remains of the mannequin. She also wore robes.

Mark struggled to his feet.

Stanley was the first to explain, "I was showing some basic magic."

Before she could say anything else, the male teacher explained the situation, "This boy," he pointed at Mark, "is a new student and he is helping him try all the subjects before the choosing this afternoon."

She looked at the mannequin, "You sure this is basic?"

Stanley nodded, "It's the spells on the list we were given."

The teacher raised one brow in response to Stanley's reply, she look at Mark, without any words to say.

The male teacher cleared his throat, "Well, I guess one mannequin needs replacing," he said, "I trust you are both done here?"

"Yes sir," Stanley replied.

Mark proceeded to pick his staff but the female teacher stopped him.

"No, leave it," she said picking it up herself.

Both Stanley and Mark went to the weapon racks where Stanley left his staff, feeling the weight of everybody's eyes on them as they made their way to the entrance and out of sight.

On the bridge, Mark let out a big sigh, "That was crazy."

Stanley chuckled, "Yeah."

Daniel and Angelina had made their way up the tower and into the Hall of Alteration. Its setting was similar to the hall of Restoration, divided into two, except that this one wasn't an infirmary, more of a greenhouse by the looks of it, filled with a lot of natural elements to it. The other half was fitted with two rows of green carpets.

Daniel was not able to make out what the learners stationed on the rows of carpets were doing. Within the quick second that he glanced in their direction, there was no visual element that drew him in. The greenhouse side of the hall was I little more interesting. Tables of plants and flowers, more colourful and appealing to the eye.

"So this is Alteration?" He asked, staring at the nearest pot plant.

"Nah, not really, there's more to it," Angelina replied, "I was also a bit skeptical the first time I entered this hall."

Daniel sighted the staves and headed to them ahead of Angelina, "I've always wanted to use something that creates magic," he said examining each one closely.

"Same here," she replied picking any random staff available, "Just pick any, they all the same," she said watching as he browsed intensively.

"This is my first staff as a wizard," he said pulling one out delicately, inspecting it as though it were a piece from a museum.

Angelina went up close to him, "Don't use the word witch or wizard around here," she whispered to him, "In fact, anywhere."

Daniel was greatly confused by her warning, "Wait," he whispered back, "Isn't that what we all are?"

Angelina shook her head slowly.

Suddenly, Daniel was interested, at even higher levels, enough to put the staff aside, "Please explain,"

Her eyes wondered all over the place, "I think it's best we speak about it in another setting," she suggested, "lets complete todays tasks first."

Daniel was way too curious now, but he was able to contain it, "Okay," he put a smile back on his face.

"Okay!" she said turning towards the rest of the hall, "Let's start with something easy."

They both headed to the greenhouse side of the hall.

"What is Alteration magic exactly?" Daniel asked.

"Well," she said finding an unoccupied wooden table, she started clearing it up while she explained, "It's kind of like, the manipulation of the world around you and other life forms," she said, "But it doesn't affect the human mind, our minds are evolved and corrupted, we have Illusion magic for that."

"Okay, I'm already interested in this," he said.

Daniel leaned his staff against the table, "What do you want me to help with?" He offered.

"Um," she responded looking around, "Sorry, give me a sec," she pulled out the piece of paper and read its contents, "Do you know what a bean looks like?'

Daniel felt this was not what she was actually asking, "Is that a trick question?"

She giggled, "No, very simple actually," she put the piece of paper back into her pocket.

Daniel was still unsure because... *who wouldn't know what a bean looks like?* So he just nodded in reply, slowly with a concerned looked on his face.

"Great," she congratulated him, "go get a few from there," she pointed at a thin long table against the wall filled with two rows of white open sacks, "I'll get the water and cotton," she went off elsewhere.

Daniel made his way to the table, inspecting all the other student's little magic tricks. He couldn't quite figure out what they were doing with the plants, but it wasn't his greatest concern, right now he had to carry out the simple task of getting the seeds.

He made it to the table.

At first he just walked up and down, looking at all the different types of seeds, some even taking very odd colours and shapes. Each one giving him wonder of what type of plant that would sprout out of it. Almost being consumed by his interests, he returned to the task at hand.

He made his way up and saw a bag of seeds that looked like beans, "That was easy," he said taking a few.

Looking at the next bag, he began to doubt the choice he'd made because the seeds occupying this one, took the form and shape of beans as well. For a few moments he stood there, unsure which to take. He decided on both so he used his other hand to pick a few from the bag.

The situation seemed solve and out of his hair until he came across another bag filled with bean shaped seeds, "Wait," he said to himself. When he put some thought to it, he didn't remember the exact look of a bean, the colours and markings on them. His head was about to explode because to him, there is only one type of bean.

At that moment, he came up with a plan that could make the situation better, and asking for help from one of the learners was not it. He placed one bean from the first bag onto the table and one from the other bag next to it. The access seeds he shoved into his pockets.

He took a bean from the third bag and placed it next to the others and made his way down the table in search for other similar seeds.

In the end, It came to be a row of six seeds.

Standing there in front of all six seeds, he realized what Angelina really meant when she asked him the question. It was a trick question, "She probably knew there was hundreds of seeds that took the shape of a bean," he said to himself.

He stood there, so very scared to pick the wrong seed, the probability was against him.

He felt a few taps on his right shoulder.

Looking over, he found no one. A little suspicious but he turned back to his seeds.

At the corner of his left eye, he noticed someone standing next to him.

It was Angelina smiling back at him.

"You fell for it," she said taking notice of the row of seeds in front of him, "What are you doing?" She began to laugh uncontrollably.

He couldn't help but giggle himself. He bent over to get a closer look at the seeds, "You knew this was going to happen, didn't you?"

"No," she continued to laugh, "You said you knew."

"I didn't think there would be hundreds of these things."

Angelina also bent over next to him, trying to calm herself.

"Well?" Daniel said turning to her.

"Well What?"

"Which one is it?" He asked.

She placed her finger above them, pointing at them one at a time. It was as if she didn't know herself. She picked one as if at random and stood up, "Let's go," she said picking more from the same bag.

"How did you know?" Daniel enquired.

Angelina chuckled, "They're all beans."

Daniels face became blank, "Oh."

She laughed.

They headed back to the table.

The desk was now prepared, with two sauces, a jug of water and cotton.

Angeline placed the pile of beans next to the saucer and began to explain, "What we are going to start with here is to simply grow a plant," she said, "to be precise, accelerate its growth... growth acceleration."

Daniel nodded, "Sweet."

She placed a bean in between the cotton and poured a bit of water over it, "Do your bit," she instructed.

"At least this is going to help me grow my garden quicker," he said pouring water over it.

"That's an upside to it."

Daniel could recall having grown some plants with a bit of cotton and water when he was younger, as some school experiment.

"For this, all you have to say is the word 'Rritet'," she said placing her staff just over her experiment, "Rritet."

A small bit of green smoke drifted from her staff and entered into the cotton. In a few seconds, a small stem sprouted from the top and a few leaves started to form.

For some odd reason, this phenomenon was surprisingly more fascinating to Daniel, what he remembers from this experiment years ago, was the fact of waiting day by day, for one tiny stem to find its way through the cotton. Seeing it happen in a matter of seconds was amazing.

"Now you turn."

Daniel was excited about it, just about to grow something, "Rritet," he said holding his staff by his experiment.

The same thing happened with the green smoke, his plant too, began to sprout from beneath the cotton. The growth of his was rather quick and was twice the size of Angelina's experiment when it stopped growing.

"Hmm," he said impressed with his one, "I'd say about twice the size of yours."

"Haha," she said sarcastically.

The plant began to grow again, and from inside the cotton, the roots as well began to show themselves.

"Woah," Angelina stepped back.

The plant was a small bush at this moment.

This did certainly draw some attention from the rest of the crowd.

The plant stopped growing, and now it seemed to be for good.

"It's not growing anymore," Daniel sounded disappointed.

"Off course," Angelina replied, "There is nothing for it to consume anymore, your spell wore off."

One of the teachers of the hall came up to them, "Impressive growth," she said admiring the plant, "For a new student, you have quite the talent."

Daniel felt flattered, "Thank you ma'am."

She moved on to assist another learner.

"How'd you do that?" Angelina asked, "We're using the simplest growth spell."

Daniel shrugged, "The teacher did say I have some talent."

"I don't think so."

"Don't be jelly."

Angelina gave him a wired look.

Daniel soon realized that, the word he just used was not appropriate, given the timeline, "Jealous, I meant jealous."

Angelina shook her head, "Yeah, yeah, let's just move on, to something a little more interesting."

"After you," he spoke like a gentleman.

"Thank you," she replied in a similar manner.

They made their way out of the natured part of the hall.

"Is there such a thing as reverse growth?" Daniel asked.

"Yeah, actually there is," she replied, "Very advanced though."

"Now that's cool."

They picked an empty carpet for which to commence with the next bit.

"What are we going to do here?"

"I'm going to paralyze you," she replied with a sinister smile.

"Wait, what?"

The rest of the day ran a bit smooth, nothing too out of the ordinary happened. The other new students did all their first tests successfully. The day seem to go on forever, thanks to the endless walks they had to go on, in between each of the towers and the flight of stairs they had to go through.

It was later in the afternoon when they found themselves done with their first day at this school. There ideal hangout place now was the study, which was not crowded at all. Most learners wondered the grounds after school.

"Today was a long day," Mia said throwing herself onto the couch, "I'm glad it's over."

"My day started off crazy," Stanley blurted out, "Mark went a bit overboard in the Hall of destruction, he is a bit too strong."

Mark started to flex, "Yup, god of destruction," he sat on one of the chairs at a table.

Mia sat up, "Wait, what happened with you?"

Stanley leaned against the couch, "Did you see the incinerated mannequin?"

"Yeah," she nodded.

"That was him," He pointed at Mark.

"James, you also caused a scene this morning," Mia turned to him, "creating a shield that big."

"What?" He said, "It was my first attempt at magic."

"You're lucky it was the Magic blocking shield, or you could have hurt someone or broken something."

"James shrugged, "Lucky me.""

Angelina stepped in, "It seems also Daniel has some talent in Alteration, according to Mrs. Fendle."

Mia had to keep asking, "William, did you do anything crazy?"

William looked at Clara and then back to Mia, he shook his head, "Nope, I'd say I'm kind of average," he replied.

"No, you did pretty good," she said putting her hand on his shoulder.

Mia turned to Opal, "You?"

Opal shook her head from shoulder to shoulder with a smile.

"Claude?"

"Let me see," he place his hand on his chin, "Nope, don't recall turning any mannequins to ash."

Mia sat back again, "At least it was only in the morning, I was afraid you were going to cause a scene in every subject."

Mark rubbed his hands together, excited, "When do we get to choose?"

"Just before supper," Clara replied.

"Choose wisely guys," Mia said, "Not just because you caused damage in the one subject, doesn't mean it's your ideal."

"Fine by me," Mark said, "Now who's up for another chess match?"

Later, at a dimmer time of the afternoon, Mrs. Mannikral walked into their dormitory study. Most of the students silenced themselves in her presence, it seemed a tad bit rare for a teacher to be entering a dorm.

"May I please have the new students follow me," she requested.

This was the moment of truth for all of them, after the great and fun day of discovering magic, it was time for them to start making a choice. In the undying silence of the study they made their way to the door, very quietly with the regulars staring at them.

Mrs. Mannikral had another quick announcement to make, "And for the rest of you, it is almost supper," she stepped out the room, "Please follow."

Down the echoing and almost empty corridors they walked, only coming across a few students lurking about.

"So how was your day of testing?" She asked.

"It went well," William replied.

The others agreed with him.

"Well, I hope you have made up your mind about the field you will choose to take, it'll just take a few minutes," she explained.

"Is subject changing a thing here?" Mark asked.

"I'm afraid not," she replied, "After today... after your choice, you will be bound to that field till you're done," she said, "It is why we got our volunteers to explain to you a bit about the subject."

They made it to another hallway that lead to another door, about the size of your average. This door was ordinary, nothing special was carved on to or put there to make it look intriguing.

She stood at the door and turned back to the learners, "I hope you've had your time to think about it," she gave a slight nod and opened the doors.

There was not a sound, with only the door's creek to fill their ears, it made it a very nerving moment.

They stepped into a dark room with closed curtains, thick enough to keep every bit of light from entering, not even through the fabric. It was kind of stuffy and warm.

Mrs. Mannikral closed the doors, and for a moment there was complete darkness, with only the sound of her footsteps that could be picked up by their senses.

The centre of the room lit up in five different colours. It was the same transparent orbs, each bearing a simplified but still recognizable version of the symbols of magic. They floated in midair with a bit of an aura about them.

Mrs. Mannikral stood beside the orbs, "This here is where your choice will be made," she began, "The reason why we don't allow subject changing, is because whichever choice you make here, you will gain a certain amount of special properties that come with that subject."

James's interest lay with the layout of the room, wondering why it was made to be so dark. It did allow for the orbs to create a beautiful and aesthetic feel, which he did fancy.

"Let's say it is some type of enchantment that is placed upon you when you gain the badge," she continued, "It will allow you to do better in that chosen subject than the others you didn't decide on."

None of this made much sense to Mark, he was just lost in the colours the orbs were giving off.

"Ok, I will not waste anymore of your time, it is time to make your choice," she smiled and gave a light nod, "I will call you up," she pulled out a small piece of paper, "First we have Opal."

Opal was really nervous, being the first one to make her choice, and above all that, she did not know what to do. Sure she saw these floating spheres in front of her but that was it.

She stepped forward and stood in front of them.

"Now please place your hand into one," Mrs. Mannikral explained.

She was saved, it was all she wanted to hear. She raised her hand slowly, trying hard to keep it together, heart pounding, feeling a little unsure of her irreversible choice. Still she didn't want to be wasting everybody's time so she placed her hand into the purple sphere.

"Conjuration," Mrs. Mannikral said.

Opal was expecting something drastic to happen.

While her hand remained in the orb, she noticed a purple light appear on her blazer, just beneath the school badge, it seemed to be stitching together her conjuration emblem and when it was complete, Mrs. Mannikral congratulated her on her choice and was asked to step aside.

"Mark, if you may," she read the next name.

Mark didn't seem to be nervous at all. At first his choice was going to be Destruction, but then he started to think about it a bit more, and took into account what Mia said, so he made a wise decision, one base on the ability of his diamond, which was protection. He placed his hand into the yellow sphere. He chose Restoration.

This came as a surprise to both James and Daniel, not too long ago he was boasting about being the 'god of destruction'.

When his badge was formed he stepped aside and stood next to Opal.

"James."

James went forward and decided on the subject of Destruction. His choice was not base on anything really, he felt that if there is a healer in the group, someone who can use destruction spells may be a necessity.

Daniel was called up next and he picked Illusion.

Claude fancied himself Alteration and William decided on Restoration as well.

"And that's it," Mrs. Mannikral announced, "I thank you for you cooperation and hope that you excel in the subjects that you have chosen."

They thanked her.

"You are now students of Marridor," she smiled making her way to the door, "Now I hope you know your way to the hall."

They didn't.

"It's almost supper, ask around if you get lost," she said, "don't be shy, it's time you get to know some of our students and prefects," she pushed open the doors and the spheres disappeared again.

Mrs. Mannikral made her way elsewhere and they were left alone in some corner of the school to fend for themselves.

At the main hall that evening, All the new students eventually found their way to the hall, but from their experience, tagging along with the regulars is a much better idea when mapping out the maze of the school. No one had begun to consume their food, waiting for Mr. Patchwalker to walk in and give the announcements. While they waited, everyone continued to communicate about their previous holiday or how hard their first day was.

"That choosing room is scary," Opal said.

"It's just an empty room," Mark replied, confused.

"A dark empty room," she add, "Why is it like that anyway?"

Clara shrugged, "No one knows or cares, you just go in there for your choosing, and never go in there ever again," she explained.

Mia looked at their badges, "Great choices, what was your motivation?"

"What was your motivation?" Mark redirected the question.

"Nothing really," she replied, "Jake suggested I take it."

"Huh," James said, "Jake said take Alteration?"

She nodded.

"Hmm, I'm guessing he didn't mention why?" Daniel predicted.

Mia shook her head.

It was a few minutes after all the students had made their way to the hall and all the staff was seated that Mr. Patchwalker made his presences clear. He went and stood behind the announcement stand and asked the learners to silence themselves.

"Good Evening Marridor," he greeted, "As you may very well know, today was our new student's choosing day," he began, "I hear that some of them already have exceptional talent and am very excited about that," he said without excitement, he paused for a moment, looking at something on his stand, "I would like for all the new students to stand in their places," he instructed.

Another embarrassing moment. Most of them thought, but they did as they were told and stood up, standing out from the majority that sat and watched.

"I hope you found it to be a welcoming place and that you have made a wise decision with you subject choice," he paused again for a moment, "I look forward to seeing you excel in your chosen fields and discover many hidden talents."

Everyone listened in silence, and the ones standing up couldn't wait to be ordered to sit down again.

"I, Mr. Patchwalker, the staff and fellow students give you all a warm welcome, as students of Marridor," he gave a slight nod and began to clap.

The rest of the hall joined in with the applause.

"You may be seated," he instructed.

James didn't waste his time following this instruction.

Mr. Patchwalker's expression turned dim, "Now."

Every student turned to him again.

"I feel I was a bit mysterious about the new rule I set in motion yesterday, about halting your freedom to leave the school grounds," he switched some papers on his stand, "I believe it is best to explain it now."

Silence came about by itself as everyone began to listen attentively.

Mr. Patchwalker took a deep breath, "We have been told about a group of very dangerous individuals, three to be exact, whom have stolen some dangerous magical objects and have even threatened to kill with them. This was just a few days ago" he explained, "and one of these victims to their threats was a Dead Crow."

The hall gasped as they heard mention of the name 'Dead Crow'.

James's heart skipped a beat, and repeated in his mind, the information Mr. Patchwalker just revealed. *Three individuals, Dangerous objects, a few days ago.*

James couldn't help but exchange glances with Mark and Daniel, whom were also locked in the same thoughts.

He turned his attention to the silver plate in front of him, stared into the many reflections that bounced off it. If it were really them that Mr. Patchwalker was talking about, then his information was false. He didn't recall making any threats, unless by threat, he means when he lost control of his body and raised his sword against the thief that happened to be a Dead Crow. *Stolen* was another word that stood out, the way he remember it was different. It was the Dead Crow thief that tried to steal the *dangerous magical objects*. Jake himself said that these objects only came into existence during their time, in the present. Now the new question engraving itself in his mind had to do with this Dead Crow. Who were hey exactly?

"Right now, the Dead Crow will be searching the whole city for these three criminals as they believe that these individuals have taken refuge here, and do not want any of us to interfere by entering and leaving the school as we please," he explained, "I am sorry but it is for your own safety and ordered by the Dead Crow themselves," he neatened up the papers on his stand, "Enjoy your evening," he concluded.

Mark sighed out loud, "Well, that was welcoming," he said sarcastically, "It was good until he told us to sit down," he said filling his plate with food.

Daniel nodded in agreement.

"What is this Dead Crow group exactly?" Mark enquired seeking an answer from someone other than Jake.

That question came as a surprise to everyone except him. Daniel and James were just as clueless as him but asking it that way was not very clever at all. But he himself didn't see any problem with the question.

"You don't know the Dead Crow?" Claude asked with a very concerned look on his face.

Mark shook his head very casually.

Daniel came in to save the day, "Where we come from, it's very secluded, no Dead Crow, nothing," he explained, "We've only heard rumors."

Mia smiled and shook her head at the incredible lie Daniel came up with.

"Well," William began, "To put it simple, they are our protectors, more important than even the lords protectors," he took a sip from his goblet, "they are the judges, juries and executioners, symbols of Justice, they make the wanted posters, pay the bounty hunters, a lot of things," he explained.

Similar to Jake's answer it seemed.

Well, that would explain the false story they have given out, James thought.

"Dead Crow," Mark repeated.

William nodded.

"That name doesn't fit the description you just gave me."

"But I'm surprised you don't know about them," Clara said.

Mark shook his head, "Never cared."

Opal change the mood, made it a bit more serious, "That's because you live the good life."

"What?" Mark asked surprised by her reaction.

She never made eye contact with anyone, kept her eye one her plate.

Mark was confused by her sudden change in mood, but didn't say anything about it in fear of making it worst.

"What's wrong?" Daniel asked.

"Nothing," she replied.

The atmosphere was unbearable.

"So this Dead Crow," James began, "what makes them so famous, who is the leader?"

"That's a long story," Clara replied, "you will have to catch up in history, as for the leader..." she shrugged, "but they earned their reputation by bringing in the system of justice and by implementing it in exchange for nothing," she explained, "From what I hear, they have helped a lot of people and have brought in some better times."

"'Favour is our Duty' they say," William added.

Everything James was hearing right now was selling a very good name to these Dead Crows. Their most recent actions in trying to steal from them was very puzzling. The name itself does not have a welcoming ring to it. Now this talk about them being these good people that have created a system that has helped many. This most definitely needed some digging in to.

"Be glad this happened right after you joined this school," Angelina added, "You would be trapped out there with these dangerous people."

James raised a brow, knowing very well that this lockdown is partially their fault.

"I guess we dodged a bullet as they say," Mark said.

James frowned at him and shook his head.

Mark was very bad at this blending in verbally part, mentioning things of the modern age in the presence of these people.

"Bullet?" Claude asked.

"He meant to say 'arrow'" Daniel lied.

"How can you possibly mistaken the one word for the other, they don't even sound the same?" He asked.

Daniel just shrugged in return.

Mark didn't seem bothered about what he just said. He just continued with his meal.

"Yeah," Angelina agreed with suspicion, "I guess you're right."

The hall emptied out much faster today, people going to get themselves a good and long night sleep. First learning day really does upset the schedule you have set for the holiday, you have to change it at a moment's notice.

The very next day was to operate as a normal school day for everyone, though the first lessons were not over just yet. They had to pack a few of their books into their school bags before leaving.

It was a game of follow the leader. Finding a class was impossible. As for this being their official first day. The excitement was quite high.

A few lessons into the day, they found themselves in a more interesting class, that taught the subject of Enchanting and a familiar face, Mrs. Mannikral was the teacher of this class.

The setting was more like a display room, around the tables and chairs, with a lot of medieval objects included in the variety of inventory. What really stood out was the small very bright coloured cubes that were placed on higher shelves.

In front of each of the learners was a small block of wood and a dagger.

Placed behind Mrs. Mannikral was a very large chalk board stand.

"Good morning learners," She greeted, "Now for the new students, joining us this term, I'll give a brief explanation of what this subject is about," she began the explain, "Enchantment is a sought of magical art that allows you to brand or engrave an object or living organism with magic, for example, a curse," she walked around the class slowly, "Last term we did the theory of Enchanting, which I suggest you look over and give a bit of studying in your free time to be on board with the rest of the class."

The horrors of arriving late or missing quite a bit of school has always been putting the extra hours to catch up to the rest of the class.

"This term we will begin with the practical side of enchanting, using what we call enchantment cubes," she picked a light blue cube with an inner glow, about the size of her palm, with runes engrave to the near edges of the sides that held a darker blue shade, "Now, these come in different colours and rune markings to serve an incredible variety of purposes, some even crafted with many properties," she placed it back on the table, "Okay, in front of you is a block of wood and dagger," she said picking a box filled with these enchantment cubes, same colour as the one she showed but much smaller, about the size of an eraser.

She handed one to each learner.

In front, with the same objects as the learners on the small table, she began to explain what was to be done, "I have given you a smaller sized enchantment cube and will demonstrate what you are to do with it," she explained picking up the dagger, "These are not sharp so no need to worry about cutting yourself," she said placing the blade on her palm, "you are to place the cube on the blade and press down against it," she closed her palm for a few seconds and opened it again.

The cube had disappeared.

The class was surprised by her magic trick.

"Now if you look closely, you will start to see the runes just a bit faintly," she held the dagger forward, "This just means it is enchanted, the cube has merged with the dagger and has given it special properties," she then picked up the piece of wood and held it up as well, "What I want you to do next is simple, just drive the dagger along the wooden surface and witness how it begins to freeze it and give it a minor shade of blue," she demonstrated, "Now remember, that it is important that you do not cut yourself with the blade once enchanted, the effects will hurt," she explained placing both the dagger and wood back on the table, "Now it's your turn."

Everyone picked up the cube of ice and followed exactly what Mrs. Mannikral instructed.

James was a tad bit curious of how it disappeared, and decided to do things differently. Instead of closing his palm around the blade, he placed the dagger on the piece of wood, then the enchantment cube steadily on it. With his forefinger he pressed down the cube onto the blade and witnessed what really happened. The cube began to melt quickly into some type of thick liquid and slowly disappear into the object.

"Hmm, that's interesting."

The girl sitting on the desk to the left found his experiment interesting, but was unable to implement it herself, having already done it the way Mrs. Mannikral demonstrated.

James picked it by the handle and placed the edged tip onto the block of wood with a bit of force. The same blue effect occurred, just as Mrs. Mannikral showed. He touched the wood out of curiosity and found the texture very smooth and kind of sticky, like dry ice. This was definitely a subject he wouldn't mind catching up with. This was way more interesting than you average topic.

One of their final classes of the day was P.E, taking place around one in the afternoon. It was outside, on one of the school grounds, in front of another building, there were a lot of targets and hay stacks against the wall of the building. No teacher had arrived yet to tend to the learners so socializing is what they did.

"So what kinds of sports are there?" Daniel asked.

"Oh nothing much," Mia replied, "For P.E it is just Archery, sword fighting and what you may call parkour."

They stood in a small circle, as the others did.

"What are they training us for? War?" Mark Asked.

Mia shrugged.

"They might," Clara replied, "A lot of bad things have happened in the past, war being one of them, they probably just preparing us for the worst."

"So it's not just for sport?"

"I don't think so, I mean most people who leave after their final year join the Dead Crow."

The mention of the Dead Crow again, and by the looks of it, if most of its inhabitants are scholars from here, then it cannot be bad. Maybe this thief was just a bad apple trying to cause some trouble.

"Is it choice?" James asked, "That they join the Dead Crow."

No one knew the answer to that question.

"You seem to distrust the Dead Crow James, why is that?" Opal asked.

"Uhm," James was not sure how to reply, so he pulled out the oldest reply in the book, "Just curious is all."

"The library has a lot of history on them," she suggested, "maybe you should have a look."

"I'll be sure to do that," he replied. Just then, he remembered Jake mentioned that a lot of the history was re-written to bestow some kind of new order in the new world and that they should pay a bit more attention to the difference in history now and what is being taught in the present. Just for the sake of knowing, he realized he was going to have to enjoy the subject of history now. Maybe finding the modifications would make it more bearable and possibly fascinating.

The teacher arrived finally.

He was a tall man with short brown hair and a trimmed beard. He looked forty, wearing a cloak over his clothing.

He stood in front of the students, "Afternoon, learners," he greeted.

The learners gathered around him.

"Who is that?" Mia asked.

"No idea," Angelina replied.

"Shouldn't that be us asking that question?" Mark giggled.

"I am Mr. Padgett, your new teacher."

"Oh," Mark realized.

Everyone remained quiet. They all had surprised looks on their faces.

Mr. Padgett tried to put a smile on his face, "I will be replacing your previous teacher, he seems to have fallen sick, something that will keep me here permanently," he explained, "Today we won't be doing anything…physical, that's why I requested that you do not change, instead I suggest that we get to know each other," he said putting a big smile on his face, from cheek to cheek.

CHAPTER 10

The Dead Crow's Watch list

At about a similar time, far down to the south in the same village James and his friend awoke. An unexpected event had come into occurrence, we are now about to meet with a new group of people that also found themselves in the wrong place. In a further part of the village, in an area of abandoned houses. A place very few people ventured to.

Upstairs, of one of the forgotten homes, in a small bedroom with a single bed of white sheets, lay someone in a deep slumber, since the moment she last saw her own present. Lay straight on her back as if a patient in some hospital.

We have met her before.

Her name was Jane Olivia Lamaine, mother of James.

Under the covers of the bed sheets, in the room long settled by dust.

It was round about this moment that she came about, regaining her consciousness. Her eyes opened to an unfamiliar sight, an old wooden ceiling. Still drowsy and a little light headed, she was unable to react to the unknown situation. Her body ached and didn't want to move. This realization brought her back to her senses, her neck had trouble turning, so for the moment, she just moved her eyes, trying to map out as much as she could, even though it was a majority of the ceiling, on the one corner she was able to catch sight of a wardrobe and the other a curtained window.

Her inability to move was starting to scare her so she tried to force it. For starters, she had to move her neck, she sealed her eyes shut and started turning her head to the left. The pain was almost unbearable. As soon as she was sure she would be able to see a lot more than just a ceiling, she stopped and opened her eyes.

Nothing was even remotely familiar except for the fact that she knew what she was looking at. There was a bedside drawer next to her with a candle stand, everything else coloured by dust. It was the first thing her eyes were drawn to, then there was a large closed wardrobe, it was not too interesting so she moved on to the next thing, which was just an open door way.

The dust on the covers was entering her nose as she took in air. This forced her to sneeze and send a wave of pain all over her body, "Ow!" She exclaimed.

Then the thoughts of being held captive for some odd reason came flying in, which alerted her greatly. The setting was definitely not in the wrong, so with further hesitation and less regard for the pain she was in she forced herself to sit up.

She gave a loud shriek.

In front of her was a person staring right back.

She then sighed in great relief, after realizing that it was just her own reflection. A reflection created by a mirror that stood on a dressing table across the room.

The freight took its toll, she placed her hand on her chest, checking how fast her heart was beating. Trying to calm herself, she realized the situation she was in again, so she silenced herself and listened for any activity that might be occurring nearby.

Silence.

While doing so she examined more of the room.

The walls were a faded white paint that was peeling off from the corners. There were a few items on the dressing table, but that was it. The room was empty.

Another thing she noticed was the smell of the room, over the dust and obvious aging scent, there was a particular odor that stood out, strong and awfully sickening.

She didn't like the feeling of being stared at, even if it was just by herself in the mirror, so she removed the covers from over her legs and proceeded to move them. It felt like they were locked in place for years. Her left leg was the first she moved, using her hands to help place it over the edge.

The bed squeaked and creaked every time she budged.

The other leg followed and soon she was in a proper seated position, panting from the tiredness her muscles felt after that little struggle.

The floor was soft with dust.

She picked up her feet and saw there was a footprint in its wake.

Next to her feet was a pair of brown leather boots, without a second though, she picked up one, also recoloured by the dust. Bringing the boot to her face, she blew away some, that wasn't too attached and with the rest she wiped off with the covers till it was almost spotless.

She examined the inside of each boot and found a pair of socks stuffed in them.

At first she did not want to even touch them, for hygienic reasons. But they were white, and made it easier to notice if they were soiled by someone. Fortunately they were not. So she took the next step in the process and picked one up carefully and brought it to her nose.

They were clean.

Without further ordo she cleansed herself from the dust she'd picked up from under her feet and wore the boots. It was then when she took notice of her attire. She wore a white long sleeved buttoned T-shirt and dark brown belted pants.

She slowly made it to her feet and stretched her arms and legs.

Her first heading was the dressing table, to examine the contents on it, the only items of interest that were in the room. In front of the mirror she stood, staring at herself for a moment, wondering what in this world was happening. Her initial thought of being kidnapped and held hostage, slowly dispersed as she looked down at the table, finding a leather belt with a sheathed dagger strapped to it.

"Hmm," she said, picking up the sheath.

The blade inside was shiny and looked very sharp, it didn't give off a secondhand vibe.

It was a very appealing belt, with a brand new dagger to go with it. She felt bad leaving it in such a dust infected place, so she strapped it on.

As time passed, second by second she began to feel a little calmer, off course still clueless of her situation. Naturally, she began to explore the place a bit more. First heading to the window and opening the curtains. The light blinded her vision for a few moments.

The outside view was beautiful to her eyes. A green hill lay before her, with an oak tree positioned right on top, with leaves dancing slowly in the wind.

She looked to the one side and could only see some trees and tall grass, the other side was similar. Looking down, she could spot a small picket fence hiding in the tall grass, also realizing that she was on the second floor.

The view was a sight to see and all, but now she was asking herself where she was. *Was it a Farm?*

Her surroundings were not speaking 'modern' at all, even for a farm, but the place was abandoned anyway. Someone clearly left the knife and shoes here, and her attire was not as she remembered before waking up.

When she turned away from the window, an old face appeared in her mind, the old man that visited James. She sighed, "This must be that old man's fault," she said, "Jake was his name if I remember."

She placed her hand on her forehead and took a deep breath.

She jumped, and held her breath almost immediately.

The stench was still present. She covered her nose, pulling a disgusted face, "What is that?" She asked herself.

Investigating for the source, her gaze locked itself onto the only mysterious object left in the room, the wardrobe that stood against the wall across from her. Her curiosity grew strong, *no doors should be left unchecked.* Something was telling her not to check, but her legs were moving toward it without consent.

Now that she was thinking about the odor, it seemed to smell a lot stronger than before, even with her hand providing some cover.

Standing in front of the doors, she realized she was there, about to reveal what it was that stood behind.

Her heart started to race. Ringing in her head a bit too loud for her liking.

She turned to the door handles, designed in a floral and soiled with dust. She placed her hands on them.

She decided to waste no more time and pulled the doors open.

She looked up.

There was nothing to be seen.

One thing that almost killed her was the smell. It was concentrated.

She lowered gaze to the bottom of the drawer.

Her heart fell, let out a shriek and collapsed to the floor. She moved herself away till she was against the bed, panting, out of breath and light headed. Her eyes bulged and unable close or look away from the gruesome scene.

She shook from the shock and fear.

It was a body.

The corpse a little girl, about eight years in age, sitting, leaned against the wardrobe wearing a white dress, stained with dry blood around her chest and hands. Her eyes staring lifelessly down at her lap with an indication of dry tears on each cheek. Her black hair still tied back hanging over one shoulder.

By the looks of blood stains, she'd been cut along the throat and left here to decay.

Jane couldn't help but start tearing up. She felt nauseous and regretted her curiosity. She stretch out her right leg and kicked the door closed.

This was followed by an emotional breakdown, the shaking didn't stop, crying and breathing unevenly as she hugged her legs and stared at her one shaking hand. The traumatic experience shut down some of her senses, she was frozen.

Closing the door didn't seem to hide away the image now branded in her mind. The other door that remained opened kept her feet visible. The little girl wore open shoes.

She turned her sights away from the wardrobe.

After some time, sitting there, she slowly started to regain some of her strength again. The first thing she did was wipe her face clean of her tears and get up. She closed the other wardrobe door. Her body still in some shock, but she felt it was now time to leave the room and find out what's really happening.

The door out of the room was her next heading. It was already open and it lead to some stairs.

The house was quite small, a cottage, but had long since seen the company of people. The people who last called this their residence had left it a complete mess. Dishes were still on the table and in the sink, some finding their way to the floor, all shattered beyond repair. Chairs lay on the floor. The hearth lonely for some fresh firewood, candles that had fallen over and cupboards left wide open. The curtains were slightly opened, letting in a bright ray of sunlight into the room, making visible the tiny dust particles that floated in the air.

She made her way to the kitchen, tiptoed across the floor, avoiding anything sharp or that could potentially make some noise.

Standing in front of the curtains, she started to hear a faint voice, which jumpstarted her fear but figuring who it might be was more important so she peeped through the gap allowing in the sunlight. Before further examination of her surroundings, she caught sight of a group of three men standing just outside the house in a circle, on the gravel road, chatting about something.

What stood out about the men was their clothing, it was similar, except for the one, he wore some kind of robe uniform. The funny thing was, that she'd seen this in a book before, their attire, it was in a history book. Though she recognized the uniform, she could not remember which group it belonged to, "Where am I?" She whispered to herself.

Asking herself wasn't going to solve anything at the moment, so in the situation she decided to listen in on these men.

"Ok, how much longer are we going to be assigned here?" One of the men asked.

"Until we find the rest of them," the second man replied.

The first man decided to continue complaining, "Why didn't the ones before us complete the task?" He asked, "I mean, this is not fun at all."

The third man joined in, "They arrived at a different time, and according to our orders, the women are in this village with another group."

"It's been a full month."

"I know," the second man spoke, "No one knows when they might arrive, our job is to keep watch, and kill on sight."

Whatever Jane was listening to was not making any sense at all. None of their words gave away any information that she wanted. But she couldn't complain about what she was getting right now. She now knew these uniformed men were looking for her, so she was unknown to them at the moment and this part about arriving was not quite clear to her. Has someone brought her here. The men continued to speaking.

"But how can someone do that?" The third man asked.

The second man shrugged.

The first was clueless, "What do you mean?"

"Time travel," he replied, "I here only the-."

"You speaking about it again," the first man interrupted, "Why, you know we're not allowed to mention that?"

"I just want someone to hear us," he smile, "It gets boring around here."

The next few words that escaped from their mouths were more reasonable, they gave her a headache. This talk about time travel was clinging to her mind like a leech, it was something she had never heard of in her entire life, not something that was ever deemed possible in any timeline. Her surroundings started to make a bit more sense.

"Do you remember this house?" The third man asked turning his sights toward it.

The first man shook his head, "It's the same every other house."

"Oh come on," the second man crossed his arms, "This is area where we found that little girl skulking around."

The third man nodded, "And unfortunately she may have heard of what we were talking about," he giggled.

The first man laughed, "Oh, I remember now," he cringed, "Must have been about a month ago, how do you expect me to remember that?"

The conversation suddenly turned too sour to bear, Jane became disgusted and angry.

"I even remember her plea," the second man said, "how she promised she would not tell anyone about our conversation," he chuckled.

The third man pulled out his dagger and threw it up and down, "The slow gentle slit around her throat was most satisfying."

"Perfect," the second man compliment.

"I loved the silence that fell as soon as she was cut," the first explained, "she couldn't cry for help, not as if she was going to get any," he laughed.

A tear ran down her left cheek as she stared blankly at them, unable to move and in disbelief. Jane was encountered with every bad emotion, rendering her paralyzed, with nothing more to do but listen to these people. In those few moments, her mind became clouded by malice.

"It was our little experiment," the third man said.

The first man agreed with him, "Yes, I have never seen a decaying body before, it will kill our boredom for at least ten minutes."

The third man sighed, "Great, I need to go get something, go on in, I'll be back in while," he started to walk down the road.

Jane wasted no time. She pulled herself together and tiptoed away from the window. She climbed the stairs as quickly and quietly as she could. In the distance she could still hear some murmurs.

"Remember, we left it in the closet!" The third man shouted.

"Yes!"

Jane found herself stuck in the doorway to the room, there was no place to hide. The closet was occupied and there was nothing else about.

The front door opened.

She began to panic, her eyes looking for what wasn't there.

The men downstairs were laughing and destroying the cutlery.

She stepped into the room and found that the only place that would keep her out of sight was the bed. She made her way to the other side and lay down on her stomach. She attempted to go under the bed but the legs were too short.

Laying there was very risky, *the men could try open the window because of the smell.* There were many other scenarios playing in her head, none of them good, but this was where she was at this moment so she had to take it, no matter how terrifying it was.

Her breathing was blowing away the dust from beneath her mouth, her eyes watching from under the bed for any feet that may appear and ears listening very carefully, at every sound they were making.

Shifting to a more comfortable position she heard a clank on the wood by her waist, she realized it was the dagger she just picked it up. Both sides of her mind were in argument, debating on whether it would be more viable to have it sheathed or pulled out. The choice suddenly became what clouded her mind, was she going to need it at some point or should she just hope that they do not find her. Hoping they just leave was playing it a bit more on chance which does not favour anyone because it is fair, pulling out the dagger gives her a better chance of survival, giving her a head start against them should chance decide to favour them.

After looking into some predictions, pulling it out and having it in her hand at all times was her concluded choice.

"Come on, let's go upstairs," one of them said.

Their footsteps could be heard racketing up.

"I can already smell it," he giggled.

They made their way to the wardrobe door. Jane's only visual was their black leather boots. She had never been so frightened before.

"Open it," one of them ordered.

"Hmm," the other replied, "Scared of a dead body."

"Well, one of us has got to open it, and I don't want to dusty my hands."

"Off course," he replied with a chuckle. He then proceed to open the doors

The both cringed in disgust at the sight of the girl's lifeless body, making horrible comments about the smell and her decaying state while laughing and joking about it.

Jane felt that one such type of person should not exist. Never has she ever encountered a group of people who find pleasure in this, especially on children and would proceed to laugh over her dead body.

One of the men crouched down, getting closer to her. Starting to examine her face and fiddle with her hair, trying to get a better look at the wound.

"No maggots yet," the crouched man said, "strange."

"Maybe they're inside?" The other said unsure.

Jane looked at her hand, the one wielding the dagger. It was trembling. There was no way she was going to be able to do it. Right now she wanted nothing more than to end their cursed lives, feeling that if they were to continue taking in the fresh air, another like that girl will disappear one day and never be found again.

Her mind had decided to soil the dagger with their blood, a choice she felt she didn't have an alternative to.

The one problem she faced now was the fact that there were two of them, right next to each other and only one of her, trembling in fear. Listening to them made her stomach turn, made her nauseous. Lost in these emotions, she forgot to breath and could feel herself getting weaker, and light headed.

"Let me open a window, this is a horrible smell," the man standing said, "I'm getting a headache."

"Go ahead, I'll be checking the throat, haven't seen the inside of a person before."

Jane's heart nearly stopped. One of her predictions came to life, chance favoured them, meaning the next few moments should be decided by her.

The man standing hurried around the bed and to the window.

His speed helped out Jane, he didn't see her, even in the corner of his eye. The smell was priority.

The man opened the curtains.

A bit more fortune seemed to favour Jane, the sun only set to the west and this window was facing east. Her shadow would be hidden.

All of sudden, Jane felt she couldn't do it anymore. Now that it came to the moment, the choices came back to her, even though the other ones meant imminent death, they returned. She looked up at the man, searching for a means to open the window.

She took a slow, silent deep breath and used her arms to lift her body and then allow her legs to do the rest.

She took a single step in the man's direction.

Her mind replaying the next few seconds over and over again.

The man figure out how the wind was to be opened, and did so.

She took another step.

Then another.

Right behind the man she now stood, still trapped in her thoughts.

The man was done. The window was opened and a strong gust of wind blew right in. He took in the fresh air.

Jane's mind went blank. She raised both her arms. Her left went around the man's head and covered both his mouth and nose and the other, holding the dagger, found itself driving into the man's neck.

The man was only able to struggle for about a second, before he lost all his strength and dropped his arms. His body began to weigh a ton in her arms. She let go of the dagger and helped the man lie down silently on his back.

When the first bit was over, she pulled out the dagger and stood to her feet and looked down at the other man as he continued to defile the little girl's body. Without wasting any amount of time, she made her way around the bed, dagger dripping with red.

The man was still unaware of any event that occurred.

Jane found herself behind him in almost no time at all. And without another thought to tend to, she drove the dagger into the other man throat.

This time it went a lot differently than the first man, this one reacted with haste, though he was cut, he did not die immediately. He used one of his hands to cover his wound and the other to drag himself up against the wall. The horror in his eyes as he sat there looking up at Jane for the first time. His jaw dropped and shook in shock.

Jane took a step closer to him and crouched, as terrified as she was, but without thought of any kind of sympathy. It was all deserved for the dead girl, that didn't deserve such a fate.

The puncture was leaking rapidly, seeping its way through his fingers like water.

Jane couldn't look away from his suffering, unsure whether this experience was traumatizing or not. Her mind hadn't gained its sanity yet.

The man struggled to breath, "You're...you're-," he uttered, followed by a cough that brought blood to his lips. He tried to speak again, as his strength in life faded away, "you're...her," those were the last words he spoke before the horror in his eyes disappear, the shaking in his jaw came to a halt and the strength in the arm that kept him alive faded and fell to his lap.

Jane blinked and found herself there again. Well aware that she had taken two lives. She brought her dagger wielding hand into view. The blood was so red upon the sharp edges of it, some of it had found it's was to her hand and a drop or two on her white shirt. She stood up straight without letting the dagger in her hand out of her sights.

Her hand opened up and the dagger fell to the floor, making a loud noise. Unable to immediately comprehend with the last minute of her life, she sat on the bed, incapable of stopping the quivering her whole body was experiencing.

She sat there as the only living being, surrounded by bodies, one innocent and the rest guilty, all dead.

A short while passed, Jane still remained seated in the middle of a murder scene, trying to piece together all the information she had heard, trying to figure out who these men were, what the uniform stood for.

Something did occur to her, while she sat there thinking. Searching the bodies could not be a bad idea.

She got up and started with the man seated against the wall. In one of his pockets she found a small folded piece of paper, that she didn't bother opening, since what she saw next took away her interest in it. The folder piece of paper was put into her pocket and she pulled out the dagger this man had.

It was an interesting one, wide and short in size, with black carved runes into the blade itself. She held it by the hand which also had an interesting design.

Something about it was off, and this was just by her instinct. She brought it closer to her face for a better look caught a strange smell from it. Under her nose she placed it and sniffed it in.

It gave her a sharp pain in the head. She threw it aside and shook her head. It seemed she would have to take custody of the same dagger she had just used because she was not going to trust what her nose was afraid of

She picked up her dagger and wiped it against the man's uniform.

Her gaze turned to the little girl. She felt it was not right leaving her here to decay so she took the covers off the bed and used them to pick her up from the closet and lay her on her back. Then she wrapped the little girl with the thin white sheets that she now lay on.

After completion, she picked her up in both arms and headed out the room. Carrying her body brought water to her eyes as she made her way down stairs. She carefully placed her onto the table.

The door was left wide open, with sunlight pouring in, heating up the room.

She left for the door, but came to a sudden stop and gasp for breath.

Just outside, was the third man, making his way to the door.

Jane was frozen, afraid to make any sudden movements.

The man looked up as soon as he was at the doorway. He too was shocked to see her.

Jane caught sight of what the man was wielding in his right hand, a long wooden stick. She wasn't too sure why a young man would need it, but it was not the important matter right now, the stare down was.

She didn't want to break eye contact and let things escalate quickly, so she kept them locked on his.

The man's sights turned to the table, where the girl lay.

In that window of time, Jane went for her dagger.

The man noticed immediately and hit his wooden stick against the ground with a loud thud.

Jane was unable to move. Not even shake, or even blink.

The man began to smile.

What is happening? She asked herself, standing there, only able to watch as this man smirked at her. Any amount of struggle came to nothing. Then she realized what the supposed walking stick could have been, and that realization was the worst thought to come up in her mind. Being paralyzed is the most vulnerable you can be.

She grew terrified. With her eyes still being able to see him standing right in front of her.

The man began to speak, "You know, most people overlook the effectiveness of Alteration," he stepped closer to her, "I mean, I've paralyzed you, there is nothing you can do about it," he gave a sinister laugh and his eyes began to water.

He leaned forward and looked closely into Jane's eyes, "I wonder what's going on inside that pretty little head of yours," he said giving her a little tap on the forehead.

Jane was struggling inside, really trying to move, even flinch, in hopes to break free of this bond.

The man stood up straight again and turned his sights to the body on the table, "Judging by the smell," he pinched his nose for a moment,

"That's the little girl," he giggled and this time a tear came rushing down his cheek, "Where're my friends?" He turned back to her.

Jane was not understanding this man's emotions, they did not seem to be sane. *Were the tears shed for his friends? Were they of some kind of joy, being accompanied by the smile he never took off?* Jane was sure this man was not in his right mind, and that did not speak any good for her.

"Sorry for asking," he apologized, "I am rude to make fun of your paralyzed state," he said placing his hand on his chest, giving a slight bow, "but It's fine you know, my friends, I will just take all credit for your, soon to be, unbearable suffering," he gave her a gentle touch on the chin.

Jane's eyes began to shine with the water build up reflecting the light of the sun. This felt like her fate, dying in the hands of this man.

"The only problem now, is finding the others without extra hands," he said, "Well… that will come later."

The man nudged forward and his smile disappeared. He gasped for breath, his eyes popping out of their sockets.

Jane couldn't react to this sudden change in atmosphere, she could only watch and listen as he suffered.

The staff in his hand fell to the ground and rapidly, Jane was able to move again, she stepped back, gasping for breath, with her hand on her chest, so relieved she could move again. Without any additional thoughts she pulled out her dagger and held it up with both hands, shaking from the experience of being paralyzed.

The man fell to his knees, already without life in his eyes and behind him, two people, both of them females.

They both stepped forward toward Jane.

Jane lowered her dagger, recognizing the two women. She fell into the arms of the one closest to her, "Thank you, thank you," she was so grateful to them.

The woman stepped back and held Jane by the shoulders, "What happened?" She asked with a worried expression.

The two women went by the names Mary and Denice.

Jane sheathed her dagger, and calmed herself down, never so relieved before in her life, but still shaken from the disturbing experience. She sighed, placing her hand on her forehead.

Denice stepped forward to give her a rub on the back, "We're here now."

"He paralyzed me," Jane managed to utter, "Magic... he used magic."

Mary let go of her shoulders and stood over the man lying on the floor, face first, with a dagger in his back. She picked up the wooden stick that lay next to him, "With this wooden stick?"

"It's a staff."

Denice frowned in confusion, "What is going on?" she asked, "I just woke up an hour ago in some abandoned house."

"Yeah, we found each other by luck," Mary said, "especially you, another minute and you could've died."

Jane shrugged.

Mary threw the staff aside, "Where are we?" She asked, "This place looks a little outdated."

"And there's magic," Denice added.

"Jane... any ideas?" Mary asked.

She nodded in return.

Mary stood up a chair and sat on it.

"This place is outdated," Jane began, "and magic is not banned."

Denice picked up the staff and examined it, "What do you mean?"

"I overheard these men talking, and apparently, we're in the past," she explained.

Mary's face turned straight, "Hmm, that's not possible, not even remotely."

"Look around you."

"She kind of has a point," Denice said, "I mean, this doesn't look like anything in the present."

"I think I know whose fault it is," Jane sighed, "There was an old man that visited me, on a random day, your children were there as well," she explain, "He asked to see them, and that it was important, he said was from the GM government... and before I knew it, he was giving them these diamonds."

"This is just confusing me even more," Mary replied.

Denice agreed with her.

"I think he is the source."

Denice tapped the man with the staff, "And this man?"

"They were sent to find and kill us," Jane answered.

"They?"

"There were two others...I had to take their lives, and judging by what I heard, there are others, and by others they probably meant, James, Mark and Daniel," she said.

"What!" Mary got angry, "They are being hunted by them?"

"It would seem," Jane shrugged with uncertainty.

Denice shook her head continuously, "No, that is not on, that's madness."

Jane took a deep breath, and tried to calm their growing anger, "What we must do, is find out more and if my assumption is actually true," she stared at the dead man, "Haven't been here for more than an hour and have witnessed the cruelty of this time," she rubbed her arms.

Mary and Denice assumed she was talking about her near death experience.

"It's okay Jane, we got here in time," Denice smiled.

"Oh, it's not that," she replied, "worse."

Mary and Denice exchanged glances.

"Come here," Jane walked over to the kitchen table.

They all stood around the table looking down at the sheets.

"What is this?" Denice enquired seriously.

Jane slowly uncovered the sheets around the little girls face.

Both Mary and Denice picked up on the gruesome scent.

Jane revealed the girls pale dead face to them.

Denice stepped back into the kitchen counter with a frightened look on her face, knocking over a cup, "Oh my god."

Mary covered her mouth in shock, "Wh-what," she stuttered.

"They happened," Jane replied pointing a finger at the dead man lying on the floor, "these men murdered this helpless little girl, in cold blood," she explained, "they found it amusing that she had begged for help, so what they did, was drag her upstairs, slit her throat and leave her body to decay in the wardrobe...this was a month ago."

Mary and Denice were horrified, even more after the story.

Jane continued, "They also thought it hilarious to visit the body, and check how much it had decayed."

Denice shook her head in disgust, "These are not people."

Mary shook her head, "But why would they do it?" She asked, "Them specifically."

"Specifically?"

"Don't you recognize that uniform?"

Jane shook her head, "Who are they?"

"The Dead Crow."

Jane's jaw dropped, "Wait, The Dead Crow?"

Denice nodded.

"The ones who saved the world, according to history," Mary said, "The group people looked up to for aid."

Denice stepped forward, "She's right, and we can't stay here any longer, we have killed three cops basically."

Jane looked at the little girls face and covered it again, "I want to bury her first," she proposed, "I am not sure if she was orphaned or had someone, but we must lay her to rest, she did not deserve any of this brought upon her."

Denice agreed, "Ok."

"I'll look for a shovel," Mary volunteered, heading out of the house.

As the sun neared itself to the horizon far to the west, Jane, Mary and Denice found themselves on top of the hill that had the one oak tree growing on it, overlooking most of the abandoned area of the village. The wind was still blowing strong and cool.

Jane had carried the little girl up top and placed her under the tree, she had removed the girl's shoes and placed them next to her. Mary had been busy with an old rusted shovel unearthing the grass and digging a small grave. Denice had found some wooden planks which she tied together, making a memorial.

Most of this task was achieved with silence.

Denice became curious about this time travel, "Do you think people will notice we are gone?" She asked.

"They don't even know we exist," Mary replied.

"No, I mean the present."

Jane shrugged, leaning against the oak tree, watching Mary as she picked the dirt and heaved it onto the growing pile, "I don't know, I never knew such a thing existed till today."

"Maybe," Mary replied, "I mean, the only thing we know now is that it exists, we're proof I guess," she flung the shovel aside, "Done."

"Thank you," Jane said picking up the girl and carefully placing her down.

Denice was the one to fill the grave, using the shovel. After she was done Jane took the memorial and stuck it into the ground, and with the little girl's shoes, placed beneath it.

All three of them stood in front of the grave.

"May you be at peace," Jane spoke.

Having buried her, they were able to move on with their current problems, waking in this unknown place, as if kidnapped.

The orange light of the sun made everything look beautiful and rustic.

"Beautiful, isn't it," Denice admired, "The sunset," she looked into the far distance.

Mary and Jane stood next to her taking in the view, as they enjoyed, what would seem to be their last moment of peace. In this completely new world as travelers without a guide.

"Yeah it is," Jane replied.

"What do we do now?" Mary asked, removing the hair from her face.

"I suggest we go meet the locals, get to know people, places… blend in," Denice said.

At that moment, Jane remember she had picked a note from one of the Dead Crow agents. She pulled it out of her pocket.

"What's that?" Denice noticed.

"A paper I picked from one of the Dead Crow agents," she replied unfolding it, "Hmm, 'Dead Crow's Watch List'," she read the title of the paper.

The contents of this piece of paper consisted of a list of names, ranging from one till twenty.

"Is it some kind of wanted list?" Mary enquired.

"Maybe."

She looked at the first bit of names that were listed.

1. *Levina*
2. *Henry Skycreek*
3. *Silvia Batch*

*4. **Vincent Roald***
*5. **Leonard Lacehowld***

The only thing that seemed odd about this list, which stood out quite a bit was the very first name, *Levina*. It was not at all familiar to them, but it was the only name listed without a surname.

"Hmm, wonder why she doesn't have a surname," she said folding the piece of paper and shoving into her pocket, "Let's go, we need to get some answers.

CHAPTER 11

Wanted Girl

A few weeks passed since the official first day for the new students of Marridor. Becoming settled in was easy enough, everyone being so welcoming, and as the biggest contributor, they hung with each other most of the time, during breaks and weekends. One thing that was still a little challenging, was mapping out this maze of a school. The Main hall and the magic towers were an easy find, but the classes were still a bit hazy in their minds. Most of them have stuck to one root for making it from point A to point B. Exploration was left mostly for the weekends since they weren't permitted to exit the school grounds anymore.

James's age group was now currently at the class of P.E.

They were at the same place, outside near the building with the wall rowed with archery targets and piled hay stacks, keeping the arrows from being dulled by the stone.

The students used long bows, made light for easy handling, and shot with arrows without any dangerous metal heads, just a sharpened edge like a pencil.

All the students were scored according to their accuracy. The targets which they shot at were divided into red and blue circular points, similar to a dart board.

Most of the students were still inexperienced at archery, this being the very first year for all of them. It was an activity for their age group and up. Still the new comers fell short, so Mr. Padgett, the teacher, marked with a little more leniency when it came to them, but it was not to last. For the students that scored horribly, despite having started at the beginning of the year, weren't so lucky, Mr. Padgett showed no mercy.

He was no joke. Mr. Padgett was a true marksman, never missing his target's mark. Every time he demonstrates his skills, he never failed to impress, hitting the centre mark was just like breathing to him. Certainly better than the teacher he replaced, some learners were claiming that he uses some kind of enchantment to be that good. He was kind of ill-tempered at times, his emotions changed with every step he took, but the students didn't hate him for it, being a great teacher at most times. He rose in the ranks, becoming one of the students favourite teachers.

Today he was a military instructor, motivating and inspiring them with old tales of history, the wars that he fought and the heroes who lived in them, preparing them as new recruits for an unknown threat or for the perks of hunting in the endless wilds that tainted Maramel.

"Ready!" he shouted from behind a small table filled with papers.

There was a row of about ten students, each lined up behind a target, about fifteen metres away from them, with arrows drawn and ready to be released. Each learner was given a quiver, strapped around their backs, to familiarize themselves with reloading.

"Remember, use the eye closest to your arrow when aiming," he reminded them.

The other students stood in a group nearby, waiting to see who will excel in the next shot, or miss the target completely.

"Fire!" He gave order.

The arrows were released, and as expected, quite a few of them missed their mark completely, burying their arrows deep into the hay, some arrows didn't even make it to the other end, which was what got the learners watching all amused.

After every student had been given at least five shots under supervision for marks, Mr. Padgett would give them the rest of the period off to do whatever they pleased. Some of them would continue firing arrows at the targets for their own competitiveness and amusement, but most decided it was best to just socialize for the rest of their given time.

One thing that was very odd about the school was the obvious time gap that was very clear if you're from outside the city or a different time. For instances, their training uniform was very much like the tracksuit that you see today.

"Is it me, or is this clothing a little up to date as in, should not be in date...yet?" Mia asked examining it.

The tracksuit jacket was black with a large white and a purple diagonal strip down the right side and the badge on the left, the shirts were designed in a similar way. The shorts and pants were just black.

No one really understood what Mia was saying, but Mark had something with more sense to say, "I don't think this kind of clothing should exist yet," he said.

"What are you talking about?" Clara asked, "I mean, sure this clothing is very different compared to outside the school, but not exist yet, I'm not following."

Once again, Mark felt comfortable saying anything that could expose their actual identities.

"It's comfortable," William complemented, "Better than anything I've ever worn, and light."

"Why hasn't the rest of the city made these, I'm sure they would like it?" Daniel asked.

"Not allowed," Clara replied, "you can't leave with anything that is school property, or made by the school."

After the period had ended, they were to return their bows and quivers back into the massive armory, it was the building the archery targets and piled up haystacks were placed against, a building of about four floors of just weapons.

It was now break, free time for the learners to tend to whatever it was that interested them. James, Mark and Daniel had a knack for exploring the school, venturing into places they may have yet to see, even after the several weeks into the term, it wasn't too easy to do as they pleased, having missed a whole term, they had to catch up in every subject, one in particular was history, which off course was also compulsory in this time. And break wasn't too large of a window for getting lost. No magic was allowed outside the halls, and without supervision. Using magic freely in the halls was only permitted during the weekends now, as a way for the learners to better themselves in each of their subjects, and to fill their minds with a fun alternative than to complain about the lockdown. The teachers were given permission to carry around staves on their persons, but most of them chose not to.

The exploration of the three musketeers and their friends was put on halt for this break in particular. Mia had wished to speak to them about something. Something nobody else should be around to hear. So they met at a small circle of stone benches, quite some distance from the nearest learner, under a tree.

Mark sighed, "Why do I feel like we're about to have an important conversation during the only free time we get," He opened up with a complaint.

"Oh come on Mark," Mia said sitting across him, "You get plenty of free time in the afternoon."

Mark put on a straight face, knowing he was defeated.

Mia smiled in return, "I have noticed something."

James shrugged and shook his arms, "What?"

"I'll get to that now."

"Huh?" Mark responded, surprised.

"Just hear me out," she began, "How well have you been doing in you magic classes?"

James stepped in first, "I've been doing well, almost top of the class," he said with confidence, "I'm the fastest exceling student so far."

"Yup," Daniel agreed, "Words stolen out of my mouth."

"Same," Mark said.

"Don't lie Mark," said Daniel.

"Shut up," he shot back.

James moved on to the spells, "We working on the Repetitive Strike spell, they become better every time we move on to the next."

"I like Unreal Existence," Daniel said, "Not like you know what it does."

Mia did, "I do, I used it on James when we first met."

"Ah, you were there but not there," James explained, "Pretty neat trick."

Daniel turned to Mark, "How far have you come with Restoration?"

"We are busy with a spell called Rejuvenate," he replied, "Restoring your or someone else's energy and strength."

"Mia, what about you and Alteration?" James asked.

"We working the simplest form of Obey," she replied, "getting small animals, for instance birds to do what we command.

"That's cool," Mark said.

"Anyway, why we here," she pulled everyone away from the conversation, "I think I know how you have been doing so well when it comes to your magic fields."

"Natural talent?" Mark guessed.

"Nooo," she replied, "Not even close," she took a deep breath, "I understand you've been keeping your diamonds on you this whole time."

"And?" Mark enquired.

"They are increasing your power and ability to use magic," she finished.

Mark chuckled.

"Oh," James replied with a bit of concern in the mix, well aware of what Mia might suggest in the next few minutes, "I'm still keeping mine on…for safety…off course."

Mark and Daniel backed him on that claim.

"I was not going to suggest taking them off," she made it clear, "They far safer with you guys, I wanted to make you aware that they may carry some additional properties with the abilities they give you."

James then remember the first day, when they were testing out the different subjects, "Wait a moment, I know you said I must not say anything about it but how come you have a special ability?" he asked, "You don't have a diamond, yet you can use magic without a staff."

Mia took a deep breath, "I guess you deserve some sought of explanation,"

"Yessss," Mark frowned, remembering the past, "You froze us without a staff."

They silenced themselves, anxious to hear the answer.

Mia sighed, "I'm different," she started, "I seem to be the only one able to do so, she explained, "Jake told me that I was very special, I don't know why or what I am, because Jake felt no need to mention it, but he gave me strict order not to mention it to anyone in this time…at all."

"I wonder why," James said.

"I searched through a lot books here in the school, but haven't found any reference to my ability, why I am like this, I do think that something may be in the library in the city, but we are unable to go there at the current moment."

"Maybe your ability came when the diamonds were made," Daniel suggested.

"Maybe, but then why would it be a danger?" She asked.

"We are not allowed to mention the Diamonds," Mark added.

Mia sighed, "True."

Their conversation was broken by a teacher, ordering all the students to head straight for the hall at once.

This was some good news for a few learners as it was not the end of the school day yet.

"Settle down," Mr. Patchwalker ordered from behind the announcement stand.

There were some new faces up on the stage. A man, dressed in the clothing of a Dead Crow. This had the learners interested in what was to be happening next, they also kept themselves silent, out of respect.

Mr. Patchwalker cleared his throat, "We have received some rather troubling news recently," he started, "it may seem that the thieves we spoke about a few weeks ago, have entered the school premises."

Every student started murmuring.

James, Mark and Daniel were greatly surprised by this fact, it was kind of hard, acting normal in this situation, but blowing their cover was not any option available to them. Their exchange in glances stood out from the shock in realization the other learners were feeling and acting. Mia tried not to make any eye contact, keeping her eyes on the table, tapping her fingers.

"Settle down," he ordered again, "Now it is said that they are amongst you, as learners."

"OH," James said quite loud.

This was not very good at all, James had in mind, the incident that occurred at Lonestar Inn. But the one thing he could not wrap himself around was how or what lead to those events. Unless, it was the crazy blind man that spoke to the Dead Crow, he seemed to know that they had diamonds. Either way, their faces have been seen at least once, and hiding was just as bad as trying to conceal a wine stain on a ladies white dress. No one had access to anything that could be of any aid. The thoughts were overwhelming.

Mia as well started to feel a little worried.

"That is why we are joined here today by a member of the Dead Crow, a mage, Edward Macovy," he introduced the man next to him.

Edward greeted with a small bow and smile.

His attire is different from your ordinary Dead Crow soldier, with the title 'mage', he wore dark red decorated robes, on each shoulder, a black pad and over the arms, above the robes, were silver gauntlets bearing their mark. He was hooded so his face wasn't so visible.

Mr. Patchwalker continued, "Right now, they are going to inspect each of you, just to see if they will be able to recognize the culprits."

And things just got worse, there was no doubt they knew their faces.

Everyone started to engage in conversation again, each of them making fun, obviously in the notion that they weren't the thieves.

The actual culprits didn't know how to react to this near end situation, the only upside to the inspection was the fact that it was only facial recognition, if it was a full on search, the Diamonds would be found.

Mark started fidgeting, playing with his hands, wearing a very worried expression on his face.

This surprise search was really shocking.

"I will allow the rest of the Dead Crow mages in, and will commence with the inspection," Mr. Patchwalker said, signaling for them to come in.

From the hall entrance, another eight mages entered the hall, their entry brought about a dead silence. Two mages assigned to a row.

"Now, I ask that you all get up and stand behind your benches," Mr. Patchwalker instructed.

The learners did as they were told.

"Now turn and face the back of the hall, keep in your straight lines."

They stood there like robots, afraid to even turn their heads, each learner staring at the next.

This group of Dead Crow's did not have any staves in their possessions. James was confused. How is it that they all knew his face, without any drawings of him to support their search. He guessed that they were following the rule that no magic is allowed except for the halls.

"Please remain calm as they identify your faces," Mr. Patchwalker said, "You may begin," he gave the order.

They all started down the hall, examining every child before moving on to the next. The scary part was the fact that they were rather quick with the learners, moving on to the next as if they were already aware of the thieves.

James started shaking from the fear of being caught, heating up like an oven under his uniform. He looked across the table, at Mark, who was in a panicked state, fiddling way too much with his hands, even if they did not recognize him, he would bring attention to himself. He looked at Daniel, whom was in front of him. He stood up straight with his hands behind his back, looking normal and calm as ever. He was doing better than the people who knew weren't the culprits. Had he accepted this end so calmly?

Mia was standing behind James, and despite the irreversible situations, she was trying to think of an idea, something that would work, even if it had a one percent chance of success, but nothing came to mind. This was an unexpected turn of events, just as they were starting to get very comfortable, this happens. Though she was not in the frying pan, she was a part of all this, and in just a few more moments, everything would be lost, the diamonds, and any hope of figuring out what their task was, along with the unknown reason for their presence in this time. And from what she has heard, prisoners of this era are not treated at all with any kind of respect.

She checked the inspection progress.

The situation wasn't changing, panicking and thinking at the same time, for any open windows.

She gasped for breath, louder than she expected.

There was an open window.

It was of great risk but it was letting in a breeze of fresh air, it was worth a shot. The only problem to the idea was their traumatized expressions, so she calmed herself and detached from her surroundings, took a deep breath and closed her eyes for a moment. In her concentration, every sound rung loud in her ears, especially the multiple footsteps that made their way down the hall and her drumming heart that echoed all round her body.

As the footsteps were only a few metres away from any of them she began to whisper, a whisper that she too couldn't hear, but aware of the words that she spoke. When these mages were too close for comfort, she stopped speaking and opened her eyes again.

Daniel was the first to be check, he stood there with a straight face, looking at the mage. He was feeling sick from the suspension created between the two. But to his godly fortune, the mage moved on from him, and onto Mark, who was a nervous wreck. The Dead Crow looked at him with concern, but his face didn't for once grow the look of suspicion, he looked more worried. And to his luck as well, the mage moved on.

On Mia's side of the bench, James was up for inspect, he stood there trying his hardest not to make any sought of eye contact, and just like Mark and Daniel, he moved on. James raised a brow, confused about this stroke of luck, but at the same time very happy.

Mia wasn't a problem, she wasn't one of the culprits, so when she was being check, there was a little less tension build up. She just gave a faint smile and it was over. It was followed by a sigh of relief, it was a close one, too close.

James, Mark and Daniel were really puzzled, they looked at each other, more relieved than ever.

Upon completion of the inspection, Mr. Patchwalker ordered the students to be seated once again. He was not done with his announcements just yet.

But first, he stepped away from the stand and had a little whisper with the Dead Crows for a moment, this was another opportunity for the learners to chatter about what was happening.

"I guess the culprit wasn't among us," Angelina whispered, "missing my magic class thanks to this inspection."

Clara agreed, "Yeah, it's the subjects we actually enjoy."

Mark would often have some kind of comment on this, but his nerves were killing him right now. His fidgeting hadn't yet stopped, the relief had only lasted for about a moment, but being the one who is being hunted down, brings upon its own kind of nerve breaking feel. Having to keep alert at all times.

James wanted so badly to ask why he was not recognized by them, "That was pretty scary," he confessed.

Daniel nodded in return.

"Any inspection is scary, no matter how innocent you are," Angelina said, "Though," she turned to Mark, "Why the pale face?"

"Scary, like James said," he replied.

"Mark doesn't know how to handle these situations...I guess?" James supported his answer.

After some time, Mr. Patchwalker made his way back to the stand and asked for silence, "Thank you for your cooperation," he started, "We appear to be still in the dark, but this does not mean that we have given up on this search, so I have a list of new effects that will be put into place as from this moment."

The Dead Crows stood behind Mr. Patchwalker in a straight row, looking very formal.

"New rules, that's convenient," Mark said sarcastically.

"We need them," Opal whispered back, "I'm not living with a criminal here."

You're talking to one. The words Mark really wanted to reply with.

Mr. Patchwalker continued, "As from this day, this school will play host to a number of the members of the Dead Crow, here to keep you safe and off course, on the lookout for whom they are searching for and the objects that may be anywhere on school grounds...which brings us to our next changes," he explained, "The school has been promoted to total lockdown from the outside, meaning that, even between school terms, every learner will be kept here in this school."

The world shook right after that rule was spoken. The children did not except this regulation at all.

"Okay that's a bit too much now," Clara said, "I know this place is big and all, but the idea of being trapped here makes it seem small."

"It is prison," James said, well aware that now, they can't even contact Jake anymore, or leave for that matter, and when left in one place, the rot is slowly going to start smelling real strong, they will be snuffed out eventually.

Mia sighed, "There is nothing we can do about it, they are the Dead Crow."

"Silence!" Mr. Patchwalker shouted, "I'm not done."

Everyone turned back to him, faces now filled with more anger than fear.

"One more thing, once a week, there will be a full inspection of every student and any of the Dead Crows will have full clearance to search your belongings at any time they see fit, this rule of examination will be in composition till further notice," he explained, "You're dismissed," he stepped away from the announcement stand.

While every student stood up, chattering and complaining to their next classes, Mia caught sight of one of the Dead Crow mages Pulling out a small folded piece of paper from her robe pockets, a paper she examined and showed to the others standing by her. Having next to no knowledge about this organization, the small piece of paper began to look more prized. And anyone would be interested in even a gaze of what value inside is hid.

The announcement had now made everyone feel a very high level of safety, but with that safety came at the price of privacy, which was not at all what a person would want to pay in return for anything. Right after the dismissal of the students from the hall, Dead Crow guards were spotted in a lot of places, with a few mages amongst them, wielding staves. The school was now turned into a military protected compound, with regular patrols down the halls, making the learners feel a little less happy with all the excess adult supervision, this had turned into kindergarten.

Daniel had some things he too wanted to find out, so before heading to the next class he caught up to Angelina.

"Hey," he greeted, catching up to her.

"Hi," she smiled, "How you doing?"

They made their way down the hall.

"Great thanks," he replied, he felt a little nervous, "Uh, I wanted to ask you about the thing you wanted to tell me about."

Angelina's face turned confused, "What?"

Daniel lowered his voice to a whisper, "The witch thing."

Angelina didn't catch anything he said, "What?" She tilted towards him.

"Why we not allowed to say the 'witch' word," he whispered a little louder.

"Ohhhhh," she realized, "I forgot about that, meet me at the library after school."

"Shot thanks, I'll see you there."

"See you," she replied cheerfully.

"Okay, class is that way so... bye," he started at the opposite direction.

At a sudden realization, he came to stop and turned around, "Angelina!" He called.

She turned around wielding the same beautiful smile.

His heart skipped a beat, "What time, exactly?"

She gave a second to think, "Um, three would do."

"Got it."

She waved goodbye.

After school came by, taking its time as if there weren't any important schedules. School was over at around half past two. Mia was so keen on figuring out what the piece of paper was about, since the moment she saw it, so she decide to catch up with one of her friends, Angelina. Mia knew her last magic class and it was closest to hers so she scurried down the corridors in search for her, waiting till later was not an option right now, in fear of forgetting.

Her search was cut quickly, she was heading down a corridor near the one of the grounds. She stopped her in her tracks.

"Hey Angelina," she greeted almost out of breath, "Finally found you."

"Mia," she said with a surprised look, "What are you doing, running up and down?"

She slowed her breathing, "I was looking for you."

Angelina had a place to be heading to but she was willing to hear her out, "What is it?"

They both started down the corridor slowly.

"I saw something of interest whilst we were in the hall during the search," she started.

"Yes..."

"One of the Dead Crow people had some paper on them, I know it could be anything, but might you have an idea what it might...could be?" She asked.

"OH, that's pretty hard to answer, but it may be an order, or list of names," she replied.

"Names?"

"You know, the people they looking for," she explained, "It could be any, I'm sorry."

"It's fine, I was just a little curious, these Dead Crows are invading this place," she replied, "Anyways, where you headed?"

"Um, the library," she replied, "I'm supposed to meet with Daniel, he needs help with something."

"Hmmhmm," she smiled, "I'll leave you two to it then."

From there they went their separate ways.

The school library was quite the size, off course nothing in comparison to the city library. It was stacked to the brim with bookshelves and sitting areas. The library was a pretty common place for the students to be.

The place of meet that Angelina picked was quite secluded, a round table at a corner created by two bookshelves.

She had an A4 sized dictionary book, designed by some craftsman.

Daniel had arrived shortly after the given time, with nothing but himself, really surprised by his surroundings, which brought him up for questioning.

"Why the surprised face" she asked as he took a seat at the round table.

"Oh, never been here before," he confessed, "Pretty library."

"You've never been here?"

He smile and shook his head slowly, "I mean I've seen the entrance, but never stepped in."

"Hmm, a few weeks into school, the library should be your best place to visit, you supposed to be catching up anyway."

"I listen in class," he replied, "Besides, this library is much too big, I'd be spending half my time trying to find a book."

Angelina nodded, "Excuses."

"No," he disagreed, "Look at this place, I would need some kind of guide."

"I'll pretend you didn't disagree, but if the place is really the problem, I could help you," she suggested.

Daniel did not hate the idea at all, the thought about being around books all day was kind of boring, but the company was going to make up for it. And she suggested it, on top of all things. Was he prepared to pay the price of books?, "Great idea," he replied, "I guess, I mean, these books are pretty looking…," he paused, "I'll do it."

"Okay, that settles that," she said placing her hand on the book she brought.

Daniel looked at it with interest, "What is this ancient book about?"

It had carvings on it, the primary was a large symbol.

"You know this symbol right?" She asked.

I was familiar, as if he had just recently seen it, the image popped up into his head, "These Dead Crow people have it," he replied, "Why are you showing me that?"

"All that I know is that they are the main reason, why the word… witch…is not supposed to be used," she whispered.

"I am not surprised," he said, "They are allowed to do anything by the looks of it."

"Shh, there is a 'why' in this matter," she silenced him.

"Okay," he decided to listen, "Ears open."

She took a deep breath, "First things first, there are two races… well were," she started.

"Which are…?"

"Well… the classification is kind of strange, being witches and humans," she explained.

Daniel fell into confusion, unable to decide whether he was a human or a witch, he was using magic, but he was quite sure he was human, "So we are witches?"

She shook her head, "No, we fall under 'human'."

"But we are using magic."

"Okay, that's a different story, let's stay on topic, why it is not used anymore."

He nodded.

"Okay, for reasons, I soon want to discover, both races were living together in peace, and then apparently, the witches did something very bad, something that brought upon a war that led to their extinction, taken care of, by the Dead Crow," she explained.

"So that's why they are respected, the murder of a whole race?"

Angelina shrugged, "Maybe, but one thing is certain, the witches had an evolved advantage, which may have upset the humans."

Daniel could not think of this advantage as he sat there. His first thought was magic, but everyone is using it, "What is it?"

"To use magic without an object," she replied.

Daniel squinted, "Use magic without any objects," he repeated slowly.

Angelina nodded, "As you may have noticed here at school, without staves or enchantment cubes we possess no magical abilities."

Daniel jumped, "Huh?"

Angelina was confused, "What?"

"Repeat the first bit," he requested, unsure of himself.

"What you mean about being able to use magic without objects?"

He nodded in return, staring into space.

She could see him drifting away so she clapped in his face.

"Sorry."

"Anyway, that's what made them so dangerous, and I hear, the last one was killed ten years ago," she said, "Kind of sad if you ask me, and now the Dead Crow wants to remove them from history."

Daniel frowned at her, "How do you know this?"

"Uhm, an old man told me," she replied, "They at least know about this stuff, it's not written in any book, believe me, I've searched."

His expression turned worried, "Thanks for the heads up."

"Anytime," she smiled, "We live in strange times."

Daniel pulled the book from under her hand, "Doesn't this say anything about what you just told me?" He opened it up at a random page. The writing needed a magnifying glass to be read, he cringed at the sight of it.

Angelina giggled, "No it doesn't, like I said, they are trying to hide it, all that stuff has probably been changed by whomever writes these books."

Daniel sighed, things were happening so fast, Jake had told them to learn about the history of this day and age because what they were learning in the present was completely different. These differences had already started. History is already being altered.

Daniel closed the book and started to brush his hand of the cover, all the smooth textures he could feel, dominated by the leather.

"Anyways," Angelina decided to change the subject.

Mrs. Mannikral was not available for her Enchantment class, the next day. There was another teacher filling in her place for the time being, so it was a free period.

This was good for some of the learners, to get in a bit of studying in the time that was given to them, Mia among them.

Most of the class was socializing and some engaged in some chess matches. At a table near the back of the class, James and Mark were enjoying a bit of chess, using one table and three chairs around it. Daniel stood leaning on the third chair, for a good aerial view of the bored. Claude and William were doing the same with some other kids at another table. Some of the learners were more interested in the contents of the classroom, all the weapons, objects and the rainbow of enchantment cubes displayed behind small glass domes. The class was not too loud, under the supervision of the teacher, as she was busy with some work herself.

Mia closed her books and put them in her bag, she then scanned the area for James and the others. Upon detecting them, she noticed Daniel looking right back at her. It created a weird vibe between the two.

Daniel nodded at her as a sign of greeting.

Mia returned it.

Daniel returned his focus to the game James and Mark were having.

She stood up from her seat, picked up the chair and brought it to the chess table. Whilst doing so, Mia noticed Daniel watching him again, "What?" She asked placing her chair at the table.

"Nothing," he turned to the match again.

"Hey Mia," James greeted, ending his turn.

Mia took a seat, "What are you guys doing?"

"Hmmmmmm, I don't know," James answered giggling

Mia rolled her eye.

"Just jamming," Mark replied, "You lose, you out, want to join?"

"Yes," she replied, though her interest was primarily on the contents of the page.

It was not but a few moments, when Mia again decided to draw them away from the chess match, "Listen guys."

Mark turned to her with a straight face, "Have you ever been near a chess board before?"

Mia didn't understand the relevance of this question, but she nodded in reply.

"Then you should know that concentration is key here," he turned back to the board.

James pointed at Mark, "Pause," then turned to Mia, "Yes Mia."

"Thank you," she lowered her voice, "Okay, so I found something of interest that the Dead Crow guards have, a paper that might have some important information."

"Yes?" James said.

"I want to take it."

"OH," Mark chuckled, "You're funny."

"I don't think that's clever Mia," Daniel added his input.

James agreed, "We dodged a shower of bullets yesterday-,"

Mia interrupted him, "Because of me."

"Wait what?" James sounded confused.

"Oh come on," Mia shot at him, "You know I can use magic without a staff," she whispered.

What Mia just said was confirmation for Daniel, he was now very sure that Mia is what Angelina described, now a matter of telling her.

"How?" Mark enquired with great interest.

"It's a simple cloaking spell," she replied, "I gave you different faces, but only to the Dead Crow."

"Sweet," James said.

"I just thought they didn't know us," Mark giggled.

Mia wasn't at all happy with Marks response, "Oh really, they don't know your faces?" She shook her head.

Before Mark could make things worse, Daniel stepped in, "Thanks," he said

James and Mark said the same.

Mark's thanks didn't seem too grateful, and Mia could tell, she chuckled, trying to hide her anger, "Mark."

"What Mia?"

"Will you allow me to speak now?"

"No, we already agreed your idea is bad," he replied.

Her jaw dropped, gasped in shock, "Well, if you are not willing to prepare for any possibility, maybe I should just remove the hex," she said messing up the chess board

"No, please don't," Daniel said taking a seat.

"What are you doing!" Mark raised his voice, trying to reposition the pieces, "And Daniel, she's bluffing," Mark added a bit more salt

"Don't test me Mark," she spoke a little calmer.

"I'm testing you," he shot back.

Before anything else, James stepped in, "Okay, that's enough," he raised his voice, "Mark, she is right, Jake sent us here for a reason," he lowered his voice, "I'm open to any suggestions that may lead us forward, even if it is pickpocketing a Dead Crow," his face turned to fear, "How is this a good idea exactly?" He asked, very concerned.

"It's not, but it's a step forward," she replied, "First I need to know if you are on board," she placed both her hands on the table.

"I'm in," James said.

"Yes," Daniel agreed.

Mark nodded.

There was a bit of a stare between the two.

"Okay...but first, do not, by any circumstance come across a Dead Crow while I'm asleep, the hex doesn't work during that period of time," she explained.

They nodded in return.

"Moving on," she started, "I heard the Dead Crow keep a separate list of names that they keep exclusive to themselves, these names are apparently the worst this world has to offer, no bounties, nothing," she explained, "I'm saying you might be on that list, seeing as there are no bounties and they came here themselves."

"What are you saying?" Daniel asked, "We lucky and unlucky?"

She nodded in response, still a bit unsure about the second question.

Mark took a deep breath. "Is this a panic matter?"

"No, at least not yet," she replied, "We must take this piece of paper, and we will decide from then."

"We are starting a fire we won't be able to put out," James said flicking away a chess piece.

"We need to, we have to burn down the forest and see what's hiding in it."

"Nice one," Daniel complimented

"I've already taken some steps, and we have a target."

"Okay, when do we do this?" Daniel asked.

"Today."

Motivation was greatly decreased.

The time was here, it was break and the school grounds occupied, and their Dead Crow target was standing steadily against a wall under one of the corridors. This guard stood there, bolted in place, just observing with the eyes of a hawk, whilst everything around him acted as if he was not there, children sitting, socializing on the grass and younger ones playing games.

Not too far from him was our party, seated on a set of stone benches under a tree.

"Day two and the agent is already bored out of his mind," James pointed out.

"Off course, standing around like that is no joke, I feel his pain," Mark added.

They both didn't stop staring at him.

Mia brought them back to the situation, "Guys, you want this to fail before it begins?"

Mark turned to her, "Why today, why me?"

"It was a dice roll," Daniel said, "you got the lowest number, it was fair."

"Don't worry Mark, your visuals won't be compromised, I have practiced quite a bit," Mia said, "But you have to be quick, I'm not very good in terms of duration."

As you may know now, the only people apart of the plan are Mark and Mia, Mark will be the errand boy, and Mia's magic, the necessity.

Mark was starting to panic, this idea was throwing him out of proportion. His fiddling had returned, thinking of some way this could be postponed, "How quick?" He asked, panting.

"Two minutes tops."

"What!?" He uttered, "That's not going to work."

"She is turning you into a twelve year old curious boy, you should be happy," Daniel said trying to uplift him.

"Then you should do it."

Mia sighed, "Unfortunately, I don't have the power to change your emotions, so please stop panicking."

"Don't tell me to stop panicking," he gave her a sour look.

"Why do you look like a red flag," James giggled.

"Shut it!" Mark shot at him.

"Guys, let's be serious here, Mark is about to talk to someone," he tried to keep a straight face, he burst out laughing.

"Haha," Mark laughed sarcastically, "You guys are not being friends right now."

Mia cut in, "Time is valuable right now."

Mark calmed himself with a few deep breaths and loosened his body. James gave him a hard pat on the back, "You got this."

He stood up, "I'm ready," he announced, "Let's do this before I start panicking again."

Mia held her hand up at him and closed her eyes.

A few moments passed, she lowered her hand, "I'm done," she said, keeping her eyes closed.

Mark didn't feel any different, a thought came to his mind that this might have not worked, "You sure, I don't look any different."

"The hex will only affect him, just go," she insisted.

He stood right in front of him, heart trying to give out from fear. The agent had just noticed him staring back at him. Another second would have brought upon a strange awkwardness that was going to make him feel uncomfortable, if not already, so Mark gave him a pearl white smile. Off course, now he was acting as the twelve year old he was hexed into looking like.

The agent was greeted with a whole lot of mixed feelings, confused by this child's presence, and his smile. Those first few seconds had made him feel a little too uncomfortable, so he started pretending the boy didn't exist.

"Hello mister," Mark greeted.

The greeting allowed his nerves to calm, his biggest fear was communicating with the guy, now that it was out of the way and the agent greeted back, it was time for him to start up a random conversation with him.

At first he began by giving compliments to the uniform, which was, undoubtable very appealing to look at. This was just to remove the awkwardness that was created by the unnecessary stare. It didn't seem to be working too well so he moved on to the question him about their jobs and how one goes about joining the Dead Crow.

The agent became a bit too comfortable, explaining a lot of things, the two minute window thinning with every second this agent spoke.

Mark decided to try cut him off, nicely, and move closer to mentioning the piece of paper. Fibbing a tale, that he had seen one of the agents with a piece of paper. This led to the questions about it.

"Is it a secret paper?" He asked.

The agent nodded, "Yes little boy."

"Can I take a peek?" he asked with the most cheerful face ever, "I promise I won't tell anyone."

The agent shook his head, "No, little boy, it is top secret."

"Pretty please."

"No can do," he replied, "So please go play with your friends, or I'll get in trouble."

Mark blew up his face, "Fine," he turned away from him and headed out of his line of sight, carrying a disappointed face.

James tapped Mia on the soldier, "He's done."

Mia opened her eyes, panting, "I hope he is successful."

"Uhm, how is he supposed to steal it again?" James asked, "I didn't catch that bit."

"Not steal, as in pickpocket," Mia replied, "The reason why there was only a two minute window, wasn't because of the transformation, it's an illusion so it does take much from me," she explained, "It is because I gave him a different hex-,"

Mark walked up to them, "Sorry Mia, he was very defensive about it," he took a seat.

"What," Mia was surprised, "Not even a small peek at it?"

He shook his head in disappointment, "He said it was very secret and that he would get into trouble, so he told me to leave."

Mia noticed the agent being very observant, "It's fine, it just means that this piece of paper is more important than we thought, we going to have to come up with something else," she stood up, "Let's go, there will be another chance."

James sat there, already trying to think of more ways to gain the piece of paper, but this was no game, and a pickpocket is not going to work. While lost in thought, he couldn't help but stare at this Dead Crow agent, while he minded his own business.

Something happened, that caught his attention, there was another person.

Someone else stood next to the agent.

Mia tapped him on the shoulder, "James?" She asked, "What are you doing?"

"I'll catch up with you guys later," he replied, keeping his eyes on the person.

They left, one by one.

James decided to stop Mark, as he was the last one to leave, "Mark," he called.

"What?"

"Do you see anything strange near that agent?"

Mark looked up at him, "Hmmmm, now that you mention it yes," he placed his hand on his chin.

Maybe James wasn't going crazy after all, "What?"

"There's a hole in that bench," he chuckled

James shook his head and sighed in disappointment, "Okay, whatever."

"See ya," he left.

So maybe he was going crazy. He decided to rub his deceptive eyes, just to make sure.

He opened them.

The person was still there, looking exactly as she did before. It was the same ghost from before.

He kept a close watch of her actions. The ghost took a peek into the agent's pocket and proceed to shove her hand into the pocket.

To James's surprise, the agent continued on unfazed. He did not notice this girl carelessly pickpocket him. A moment after, she pulled out the paper and examined it with a curious face. She then turned her gaze to James.

James received a long cold chill down his spine, unable to break off from her stare. The fear was followed by a bit of confusion, when he noticed her smiling at him. He tried hard, but was only able to pull a faint smile.

The little girl then started walking, walking toward him.

He started looking around, wondering why no one else was noticing this strange phenomenon.

It wasn't long before she was standing right in front of him.

He was shivering as if it was winter, "Hi," he uttered.

The little girl smiled at him again, with her adorable face. She then held out her hand, the one holding the folded piece of paper she had just stolen from the agent. The paper was also transparent, like her.

James lifted his shaking arm, thinking, *how am I supposed to take this paper?*, it was also transparent, but he just went with it. Upon coming into contact with it, he could feel it, it was an actual piece of paper. He grabbed a hold of it.

As soon as the little girl let go, it lost its transparency, the only odd thing about it had disappeared.

James was shocked, still shaken by this moment, he was able to force at a couple of words, "Thank you."

The little girl just smiled and waved at him, before fading away from existence.

He looked at the paper for a moment, afraid to open it, he cleared his throat and scanned the area for any prying eyes. Once he knew it was safe, he proceed to unfold it and read the bold letters on top : **DEAD CROW'S WATCHLIST.**

He folded it again, before reading anything else, really surprised that he was actually holding the piece of paper owned by the Dead Crows, given to him by the ghost.

He still couldn't believe what just happened. Was this ghost here to help?

Was this a tale for his friends? No. Mark was proof that she is only visible to him. So this walk to rejoin his friends would be spent thinking of a way to tell them how he came to possess this list, or he could just try brush it off.

It did not take much convincing, but they all agreed to meet at the library later after school. James hadn't disclosed anything to them just yet, only that it was important.

A nice place to have such conversations, not many Dead Crow agents explored the library, so their discussion would go unnoticed. A quiet corner was still essential, just to be sure.

Mark sighed, taking a seat at the round table, "Okay, James, what is it, we're in enemy territory here."

Mia and Daniel just studied his unsure facial expression, wondering, what could be of such importance.

James kept silent, reached into his blazer pocket, pulled out the folded piece of paper and placed it down on the table right in front of him, "I haven't looked at it yet," he said.

Mia was the first to pick it up, glancing at James whilst doing so, "What is it?"

"The list," James whispered.

"What?" She halted the unfolding process.

"Open it."

She then did so quickly, but upon reading the heading of the paper, she did not show any bit of excitement at all, she frowned, "Where'd you get this?"

And the part came, where explaining how he got the paper was more important than having it. Winging a story was not going to help, telling the truth either. Mia was smart enough to tell if it were a lie but the truth was going to sound even crazier.

Mark went on and grabbed the piece of paper from Mia, "What is this?" His examination ended up with the same question, but with a bit more persona, "How were you able to get this?"

Daniel wanted to know as well, "Can someone just tell me."

"He got the list," Mia replied.

"Luck I guess," James replied, "Look, we have it, let's just move on, I'm sure you don't want to spend any more time here than I do."

Mark was the first to agree with him, "You read my mind," he looked at the paper.

Mia held out her hand, right in front of Mark.

"What?"

Mia looked at the paper, then up at him again.

"Yeah, whatever," he handed it back to her.

James and Daniel leaned over to view the contents of the piece of paper while Mark sunk into his wooden chair and placed both his hands behind his head.

They went down every name on the list and found nothing, their names were not present. Which meant that they had reached a road block, one with no answers.

This was a great disappointment, but not entirely.

"Nothing," Mia announced, placing the paper on the table.

"Well, that sucks, I guess," Mark said.

Daniel took the paper, "Well, I guess that's why they didn't call us out during inspection, they don't know our names yet."

"That's a good thing," James replied.

"So the most dangerous person here is Levina," Daniel read, "No surname for her."

"What?" Mia took interest, "I wonder why."

"Levina…" Mark repeated, "Nice name, wonder what she did."

"Should we start looking at wanted posters?" James suggested.

Mia shook her head, "The newspapers that come here don't have poster in them."

Mark took a deep breath, "They don't know our names, so there won't be any wanted posters."

"That's not entirely true Mark, if they have your faces, it's all they need," Mia corrected him.

"Okay," he sat up straight again, "The only place I saw these posters was the inns and that library, and in case anyone hasn't noticed, we stuck here, forever, or at least until we get caught."

"Leaving the school is asking for it," James said.

Mia took the list from Daniel and folded it up, "Leaving is not a possibility, too big a risk just to find out whether or not you're on the wanted posters, I have a better idea, not good, but it's an idea, one that can't afford failure."

Mark hit the table softly, "We just came from a failure we could afford," Mark sighed, "How bad is this idea?"

"Well if you have a good one, I'd be happy to hear it."

"I'm listening to yours."

Mia sat back, "I know that Mr. Patchwalker has these posters…in his office," she gave a sly smile.

"You know everything, how is it?" James enquired.

"I've been here a term longer than you people," she replied.

"Okay, fair enough, so how is this going to work?"

Mia sat there for a moment, "It will be fair, oh, and someone has to get hurt," she glanced from one to the next, "But first I will have to check a few things before we can actually carry it out."

Mark shifted to the idea, "Someone has to get hurt?"

Mia nodded.

"Not happening," he sat back, "I have already been a part of these plans, it's your turn guys, I plan on sitting this one out."

"You will, if you don't roll the lowest number," Daniel said.

"That's not fair," he raised his voice.

"What do you mean," James stepped in, "You were chosen fairly the first time, now is another chance to try your luck."

He ignored him, "Mia, when is this happening?"

"Today."

Mark's jaw dropped, "What is it with you and today?"

She shrugged.

By the time it was supper, their plan was just about ready to be set in motion. The evening announcements had already been said by Mr. Patchwalker and the students already enjoying their dinner.

This was a very tense dinner, in their minds, the plan only drawing nearer to its execution. The one person who seemed more cheerful was Mark, he was somewhat relieved. The fearful one this time was James, the food didn't taste as good tonight. The feeling of knowing he was about to get hurt was not nice at all, and the thing is, this was all going to be unknown to him. Mia did not mention how it was going to happen.

"Oooh, this is bad," James said with a shaking voice, "bad luck."

"It was fair and square," Mark replied.

Angelina leaned over to Daniel next to him and whispered, "What's wrong with him?"

"Oh, he lost a bet is all," he replied, "We don't really talk about it."

She nodded in response.

It was some time, before a few of the learners had started to make their way out of the hall. This was the best time to start acting, all suspicion was minimized, leaving the place with the rest of the evacuees.

They fabricated an excuse for their early departure, to ensure none of their other friends followed. Mark stuffed his mouth a bit and James left his plate barely touched. All four stood from their places and headed out the hall. James gave his blazer to Daniel for insurance.

The great part was the fact that there weren't many Dead Crows in the school, that or this place was way too big and they were all stretched out thin.

When they neared Mr. Patchwalker's office, they split up into their designated areas.

Distracting a couple of the patrols was the job Daniel and Mark were assigned to, creating simple conversation with them just to keep them in place. Mia had given them the special twelve year old look, just to make things a whole lot less suspicious. The same topics used on the agent earlier today was to be put into effect.

James and Mia stayed together, they were both needed for this part of the plan. The agent James had to distract was standing at the door they needed to get into. He was going to need more than a simple conversation to pull him away. This was the reason for the dice roll.

Far down a long corridor they stood, just behind a corner. The door stood on the other side of a T-junction.

Mia peaked from behind the corner and saw the agent standing up straight and still. She hid herself again quickly and turned to James, "Okay, this plan might and might not work."

"What?" James said surprised, "Am I going to get hurt for nothing?"

James was a nervous wreck at this moment. And this new bit of information had just made it worse.

"Shh," she whispered, "There is a fifty percent chance that Mr. Patchwalker might be there."

"That's convenient."

"Don't worry, I will use Perceive Life before entering," she replied.

"I meant me," he said.

She put on a straight face, "We don't have time, Just make your way down the corridor, I'll take care of the rest."

James took a deep breath and nodded.

"Okay," she signaled for him to go, "Make it quick."

James made his way around the corner, his heart beating faster than the rate of his footsteps.

The agent took notice of him immediately, it was quite common for students to come by Mr. Patchwalker's office so it was no big deal that he was headed in the same direction. The one thing James couldn't take off his mind was the final step he was going to take. He wanted it over with and yet wished for another step. Acting normal was not very hard, he was only breaking down on the inside.

Mia would take a small peek every few moments, and when the time was about right, she summoned the same blue mist in her one palm, and with careful concentration, she was able to whither the floor before James with a thin layer of ice, that was very reflective, simulating a mirror, cloning the light from the chandelier.

James was way too close, he didn't have enough time to detect the ice and took his first step onto it.

One who did notice however, was the agent watching him as he drew nearer, but fortunately, his reaction was a bit too late, having had to process everything in his mind first before eventually realizing. He took a step forward, "Watch out!"

James was distracted by his gesture and turned his attention to him, which took his focus away from everything else. It happened as if Mia knew he was going to try give him warning.

He lost his balance and slipped forward.

It was an unexpected way to go down, the floor being so clear, the thought of slipping died as soon as he took his first step down the corridor.

His reflexes tried to save him from the matter but they weren't fast enough, and in this situation, he was definitely getting hurt. And it was his left arm first, to suffer from the frozen stone floor. This was followed by a loud cry in pain.

Mia watch as her plan fall into place with a cringed expression, "Sorry," she whispered to herself.

As hoped, the Dead Crow agent rushed over to help him.

Mia melted away the ice, to minimize the risk of the agent getting hurt.

James didn't stop fidgeting around on the floor, with a face frozen in shock as he look at his arm.

The agent first check for any ice on the floor, but to his surprise, there was none, then he proceeded to help James, "Are you okay?" He asked.

James was shaken from shock, "It's not moving," he muttered, "My hand's not moving."

The agent decided to check his forearm and saw the centre was red and swelling, "Oh, I think we might have a broken arm here," he said.

James started to panic, "It's painful," he started to hyperventilate.

Without any hesitation, the agent picked up James and hurried down the hall, "I'm taking you to the infirmary."

Mia moved from the one corner and hid away behind another for the duration it took for the agent to carry James away and out of sight. Afterwards, hurried away down the hall, pacing quickly till she reached the doorway, checking both sides for any signs of people.

It was clear.

She closed her eyes for a moment and opened them again, her irises were both a slightly bright, light green colour. The ability allowed her to see passed all non-living things and see the aura of all that was alive. She looked in all directions in front of her, just in case the office had any additional rooms that Mr. Patchwalker might be in.

The coast was clear and her eyes went back to their normal state.

The next step was getting the door open, she turned the door, expecting it to be locked. To her luck, it pushed open.

Door unlocked? Well it did make sense for there be an agent here then. Without a second to waste, she stepped in and left the door just barely closed.

She stepped into a rather large room, dimmed out a bit, with only one chandelier hanging down the centre, not too many other sources of light.

Mr. Patchwalker's office was a sanctuary with many interesting things put on display, from well-designed weapons and staves to other objects of interest like jewelry that looked aged, locked away behind glass display cases. She noticed very interesting enchantment cubes, that glowed and floated in their cylinder displays.

Mia loved the room, also having some exotic plants placed in random places. But this wasn't the time to be browsing, she headed straight for his main desk, which was well-organized as if it were untouched, papers and books stacked properly, and a few potions as well placed near them.

Her first place of interest was the drawers, she started on the left side, searching through all three with haste, knowing what she was looking for. No posters were found so she moved on to the right side of her desk.

And the right side was right. She found the posters, right on top, the very first drawer.

She pick them all up and scanned through them as fast as she could, as the pile thinned, her luck was increased. If they weren't on the posters either, then it was a good thing, but then just another dead end.

None of the faces in the pile matched, a relief. Making sure the list was in the same order she attained it, she neatly straitened the pile. Before putting it back where she found it, she realized she hadn't taken all the posters out, so she placed the pile she had already examined on the desk and pick the posters still in the drawer.

Luckily it was only one.

But the contents of this poster were very interesting.

It was a picture of a young girl, with long black hair, looking about the same age as her.

She lowered her sights to the name and it read : **LEVINA.**

This came to Mia as a surprise, "She is on the list and a Wanted poster," she muttered to herself, "It's just a teenager."

Mia wanted so badly to take the poster but that would raise questions, should Mr. Patchwalker find out it was missing. She placed it back into the drawer, along with the rest of the posters, "How is she the most dangerous person?" She asked herself.

There was no time to dilly-dally so she made her way to the door and use Perceive Life again before opening it.

After the mission was a success, she headed back to the study, with more questions about this girl, Levina. Why she would be the most dangerous and yet just pass as a teenager.

James had been sent to the infirmary, where the nurses had treated him with a cast and a sling. He was also given a few vials of potion to help with the pain, placed on a small desk beside the bed.

He was spending the night there, in the hall-sized infirmary, alone, just surrounded by rows of beds and medical supplies.

Later that night, he was awoken by the pain in his arm. Opening his eyes, he remembered that he wasn't in the dorms, but alone in a dark room. The thought alone gave him the jitters. Being a person who has been exposed to many horror movies in his time, this setting brought to him a lot of fear.

He turned to the table on his right and picked up a small vail, sealed with a tiny cork. With only one hand, he was able unseal it with his teeth and drink the solution. The taste was not pleasing but it did the job.

As he finished the potion, he place the empty vail next to the others. His gaze turned to the bedside near his feet.

He received another heart stopping fright.

Sitting there was the little ghost again, swaying her legs back and forth. She turned to him and smiled.

James sighed in relief after recognizing her, "Hi," he uttered, trying to lower his breathing back to normal.

"Hi," she replied, "what happened to your arm."

James was surprised by her sudden interest to speak, "Oh... just fell over and broke it," he replied.

She giggled, "Silly."

"Uhm...thank you for helping me get the list," he spoke calmly.

She nodded with her cute smile, "It's a pleasure mister," she replied, "Might I ask your name?"

The more James was in her presence, the more he felt as if he were just talking to a normal person, "Sure, my name is James," he answered, followed by a similar question, "Who are you?"

She became a little hesitant after the question was directed to her.

James noticed her expression change from cheerful. He felt bad for asking, she may not trust him yet. After all, she was a ghost.

"Promise you won't tell anyone," she said.

That sparked a whole lot more interest in James, why would she want it kept a secret, he was the only one able to see her. Was her name very important before she died? Nonetheless, he wanted to call her by something so he agreed to the promise.

"I promise."

She smiled again and replied, "Levina," before fading away again.

CHAPTER 12

A Rainy Day

The next day arrived, a beautiful Friday morning and an especially good one for our friend James. Since the injury that was concocted the night before, he was able to earn himself a day off from school. Waking up at his own desired time was also another perk that came with this injury.

He was greeted by one of the nurses, busy with something on the table beside his bed.

"Morning Mr. Lamaine," she greeted.

James sat up, "Morning."

"How is your arm feeling?" She enquired.

He turned to his arm and the pain slowly started to come back again, "Painful," he replied.

She picked up another one of the vials and handed it over to him, "Drink this," she opened it for him.

While James took in the horrible taste, she explained what was to happen.

"Okay James, what happened to you yesterday was unfortunate, somehow you managed to crack the Radius during your little fall reaching about half way through the bone," she said taking the vial from him, "so for today you will remain here in the infirmary for the day and we will be mending that arm together, which it why I need you to take another vial of that potion so we can start right away," she said picking up a staff she had placed aside.

She fetched a nearby chair, placed it beside his bed and sat down, "this may hurt so be prepared."

Another warning of pain that is about to occur, James felt scared again, but figured it won't be as bad because it's the healing process and he just took another vail of that painkilling potion.

He had never been so wrong in his life.

She stood her staff up straight and spoke the words, "Riparim."

From the head of the staff a bright yellow aura of mist emerged and slowly drifted from the staff to his bandaged arm.

James stared at it with both interest and fear, it looked pretty but it was about to do its job. The mist drifted around his arm for a moment before the a sharp pain sparked out of nowhere.

He closed tight his teeth, trying hard not to cry out loud.

Moments later it decreased but still felt unbearable. Not enough to make him scream.

The nurse spoke up another spell, "Romandre," before she let go of the staff.

To James's surprise the staff remained still and standing on its own whilst projecting the spell. He expected it to put the hex to a stop or the staff to fall over.

She stood up from her seat, "You may have another vial of this potion should the pain get worse," she explained, "but don't have them consistently."

He nodded in return and turned back to the staff again.

"I'll be back in a few minutes," she said heading for the door.

Alone again.

Midday came by in about a century. The nurse had long since removed the spell from his arm and was told to remain in bed because of the potion's minor side effects that numbed most of his body.

This day off was not at all as he expected, but then again it was visible from a mile away that sitting in bed alone all day was going to be terribly boring. It was a murderous kind of boredom that left him literally just staring into the abyss, or attempting to move is arm, or hum away at some tunes.

He was given something to consume at midday, so that was something he could count as productive.

Looking at the empty room, he wondered why it was unfilled, all the beds neatly made, only his small area that seemed out of place.

Break came after shortly, James could hear some of the younger children shouting in the far distance. He half expected a little visit from his friends in the few minutes he waited, but nobody showed up. Not all hope was lost, he envisioned they would be busy at first, but at least find even a spec of time to greet him.

In this dead room, he kind of wished to be visited by his new friend Levina. She seemed a friendly young lass since her last visit. If only she had allowed him to ask her a few more questions instead of just fading away with that horrible cliffhanger. Even a visit from his friends won't get any answers because his lips had been sealed shut by his promise.

Dwelling on his thoughts wasn't enough to keep him alive so he attempted to peer through the window closest to his bed, but leaning from the bed was not enough. Upon this failed attempt he tried to get out of bed.

"What are you doing?" A female voice echoed across the room.

James received a fright and nearly fell over again, thinking it was the nurse checking up on him. Lucky his right arm was still good... mostly, but it did the job.

He turned back to see that it was only Mia, "Oh, it's you," he smiled, positioning himself properly on the bed again.

"How are you?" She asked sitting down on the bed.

He looked at his arm for a second, "Fine I guess."

"Well," she took a deep breath, "I'm sorry for..." she paused raised her eyebrows expecting an answer from him.

It took a moment for James to catch on, "Oh, cracking my Radius in half," he replied.

"Huh?" Her expression turn confused.

He put things a little simpler, "Breaking my arm."

She nodded, "Sorry for breaking your arm," she apologized, "Though I didn't expect anything to brake, I just-,"

"-Iced the whole floored?" He completed her sentenced.

She looked at his arm, "If you put it that way, I kind of get it."

James shook his head, "You turn the floor into an ice rink," he turned his sights to the door and saw nothing, "Are there any others showing up."

Mia turned to the door and shook her head, "They busy betting on something."

James jaw dropped, but there was still a smile, "Oh!" he blurted out, "Okay, I see how it is," he shook his head continuously, "Gambling is more important, I'll be sure to check that on the list, I'll remember this day," he nodded.

"What list you talking about now?" Mia asked.

"Never mind," he replied, "Now please tell me that my arm didn't break in vain."

"I'm not sure what 'vain' would be."

"Did you find anything?"

She shook head in return.

"It broke in vain."

"No," she disagreed, "It's actually a good thing that your posters are not there."

"I broke my arm for nothing," he said, "I pretty sure that the word 'vain' can be used in this matter."

Mia was confused, "So wait, you wanted me to find posters of you guys?"

"I kind of wish that now, yes."

"Ugh," she rolled her eyes.

At the tip of his tongue, James had this secret he wanted so badly to slip out, even by accident. But being full aware of it, there was no way this could slip out by accident and deep down in the back of his head, he imagined Levina was lurking about nearby listening to them in her invisible state, waiting for him to slip up.

Mia sighed, "Down to business, I found something strange though."

"Go on."

"I found a poster of the girl Levina in the pile that I searched through," she started, "Her name was the only one on the list that appeared on a wanted poster as well."

"Didn't you say the list was secret only to the Dead Crow?"

She nodded, "Mostly, I'm sure that lots of people know the list of criminals, but in her case it was different, and get this, she is just a teenager, about our age by my guess."

"A teenager being the most wanted person," he squinted suspiciously at her, "hmm."

"I'm serious."

James had to get some features, "What does she look like?"

Mia tried to remember the image, "She has long black hair, it's all I can describe, why you want to know?"

"Just curious," he replied.

She didn't trust his answer. She place her hand on his leg, "I have to go now...get well soon."

"Thanks, but I'll be out tomorrow, we can talk about this better then."

"Okay, bye," she stood up and headed for the door.

James watched as she made her way out and nodded slowly, lost in thought once again.

Back to the description. Long black hair, that was the exact same as the little ghost Levina. The thought alone was confusing. *How is it the ghost has the same name as her and same hair?* This was not much to go on about, he had to see the poster by himself.

Saturday sure did take its time, but it did arrive and it was time for James to take his leave of the infirmary. His morning was quite early for someone waking to a Saturday. The nurse had arrive to check up on him early and ordered that he cleaned himself up and change to his casual clothing, and by doing so, return the patient clothing that was given to him during his time there. He was also given a few more vials of the painkilling potion just for some insurance.

The morning was quite gloomy outside, a lot of clouds gathering, greying out everything. There was sure to be some rain today.

James started wondering the halls at around nine in the morning, all done with his errands and now on the hunt for his friends. Wearing a pair of jeans and a hoody, his sling above everything.

His clothing stood out from everyone's, but then again, everyone's clothing in this city stood out uniquely. It was as if each person had their own tailor or dressmaker.

The corridors were filled today with a lot of students, keeping away from the school grounds where it had recently started to drizzle a bit. It was common for learners to spend their time in the library, or the magic halls, studying or socializing in the main hall was also common in such weather cases, so James's search was going to be a little simpler, depending on his detection skills.

The morning trip to their study was met with none of his friends, so his next visit was to the hall, which looked promising but no one was there. On his way to the closest magic hall, he ran into a couple of his friends, William and Clara.

"Clara!" He called jogging toward them.

They both turned to him.

"James, you're back," she said, "We didn't see you yesterday in class."

"Yes, had a little accident," he held up his broken arm.

"How did that happen?" William asked.

James was in no interest in telling the story so he just kept it short, "I just tripped and fell," he took a deep breath, "Do guys perhaps know where Mia is?"

Clara nodded, "I heard her speak about going up to the library or something like that."

"Thanks," James replied, quickly turning away from them, heading to the library with haste.

Aisle by aisle he checked for their presence, in the forever occupied library. His source was correct to send him here, he found all of them hanging around a table having what seemed to be a serious conversation.

"Hey guys," he greeted, "Oh and thanks for the visit yesterday you two," he pointed at Mark and Daniel.

"Hey, they gave you a sling," Mark pointed out, "How bad was it?"

James ignored his voice and just sat down at the table.

Daniel was leaning against a book shelf up against the wall, "Sorry James, we were kind of hung up."

James laughed, knowing full well that whatever kept them busy was not important, "Sure sure, I understand," he decided to let it go.

Mia was also the only one seated at the table, "How much longer do you have to wear that?" She asked.

"Just a few more days," he replied.

"Oh so it wasn't that bad?" Mark figured.

Mia shook her head, "Not good at all, apparently I nearly snapped it, it broke till half way, or something along those lines."

"That's not possible," Mark disagreed, "A simple fracture can take many weeks to fix up."

James shook his head in disbelief, "They use magic Mark, and you are studying restoration," he sighed.

"I know, and this was banned in the present," He shook his head, "That is stupid, people doing this medical stuff manually."

James was getting a little sidetracked now, forgetting the reason why he was looking for them in the first place. He had to close off this conversation, "So what were you guys talking about before I came here?"

"Oh, just magic stuff," Daniel replied, "We wanted to check the newspaper for this week."

"I presume, you told them about Levina right?" He asked Mia.

She nodded in return.

"Yeah," Mark replied, "Some very dangerous teenager that has done something for some reason, not important if you ask me," he started pacing back and forth, "The important thing is that we are not on the list or any of those wanted posters."

"But that girl is on both," James said.

"So," he replied, "She is not important, we don't even know her."

"What are you trying to say James?" Daniel asked, "It sounds like you have something in mind."

He nodded in response, "We must find out more about her," he suggested.

Mark stopped pacing, "What?"

"You heard me," he replied.

"You are not thinking straight," he said, "We just found out we are clean, no posters or list-,"

"Yeah, and why is that?" he raised his voice a bit, "It's clear they are looking for us, they have seen our faces, so why make it so hard on themselves?"

Mark was quite caught between a ditch after getting asked that question, which made him think a little more about the situation.

Daniel stepped away from the book shelf, "You have a point there, they could've just printed our faces anywhere and we would be caught immediately."

"Yeah, I wouldn't be able to create a hex large enough to protect you from everyone, and besides, your faces a very common here except to the Dead Crow, so even hiding them would depict you are missing, and then your names would be known as well," Mia added.

"But how does this girl fit in to the picture?" Mark enquired.

James would have had it way easier, if he was able to mention the ghost. Though he was still unsure if there was some kind of link between her and the teenage girl in the posters, he had to follow this new lead, because in the back of his head, he still remembered the very first time he met with this girl.

He had to answer this question fast, "I have a feeling…I guess."

"Hmm."

"I mean, she is the only one standing out here, and she is our age, that to me is something worth checking out," he added, "And remember, Jake said we should keep an eye out for anything potential."

It was a great pitch, it got them thinking about it, probably considering it.

Mia looked up at James, "To be honest, she did have me thinking, when I found out she was on both the list and posters, and so young."

James smiled, one person was on board.

"I asked around," Mia continued, "Inside here, it seems no one knows anything about her, they just recognize the name."

"Daniel, Mark, I'm sure you also think this is fishy."

"I hate you James," Daniel decided to agree with him.

Mark was the last one, trying hard to get himself out of this situation. Eventually he let out a sigh, "Why do we have so much responsibility?" He shook his head.

"Well, I guess we signed up for this the day we took those diamonds from Jake," James said.

"We're just kids," Mark got a bit frustrated, "He forced us."

"Mark, calm yourself," Mia said, "If we really going forward with this, we're not going to find any information here in this school, this has to be accomplished outside the school."

Mark started pacing back and forth again, getting a little on edge, "And I thought breaking into Mr. Patchwalker's office was as dangerous as we can get."

"We forget that we are trapped here for an eternity," Daniel Pointed out.

Mia gained herself a sly smile, "Not quite."

James wanted to give a drum roll before Mia revealed another great plan, but his condition made it impossible to do it proper, "What do you have for us this time Mia," he smiled.

Daniel pulled a chair and sat down, really anxious to hear about the other way out of the school.

"What clever plan do you have this time, Mia?" Mark asked pulling out a random book from the shelf and examining it.

"Well, it wasn't exactly cleverness that got me to find this place," she started, "I stumbled across it out of curiosity, I too was a bit of an explorer when I first arrive at this school. Clara, Angelina and I went around the school grounds after school and on one of those days we came across this small tower somewhere behind the school, and in it, was nothing but a trap door and a few steps leading to the top."

Mark stopped checking the book he picked up, "Trapdoor?"

Mia nodded.

Mark shook his head, "Oh no, that's not a good idea at all."

"Have any of my ideas been good?"

"Well... they good compared to this new madness," he place the book back and pulled out another, "You talking about going down a sewer."

"According my friends, it is more than just a sewer."

"I've been down sewers before, and it never goes well down there."

Mia raised her browse, not believing a word he said.

"Ok, in games," He confessed, "I meant to say 'in games'."

"Hmm, this might work," James replied, only thinking about helping the ghost, "Crazy dangerous though."

Daniel pointed at James's bandaged up arm, "If we going, you're not coming with us."

"Now I wish I had the broken arm," Mark said.

James was hell bent on tagging along with them, he had to ask questions for himself as well as collect something, "I'm going."

Mark dropped the book onto the table, "James, you are literally blessed with a broken arm, why do you have to act so rash?"

"James, I think Mark's right," Mia agreed.

James couldn't take no for an answer, "I have some questions that I have to ask Galvani, besides, I suggested this, I'm not going to sit it out."

There was no changing his mind, no matter what anyone tried to say, no amount of convincing got through to him. He wouldn't miss this opportunity to get something done. He had his own set of questions he wanted to slip in.

"Ok James, Have it your way," Mia gave in to this unending argument.

"Thank you."

"It's going to have to be carried out today though," she announced.

This obviously came as a shocker to all of them.

Mark chuckled, "'Today' again, that's funny, jokes aside please Mia."

Mia's expression didn't change which made them all uneasy, "What joke?"

Mark frowned, "You aren't being serious?"

"Guys, we are running out of time as it is, and tomorrow is the apparent inspection."

"Oh, so you are serious," Mark was disappointed, "Why, may I ask?"

"It's raining, meaning less prying eyes, and I have already seen a draft of the place, so I'm going to put the directions on a piece of paper."

This was coming way too stressful, they were expecting a more postponed time, but the more she spoke and the closer they listened, the more sense she was making, and the more reason this had to be carried out on the day.

Mark shook his head and let out a long sigh, "It's as if you knew James was going to suggest this, did you speak about it yesterday or something?"

James declined, "I only thought about this right now."

Mark looked into Mia's eyes as if looking for something, "You're psychic aren't you?" He asked tilting his head.

She burst out laughing, "No."

Mark suggested something a little more understandable, "You have some kind of mind reading power then."

Mia shook her head, "No such magic exists."

James's eyes started to wonder all over the place, "Is there a clock around here, I want to check the time."

"It should be about ten now," Mia replied, "Meaning we have to start acting now...I will start mapping out our route and you three check the perimeter if it's clear, by the trapdoor entrance."

Daniel stood up, "I think directions to this place are needed."

Mia sighed, "Okay, just ask Angelina or Clara, they should have no problem helping you out."

The next part in their investigation was to begin.

On the hour they met at this tower, a place that seemed to be empty at all times and down the hill from the main buildings. The tower looked forgotten, standing as tall as your average windmill, it was built from stone, which now harbored vegetation. Inside was just a wooden trapdoor surrounded by nothing but earth and grass, the staircase seemed dangerous to even attempt climbing.

Everybody had put on a rain coat. Mia had brought the piece of paper showing them the directions they needed to take.

James had removed his sling for better mobility, "How big is this place we going into?"

"About the size of the city," Mia replied, "If you saw the map, you would be surprised, it's a whole maze down there."

Mark was afraid, "Isn't anyone else scared right now?"

"Sought of, yeah," Mia replied, "But we have decided on it, so let's do it," she crouched down in front of the trapdoor.

It was sealed shut with a lock and chains.

The placed her hand just above the lock, "Hapur," she said as the lock opened.

"Nice," James complimented.

She removed the chain and lifted the trapdoor open.

Everyone's head hovered above the entrance, staring down into what seemed a bottomless hole. The ladder was made of cylinder metal bars and made orange because of the rust.

"I'm having regrets," Mark blurted out.

Daniel placed his hand on his shoulder, "The school's that way," he pointed with the other.

He slapped his hand away and leaned forward, hoping to see more than just nothing. He took a deep breath.

"I will go down first," Mia volunteered, "Since I'm the only one here capable of making light."

Everyone else agreed without any second thought.

She placed her boot onto the first metal bar and stomped it, just to ensure it was safe and still stable despite its hoary age. After the successful test, she lowered herself down the ladder, step by step, testing each rusted metal bar, till she was not visible to the others standing there, waiting for clearance.

In the darkness, as Mia lowered herself, the light above her being the only source of visibility. The surrounding walls were murky with moss growth everywhere, water dripping onto her raincoat and off course the air, thick and warm, carrying an ever growing sour smell, getting stronger the lower she went.

The climb down was taking forever, the light above her was decreasing and she feared no one would hear her if she waited till she reached the bottom before calling them down, so she called for them to start climbing down as well.

The first to reach the bottom, Mia looked around and saw a very faint red light, glowing on the ceiling of this sewer. It wasn't enough to see anything so she conjured a very bright light on the palm of her left hand.

The light covered a pretty large radius, revealing to her quite a lot. For one, there was a still murky river in between two sides of the really large tunnels, shaped like a cylinder. They were lowered onto the left side of the river.

There was a railing, clearly there to protect people from falling, but in this case, it was the railing itself that was falling apart, and only standing in a few spots so its purpose was long since used and now it was just as dangerous as having no railing at all.

The walls were wet, reflecting the light like tiny mirrors, with even more moss growth, everywhere, hanging from above them as well. The floors were riddled with puddles and slippery at some places, but it was all bearable to look at. The only thing that would need getting used to was the stench. It reeked with the absence of fresh air, it was really hard, taking it in with each breath.

"This is really unpleasant," she murmured to herself.

"Wow, this is taking forever," James complained, "Is this some kind of mine," his voice sounded down the small space they were in.

Mark and Daniel made it down rather quick.

"Hate small spaces," Daniel said, jumping off the last step.

"Oh, that smell," Mark said covering his mouth.

"Did you close the trapdoor?" Mia asked.

Mark nodded, "Somehow, James managed to do it, he's on his way."

It was some time, but James made it to the bottom eventually.

"Yeah this is not creepy at all," He commented on his surroundings, "And what's with that creepy red light?"

"Shh," Mark silenced him, "Whisper, we don't want to wake up anything that may live down here."

Everyone stayed close to Mia, the only source of light in these dark tunnels.

She pulled out the paper that had the directions written on, she started down the tunnel, "Let's go, we've got a long way to walk."

They headed down the tunnel, the river forever beside them as they walked. Daniel couldn't take his eyes off it, it wasn't a pretty sight, but his eyes just didn't want to stop examining.

Mark was way too jittery in this situation, always looking over his shoulder for anything he hoped not to be watching, or following just beyond the radius of light, "Oh man, I wish I could use my diamond, I would have my shield up at all times."

They made their first turn left, and continued down the path. Mia had to constantly check the map, there were many different turns that led to other unknown places, and every so often, they would come across these faint glowing lights that just hovered. They figured they were there to help show the way, but not doing a good job.

As they went deeper into the tunnels, they began to notice a few arrows and signs, pointing and naming destinations.

"So now there's signs," James nodded, "Was this some kind of travel route?"

"Maybe," Daniel replied, "But you can tell it's been out of business for a while."

"It seems so," Mia agreed.

This venture down into the sewers was not at all bad after a while. The horrible stench was more bearable than the first few moments. Mark had stopped checking over his shoulder for anything that may not have been there to begin with.

There were many ceiled doors and staircases to be seen, all leading to places they did not at all feel curious about seeing.

Their little walk came to an end when Mia came to a stop in front of a ladder, similar to the one they had come down from.

"This is our que out," she said shoving the paper back into her pocket.

She dispelled the light and brought back the darkness as she started climbing the ladder.

The trapdoor up top was unlocked, but a bit heavier to lift than the other.

Pushing it open, she was greeted by the rain which was now pouring heavier than before, she stepped up into an alley and took this moment to have a feel of the fresh air brought by the rain and the relief of a better smell.

She immediately started to study her surroundings, the alley in which they emerged into was pasted with wanted posters all round, all soaked with a few that had faded ink or been torn. The ground was puddled with water. There wasn't much more to see, except for the garbage.

The posters were what she was drawn to, looking for a poster of Levina, and to her luck, it was among them.

One by one they emerge from the trapdoor. Daniel gave James a hand getting out.

"Thanks," he said wiping away some dirt soiling his raincoat, "Phew, at least that part is over," he rejoiced.

"It's our way back you know," Daniel reminded him as he closed the trapdoor. This one had metal plates over the wood.

"Guys, here's a poster if you want to see," Mia called them over.

James was first to get there, eager to make with some kind of resemblance. She had the black hair alright, the face was very hard to match, since the ghost was only around six years in age and this picture showed a teenager, ten years older perhaps. The names were a match at least.

And the hair.

And the sex.

"Wow!" Mark blurted out, he placed his finger on the bounty, "that is a lot of gold coins, a hundred thousand, that's way too much if you ask me...I mean look at all the others, the highest is one thousand."

"Yeah," James agreed, "Maybe it's a mistake."

Mia shook her head, "It's right, even the poster in Mr. Patchwalker's office said the same."

"What did she do, kill a king or something?"

Mia shrugged, "I guess we might find out," she turned to the streets, "Come on, let's go, I don't want to get in trouble."

The streets were crowded as usual, rain didn't seem to slow down business, here in the Market district. Raincoats did the trick. The street safety seemed to be upgraded a lot. It was not only the city guards that now watched over them, they were now infested with Dead Crow agents everywhere. Both mages and soldiers were posted on ground level, helping with patrols as well, and on the rooftops, archers stood guard with a good aerial view of the streets.

Their first stop to gaining information was at the library, the massive house of knowledge was probably their best bet for gaining any sort of information.

"Okay, ask around about Levina and see if you can get any answers from anyone, I will be in the books searching for some," Mia instructed.

"Me too," Daniel said, "There is something I got to find that might be in this library."

"Okay...," Mia gave him a concerned look, "Meet by the hour, if not earlier."

They split into their different directions. Mia and Daniel losing themselves in the endless aisles whilst Mark and James just headed over to the notice boards.

Mark wasted no time heading over to newspaper section, picking out the oldest newspapers placed on the shelves and heading to a seat where he could start concentrating and possibly find a story.

James went on to the notice boards containing the wanted posters and various bounties about missing people or animals and objects.

Upon finding the poster of Levina, he started reading up on other bounties that he found interesting.

A few minutes into his examination, a tall middle-aged man with a small backpack and weapons, wearing what look to be a travelers attire, walked up to the board and stood beside him. He looked at James for a quick moment, "Aren't you a bit too you to be bounty hunting boy?" He turned back to the board.

James chuckled, "Yeah I am, just looking to gain some information about someone here."

"And who might that be?' he asked, "I've been in the bounty hunting business for a while now."

James put his finger on the poster of Levina, "This girl."

The bounty hunter cleared his throat, "Levina, one of the very few bounties I am not even tempted to find."

"Why is that? Why is she so dangerous?"

"Well, don't be fooled by that pretty face…she is a curse," he man replied, "someone earning such a high price is a first."

"She is a curse?" He repeated.

The man nodded, "Yes, folk all over call her A living curse or The living curse, even the Dead Crow themselves are unable to catch her."

This man had some information alright, so James decided on asking further questions, "Do you know why she is called 'The living curse'?"

He shrugged in return, "From what I hear, it's from an incident that took place ten years ago."

"Might you know about the incident?"

"No, I missed that part of the news," he replied, "I don't think I want to know either, I mean, what can a little girl possibly do, to be dangerous enough to be only wanted dead," he pointed out on the poster, "the others give you the option 'Dead or Alive' some just 'Alive'."

James looked at the other posters and began to notice the different texts. Levina's poster had only 'Dead'.

"I don't care what she did, I am not going to kill a little girl."

James just nodded, "Thank you."

"Anytime kid."

James decided to join Mark in his newspaper search.

Mia and Daniel found nothing and decided it was best to search for recent events about her, so they joined in the newspaper search, allowing for the search to be carried out swiftly.

After some time had passed and every newspaper read, it was only after looking into the newest addition that they found something written about her.

"Great," Mark shook his head, "If only I looked at the newest paper, I wouldn't have wasted so much time."

"Let me see," Mia said pulling the newspaper from him.

Both James and Daniel hurried over to the paper. Mark was way too tired to even look into another newspaper so he sat back and waited for them to read over it.

Daniel read the headline, "Levina Vanishes into Thin Air."

Mia proceeded to read a bit of the information under the heading, "Levina, the living curse, was sighted in a small town south of Terratoar Mountain. Upon her immediate appearance, the Dead Crow took action," she skimmed over the unimportant information, "when she had destroyed the city, she then vanished without a trace, the Dead Crow are still on the search."

"Hmm, sounds dangerous to me... very," Mark said.

James shook his head, "Doesn't seem believable."

"It's in black and white," Mark replied.

James leaned over and whispered, "Do you believe we stole the objects and threatened a man's life?"

Mark look at the newspaper and then shook his head, "No I don't."

Mia took a deep breath, "We going to have to speak to Galvani about her," she suggested, "I mean, being Jake's friend he must know something."

"Sounds good," Daniel agreed.

They packed the newspapers back onto the shelves with no care to which date came before which and headed to the entrance of the library.

"Which way was his house again," Mark said with arms crossed, looking left and right.

"Follow me," Mia said heading out.

This was James's time to speak up, "Ah...guys,' he stopped them.

"I can't come with you, there is something I have to check out."

"Huh?" Mark turned to him.

"What is it James?" Mia asked.

He thought quick for a valid and believable excuse, "The man inside I was talking to told me about something, I just want to find out if it was true," he lied, "Mark you saw the bounty hunter I was talking to right?"

Mark nodded slowly, "Yeah, you were talking about someone."

James turned to Mia and Daniel, "I won't be long, I know where Galvani's house is."

"James splitting up is not a good idea," Mia pointed out, "We don't want to be searching for you."

"Don't worry, I'll be quick and careful, we don't want to be wasting time, I'm going either way."

Mia gave him a concerned look, "Okay... but only because you are hexed."

"Thank you."

They agreed to split up and wait at Galvani should he take a while longer to find his way.

Mark knocked on the door of Galvani's place.

No one responded.

He gave it another go, a little louder this time.

No response came from inside again.

Mark turned to his friends, "Maybe he is out somewhere... the market?" He raised his brows.

Daniel leaned against the railing and sighed, "I don't want to search," he shook his head continuously.

"On my way," A faint voice filled their ears.

Moments later, they heard the door knob turn. He decided to peak before opening the door any further. His eyes bulged, almost popping out of their sockets at the sight of the children.

His first reaction was to close the door.

"Galvani, it's me, Mia," She identified herself.

"I know," he replied from the other side.

"Then... may we enter please?" She asked politely

The door opened slowly again. This time it was opened wide. He peeked his head out and scanned the area, after his weird little act, he stood away from the doorway and allowed them in.

He closed the door with a loud bang, scaring the guests.

Galvani turned to them, "What are you doing here!" He whispered aloud with a worried tone.

They chose to get themselves comfortable first as if they were expected visitors, removing their coats and hanging them on the coat hangers.

"What are you doing here?" He repeated himself

"We have questions," Mia replied.

"You do know that the Dead Crow is looking for you right?" he asked, "And I know your school is not allowing anyone in or out."

They all nodded in response.

Mark headed over to the hearth.

"Speaking of which... how did you get out?" He continued with the questions.

"The sewers," Mia replied, "but that's not important right now."

"The sewers!" He raised his voice, "Are you trying to get yourselves killed?" He took a seat at the table.

Mark turned to him with a scared face, "Okay, now I'm scared of the sewers."

Galvani did a head count, "Where's James?"

Mia hesitated, "He had to go somewhere, he'll be here in a few."

Galvani's jaw dropped, he shook his head in disappointment, "Mia, you're safe, but these two and James, they will die if they are found."

"Don't worry," Mia said.

Galvani was shocked with her request, "Don't worry."

"I've put a spell them, they will have different faces to the Dead Crow," she explained.

"Jake specifically said to not use your magic!"

"They'd be caught if I hadn't."

Daniel stepped in, "She's right, the Dead Crow already know what we look like."

"And how is that, may I ask?"

"That story, that they are using about us... is not entirely false," Daniel replied.

"Oh my," he took a deep breath.

"Listen," Mia said taking a seat across from him, "We don't have much time."

Galvani nodded, finally excepting the fact that they were here, "What is it?"

Mia placed onto the table, the Dead Crow's watch list and a poster of the girl Levina.

Meanwhile, James had made his way swiftly through the crowded market district, making sure to blend in at the same time.

Now he was passing through the inner gates, making his way down the small hill of decorated gardens, nearing the shanty town that lay just outside the city.

The road turned from brick to gravel and dirt as soon as he made it passed the gardens. The decreasing hill became a bit more slippery, so he made his way into the village carefully, keeping his head down and hands in pockets, reducing any chance of getting wet.

Galvani pulled the list towards him first, he recognized it, "Where did you get this?" He frowned at her.

Mia was hesitant to reply, she looked at Mark and Daniel.

"Where'd you get this?" he picked it up and showed it to both Mark and Daniel.

"We stole it," She answered, "from one of the Dead Crow agents," she force a smile.

Galvani chuckled in disbelief, "You guys have been up to know good, you going to give this old man a heart attack."

"Sorry, but we really need to know," Mia apologized.

Daniel came to the table.

Galvani sighed, "Okay, what do you want to know?"

Mia tapped the poster, "This girl is on both the list and the poster."

Daniel nodded, "We wanted to know why, and what is this term, 'The living curse' mean, we read it in an article?"

Galvani's eyes jumped from Daniel to Mia, "She is very dangerous… yes," he replied.

"She's just a teenager though," Mia pointed out.

"Yes, she is but…-,"

"But what?" She interrupted him.

Mark decided to take interest in this conversation, so he turned the direction of his chair.

"-but why the interest, you don't know her at all, you just playing with fire," he finished his sentence.

Mia realized there was no valid motive for this questioning, they were all driven here by James and their own interests and curiosity.

Galvani stood up from the table and went to the kitchen counter and pulled out three mugs.

"I guess we are just interested, I mean, since when is a teenager the most dangerous person, and by such a large number," she replied honestly, referring to her bounty.

Even though Mia did not know a single thing about this girl but her name and the nickname the article gave her, she still felt it was important she found out. It was the reason they left the school, so she had to get something out of it, and allow this trouble of escaping be very worth it.

The thought James gave to them that this might as well be their very first task, made it more important that they figure out more, even thought they were still in the dark.

"Interests, huh?" Galvani mumbled to himself.

"Mia's right, this is very odd," Mark added.

"So it is curiosity that is going to get you killed," Galvani turned to them, "That's not very responsible," he poured hot water into the cups, "but you're here, and that can't be changed, so I'll tell you what I know," he said bringing the cups of tea to the table and calling Mark to fetch his.

The town outside the wall was a lot more empty due to the current whether. The stalls were out of business, all goods packed and stored away. The inn would definitely get a lot more business on a day like this. Only a few people remained outside amongst the Dead Crow agents that were stationed there, people working under shelter had no excuse to be closed, the blacksmiths included.

The ground was plagued with puddles and small streams that had formed by the shaping of the sands and the gutters that had formed over some time on the side of the road.

He made his way passed the market centre and into the residential area, keeping on the main road.

The rain did not stop the younger ones from playing outside, just a few coats and boots and they were good to go, continuing with their mischievous ideas and games.

The peaceful walk in the rain, brought to James a lot of good thoughts for once, the little ghost still present in his mind, wondering when again she would appear to him. For once, he really did feel in place, despite his obvious lack in understanding for his life that has taken such an unexpected turn. Though stuck in this past time, it started to feel normal, getting used to things in a magical world was very hard, coming from a time where technology was the new magic, everything here remained just as fascinating.

One thing that kept him sane was the presence of his friends and the new person that has entered into his life, Mia.

But at this moment, his mind was on the first thing of value he saw the first time he entered into the city. All he hoped was that it was still there, doubtful, but he just wanted to be sure.

Everyone waited eagerly, waiting in silence for Galvani to start saying something. Sipping away at the tea he had made for them, with the sound of the rain getting louder. It felt as if an old tale was about to be told.

"Okay," he sighed, "I don't know much but-,"

"Ahhhh, what," Mark stepped in, "You going to be like Jake aren't you?"

Galvani was confused, "What do you mean?"

"Mark, shh," Mia silenced him.

"What can I say, she's a mystery," Galvani said.

"Why doesn't anyone know anything about her anyway," Daniel asked.

Galvani shrugged, "One minute she doesn't exist and the next she is the most wanted."

"Hmm, when did this start?' He asked.

This was starting to copy there tale, in a way, the one minute they don't exist in this time line and the next, find themselves waking up in this place.

"It happened about ten years ago, that's when the first wanted posters of her were made."

Mark nodded, "Ten years, that's impressive."

"Wait, she was just a little kid back then," Mia pointed out, "none of this is making sense, a what, seven year old with the highest bounty... that's just crass."

Galvani agreed, "I do admit it's kind of rash, but look at that price, the Dead Crow really wants her dead."

Mia pulled the poster toward her, "I'm guessing you don't know why then?"

Galvani shook his head, "Like I said, one minute she is not known to anyone, and the next she has that bounty, though it wasn't always that high."

Mia looked at the list again, "There's no last name, might you know what it is?"

Galvani didn't know her last name.

Daniel sighed, "Another dead end."

"Would you like something to go with that tea of yours?"

"Yes please," Mia replied.

Some few minutes had passed since the town and James was now ahead of the small village, now walking in the centre of what was miles of fields and secluded farmhouses. It was at this point when he started to slow his pace and walk on the right side of the road. His eyes searching the gravel gutter which was flooded with water.

It didn't take a lot of time to find what he was looking for, but he was greatly surprised that it was still there. To his thought, anyone would pick it up at first sight and exchange it for some bit of money. This was the main road, meaning a lot of travelers and most traders would pass by here. He thought surely someone would've stumbled by it by chance, in the time since he was here.

There wasn't time to worry about any probability calculations, he had to get back as soon as possible so he crouched himself on the edge of the stream and picked up the amulet.

He looked at it again, remembered the mark and the reason why he left it behind. Since no one has yet found it, he decided to be the one to take it. He stood up, holding it by the blue ribbon in his face, thinking it would hypnotize or bewitch him at any moment. But it was just his imagination, this object was just a trinket of gold, worth some money if sold, though he wasn't at all interested in trading it, he would spend his next days trying to open it first.

Down into his pocket the amulet went, he looked up ahead, and for the first time since he came here, witnessed the beauty of his surroundings. He wanted to remain there, till the rain stopped, just to watch as it poured over the world, and see the greens dance in the wind as it passed. Lose himself in time, but the luxury had to end before he became lost in it.

He headed back up the road toward the city again.

Back at Galvani's place, everyone was indulging in some tea and biscuits, enjoying what little time they had outside the school.

It was in just a few minutes when they heard a loud knock on the door.

At first everyone was worried, but calmed by the sound of James's voice.

"Hello!" He shouted.

"I'll get it," Galvani whispered.

"Okay, he's back in one piece," Mia sighed in relief.

Galvani unlocked and opened the door, "James, you're late," he greeted.

"F-for what," He stuttered stepping into the house, removing his coat.

"You're back, did you find what you were looking for?" Mia asked.

James hadn't really thought a good story to tell upon arrival, "Nope, just a dead end."

"Oh."

Galvani helped a great deal in preventing any further questions when he noticed the cast over James's palm.

"What happened to your arm?" He asked.

"Oh," he looked at it, "Just an accident, I'll be wearing this for a few more days."

"You children can't sit still can you?" He asked, making another cup of tea for James.

James picked up a biscuit from the table, "Thank you for having us," he took a bite.

He sighed, "Yeah well, I was supposed to look after you during the weekends, should you want to see the city and all, but that's not the case anymore."

"Anyway, what happened while I was gone?" He sat at the table.

"Another dead end," Mark replied shoving a whole biscuit into his mouth, "All this time, detective work is not for me."

"We were only able to find out that these posters showed up ten years ago," Mia added.

"Hmm," James thought, "Is that it, nothing else Galvani?"

He shook his head, "As I've said to them, she just appeared from nowhere and earned herself that nickname and bounty."

"Then that means she was just a little-,"

"Yes James," Mark interrupted, "We've been through that, it's a dead end."

The image of the ghost and the picture on the wanted poster stood next to each other in his head. The age difference was there alright, another dot connected. As of right now, James was to assume that the person the ghost wants him to help is the girl in the poster. It's been well over a month since they started school, and longer since they were brought here. It was probably about time they acted on something.

"Surname?"

Mark shook his head real slowly.

"She a ghost," Mia replied.

"And 'a living curse'," Daniel added, "Whatever that means."

Galvani handed James his cup of tea.

He thanked him for it.

He took a sip, "A good reason why we must find her."

Mark burst out laughing and clap once, "Shut up James."

James was indeed muddled by his reaction, "What?"

"You're crazy," he replied, "I don't want to hear another word from you."

Daniel was caught by surprise but he decide to silence himself from this one.

Mia had the same feelings, but was honestly feeling a little considerate. Hiding in the school waiting for them to be caught was way scarier than breaking the rules and doing something that could be of help to them. Her thoughts and consideration on this matter were driven by a completely different assumption. One she wanted to figure out first before letting anyone else know.

"Why?" James asked.

"You know how crazy you sound right," he turned to Daniel and Mia and was confused at their expressionless reactions, "You guys are not considering… right?"

Galvani just stood there, leaning against the kitchen counter with his arms crossed, just listening and watching.

Mia smiled and shrugged in response.

"I'm sitting this one out," Daniel replied.

James came with an idea to solve this quick, without any complications, "Great, since Daniel is sitting this one out, we'll vote on it."

Mark nodded in defeat, "I know I've lost this one, but what the heck."

James hosted the vote, "In favour of the plan?" He put his hand up.

It took a moment for her but she put it up, "I guess trying doesn't hurt."

"In favour-,"

"Don't be an asshole James," he frowned at him.

Galvani stepped in, "If that's what you have decided upon, I will not stop you."

"Why?" Mark asked.

"I don't know much but Jake said to help you with whatever decisions you make."

"Mark, I can't hex you forever," Mia said, "The Dead Crow is going to find you, we won't stay hidden forever."

Mark took a deep breath and rubbed his forehead, "I guess you may be right there."

"I guess we'd better head back… now that we have decided on something," James suggested.

"Yeah, but how will you help us Galvani?" Daniel asked, "They won't allow you in."

"About that, I may be able to help you… I can send you any information I get about this girl through the sewers," he explained, "Every Saturday you will have to check the sewer entrance, I'll leave something at the bottom of the ladder, assuming off course I find something."

"Great, we'll wait till you get something," James said getting out of his chair, "Thanks for the tea."

"Anytime," he smiled.

Mia took the poster and list with her.

James felt he had accomplished another step, though now he had to wait a week, or maybe more for anything else to be done, though he was still happy with what he'd done by helping the ghost.

They got into their raincoats.

"Now be hasty before someone starts looking for you," He said.

They said their goodbyes and headed out the house.

To the same sewer entrance they went and climbed the ladder down. The stench smelt new and unbearable again as if it were there first time being exposed to it. Their time down there was reduced, thanks to their fear of being caught. The map was still needed, this maze was not to be played with. Getting lost would mean never finding their way back since Mia only copied the route, not the whole map.

Making it back was a success, Mia shut the trapdoor and locked it again.

They immediately headed back to the study, which was quite busy at this time. It was as if they had never left, even with their raincoats and a bit of the sewer smell latched onto them, no one seemed to be bothered by it.

After cleaning off the smell, it was back to doing whatever they pleased.

Mia hung up her coat inside her drawer and headed back down into the study, there wasn't any place for them to speak without being interrupted or listened to. They took to the hallways and corridors where it was less occupied and just walked from passage to passage.

"Congrats guys," Mia said, "We are moving forward," she blurted out cheerfully.

Mark didn't have any enthusiasm, just more negativity, "Ugh, we missed lunch," he shook his head.

"You really have to dim everything, don't you?" Mia turned to him.

He nodded.

"At least we have our task," James shrugged, "And you did get something to eat Mark."

Mia punched Mark on the shoulder, "James is right, and wake up, you acting like a zombie."

Mark rubbed his shoulder, "Ow, and why wake up, it's Saturday, I was supposed to be sitting enjoying the day, playing some chess, chilling in the restoration tower, but no, I've been sneaking out, traveling in the sewers and reading newspapers," he said, "I had to bath twice today."

Daniel couldn't help but laugh at his endless complaints, strolling among them in silence.

"Blah blah blah... that's all I hear," Mia replied.

"You seem excited about this," James pointed out, "Why?"

She shrugged, "I guess using this spell on you guys 24/7 is tiring," she said, "I have my own reasons."

"We all excited now, but no one has thought, 'How will we find this person, she has been missing for ten years'," Mark pointed out.

Daniel pointed at him, "Clever thought, we are chasing a ghost."

"Thank you, thank you," He raised his hands.

"This is not at all going to easy," Daniel added.

"When we signed up for this, no one said it would be any easy," Mia pointed out.

Mark reacted with a full negative force to that statement, "Signed up?" he repeated, "If only I knew we were signing up for this."

"Really?" Mia shot back, "You would've said no to a magical diamond and a chance to travel back in time?"

Mark was second guessing what he'd just said, "Yeah... I probably would've, but there was no choice" he replied.

"The thing is, Jake posed as a government official, we just took those diamonds without a thought," James said, "How did he sell this this to you, with no diamond?"

"He just showed me I could use magic, just as some governmental experiment... I also did not have a choice in the matter, next thing I'm here."

"He is a mystery, that man," Daniel said shoving his hands into his pockets.

James started feeling a little pain in his broken arm, and remembered he had left the medicine in the dorm room with his sling. It was time to put it back on, "Okay," he declared, "I have to go to the dorm, forgot to put on my sling and bring along my painkillers, see you later," he turned away and headed back.

That night, after dinner they were able to keep up after hours, outside their dorms. Some people cared about their sleep and headed straight for bed. Many of the students remained in the hall, or chose to head to the library.

James found out he was allowed to head out front of the school, in need for some time to just think and listen to the rain again, he headed up to the Entrance bridge of the school, where he knew no body would be skulking about. The Entrance tower was sealed shut by a magic barrier since there was no door in the doorway.

Mia hadn't seen where James had carried himself off too, so she headed up to the Restoration Tower and into the hall which was currently uninhabited, unlike the other halls, the lights were off and the view outside more visible. She stood at one windows, on the side that overlooked the school grounds in front of the main doors and watched as the rain drops raced down the glass, also giving herself some time to think, trying to figure what is it that must happen next, reflecting on the decision she had in deciding to help the most dangerous person in the world. Her reason was kind of a stretch but it could be possible, the girl did just appear from nowhere.

Mark was with Claude, Opal, Clara and William, just busy enjoying some board games up in the library, trying their hardest not to make a noise. Mark starting right now, enjoying the last few weekends he had left before his life became a little harder.

Daniel was hanging out with Angelina, just taking walks down the loneliest hallways, engaging in random conversations, just enjoying each other's company on the gloomy, rainy night, but forever in the back of his mind, the fact that he knew about Mia's special abilities, the reason she had them.

He leaned against the railing of the very high bridge, taking in the cold fresh air that came with the rain.

From up the bridge he could again see the whole school, a bit dark, but the lights from inside helped. Though it wasn't really what he was up there for, he thought maybe a few seconds wouldn't mean anything. He pulled out the amulet from his pocket and gave it another look.

So curious to find out what treasure inside was hid. In his palm, it weighed too light to be solid, but when he shook it, there was nothing to be felt, when placed near his ear, no sound to be heard. Was this empty?

He attempted at opening it again, but fell short due to his arm, he hit it hard against the railing, trying to dent it or break it open, but nothing was successful.

"Useless amulet," he said shoving it back into his pocket.

He leaned against the railing again, now unhappy that he couldn't open the object and at the same time, the wind had started to pick up, making it really chilly up there for him, wearing only a hoodie. His negative mood made it a bad place for him to be so he decided it was best to leave the bridge and get inside where it was warm.

On the stepping stones he was, heading back to the main entrance, finding it harder to see since the wind was now blowing the rain at an angle. He reached the tower that stood to his right and stared at it. An idea popped into his head, one to give a shot before he became visible to the Dead Crow agent standing at the main entrance.

He pulled out the amulet and looked at the symbol for a moment, he looked at the wall and with all his strength, flung it at the wall, hoping maybe it would break open.

Looked at it, laying on the grass, not even a mark.

He stepped forward to pick it up.

Something strange happened which rendered him paralyzed.

The amulet clipped open by itself, and from inside emerge a black, thick smoke.

"Huh?" He blurted out in shock.

The smoke slowly grew out of the amulet.

James couldn't move, wouldn't move. He wanted to see this to the end. He was trying to open it anyway.

The thick smoke was just a bit higher than him when it suddenly dispersed into nothing and in its place stood a man.

"Ta-da!" he shouted with his hands wide open, and the biggest smile he could make.

James almost screamed, but his voice box was not responsive.

It was the crazy blind man.

James remembered the first encounter with this man. Jake was not at all happy to see him. He didn't know how to react in this situation, because in his own opinion, this man was just crazy. Even his entrance right now was a bit off.

The man's smile disappear quickly, "No applause," he sounded sad, "I thought you would like that little magic trick."

James was not responsive, he just stared at him. There wasn't much fear in it, he was more concerned.

The man sighed, "Good evening," he greeted politely.

James turned his sights to the main entrance.

The crazy man was curious to what he was looking at, he took a little peek, "Oh, don't worry, the Dead Crow won't know we are having this conversation," he explained, "Even if I shout!" He raised his voice, "They won't hear."

James was counting on being saved by the guard, but the man made it clear that he could not be heard, he turned back to the man.

He cleared his throat, "Let's try again," he put on a cheerful smile, "Good evening."

James had no choice in the matter it seemed, so he decided to be polite as well, "Good evening," he greeted back.

"Don't be afraid," he said calmly, "I'm a friendly person."

James was afraid, even more so after the man just told him not to be, but he decided to try make best of this odd situation, "Ah, wh-who are you?"

He gasped for breath, "Oh, how rude of me," he was surprised, "The first time we met, I failed to give you my name... my apologies," he placed his right hand on his chest and gave small bow, "My name is Diadora."

Okay, this man just apologized and gave away his name as if he were some common stranger. James was confused, should he fear this guy or not. His appearances were not very friendly though, and if he remembered correctly, he had a symbol on his back, of a bomb with a smiley face and crosses for eyes. He didn't know if he should give him his name or not.

"I'm James," he replied out of fear, without consent.

"Nice to meet you James," he held out his right hand.

James reached out his right as well and shook it.

"Are you fitting in?" He smiled again.

He gave him a slow nodded.

At this point, James was just being nice to him, as he was back to him, but in his mind, he wondered if this man was blind.

"Good, good, nice to hear that," he nodded, "Now I'm sure you're wondering why the little visit, I've got a little secret to tell you," he leaned forward.

James didn't know where to look, the man's eyes were covered, and was going back and forth on whether he was looking at him or not. He decided to look at the mark inked onto the cloth.

Diadora began to whisper, "Listen to my voice... and hear the sweet sound of my... curse," he put on his big smile again.

"Wha-," James felt dizzy and unable to breath. He fell onto the wet ground, the rain dripping onto face, his eyes struggling to remain open. He grew weak, unable to move and watch as his eyelids closed shut.

CHAPTER 13

Begin the Hunt

Quite some time had passed since the burial, and now on this cloudless, starlit night, in a place you have been to before, Lonestar Inn. The party of Jane, Denice and Mary were occupying a table, waiting for some food to eat. They did, however, have something to drink out of the tankards on the table.

Their last couple of weeks have been quite hard, being introduced to a new place without any amount of money to help sustain them. They have been taking small jobs and completing tasks placed on the notice boards to keep going.

It was their first night in this small town and probably another place they would be spending some time in. Still trying to understand the situation, as well as try figure out where their children might have went.

"It's been a few weeks since we awoke on that day," Jane said, "and still we have figured out nothing about this Dead Crow Organization and what they have against us."

Mary took a sip from her tankard, "We know people say they are great symbols of justice, just as we were taught," she spotted a group of them sitting around at a table in the corner, "Quite accurate actually, these guys are everywhere."

"Yes," Denice agreed, "They control bounties and basically the law, like you said, police."

Jane took a deep breath, "Do I really have to remind you about the funeral?"

Denice shook her head, "You just did but... the actions of one don't necessarily mean that they all sadistic, murderous bastards," she leaned forward, "I mean, since then, there has been nothing bad, just a bunch of police doing their jobs."

Jane didn't want to agree with her, "Why don't we just show them the list then, or just give it back, maybe ask them some questions."

"You know that's not an option Jane," Mary said, "Even if they are saints, we can't raise any suspicion or attention towards us."

"Yes I know," she took a sip.

A few minutes passed and the little girl serving them brought to their table a small wooden tray with baked bread and placed it on the centre of their table, a few seconds later, she brought a tray with three large bowls of soup. She wore an apron over her clothing with a pocket, containing a table cloth in it.

Jane thanked her.

After serving them their food she proceeded to clean the closest table.

Mary was the first to pick the bread, "We are facing quite a problem," she mixed the soup with a ladle, "I mean, where do we start searching, Mark could've awoke and wondered off anywhere, I mean... we found each other by luck, what if they didn't and are scattered?"

"We have to stay positive about this," Denice said.

"Yeah, thanks a lot," Mary replied sarcastically, "I mean, how are they surviving, we are barely making it."

Denice just decided to stuff her mouth, try to divert her attention from the problem.

"It's just stressful talking about it," Jane added, "let's just try get some rest today and see what this town has for us," she brought the ladle to her mouth.

"One person, I'm going to take my stress out on is that old trickster, Jake," Mary raised her voice.

The little girl wiping away at the table came to a sudden stop and turned to their table. She went and stood right in front of them with a surprised smirk on her face.

It was hard not to notice or ignore her.

"Hello," she greeted waving her hand, "My name is Bertha."

Denice nodded, "Hi Bertha, what brings you to us," she spoke with a friendly tone.

Her expression turned to excitement, "I thought I was going crazy."

They looked at her with as much confusion as they could muster.

Bertha leaned forward and whispered to them, "You're time travelers."

They exchanged glances, very sure that they never mentioned anything about time since they set foot into this inn, so now, the question was, How in this world did she know about such?

Jane giggled, "What are you talking about little girl, there's no such thing as time travel."

Both Denice and Mary supported her lie, hoping that she would believe and drop it before she mentions it to another soul that would take this seriously.

Her face turned to sadness and disappointment, "Oh."

For a moment there, Jane felt she succeeded.

"When I heard you say Jake's name, I was sure it wasn't just me," She said.

This could be some kind of discovery.

"Please tell us what you wanted to say," Denice said placing her hand on her shoulder.

Bertha cleared her throat, "Jake was here about two months ago," she started, "with three boys."

A stroke of luck. Could this be the answers they were searching for? They did not allow for this chance to slip away so Denice pulled back the empty chair in front of Bertha, "Please sit with us."

"I knew it," her face lit up again.

As soon as she sat down, the questioning started.

"Do you know what these boys look like?" Mary asked, "Can you describe them for me?"

She shook her head, "No, I don't really remember, I didn't see them properly, just happened to be listening to what they were saying and time traveling was one of the things they mentioned, and what happened the night they were here."

Jane's heart started to race, excited and really glad that she had eavesdropped on them and Jake, "What happened?" She asked.

Bertha placed her hands between her legs and took a deep breath, before beginning the tale, "They arrived here at the inn in the evening, with Jake, they ordered some food... they started talking about time and their parents, which I would assume would be you?"

Denice nodded.

"It's strange... Jake said that you didn't time travel, only them."

That bit of information caught them unexpectedly.

"Jake was probably trying to stop them from worrying," Jane suggested.

Bertha shrugged, "Maybe... anyway, I then noticed one of them wearing a necklace, with a diamond, which he hid as soon as he noticed it was visible," she paused for a moment, remembering what happened next.

All three mothers listened diligently, waiting for her to continue.

She went on, "What I think is that, if I had noticed the diamond, maybe someone else did as well, and I was right," she explained, "That very same night, someone attempted to steal the diamond from them."

They were getting a little worried, "Do you know who it was?" Jane asked.

Bertha's stomach growled, loud and clearly.

"Oh," Denice pushed her bowl of soup to her, "You can have some."

"Thanks," she took the offer.

"So do you know?" Mary asked.

Bertha sipped up some of the hot soup, she shook her head, "I never saw them."

"Well, thank you for the help Bertha," Jane said.

She smiled in return, "If you guys are really from the future, I can tell you some things that I may know, this place is the centre of all news, you won't believe some of things I've heard," she took some bread, "Well... not as crazy as you, but good enough."

They were not going to pass a chance to hear the latest gossip. It's always helpful to be kept updated.

"Okay," Jane thought, "Do you know anything about the Dead Crow?"

"Wait," she frowned, "They don't exist in you time?"

Jane wasn't too sure because she only learnt about them, "I don't think so," she replied unsure, "But we just want to know if you know anything out of the ordinary?"

"Not really," she replied, "The only thing that was strange and scared me was their name, 'The Dead Crow', I asked my mom why that name, it's kind of scary, she told me that they weren't always called that."

"What were they called?" Mary asked, her eyes wide open.

"She never said," she replied.

That reply was a downer. It could've been their very first lead, to discovering more about this organization. Well… at least now that they know they had a different name in the past, it was kind of a heads up.

"It's the only thing I know about them that it is strange… I guess," she said, "Other than that, they do their jobs, do whatever it takes."

"Thank you," Jane said pulling out a gold coin from her pocket, "Here."

She gasped, surprised, "Thank you," she said before taking her leave.

Mary sighed, "At least we know the old man is a good sitter."

"Now just to figure out where they may have went next," Jane said sitting back on her chair.

Denice stood up from her table, "I'll get the rooms," she walked off.

Mary observed her surroundings and her sights locked onto the group of Dead Crow agents sitting in the corner, "These people are everywhere," she whispered to Jane, "After seeing them try to kill you and what they did to the girl, I don't think I can ever trust them."

Jane nodded, "Same here."

A few hours passed since the conversation with Bertha. The inn was not as packed anymore, people headed to their homes or rented out rooms, like Jane and her friends. They rented out one big room.

Each of them had a rucksack, for which they carried what little belongings they had. They were placed beside their beds.

Janes was sleeping closest to the door, before trying to get some shut eye, she placed her now trusty dagger on the table next to the candle stand with her new broad sword, short, thin and edged.

It wasn't long before Mary and Denice drifted off into their own dreams, resting both their minds and bodies.

Jane was under the covers but unable to fall asleep, for most of the time she would just stare up at the ceiling, or gaze into the entering moonlight from the window, hoping no one would pass by creating a scary shadow. The door to their room was closed so no worries there. Everything was visible, her eyes well-adjusted to the darkness.

After figuring out Jake was taking care of her son, she felt some bit of closure, the weight of her worry was greatly decreased, but still there, since she did not trust him or this situation he had placed them in, so the primary task was still finding out where they were actually and then questioning the old chap, hopefully providing them with some valid explanations and answers. What was secondary and not as important, was figuring out the motives of the Dead Crow Organization.

She turned to the side and covered her head with the blanket, leave it open for her eyes and nose to breath. Her eyes locked onto the door, trying to drift away and wake up to the light of the day.

She closed her eyes.

The door knob turned, slowly.

She heard it loud and clear, in the dead silence of the room. Her heart jumped as she entered into an alerted state that removed all symptoms of sleep. Her body started to shake and her breathing became uneven. The door was about to be opened, she couldn't stop glaring, or even move.

It opened slowly. Behind it, total darkness.

After a few moments, the door was wide open and the hand pushing it open visible.

It was a gloved hand.

It leapt into the darkness again.

Jane looked up, saw her blade resting right next to her, waiting to be wielded, but she was in shock, afraid to make any sudden movements. She just turned her sights back to the door.

Out of the darkness, stepped in a tall figure, a man wearing a hooded cloak.

Her first assumption, judging by the clothing was that this man was a Dead Crow, unable to make out the colours, it was her best guess.

In the man's right hand, she spotted a dagger, and knew immediately that this was some kind of assassination.

Even with all this figured out, she still lay there still.

This man stepped closer to her bed.

It seemed he was unaware that Jane was awake, staring right up at him, which counted as some fortune towards her, but it didn't help much because of her shock. Right now she felt the same way she did when she killed the other two in the room. She waited for the perfect moment to act, knowing where her sword was and having the element of surprise.

As he took each step carefully towards her, time seemed to move slow, making it look like he was never going to reach her but at the same time, having close to no time to react.

The man now stood right up against the bed, looking down at her as he slowly raised his dagger.

It was time to act, this was her moment of opportunity, while he raises his dagger, preparing to strike, the moment he thinks he is about to succeed, the moment just before death.

Without a single moment to hesitate, she reached out and pulled her sword from its sheath as if planned, and with great speed, she dug the sword in from the side, into his abdomen, she let go of the sword and rolled out of bed with the blanket.

The man cringed in pain trying not to scream and attempted to stab Jane with the dagger, but it was too late, his dagger only tasted the innards of the mattress she had laid on.

Jane began to hyperventilate as she watched. She turned and gave Mary a very hard shove, "Wake up."

She awoke, "What?!" She asked furiously. Her eyes turned to her bed as she noticed the man struggling for his life on Jane's bed, "Oh my god," she grabbed her sword.

Jane was still shocked, "They tried to kill-, they tried to-"

Mary got out of bed swiftly and alerted Denice.

Jane turned to the man and watched as he fell to his knees, staring right back at her, blood seeping through his closed teeth... he smiled, which scared Jane a lot. She watched as he fell face first onto her bed, dagger still in his hand.

To be safe, she threw her blanket aside and got up. She went up to the man and pressed on his back hard, while her left hand grabbed a hold of her sword. She pulled it out and stepped away from him again, her jaw shaking, just realizing again that she was close to death.

Mary came up to her, "Who is this?" She asked giving her a hug.

Jane tapped the man's back with her sword, "He's Dead Crow."

"Ah…guys," Denice called, pointing at the doorway.

Two more Dead Crows stepped into the room with haste.

They caught sight of their dead comrade, and pulled out their daggers.

"Oh, it seems being all sneaky like did not help," one of them said, he chuckled, "I did tell him, but he said, 'No we might alert the others," he impersonated another voice.

Mary and Denice held up their swords. Jane remained in her place, staring at them, holding up a confused face.

"What should we do, it's three against two?" The other one asked.

"No it's not, the one over there is still shaken," he replied, "We kill these two first I say," he pointed his dagger at Mary and Denice.

They both charged in with their daggers without thought.

All four of them were led into a fight. The Dead Crow agents swinging their daggers carelessly at Mary and Denice while they took to the defensive, dodging and blocking every strike.

Mary decided to use her legs as well and heel kicked her attacker in the diaphragm, stumbling him back.

He giggled, "Don't think you're not going to die here, we have these," he held up his dagger at her.

Jane recognized the dagger, it was the one with all the rune markings. She looked at the dead body lying on the bed, then she turned to the agent speaking about it.

Denice was able to play defensive for a while, stepping back every time her attacker struck at her. It continued till her back hit against the wall, with no more room to step back.

"Time to die," the man declared as he went for the final strike.

This was Denice's first moment before death, she could see it coming, but at the moment, her reflexes shifted her to the side as the man's dagger drove into the wooden wall.

Denice couldn't decide what to do but she acted immediately, before he could pull out the dagger. Her sword found its way into the man's back, she let go of it, terrified, watching the first man she ever stabbed die right in front of her.

The agent against Mary charged at her. She prepared to block but Jane stepped in and swung her sword at his arm cutting it clean, off from his forearm.

Mary took a step back, surprised by the unexpected turn.

The Dead Crow agent held it tight as an endless stream of blood squirted from the open wound. He turned to Jane, "You cheated."

She shook her head, "This is no game," she said looking at him with disgust.

He smiled as if there was no pain at all, "Oh but it is, and even thought you cheated, you will still lose… everything."

Mary pointed her sword at him, "What are you talking about?"

"I'm talking about you," he looked at his arm with a disappointed face, "Well this sucks," he smiled, "at least every bad situation has some good in it," he nodded, "Now I can get a hook for a hand," he chuckled.

"You're mad," Jane pointed out.

He turned to her with a furious expression, "No, don't say that," he turned to his arm again and smile at it, "I-I just look at every situation positively, though… I am guessing… you guys are not going to let me live to see my pirate hook," he looked at them, "Am I right," His expression turned cheerful.

Mary became furious at this agent, he didn't care at all of what he'd just done, "You're going to tell us why you're on our case, while you bleed."

"I'm sorry, but that's not for me to say," he replied.

"You will tell us," she spoke calmly, hiding her rage, "Why were you sent to kill us?"

The agent started to laugh, silently as his eyes started to water, "I-I wish I could tell you," he took a deep breath, "but look at this situation, you didn't die… we died."

This man was hard to take seriously, Jane saw no answered coming out of him, he was just switching from one emotion to the next, laughing, getting furious or looking sad.

He fell to the ground, looking a little drowsy, "I guess it's my time to say goodbye," he let go of his arm and gave them a salute, "See ya," he fell back and lost consciousness.

Mary sighed in relief, "Killing us in our sleep... this is not good at all," she shut the door.

Denice sat on the bed and rubbed her arms, looking at the man she just killed, "Never taken a life before," she murmured.

"I know, it's crazy," Mary replied, "We've taken now, and I don't think this will be the last time we do so... if we wish to stay alive."

Jane kept staring at the body lying on her bed, replaying, in her mind the smirk he pulled before dying, as if he had accomplished something. That thought didn't remain too long, after witnessing the insane nature of the man without the arm she figured they were just crazy, enough to give no damn about dying.

Mary proceeded to the arm lying on the floor, "This is a very interesting blade," she crouched in front of it.

"Don't touch it!" Jane blurted out.

Mary froze.

"Look at what it does," she pointed at her bed at the dagger that pierced the mattress.

Mary came to examine, "Eww, its turning black."

"It's some kind of poison, and by the looks of it, the stuff spreads on anything," she explained.

The mattress and sheet above it were turning black in a small radius around the knife. It was like the mattress was decaying.

"It's probably why some of them only carry the dagger, one cut and you gone."

Jane nodded, "They don't get killed often either, many people fear this group."

"Yeah, I bet, and we just hopped back in time and took the life of six," she added, "There is no way out of this one, people will know it was us."

Jane shrugged and took a seat on Mary's bed, "No one would believe they attacked us first either, they are the ones lying dead," she turned to Denice, "Are you doing alright?"

"Yeah, just need a minute."

Mary sat next to Jane, "I cannot believe we almost died, if it weren't for the few lessons we took from the shop owner down south, we could have died... and from poison."

"Don't forget the XP pills we found in our pockets," Jane added, "I didn't think they existed."

"That too," she sheathed her sword.

Jane used the white sheets to clean her blade, "I don't think staying here is wise."

"Off course, we have to leave now," she stood up and went over to help out Denice.

A few minutes passed and they were ready to be heading out. They did not try to conceal the bodies, there was way too much blood as evidence, and fidgeting around in a silent place can be quite alarming for some who were not heavy sleepers.

Denice stood at the window and moved the curtain up just a bit, to get a view of the whole place just outside, "It's clear," she reported, opening the curtains.

"Good," Mary whispered back, "Open the window."

Denice did as she was told and climbed out through it. The earth was only about two metres from the window so she was able to make a quiet landing. She immediately went into a crouched positon, eyes forever scanning the area for any patrolling guards.

She knocked on the wooden wall, signaling that it was clear and safe to step out.

They Jumped out the window and Jane tried her best to close it again but it wasn't possible.

The inn was very big and stood right up against one of the roads, which had lanterns lighting the way. The nearest alleyway was not near at all, it was around the corner of this inn.

Before moving stealthy, Mary stopped them, "Guys, I think we should look more normal, not as if we just stole something."

Jane gave it a bit of though, "Okay, just impersonate a group of travelers," she stood up straight and started walking a little more casually, still keeping her footsteps as silent as possible.

Mary and Denice did the same, very nervous about their current actions, hoping to get as far away from their room window as possible before getting caught, so that telling their lie could be accomplished easily.

They reached the edge of the inn block and turned the corner into the shadows.

"Hey!" A man shouted from a distance.

They froze in their tracks, the small victory snatched away.

"Oh crap," Mary whispered, "Do we run?"

"No!" Denice whispered back, "That would mean we are caught."

"What if he knows about our assassination?" Mary asked.

"Then we're caught anyway," Jane replied.

Mary turned to the direction of the voice, it was a normal city guard. She sighed in relief, "Just a normal guard."

"Step out of the shadows," he ordered walking up to them.

He held a wooden torch in one hand.

All three of them made their way onto the road, already playing out this scenario in their minds.

He stood in front of them and examined their attire, "What are you doing outside at this late hour?" He asked.

Denice gave him an awkward smile.

"Oh, we're so very sorry, mister," Jane stepped in with a smile, "We're just heading out of town, we haven't the money to stay at the inn so we decided it was best to leave now."

"We're sorry to have startled you," Mary added.

He didn't seem to be believing this story they fabricated, "You'd better not be lying, we get people causing mischief around this time, giving us trouble," he explained, "If you're heading out of town, then remain on the main road where I can see you, don't be going into the shadows."

"We'll remember that," Jane replied.

He nodded, "Okay, hope you ladies have safe travels ahead."

That was surprisingly simpler than any of them thought. Off course, now they had to use the main road, but the convincing part needed no more work.

"Thank you," Denice said.

He smiled back at her.

Before anything could happen, before any sigh of relief or minor celebration within, another voice sounded out nearby.

"Hey!"

Everybody turned toward it and all manner of luck disappeared from there. It was an agent.

"What's this here?' He asked stopping in front of them.

To some manner of luck, he didn't seem to recognize their face... hopefully.

The guardsman held the torch up near the ladies, "These here ladies are travelers passing by," he explained.

The agent was not at all happy with the explanation the guard had given him, "How do you know," he smile at the guard.

"I just spoke to them" he replied.

The agent turned to them and gave them a head-to-toe look, "I don't believe that... they may be thieves," he stepped closer to them, "You will leave them with me, I will take them to the Jarl's hall where they'll be searched," he smiled.

The guardsman gave a small bow in front of the agent before heading back to his post.

This was an unexpected turn, just as they were about to leave, this Dead Crow had to show up. Being searched was not the problem they were facing now, it was the discovery of the bodies in the inn. Escaping from this agent and becoming fugitives from this very moment started to come across as a very good idea, but how far would they get.

They had to play this one safe and follow this agent to wherever he wanted to take them.

It was a cold, long walk. The town was a lot larger than they initially expected. The main road passing through was much shorter.

They started up the stone steps, guards posted at the bottom and the top. The Dead Crows seemed to have a much higher authority than these guards, asking no questions at all about the people he was bringing in.

Up top they reached an open passage way leading to the main doors, which was most likely where this hall was.

He pushed the doors open and stepped in.

It was too late for the escape plan now, there were no other options open to them.

The jarl's hall was much smaller and less expensive. Both sides of the hall had tables and benches placed beneath the first floor which was held up by wooden pillars, each having a torch placed to light up the area making the place look much more appealing. Weapon racks were places against the walls with mannequins wearing different kinds of armors for decoration. There weren't any windows due to the extra rooms on both sides of the hall.

The agent called upon two female agents to come search them. He attempted at Jane but she stepped back.

"No, I'll wait," she took of her bag and threw it at him.

"As you wish," he said placing her rucksack on the table and beginning his search there.

She waited for one of the females to conduct the search.

None of them had anything except for a few blades, food and other travel equipment which they were allowed to keep. The potions and medical supplies were untouched and appeared new, so those were confiscated from them, it just seemed like this agent wanted to take from them, and any kind of resistance would have only resulted in a worse situation, so they just let them have the things.

Jane was never more happy that she decided to clean her blade, as well as Denice's.

The agent gave the others the medical supplies and told them to take them to other rooms.

After it was all done, Jane was the first to ask, "Can we leave now?"

He gave it a bit of thought, "I think not," he replied.

"You're done searching us," she started losing her patience.

He smiled at her, "We wouldn't want you to steal anymore goods now would we?" He faked a sad face.

Mary came up with a suggestion, "You can take us to the edge of town, we won't come back."

He giggled, "That's way too far, and I need some rest."

"Then order someone else."

"And inconvenience them?" he crossed his arms, "I'm not letting you go till first light, you will sit here until the guards let you go."

This agent was just trying to make them angry, and it worked. It was anger they were not willing to show, again to keep the situation from getting worse. They just excepted his wishes and took a seat at one of the tables.

Leaving at first light was very dangerous, their chances of being caught and accused for the deaths would be imminent. But there was nothing they could do to change that, the bridge would have to be crossed when they got to it.

It seemed only a few minutes had passed before they were shaken awake by one of the guards tasked at setting them free in the morning. It was uncomfortable to sleep at the table but they got their bit of needed rest.

Their morning was not sluggish at all, as soon as their eyes were opened, the realization of the night before popped into their minds. Judging by the calmness of the atmosphere, the bodies hadn't been discovered yet.

They picked what was left of their belongings and thank the guard that woke them up before being let go.

Jane took the lead and went straight for the door, trying not to make eye with anyone. Before she could pull open the main doors, someone else did, from the other side, which had her jump and move out of the way.

I was an agent, rushing in, panting from a run he'd just taken.

They took little notice of him, their minds set on leaving the place.

Jane stepped out first and was met by the shining light of the sun which she shielded her eyes from till they were adjusted.

Mary pulled the main doors closed, "Okay, let's get out of here," she picked up her pace, also hiding from the suns blinding flare.

"That agent seemed quite worried," Denice pointed out catching up to them.

"Probably late for work," Mary replied starting down the steps.

Behind them, the main doors opened up again, followed by a man's voice, "Hey!" He shouted.

Jane stopped in her tracks, wondering why she had stopped, when the next words could be their doom.

"Stop those three women!" He shouted.

Those next words were their ticket to start running without a second thought.

"Murderers!" The man continued to scream.

This was the guards que to draw their swords and use any means necessary to apprehend them.

A bell was rung in the near distance, loud enough to wake up anyone that was asleep. It was heard from all corners of this town. The citizens that were already wondering about on the streets preparing for work became alerted by the sound and went into panic, running away, hiding from plain sight or returning indoors.

Jane, Mary and Denice were in plain sight, impossible to go into any hiding as the guards were tailing just behind them, their faces already identified by a lot of them. Running seemed to just prolong the inevitable, but prolonging it gave them the smallest of chances of escaping. Their crime was quite extensive.

Turning at every given corner, trying to lose the guards, they headed straight for the main road so as to find the way out of this town. The night before was dark, the directions to the road out of town was not clear to them.

As time progressed, the town guards began to lose ground, slowed down by their armour... for a moment they were gaining ground but then the agents started popping out, joining the chase.

Mary was the first to realize that their rucksacks were playing a part in getting them caught so she took it off and with a strong swing, turned around and flung it at the Dead Crow agents. She succeeded in hit one in the legs, toppling him over before continuing the escape.

Jane and Denice caught on what she was doing and both ditched their bags as well.

This effort allowed them to gain a bit more speed but at this point, there were agents and guards appearing from every direction, the late comers from the other side of town.

All three of them turned to using their surroundings as an attempt to distract their pursuers, climbing over haystacks to avoid the edge of the blade or toppling over barrels to slow them and throwing buckets to scare them.

Their efforts allowed them to get far, but as soon as they were on the main road they found themselves overwhelmed by the amount of guards and agents there were and found themselves surrounded before long.

Jane, Mary and Denice stood back-to-back all with the view of swords pointed right at them.

The town guards were tired, as if this was their first chase in long years, that or they needed to get lighter armour.

Jane sighed, thinking they would have made it out if there were just guards, they would be far away from this town by now.

For a while there was silence and a stillness in the air. The townsfolk were appearing from hiding and showing up to be witnesses.

The edged fence containing them in, opened up on one side, allowing someone to step into the circle. It was an agent, wearing the mages attire.

Mary and Denice turned to him as well, afraid of what was to happen next.

This mage seemed much older than the other agents, he smiled at them, "Good morning," he greeted with a deep and raspy voice.

None of them replied.

Jane's heart wanted to escape from all this, there was no way out this one, and now this agent, standing out as the leader was ready to start blaming and placing judgement.

The mage seemed surprised they didn't greet him back, "Perhaps you're a little scared...no?" he looked around, "Come on everybody, put away your swords, can't you see you're scaring the ladies," he ordered.

All the guards and agents sheathed their weapons.

He was happy they all complied, then he turned back to Jane, "Let's try this again shall we... good morning," he greeted, and this time gave a small bow.

Mary and Denice gave him a confused look, wondering if this was really part of the confrontation. Jane's expression didn't shift, it remained straight, only her eyes following his. Seeing the same kind of crazy in him, quite similar to the ones they killed the night before.

"Oh," he seemed surprised again, "I guess you weren't scared at all, just no manners."

Almost everybody in town was here, watching and listening in silence.

The mage started to pace back and forth slowly, "You ladies know why you're in this position right?" he asked aloud shaking his head, "Off course you know, that was unwise of me to ask," he sighed and turned to them, "You're in this position because you murdered!" He announced.

The towns people were surprised to hear this, turning to each other and whispering.

The mage turned to the left, just behind him, "Does that place look familiar to you?' he pointed to the inn, "It is where you decided to take the lives of three Dead Crows, YOUR protectors!" He turned angry.

They saw the inn's front porch and entrance, Mabel standing there in shock with her daughter, Bertha standing right next to her. Jane didn't want her to witness all this, but there was nothing she could do about it.

The agent stole their attention again, "Now why would you be driven to do such?' He smiled waiting for a response.

Jane looked at Mary and gave a slight nod.

"Nothing?"

Mary took a deep breath, "It was self-defense."

The mage laughed, "Self-defence!" he said aloud, "did you hear that," he paused for a moment, "Your definition of self-defence is ruthless."

Jane knew that this was pointless, this man was just trying to give them an even worse name, now they could be labeled as liars, but she felt the need to speak, "We were about to be assassinated by those agents last night, we-,"

"Assassinated," he whispered, his smile faded, "Assassinated?" he smiled again, "If that were even remotely true, why hide it, why attempt to leave town at midnight?"

She saw that question coming, they were in a corner now, the people as well now thought they were liars and murderers. Their actions could not be justified at all, only they knew they were innocent, but couldn't deny killing them, it was committed in the rooms they rented out. Keeping quite was the best thing they could do know, and await the inevitable sentence.

"We can call upon the guard that caught you trying to make your escape last night, let's see what he has to say," the mage continued to speak.

Moments later, the same guard was called upon.

Jane turned to the inn again, she looked down at Bertha, whom was making some gestures. She decided to take interest instead of listen to this nonsense.

Bertha pointed down at her hip. She then acted like she was pulling something out of a pocket. Though, wearing a dress it made sense.

She then acted as if she were throwing something onto the ground, after she used both hands to gesture an explosion.

No one paid attention to her, too busy listening to the witnesses.

Jane turned back to the leader of this group of agents just in time for the sentence to be given.

"You will be sentenced to die right here," He announced, "Right now," he looked around, "Ugh, didn't bring my staff... oh well, you will die by the edge of the sword," he turned away and signaled an agent to carry out the deed.

"That's not fair," Mary blurted out.

He turned back and walked up to her, "What's not fair, is thinking you have the power to take the life of a Dead Crow," he smiled, "This is justice for them."

Jane decided to have a feel for her pockets, there was something, a small round object, two of them, having no recollection of how they came to be there. According to Bertha, they were supposed to explode, which gave her a whole bunch of unsettling thoughts. *Were these going to kill people? Them amongst the victims?* She had no time to think it through, the agent had already unsheathed his weapon so she put her hand into her pocket and glanced over at Bertha again.

She gave a slight nodded.

Taking a deep breath she pulled out the two objects and threw them towards the ground hard before anyone could react or stop her from doing so.

A great black cloud of smoke was created on impact, spreading in every direction like a powerful wind, it's radius continued to grow with no slowing down.

It was impossible to see in it but a lot of panic could be heard from all around. Escaping was not possible in their blinded state. Something strange was beginning to happen as they listened, the voices of the people started to disappear, instead of an increase in noise and panic, there was a decrease, and around them they could start to hear loud thuds and metal clinking, it seemed the people around them were collapsing, everyone while they stood their helplessly waiting to regain their sight again.

It was but a few minutes when the smoke had cleared away completely. All the silence was explained immediately as they opened their eyes.

Everyone was lying on the ground, unconscious.

"Woah," Denice blurted out, "How'd you do that?"

Jane shrugged, "something I had in my pocket... somehow."

Mary crouched near the mages body and gave it a shook, "Hm," she smiled, "Next time please let us in on your plan, I was terrified."

Denice agreed, "That was a close call."

Jane turned to the patio, where Bertha stood. She was still standing, unaffected like them. She riddled her way through the bodies to her. Both Denice and Mary followed behind.

"Hi Bertha," Jane greeted.

Denice pointed out the obvious, "You're still awake."

She nodded.

"It's thanks to her we are still alive," Jane said, "She told me what to do."

"Yes, and it's thanks to you I am still awake," she smiled.

"What are you talking about?" Jane asked confused, "How, we did nothing?"

"You shared," she replied.

Confusion clouded their minds.

"How are we unaffected?" Jane continued with the questions, "When did you give me the explosives?"

She just smile, "They going to wake up soon, they will remember what just happened, I suggest you get away as far as you can."

"She's right," Mary agreed, "They could wake at any moment."

Jane placed her hand on Bertha's shoulder, "Thanks for your help, and we're very sorry about the room."

"Please go!" she raised her voice, "I'm serious, you don't have much time."

"Okay, bye." Jane said taking the stairs.

Denice and Mary thanked her.

Bertha shouted after them, "Wait, I forgot to tell you something."

They stopped to listen.

"Head to the magic school in Marridor north from here, you may find them there!"

"Thank you!" Jane replied.

Just outside the town they stood, taking in the light of the sun and morning wind, staring at a sign board which gave direction to the other towns and cities closest to this one.

"So Marridor it is," Denice declared.

"Yes," Jane replied, "I think Jake would've sent them there, the school is probably the safest place for them."

Mary took a deep breath, "Can't wait to see my Mark."

"That can't happen Mary," Jane said, "Doing that would put them in danger, in a few days, we are going to be known everywhere," she explained, "I think it's best that for now they don't know we are here."

"Then why don't we head on elsewhere?" Denice suggested.

"We have to find out more about this place and maybe meet with Jake there before we become known to the public... something isn't right here, I have another plan."

"Enlighten us," Mary said.

"The Dead Crow."

CHAPTER 14

Levina's Whereabouts

Early in the morning, just before another sunrise, back in the infirmary, James again being the only patient of this clean hall of medical appliances. He lay in the same bed for quite some time, unknown to him.

He opened his eyes, greeted by the sight of the ceiling above him. Nothing was at all clear to him at this moment, his current place of rest was not given away until he turned to the side and saw a row of beds, covered in white sheets and the bedside desk he found familiar.

He raised his arm to his forehead, it ached. He looked to his hand and realized it was his left, the cast had been removed. He twisted his wrist and stretched it out.

No pain.

It was something he thought really strange, last he remembered, it was to take a few days before the nurse removed it, but here it was all good and ready to continue doing its job.

Everything was a little hazy, a blur in his mind, trying to remember the last thing that happened to him before he passed out.

"Diadora!" he blurted out as it all came back to him.

It was all clear all of a sudden, the amulet, the smoke and the crazy blind man, Diadora. He was put into alert and almost wide awake as soon as the thought came to him.

Still unsure about his arm, he hit it against the bed and put some pressure on it. It was as if it never suffered injury. He decided to sit up and gain a bit more of his surroundings.

He let out a frightening cry.

There was a little girl sitting on the bed.

"Oh, it's you," he sighed in relief.

It was Levina and she was kicking her legs, "Morning sleepy," she greeted.

It took a moment for James to find his ground again, "You gave me a freight," he said.

"Sorry," her face turned sad and looked down at her hands, "I must look kind of scary," she shook the cuffs and made them rattle.

"No!" He replied, "You not... It's just- It's just I wasn't expecting to see someone here, thought it was just me."

That was a good save, she turned happy again.

"Anyways," he changed the subject, "What brings you here?"

"Oh, I was worried about you," she replied, "you're in the hospital again."

James nodded, "Yeah, something happened yesterday."

"What do you mean 'Yesterday'?" She asked, "You've been sleeping for five days."

"Wait what," he didn't believe, "five days?"

She nodded, "I showed up every morning to see if you would wake up."

James frowned and looked at his left hand, "I could've sworn it happened yesterday," he murmured, "But then again, my arm's all good."

"Yup, they took it off in your sleep," she explained, "But how you ended up all sleepy I don't know... I only saw them bringing you up on that night and when they tried to see what was wrong, they said it was something you breathed in."

"What do you mean... like poison?"

She nodded, "Were you poisoned by something?"

James didn't remember the smoke from the amulet being any poisonous, it just made Diadora appear, he shrugged, "I'm not sure."

"Do you remember anything?"

He took a deep breath "Yeah, I was walking back to the school," he started, "When out of this amulet I had, this crazy blind man, Diadora, showed up from nowhere."

Levina's eyes widened and her jaw dropped, "Diadora... are you sure?"

"Yeah... do you know him?"

She nodded, "I know the name, what did he want?"

"I don't know, he was nice to me, introducing himself and apologizing, the last thing he said was about some curse or something before I passed out, he was about to give me something as well," he explained.

Levina became jumpy, "Quick, show me your arm."

"Why?"

"Just do it!"

James held out his right arm. She grabbed it before he could pull up the sleeves. She did it herself and examined it.

"The other one please."

He did as she said.

James was more surprised by the fact that they were able to interact with each other, "I didn't think you could touch me."

"hmmhmm," she check the other arm, "Nothing, that's good."

James checked his arms, "What were you looking for?"

"A mark, I thought he gave you a curse," she replied, "I guess you really are protected," she smiled.

"What?" James got thrown into confusion.

Levina turned her attention to the entrance, it was the sound of footsteps in the distance.

"Please tell me what's going on?"

"I'm sorry, I have to go, someone's coming."

"Oh," he sounded disappointed, but then remembered the time when she walked right passed everyone on the school grounds unnoticed, "Wait, but no one can see you."

"But they can see you," she smiled and waved goodbye before fading away, "See ya."

"Bye."

"James?" A female voice filled the room, "Who you talking too?"

James turned to see Mia standing in the doorway looking back at him with concern, "Uhmmmmm," he couldn't come with an answer, "Myself," he force a smile.

She made her way to him, already dressed and ready for school with her backpack, she had an excited look on her face, "You're awake!"

"Yup, finally awake."

"You know you've been asleep for a few days?" she asked.

"Yeah," he answered unsure as to how he would know. He raised his left arm, "This things off so I sure it's been a few days."

She sat down, "How are you feeling?" she questioned, "I was the one that found you lying there in the rain unconscious."

"Oh, you saw what happened?"

She shook her head, "Only you lying there."

"Thanks, I'm fine, just a minor headache," he replied, "What day is it?"

"Friday."

"Wow, it's already the weekend, missed a whole week of school."

"Yeah," she said, "I volunteered to help you catch up... but not with your magic subject."

"Thanks," he smiled, "I've been getting into way too much trouble lately," he scratched his head.

She agreed, "Anyways, how did you end up in this state, you might be lucky I found you before anyone else."

"Because...,"

"Just tell the story."

"Well... I had this amulet, which I seem to have lost," he started, "I'm not sure if it's fortunate or unfortunate."

Mia pulled it out of her blazer pocket, "You mean this?" She held it up.

James nodded, "Where'd you get-,"

"Like I said dummy, I found you first," she opened it, "It was right beside you and the mark on it was peculiar so I decided to keep it."

"How did you find me first?" He enquired.

"I was up in the Hall of Restoration, I noticed someone by the building, I didn't know it was you, but I thought I saw another man by the wall, but it was just my eyes playing tricks on me because he disappear and you collapsed... that's when I decided to investigate," she explained.

James remembered Diadora saying that they were not visible to anyone else, he even demonstrated it by showing his face and shouting at the guard right by the entrance, but apparently Mia was able to witness it.

"Did you see what happened?"

"It was dark, I thought I was seeing things... was I?"

James shook his head.

"I'm guessing this little thing was the cause of your long sleep?"

"Not really, it was the man," he said, "He came out of that amulet... it was the crazy blind guy, you know with the bomb on his back.

Mia turned worried, "What did he want?"

"Nothing," he replied, "He was just introducing himself to me, his name is Diadora," he felt no need to mention anything about the curse because of Levina's check, she clarified that he wasn't.

"Do you know him, heard of him?" He asked.

She sighed, "Nope, but it's weird that he would just show up to give you a name and nothing else."

James couldn't take it anymore, "God I'm confused," he said with anger, "How can you just give us diamonds with powers and throw us into the past for no apparent reason and ditch us to be hunted by Dead Crows."

"Shhh, someone will hear" she tried to calm him down, "I know it's frustrating, but it's happened to all of us, and another ten whom we don't know of yet."

"It's so messed up," he giggled.

Mia had to keep him silent before someone walked in, "We'll figure it out."

"How?!" He shouted.

Mia just remained silent, surprised to see James lose it.

He took a deep breath, "Sorry."

There was a moment of silence thereafter, the sun started to reveal itself, shining rays of its colour into the hall.

"Listen, no one knows about the amulet so I'll keep it with me for now and come up with some story that they will buy, or just say you forgot everything," she stood up, "I've got to go to class now, see you when you get out," she left the room.

"See ya."

James felt a little bad for the outburst, if someone had stepped in or eavesdropped on the conversation, this would've been the end.

Later that morning, the nurse visited again to check up on him. After a few questions about his condition and the incident, which he passed off as memory loss, she gave him something to help with his headache and was good to go. He was sent back to his dorm to change and clean up. The rest of the day was his to do as he pleased so he spent most of the morning in the empty study, in his casuals and later on headed up to the library to read up on some things.

It wasn't long before it was break time and the library became a bit too crowded than usual, it was the autumn season, and this terms exams crawling closer to their expiration date. There he met some of his friends, Claude, William, Clara and Opal among them, they did, off course check up on him to see if he was fine.

It was no surprise that Mia had shown up to the library, but her intentions were not to read and study, but to fetch James and take him to the school grounds where Daniel and Mark were at.

She led him to some benches located outside near the archery section. As from now they were planning on what they were to do in the time being, while they wait for a response from Galvani.

"Hey, you get to wear civvies," Mark said as he sat down.

Daniel punched him on the shoulder.

"What are you doing?" He punched him back.

"Welcome back buddy," Daniel said, "How are you doing?"

"Better, thanks," he replied.

The weather was perfect, windy and cool, with many clouds passing by. The school grounds were still occupied by many learners, the younger ones at most. No one was permitted to do any P.E activities during the breaks, but after school was, as long as there was teacher present.

"Okay," Mia started, "Now that we are all here, we can talk about plans before we leave this place."

Mark put his hand up, as if he were in class, "I want to take a guess… study?"

Mia saw no problem in his guess, she actually found it a quite intelligent answer, "Yeah, that's a good idea."

"Knew it!" He shouted out.

Daniel and James were lost, giving him confused glares.

"What's wrong with that?" Mia asked.

Mark placed his hand on his chest, "Me, I'm planning on leaving before we writing exams… I'm not studying," he turned to James, "Ever since Mr. Patchwalker announced the exams on Monday, she's been paranoid."

Mia didn't take that kindly, "Paranoid?"

Mark nodded, "I was a bit off board with this idea of leaving until I found out I will be missing the exams… and now, I think it is a brilliant idea," he spoke proudly, "Besides we are not a part of this time, so why care."

James ignored all of Mark's preaching and turned to Daniel. Mia, however, had something to say about.

"Daniel, do you have my diamond?"

"Ohh yeah, it's safe, I'll give it to you when we get the time."

Mia was not too happy, "It is always good to know more Mark, especially in this place, it's not going to kill you by getting to know a bit more."

"I'm not going to die either way, I just picked my side," he replied.

"Guys!" Daniel stepped in, "Why are we here?"

"Yes, we need to get this over with," James agreed.

It was something everyone agreed on.

"Okay, I have an idea," Daniel started, "I suggest we train everyday afterschool in the meantime."

Mark clapped once, "Now that's an idea I can agree on, it's more useful," he glanced at Mia.

"Okay," Mia agreed, "You guys can play swords and target practice while I go to the library," she smiled at Mark.

"And there we go again," Mark added, "You're not going to write exams Mia."

"Mark, shhhh," James silenced him.

Mark continued to speak, "I'm guessing you'll want us to protect you, you have no diamond and did Jake even give you a weapon?"

"You think this is one of your PC games don't you?"

Mark shrugged, "I'm just being realistic, we stuck in the medieval times, outside this school we enter the real world."

"And you think it's not realistic to find out more about it!?"

Mark shrugged and shook his head.

Daniel had to step in again, "Okay!" he shouted over them, "You're both right, is that what you want us to say?"

"I'm not saying he's wrong," Mia replied, "I'm just saying I'm not wrong either."

James just laughed to himself as the commotion escalated.

Daniel continued with the peace solution, "I think it's a good idea for Mia to spend some time at the library, unless one of you did geography and are experts at it."

"Just give me a map, I'll know where to go," Mark replied.

James laughed to himself again, it was a great way he could destress, just watching them go at it, "You guys are stupid."

"What are you talking about?" Mark asked, "Where's your input? Calling us stupid."

He sighed, "Never mind, don't let me disturb you, still recovering from my headache."

"Mark, I'm not just their for geographical purposes, there's a lot that we need to find out," She pulled out the amulet, "This, for example, is one of them."

Mark gave it a closer look, "Wait, I know that thing," He turned to James, "So this was what you were fetching last week, wanted to keep it for yourself hey?"

James shook his head.

"Hmm," Mark didn't believe him, "Were you able to open it?"

"It's empty," he replied, "but maybe the symbol might mean something."

Mia put it back into her pocket.

James was not at his right mind at this moment, as usual he was lost in his thoughts, but this time he was just thinking of the very Saturday, at the park, he heard a crack in the sky and then darkness. His mind had already decided to stop trying so hard to piece everything together and just take everything slowly, one lead at a time, but now his mind was thinking about nothing else, making him really unhappy that he couldn't control his thoughts.

"James, are you on board with the training?" Daniel asked.

He nodded in agreement, "And about Levina, our first check is tomorrow, if there is nothing, we will commence with what we have discussed, let's hope we get an extra week to prepare, at least," he explained, "Sound good?"

They all agreed with the terms and ideas.

Mia stood up from the bench, "Okay, see you guys later," she headed back indoors.

Daniel took a deep breath, "As for me, I have the diamond of flight, seems only relevant that I get better at archery... I think I'm going to start using the crossbow as well."

"I guess I'll train with James with swords and better ourselves there," Mark said, "I'm protection and he's speed."

James put a faint smile on his face, "Sounds fun."

The opportunity to visit the past, despite all the other complications, gave him some bit of joy, being someone who loved fantasy and magic.

Mark stood up and held out his hand, helping James up, "Come on bro, let's go back inside."

Daniel stood up as well, "Yeah, let me give you your diamond back, it's stressful keeping an eye on both."

They headed back to their dorms.

That afternoon, they started with their training, the school grounds weren't filled with people so Mr. Padgett allowed Daniel to practice with his archery skills on his own. Mark and James were on the rooftop of the armory building, where all the things they needed to train with swords were provided, this is where Mr. Padgett was needed, to help teach them the basics and different techniques. Before any of this was agreed upon, many questions were asked, but with a bit of convincing, Mr. Padgett had agreed to train them every day because of their dedication. Mia wasted no time figuring out what was needed to be figured out, with the help of his friends, Angelina and Clara, off course only helping out with the more basic things that wouldn't give away any ideas. She was also familiarizing herself with the class of Alteration, learning more about it.

The first Saturday was finally upon them and the day started really slow, the thought of waiting till afternoon just made it seem as if the time would never arrive. This day was as well spent with a lot of practicing in their different fields. The hardest was for James and Mark, they needed a lot of supervision. Their sessions with Mr. Padgett were not that long, since he wanted to spend his Saturday with a bit of rest, and since the weapons they used were not dangerous, he left them to continue with their practice, and nobody ever did wander up the armory building. Daniel was still at the archery range shooting away with a bow, testing his reload speed and firing rate with accuracy. Most of his time there wasn't spent alone, William had decided to shoot a few as well and get a little competitive.

The afternoon seemed to arrive after a long time, the days were turned very cloudy and windy since the beginning of the shift in seasons. Heading to the tower in the late afternoon was not at all going to be hard this time, only two people had to go down to the abandoned tower, Mia as an essential to unlock the trapdoor with her magic and the other was to go down the sewer and check for anything. The other two would just stay at the building and watch out for any prying eyes.

This week was empty, there was nothing, no note from Galvani, it was good that they didn't receive anything this week since James had just come out from his sleep and only one day had been put into their training and knowledge seeking, it just meant they had another week to prepare should the information arrive then. The newspapers weren't so helpful either.

This played well in their favour as in the next few days they were introduced to something quite interesting during one of the classes they attended.

It was yet another gloomy day, covered with clouds. The class which they were attending at this time was Alchemy. A class that took the shape of a lab, the front was typical, the back filled with all that one needed to mix up any kind of ingredients and create mixtures. Shelves and shelves filled with potions on display in their varieties of flasks, it was a bit unorderly though, but no one seemed to care.

Today they were busy with the theory side of it which seemed to be really boring as opposed to the practical where they can make and experiment. The teacher of this class went by the name Mrs. Kendilworth, she wasn't an old and cranky educator like some of the other staff, she look to be in her late twenties at least and quite a fun teacher. Most of the learners liked her and she was able to make the theory of alchemy somewhat bearable for those who weren't interested in reading about plants and nature. Today, however, she had something a bit more different to show the students, handing out a different textbook to the learners titled : Advanced Potions and Poisons.

This heighten there spirits a bit, nothing is more exciting than learning about poisons.

She stood in front of her class, "Okay, now that we have learnt quite a bit about our plant life, we are now going to start looking into what they may be useful for," she spoke, "But know that there is still an endless variety that we still must learn about."

This was a book most of the learners wasted no time opening up and examining, mostly for the images.

Mrs. Kendilworth was busy drawing an image on the chalk board.

James sat with Mark in this class and both didn't find plant life too interesting, today wasn't as boring, it was as if they were in some kind of game with a cook book for poisons. A new book to explore since they started here.

"Hmm, poisons," Mark murmured to himself, "Poisons that can do all kids of crazy things to you," he said paging through it.

"Yeah," James agreed, "Now I wish I paid attention when ma'am was teaching us about the plants."

"Nah, not really, each potion here has a recipe," he pointed out.

"Yeah, but do you know what...," he looked for a complicated name in the recipe on his page, "an Avaerian Puff Plant is?" He showed Mark the words.

Mark stared at the word for a couple of seconds, giving it a bit of thought.

James was confused by the expression he was making, "Dude stop thinking," He gave him a pat on the back, "You and I both know, you never even knew the word existed… you just going to give yourself a headache," he laughed.

"I know it's a plant and it grows out of the ground," he replied.

"Okay…okay," he said slowly.

"Relax bro, now I just need a picture," he added, "In fact, if there was just a picture of that flower or whatever, I'd be perfectly fine."

"Hmmhmm, sure," he replied sarcastically.

Mark looked around the class, just checking what other people were up to, "Hey, how much you want to bet someone is searching for a love potion in here," he whispered him.

James thought for a moment, "Nothing, but I'm sure there is, they are the pinnacle of potions, they everywhere."

The free talking session was over when Mrs. Kendilworth was done with the board.

"Okay, learners, listen up," she silenced them, "In previous years, you've been taught about bottled potions, liquids, ones you have to drink in order for them to take effect, this year we'll learn about inhalable types and pills."

"Pills?" Mark said with a confused frown.

One think he didn't realize was that he had spoken a bit too loud, the class was staring at him, including Mrs. Kendilworth whom was now interrupted.

"Yes Mark, pills, a small round sweet of compressed ingredients."

He nodded in return, "Sorry."

The class was able to return their attention to Mrs. Kendilworth again.

"I didn't know they existed in this time," Mark whispered to James with curiosity.

James frowned at him and shook his head as if trying to clear it, "Bro… pills have been around for thousands of years."

"Oh…"

They both turned to ma'am and decided to listen.

"Now… inhalable mixtures like aromas are mostly designed to immediately affect the lungs and brain, more dangerous in the sense that it is very easy to breath in, as soon as you smell it, the inhalable may have already started taking its effect on you," she explained, "Pills act much slower and are supposed to last for long periods of time, these are also the most complicated to craft as some of them have interesting effects on you… for example, if you will please turn to page 284, there you will find the XP pill."

Pages flapped all around the class as the learners searched for the page.

James noticed this image of the pill. It had the exact same look as the foul tasting sweets that Jake had given them on their way here.

"Hey… these are the same horrible sweets Jake gave us," Mark whispered aloud.

"Shut up," James silenced him.

"Mrs. Kendilworth continued explaining, "These pills in particular are very rare and extremely hard to create. They are able to, after consumption, give the host experience in a specific type of field… say archery, for example, this pill will have a permanent effect."

The pill caught everyone's interests.

"Okay," Mark whispered, "Drugs… Jake gave us drugs."

A girl from the front put her hand up, "Ma'am, there's no recipe."

"Yes, off course, such a pill is forbidden to create for various reasons which I'm sure you don't want to know," she explain, "Some of those reasons include the use of dark magic and it's horrible side effects."

"Sorry Heleny, there is no cheating your way to the top," another learner said aloud.

"Shut up," she shot back, "I was just asking."

Mrs. Kendilworth raised her voice, "Okay, lets continue, no one is going to be making any XP pills, you will be arrested even if you try."

"Woah," Mark was surprised, "An old man gave us some kind of forbidden drug and we didn't know about it."

James nodded, just as surprised, "I wonder what the ones Jake gave us did."

Mark looked at his palms and shrugged, "Did you feel any different since that day."

"Nope, I wonder what the side effects are, I don't feel any different."

"Maybe we should ask ma'am about the side effects," Mark suggested.

James shook his head, "Best not dig into this, we'll find out when we find out, maybe Galvani might know a thing or two."

School was over for the day and a lot of students were again using the time they had to fill up the library and prepare for the upcoming exams and off course there was quite a number of learners that didn't care too much.

Mia and her friends Angelina and Clara had decided to take some time away from the library and just take in the air. Their choice of hang out this time was through the main entrance to the school buildings and down by the entrance bridge. They didn't climb the flight of steps to the top but instead decided to hang around beneath it.

Angelina took a deep breath, "Fresh air."

"Yeah, let's enjoy some fresh air, away from the stuffiness of that packed library," Mia added, brushing hair away from her face.

"Anyways, how have your magic subjects been treating you," Clara asked.

"I'm doing well, sometimes I just wish I could bring the staff outside the hall for a while," Angelina replied, "It sucks that we not allowed to."

This brought to mind, Mia's ability to use magic at will, without the use of a staff or any other magical object.

"I guess they thought children would get into all kinds of mischief," Mia added, "I mean look at the spells we learning, I'm pretty sure that there would be chaos all the time."

Clara agreed, "Safety comes first."

"That I understand," Angelina said, "But this Dead Crow thing is making it a bit to safe, I mean, they should have found out who the culprits are by now, especially since they brought in some mages."

It was a good time to bring up someone in particular, "Maybe they are playing things really safe because of that girl Levina."

"Who?" Angelina asked.

"Levina," she repeated.

She shook her head, "Never heard of her."

"She's the most wanted person right now," Mia added.

"I only know her name," Clara added.

"Nothing else?"

She gave it some thought, "The only thing I recall, was about some incident that occurred about ten years ago, there was a lot of commotion about a little girl," she explained, "other than that, I got nothing... no one really knows much, except that people call her 'The Living Curse'."

"Hmm, interesting," Angelina said.

Another quick dead end, no one knows anything about her, she also felt quite tempted to ask one of the Dead Crow agents, but that could be pushing the wrong buttons.

"Anyways, how did you guys feel about the XP pills?' Mia asked, "Do you thing Mrs. Kendilworth might have them?"

Angelina gave her a surprised looked, "Looks like somebody's trying to get themselves some XP pills."

Mia chuckled, "No, off course not, I wouldn't cheat... I was just curious."

"Well... if you're just curious," she gave her a sly smile, "I would go looking for them in her store room near the enchantment chamber."

"You just gave me the location of her store room... why'd you just give me the location of her store room?"

She shrugged, "I don't know, isn't that what curious people do?... they go check out whatever it is they find curious."

"I guess but-,"

"You guys aren't serious about this right," Clara stepped in, "Because it sounds like you're already planning to go there."

"Maybe...," Angelina replied.

Clara looked at her with great concern.

"I'm joking," she announced, "The room is always looked, with a key, which is probably why we aren't allowed to use magic freely, children would be breaking in and entering places."

Clara sighed, "I thought you'd be bringing trouble to yourself, it's only second term."

Mia looked up at the sky, the clouds were shifting passed quite fast.

Angelina brought her back to reality with a different subject, "I've noticed you hanging out with James, Mark and Daniel a lot... Mia," she nudged her on the shoulder, "So which one is it?"

Mia stared at them, unable to process the question while they both waited for an answer.

She cleared her head, "It's not like that guys, not even a thought," she replied with a very unconvincing expression.

"Just tell us as a surprise," Clara suggested.

To her honesty, Mia had not thought about anything, she was hell-bent on figuring out the situation first. To her, figuring out this task that they must carry out would mean going back to the present time… at least that's what she'd hoped, to see the people she had left without saying goodbye. Another thing that was keeping her on edge was the weight placed upon her shoulders as being the only one able to use magic and the person they relied on the most. Finding the other kids trapped in this time was also on her list, maybe Jake had given them tasks to do as well and their part in any of this would go unnoticed to them, having their hands full with their little investigation.

Off course this had to be kept to herself, just blending in was the essential, "Trust me guys," she giggle, "It's mostly academic, I was told to help them out."

"Okay, we believe you," she replied sarcastically.

Clara rubbed her arms, "It's getting a bit chilly guys, let's go back inside."

They both agreed and headed back to the school, the day was nearly over anyway and just about time for some supper.

This week had passed with a lot of effort and training in all their designated fields, though it was only one week, a lot of progress was made in the part that Mia played in getting the necessary information. Mark and James, still under the supervision of Mr. Padgett were getting the hang of all the basics and simple techniques, still beginners for most of their part, but progressed like men training for an upcoming war. Daniel was doing his part pretty well, gaining experience in both bow and crossbow.

It was now the second Saturday since their visit to Galvani's place, and about the right time to head down to the tower and check for any findings. Mia headed down to the place with Daniel this week.

The sun was peeking through the clouds today, providing some bit of warmth to the world beneath it.

Mia unlocked the trapdoor with her magic and allowed Daniel to climb down the dark hole and have a check.

"I think this place smells worse now," he exclaimed.

"It's been two weeks, off course it's going to smell bad," Mia replied, "And make it quick, don't want to be caught."

"Hey, I'm doing my best here, I would've happily opted for guard duty than climb down this infected ladder," he said, "Besides, you have the light."

"You have your flight powers... apparently, I haven't seen you so much as jump from you."

"Ha...ha, just let me concentrate please," he said as he reached touchdown.

He looked up the ladder, the light seemed so far away, his sights quickly turned to scan the area, the fear of any kind of monster living down here was still present, even after the successful run last time.

Mia crouched and put her head closer to the hole so as to reduce the spread of sound when she spoke, "Did you find anything?" Her voice echoed down to him.

Daniel turned to the floor and searched, "It's dark down here, give me a sec," his eyes scurried the murky floors

"Please give me some good news," she called.

"Ah... do you want good news or bad news?" He asked.

Mia didn't understand the question. To her, there was only one, the good news or the bad news, "What do you mean?" She asked unsure.

"Just pick one."

"Ugh, fine, bad news... I guess."

"There's nothing down here," he broke the bad news.

"What could possibly be the good news then?"

"More training."

Mia got a bit impatient, "I'm going to lock you down there."

"Okay, I'm climbing up," he started the climb.

Up top, Mia locked up as soon as Daniel was up and out.

"Well... that was disappointing," Daniel said checking his clothes for any dirt marks, "Had to sniff up the sewer for nothing."

Mia nodded, "It isn't too surprising, she has been avoiding people her whole life," she had a disappointed look on her face, "I guess we might never find out where she is."

Daniel pulled out something from his hoodie pocket, "Do you think this might help, I found it?" He laughed silently, waiting for her reaction.

She turned to him and her eyes locked onto the envelope and newspaper roll in Daniels hand, "What!" she snatched them out of his hands, a little soiled from the sewer floor, "That's not funny."

"You should've seen your face, all disappointed, as if you had given up," he laughed.

Mia decided to play a little joke of her own, she summoned the same blue mist and tapped Daniel on the shoulder making him feel really cold.

Daniel jumped back as soon as he felt the winter cold all over his skin, he grabbed a hold of his jacket tightly, trying to get rid of it, "Jeez!, it was just a joke... make it stop!"

Mia didn't turn to him, she just examined the envelope, sealed with wax. She didn't unseal anything, she just handed it over to Daniel again since she didn't have any pockets big enough for either the newspaper or letter, "Here."

Daniel took them with his shaking hand, "Are you going to do anything about this cold?"

"It'll wear off," she stepped out of the tower, "Let's go back."

"How long will it take to wear off," he asked putting the letter and paper into his pockets.

"A few minutes."

They wasted no time heading up to the library to examine the goods brought to them by Galvani. The Saturday was not filled with endless studying so the library was not as crowded as on most weekdays. They picked the most secluded spot to read the contents, all filled with a mixture of many feelings, really anxious to find out what Galvani has for them.

"Time to find out this girls whereabouts," Mark announced as he sat at the table.

Daniel took them out of his pocket and placed them on the table.

James picked up the note, "I'll read this first," he unsealed it.

Mark picked up the newspaper and untied the string keeping it rolled together, he place it flat on the table for everyone to see.

"Let's hope this is straight forward," he pulled out the piece of paper and unfolded it. He cleared his throat, "It reads : I have given you a newspaper," he began, "Turn to page 2."

"Okay," Mark paged through.

James continued, "There you will find an article about her current location."

Mark put his finger on the article title, "Found it."

The title read : The Curse is a Ghost

"Continue James," Daniel said.

"Oh, it says : I was unable to figure out her exact location, but I am certain it is to the north, maybe with your resources, you might be able to pinpoint it," James dropped the letter.

"Great," Mark said sarcastically, "That's as accurate as he can get."

"Let me see the article," Mia turned the newspaper and read it to herself silently.

"It speaks about her being impossible to find," she continued to read.

"I wonder how she's hiding?" James said turning the letter around and folding it backwards.

Mia shrugged as she read, "It also says that she has been the cause of a lot of deaths that have occurred recently in the north, even innocent children have fallen victim..."

Mark stopped her, "Okay, wait just a minute... why are we looking for her, this clearly states she must be apprehended," he sat back on his seat, "I actually think writing exams may be an option for me now."

"Why?" James asked.

"Um, maybe it's because I don't want to be looking for someone who murders children."

"I don't think it's true," James defended her, "I mean... what would a teenager want out of killing a lot of people?" He looked around for someone with a valid answer.

Mark just shrugged, "I didn't say I was dispelling this, exams are still a bit scarier... I don't think this is true either," he said, it was just about the nicest thing he'd said about this mission since it grew out of the dirt.

James turned to him, "I don't think I've ever heard you agreed with us before."

"Shhh, I'm doing it for the exam," he whispered.

"Anyways, is there anything there that could help us be more accurate," Daniel asked.

Mia shook her head skimming through the article again, "It just says north here... I mean it could be a city, since they said a lot of people were killed."

She paged through the paper and came across another article that caught her interest entitled : The Hunt Grows. She began to read it out of curiosity, "Guys, there is a group of people who have just been accused for the murder of a few Dead Crow agents...it happened three days ago at some Lonestar Inn."

"Yeah, we know that place," Daniel said, "We passed by there on our way to the school."

"Wow, they killed some Dead Crows, that's very dangerous," James added.

Mia agreed, "Yeah, their bounties will be issued in some days it says."

"And there faces are known," Mark laughed, "That must be very bad on them, every bounty hunter and Dead Crow will be on their tails."

"Okay," James stood up, "Our priority right now is figuring out her location... I'm sick of this library, I'm going to play with some magic."

"And quickly too," Mia added rolling up the newspaper and taking the note.

Mark stood up as well, "Okay, we'll keep that in mind," he turned to James, "Let's go to the destruction tower," he suggested.

It wasn't long before they all left the library.

It was round about midnight in the boys dormitory, Moonlight shining through the windows creating beautiful light rays. Not one single person was awake, which was strange for a Saturday... at least no one in the dorms.

"Wake up," A voice whispered in the room.

"Wake up," this time it sung it out.

James let out a gasp and opened his eyes.

It wasn't loud enough to wake the dorm, but one of the boys, quite a few beds from where he was heard him, "Keep your dreams to yourself please, you waking us up," he murmured as he drifted away almost immediately.

James sat up only to see Levina sitting on his bed, "Oh, Levina," he said, looking around the room, "It's sleepy time, why are you here?"

"Shh!" She exclaimed, "Don't say my name out loud dummy!"

James's bulged his eyes, "Why you shouting," he whispered, "You heard him, you mustn't wake him, he's trying to sleep."

Levina looked at him with a straight face, "No one can hear me... dummy, they can only hear and see you," she poked him.

"I'll-I'll never get the hang of that," he shook his head, "I can hear you loud and clear, and touch you, and see you."

She nodded as if to the beat of a song, "I understand, but right now, if anyone sees you, you will be talking to yourself, they'll think you crazy," she giggled.

James really wanted to find out more about her and current state.

"So what brings you here, at midnight?" He asked.

"Oh," she became excited, "I found her... that girl you've been looking for."

"Wait what?" He hadn't processed anything she had just said.

"That girl you've been looking for," she gave some thought, "Levina, yes, that's her name."

James looked at her with some bit of concern, "Yes... the girl with the same name as you..."

Levina just nodded in return, "You're right, she does have the same name as me."

James was unable to realize the first thing that she'd said so he asked again, "You said what?"

"I found her," she replied.

Only then did James react like he was supposed to, with a bit of excitement and shock, "How?"

"I read that newspaper that you found today and went to go check the places in the north," she explained.

"Well done," James congratulated her.

She became so happy, "Thank you," she spoke excitedly, "she is in a place called Ad-Adornfell," she struggled to pronounce it.

James felt excited, receiving the name of the place at which they must head to, but also afraid, now that it came to it. The comforts of the school have made him second guess, but he still knew that he had to find her and figure out why she is so dangerous.

Levina continued to speak, "You going to have to go there very quickly though, a lot of bad stuff is happening there and she might leave again."

James nodded, just as he realized another block, "How do I convince these people?"

"Make up something, but you must be quick."

"How soon do you think we should leave?"

"Tomorrow," she replied a bit unsure. She looked at the clock, it was after midnight, "Today," she changed her answer, "Because when school starts, you won't be able."

James suddenly lost all the sleep he had in him, he wasn't surprised that it had to be today, Monday is the inspection. Giving themselves a day's head start was going to be of great help. He nodded, "I'll make a plan, thanks for your help."

"Anytime," she smiled.

"Good night."

"Bye," she waved and faded away.

James lay back on his bed and stared up at the ceiling, this was the time to act, he had to come up with some kind of idea or plan to make sure that this happens today. If she really vanishes at a moment's notice, leaving in a week's times would mean that she would be long gone by then.

It was an early morning for James and he had made it so for both Mark and Daniel, whom didn't take the disturbance well.

Down at the study, Mia was not around to be seen, she was still asleep apparently, James asked one of the girls to wake her up.

Straight after breakfast, which James didn't seem to enjoy, rushing through his meal under the eyes of Mark, Daniel and Mia, whom were very concerned for his well-being as he looked over at the clock from time to time, James took them to a quieter place at which he could reveal his findings. It was just at a random spot outside on the school grounds.

"James, this had better be really, really, really good, because if it isn't, I'm out of here," Mark said.

"Don't worry, it is."

"Okay, spill it out," Mia got a bit impatient, "I got some digging to do about Levina's location."

James took a deep breath, "I know where to go," he announced.

No one replied or reacted.

"Guys!" He said a little louder, "I know where she is."

Mia shook her head in disbelief, "Wait what?"

"I know where-," He was interrupted by Mark.

"Okay, explain...how did you find out?"

The predicted response : Too good to be true.

"Yes, enlighten us," Daniel agreed with Mark.

Time to tell a short story, "I overheard some teachers speaking about this place where, it's chaos right now, fights, people dying and the such," the end.

Again, no reply or reaction.

"Okay...," he glanced over at each of them.

Mark shook his head, "Where's the place?"

"There's a city north from here, a place called Adornfell," he replied.

Mia nodded, "You may be right," she said.

Everyone turned to Mia, the person Mark and Daniel would most likely believe.

"I did check the map yesterday," It's the only closest city directly north of here, the other places count as villages or towns."

"Oh great, we figured out the place," Mark blurted out, "And now the stress settles in."

James agreed, "Yeah, a lot of it, and even more when you figure out when we must leave."

Mark looked at James, "Please don't say that word Mia loves."

James nodded, "Today."

"Okay, I'm out," Mark turned away.

Daniel grabbed him by the arm, "You're staying."

"Guys," He turned back, "We're breaking out of the school... today, nah, I don't believe it."

"Why?" James asked.

"I wish I knew why... I wish I had a valid reason that would keep us here," he shook his head, "Breaking rules is not what I'm up for, and worse of all, the Dead Crow will be on us... I can't."

"I'm also scared bro," James admitted, "As soon as I figured out the place, I wished that I hadn't heard anything, but we got too do it today."

Mia agreed, "Yes, we must leave as soon as possible in the hope that we find her, that or we won't have any motive here in this time."

"And it's a whole day before inspection, before they find out that we're gone," James added.

Mark glanced at each of them and stepped closer, "Okay, what the heck, let's get it over and done with before I realize what I'm actually doing."

Daniel brought up another matter, "What about training, we are sitting ducks if we get caught, I don't even know how to activate my powers properly."

Mia snapped her fingers, "I know of a way to help with that, don't worry about it, I'll let you in on it later, right now we going to have to smuggle out our things."

Daniel was also getting hit with the realization, "I can't believe we're about to break out of school."

Mark tried to enlighten him, "Think of it as a game... where every outcome, no matter what, death, imprisonment, torture," he listed all the worst things, it even scared him in the process, "You cannot respawn."

"Thanks," he replied sarcastically, "I'll be sure to remember that."

"This is starting to worry me," Mia admitted as well.

James turned to her, "We'll be fine, we got you on our side... master of magic."

She felt a little better.

"Yes, you can hide us," Mark sighed.

Daniel agreed, "No one else can use magic the way you do, you don't even need a staff."

Mia realized something, "Speaking of which... when was the last time you guys attempted to activate your abilities?"

None of them had any specific date, which was kind of worrying.

James shrugged, "I don't know, months ago, when Jake was trying to teach us," he fibbed.

"We'll have to train outside the city," Daniel suggested.

The wind started to pick up.

Mia sighed, "Okay, it's now or never, we need to get ready… I for one have a lot to do."

Mark stopped them from leaving, "Let me get this straight… we're about to become high school dropouts?"

Mia nodded, "Yeah, pretty much."

He snapped his fingers, "No pressure."

Mia headed straight for the library with her backpack and immediately started searching through many books and secretly using her magic to copy some of the more important pages onto blank pieces of paper she had brought with her. Some of the information she imprinted onto a diary that she owned. She had been doing it for quite some time, but now was time to rush and gather as much information as she could. Mostly useful alchemy recipes and spells that she hadn't come to learn of yet.

James, Mark and Daniel didn't have much to do, they just packed their bags with as much essentials as they could bring. They did get some curious birds pop up and ask some questions but they were easily brushed away.

Most of their day was now spent trying to keep their nerves in check, just wandering about like normal people. The clock was moving quite fast this time.

Their last lunch was spent in silence, unable to speak as the fear started to settle in. Even the Dead Crows seemed to be watching their every move, waiting for them to do something… it was one of the many different scenarios that haunted them for the rest of the day.

The evening arrived, and everything was set.

Nerves trying to kill them… check.

About to try something new… check.

The reality of the situation weighing a ton… check.

The feeling of all eyes on them… check.

Sitting in the hall was one of the most stressful moment of their entire lives.

The food was impossible to swallow, but their job in this school was not done yet, there was one more pick up left to do, one that could only be done at this time of night before their disappearance.

Again, they waited for people to start heading out of the hall before they commenced with the plan. They stood up and left the hall, plates empty as this was probably their last good meal.

Corridor to corridor they headed down, traveling close as a group, drawing as little attention as possible.

The passage in which the store room was located was clear, not one Dead Crow in sight, off course this could have been for just the few moments that they were there, their patrol patterns were unknown to them.

"No one on patrol on this passage," Mia declared, "But still keep a keen eye, I might be a while," she ordered.

James went on and seated himself on the short staircase that lead to this section of corridors. Mark and Daniel kept an eye on any other corners that could surprise them.

It felt a little exciting, breaking the rules. The adrenaline rush that settled, knowing that they may be caught or implement some of their stalling tactics.

Mia headed down the empty corridor, with the light of the moon seeping through the tall arched windows. The door was reached within a few seconds, older than most of the others.

At first she check if it was really locked before using her magic to unseal it. Opening it made a loud creak that echoed away in the emptiness, she tried opening it slower but it only made it worse.

She slipped in without opening it completely and closing it again would amount to more unnecessary noise so she held it in place and looked around the room for something to act as a door stopper.

Nearby, she came to see a small wooden box, something that could keep the door. She crouched down and tried to reach for it with her other hand while the other kept the door from waking up the place. It was unsuccessful unfortunately.

A second attempt was in play, and this time she stretched out her leg. Successful in reaching the box, she place her foot on top of it and shifted it till it was at arm's reach before picking it up and placing it as a doorstopper. Fortunately the box was heavy enough to do the job.

When problem one was dealt with, she stood up to face another, the store room was packed to the brim with what seemed to be an endless amount of ingredients and finished recipes. The room itself was not big, just having four shelves placed against each wall.

She let a sigh, "This is going to be fun," she said to herself sarcastically.

The only upside to this search was the fact that what she was looking for stood out quite a bit. It wasn't some random potion among the many flasks that plagued most of this room.

Mark and Daniel patrolled the area.

"We're going camping for real this time," Mark mentioned, "No teachers or supervisors, just us... it might be fun," he tried to lighten up the mood.

Daniel agreed, "Yup, but with those teachers and supervisors, the many endless camp trips we went to... I still don't think we know how to build a fire."

Mark stopped in his tracks for a moment, "Crap, that must have slipped my mind, I kind of remember being shown quite a few times before...I guess."

"I remember not seeing much of a point in all this because... why?" Daniel replied.

Mark nodded in return, "It's whatever."

"We're in trouble, no fire skills and we don't have tents," he giggled.

Mark stopped him from saying anything else, "Stop trying to make me rethink my decision to leave... now... I'm going to patrol elsewhere in peace."

James had started to relax himself on the steps as the seconds stacked into minutes. His fear of having to confront someone in this lonely place reduced.

Something appeared from the corner of the corridor.

He sat up, ready to start implementing his tactics, till he realized it was just a student.

"James?" She called as she picked up her pace.

It was Angelina.

James stood up and went down the stairs, to stop her before she got too close for comfort.

"What are you doing here?" She started with the interrogation.

James came up with the most sought after excuse, "Oh, you know, just chilling."

"Chilling?" She frowned in disbelief.

James nodded, "Yeah, just sitting...enjoying the silence," he replied, "What are you doing here?"

"Looking for Mia," she answered.

"What makes you think that she's here?"

"Because you're here," she replied, "And I noticed you coming this way, the alchemy storage room is here and it's something we just recently spoke about," she crossed her arms.

James was confused and in the dark with whatever she was talking about at the moment. A Dead Crow agent was what he wished for now, "I don't know what you're talking about but like I said, it's just me here."

Not one word that came out of his mouth was believed, "Okay... I believe you," she decided to play along, "She's probably at the study or something."

James main mission was to stall for as long as he could and right now he was led to believe that he was successful, "Yes, you can check there, I'm sure you'll find her," he smiled.

She nodded in return, "Okay... alone right?"

He nodded.

"Then don't mind me, I am just taking an evening stroll," she tried to make her way passed him.

He had no choice but to stand in her way.

"So you are stuck in this passage way," she figured.

James had to think of a way to outsmart her, which was impossible at this point, "A Dead Crow agent told me to keep watch while he went off some-,"

She placed her finger on her lips, "Shh," she silenced him, "You are really bad at this, I'm telling you... you are really bad at this," she chuckled, "Now I'm going to see what she is up to and you're not going to stop me," she spoke calmly.

James was defeat, this was not what he had expected or signed up for.

She walked right passed him and started up the stairs.

James followed her closely behind.

Angelina headed down the corridor and notice the store room door was slightly opened. She picked up her pace and peered in, "Mia?"

Mia received the most unexpected fright, almost dropping the small crate of potions in her hand.

James didn't show his face. He stood just out of sight… remaining here was not going to do him much use so he headed back to his post.

Mia sighed in relief as she placed the crate back onto the shelf, "It's only you."

Angelina stepped into the room carefully, "What are you doing?!" She whispered aloud, "You know I was just joking right?"

"Yes I know you were joking," she replied, still searching, "And I'm looking for the XP pills."

"You're stealing XP pills?" she was in disbelief, "Even after the talk about them in class with Mrs. Kendilworth?"

She continued to search, "It's not why I'm stealing them."

"What other purpose could you possibly have?" She continued with the questions, "You're being really strange Mia."

Mia stopped what she was doing and turned to her, placing her hands on her shoulders she said, "I'm sorry… but we're leaving."

Angelina turned really confused, "Leaving?"

Mia nodded, "Yes… please help me find the pills, we have no time," she turned back to the shelves.

Angelina just stared at her, really concerned with what she'd just said. But she did eventually decide to make her way to one of the shelves and start searching as well.

"Leaving school?"

Mia took a deep breath, "Yeah," she replied.

Before another question could be asked, Mia continued, "We have to find someone."

"I don't understand."

"I don't expect you to at the moment but please promise me you will tell no one about our motives," she stopped and turned to her, "Look at me."

Angelina turned to her.

"Promise me, you will tell no one of this."

Angelina was her closest friend and she was not about to sever that little bond created since their first day here, "I promise."

"Thank you, and I'm sorry," she turned to the shelves again.

It was about a minute later that Angelina found them in a small box labeled : Basic XP pills.

Inside they were categorized into small corked glass bottles.

Mia picked one from category Alteration and Archery and two from swordsmanship. She place the box back onto the shelf that Angelina picked it from.

"Let's get out of here before somebody finds us," she said exiting the room.

Mia remover the doorstopper and closed the door.

"You have no keys," Angelina realized.

Mia didn't want her to see that she was able to use magic without a staff, but there was no imaginary key around. She was faced with the choice of either having to leave the door unlocked and give the Dead Crow agents her identity and worse, Angelina's identity would be all over that storage room as well, it could get her into some serious trouble with the agents. It was that or trust her to keep another secret.

To her, it was a bit obvious what the choice was. Allowing her friend to take the fall for something she wasn't even a part of was not right to do, on her part.

She placed her hand over the handle and used her spell to lock it up.

Angelina's eyes almost popped out of their sockets and her jaw nearly fell off, "Y-you can-."

Mia nodded, "I can use magic without a staff," she turned to her again, "Please don't mention that to anyone."

Angelina smiled, "Don't worry, your secret's safe with me," she couldn't help but ask, "Can James, Mark and Daniel...?"

"No, it's just me," she replied, "Please call James, I'll fetch Mark and Daniel."

They were all back together, mission accomplished, with Mark and Daniel confused about Angelina's presence in the mix.

"Let's go before something bad happens," Mia whispered making her way to the closest exit leading to the sewers.

Naturally, Mark and Daniel enquired about Angelina but Mia just said that she would help them out if they were to get into a sticky situation.

To their luck, every corridor they went down was clear.

Just before they could head down the last corridor out, and by happy chance, they spotted a Dead Crow agent before they revealed themselves. He just stood there, fiddling with a piece of paper. He was in the way.

"Oh, no," Mark whispered, "He's not patrolling, we can't just slip passed him."

Mia tried to find an alternate way to get passed this agent, but there was no luck. His spot covered a large radius.

"I have an idea," Angelina whispered to them.

Everyone moved away from the corner and heard her out.

"I can sneak around this block to the other side, I'll draw his attention from the corridor on the other side," she started, "He will come check on me and that will be your way out."

Daniel nodded, "That's a good idea."

"Anyone could have thought of that," she added, "You lucky I found you when I did, even with James's horrible stalling strategies," she giggled.

The Dead Crow agent let out a cough which stunned everyone.

"Okay, let me give you the way out," she turned.

"Wait," Mia stopped her and gave her a hug, "Thanks for helping us."

"No problem."

"I hope to see you again."

She chuckled, "Oh, I will see you again, trust me," she turned away and hurried to the other side.

It was moments later when a loud scream sounded from the corridor on the other side. The agent was immediately pulled away from his boredom and alerted. He hurried away to the source of the sound.

As soon as he was out of sight, they all headed down the passage way as stealthily at possible.

Angelina was explaining the longest story to the agent. Unable to see their progress, she saw it best to stall for as long as she could.

Into the dark moonlit night they went, picking up their pace as they started down the hill.

Everything was already at the tower waiting for them. The only thing that had kept them from leaving was the pills they had just stolen. Their rucksacks were placed in the tower under the rotting staircase.

James, Daniel and Mark put on their robes. Mia didn't have one so she remained with her casual clothing on show, she wasn't the problem anyway, the people in danger were James, Mark and Daniel.

"Didn't Jake give you a robe?" Mark asked.

Mia shook he head, "I arrived here safely, with only Diadora having given us a little visit, and I'm not one for old people robes."

They wore their backpacks and Mia unlocked the trapdoor.

She allowed everyone to go down the tunnel first, but before James could have his turn, she came to notice something on the back of his neck.

"I didn't know you had a tattoo," she blurted out.

"Wait what," he turned to her, "Tattoo?"

"On the back of your neck, there's a tattoo."

James placed his hand there, as if hoping to feel something. He never recalled ever getting a tattoo. He was sure about this one.

"Tattoo?" He asked again.

Mia nodded, "It's some kind of symbol... I guess."

James really wanted to see this tattoo, but its position made it impossible. He shrugged, "It's whatever, we have to leave now."

"Off course."

James started his climb down to the sewers, now thinking about this tattoo that he now has.

CHAPTER 15

Into the Wilds

James held his nose shut. The scent of the sewer tunnels was not something to be reckoned with, "I forgot the smell of this place."

Mark agreed, "I am no fan of this creepy place, I want to get out now."

Daniel chuckled, "I guess having my turn yesterday made me quite familiar with this smell again... not saying that it's any less bad though."

The red dim lights of the tunnels were still lit.

Mia lit the way again and pulled out the little sketch she had made a few weeks ago.

"At least it's the last time we will be in this place," she added.

They all started down the tunnel.

Mark was quick to get bored. The tunnels hadn't scared him the first time so this time around he was more casual and unafraid to make noise or kick something into the water. He pulled out a potion, "Hey, do you remember this?" He held the potion up at them.

"Yeah, the potions Jake bought for us," James replied, "They supposed to help with poison or something."

Mark pulled off the cork and sniffed the contents, "Not bad, not bad."

"Did you just drink that stuff?" Daniel turned to him.

"No, but I'm about to," he replied, "Nothing wrong with a little taste."

Daniel shrugged, "Up to you, don't complain if you don't feel well afterwards."

"It's a healing potion," he said with a straight face.

Mark certainly was tempted to give it a little bit of a taste, but didn't bring himself to, he just placed the cork back and put it away.

"Something is telling me I should get poisoned," Mark continued, "Then the potion would come in handy."

Mia sighed, "It is clear you don't like alchemy, that potion is not a cure for every poison… so it's best you don't listen to whatever it is that is telling you to poison yourself."

"You're right, alchemy was not nice," he replied, "Enchanting was way better, giving your weapons all those special abilities… I would even keep a bunch of those cubes on display, they bright with colour," he stepped into a puddled intentionally, "Too bad we were too young to be taught how they were actually made, that would be a class I'd pass."

Mia brightened her light and picked up the pace just a little.

Mark started to whistle up a tune.

"Will you please stop whistling Mark," Mia requested.

"Why, it's kind of boring down here."

"I don't want you alerting anything that could be living down here," she replied.

"Thing," he raised his voice, "What are you talking about now?… our last trip was smooth, nothing was about."

"Please stop making things harder than they already are."

"What, I'm lightening up the mood… just making this place a little less creepy."

"There are doors and stairs leading to places we don't know about, I'm pretty sure this place is not empty so I suggest we do things quietly like last time."

"Fine… no more whistling," he said.

They made another turn, down into a long tunnel.

"So how was your archery training Daniel?" Mark started again.

"It was pretty good," he replied, "Though I did better with the crossbow," Daniel came to realize something, "I've been training in archery this whole time but have no bow."

Mark laughed, "Maybe you should have stolen one, we had the whole day."

James agreed, "Now you going to be stuck with a sword… ask Galvani, he might have."

"Guys," Mia called, "We are going to be as stealthy as possible out there, avoid as many fights as we can… we're just children."

"Children that are being accused for crimes we didn't commit," Mark added, "Is that why you didn't train?'

"Mia's got magic," James reminded him. "You probably don't need some sword or bow."

They made another turn, right this time.

She sighed again, "Can we just keep it down please."

It was like no one heard her.

"Speaking of training, did you find the XP pills?" Daniel asked.

"Oh, yes I did," she stopped and gave the map sketch to James. She pulled them out of her pocket, each one in a wrapping with a label of the category, "I got two sword one's for you Mark and James," she handed them over to them, "And an archery one for you Daniel, mine is for Alteration."

"Sweet," said James.

They consumed the pills on the spot.

Daniel made a sick face, "Woah, I forgot that these things were so disgusting."

"Why'd you forget!" Mark shouted at him, "You useless thing, now I have that taste in my mouth."

The insult pierced Daniel, "Thing!" He also raised his voice, "Did you just call me-."

Mark was happy to interrupt him in the middle of the most predictable line, "Yes," he nodded, "It's about time you realized what you were," he gave him a sick stare.

Daniel chuckled and turned to James, "Did you hear that?" He stepped forward and pushed Mark by the chest.

Before he could react James stepped in between them both, "Aye!" he held them apart with his hands, "I don't want to see two little girls fighting over their stupidity right now!"

"Guys!" Mia stepped in, "Shut the hell up, you're like five year olds!"

"What!" James turned to her, "It's your fault they're like this, I'm just fixing up your mess!"

Mia raised her left hand and allowed for the mist to form around it, "I am a second away from freezing you to death," she spoke calmly, "So I suggest you take a step back."

James closed his hand to a fist, "I dare you," he whispered to her.

Mark shoved James by the shoulder and grabbed him by the neck, "You just insulted me didn't you?"

"You're not important right now Mark, you're not needed," he replied swatting away his hand, "I have to deal with her first."

Mark didn't allow him to confront Mia, "Apologies first, maybe then I will overlook your sickening tone... it belongs down here."

Daniel joined in the madness that was happening out of nowhere. Everyone just started insulting each other and the need to hurt the other grew stronger as more words bled.

No one understood why they were feeling so angry and ticked off by even the slightest gesture, but it didn't go on forever. Mia was the first to clear her head, only moments away from killing someone she undid the magic she was creating and shook her head, feeling a little hazy.

She looked up to see the others still going at it. The only benefit in their situation was the fact that there was three and each ones attention did not remain on one person... and the fact that none of them had any magic skills or weapons to pull on each other.

Her first realization was the noise that they were making, it echoed across the tunnels.

"Guys!" she shouted again, this time it was her, "Please keep quiet!" she had no choice but to scream louder than they barked.

Luckily they turned quiet and also came to the realization.

"Woah, that was unexpected," James murmured, "what in this world just happened?"

"Are you guys back?" Mia asked, just to be a hundred.

Mark was a little unsure, since his head was as well a little hazy, "I'm not angry anymore, if that's what you want to know," he placed both hands onto his forehead.

"I'm good," Daniel confirmed.

Mia brightened her light, "I think it's these pills," Mia suggested, "They are some kind of evil... remind me never to have them again."

She closed her eyes, trying to straighten up her head so that she could think clearly again.

"I had completely forgotten what these pills do to you," Daniel mentioned, "It was the same when Jake gave them to us, but then, the effects weren't as bad as this."

Mia looked up, surprised, "Wait, you've had these?"

He nodded, "He didn't give you?"

"No!" she raised her voice, "If I knew this was the case, I wouldn't have even thought about it."

Mark looked over the edge into the river and noticed something floating in the water. It was newly stained and white. It took him a moment to realize that it was a piece of paper, and in the midst of his haziness, the thought of not being alone down here started to crawl back into his mind. He looked around in search for something he didn't want to be there.

"Guys," he pointed into the water, "I don't think we're alone."

Everyone stopped and investigated the piece of paper floating in the water.

"It looks like it was dropped recently," he continued.

"And we just made a lot of noise," Mia added, "I hope not to see whatever that may be down here, not even people," she held out her hand, "The map please."

James started searching his robe pockets and pants for the map.

Both places were empty.

He looked at the piece of paper in the river. His heart started to race.

He continued to search, his whole body now, wishing in his mind over and over again that it was somewhere on him.

Mia gave him a weird look, "What are you doing?" She asked, "We need to get out of here now."

James did another quick search.

He was now ready to confess.

"I think-...," he struggled to bring the words out of his voice box, almost choking on them.

Mia shook her head, "What!"

He couldn't take his eyes from the piece of paper. Clearing his throat he attempted again, "I think-I think that that's our map," he lead his shaking hand and pointed at the piece of paper.

She turned to the tainted piece of paper, "No... You didn't," she moaned.

James was quick to say that he can't be blamed, "It's not my fault, the pills did that."

Mark and Daniel were not at all pleased with this stunt and were happy to blame him instead of the medicine.

"Okay," she took a deep breath, "I can't believe I just took a deep breath down here... I don't know the rest of the way."

"What do we do now?" Daniel asked.

Mia heard something, "Shh," she raised her finger.

"What-,"

"Shh," she silenced him again, "Can you hear that?" She whispered.

The sound she heard was of someone struggling for breath. It was uneven, clearly suffering.

Mark realized as well and gasped, covering his mouth, "What the hell was that?" He was in shock.

Mia detected it was coming from around the corner they had just turned.

Another sound came into existence, this one a dying moan.

Everyone remained as silent as a cemetery, growing in fear of what unknown thing was around the corner.

Mia decided to investigate and made her way quietly to the corner. Daniel and James were as well curious.

"What are you doing?" Mark whispered taking a step in the same direction as the others. He felt much safer with them than alone, even though they were heading in the most unsafe direction.

Mia dimmed the light of her spell greatly as she drew closer to the corner and the noises grew louder.

They all stood on the edge, paralyzed and afraid to take a peek. At this point they were just listening.

Another sound emerged from nowhere, which confirmed that it was just around the corner, it was vomiting, it was pouring into the river by the sounds of it.

It didn't sound pleasant at all.

James, probably the bravest soul amongst them at the moment decided to take a look.

Mia, was closest to the wall, but barely touching, then followed Daniel. Mark, the one totally against this, without even a pinch of curiosity in his blood was furthest away, having all kinds of feelings, even ones of ditching his crazy friends and saving his own life because nothing about this situation had a good smell to it.

But again, he was stuck with them no matter what, it wasn't like he had the map out of this place and being alone in the dark was not an option.

James's head peeked, then he retracted it immediately.

Mia shrugged, asking what it was but James hadn't given himself the time to examine.

He peeked again and this time to inspect.

The sight was revolting. It was people, that part was easy to deduct, but something was really wrong with them. They weren't just sick.

The first person he inspected was a man, just wondering around in circles with his hands pressed against his chest. His clothing was ragged, stained with the worst of marks. With a few flies making themselves at home around him. His eyes were glued to the ground as if he was searching for something. It was clear he'd been here for an age, but that wasn't the worst of it. That wasn't what gave the word *revolting*.

Their skin was cover in small black leeches sucking away at their blood. They did not even care that these things were on them.

James felt sick just watching, his face turned to disgust

Another one came out from another passage, a women with a similar look, all skin and bone she was, wandering undead.

By now, both Mia and Daniel were also peeking, unable to stop watching.

James felt something tap him on the shoulder, which caused a fright. He turned around only to see it was Mark who hadn't pulled the courage to show his head yet.

"What is it?' He whispered.

"Sick people," James turned back, "What's wrong with them?" He asked both Mia and Daniel.

The both just shrugged in return.

Mark's head came into view as well.

Just at that moment, something unexpected happen.

One of the sick men looked up.

His eye were locked on theirs.

For a moment, it was like time itself had fallen paralyzed by the fear created. No one was able the move. Afraid to move, scared any sudden movements might result in an unwanted quarrel.

One of them clearly didn't sync with them... and it wasn't Mark. This time it was Daniel who was terrified. He turned away and started sprinting down the tunnel. Even though he did this right in front of them, it took a while for them to figure he had given himself a head start.

The man moaned and started to jog towards them, hands still pressed against his chest.

"We need to go, we need to go, we need to go," Mia whispered unable to move.

The others noticed them and came their way.

Mark tugged at their shoulders, "Let's go!" He shouted.

Unable to keep the light up, Mia dismissed her spell allowing herself to run properly and at full speed.

Daniel was quite some distance away, a little faint from their current position. He was just heading dead straight.

"They chasing us," James pointed out, "Why?"

No one replied, being out of breath already with their hearts trying not to give out from the freight of their lives.

"Daniel!" Mia called, "Do you know where you're going!"

"Off course not!" He shouted back.

James and Mia caught up with Mark, who wasn't a fast runner.

Daniel seemed to be looking for any ladder that would lead him up and away from here. He made a sharp turn at an area closed off by the river.

Mia picked up her pace, hearing the sick people behind her. Her concern was more on Daniel at this point because he'd made a turn and was now out of sight.

James took a quick look over his shoulder and let out a shriek. The sick people were only a few metres away from them, running so fast without using their arms. He tried to pick up his pace.

"Guys, watch out, there's a turn, don't slip," Mia warned them.

Their footsteps gave Mia an idea. The whole floor was moist with many puddles, this was a dangerous plan so she gave them a bit of a heads up, "Guys use the railing to turn!"

"What?" Mark shouted, out of breath.

"Just trust me."

The turn was just a few metres away and they weren't slowing down to allow for a safe turn, given the wet floors. There wasn't much of a choice for them either.

Mia summoned the mist around her right hand. She hoped they would comply with what she had instructed, since she was ahead of them both. As she was about to make her turn, she swung her arm forward as if throwing a bowling ball and the wet floor quickly solidify.

She made her turn safely and saw Daniel just ahead. She turned back, waiting for them to appear around the corner and hopefully have them use the railing instead of being tripped by it. It was a risk yes, but she had to at least slow down their pursuers.

She was panicking, her very own idea could be the end.

James was the first to appear, using the slippery ice as a slide and grabbing the railing, having the top half of his body throw it's over the edge almost bringing his legs along with him.

He was safe. He'd made it, out of the iced area.

One less person to worry about.

Mark appeared immediately after, looking as clumsy as a clown. Grabbing the railing was the first thing he did, but he wasn't safe as his pursuer was right behind him. He stopped himself from falling over but the person behind him had lost control.

Mark turned back, and with the reflexes of a cat, ducked down really low, tripping the sick man, sending him diving straight into the river.

Mark crawled away and got to his feet, "Good idea," he said starting with his run again.

Mia started to run as well, after the panic was relieved by their survival. She looked over her shoulder, examining the effectiveness of her idea. It certainly did slow them down and quite a few of them were tripped by the rail. Unfortunately, two of them were saved by it as well and regained control, the chase wasn't over yet.

The path which they were on was a one way, without any turns, at least not on their side of the river.

It was thanks to the robes James and Mark were wearing, the reason why they were falling behind again. These people were really fast and didn't seem to be getting any tired.

James's chest was burning in pain, forcing him to slow down, no matter how much he forced his legs to keep carrying him.

The woman that was right behind him reached out her arm.

He felt something grab him.

At this moment, he saw the only future, and that was his death. He had never been so afraid before in his entire life. His heart stopped and he blanked out.

He opened his eyes.

He was still in the tunnel.

He looked around and saw only darkness.

He heard footsteps behind him and turned to them.

It was Daniel, running towards him.

This had his mind in a twist, he could see Mia and Mark still running... towards him.

The woman that had grabbed him had fallen down hard and probably knocked out since she wasn't in motion anymore.

The man was still on Marks tail.

"What!" Daniel stopped in front of him. He did not bother to ask because right next to James was a ladder leading to the top, he turned to the others, "There's a ladder here!" He screamed.

It was a few seconds before Mia reached them and turned to Mark, "Run faster!" She shouted.

Daniel was already making his way to the top, with James following him behind.

Mia summoned the mist again, this time on both her hands, creating small orbs above her palms.

Mark was doing his best, trying not to get caught but was unsuccessful.

The man grabbed a hold of Marks shoulder and jerked it, turning him around by force.

He closed his eyes and protected himself with his arms.

Before Mia could do something to help him, something phenomenal happened.

Around Mark, a blue transparent sphere grew out of him, glowing with little stars. The sphere grew so fast and so big that it threw the sick man back.

James had witnessed it as well.

Mark stood still, eyes still closed, only hearing a loud thud and splat.

He was waiting for something terrible to happen.

Nothing.

A moment passed.

Nothing.

He opened his eyes and lowered his arms.

The shield around him gave him a freight, he'd never seen anything quite gripping before. He looked down and saw the man squirming on the ground.

Mia hurried over to him. She stopped just outside the barrier, dispelled the mist from one hand and tried to touch it.

Her hand passed right through it.

She stepped into the barrier and out the other side, swinger her arm forward and let ice freeze everything up to the man. It was more powerful, creating crystals in its wake and over the man.

The shield disappeared, making the place all the more darker.

Mia grabbed a hold of his arm and pulled him, "Come on, we got to go."

Mark was in shock, but able to move his legs.

James continued up the ladder.

The trapdoor up top was not locked so there was no need for Mia's magic. This time, without a map, they found themselves emerging into a completely different alley. This place in which they found themselves didn't deserve the name 'alley', it was almost spotless. The ground was made from perfectly carved stone and looked as if no one had set foot back here before. The overlapping and faded wanted posters were missing. Not trash anywhere. The place that they found was not what they expected.

"Woah, we're lucky," Daniel said, "I thought were would have come up in the middle of the streets and be caught same time."

"What!" Mark burst into anger, but then quickly shook his head, he didn't want to waste his energy.

"Here I was thinking you'd say we were lucky to have survived that," James said.

"I was expecting the same," Mark added, "But then again, he took off without us."

Mia was already scouting the area, checking for their exact location.

"I'm not going down there anymore, one of them touched me... I'm still shaking," James looked at his hand, "that was disgusting."

"So we're all going to remain quiet, after being chased by zombies?" Mark asked taking a sit on the spotless floors.

Daniel chuckled, "Zombies, that's a little...," he couldn't finish his sentence.

"What?" he looked up at him, "It's a sewer, and what do sewers have in common?... zombies."

James cringed, "They had leeches all over them, I can't take that image out of my head."

"Maybe it was just a bunch of sick people?" Daniel suggested.

"Keep quiet Daniel," Mark silenced him, "Don't want to debate about it."

It was clear that he was still in some kind of shock. Not a lot of people have been faced with this near death situation. Mark on the other hand, felt it best to just think that he was in one of his games.

Mia came back from her little scout, "Now we know why it's important to stay quiet in quiet places," she said, "That place down there has many pathways and rooms, I wouldn't be surprised if it was some kind of travel route way back."

Mark nodded, "Thanks to you we survived."

Mia crossed her arms, "It was more like you saved yourselves, how did you activate your abilities, it thought you said you couldn't?"

Daniel stepped in, "Yeah, James was in front of me standing next to the exit when I arrived."

"I didn't," James replied, "I blanked out and found myself where I was," he explained.

"Same here," Mark added, "When he was about to get me, the barrier protected me, I didn't even know it was out till I opened my eyes... it was really different as well."

"Wait, you used your shield?" Daniel asked, surprised to have not seen it.

"It's strange, but it helped," Mia held out her hand above Mark.

She helped him up.

"Thanks."

"We need to go," she declared, "this is a Dead Crow hive, not as much as the other district, but they're about."

"Do you know this place?" James asked, "It's very clean."

"Yes, it's one of the richer districts," she replied, "The market district that we need to go to is not too far from here."

Their sneaking about was successful so far, being sure to keep in the shadows between the houses and shops, keeping an eye on the guards and watching their patrol patterns, a trait they needed to look out for in this part of town because these ones were not slackers, they love their posts and patrolled like guard dogs on the streets.

Mia's intuition was wrong, this place didn't have much agents, it seemed that they took care of the more chaotic areas of the cities. This side, there were only a few mages posted and stretched out thin. There weren't any rooftop archers or your standard Dead Crow agent walking about, they relied on the amount of city guards that were stationed there, and more disciplined than the ones at the market district.

The light of the moon had made everything really clear and visible, which worked against their favor.

It was really strange, this place was peaceful and always quiet, surely it hasn't seen crime in many days, yet the guards act so formal. She had expected they'd be the ones slacking or engaging in conversation. On the other hand, the market and poorer districts... districts with higher crime rates had security that slacked on a daily basis, as if they were regular members of the city, communicating and doing other activities.

Most of the ones posted here had helmets on, which meant that most of their sight had been blocked.

Fortunately, for the escapees, Mia was familiar with this area of the city so she took the lead and made sure no one would get caught or lost. One thing that did worry her to an extent was the entrance to their destination, from where they were, she could see the wall towering above everything, this city did love its walls, dividing each district, each entrance having its own guards standing by it. It was never part of the plan, losing the map and being chase by the sick people.

Everything remained successful thanks to Mia, but the problem of this path into the market district was still there. They now stood between two double-story homes just a short distance away from the gateway to the other side. There was a small wooden house with one small window place just beside the gateway. The entrance was guarded by two guards with pikes as weapons. These ones at least seemed the type to be reasoned with. They didn't take this job seriously and were chattering about something.

"This is a dead end," Mark declared, "there is literally no way we can get through unseen," he started to pace.

Daniel gave it some thought and came up with something, "Guys, I think I've discovered something."

Everybody turn to him.

"Is it an idea?" Mark asked.

Daniel nodded, "We are wanted by the Dead Crow right?" he started, "it is only them who know who we are or may suspect something, other than that, no one else would guess."

"Meaning?" Mia asked.

"Why don't we just act like normal citizens," he replied.

"So you suggesting right...," Mark couldn't help but giggle, "that we walk right up to them, wish them a good night and be on our way?... have you been with us these last few hours?"

"It's just a thought Mark... Please."

"I don't think that would work," James agreed.

"Yeah, especially now that we are in the richer district, they'll think we stole something and take us in to be searched," Mia explained, "That would be the end," she sat down, leaned against the wall and stared into the starry night.

The ideas were not coming in.

Mark leaned against the wall and took a deep breath, "Waiting until morning is not an option right?"

"Off course not," Daniel replied, "That's when they notice we're gone."

James laughed quietly, "How can you even think that?"

Mia stared at her palms, thinking and scheming in her head, looking for any possibilities that could prove themselves successful at this moment.

"I don't suppose there's any kind of invisibility spell?" Mark asked.

Mia shook her head.

"There is," Daniel replied, "But it's very advanced stuff."

With only the basics at her disposal, Mia did come up with something that could serve some purpose.

"Guys, I may have a way to pass them," she tapped her forehead.

Nobody said anything, they just stood there an listened.

"We going to have to do it really quickly though," she mention taking a deep breath, "I am going to hex those two guards keeping watch," she started, "I am going to use what Daniel just said about being citizens, I'm going to try make them feel remorseful."

"How?" James asked.

"They will see us as homeless."

Daniel nodded, "That could work, no one would want a homeless in this part of town."

"Listen, we going to have to be quick," she flicked away a small pebble, "because I'm not just going to be changing your faces, it will be everything, a lot of magic will be needed."

"This will be weird, acting as something we're not," James added.

"Acting..." Mark dragged it out.

Mia stood up, "Okay, let's make this quick... oh and don't act, that's something everybody seems to get wrong."

She made her way to the edge and peeked. The guards were still having a conversation.

She raised her left hand and from her fingertips, they gained a faint dark blue colour, she started moving her fingers in a crooked motion and whispered the words, "Aldatu Videnie," her fingers turned normal again, "Okay, it's done, we must leave now!" She whispered loudly.

Mia was first to step into the light with the others following behind. She was walking toward them pretty fast, as if in a hurry.

The guards noticed them, "Halt!"

"Ye-yes sir," Mia said with a concerned and saddened expression.

The guard realized he was talking to some kids, his expression didn't change, "What are you youngsters doing here?" He asked rather seriously.

"We accidentally found our way into this district," Daniel replied.

"Now how did something like that happen?" He enquired.

That part of the story was not clear to them, mentioning the sewers could be really dangerous, the guards might think they may be sick.

Every second that passed, made the guard a bit more impatient, "Well?"

"We snuck into a carriage looking for food," James came up with something, "When we got out, this was the place the carriage had led us to."

This approach was the most understandable, by far, but it had dire consequences.

"Thieves hey?"

"We're sorry, we promise not to do such a thing again," Daniel added.

The guard gave them a real suspicious look.

Mia wasn't feeling good anymore, she became a little dizzy and her vision blurred, "We sorry," she whispered, as she started to lose her balance.

She fell to the side.

James, standing beside her, caught her.

This wasn't good, as she had said, there is a lot of magic in hexing someone to this extent.

"What's wrong with her," the guard turned worried.

"I think she is hungry," James replied.

It was at this point that the guard felt some remorse, "Wait here," he order as he went back and into the small wooden house.

"What's wrong?" James whispered to her.

"We're out of time," she started panting, "If I pass out, you will be seen."

"Hold on, we're almost there."

The Guard came out of the house, holding a wrapped package in one hand, "Here's some food for you lot," he handed it over to them, "Please don't be getting yourselves into trouble," he allowed them to pass.

Daniel nodded, "Thank you, we won't."

James helped Mia make her way passed the entrance, but then she was unable to even take a step. Daniel handed Mark the food and helped.

On the other side they found their way to another hidden alley nearby. It was funny, as soon as they had passed through the other gate, everything felt a little normal again, it didn't have that wealthy vibe to it, and the alley that they came too first had wanted posters. It was a mystery how these posters found their way into places people barely go.

The walls really did create this kind of divide, but the Market district served more as the centre of the city. It was where a lot of people from the other districts would come together.

Mia removed the spell as soon as there weren't any eyes prying.

James and Daniel seated her on a wooden crate placed randomly against the wall.

Mark went on to check around the area for anything.

"You saved us again," Daniel said, "Thanks."

Mia didn't respond, she just sat back and closed her eyes. So tired but able to move since the hex was removed.

Mark grew an interest to the package that the guards had given them. He started to unwrap it and see what kind of food they were given, "hmm, sandwiches."

Mia immediately held out her hand, "Give me some," she whispered.

Mark pulled out half a sandwich and handed it over to her. She wasted no time consuming it, didn't even check what was put in it.

"Woah," Mark was surprised, "We just had dinner."

"Is it the magic?" James asked.

"I guess," she replied, "But Jake said, the more I better myself, It won't put as much strain or eat as much energy."

Mark wrapped up the food again, "You know, I wonder where that old man is right now?"

"Don't think about it," Daniel suggested, "It'll just make you angry."

"At least we've got Galvani," James shrugged.

"Yeah, but he's also just doing what Jake told him," Mia added turning to Mark, "Give me that food," she held out her hand, "I'll be a few minutes before we can continue, keep an eye out," she order opening up the pack.

"Shot," Mark replied, "I have this side," Mark headed to the far end.

James and Daniel went over to the side closest to the gate. They both stood at each corner and observed.

This part of the market district wasn't as cramped, less shops compared to the southern entrance with all the small shops. This side had a large open road and broader buildings. Shops that stood on their own, with even fancier sign boards. There were only a few lurkers around this place, wondering about at night, it didn't seem like the area had places of entertainment anyway. It was much clearer.

The Dead Crows and guards were tending to their boredom at least, so them standing in that alley way was not much of a problem at all. It seemed the sneaking part of this detour was over, the more relaxing part had begun.

James couldn't help but think of this situation, he shook his head looking up into the clean night sky, "What have we done?" He asked Daniel

Daniel took a deep breath, his eyes glued to the ground, "I have no idea, I am thinking the exact same think this side man."

"I know this is real and all, but sometimes I think it's one of those realistic dreams, that I would just wake up… and probably be angry that it was just a dream," he giggled.

"Relatable," He replied, "Ever since we jumped back, I've read into some history, and I haven't found anything that explains why the use of magic was banned, have you?"

James shook his head, "To be honest, I haven't picked up a book… so you found nothing about any wars or politics?"

"No, nothing, and yet we're so close to the time of the 100 year shift."

James shrugged, "It's like Jake said, history is different."

"Yeah, that's just strange… I wish I had a chance to interview the owners of the school."

"Who?" James asked.

"Didn't you hear, the school is own by this other family… The Maithindor family if I'm right," he explained.

"Oh, I heard that name from someone in the school."

Though their current job right now was to keep watch, it was very peaceful, able to just stand and look into the stars. For those few moments, it was as if no one was after them, as if all problems had fallen away.

But it was only just a few minutes. Mia was ready to go again, she pulled James and Daniel out of their peace first.

"Okay guys, it's time to go," she called them, "we'll leave by Mark's side."

They followed her to Mark who was standing against the wall, trying hard to stay awake.

"Time to go Mark," James tapped him on the shoulder.

"Oh, you good to go?" He woke up.

Mia nodded, "Please wear your hoods," she requested, "Your faces mustn't be on display, we got quite a bit of Dead Crow agents here," she said, "Try to avoid the mages at most, they can be a problem."

They did as she said before stepping out into the streets.

This side of town had quite a lot of people that wandered around at this time, which was what dispelled the reason to sneak and hide. The robe which James, Mark and Daniel had worn helped them blend in as average travelers which were a common sight in this place, it was only Mia that had the different and modern attire on, but no one could care less, this place was known for its visitors. Some people were only just closing up shop, some bartering for the last few customers, then there was your average lurker or random drunk here and there.

For James, Mark and Daniel, this place was still new to them, they wouldn't have known where to go, having seen only the one road that passed through the city.

It wasn't long before they had reached the library, and from there, the way was easy.

"Wow, how far off course were we?" Mark asked, "You lead us to some other place Daniel," he chuckled.

After the library, they headed down to the residential area that Galvani lived in.

They headed down the road and from there could see the lights of the school's towers and high buildings.

They reached Galvani's residence.

Mark stood in the middle of the road and stared into the distance, he gave a slight wave, "Bye school."

"What are you doing?" James walked up to him.

"We had some good times," Mark continued to speak, "Now we'll never again be welcomed," he sighed.

James put his arm around him, "I hear you bro, best school ever."

Mia and Daniel were already up on the porch.

Daniel gave the door a loud knock.

After seeing enough of the school's exteriors, Mark and James came up the stairs as well.

"Hey, what are you children up to!" An old man's voice came from behind them.

Alerted by the tone, they jumped in its direction.

It was another old man, perhaps in his 70's by the looks of it, carrying a lantern in one hand and a walking stick in the other.

"Well!?" He demanded, "Answer the question."

"We're here to visit Galvani," Mia stepped forward.

"Galvani, with visitors your age, that's most unusual," he said, "Especially at this late hour."

"He asked for us," James said.

"Hmm!" he didn't believe them, "You three boys look the type to be wanting trouble, don't be bothering him or I'll report you!"

This was getting a little problematic.

"They won't," Mia said, "We are friends of Galvani, we won't cause any trouble, just please don't report us."

The old man gave it a bit of thought, "Oh alright, as long as you youngsters don't cause any trouble," the man started down the road again.

"Thank you," Mia said.

Daniel continued with his knocking.

A few seconds later they heard a voice from the other side of the door, "Who is it?"

"It's us again," Daniel spoke.

Galvani unlocked the door and opened it up. He sighed at the sight of these children and let them in.

Closing the door behind him, he began to speak, "What are you children doing here at this time?"

They took off their bags and placed them on the floor against the wall.

"We received your letter yesterday," Mia replied.

"And the very next day, you decided to pull this trick again?"

Mark sat at the dining table, "We've already figured the place that we must go, to start our search... Adornfell."

"You figured all this in one day?" Asked Galvani, he did not believe this.

"Yes, with some luck," James replied, "Besides, today was the best time to leave."

Galvani shook his head, pacing up and down, really worried about what was happening, "This is crazy, four children heading out into the wilds," he took a deep breath, "I'm not sure if I can allow this."

Everyone else joined Mark at the table.

"What?" Mark was surprised, "You gave us the information."

Galvani stopped, "I was thinking you would wait for Jake or something, gain his approval."

Mia stepped in, "You said Jake told you to help us."

"You have good memory don't you," Galvani sighed, he didn't want to be responsible for anything bad happening to these children, now that the time had come for them to actually leave.

"We are only doing what Jake told us," Mia said, "It's all we know since we came to this time."

Galvani looked at them with his thinking expression, hoping to gain some kind of way to sway them out of it, "Don't you want to wait for him?"

"Not possible," James replied.

"He's right," Mia said, "It's not possible to head back at this time and by tomorrow the Dead Crow will know who we are, which brings us to why it is essential to leave tonight, because as soon as the sun rises everyone will know who we really are."

Galvani was put into a really tight situation, "So they don't know who you really are."

"Not really," Mia replied, "When I hexed them, it was only the Dead Crow that knew who they were looking for, I changed their faces so that they wouldn't match, the problem is that everyone else that they have come across knows their real faces but didn't know who they were looking for which would mean that if they were to be known as criminals, everyone would be looking for them, not just a few Dead Crows, and that's going to be impossible to hex," she explained, "Make sense?"

Galvani was lost but he didn't want Mia to re-explain it all to him again so he just took her word for it, "Yes, I guess you're right," he continued to think, "So there's no way out," he sighed, "You're going to have to leave this night."

For a moment everything was silent. Everybody was thinking of their situation, they had started it and there was no way back, it was the choices they made and could only hope that they were the right ones.

James thought he was the source of all this, being the only one who knew about the little ghost that had asked him to help her.

Mia was the one whom noticed the paper being held by one of the Dead Crow mages which lead to the discovery of this girl Levina.

Daniel had done some digging into the past and discovered some things that he still hasn't unearthed yet. The reason why he has kept it to himself is not known.

Mark has probably been their lifeline thus far, though he hadn't meddled into these matters, he has questioned a lot of the irrational decisions that everyone else seems to be making, jumping into the fire without the extinguisher.

Galvani joined them at the table, "So, what's your plan, summed up?"

"Make it to this city, Adornfell as soon as possible," Mia replied, "Hopefully find her before she leaves."

Galvani tapped the table with his finger and cleared his throat, "You do know that she has evaded the world for ten years?"

Daniel nodded in return, thinking, how in this world are they going to be able to flush the person out, if the Dead Crow has failed for ten years, from since she was a young girl.

"She trusts no one, that much I can tell you," Galvani said.

"So she has no one?" James asked, "Not a single person?"

Galvani shrugged, "With no last name, I would presume so, there's nothing that even the Dead Crow can hold against her," he sighed, "I suppose you have chosen this as your task, I guess it would be wise to tell you about that morning ten years ago."

"So you know?" Mark blurted out, "That's good to know," he nodded continuously.

"I was not sure you would actually go through with it, but if you know even a little, then maybe if you find her, you might be able to choose your approach," he said.

"Okay, what do you know about ten years ago?" Mark asked.

"Okay... but this won't tell you where she came from, that's still not known," he stared, "on the day before she earned her price, she was found wandering the streets of a small village, on a rainy morning, knocking door to door asking the locals of that town for shelter and food, but the lot of them rejected her, despite her age and current state... what followed after was terrible, and how most people say she earned the name 'A Living Curse'."

The room was silent, with the exception of Galvani's voice telling the tale.

"While she begged and asked for help, she came across a group of Dead Crows, that immediately started to abuse her as if she'd committed the most inhumane of crimes... the towns people made themselves present and just watched as these agents hit her and cursed at her, "He took a deep breath, "they called her a sin, something that shouldn't have existed... off course being so young, she didn't see or understand why the world was so cruel to her, but that didn't give them a heart, even the citizens had come to join and cheer on like it was some kind of sport...,"

Mia did not take it lightly, her eyes had begun to water.

"Now it was the next bit that surprised everyone that morning," he continued, "During this act displayed by everyone else, she just disappear... from being in the centre of everything, she just vanished... this was another thing that surprised everyone, and gave that name," he concluded.

"So, how she vanished is still a mystery?" James asked.

Galvani nodded, "Now that you know what kind of person she might be towards other people, how are you going to go about doing this?"

Mia sniffed, "We going to help her, we going to find her and we're going to help her."

"Okay," he nodded, "Now this place you are going to is currently in chaos, so it's your best bet," he stood up from his chair and went to another room.

The four just sat there and exchanged glances. Really nervous about what they had just really gotten themselves into.

Mark sighed, he was really stressed, "This is... real."

Mia nodded, "Yes."

James wondered to himself, thinking really hard, trying to figure out why people would come to hurt a little seven year old girl. Maybe if he'd decided to listen and look into some history or learn more instead of have fun, something might have made sense to him.

"Let's hope that she is our first task," Mark broke the silence.

Mia got upset, "Whether or not she is, we are helping this person."

"Okay, okay," Mark backed away, "I didn't say we should abort."

"No one should have to suffer that way."

James was just a little happier that now, everyone was on board with this without any doubts, the little ghost would be happy.

"The only road block we have now is how we are going to find her," Daniel pointed out.

"Let's not worry about our last step yet... we first need to make it there," James said.

Mia agreed, "Yeah, we must get there first."

Galvani came out from the other room carrying three belts with swords sheathed and placed them on the table. He also place a small pouch, "Some money for the road.

"Thanks," Mia took the pouch.

James, Mark and Daniel got up from their seats and started strapping the belts on, under their robes.

Galvani disappeared again and came out with a small rucksack with a sleeping back tied to it, "It seems Jake had already known you were going to leave the school sooner or later," he said putting down and heading out to fetch the others.

"Oh, nice," Mark said picking up the bag, "sleeping bags," he put it on, "this I can work with."

Mia was busy examining the contents of the pouch, it was all gold coins.

Everyone began by transferring the contents of their other bags and into their new ones. They didn't have much of anything. Only Mia, having the few extra books and flasks for alchemy.

Galvani had also handed over to them a copy of the map and a compass along with some other necessities.

"Okay, let's get going, all the other essentials we'll get on the way there," he declared, "I will drop you off at the north gate."

"Ah, Galvani?" Mia said.

"Yes Mia?"

"My staff."

"Oh!" he jumped, "Nearly forgot," he ran off into the other room.

"Hmmhmm, so you do get yourself a weapon," Mark nodded, "Blasting people all over the place hey?"

Galvani came back with the staff.

Everyone's jaws dropped, all except Mia and Galvani.

The staff was made of metal, it was black and silver in colour. It had a smooth and reflective surface, making it appear to be a kings weapon.

Galvani handed it over to her.

"Thanks."

"Woah, where'd you get that?" Mark asked moving in for a closer look.

"Jake," she replied, "He called it Vicissitude."

"Huh?" he was thrown away by the word, "What does that mean?"

"It's another word for change."

"Hmm."

"Why is it called Change?" James asked.

"Let me show you, please step back Mark," she instructed.

Mark took a small step back, eyes glued to the beauty of this staff.

"As you can see, this is a staff right?" She turned to Mark.

He nodded.

Mia held the staff up horizontally in front of her, with both hands in the centre. The very next moment, by some magic trick, the staff split into two equal parts with each in one hand. Then the two halves morphed into two silver broad swords.

Everyone was quiet for a moment. James couldn't stop blinking continuously.

"I want that," Mark whispered pointing at it.

"There's only one of its kind apparently," Mia replied morphing the two swords into a crossbow.

"No way," Daniel came up to her, "Now it's a crossbow," he held out both his hands, "May I?"

She gave to him.

Daniel held it up to his face and aimed it at random objects, "It's light," he handed it back to her.

"So that staff can change into any weapon?" James asked.

She nodded, "Check this," she morphed the crossbow into a giant scythe, "I'm the reaper," she made an evil smile.

"I'm sorry, that's too cool, can I try?"

Mia shook her head, "Only I can morph it, Not even Jake could."

James was disappointed.

Mark seemed down, "Jake only gave us swords."

Mia cough, "Excuse me, you have diamonds."

Galvani interrupted their little session, "Come on, we have to leave, it's a long walk to the North Gate."

Mia morphed the staff to the length of her forearm.

Galvani also handed Mia the sheath for Vicissitude, it was like a bolt quiver. She strapped the belt on.

"Are we ready?" Galvani asked unlocking the door.

Mark took a deep breath and stretched his neck, "Yes."

"Ok, as you can see, It's 1 am, we must hurry, four hours till dawn," he looked up at the clock.

He opened the door and let them out.

The early morning was a bit chilly with a light breeze.

Galvani was leading them to the western entrance, taking them to the western section of the city which they hadn't ventured into yet. It was known to most people as the poor district.

Getting through the guards was not a problem at all, the only time, it seemed, that these city guards would care about who passed through was if it was into the richer districts. Galvani was also known by quite a lot of people around this city.

"You seem to be famous amongst the guards," Mark pointed out, "The ones at the gate were very happy to see you."

"Yes," he replied, "I've helped out quite a bit in this town, caught some thieves and outlaws in the past, found missing items and the lot… you can say I've done quite a bit on the local notice board."

Passing through the entrance to this new section of the city was the same as when they had made it from the richer district to the markets. It was a complete make over, and definitely not for the better. The lower district wasn't a very pleasant place to look at, not too happy for the nose either. It was as if nobody cared much for this part of the city. It looked like there was never a sweep through in the alleyways that were filled with unemptied dustbins surrounded by other garbage, it was a heaven for rats. Even some of the alleys had open trapdoors to the sewers, bringing up the stench to ground level. At least this wasn't the case for a lot of the places here, some of the streets seemed to be looked after by a few people.

None of the buildings seemed to be structured in a formal way, that or they were old and in a state of decay.

Another thing that was more surprising was the presence of people on the streets, it was way past midnight and they filled the streets, wandering about as if it was day time. Maybe most of the people on this side preferred to be night owls.

The guards posted here seemed to co-exist with folk very well, these ones were not at all bored, they looked to be enjoying themselves.

It was one of the alleys that reminded Mia about the crazy incident and saw fit to ask about it, "Oh, Galvani, I was meaning to ask you about the sewers."

"Ask away."

"When we went down there earlier on, we came across some people that looked sick with leeches all over them," she explained, "They chased us."

Galvani grew a worried look, "My word, I did say that place was dangerous, did any of them get a hold of you?"

"No, we were able to get away... what's wrong with them?"

"Folk up here call them Leechers," he replied, "It's people who have been infected by the leeches that came to live in the sewers, the disease is very dangerous and doesn't have any cure, not even magic," he explained.

"But those people also acted crazy and tried to get us," Mark pointed out.

Galvani nodded, "It's the virus, I heard that when you a bitten by the leech, it will obviously enter the bloodstream and spread rapidly all over the body using the heart, then it will enter the hosts brain and alter it, basically making the infected a slave to the virus and will search for fresh blood... as leeches do," he explained, "the leeches all over them just attach until they can jump to the next host."

Mark cringed, "And to think of it, we were nearly caught, if it wasn't for my powers activating at that moment, I would be a one of them."

James agreed on that bit, "Same here... and we didn't do it ourselves, it was as if they switched on themselves... any ideas how Galvani?"

"Well, Jake never said anything about those objects you carry," he replied, "My guess would be that they can protect you... I guess."

Mark burst out laughing quietly, "Makes sense, that a rock can tell when you're about die," he replied sarcastically.

"It's my guess," Galvani defended himself.

Daniel sighed, "It's a magic place, at this point, after seeing those people in the sewer, I would expect anything as bizarre as that to be the reason for anything."

Galvani had to make a few stops before continuing on to the north side of the city, one of the places was a small inn that seemed open for most of the night. Being so packed with a lot of people, most of which were in over their heads, Galvani ordered that the children waited outside while he tended to his business inside.

From the very moment that Galvani disappeared into the noisy pub, everyone became a bit on edge, observing every bit of movement that took place all around them. They stood close to the door, but not in the doorway, people were leaving as much as they were entering.

Almost every single body that exited had lost the ability to walk and reeked of all that he or she had tanked-up.

As the only ones around, unfamiliar to this place, it was really uncomfortable, but at least there wasn't anyone that felt, for any reason, the need to bother them. Nearby was a group of guards who had their bit for the night, they didn't take notice of anything that was happing around them, sitting on some crates in a circle using a bigger one as their table to play some sought of game.

Some people that lurked in the shadows had given off a scary kind of vibe, one in particular appeared to be some kind of assassin or thief, she was clothed in matching attire, consisting of a leather vest, leather gauntlets, pants and thigh boots, with some weapons at her disposal and purses on her belt. She looked like a bounty hunter, waiting for her prey to step out. This place did seem a haven for a lot of small time wanted thieves. A good place to hide, since even the guards were acting unprofessionally.

Another thing that was clear was the fact that some of these people had no place to call home, seeing some of them pick a haystack to sleep on or just sit on a barrel and hopefully get into their sleep so that they can continue with their cycle of hardship, struggle and hustling the next day to keep alive. It's no surprise some would find their way into groups or gangs just to belong somewhere or have life support.

One thing on this side of town that was noticed compared to the richer districts was that people on this side actually knew each other, be it for good or bad reasons, they still kept to each other instead of themselves.

Back to our party, their wait wasn't too long. Galvani had found his way out in about ten minutes carrying four wrapped packages stacked right on top of each other.

He gave each of them one to place in their hollow bags.

"This is food for the next few days," he explained "It's dried meat."

They thanked him for the food.

Galvani had also given them leather water flasks already filled with fresh water.

It was some time before they passed through the entrance that lead to the northern section of the city. It took a little more convincing at the entrance before they were allowed to step through. They were right to be questioned too because this part of the city was no joke, making the richer district look somewhat poor.

Even though Galvani was known in this city, he was only allowed to travel on the main road at this hour.

Every house was designed for a family of royalty, and every shop would probably need payment as entrance fee.

The place was riddled small gardens of perfectly trimmed hedges and the most ordered flowers. The flower pots and vases were crafted by the best of hands, having taken care of the smallest details which seemed to be telling their own tales.

The place didn't lack any guards either, and the ones posted here wore a more royal type of armour with red capes.

"Welcome to the palace district," Galvani spoke in the undying silence.

"Palace?" James asked, "There's a king here?"

Galvani shook his head, "No, I wouldn't call it that, but it's home to some very important people," he said turning to the right, "You see that castle there, bigger than the school?"

They saw the building, Galvani wasn't lying, it was larger than the school. It was faraway though, to notice any details, but atop each conical roof was a flag that lay still, the winds were not strong enough.

"I did not know that was there," Mia said.

"It's right behind the school, but divided by the walls of the city," he explained continuing up the main road.

"Important people," Mia repeated, "How come I've never heard of them."

"Oh, I'm sure you've heard of them," he said, "That palace over their is home to some of the members of the Maithindor and Ghordiitry family."

"Ghordiitry? I've heard of the Maithindor family but not Ghordiitry," Mia said.

"Yes, well, you are new to this place so I wouldn't expect that you would know them."

Mark couldn't take his eyes off it, the first time he's ever seen a palace before, "So these people run the world basically?"

"I would guess yes, there's no doubt that they are the wealthiest and most respected... they have helped grow this world, building the school, putting people first and sharing a lot with them."

"So that's where they live?" James asked.

"Oh, no, only some of them are stationed here, the leaders are far to north."

"Oh, I would've really like to see them, maybe we can explain to them how we were framed by the Dead Crow," he suggested.

"That wouldn't be a good idea at all," Galvani said, "They too have the Dead Crow protecting them... but anyways, we shouldn't speak about such things around here, we should stop," he took a deep breath, "If you want help from them you going to have to find them elsewhere, but that's not your mission right now."

They made it to the outer section of the city, where all the farming took place, this area wasn't any different no matter which section you came from.

This was always a good sight to see, and a nice place to just breath.

The closer they drew to the main gate, the less safer they felt. They were about to enter unknown territory, a place that they have never seen before and of a different time, no more walls to make them feel secure.

Galvani was still unsure about this, letting these four enter into the real world by themselves, but it was not his place to decide anything for them and all this is a part of something that he may never come to understand.

"Do you have everything you need?" He asked.

"Yes, I believe so," Mia replied, "You gave us the map and compass to find our way."

"You have food?" he realized he had just given them, "Oh, off course you do," he murmured to himself.

He was getting really worried about this, "Boys, please learn how to use those objects, they will be the ones to keep you safe."

"We will," Daniel said, "I'm sure we'll be able to train outside."

"Mia, train yourself in magic, it's a gift that you have, it will help you a lot as well," he continued to speak, "And don't be going around looking for trouble, stay hidden till you reach the city... it will be about two weeks on foot so I hope you know how to hunt."

"We've done a lot of outdoor training and camping in our time," James mentioned.

"Okay good, and there are small towns around that you may use to rest or stock up on food," he didn't stop talking, "Oh, and remember that you will be wanted criminals from this point on, there will be a lot of trouble if you come across bounty hunters or guards... I don't know how it is in your time but here, if you are a criminal with a bounty, death is the outcome for most so please be careful."

"We will," Mia sighed.

Mark was starting to feel the gravity of the situation they were in, he was now realizing what he was doing and it did not settle his organs at all.

They made it to the gate, it was the same as the one in the south. The guards stopped them. One of them recognized Galvani, "What brings you out at this time, Galvani?"

"I'm escorting my visitors out of the city," He replied, "they have a long road ahead and wish to cover more ground."

He ordered for the gate to be opened, "We hope your stay was great young travelers."

Galvani walked them to the other side, "Your journey will be long so please remember to stock on some other supplies in villages and stay off the main road, it's often patrolled," he said again.

This time they just nodded.

"Come here," he opened his arms and gave them all a hug, "Be safe, and I hope you find her and the answers you seek, I will be waiting here for Jake's return."

After their farewells, Galvani moved to back to the other side of the wall and allowed for the guards to close the gate.

They waved goodbye for the last time before it was sealed completely.

James looked up at the light spheres that floated above the gates, "So pretty at night," complimented.

"Yup," Daniel agreed.

Mia looked ahead and could see the forest that surrounded the city, "Okay," she took a deep breath, "Let's go." She followed the main road.

Everyone else joined her.

From the safety and comforts that came with the city and school of Marridor to the great unknown that now lay before them.

Into the wilds.

CHAPTER 16

Becoming Rogue

Far down south, on the road that cuts through the forest, a road that leads to the city of Marridor, traveled the company of Jane, Mary and Denice, making their way on foot. It had been two days since the little incident that had occurred on the morning outside Lonestar inn.

They were currently venturing through a forest of tall trees, that stretched out for many miles. It was midday and the sun was right above them.

"I still think we should've waited a little longer for the horses to wake up," Mary said, "We would've been there by now."

Jane jumped over a log that was blocking the road, "You heard Bertha, those people were going to wake up, I'm sorry the bomb also affected the animals, they might have taken longer to wake up."

"I wonder where she got a hold of that bomb," Denice added, "For a kid, she really did save us," she pulled out her dagger and examined it, "But I agree with Mary, the horses could've helped."

Jane stopped in her tracks and turned to the them, "Yes, the horses could've helped and we'd be there by now, but do you think taking that kind of risk would be worth it?" she continued down the road, "don't answer that... besides do you really want to add animal theft to our heads?"

"Might as well," Mary replied, "We were accused of murder not two days ago," she turned to Denice, "Is it still murder if it was all just self-defense?"

Denice shook her head, "No, murder suggests that we planned to kill those Dead Crow agents when in reality it was attempted murder on their part."

"See, we were wrongly accused for their murder, and Dead Crows on top of that," she turned to Jane, "So a few missing horses might have been nothing, it just can't get worse than that."

Jane gave it a bit of thought, "Think of it this way… since they were able to easily accuse us of murder, just think of how they could have twisted that story into their favour," she explained, "The next story could've been something like, 'Three murderers steal a lowly farmers horses', that would not work well for us."

"You really do want to save our non-existent good reputation do you?" Mary asked.

Jane took a deep breath, "Just because people think we are bad and see it in this case, doesn't mean we should now act the type."

"This is the medieval times, just before the hundred year shift if I presume, people hated anything they didn't understand, I don't think the justice system is as ordered and chaotic as the present… here if you are accused, you died," Denice added, "It's going to be hard, maybe even impossible to clear our names."

Mary disagreed with Denice, "There is no 'maybe' there, it's just impossible, these Dead Crows have been wanting us dead since the day we woke up here, like they know where we're from, so if they are able to get everybody else to hunt us down that just means less work for them."

"Yeah, I don't understand how they know about us, that bit is kind of strange," Jane added.

"Waking up in this place is kind of strange," Mary added.

Denice giggled kicking away a small branch that lay in her way, "I still hope we're going the right way."

Mary sighed, "Denice there is only one road that we've been following, we haven't had to pick and choose which direction to go since the other sign yesterday."

"I was just wondering, maybe some Dead Crows or travelers would have passed by since then."

"They probably use the other routes," Jane suggested, "Not a lot of people think traveling in forests is very wise."

Denice shrugged, "I guess."

It was some time that had passed when Mary heard her stomach growl, she place her hands over it and groaned, "My stomach just reminded me... I'm starving," she announced.

"We all are Mary!" She threw her hands in the air.

Denice took notice of her surroundings and found what she saw very surprising, "Ladies!" She called, "We're in the forest."

"Yeah," Mary nodded, "Thanks for making me aware of that."

"Shh... we can look for food," she suggested with a cheerful smile, "Put our rusty outdoor skills to the test."

"Dead outdoor skills," Mary corrected her.

Jane stopped and turned to face the western side of the forest. She just stared into it, thinking, as it stood still.

The wind started to pick up.

Mary and Denice were concerned with her sudden interest to stare deep into the forest.

Jane continued to stare as if it was some kind of game, she finally opened her mouth, "Hmm, looks scary as hell... but I don't want to die of starvation," she place her hand on her stomach. She sighed, "Let's just do it."

Both Mary and Denice turned to the forest as well.

"Gives that horror movie feel doesn't it?" Mary asked.

Denice nodded, "But that's not real, it's just a bunch of trees that decided to grow together."

"You're right," Jane agreed, "I still know of some foods that can be eaten, let's collect for now and sought it out later," she instructed, "And we should stay close, we don't want anybody getting lost now," she tied up her hair.

"Okay," Mary agreed, "We got no other choice, let's go before I run out of energy," she pulled out her dagger.

After laying down the basic rules and conditions they stepped away from the road and into the forest they went.

It was a few hours of exploring that only attained them quite a small amount of what was edible. They had come across and only picked the basics, which consisted of aggregated fruits and berries, only trusting the ones they could recognize such as rasp, salmon and thimbleberries. Everything else to them was considered poison, since their skills were not as fresh anymore. They remembered more on what the different poisons did than what was actually edible, like wild nuts for example, all of them seemed to have the scent of almonds, which meant that they were extremely dangerous since they contain hydrogen cyanide. Mushrooms or fungi were well out of the picture.

As for the wild life that took residence in this forest, they were impossible to catch with what they had right now, only a dagger and sword as their weapons. It would have worked much more in their favour if they knew they were going to be in this situation and maybe taken a bow and some arrows with.

But that was not the case and every little animal they caught sight of would immediately go into hiding as soon as it spotted them.

It was later that afternoon that their miserable day had come to some light. As they had traveled down, further into the forest, they came across a small river. Not only could this snake of water help them get their food cleaned up and edible, but as soon as they had heard it, realized that they also had a thirst.

Down to the stream they headed and right beside it, dropped their disappointing loot on a rock. The first thing they did without any thought was have some of the water.

It was a fast stream and transparent at the least so they felt it safe to have just enough to keep them going.

Jane was allowing the cold water to pass through her fingers when she caught sight of small fish, about the size of her hand swimming against the current, rendering it stuck in one place as it struggled continuously. It was a bluegill.

The fish was awfully close to her, and as soon as it was spotted she froze, pulled her hands out of the water and kept her eyes locked onto it.

It was a surprise to her that it didn't care for her presence or perhaps didn't notice at all.

She made herself comfortable and slowly moved both her hands over the water, it didn't look too close to the top so this was definitely going to be a challenge.

Mary and Denice didn't notice what she was doing, they were busy by the rock sorting out their scavenged food, separating the scraps from what could actually be eaten.

Jane was very sure that she was going to get soaked no matter what, so her mood was only going to be determined after her attempt.

She took a deep breath and held it in.

This was the moment of truth, between predator and prey.

Crouched and ready, she pounced forward into the water.

Denice was alerted by the loud splashing sound and halted her actions to inspect the noise. Mary was facing her and really confused with what she was up to, with a berry just about to enter her mouth, she just stared.

With about half her body submerged under water, her attempt was a success but still incomplete. Holding the fish tightly between her hands, ensuring that it didn't slip away as it squirmed. She was unable to get up since both her hands were occupied and amidst the struggle and her fast heart, she ran out of breath really quickly.

With some quick thought, she turned to her backside, raised both her hands above the water and cast the fish out onto land before turning around again and lifting herself out for breath.

"Wow," Mary complimented, "You noodled it, you got some skills."

Jane stood up, the top half of her body soaked, "That was luck," she replied, "100% luck, I don't think there was any skill there," she laughed walking over to the fish.

"Congratulation," Denice said.

Mary looked at the berry she was about to eat, then she looked at the fish Jane had in her hand. She turned back to the berry and gave it a sour look before flicking it away. She stood up, "I want fish."

"Yeah," Jane agreed, "I think fish are better... I think there's a slower current up that way," she pointed upstream.

"Clever idea," Denice said, "Let's go check upstream, we can use our swords as spears I guess," she chuckled.

"Yeah, it don't think I can catch a fish with my hands."

Jane found a good spot to sit, a log that had direct light from the sun, "You guys go on ahead, and take this," she handed Denice the fish, "I'll join you in a bit."

Mary and Denice started their walk up the stream. Their spot was still in Jane's sight.

The shirt was really cold due to the wind, even in the sunlight. Wearing a breast band underneath, she unbutton her shirt, took it off and held it up in the sun and wind to help it dry quicker.

Meanwhile, Mary and Denice had found a good spot to start their hunt for fish. It was a wider and more shallow pool of water. They had both removed their boots and socks.

Mary was already in the cold water with her thin sword drawn out. The water was up to her knees so she had her pants folded up just above the knees. Denice was sitting on a small log with her sword drawn, she was sharpening it against another rock to increase her success rate when spearing the fish. The fish Jane had caught lay dead on a rock that she had rinsed with water before placing it.

"You sure you don't want me to sharpen your sword first?" She asked.

"We will swop once that one is sharp," she suggested, "Then you can do mine."

"Oh, so you want to do all the catching?" Denice asked.

"I don't want to do the sharpening," she replied observing the waters carefully.

She stopped sharpening her sword for a moment, "You'd better be catching something if that's the case... don't want to be starving thanks to you."

"Trying to concentrate here," she replied.

Denice continued with her sharpening and kept quiet.

It was a few minutes later when Jane came up to join them, she had left her shirt to dry on the log.

Mary and Denice had already swopped blades by now.

"Any progress?" She asked, standing next to Denice.

"No," she replied, "It's only been a few minutes."

"Yes," Mary agreed, "You could help by surfing up that way."

Jane shook her head, "I'm going into the woods... going to be collecting some wood to build the fire."

Mary shrugged, "Sounds good."

"Don't go too far away," Denice said examining the sword she was sharpening.

"Okay, I'll see you guys later," she turned away and headed into the woods.

About an hour had passed since Jane had started collecting for the fire. Her twig pile and grown quite big, placing her findings next to the rock that carried their dinner. She was not done yet though, now she was to begin her search for larger wood and dead branches to keep the fire going for a much longer period of time.

Their current position near the river ensured that they wouldn't get lost in this forest as the river itself was parallel to the road.

Finding the larger wood and dead branches was a more challenging task to execute, they lay at random places, sometimes hiding in the grass or bushes, and a lot of the trees stood quite tall to reach, so it was clear she had to expand her search radius.

Another hour had passed and she was now satisfied with her salvage. The wind had begun to settle a bit and the sky started to dim itself. It was late in the afternoon and probably the best time to join up with the others and see their progress.

She headed back up the river first with both her arms filled with dead branches and small logs. It was some time but she made it back to the stream, but not at the place they were fishing at, it had seemed she had travelled a little too far south.

Taking a deep breath, her sights turned south, spotting something that startled her. She froze in her tracks.

It was some kind of creature, sipping away by the river.

It was deer.

This would have been a good catch if the situation was different, but with her hands full and legs weary from the circles she'd been walking, all she wanted was a closer look at the creature, so she turned to it steadily and started towards it silently.

The sneaking and remaining under the volume of nature around her was quite hard and even more tiring. Her progress was great, she could see it quite clearly from where she was. It wasn't enough, she now wanted to see how close she could get to it.

With her eyes locked on the target, she was unable to take notice of anything else, and that's where the problem started, that gave her away. In her arms, one of the logs she was carrying had slipped out and landed on the ground quite loudly.

She froze as soon as it hit the ground, hoping that the deer wouldn't care or notice, but it had the sharpest ears and was startled.

It looked up at her for a few moments and began to trot in the opposite direction.

"Ugh, bloody log," she was disappointed at her loss and started up in the opposite direction, going back up to the fishing area.

The trip back was easy, stopping on the way to get her shirt. Turned out she was not as far as she thought. Back at the spot, she found there was no one.

She place the wood next to the twig pile and scanned the area for any sign of them. Their shoes were gone which meant that they had left intentionally.

Their catch wasn't at all that bad, five fish. And all about the same size lay on the rock.

"Mary!" She called, "Denice?!"

No one responded.

"Oh my… now I have to look for them," She murmured to herself.

Jane headed up the stream for a short while before calling their names out again, but again there was no response.

"Mary!" She called again, a little louder.

In the distance just behind her she heard another faint voice, "Over here!"

It was Mary.

Jane sighed in relief, just as she was about to start worrying. She turned and hurried off in the direction of her voice.

She could see them standing in the distance right beside each other in an open space of the woods.

"Guys what are you doing just standing here?"

They didn't respond.

They seemed to be stolen away by something.

Jane jogged up to them and almost freaked at the sight of what they were glaring at.

Her face turned disgusted, "What is that?"

They were staring at a statue that looked like some kind of shrine. It was of a bold man standing, covered in long robes, holding a large flat bowl in both hands. The man wore a necklace consisting of bones, mainly the jaws and teeth. The bowl that he carried was filled with blood, aged and thick on the surface, consisting of dark and lighter shades of red. The ground around this statue was dead with bone, different kinds of skulls, some crushed and scattered all over. The dead grass was as well stained in dry red.

Mary shrugged, "I don't know, I'm guessing it's a shrine."

"Yes," Denice agreed with uncertainty, "Now I'm afraid of this majestic place."

"Who would do this," Jane took a step closer, examining the bones on the ground, "Some of these are human," she pointed out.

Jane turned her attention to the statue and notice that it was wearing some kind of crown, but that didn't interest her as much as the small marking that was on the man's forehead. It was a symbol of some kind of eye, marked with illusion patterns and small spikes around it.

She stepped away as soon as the smell became too strong to bear.

She started noticing the symbol everywhere, marked on the skulls that lay in the grass.

"What is that symbol?" She pointed it out, "Any of you seen it before?"

Both of them declined.

"I think we should leave," Jane suggested.

"No need to repeat yourself there," Denice agreed.

"We will make camp closer to the road, far away from whatever this thing is."

They headed back to the river and collected their catch and firewood. Denice saw it useful to also get the fruits they had collected.

Near the road, they found a great place which they would be able to spend the night. In their current case, setting up camp just meant that they built the fire and found a place with soft ground to sit.

Ever since their little visit to the shrine, night time had decided to come upon them rather quickly.

The fire had already been started and was now their only source of light, flickering in the darkness. They had gathered some stones and placed them around the wood to prevent it from spreading and setting the forest a light.

All three of them had gathered closely around the flames, simmering their dinner over the fire. They were glad to be set for the night and morning.

"Night time is the worst," Denice said looking around into the darkness, "And especially in the forest."

"What do you mean," May asked, "I'm sure you also spent all those school trips camping and learning about the wilds."

"Yeah, I'm still no friend of the night, and those camping trips were spent with other people, and instructors... it's just us here."

Jane joined in, "Yeah I remember them as well... they were fun before the teenage years began, after that, I didn't want anything to do with the wilderness."

Mary nodded, "But it was compulsory for everyone," she took a deep breath, "I never thought I'd say this but, it sure did pay off... for us at least."

"I still wonder why we did so many camping trips, they taught us everything about the wilds and how to survive as if we were going to live there," Jane said turning her fish around.

Denice heard an annoying sound buzzing just around his ear, she swatted it away, "Mosquitoes!"

Mary laughed, "Just relax Denice, we going to get bit, don't fight it."

"They are just annoying, sometimes I just wish that they would just bite me and be on their way, not hang around my ear."

Jane giggle and changed the topic of camping, "You remember in history, when we were taught that magic was evil and the reason for every war that ever happened, so the leaders decided to ban it's use?"

Mary nodded, "Yeah I remember"

"Is the war still going to happen?" she asked, "The one that finally ends the use of magic, because I still see people using it... that Dead Crow in that abandoned village and I'm sure there will be magic in the city we're going to."

The both shrugged.

"Try not to dwell on it," Denice suggested, "It'll just confuse you."

Jane took that advice, "You're right, I guess history is a tale we have to believe, not being physically there you know, maybe trips to museums and shrines would've have done us better."

"Thanks for the heads up Jane," Denice sighed, "Now I have that image in my head again, that shrine was creepy, the stuff out of horrors."

Jane sighed, "Those were just movies... I don't think anything is going to show up," she too started to scan the area, she didn't trust her own words.

"Those movies were mostly driven by witchcraft and guess what, we're in a place of witchcraft."

"Denice please," Mary stopped her, "I don't want to think about it, we going to have enough trouble dealing with these insects, I don't want anything else to deal with when I'm trying to sleep."

"Sorry," she apologized.

Later, after consuming their rations for the night, they left their other fish on small sticks to prevent them from soiling.

It was their plan to fall asleep while the fire was still very much alive to make the drifting better. And it worked, after their long day of scavenging had now come to an end, they were exhausted and no effort was needed to go into a deep sleep.

"Wake up," a faint voice sounded, as if from a far.

"Wake up."

This time the voice was much closer.

Jane slowly opened her eyes to meet Denice's, her face was right above hers.

"Finally, you're awake," she stood up.

Jane sluggishly sat up and gave her back a good stretch, "What time is it?"

"Morning time," Denice replied.

Jane place her hand around the back of her neck and tried to click it. She looked around and saw no sign of Mary, "Where's Mary?"

"Oh, she's by the river, getting a little clean, she already ate," She explained, "You should too, we must start moving as soon as possible, we can't afford to waste any energy."

Denice had started another fire and warmed up Jane's fish. She handed it over to her.

Jane looked at it with concern.

Denice noticed her expression and smiled, "It doesn't look as appetizing in the light I know, but it's still edible... it's all we have, including the berries we found yesterday."

Jane broke off a piece and put it in her mouth, she chewed the contents slowly.

"The faster you eat the better," Denice suggested, "I'm going down to the river as well, I'll see you there if you're quick," she was off.

It was easy for them to continue with their journey, with nothing to pack or carry but themselves. It was the only perk they had.

The morning wasn't too harsh in terms of weather, the sun wasn't there thanks to the trees but the morning breeze wasn't a freezer.

Jane, being the last one to wake up, was still busy tying up her hair whilst they made their way onto the path.

Mary was tired of her repetitive surroundings, "I hope we make it out of this infestation today," she said grumpily, "I'm sick of the sight of trees all around me."

Denice chuckled, "This forest that you hate so much is our source of food, what do you think is going to happen once we make it out and it's nothing but plains everywhere?"

Mary shrugged, she kicked away a wooden stick, "I don't think this path ends."

Their morning was all silent and grumpy for most of its part, it was only around about midday that their fortunes decided to take a turn.

They still continued on the forest road, an infinite path with no end. And at this time, the hunger had started to sink in again.

"Guys, I think this is going to become a part of our daily routine," Mary broke the silence, "I'm hungry again,"

"If only we had some kind of container which we could use to store some of our food, that could be very helpful," Denice said.

Jane stopped and turned to them, "Do you still have the berries from this morning?" she asked Denice.

The problem of having to deal with hunger had made them stray from their primary task of reaching the city. Walking the whole day really did take its toll on them, it consumed quite a lot of energy.

It took a while for Denice to react to the question Jane had asked, she just smiled from cheek to cheek and slowly shook her head.

Jane turned to disappointment, "I really don't want to do this again."

Mary acted all surprised when Denice shook her head, "Great, you ate all that we had instead of keeping it for a time like this," she placed her hands on her hips and started to giggle, "We never going to get to the city are we?"

Denice became a little defensive, "There was no place to put the food… I'd like to remind you that we've got nothing."

This was all new to them, for people who haven't really had been a day without anything to consume, this was a real challenge that they faced.

"We going to make it to the city, we would just have to skip the fishing part, because wasting half the day looking for food is getting us nowhere," Jane said, looking into the forest.

Mary stood there, thinking of a way out of this, she shook her head, "I got nothing."

"How did we get into this situation?" Denice asked, "We have nothing."

This situation was really weighing a bit on their shoulders, since their arrival into this timeline, they have made it by doing small jobs and earning enough to get by. Now, suddenly, by the will of misfortune, they were with nothing and now hunted down by the Dead Crow… though this was the case from the beginning, now it had gone a bit too far since the accusation that pointed right at them.

Jane took a deep breath, "We need to make it their as soon as possible… I don't know how fast news travels or how long it takes for the posters to be made, but I'm sure our faces will be on notice boards all around."

A few seconds passed, and thanks to their little silent thought session, they were able to catch the sound of something nearby approaching them.

Mary turned back, "What is that?"

They all listened quietly.

"Sounds like-," Jane couldn't decide.

Mary interrupted her thoughts, "Galloping," she whispered as her face lit up.

As the galloping drew near, Mary suggested that they hid behind the trees.

They scurried away and waited there quietly.

Their guess was right, the sound was of a horse galloping along the path.

Jane couldn't get a good look at the rider, "Who is it?" She whispered aloud.

Denice watched as the horse approached, she gasped, "It's a Dead Crow."

Mary disagreed with her, "No, it's our lucky day… let's stop him."

"What!?" Jane blurted out, right before she covered her mouth.

It was too late, Mary had made herself visible by stepping out from behind the tree and into the road.

Jane's attempt at stopping her was unsuccessful, so she and Denice had no choice but to join her and back her up in whatever crazy idea she had.

The horse slowed to a trot and finally stopped a few metres in front of them.

It was quite the stared down for only a moment, before the Dead Crow agent decided to speak, and really cheerfully, "Hey! It's you three," he recognized them, "How has it been?"

The greeting was…odd. Why was this agent giving them the warmest of welcomes. None of them felt the need to give it to him in return.

"You know who we are?" Jane asked.

He gasped in disbelief, "How could I forget, off course I know you three, we were about to kill you for murder before you played that little magic trick of yours and put us all to sleep," he explained.

It seemed he was one of the agents involved in the confrontation that took place three days ago.

Denice tried to clear their names, "We didn't murder those agents, they tried to assassinate us in our sleep."

The agent laughed, "Oh! It seems my facts are a little muddled up, was it you who killed them or did they kill you?" He asked.

It was hopeless, but worth a shot. But it seemed all of them acted in this manner.

None of them answered that question, knowing full well that he too knew the answer.

"So-so, I'm not wrong?" he started acting surprised, "For a second there I thought I was wrong."

Mary didn't like this man's tone, it made her upset.

The agent rubbed his chin, "Assassinate," he giggled, "I wonder why we would want to assassinate."

Jane had to try to get something out of this man, "Why are you trying to kill us."

"You guys are murders!" He shouted, "I thought you already knew that."

"No!" Jane raised her voice, "This is not the first time this has happened, you have attempted before."

"Oh?" he looked at them with concern, "So this isn't the first time you've killed?"

Jane's patience was being tested, this reminded her of the little girl in the wardrobe that she had to bury because of those sadistic agents, "You will speak,"

"Or you will die," the agent said, "Was that the next part of your sentence?" he looked at them with disgust, "You guys really do find it enjoyable killing us...tell me, is that how all of them died, interrogation?"

Denice could see there was no getting through to this man, he was just as crazy as the other agents they have encountered.

Again, they did not embrace that question with an answer.

The agent then came to a realization, "Oh, ladies, before I forget, I have something to show you," he jumped off his horse.

They were alerted immediately.

The agent looked at them with concern, "You not going to get all murderous now are you? I just want to give you something," he started looking through a pouch hanging from the horses saddle.

After his little search while the ladies waited, he pulled out some papers. He held them up.

These were wanted posters, with their faces on them.

Now this agent was just rubbing it in, "They have been sent to many other towns and cities, I'm going to Marridor," he smiled at them, "Or maybe you turn yourselves in or let me kill you," he laid down the options, "Most people don't defy the Dead Crow."

The posters were a horrible turn, this was definitely going to make life increasingly hard, much harder than the petty struggle they had been going through the past couple of days. Their faces on every notice board in every town, and now this agent says he is heading straight to Marridor with them. Was this a stroke of luck?

"I'm joking, I know I can't do much in this situation," he walked up to them.

Mary was ready to act if he was to make any sudden movements, she had her dagger out, gripped tightly in her right hand. She was really angry inside and trying hard to keep it in.

The Dead Crow agent was unsure about his approach, but he did it anyway, "Here's one for you," he handed to Mary a wanted poster of her.

She grabbed, keeping eye contact with the agent.

He stepped aside handing to Jane, her one. Her mind was filled with all the motivation to stop this man right now, without having any kind of regrets.

The agent didn't step over to Denice, he had something to say, "I have something else for you," he smiled.

Mary could see the dagger with the marked runes hiding under his cloak, thanks to her observation, she knew what it was that he had for her friend.

The agent pulled out his dagger, but it was too late for him to do anything, Mary had swiftly used hers at a moment's notice and drove it into his neck, in from the side and let go of the dagger.

Jane's reaction was a little late, she jumped back.

Mary remained quiet, she sighed and began to tap her forehead, closing her eyes.

The Dead Crow fell to his knees and dropped his dagger, he held the dagger stuck in his lower neck, his mouth filling up with blood and in his last moments, he chuckled, "I'm dying," he uttered, "You win...you-you saw that coming," he coughed, "enjoy your bounty filled lives," He fell to the ground, lifeless.

Jane turned away from the dead body and looked at Mary, "Thanks... you saved me."

Mary took a deep breath and shook her head, "Never mind that," she was trapped in her mind, this was another Dead Crow dead. The only viable reason for his death would only be known to them, this will be just seen as a murder, but the real question now had arisen. She looked at her wanted poster. *Did I just kill a man who was just doing his job?*

She brushed it off as something that she didn't want to answer, "We've bought ourselves a few days of freedom, that's what matters now, let's utilize it as best as we can," she folded her poster and walked over to the horse.

Mary found some food on it and consumed it with Jane and Denice for lunch. They kept just a little for later."

"Did you find anything on him?" Mary asked searching through the other pouches on the saddle.

Denice shook her head, "Nothing, just a compass and the watch list again," she took notice of the dagger that he had dropped and picked it up. She brought it to her face and examined the markings.

Jane was busy petting the horse.

Mary noticed Denice in her carelessness, "Denice!" She shouted.

Denice was startled by her tone and turned to her, "Huh?"

Mary stomped up to her, "Don't touch that, it's got some kind of poison on it."

She dropped it.

Mary picked it up by the handle, "Didn't you see what happened to the mattress in the inn? I don't know what it is but watch this," she walked up to the nearest tree.

Even Jane stopped to see what Mary was about to do.

She place the knife against the bark of the tree and gave it a cut, applying whatever poison that was on the dagger, "See."

The cut slowly turned black and spread a certain radius, making the poisoned region look decayed.

Mary flung it into the forest, "These people are dangerous."

Denice stepped closer and examined the decaying part of the tree, it had a sharp smell too, "What do you think happens to a human cut with this?"

"Don't have that kind of curiosity Denice," Jane said, "Let's leave the madness to them... anyways, did you get anything on the horse."

"Just wanted posters, food and more wanted posters," she replied.

Denice looked at the horse and came to notice a slight problem, "Guys... there's three of us."

Jane was unsure about what Denice was talking about, "Yes," she dragged it out.

"And one horse," she made it a little clear.

"Ugh," Mary looked up at the sky, "We won't be moving any fast than we were, the horse can only seat two at best."

Ultimately for them, being able to buy themselves a few days of freedom was good, but were those few days given to them going to be spent making their way to the city? If that was the case, nothing had changed at all, all they had now was a bit of food to keep them going for the day and a horse that they now had to take care of. There was no doubt, word of the death of this Dead Crow agent would go unnoticed. And who is to say that the latest newspaper addition won't come with the posters, just to help spread the news of these new criminals much faster.

They spent some time in that very same place, trying to break out of their position, it was starting to look like their life of poverty was just beginning. No criminal can become a bounty hunter or help the community without being hunted themselves by other bounty hunters and Dead Crows. There wasn't a way to get out of it since it was the Dead Crow who initially started this feud, and if it's the laws doing, then you cannot expect to get out of it.

Sometimes waiting can bring upon some good to a very bad situation, and in their case, it happened.

In the distance, again they heard another gallop, another horse was heading in their direction. Again they decided to hide away behind the trees, and this time, their presence was not needed to put the rider to a stop. It was another agent.

"It would seem that today is delivery day," Denice whispered.

"Lucky day," Mary replied, "Now we have two horses," she searched for her dagger but could not find it on herself. She realized it was still stuck in the neck of its first victim.

Jane was not going to take any chances this time, the first agent almost killed her. She pulled out her sword, "Let's just hope this is another flunky, we won't be able to deal with him if he can use magic."

The agent slowed to a stop in front of the stray horse.

This was their time to show themselves again. They came out, weapons drawn and stood between him and his comrade.

The agent remained silent, only shifting his sights from the girls to the horse, then his comrade, he continued on in silence.

Jane found it strange he had not given them some sought of greeting, "Are you going to say something?" She asked.

He took a deep breath, "I'm just surprised... not once, since my employment, have I ever heard of a person take the life of an agent... not once," he gave some thought, "Although, I did hear of a murder that took place in the inn of the previous town, I was told to watch out for... three ladies..." he looked at them, "Three ladies..."

"Are you delivering more wanted posters?" Mary asked.

"Oh, so that's why you killed that man, just for doing his job?"

"No, he tried to kill us, like many of the other agents," Mary replied.

"So... he was still doing his job?"

Mary could not answer that, it just made her feel a little guilty just thinking about it.

This one was not as crazy, he just continued on as a normal person would, something Jane immediately picked up from him, probably because she was expecting something messed up to leave his mouth.

"If it makes you feel any better," he smiled, "I'm not delivering wanted posters, it's something a little more important than that," he glanced over at the body, "You ladies have only bought yourselves a few days, and I'm going to report this crime to my superiors," he explained, "Though I do have a suggestion."

They remained silent and listened, this was the first normal conversation they were having with a Dead Crow.

"I am running a bit late and I don't want to get into any kind of trouble, so why don't you just let me kill you and I'll be on me way," he smiled, "If you think about it, it's not half bad, I'm saving you before your lives become unbearable... either way, we were trained not to retreat so I'm not leaving you, this world is in need of a little justice."

It all sunk away, though this man was calmer than the rest, his mind was still on the side of insanity. That is, however, to them, being the ones given the opportunity to be executed before things become really hard.

Jane decided on a different approach, "Why aren't you afraid?"

"I've faced many scum, murderers, thieves, kidnappers in my life as a Dead Crow, in the end, every different face that I've met has been the same, they all have fear, regret… and only care for their own lives, this is off course when they meet with an agent," he explained, "They know not to defy us, they know what we did, which is why seeing someone in my uniform dead doesn't make sense… have you forgotten what we did?"

None of them could give an answer to that. For once, they actually started to really feel they were in the wrong.

"Why did your friends try to assassinate us?" Jane asked, "I know you know something about this."

He took a deep breath, "This is getting nowhere, answering questions with questions… I'm not sanctioned to speak about anything to do with the Dead Crow, such a thing is punishable by death, we receive orders and jobs and execute them, so I ask again about the offer I gave you."

Mary shook her head, "That's not happening, we've done nothing wrong."

"Hmm," he sniffed, "Hard to believe."

Jane started to get impatient, "Who's your leader, we know you know something."

He jumped of his horse and pulled out his dagger, "We know everything…but that's the test," he sniffed his dagger, "I'll expect some resistance then?" he raised his eye brows, "But I do give warning, my package is really important, it is supposed to be delivered to the Maithindor and Ghordiitry house in Marridor…a tribute, not that you know what I'm talking about, if you know what I mean," he smiled, "I strongly advise you let me kill you now."

This agent was questioning every decision they were faced with. Did he know they were from another time? This was really getting to them, but now that their children were in this mess as well, things had to be done, even if they did not like it.

Jane's hand was shaking, unsure of herself anymore as this man took slow steps towards them. Once again, stuck and unable to think or come to a decision.

The next few moments caught them off guard.

The agent stopped, "I've come to a decision, since you three are trapped in your own minds," he started, "Take the horse," he smiled, "and everything on it, you would be able to make it to the city before your posters go up, and the tribute, is enough for a long time."

Jane was thrown into the ocean, her mind floated in the most confusing part of the sea. He was giving them everything they needed. Trapped in this state of mind, she just kept silent and let more unfold.

"Unfortunately, letting you go means a bad ending," he place the edge of his dagger onto the palm of his other hand, "For me off course," he gave it a small cut, and held it up for them to see as the poison started to spread, "It's the end for me," he smiled, dropping the dagger and taking a walk into the woods.

Jane, Mary and Denice could only watch. What they felt now was remorse, there was just one other thing that got to them. Why? They did not understand at all. Why would this man take his own life?

As they watched him take his little stroll, there was a moment where he just stood still and took a deep breath, as if free of something, but at the same time he was just about to die.

Jane couldn't watch anymore, this was not right. She walked up to the other horse. Mary and Denice decided not to see it through as well.

For a moment, it was as if all the sounds of nature had gone silent, as if they knew what was happening.

"What is this tribute he spoke about?" Denice asked.

"A lot of money," Jane replied, "Gold coins," she checked the other bags on the saddle, "Bags of gold."

"What!" Mary had to see for herself, "No way."

Denice looked into the woods again, looking for the man but he wasn't there anymore, the poison had done it's work, "Can we leave now."

Jane and Mary didn't hear her.

"Who do you think this house of Maithindor and Ghordiitry is?" Jane asked.

Mary shrugged, "But judging by this, they must be very important people."

Denice spoke a little louder, "I think we have to leave."

Mary looked into the woods, "I think you're right."

Jane had never witnessed such a thing in her life before, she did not know how to react to any of this, it was clear that they knew nothing about what was happening around them. There was a lot that they still needed to understand about all this. Why was it that these agents of the Dead Crow acted in this way?

"At least horse riding was part of our little camp trips," Jane giggle, trying to take her mind off everything she did not understand.

Denice nodded, "Yes, those were fun."

Mary stopped looking at the gold, "We got these last few days to stock up on everything we need."

Jane got onto the horse that carried all the money whilst Mary and Denice climbed onto the other one. This day had brought some fortune to them and a lot more on the table, but now was the time to make haste and find their way to the magic city, Marridor.

They rode for a about a day, arriving at the southern gate of Marridor the very next day at noon. After dropping off their horses they made their way to the gate. The bags of coin they had, were to be carried all the way. Since they were just visitors to the city, their cavalry was not allowed within the walls.

They made their way down the main road, Mary and Jane being the ones to carry a bags of gold, bringing it all with them was the only way to ensure safety.

"Hmm, pretty gate," Denice complimented.

Jane agreed, "Magical spheres are a nice touch."

As it was daytime, not much was asked of them at the gate, only welcomed as travelers just passing by, and to their luck, nobody recognized them.

"Enjoy your visit to the city," one of the guards welcomed them as they passed through the main gate.

In return they just bowed their heads in respect.

And as for first timers to the city, they were not impressed by the view they met as soon as they were on the other side of the wall. Like most of the people visiting for the first time.

"Impressive...I guess," Denice was let down. She looked into the distance, "Ooh, and there's a cute little village up ahead as well."

Jane pointed up ahead, "There's another wall beyond that, must be where the city is."

Mary picked up her pace, "Let's get going, it's been a day since we stopped the delivery man, we should get everything we need today, posters might show up any day from now."

Jane and Denice hurried over to her.

"No touring then?" Denice asked.

Mary shrugged, "I guess today could be that day, we are going shopping after all."

"If I'm not mistaken, this is the city that has been restricted by the government in the present right?" Jane asked.

"Yup," Denice replied, "Some base of operation... it's rumored that it's the only place where magic is still used."

They were somewhat nervous as they walked passed the small village, not because of the amount of gold in their bags, but in fear that they would be recognized by someone, they felt watched.

The real problem began when they passed through the entrances into the Market District, within all the beauty in everything they saw, from the shops, to the goods and fashion worn by the locals, they spotted a lot of Dead Crow agents, posted everywhere, the mages, regulars and rooftop archers.

It was packed, as usual so they were not the centre of attention, despite the fact that they were travelers, which was also very common, from visitors, the poorer and bounty hunters.

Unfortunately, being criminals, it was not relaxing to be around so many agents, even though unidentified yet, they had been around enough to know how unpredictable they can be.

"Well, let's go shopping, ladies," Mary declared.

Denice took a deep breath, spotting each agent around her, "Some actual fun at last," she replied with uncertainty, "though things may be a little outdated, the culture here is very diverse."

"Yes, but first we will need to gather us some essentials, travelers gear and weapons," she said, making her way through the crowds, "Since we are stuck in this time, might as well become a part of it now."

They made it out of the main street and were met by more that were not as crowded.

Jane looked down at her attire, it was not too pleasant, same went for Mary and Denice, "We need new clothing as well."

"Certainly," Denice agreed.

They picked a random street to start with their window shopping, every shop seemed to do with everything magic. Most of the things they saw were out of their understanding, alchemy shops were quite common, each of them selling potions and ingredients of a large variety, most under specified categories. Fashion was diverse and unique, most of the shops were tailored and then there were shops selling staves to those able to use them.

"Wow," Denice pointed through a window, "What are these cubes for, they so colourful"

"Come on guys, we need to ask around for directions to some non-magical shops," Mary suggested, "We don't have all day."

They started to scan the area for the city guards. They were everywhere as well, looking more approachable, some standing awfully close to the feared agents, communicating with them. Now it was just a matter of finding a guard that was away from the others, or make things easier and ask any random person.

"I'm glad we haven't been noticed yet," Denice whispered, "I guess it was only the ones sent to kill us that knew our faces."

Jane nodded slowly, lost in her own thoughts.

Denice decide to detach from them and ask around for some directions.

Mary and Jane didn't notice her departure, they just stood in their places looking around, spotting every agent.

"There's a lot more of the magic ones here," Jane pointed out.

Mary nodded, "This is the most dangerous place to be."

Nearby, on the corner of one of the streets, there was a gathering of people listening to someone else, standing on a higher level, speaking about something. He also had a notice board behind him.

"We know nothing about magic," Jane said, "if they find out about us here, we're dead."

Mary looked up and saw another archer patrolling the rooftops, "Security is tight."

Another lady, in black witches attire, passing by overheard her and decided to speak to them, "They increased it by a lot," she said.

Both Jane and Mary listened.

"Why so many," Mary asked.

"Oh, you a traveler... well, let me give you a bit of insight as to what's happening here," she started, "over a month ago, they came to this city, looking for some criminals that stole some very valuable things and threatened the life of a Dead Crow, they have been searching for these thieves ever since," she cleared her throat, "It's like the palace district where those families live."

"Which families?" Jane asked.

"The Maithindor and Ghordiitry off course, who else would have a palace in this city," she frowned at them, "But don't raise any suspicion, they are everywhere."

"Thank you," said Jane.

"Happy to help," she smiled walking off.

The names popped up again, the two families that they had now apparently stolen from. Now the question was *How famous are these people and what part do they play?*

"I'm afraid now," Jane whispered to Mary, "Who did we steal from exactly?"

Mary shrugged in return, "The agent did technically give us the money, if we are ever caught, we can just say that."

"But he's dead."

Mary took a deep breath, "You are creating problems that don't exist yet, right now, whoever they are, they don't know who we are."

"I know where we must go!" Denice announced, putting her arms around them.

"What?" Jane turned to her, "What are you talking about?"

"We were lost...," she looked at them, eyebrows to her forehead, "I went to go look for directions..."

They both just looked at her.

"Ugh, just follow me," she led the way, "And from what I hear, this place is pretty good and fancy."

They headed to another street, one with a lot less potions and staves in it. Denice led them to a shop called The Adventurer's Journal.

The name was in a large, gold, fancy font, with a small book and quill carved image next to it.

The shops interior was much larger than expect, aisle after aisle of clothing and other goods. Standing behind a counter at the other end of the store was a short, bald, black man. He walked around the counter toward them as soon as they entered the shop.

"Afternoon lovely ladies, I'm Willard," he gave a small bow, "Is there something you need me to help you with?"

They exchanged glances.

"Um, everything...I guess," Jane replied.

The owner of the shop treated them with great value, showing them everything that they needed. It was first in terms of attire and what they would need as travelers.

His variety, even of female clothing seemed endless, so Jane, Mary and Denice could pick to serve for their particular tastes.

After the picking and fitting was done, they had all concluded with their very own light weight adventurer's outfits. Something that was easy to move in and breathe, short hooded cloaks were also included.

Next, the owner showed them to the other essentials that they needed with them, including their own rucksacks to carry their goods in which came with sleeping rolls. A compass and map was also part of some of the essentials needed to survive and navigate the wilds, which they had known nothing about.

"We were also wondering if you would help us with weapons?" Mary enquired.

"Gladly."

The hunt for suitable weapons was not as long as the clothing one. Willard helped them pick out the best broadswords, the lightest and amongst the thinner, for better handling. Their current ones could now be disposed of. They also picked out new daggers.

For hunting, our party had confessed to being bad when it came to using the bow and arrow. It was not a problem for Willard, he introduced them to a completely new type of mechanical weapon, small and compatible and attachable to a gauntlet.

"This is what I like to call the Gauntlet Crossbow," he took and showed it to them, "Put it on," he gave it Jane.

Jane strapped it around her arm.

Willard held her arm and began to explain how it worked, "As you see here on top, if you press this button these two metal pieces will pull back and stick out," he demonstrated, "Now it looks like a smaller version of your average crossbow."

They were impressed by this clever contraption.

Willard pick a bolt and loaded it onto the crossbow, "Now all you have to do is aim and fire, by pressing this button again to release the bolt."

Jane held up her arm and rested her head on her shoulder. She closed one eye to better focus on what she was aiming at, "Where can I test it out?"

Willard showed them to an archery target.

Jane aimed at it and used her other hand to press the button and released the bolt.

Mary went to see how far the bolt went into the target, "It's powerful," she confirmed.

They all took one each and purchased quite a number of the bolts.

The last few things they bought were gloves and leather shoulder blades before giving thanks to the owner for assisting them and leaving the store.

Their Gauntlet Crossbows and bolts were stored in their rucksacks. Now that they were done shopping, they looked more like travelers than when they walked in, surviving in the wilds was not going to be a poverty stricken activity anymore. And the cost for all their new things was not that pricey, that or their money they had as plentiful, they still had both bags, only one was a little lighter than the other.

It was certain they had spent a lot of time in this shop, the day was dim and time for them to gather a bit of information. They were directed to the library.

It was a few minutes, but they made it. First thing they did was head to the front counter with some queries. Their first look at the library sacked away all motivation to start searching themselves.

They stood in front of one of the ladies.

"Afternoon," she greeted, "How may I be of service?"

"Um...," Jane felt unsure about it but it was this or the endless shelves, "Do you have any history books about the Dead Crow?"

She nodded in return, "I'll show what we have."

"And, is there any way we could enter the school... just to visit someone?" Mary asked.

"No," she replied, "Ever since the Dead Crow arrived, no one has been allowed in or out of the school," she made her way around the counter.

Jane was not sure whether this meant that they were safe or not, being in the school but surrounded by all these Dead Crows. It was certain that they would not be able to find out now, or see them for that matter whilst they were free.

The librarian lead them to a section of the library that had what they were looking for, history books. She never specified which book was where so they had to start searching, at least the radius was greatly lessened.

Jane started reading titles on the higher shelves. One of them was close, titled : Fall of The Crow.

Mary searched the lower shelves.

Denice decided it was best to disappear again, after a while, something of interest caught her eye.

"This is not helping," Mary closed shut a book and seated herself at the closest table to Jane's investigation shelf, "None of these give us origins or the leaders of this group."

Jane agreed, "I thought maybe we might find something in this labyrinth."

"All of this stuff is just about them saving the world," she sighed, "the only way I see us figuring out anything is if we interrogate one of them, or find this old man, maybe he might know something."

Jane picked up one of the books on the table, "You may be right... but that would mean we deserve to have those bounties."

"Do we deserve to be stuck in this place?"

Jane shrugged.

"Off course not, and I don't think we can save ourselves from this," she started staking the books, "The Dead Crow is coming for us with the intent to kill, we have to retaliate with equal force if we want to live," she lowered her voice.

Jane did not reply, she just stared at one of the symbols on a book she chose.

Mary stood next to her, "This is not some tour anymore, we have to survive, and that means doing whatever it takes."

Jane nodded, "We're in big trouble... you heard that lady, the whole city hunting a few criminals that threatened the life of a Dead Crow... we've killed seven."

"Yeah...and there's no going back now," Mary said picking up a book and returning it to the shelf.

I guess it is true what they say about survival, it always comes down to the host doing something he or she never thought they would ever do, Jane thought. Right now, these three had to become outlaws, people who would have to steal and hide away from their pursuers to survive. Nothing that they ever asked for, but now something that they had to do, and in a world they did not understand at all.

While they were returning the books back to their 'rightful' places, Denice returned to them.

"There you are," she said.

Mary turned to her, "Leaving us to search ourselves."

Denice ignored her, "Follow me, I have something that I must show you."

They left, leaving the few books still laying on table, and followed Denice all the way to the front. She lead them to the notice section where the board was and showed them something that put them in complete shock.

"What's this now," Jane took a step closer.

It was the wanted posters of James, Mark and Daniel.

Mary began to worry, "I thought they were at the school... safe," she started breathing unevenly.

"I-I don't understand... Jake was supposed to-," Jane was stopped by Denice.

"Jane, Mary, calm yourself," Denice whispered, "We cannot show that we know these people, there are bounty hunters and other ears around."

"You can't expect-,"

"Shh," Denice silenced her, "Right now, all we can do is watch, we're in the city, surrounded," she whispered, "I'm sorry, but that's what we must do."

Jane's face was blank, she did not know what to think now. At first, the only problem that was present was them and the fact that their faces were on wanted posters, now this pops up. She could hear her heart race and feel her blood boil, the Dead Crow had now gone a bit too far.

A bounty hunter came up next to her, "New posters," he said, "and all youngsters with high bounties...Well," he took a deep breath, "I know who I'm hunting."

Jane gave him a sour look, knowing there was nothing she could do about this. Everyone like him will now be looking to hunt them down.

"Better go get myself a copy," he left.

Mary pushed Denice aside, "What are they accused for?" She looked at the description.

> *This boy is charged for stealing a very*
> *Valuable item from the Dead Crow. Warning :*
> *He and his friends are very dangerous.*

"Stealing?" Mary repeated, "What did they steal?"

Denice shrugged, "No idea, it's not mentioned on any of their posters," she pointed at another poster among them that read, "Mia Milmoure."

"What's her deal?" Mary asked, "Did she get mixed up with this?"

"Maybe," Denice replied, "But look at her bounty, it's four times greater than theirs."

In the distance the librarian announced, "The library will be closing in five minutes."

"Does this mean they're not in the city?" Mary asked, "With all these agents everywhere."

Denice heard the librarian, "We'll talk later, the library is about to close, I saw an inn just outside the market district."

Denice was right, this was not the right place to speak about anything, anywhere with people was a bad idea.

They stepped outside just before the doors closed, the sun had appeared from behind the clouds, but it was too late, nightfall was near and its presence not needed anymore.

Out the market district they went, just beyond the walls. Denice lead them to an inn she had spotted on their way into the market district. Right now, their only hope was to not repeat the incident that occurred in Lonestar.

Denice pushed open the doors and they stepped into a warm and welcoming place filled with people.

Standing at the door, they looked around for a place which they could sit and eat and that's when Jane saw it.

A familiar face.

The face of a man that is probably to blame for all this.

Jake Mauntell.

CHAPTER 17

The Black River

On the horizon, far to the east of the world, the sun had just begun to peek over the distant mountains and fill the world with light. It was finally time for all the creatures of the night to burrow away from the light of day and rest till the sun disappeared again. The morning was quite cloudy, but not completely, the sky was still visible in some spots. The wind blew gentle but cold.

This was the morning of our young parties departure from the city of magic. They had long since passed the main road through the forest, after which they took Galvani's advice to stay away from the roads and rely solely on the map and compass which they now possessed.

At this point they found themselves surrounded by small hills and giant rocks, one or two taking the form of caves or just small shelters, a plain of yellow grass which stood up to their ankles.

A weary morning it was, having received no rest since the night day before, their current goal now was to just get as far as they could from the city in case of any search parties. Off course this took some of its toll on them and Mark as usual had something to say about it.

"Guys," he called, dragging his feet, "At first I thought this was a good idea," he sighed.

"What are you talking about?" Daniel asked, who was just a few metres ahead from him.

"We didn't get any sleep," He replied, shaking his head, trying to keep awake.

"Yes Mark, we know that."

"Man," he raised his eyebrows, "From escaping through the sewers, running from leechy people, to sneaking around hiding away from guards and the long walk out the city, to what?" he explained their whole night and morning, "Another walk across these plains," he adjusted his bag.

"They called leechers," Mia corrected him. She was just ahead of all of them, with her eyes buried into the map, "Besides, this is just the beginning."

"Leechers, leechy people, same thing," he replied grumpily.

"Just have some of that stuff Galvani bought us, or a fruit or something," James suggested walking up to Mia.

James's suggestion immediately turned Mark's grumpy frown upside-down, he put is bag down and opened it.

"What are you doing staring at that map?" James asked taking interest.

"Just checking where the city is from our current positon," she replied, eyes still glue to the map.

"Hmm, it's just north from here, nothing complicated about that," he tapped the name on the map.

"I didn't say it was complicated," she raised her voice a tad bit, "I'm just checking for any stops, villages."

James was a little surprised at the little elevation in tone, "Okay... I'll just leave you to it then," he picked up his pace, then slowed it again, "Are you okay?"

She looked up at him with a confused frown, "Yes, why?"

James noticed she had some sleeping bags. It seemed that everyone was on edge right now, it has been a rough night, without any sleep to top it up, "Nothing, just asking, you've been staring at that map since we left the forest," he replied.

Mark caught up with them having a few strips of dried meat in one hand, he had heard a bit of what they were saying, "Well, you shouldn't be Mia, we going to be walking for weeks," he smelt the strips and was pleased, "Maybe you don't understand the level of boredom we are going to reach… probably why you staring at that map."

Mia rolled up the map, "Happy now?"

Mark shook his head, "No… now we going to get lost," he replied.

Daniel chuckled.

Mia was not happy at all, she put away the map in a pouch located on one side of the bag.

"I'm just saying," Mark noticed her anger, "Now we don't know where we're going."

"I thought someone suggest you should stuff your mouth," she put on a fake smile.

"Okay, Okay," he said taking a bite from one of the meat strips, his face lit up, "Wow, this stuff is good, tastes like biltong."

Daniel, who was searching for rocks that he could throw into the distance, told them to calm down, "Guys, we're all tired and on edge because we haven't slept, let's just try to stay calm."

"Have some of your biltong," Mark suggested, "It's really good."

Marks grumpy mood had almost disappeared entirely since he took a bite out of his rations.

James spotted a small hill nearby with a giant rock sticking out of it, he decided it was best to climb it and check the perimeter

Up top, he acted like some kind of voyager looking into the distance.

Mia looked up at him, "What are you doing?"

"Looking for this Adornfell city."

"You not going to see it from here, we're over a week away from the place."

James squinted his eyes, "Pass the map."

Mia sighed, "Trust me, you're not going to see it, even if it was in viewing distance, it's on the other side of a mountain."

"Huh?" Mark stopped in his tracks, surprised, "Mountain?"

Mia nodded.

"Map please," James requested again.

Mia pulled it out, made it up the rock and handed it to him.

James crouched down and placed the map down. He looked up ahead.

Daniel also stopped, throwing a rock up and down in his hand, "What are you doing James?" He asked, "Times a waste."

"What is it?" Mia asked, looking up ahead.

James pointed on the map, what he guessed to be a forest, a collection of drawn trees, "This is the forest we will have to pass through to avoid the main roads that go around it right?"

Mia nodded, "Yes, it's the quickest and safest from any people."

"When I look ahead from up here, I see no forest, I think we may be heading in the wrong direction."

Mia disagreed, "We've been heading straight since the city...maybe it's a bit furtherer away."

"Maybe," he replied, "but look here," he placed his finger on Adornfell and dragged his finger down passed Marridor, "Going dead straight won't lead us to Adornfell, the place is north-north west at best."

"Yes, but I'm sure we left in this direction after we exited the forest road," she pointed out.

"Are we lost or what!?" Mark interrupted.

"That's the question!" he shouted back, then lowered his voice again, "I'm sure we should be seeing something, have you checked the compass?"

Daniel decided to join them up on the rock.

Mia shook her head.

"Take out your compass," James said.

"Wow, there's a lot of ground to cover," Daniel said looking up ahead, "We shouldn't be debating about anything."

Mia handed the compass to James which he held still in his hand.

It was not pointing north-north west.

"Oh, we're going in the wrong direction," he announced, smiling at Mia, "How did we go from north-north west to basically heading out north east?"

Mia shrugged picking up the map, "I don't know."

"I may have an idea as to why," Daniel said, "First of all, we didn't have the compass out, and second, we are not following the roads... when we left the forest around the city, we didn't follow the road which was basically heading in the right direction, we were trying to get as far away from the main roads as possible," he took a deep breath, "Meaning we are bound to lose our way."

Mark was unable to hear their muttering, "Guys can you let me in on what's going on."

Mia turned to him, "If you must know, we're going in the wrong direction."

"Don't lie," he didn't believe her, till he saw James stand up, looking at the compass.

Mia did not care that he did not believe her.

James stood up looking at the compass and turned till it pointed in the right direction, "We supposed to be heading that way, I'm sure we far from the roads now."

"Oh my, how far off course are we?" Mark asked.

"Not by much," Daniel replied, "It was just a mistake."

Mark had to bring up more tension, "But Mia was staring at the map all morning."

"Mark please keep quiet," she requested.

"I think we should be checking our course every once in a while," James suggested handing the compass back to her.

Mia nodded, "Yeah, easy to get lost without the main roads."

James squinted ahead, "Still see no forest."

"That's still some distance away," Daniel said making his way down.

Mia rolled up the map and followed him down.

Everyone was on the right path now, heading on to the forest that lay ahead.

"It's a good thing we figured this out still early," James said rubbing his eyes.

Mark looked at everyone with concern, "People," he called, "It's breakfast, aren't you all hungry?"

At that moment, they realized that they had not yet had anything to eat and decided it was time to stock up on a bit of energy again.

A few hours had passed since they had eaten some breakfast, still unrested and growing more tired at a faster rate. The sky was now completely covered with a layer of clouds but the wind had not yet gone silent.

"And now we cannot tell the time," Daniel said looking up at the sky.

"I don't really care about the time, so long as we can kill it," Mark replied, he caught sight of Mia's staff, "Mia... you did say that you're the only one that can use that staff?"

"Yes, I did."

"Ugh," he sounded annoyed, "Why is that may I ask?"

She pulled it out from its sheath and extended it to its normal sized, "It's because I can use magic without a staff," she explained, "As you can see, this one doesn't have a crystal, the magic comes from me."

"I still don't understand why you're the only able to use magic," he said.

She shrugged, "Jake just said I'm special," she replied.

"I know why," Daniel blurted out.

He felt it was time to just say it, the conversation Mark just started made it appropriate for the topic.

Mia looked at him, "What, you know why I'm..."

Daniel nodded.

Everyone else took interest in this chat.

"Go on," James fell impatient.

"Yes Daniel, spill it out," Mia rushed him, "I've been trying to figure it out for months."

"You're a witch," he finally spilled it out.

No one reacted to his answer at first.

Mark chuckled, "We all witches and wizards Daniel," he shook his head, "I thought this was going to be good."

"What are you talking about Daniel," Mia frowned at him, "Mark is making more sense right now."

Daniel held up his hand, "Please just let me explain."

"Please do so."

Everyone had stopped, just in between two giant rocks.

Daniel took a deep breath, "It started when I mentioned to Angelina that we were witches, then she told me not to use the words," he began, "Later she said that she would explain to me the differences and reasons..."

"Yes...," Mia urged him to continue.

"We met at the library and there she told me that basically, you are a different race of people, that are able to create magic themselves," he explained, "not 'human'... she said that normal 'humans' are unable to create magic, so they need staves, which allows them to use it."

"Hmm," Mark replied.

Mia was confused, but she could see a bit of sense in what Daniel was saying, a witch, being someone able to create magic, while others needed the assistance of enchanted objects to project the same thing. This was a simple thing to understand but the one thing she did not get was why Jake had urged her to speak nothing of such a thing to anyone else, why was she special, there's bound to be others... she hoped.

She looked at her staff, "Why would Jake then not tell me, or make me keep it a secret?"

Daniel shrugged, unsure if he should say any more, "Apparently witches are very dangerous... I guess."

"How can I be more dangerous?" She frowned, "Everyone can use magic."

Daniel shrugged, "That's what she told me... and she heard from some old man, this stuff is not mentioned anywhere in any books as you may have noticed."

"I still don't understand though," she said, "I wish I could ask him."

Mia morphed her staff back to its compatible size and placed it back in her sheath. Now she really wanted to find out more, but still unable to asked anyone about it and with Jake off somewhere, figuring this out was impossible, since even the books keep this a secret. She did not want this new bit of information to cloud her mind knowing she was not going to find out more so she thought it was best to push the thought away for now and bring up something else that was still a mystery.

"You guys should be trying to use those diamonds of yours while you are still out of trouble, you can't wait for a life or death situation for them to save you again," she changed the subject.

James looked at his, "You may be right... Jake said we should get used to using them more often so that we could better ourselves."

"Then do that," she suggested, "We've been walking for many hours, I think it's about time we rested a little... you guys can use your powers, I haven't seen them, especially you Daniel, you didn't have to get saved," she put down her bag.

"I don't think using our abilities would be the same as resting," Mark pointed out, "I think it's the opposite actually."

"It's just for two seconds... like a demonstration," Mia said, "Just to see if you can actually activate them."

"I'm down to try," Daniel took of his bag.

"You've already seen mine," Mark tried to avoid.

"I want to see what you can create yourself," she took a seat on a rock nearby.

"Fair enough."

"Okay, let's start with you James," she requested, "I only saw you standing by the ladder in the sewers."

"Yeah, that surprised me too," he said unstrapping his belt, "I'll see how fast I can run."

He threw his robe over his bag and jogged some distance away. He put his diamond under his clothing to keep it from moving inconveniently. After that he loosened himself, stretching his neck and jogging on the spot.

The others just watched from their places, waiting for him to start his demonstration.

When he was done preparing himself, he got down on all fours as if he were about sprint in a race. He tried to remember what Jake was telling him, how he should concentrate on using the ability and wait for signs that it has activated. At first, he kind of had to start running at a normal pace before the effects started to show, do it progressively, but this time he thought he should just go straight into his ability, from zero to a hundred. Off course this would mean he would have to concentrate more... to his guess, so he waited in that position for his heart rate to start picking up, a trigger he noticed the few times his ability activated. In his mind, he envisioning himself running at great speed.

Back on Mia's side, they had started to get tired of waiting.

"Do you think it's going to happen?" Mia asked.

Mark shrugged, "Let him take his time."

After some time, James just about to give in and do it progressively, when he felt it speed up, his heart rate, but he had not yet started to run, then his breathing started to go uneven, it felt as if he was not breathing enough. He took this as his trigger and pushed forward into a sprint.

Before he knew it, he had run a little ways passed them before he stopped.

This put strain on him, he took off the diamond just to be safe and dropped it next to him, to switch of anything that could still be making him feel so strange.

At least he could feel his heart had gone back to normal, but then felt his muscles were painful and that his vision was blurred for some moments. He did not see anything while he was running.

He turned back and saw his friends in the near distance behind him. Mia waved at him.

He took a deep breath, "This thing is killing me," he kicked the diamond away. He felt a bit of anger towards it. He did not even feel like picking it up again, shaking his head at it.

Before heading back to them, he put it on again.

Back at their place of rest, questions came flying at him.

"Well done," Daniel congratulated him, "How did that feel?"

James shook his head and waved his hand, "We need to practice," he replied, "My muscles are sore, and I couldn't see where I was going, everything was kind of blurry."

Mark nodded, "Hmm, you went fast... not disappearing fast, but fast."

"That was cool," Mai complimented, "They seem to be draining a lot from you."

James nodded, "I really need to rest," he fell to the floor.

Mia had a theory, "Judging by your muscle pain and blurred vision, your body still needs to adjust to that things power."

James leaned against his bag and looked at Daniel and Mark, "Next."

"Mark, create a shield," Mia requested.

He sighed, "Okay, let's get this over and done with."

Mark doubted he could create the shield, he wanted to mimic the one from the sewers. He stood away from the bags and held out his arms beside him, his hands wide open, following Jake's instructions exactly and closed his eyes.

For a few moments nothing happened, everybody remained silent, waiting for him to create something.

Mark could start to feel some force against his palms, as if something is pushing against them, very hard, it felt like his arms were being pushed into his neck so he decided to push back with his own amount of force.

He heard someone clapping behind him so he opened his eyes.

He had done it. Created a shield that only surrounded him, it was not as intriguing as the one in the sewers, it was just a dull, blue, transparent colour.

"You did it."

Mark was happy, but his arms growing very weak so he dropped them and took a deep breath, "Wow, my arms," he grabbed a hold of them, "The shield was pushing my arms into my neck."

"With enough practice, you will be our protector Mark," Mia said, "I sure do want to know what mine would've done," she giggled, "Anyways, Daniel, let's see you fly."

"Hmmm, that's some very high expectations there," he said putting down his bag, "I will probably just levitate."

"That'll be awesome."

"Okay," he loosened up a bit and did some small jumps on the spot. He took a deep breath, slowly, in and out, and concentrated on his ability.

He jumped.

Gravity didn't pull him down, he was levitating.

"Nice, can you go higher?" Mia asked.

"Let me try."

He allowed himself to levitate higher, now a few metres from the ground.

"Impressive," James complimented, still laid back on his bag.

Daniel could start to feel a little light headed and dizzy. His heart had suddenly started to feel heavy as if he was falling from a high place.

He tried to keep his mind clear. He was able to look over the small hill from his height.

Noticing something in the distance, he squinted his eyes.

It was some horse rider in a Dead Crows attire.

He took off his diamond and dropped it as soon as he realized it was an agent to deactivate his ability.

The fall was not pleasant at all and surprised the rest.

"Daniel, why did you take it off?" James asked getting up to help him.

Mark and James got him to his feet.

"I thought we were far from the main road," he said.

Mia stood up, "We are."

Daniel shook his head, "I just saw a Dead Crow agent riding by on a horse."

"What?" Mia decided she wanted to see this herself and made her way up the small hill, she stood on the highest point of the rock.

She saw nothing, "I don't see anything."

Everyone else made it to the top and could not spot anything as well, including Daniel.

"Thanks for scaring us Daniel," Mark said making his way back down.

"Strange…," he squinted his eyes again, "I am very sure I saw him, on the main road, heading that way," he pointed north.

"Maybe it's some side effect from using your diamond," Mia suggested.

Daniel put some thought to it, he nodded, "You could be right, I did feel all dizzy and light headed when I was levitating."

"I'm going to go have some rest before we continue on," James headed down as well.

"Yeah, I think it's best we do that now," Daniel agreed.

Down at their place of rest, they decide to regain their energy by eating, and judging by the amount of walking they had accomplished, it was safe to say that it was probably lunch time.

"Today is inspection right?" Mark asked, unsure of himself.

"Yes, it's Monday," Daniel replied taking a sip of some water, "they were done with that quite a while ago."

"I wonder if they figured us out, since we were hiding our faces and all," It was clear Mark was not in his right mind at the moment.

"Off course," Mia replied, "I told you that I only hexed the agents, everybody else in the school could see your normal faces," she explained again, "I'm not good when it comes to illusions, but is seems it is what we need most to get by right now."

James had lost all the pain, all his muscles had gone back to feeling normal really quickly. He had already excepted that he would have to suffer from stiff muscles for the next few days. He sighed, "I wonder how they reacted?"

"Yeah, I'd like to see that," Mark agreed.

"You three yes, but I wonder what they think of me... I mean, I was never part of their little search."

After some rest they continued with their little venture with haste.

It had been a full day since our group had tested out their abilities.

At this moment they had already enter into the forest that they were hoping to see the day before, consisting of a variety of foliage including Pine, Ash, Oak and Chestnut among the majority.

One of the good things about being in the forest, was the shade, not a lot of sunlight was able to seep through.

It was around midday, so Mark was busy chewing away at his biltong. The others had a sense of their current situation so they rationed it a bit, only eating enough to keep them going.

Mia was very cautious about being here, it was a really good opportunity to get lost, so she made sure not to head astray by constantly checking the compass every few minutes.

James and Daniel were little toddlers discovering the mysteries of the world, exploring and finding interest in the smallest of things they came across, looking strange or moving, it was something to investigate, though they did steer clear of the creepy stuff.

Mark walked up to Mia, "How many days do you think till we get to Adornfell?" He asked chewing on his food.

"You really are impatient are you, this is our second day."

He ignored her claim, "So, how many days."

"Depends," she replied.

"On..."

"The route we take."

"Well, that's easy, we take whichever is the shortest," he suggested.

Mia sighed, "We'd have to talk about that some other time perhaps," she looked at him take another bite from his food, "You're still eating?"

He smiled and nodded in return.

"Ugh," she shook her head, "You're going to run out."

"Uh… we're in the middle of the forest, deer and squirrels for days," he replied.

Mia frowned at him, "How are you going to hunt one?"

"We going to use your transforming staff to kill it off course," he replied, "Easy as pie, besides, Daniel was training in archery before we left."

"What about building the fire?" She enquired.

Mark sighed, "why are you even asking these questions, we have your magic to build the fire," he said, "The only annoying part would be gathering the wood… next question."

"Skinning and cooking?" She raised her eyebrows.

"We'll have the fire to do the cooking part and we've been taught how to skin and stuff since we were very young," he replied, "And Galvani gave us everything we need to cook including salts and spices."

Mia nodded, "Okay, just checking," she pulled out her staff and morphed it into a crossbow, "Here," she handed it over to him.

He weighed it, "Daniel was right, this is light… where are the bolts?"

"And that's where you need to start listening," she took the staff back and showed him the top, "As you can see here, there is already a bolt loaded and ready to be fired," she pointed at two other bolts clipped near the centre, "There are two more here."

"Only three ammo?" He looked at them, concerned.

"Listen," Mia repeated herself, "And watch closely."

Mia aimed the crossbow at a nearby tree and shot the bolt. It got stuck in the bark.

Mark walked up to it, "Nice," he wanted to pull it out.

"Don't touch it Mark," she instructed, "I just said watch and listen."

"Okay," he went back to her.

"Now watch closely," she unclipped another bolt and loaded it, "Look at that bolt," she pointed at the tree.

Mark's jaw dropped at what he was now witnessing. In just a few seconds, the bolt stuck in the tree faded away and reappear in the empty slot.

"See, as good as new."

Mark was out of words to describe his feelings right now, "Infinite ammo," he uttered, "I want one."

"Pretty cool huh?"

"Pretty cool?... what do you mean 'pretty cool', that's awesome," he gave some thought to the phenomenon he just witnessed, "Wait, what happens if you forget to reload?"

"Then it won't return until you do," she replied.

Mark nodded slowly, "I'm beyond impressed."

"Thanks," she handed the crossbow to him, "Now go find the others and see if you can catch us anything... I don't know how long we're going to be in this forest so better sooner than later, I'll be collecting some ingredients."

Mark held the crossbow in both hands imitating a proud hunter, "I'll see you after the hunt."

"Don't wonder too far," Mia instructed, "We can't get lost."

Mark was off to find James and Daniel.

Mia pulled out a note book sized almanac about alchemy ingredients and searched through the pages for any ingredients that could be found in this particular area.

"Shh, you making too much noise," Mark whispered.

"Shut up," James shot back quietly.

"Guys, I need to concentrate," Daniel tried to silence them, "We've been at it for hours."

James had accidentally stepped on a small twig, which were obviously very common, which lead to Mark's little rage in silencing him creating James's comeback that suggested Mark was the actual problem in the situation, creating the annoying distraction for Daniel, who is supposed to be taking the shot, leading to our current present.

All three of them were crouched, hiding behind a bush, peeking over it, stalking some prey with Daniel being the marksman.

Their target was a female deer, which stood quite far from their current position and a little ways down the hill sipping away at a small pond. It was their only perfect opportunity since they started a few hours ago.

James and Mark had calmed themselves after realizing they were disturbing Daniel, but at least for now, the deer was unaware of their presence.

It was only seconds later that Mark questioned Daniel's delay, "You have a clear shot, it's about to quench its thirst."

Daniel turned to him slowly with a straight face, "I'm not going to shoot its butt, it might survive."

Mark did not care about what he had to say, "Don't look at me, look at the deer."

Daniel shook his head and focused his aim again, his hands dripping.

Mark and James watched in silence, waiting for Daniel to release the bolt. The hours of scurrying up and down lay in the hands of the next shot.

The deer was finally done quenching its thirst.

"Okay, shh," Daniel whispered, preparing for it to move and expose all weak points.

The deer lifted its head from the pond and scanned the area.

Mark and James lowered themselves more, concealing themselves completely.

A few moments passed and the deer turned right and started walking.

Daniel followed it, aim pointed right for the neck. Holding his breath for no movement he released the bolts and hit the deer right in the neck.

It tried to make a run for it.

"Go!" Daniel shouted.

James and Mark jumped over the bush they were hiding behind and headed down the hill after it. Daniel followed behind much slower than the other two, relieved that his marksman skills had improved greatly since the few weeks of training he had.

James and Mark remained close behind the deer, waiting for it to give up.

It eventually lost balance and fell to the side.

Daniel then proceed to reload Mia's crossbow so as to obtain the bolt again.

James stood above it and nodded with a smile on his face, "That was fun," he turned to Daniel, "Nice shot."

Mark agreed, "Yeah, that was fun," he looked around, "Now to carry it back and for the disgusting part to begin."

James giggled, "At least we know how to do it."

It was not long before they found their way back to Mia. Daniel had collected some wood which he had held under his left arm while the right carried the crossbow.

James and Mark carried the deer by the legs.

"Hey, you pulled it off, good job," Mia congratulated them.

"What have you been doing?" James asked.

"Oh," she held her hand, carrying some plants, "Been collecting ingredients, for alchemy, potions," she replied, "And I also found a creek nearby."

That night they sat around a fire, near the creek. It was a good place to spend their first night in the forest since the small stream had provided some volume in the dark silence that was occupied by many unknown skulking creatures.

They did an excellent job with the deer, extracting all the meat and cooking some of it over the fire on a small pan. The rest of the meat was chopped into smaller pieces and preserved by means of salt.

The meat they were cooking had already gained itself some colour, it had been a few hours since it was panned under the fire.

The moon was out tonight, quite bright, providing some light for them and reflecting off the creek. Their first afternoon in the forest was not as bad as they first thought, most of it was spent doing things they actually enjoyed. But off course, being in the forest at this late hour can put anyone on edge.

"I think I like sleeping in the plains better," Mark said, eyes constantly scanning the area.

"I agree, we could see for miles and didn't even need a fire for light," James added.

Mia sat leaning against a tree, "The fire was compulsory anyway, otherwise we'd be sharing with Mark here who doesn't know how to save."

"Hey, I still have some left," He sounded upset.

"I'm just glad all those years we spent, spending our holidays camping are finally paying off," Daniel said throwing small twigs into the fire.

"Yeah, it's like the teachers knew we were going to be stuck in this time, surviving in the wilds, hiding from the Dead Crow and searching for a girl," James added.

"The thing is, they didn't," Mia said, "I don't see how surviving in the wilds was going to help us, I mean, I love nature and stuff, but every holiday..."

"I just wanted more trips, different ones," Mark said.

"If there were any other trips, we'd be rationing whatever we had as if we were in some kind of apocalypse," Daniel added.

"So this camp thing was in every school?" James asked.

"Apparently so," Mia replied.

Two days passed since they entered the forest, and still they were surrounded by trees, but now they had this feeling that they were nearing the edge of this forest. It was now just another cloudy afternoon.

James, Mark and Daniel had been able to put some practice activating their abilities during the time and were starting to understand how they worked.

It was quite hot in this place so James, Mark and Daniel had stopped with the robes and rolled them up in between their sleeping bags.

Their current plan was to keep on going till they were out and free from the enclosure of these trees, it was not part of the plan to spend another night here.

"It's much darker on a cloudy day here," Mark said staring up at the treetops.

"Don't worry, we'll be in the clear soon enough," Mia replied examining the map.

Daniel, whom also took interest in the map noticed something that lay just ahead after the forest, "The Black River," he read the small text, "Is that literal?"

Mia shrugged, "I guess we'll find out."

Mark overheard, "Don't be stupid Daniel, there are hundreds of rivers and all of them need a different name, but in the end, it's just a bunch of water running down a path."

"Mark's right," James agreed, "If they were all literal, then each river would be some kind of tourist attraction or something."

Mia rolled up the map and put it away, then she check the compass.

The bushes seemed to be getting less and less spread out and more bunched up as they proceeded. It got to the point where they had to start pushing them out of the way just get through.

"It feels like we're going deeper into the forest," James mention, pushing away some leaves from his face.

"This is annoying," Daniel added.

"Mia!" Mark called, "I think we're lost."

Mia sighed, "We're almost out, trust me."

She pushed away some more branches and leaves in her way and stepped into an open area.

They were not out of the forest, at least not yet, there was still some vegetation on the other side of this open space.

Mia gasped and froze in place.

"We're out," Mark declared before realizing as well that they were not actually free. He was also frozen in shock, eyes wide open.

James and Daniel stepped out last, and their happiness too was lost.

It would seem their majestic and peaceful venture through the forest was a little too good to be true.

They stood in silence, staring at a small encampment of what seem to be a group of bounty hunters, whom also put to a pause whatever it was they were doing and stared back at them.

They sat on small logs and benches, about four of them around a small built fire, roasting their catch with small tents already built and ready to be used.

A woman stood in the centre near the fire holding in one hand, a wanted poster, and next to her a man with a long bow and arrow loaded.

Everyone possessed all kinds of weapons and wore traveling attire, that seemed a bit more intimidating, for example, the woman holding up the paper had her sleeves ripped to the shoulder, showing off some tattoos, with a black leather vest over her shirt, another wore a bandana over his head and had one tied around his arm. They looked like a band of pirates.

Mia and the others were paralyzed, as if under some kind of hex, hoping that they would not be recognized as criminals but as fellow travelers, but this was not guaranteed since Mia had not hexed them.

The first bit of movement was from the women, her eyes bouncing from Mia's face, to the paper in her hand, back and forth.

"It's them!" She shouted.

The archer standing beside her lifted his bow and immediately released his arrow, aimed at Mia. Luckily, he did not take the time to aim and it just missed her, hitting the tree behind.

Mia's heart skipped a beat, "Let's go," she turned back and disappeared into the bushes.

"After them!" The woman shouted.

They pushed their way through the bushes violently and made it to the other side.

"Ditch the bags," Mia instructed, throwing hers down as she began to sprint away.

Everyone dropped their bags and ran for their lives.

Moments later, the hunters as well appeared from the bushes and began with their pursuit.

It was hard, running through the forest, having had so many objects to avoid and jump over. The good thing was the amount of trees that were in the way, making it quite challenging for the archer to fire at them.

It was late in the afternoon and they were tired form the long day walking, they were getting tired quickly, especially now that they had to watch their steps.

Mia looked from side to side for a split second and saw that they were close enough, she turned looked over her should to see the distance between them and her, it was quite a gap, but one that was closing really fast.

An arrow flew right passed her, scaring and forcing her to duck.

Running out of breath she instructed the others, "Run in the opposite direction...," she blurted out, "I will tell you when!"

"What!" Mark was unsure."

Mia had an idea in mind, all she hope was that the others had heard her and that they would comply when she said. She pulled out her staff and morphed it to its original size. She jumped over a stump and tapped her staff on the ground four times.

Out of her body, jumped out another, a doppelganger in spirit form that continued to run ahead of her as she slid to a stop and shouted, "Now!" before bashing the head of her staff against the ground, exploding into a massive dust cloud that spread far and wide.

She shrunk her staff again and immediately started to in the opposite direction, hoping the others had done the same.

Navigating through the cloud was difficult, each step she took, hoping she would not run into the hunters by accident. It was just a few seconds but she made it out to the other side of the cloud and so did the others.

It was not time to celebrate, but to continue running as fast as they could.

Mia looked back and was relieved to see that they had fallen for her trick.

After a while they had made it back to their bags, which they picked up before disappearing into the bushes again and out by the encampment they emerged, continuing on passed their benches and tents.

James noticed the posters laying in the dirt and decided to stop and pick them up before joining up again with the other whom had already entered into the trees again.

It was a miracle, they had made it out of the forest and into the open, met with a lot of fresh air. It was only then that they decided to slow down, after some distance from the edge.

The terrain was similar to the plains before the forest, with a lot of small hills.

All panting and out of breath, bodies trying hard to keep them from collapsing.

"That's was a close one," Mark said looking back.

"Thanks Mia, you're a lifesaver," James said dropping his bag.

Mia nodded in return, "No problem," she said faintly, dropping her bag as well, feeling a little faded, she fell face down onto the grass, with her staff next to her.

James and Daniel hurried to her aid and tried to get her to her feet.

"No," she said faintly, "Leave me like this...can't move," she tried to put on a smile.

James had forgotten how tired using magic made her, especially after the stunt she had just pulled, creating four doppelgangers to lead away the bounty hunters.

"I'll be fine in a sec," she said, "Just please put me on my back."

They did as she requested.

James sat beside her and picked the staff, "Tell me when you want to get up."

Daniel stood there and watched as Mark just stared into the forest, waiting for them to appear again.

Mark turned away after some moments and noticed Mia lying on her back, "What happened?" He walked up to them.

"She used a lot of magic," Daniel replied.

Mia remained silent and stared into the clouds as they all moved away in one direction, "We have to go," she said trying to get up.

"Daniel," James made him aware.

They both helped her to her feet, but couldn't keep her balance both Daniel and James supported her. Mark picked up her bag walked beside them.

He remember that she had to eat so he searched her bag for some of the biltong.

She was now able to keep her balance and walk on her own.

Mark handed some strips to her.

"Thanks," she turned back and so there was no one, "That was too close."

They continued on forward, putting as much distance from the forest as possible.

As they pushed on, they found themselves nearing the river. It was really late at this time.

One thing they noticed as they drew closer was the grass, it depreciated, separating into small groups and random patches.

Mark could now see that the map was not just naming it The Black River because they were out of names, but because it was literal, "This can't be real," he went on ahead, anxious to get a closer look, still unsure if it was just his eyes.

When he got there, his jaw dropped in disbelief, "Guys!" He shouted, "This is not normal!"

"Tell him not to touch it," A voice spoke from behind James.

He turned around, on high alert, thinking it was the bounty hunters.

He sighed in relief when he realized it was just Levina.

"Don't scare me like that."

She smiled back.

"What was that James?" Daniel turned back.

"Nothing, just thinking," he lied.

Luckily, Daniel was more interested in this abnormal river.

James turned back to Levina. She was walking beside him now.

"Tell him not to touch the water," she pointed at Mark.

Mark crouched right next to the water.

"Don't touch it!" James shouted at the top of his lungs.

Mark stood up again.

James picked up his pace, Levina did as well, keeping right next to him.

"You all have bounties now," she said.

"Oh," James remembered, "I took the posters," he pulled them from his hoodie pockets, all crinkled up. He straightened them up, "Hmm, they were quick to make and distribute them, nice artworks too."

"Can I see?" She asked.

He handed them to her.

"You are also bad people now, for running away from school?" She looked up at him.

James smiled and shook his head, "We were accused for stealing some things."

"The Crow people are the bad ones... I've seen them do horrible things to people," she looked at the other poster, "Maybe it's their job."

"Maybe," James agreed, "They are the law around here... but anyways, what brings you back?"

"Just visiting," She replied, "I had to save your friend as wells," she laughed

They all reached the edge of the river.

"How do we cross something we cannot touch?" Mark asked, throwing some grass he had picked from nearby into the water, "It seems to be burning everything, or dissolving for that matter."

"It's weird," Mia looked around.

The river was water, but just had a black shade to it. Another thing that was strange about the body of water was the fact that it did not flow in any directions, only creating small ripples made by the wind. It was, more than five metres wide.

Mia pulled out the map and checked to see if there were any bridges nearby, but no luck in that. The river had a start and end and the main roads went over it. This was also not an option for them because judging by its length, it would take about a day to go around to the bridges and their next stop was just straight ahead.

Levina handed the posters back to James, "Going around is the only way to get to the other side."

"Go around!" James blurted out.

Mark looked at him, "You crazy, I'm not walking in the direction that's going to make us no progress," he noticed the papers in James's hand, "Are those the wanted posters?"

"Oh, yeah, picked them from their camp," He replied.

Mark walked up to him, "Then why didn't tell us," he took them from him and distributed them, "Keeping them to yourself," he murmured.

The artworks were the very first things they complimented on, as if they were happy to be having their very own bounties.

"Wow, we have really high prices on our heads," Daniel said, "I'm five thousand gold coins."

"I'm also five thousand," James replied, "Mark?"

"Same," he turned to Mia, "What about you, I didn't think you'd get a bounty."

Mia's eyes were about to pop out of their sockets as she stared at her bounty, "How am I twenty thousand gold coins?"

"Don't lie," he went over to check.

They all gathered around her.

"What!" James was surprised, "What's in your description?"

Mia check under the bounty and read it, "This girl is cursed and very dangerous, be very cautious."

"Cursed?" Mark repeated.

Mia shrugged, "I have no idea what that means."

Let's jump back for just a little while, back to the morning after their departure from the school. The events that took place after Angelina had aided them in their escape.

The morning had arrived rather quickly and it was a new school day for the learners at Marridor. It was only the about half an hour after everyone had awoken from the girls dormitory that they started asking questions about Mia's made sheets. Most of them had not seen her enter the dorm before they had gone to sleep.

Angelina, Mia's closest friend was the only one very aware of their absence, it kept her from sleeping for most of the night, thinking of a logical explanation for their decision to just pick up and leave all of a sudden, but nothing came up. While the others wonder and worried, she kept silent, seated on her bed, putting on her tie.

Being the one to be seen with her the most, a lot of the other girls in the dorm had come to question her about her absence, but for most of them she just shrugged off.

Opal came to her, also ready to leave the dorm, she sat across from her on Mia's bed.

"Morning," She greeted politely.

Angelina put on her blazer and returned the greeting, "Hi."

Opal began to pat Mia's bed, "I'm guessing you also don't know where Mia is?"

Angelina shook her head, "I never saw her, not since dinner last night," she replied.

"Well, I hope she comes back very soon, wherever she may be because we have inspection today and I don't want her to be a prime suspect, maybe one of the thieves we were told about," she said.

"She isn't a boy," she pointed out.

"Oh, yes, I forgot that they looking for three boys," Opal remembered.

Just then Angelina realized that the amount of people that Mia had left with last night was a total of three boys. James, Mark and Daniel could possibly be the very people that the Dead Crow have been looking for these past months. What kind of connection did she have with these three and better yet, how was the Dead Crow unable to find them this whole time… unless her intuition was wrong and they are not the criminals.

Opal noticed her frozen state, "Anything wrong?" She enquired.

She jumped out of her thoughts, "No, just thinking."

Opal stood up, "Okay, I'll leave you to it, I'll see you downstairs," she headed out the dorm.

Angelina placed her bag on the bed and stared at the clock on the wall, watching the second hand jumped. For a moment, she locked out all the other sounds and voices that echoed around her and tried to think of a possible reason for all this. She had already come to notice that the Dead Crow agents had only arrived at this school shortly after they came, so they could without a doubt be the thieves, thieves that can hide. The only piece of the puzzle that did not seem to belong there was Mia and her involvement.

"Angelina," A voice called from behind.

She snapped out of it again and turned to the source of this voice calling her name. It was another girl, one of the only few left in the dorm including her.

"Come on, let's go," she said.

Leaving her bag on the bed she followed her out of the dorm.

After breakfast, everyone headed back to fetch their bags and head on to their first lessons.

Opal caught up with Angelina as she headed to class, "Hey," she greeted, "It seems that also James, Mark and Daniel are missing, also last seen yesterday.

Angelina did not act at all surprised, "That's weird."

"Yup, and they are already in big trouble."

She gave her a confused frown, "What do you mean?"

"They might as well be the thieves Mr. Patchwalker told us about," she replied, "everybody is saying it."

Angelina shrugged, "You may be right."

Opal sighed, "Though I hope not, they really did seem like nice people... unless it was all an act to blend in you know."

"Yeah," she sounded down, knowing without a doubt it was true, they did escape from the school after all, through the sewers," I guess we'll find out after this period."

"I'm not going to lie, it's kind of exciting, a little drama," she chuckled.

And off to their first lesson of the day they went.

After the first period, every student was called to the hall.

All the tables had been removed and all were lined up according to their age groups. Each group separated into a boy and girl line.

Up front, stood Mr. Patchwalker, formal as ever and behind him, a group of five Dead Crow mages wielding staves and ready to do their jobs.

"Welcome back to the hall," Mr. Patchwalker greeted, "I would like for you to remain silent while we do our routine inspection."

No one so much as coughed anyway.

Mr. Patchwalker turned to the mages and allowed them to proceed with the inspection.

Each of the inspectors headed down the steps and positioned themselves between the age groups and against the walls, with their staves held in their right hands. They raised them and stomped them on the ground with a loud thud, each creating a small white shockwave of air that passed through the first group of students. A few moments after, the mages took three steps forward and created the shockwaves again. This was all done in sync, with not even one mage out of step.

The Dead Crow mages continued down the rows, everyone else frozen in fear, unsure if they were to be called up for something they did wrong because this inspection was to check for anything that was out of place whilst trying to find the stolen object and thieves.

A full school search was conducted during the first period, searching through all dorms.

After reaching the other end of the hall, the mages made their way back to the front and had a little whisper with Mr. Patchwalker while the rest of the hall said nothing.

After the whispering had been done, Mr. Patchwalker stepped forward, "We have four missing children."

Heads started to turn left and right amongst the learners.

"James," he started to list, "Mark, Daniel and Mia."

Whispers all across the hall were heard.

"Now!" he silenced them, "I would like to ask you…What happened to them?" He put a smile on his face.

No one came to answer the question, it was just silence again.

"Must I ask again, or do you want me to be a bit more convincing, because I am not at all happy right now," he spoke calmly.

Amongst the learners stood Angelina, afraid, her heart racing and body trembling. She knew she was not going to say anything, but she could not help but react in this way. Mr. Patchwalker seemed a lot scarier now as well.

"You must understand," he continued in his tranquil tone, "If we find that you have any information regarding their absence here-," he started to show a bit of his anger, "you will be treated as equally guilty, for hiding them."

And off course, we all know that when children are told to snitch, to say even but a word on the matter, about another student… they will say nothing and just join the other five hundred innocent learners that actually know nothing for the matter. It is something that staff cannot change. Nobody wanted to be the blabbermouth.

Following the silence of Mr. Patchwalker's threat, he turned away from the hall and started whispering to the mages again.

Moments later he returned his attention, he signaled for the doors to the hall be closed shut.

"Since this is a serious matter, not just concerning the school, but the Dead Crow as well, no one is to leave this hall," He said, "You will all be questioned individually by us in the next room… make yourselves comfortable, you will be here for a while," he smiled before leaving the hall with two of the five mages.

The students broke free from the bonds they called straight lines and began to chatter and hang around. Most seemed to be quite happy they were locked up in the hall, it was just like a subs period for them, but one that was going to take much longer and not confined to a single desk with your friend sitting across the room.

Everyone but Angelina was relaxed. She had to calm herself. Right now she just stood against the wall and looked around.

"What's up with you?" Opal asked standing next to her.

She looked across the room out the window and decided to speak about whether, "It's a cloudy day, just a bit chilly," she replied.

The door opened and Mr. Patchwalker walked out with some pieces of paper containing a list of names, "Andrew Doris!" He shouted.

Angelina was really surprised, Mr. Patchwalker was starting with her age group.

About half an hour had passed since the first name had been called and Mr. Patchwalker had just stepped out of the room again and ready to call upon the next name on his list.

"Angelina Shiera!"

Scared as a mouse caught in trap, Mr. Patchwalker showed her the way in and closed the doors behind her.

All the voices from the hall disappeared.

It was her second time in this room since the age group distribution, it was an office, but a little less clean with some gathering dust on the floor, with a large table in the centre where Mr. Patchwalker sat, with the agents standing behind him. The room had shelves with books and flasks filled with potions. The table had a few books and potions on it, also the list of names next to Mr. Patchwalker.

"Please take a seat," He instructed.

Angelina sat up straight on the chair across from him.

"Okay," He took a deep breath, "Angelina, if I'm right."

Angelina nodded quickly, with her hands on her lap, palms sweating.

"We don't have time, so straight to the point," he started, "Do you know what happened to these missing students?"

Angelina looked down at the table and shook her head, she looked at Mr. Patchwalker, "No sir," she replied with a bit of confidence.

Mr. Patchwalker nodded, "Any strange activity you noticed from them?"

She replied, "No."

This seemed much easier than she thought it would be, after each lie she told, the calmer she felt. She felt it was nearly over.

After a few more questions, Mr. Patchwalker pick a small flask, with a cork, from the few that were on the table and placed it in front of Angelina, "Now, we are not sure if you are telling the truth," he smiled, "I'm sure you know children can be very good liars... do you know what this is?"

Angelina shook her head. Now she was starting to break down on the inside, trying hard not to show it.

"Good, this is some kind of truth telling serum, the actual name is a little complex, but 'truth telling serum' is something you would understand," he waited for her approval.

She nodded in return. She could hear the loud beat of her heart send shockwaves all over her body. Now she was in a horrible position, if they were to ask her to drink it then they would see that she was a liar, and the truth would obviously be out.

"This one in particular has some painful effects, should the host resist," he picked it up and examined it, "We wanted to use dark magic, would have been painless but it is forbidden and they too do not have the authority to practice it on a student," he explained, "so we have to settle for this," he smiled.

Angelina had to get out of this situation, "Isn't that also illegal?" She asked starting to get worried.

"Yes... but, they approve of it," he replied, "Now please," he gave it her.

She took it with her shacking hands and popped off the cork and drank it in one go, there was no way out of this now.

A few seconds later, the questions began again.

"Do you know what happened to these missing students?" he asked again.

Angelina said nothing, she really wanted to reply 'No' but the words did not want to leave her voice box, instead she felt a sharp pain in her head, "Ow," she murmured closing her eyes tight.

Mr. Patchwalker noticed this resistance, "Miss Shiera... the effects of this serum may have more pain on you the more you resist, so please answer the question," he smiled at her faintly.

She held her hands tight on her lap, trying to resist, but the pain worsened, "Yes," she blurted out, the pain disappeared immediately after.

"Tell me what happened."

Lying was out of the question now, every time she tried, the pain would just come back, "I helped them escape last night... I distracted one of the guards and they left through the sewers under the city."

Mr. Patchwalker remained calm and continued with the questions, "Why did you help them?"

"They are my friends," she replied as her eyes started to water.

"Do you know why they left?"

She shook her head, "No."

"Okay, did you notice any strange activity from them?"

This was the question she really did not want to answer, since Mia had trusted her with the secret and she promised not to say no matter what.

The longer she stalled, the pain slowly started to creep back into her head.

"Please answer."

A tear ran down her cheek, as the pain increased, she was about to give away her friends secret to the Dead Crow.

"Miss Shiera, please answer."

"Mia," she blurted out, "she is...she is a witch," she covered her face and sniffed.

The two mages exchanged glances, stunned by the words Angelina just spoke.

Mr. Patchwalker's eyes widened, he put a smile on his face, "Thank you."

Mia looked at the amount of gold under her portrait. In her thoughts, she wondered if Angelina would in fact tell them that she was a witch. But there was a lot of doubt in her thoughts, she trusted her.

Before they could again turn their attention back to their current problem, being the river that stood in the way of progression.

A voice came from behind, "Well, well, well."

Everyone turned to see whose voice it was.

To their surprise it was the bounty hunters again.

"I guess we have the river to thank for this loot," the woman said.

They were right about that, none of them were willing to engage with whatever substance filled the river. They were frozen again, unable to make a move since their archer had already drawn his arrow. The other hunters except the woman had their weapons drawn and ready to engage in combat, one would presume that she was the leader, since it was only her voice they had heard since the first encounter.

"I believe you took something that doesn't belong to you," she smiled at them, "the posters."

Each of them had one in their hands.

"It's wrong to steal… although, technically those have your faces on them, but they were given to us by a passing agent."

Mia was not sure whether to hand it over or just remain still, the archer had nearly hit her twice now and she was not going to take any chances. In her current stature she was able to utter a few words, "We don't want any trouble."

They all chuckled.

James looked down beside him and saw Levina was still there, hiding behind his left leg, watching the bounty hunters. She hid as if she was also visible to them.

"Trouble?" the woman repeated, "You are the trouble, we're here to stop it," she started to pace slowly, "I congratulate you… that was a nice little trick you pulled there, making us chase after your doubles," she looked at Mia, "I presume you studied at that school in the magic city…teaching children how to perform magic tricks."

Levina looked up at James, "Bounty hunters are scary."

"Shh," he silenced her, forgetting again that he was the only one able to hear her.

Everyone turned to him.

"Boy," the woman called, "Did you just silence me?"

James shook his head, "No," the attention was on him again.

"You know they can't hear me," Levina reminded him.

The woman did not believe him and Levina was just making things worse by talking and confusing him, the silence was a little awkward and scary, "Do you want the posters?" he asked without putting a single second of thought to it.

She frowned at him, confused by the question, she could not help but giggle, "You know, the courier that gave us these posters told us you four were very dangerous," she explained, "We trusted him off course, word from a Dead Crow, but when we saw your faces, we thought, 'this is some kind of joke'... it was prices on your heads that made us think twice, but we thought, maybe we would have a chance against people with bounties this high so we came to this place to begin our search and you fell right into our hands," she was quiet for a few seconds.

"Shall I shoot?" The archer asked.

"No," she replied, "I think it would be best to take them captive, if they don't force us to retaliate, besides, they're just teenagers."

The archer lowered his bow, but kept it loaded just in case the word was given.

She snapped her fingers and pointed at them, "You four are just like that girl Levina."

This brought up interest, something they actually want to listen to.

"You are teenagers... like her and have such high bounties, especially you Mia," she pointed out, "Your description suggests nothing of what you did, only that you are a danger, not to mention that it's one fifth of Levina's bounty, so I'm compelled to ask you...why the high bounty?"

Mia did not reply to her question, unsure that it was wise to mention it to them.

"Well?" she lost her patience quickly, "Quick quick, so we can get down to business."

"Are you planning on killing four school learners?" She asked.

"Depends, the three boys, maybe not," she shook her head, "You, however, have twenty thousand on your head, so I am going to be very cautious with you... but hey, I already said, only if you force us to."

Mia was really not liking the idea of having such a high bounty... anymore.

"Okay, I've lost my patience," she held one hand up, "Kill," she held up the other, "or captivity," she weighed both choices like a balancing scale, "Arrow on the girl," she ordered.

"Wait," she said, "I'm different," she decided it was best to spill it, since the Dead Crow already knew.

THE BLACK RIVER

"What do you mean?" She asked, "You have to give us more than that."

"I'm different from everybody else, that's why I have this bounty."

She signaled for the archer to lower his bow, "How?"

"They'll kill her for sure if she tells them she is a witch," Levina said.

James pulled out his sword, "Don't say it Mia, they'll kill for sure."

"Boy, our offer still stands, no matter what," the woman said.

Mark dropped both bags and walked over to her, he stood beside her, "I'll try create the shield," he whispered, "If they try anything."

Mia nodded in response.

Daniel also pulled out his sword.

"So you want to fight?" She asked.

"No," Mia replied, "I'll tell you."

"Then tell us what makes you so special!" She took a few steps forward.

Mia took a deep breath, "I'm a witch," she replied.

Mark held up one hand in front of him and generated a shield around all of them.

The woman was surprised by the shield Mark created, but her interest was in what Mia had just revealed, "Liar."

Mia held out her hand and created a bright light for a few seconds before dispelling it again, "I'm able to use magic without any magical object."

Her eyes bulged out, her face filled to the top in disbelief, "A witch?"

Mia nodded.

The woman pulled out her sword, which alerted the children, she took a few more steps closer, till she was right in front of Mark's shield. Her expression still locked away in disbelief.

She reached forward to touch the shield with her unarmed hand, but it just passed through.

Mark was now afraid that his shield was not working anymore.

James and Daniel pointed their blades at her.

The women smiled at Mia, which threw all of them into a confused state. The woman was not afraid of the swords pointed right at her, and her fellow bounty hunters did not try to stop anything from happening.

The woman stepped into the shield and place her hand on her shoulder, "10 years ago," she spoke, "I thought that last of you witches were killed," she looked at a bracelet on her arm, "My younger sister among them… I am glad to meet another that is still alive."

Mia had no idea how to feel about how unexpectedly this situation had turned, she could not keep eye contact either so she looked down.

Mark removed his shield, James and Daniel lowered their swords.

The woman turned to her comrades, "We not hunting this lot anymore," she turned back to Mia, "I won't let the Dead Crow have you too."

Her comrades sheathed their weapons.

She looked at James, Mark and Daniel, "Now I don't know what you three stole, but protect her."

Still clueless from what just happen, still carrying their vacant expressions, they just nodded in return.

This situation had turned from sour to sweet really fast, a few moments ago, archer boy was good and ready to start firing and he would have hit them, since Mark's shield had failed to protect them, the others were ready to start slicing them up and picking their bounties. All until Mia mentioned she was a witch.

Right now, the hunters were basically their friends now.

"Do you need anything before you leave?" The woman asked.

And she was offering them help.

James was the first to speak, "Yeah, do you know how to cross this river?"

She shook her head, "No one ever attempts to cross this river, people either take the western or eastern road over it."

"And how far are those roads?"

She took a deep breath and looked both ways, "Judging by your current positions, the east is farthest away," she estimated, "going west is a least one hundred kilometres, if you hurry, you might make it in the next day."

Mark cringed.

"We don't have time for that detour."

"Even if we did, I'm not walking that far," Mark added.

"I wouldn't advise that either, the Dead Crow patrol these roads."

One of the hunters came up to the woman, "I think it's best we camp outside the forest today." He said.

"Why?"

"We found some kind of shrine that speaks evil," he described, "A statue of a man holding a bowl filled with blood, and bones surrounding it."

The woman did not approve of the description, "Okay, fine," she turned back to Mia, "You lot should spend the night with us," she suggested, "it's late, best start afresh tomorrow."

She was not lying about the time, sun had set and only a limited amount of light remained.

They accepted.

"You can call me Anna," she introduced herself, "You can help us move camp up here."

The encampment was moved out of the forest and set out in the open not far from the river.

They had become familiar with each other rather quickly. Their first friends and allies since their escape from the school.

The fire was set in the centre of the encampment, with all of them seated around it, the small tents and sleeping rolls all placed.

All of Anna's comrades had already gone to sleep after having eaten their meal, the only people that remained awake in the darkness were James, Mark, Daniel, Mia and her, watching as the fire flickered away in their faces.

"Sorry again for trying to kill you the first time we met in the forest," Anna apologized.

"It's fine, though you were the first we have encountered to try kill us since we escaped," Mia said.

"You escaped from the school?"

Mia nodded, "It was full of Dead Crows."

Mark was bored, busy picking long strands of dead grass and setting them a light, watching to see how far it would burn before the fire gave out.

James had heard it from Daniel but he wanted to be very sure about it so he enquired about what Anna had mentioned, "Earlier you said that all the witches had died ten years ago, but we do not call the people in the magic city witches, even though they also use magic, why is that?"

"That's different," she replied, "All those students in Marridor are just your average human beings, with no magical abilities, the magic comes from the objects they use, it's the staves that carry those magical properties, a witch doesn't need those."

"Then why kill them if everyone is able to use magic anyway?" Daniel asked.

"That equality only came recently, and by recently, I mean about a century ago, given to us by the great Artificer, when the line between both races was as clear as black and white... the witches always had something the humans did not have, which made them feel weak and naturally grow a hate for these witches," she took a deep breath, "And as usual, you will find the few who will seek to upset that balance even more, warmongers... one thing led to another and the assassinations and murders began and before long, a war broke loose which resulted in many dying on both sides," she cleared her throat before continuing, "I don't remember much, but the witches came from nowhere, seeking peace to prevent more people from dying and somehow it worked and shortly after that, The Crow was formed."

"The Crow?" Mark repeated, "Sounds similar to a name I've heard before."

"Dead Crow," James replied.

"Yeah, that's right."

James shook his head.

Anna continued, "After the Crow was founded, a peace treaty was put in order that kept both races together for many years, everything was equal, both able to use magic, but all it took was one push and everything fell apart again."

"What happened?" Mia fell intrigued.

"An assassination attempt, on one of the wealthiest families, a human family, by a witch and member of The Crow," she explained, "The witches were then all blamed and seen as liars and deceivers, witches were then despised for that action which then became the downfall of this union called The Crow, all members that were witches were then all executed and shortly after, the name Dead Crow emerged and swore to be the saviors by exterminating all witches from this world, which forced them into hiding as all people hunted and slaughtered them…I don't believe that the actions of one person should dictate the fate of the rest but it did and it was bad because a prison was then built for the witches where they were kept to be tortured and punished, though ten years ago, it was reported that the last witch was killed… until you showed up."

Mia did not really understand her importance but one think she did know now was that she was in grave danger, "How do you know this, no book mentions it?"

"My grandfather told me…after my sister died," she replied.

"Is that why people praise the Dead Crow so much?" Daniel asked.

"I don't think so, it was everything they did after the turmoil, helping take over, keeping people safe, rebuilding everything and bringing justice to those whom deserved it," she explained, "The Dead Crow just stopped all future wars… I mean, who wouldn't praise someone who has brought upon everlasting peace, right now all we do is live our lives and there are some of us who decide to help them and catch all the outlaws, us bounty hunters, and get money in return. I hate what they did to my sister but we got to make a living, and I would rather do it by keeping the world a safe place."

James and Daniel exchanged glances.

"We were accused for doing something we didn't do… the stealing part," James mentioned, "Why would they just blame us for something we didn't do?"

Anna shrugged.

"Because you're not from here," a man's voice spoke from the darkness.

Everyone was alerted by the sound of this mysterious voice, glancing from side to side, looking for its source.

Anna stood up and pulled out her sword, "Who's there!"

Mia was next to stand up and pull out her staff, followed by the others. Mia morphed her staff.

For a few moments, they all stood there like llamas without a clue as to what to do, maybe it was all just in their heads.

The same voice gave off a sinister laugh that echoed all around them. It was impossible to pinpoint the direction it was coming from.

"Who's there!" Anna shouted again, only louder. She then awoke the others that were asleep.

"This is dangerous," a little girl's voice spoke.

James was the only one to react, she noticed Levina standing right beside him again.

"What do you mean," He whispered back.

"The Dead Crow," she replied, "They're everywhere around you."

"It's the Dead Crow," James announced to the others.

"I see nothing," Mia replied.

"James may be right," Anna agreed, "If it's the Dead Crow, then one of them is a mage."

"Okay," the voice came back, "You figured us out."

Out of nothing, appeared a whole group of about fifteen Dead Crow agents, all standing, surrounding them with no way out. The last one being the mage whom stepped forward from the rest.

"Congratulations James," he applaud, "How ever did you see through my illusion?"

Everyone turned their attention to this mage, all their weapons drawn. He was the only Dead Crow here that carried a staff and wore a different attire, he was also quite young, as if he had just become a mage. The rest were standard, with two or three archers in the mix.

"It's finally nice to meet," he smiled, "The three thieves and their fellow witch," he gave Mia a hateful look which made her feel a little uneasy.

The mage then looked at Anna, "And you, Anna, how disappointing, you befriend the outlaws, I thought I knew you better," he wore a worried looked.

Anna shook her head and leaned it back, "I don't know who you are."

"Now I'm really offended," The mage replied, "How can you not remember me?"

James and Daniel had turned their attention to the rest of the agents, they just stood there and stared right back at them. Both were looking for a way out of this situation.

James looked down beside him, Levina was still standing there as if she was not able to escape from this.

She looked up at him, "I have to go," she faded away.

At least she was off his chest now, one less person to worry about.

The mage looked at Mia's staff, "That's a nice staff, stolen?" He asked, "Where'd you get it?" His expression turned serious.

Mia did not reply, both because of fear and because she did not want to mention Jake's name, and to her, telling the truth did not matter because, in the end, they were just going to accuse her of stealing it anyway.

The mage smiled, "Hmm, so you're not only a witch. You're also a thief... guess we'll have to update your wanted poster," he looked at all four of them and took a deep breath as if he were bored to death, "Only a few days since your posters and there's already so much commotion because of you four... you not even from here," he shook his head, "Can you please tell me from where it is you reside?"

Mark was the first to allow his voice to be heard, "We're from Marridor, the school."

"Liar!" He shouted.

His sudden change in mood and temper gave them quite the scare.

Daniel had some things to say as well, "You lied as well, we stole nothing."

The mage chuckled, "Our sources are very accurate, this one in particular would like to remain anonymous, he told us you had something that did not belong to you, something dangerous, we were never told what it was but shortly after, we received orders to hunt you down," he explained, "It took a few months to figure out your identities and then came out your posters, the witch was the only one that caught us by surprise, you're a special one aren't you?" His face turned cold.

Mia felt intimidated, now coming to realize the reason why Jake did not want her secret to be spilled out. Her hands felt a little shaky, especially now that she had heard the history tale from Anna. In her fear, she fell unable to assess the situation, the feeling of being hated or wanted dead by almost everyone was traumatizing, her breathing became unstable, hoping for something to happen but at the same time for nothing. Her mind was now just a compilation of scenarios with fatal outcomes.

The only thing she felt was a bit of luck right now, all this was being postponed, the mage loved talking.

"Now back to you Anna," he took a step forward, "Why is it a group of bounty hunters having a little get together with their bounty, huh?"

She did not reply to the question, she was really caught in a tight position.

"Tell you what," he interrupted the silence, "I'll give you the power today, the power to choose, yes?" he put on a cheerful smile, "Join us in killing them, or die with them," he gave them that simple choice, but felt the need to go a little further, "You will get your bounty prize as well, we are reasonable."

Was this really happening? James could not comprehend with the chaos of what was taking place. In his present, none of this existed, there was a court with judges, people actually had the chance to prove themselves innocent. Right now, the Dead Crow was right and everybody else wrong. There were no arrests, nothing, they were just going to die where they stood.

This little uneven balance in choice given to Anna was making him feel a little doubtful, but there was a bit more hope in there.

Anna shook her head in shame and then looked up at the mage in disgust, "This is not something that I can become a part of," she said, "You can't kill someone because of their race or wrongly accuse them for crimes they did not commit."

"Okay," he shrugged, "Then you die," he smiled.

The agents surrounding them drew their swords and arrows.

"Agents, kill without mercy, we have blood traitors and criminals in our presence," he turned his gaze to Mia, "I'll kill the witch."

Everyone surrounded Mia, to protect her.

In that moment she felt safe.

The archer began firing as the agents charged.

Before James, Mark and Daniel could hopelessly attempt to defend themselves from the agents, they began to feel a little strange all round their bodies, they were stiff and unable to move. Their minds had lost total control over their bodies.

They all began to panic as they watched everybody else engage in combat.

"I can't move!" James shouted.

"Same here," Mark shouted, "Is the mage using magic on us!"

Mia noticed their statue stances, "I'll try something," said Mia, holding up her staff.

James watched as one of the agents walked up to him with the smirk of insanity smeared all over his face, he watched helplessly as he raised his sword above his head and swing it down at him, he observed as he was about to be cut open. He was terrified.

He disappeared right before it was able to touch him and found himself standing behind this man, still unable to control his movements.

The man on the other hand was lost in confusion and terrified at the same time, afraid of the fact that his target had just mysteriously disappeared. He stood up straight looking around for any sign of James, but before he could go 360°, he felt a sharp pain in his back. It was James, his sword had made its way into the agent's back.

The agent struggled to breathe as he watched the blade emerge from his abdomen.

James pulled it out.

The agent fell to his knees, "How…?" He utter before falling to his face.

James let out a pitched cry in terror, realizing that he had just killed. His hands, gripping the blade tightly, would not stop shaking. Even though his body was not in his control, he could feel everything and could see it happen. He could feel his ability.

Some agents noticed his little magic trick and went after him.

Mark's actions were a little out of his box. Unable to control the actions of his body, he too was preparing to die, he just waited for it to be over and done with.

But just then, his body decided to drop the only thing protecting him, his sword.

"What!" He cried out loud.

Two pursuers saw him as an easy target the second he let go of his blade, they came after him with haste.

As he watched them approach, he tried with all his might to reach for it, but he did not budge. Right now he was hoping for some kind of phenomenon, to save him from this oncoming death.

Mark's right arm lifted up beside him when the agents were just a couple of metres away. A barrier formed right next the men, a high wall and as Mark swung his arm to the left, the wall followed with swift speed and swatted away the two agents. The wall pushed them away and when it stopped, sent them flying into the black river.

A moment later, everyone heard their screams in pain as they drowned into the black water.

Mark, watching in horror whilst everybody else turned to him with the look of fear.

The agents continued to attack.

Mark's arms then pushed out beside him, creating a growing shield that pushed away everybody except his friends and the bounty hunters.

All the agents were thrown to the ground, in shock as they watched the sphere shrink and disappear around Mark.

Even his friends were surprised by the power he was using.

As Daniel's powers activated, they had him jump very high into the air and land right in front of one of these fallen agents, and without his consent, stabbed them, unable to gain the time to react to this terror, his body moved onto the next agent that still drew breath.

Some of the Dead Crow agents that were left decided to retreat, but James did not allow that, he would disappear and appear right before he killed them.

The mage, being the only one left alive, watched in dread as all his soldiers fall and by the hands of just a few children.

He took a step back, he too was not ready for this madness.

Mia had her sights on the mage and stepped closer to him.

The mage noticed and was placed into a prison of fear, he cast upon the same spell to turn himself invisible in an attempt to escape, but Mia was a few steps ahead of him.

She grabbed her staff with both hands, "Oh no you don't," she said swinging it like a bat, with full force creating a large gust of mist, freezing the mage in place and everything around him.

Mia ran up to him as his spell wore off.

He was still alive and unable to move.

She stood right in front of him, watching him suffer from the ice, she had one question, "Who is your leader, who decides what goes!?" she shouted at him, "Who decides the extermination of an entire race!"

The others came up to Mia. The area around her was cold, with a small amount of mist drifting along the ground.

The mage just stared back at her.

"I think he's dead," said James.

Anna sheathed her weapon, "You children are something else, what are you, because what you just did is not magic," she looked at all the dead bodies behind her, "What do you have?"

"I'm sorry but we cannot say," Daniel replied.

She accepted that, "Nonetheless, we have to leave immediately before they find out their party has been massacred," she returned to the campsite.

The others followed.

Mia remained for some moment. The mage's cold dead eyes were like headlights to a deer, she was paralyzed.

After packing everything, they said their farewells.

"I hope you make it to your destination," Anna waved them goodbye, "stay safe."

Mia waved back, "Thank you."

Anna and her group headed into the forest.

Our party was still stuck, unable to cross the river.

"Okay," Mark sighed out loud, "How do we cross this thing, I don't want any more Dead Crows to fight."

"It burns people to death," James said, "That was horrible Mark."

"It wasn't me!" He shot back.

"That was really strange," Daniel said moving is hand, "I couldn't control my body."

"Guys," Mia called, "We will have time to discuss those problems after we find a way to cross this river, we're not safe here and going around is a bad idea too, we are bound to meet more agents."

Levina appeared again, "Hi," she greeted.

James smiled and nodded in response.

"Try freezing the river and walk on the ice," she suggested.

James looked at the water, "That could work," he blurted out.

"Huh?" Mia turned to him.

"Spill it James," said Mark.

"We could freeze it and just walk over the ice."

"Hmm," Mia thought about it, "It might not work, if this solution is some kind of acid it won't freeze solid."

"Please try Mia," Mark insisted, "We are not in the land of science and reality anymore, this could be just some kind of magic water."

"That too," she agreed, "I'll give it a go."

She pulled out her staff but kept it small and went to the edge of the river. She then swung under and slowly froze the surface of the water, "Great, it works," she said morphing her staff to its normal size. She froze a solid path from the one side to the other.

James gave Levina a pat on the shoulder, "Good idea," he whispered.

He held his hand up for a high five and she returned it.

Everyone else was too busy testing out the frozen water to notice.

Mark was the first to cross over to the other side, then it was Mia.

"Bye," said Levina.

"Cheers."

She faded away.

James hurried over to join the others.

"Yay, we made it across the river," Mark declared, "Now we can leave."

Mia pulled out the map, "Where to next..."

Sleep was not in them anymore, right now, getting as far away from this place as possible was their goal.

"If we keep going we will reach a small town and then a mountain."

"Great, let's go and put some distance between us and that river," James gave it one last look.

Mia put away her map, created some light and lead the way.

CHAPTER 18

Sealed Door

"Explain yourself!" Shouted Jane.

Jake was really surprised to see them, "What is it that you're asking?" He sighed.

They were outside the inn right now heading up into the Market District. Jake had initially wanted to spend the night there but since the appearance of Jane, Mary, Denice and their commotion, it was going to draw too many listeners. Outside was even more unsafe, having all the guards patrolling up and down, it was more silent there as well, making even the normal volume too loud.

Jane was speaking at the top of her voice trying to get answers out of him, blocking his way.

"Why are we here?" Mary stepped into the interrogation.

Jake tried to be as shallow as possible, "I don't know," he stepped around Jane, "Can I please just walk."

Denice was the only one with sense and the eyes to observe her surroundings, "Guys, keep quiet, I'm sure we don't want to be talking so loud."

"I agree with her," said Jake, then he studied their faces for a moment, "Who are you people?"

Jane raised her finger at him, "Oh no, you did not just ask that."

"Can we please just talk somewhere else, then you can explain yourselves properly," He said, making his way passed the entrance, greeting the guards posted over there.

Jane was able to keep in the questions, the important ones at least, "Where you taking us, there's Dead Crows everywhere here?"

"Galvani," he replied, "He will be our host for the interrogation."

"Who is this Galvani?" asked Mary, eyeballing every Dead Crow agents she passed by.

"He is a friend of mine."

Jake was not too sure about these ladies, but as soon as he heard them speak about time, he knew the inn was not the right place to be. For some odd reason he did not recognize them, how could they be back here if he was not the escort. One thing he did notice was their attire and gear, it looked very expensive. It was clear they were able to fit into this place and without getting into any trouble.

"You three have done a great job living here, did you get jobs or something, bounty hunting?" Asked Jake.

"Yes, for a while," replied Jane.

"Hmm, that would explain your expensive clothing and gear."

Jane looked at her clothes, "Oh."

It was a while before they reach the porch of Galvani's residence.

Jake knocked on the door.

There was no response for a while.

Jake attempted a second time, but nothing.

"I think it's clear your friend is not around," whispered Mary.

Jake knocked a little louder.

"Who is it!" A voice came from the other side.

"It's Jake," he replied.

Galvani unlocked the door immediately and opened it. He had a really worried expression, "What a surprise," he force a smile, "And three ladies... what's the occasion?"

Jake shrugged, also wearing a worried expression on his face, "May we enter?"

"Off course, off course," he opened up for them, greeting the women as they entered.

He locked the door and showed them to the couches.

"It's been a while since I've seen you Jake," said Galvani, working at the kitchen counter, "Not since you dropped of the boys at the school."

"Boys!" Mary repeated, "I presume that he's talking about our boys?" She leaned forward.

"He is speaking about James, Mark and Daniel," replied Jake.

Jane nodded really quickly with a smile on her face, "Yes, we're their parents."

Jake nodded really slowly, this was starting to make a little sense. Why they were able to recognize him, the anger that they may be feeling right now. But the only thing bothering him was their presence here.

Galvani made sure to be busy at the table, he too was quite surprised to hear that these women were their parents, now his mind was filling up with storm clouds.

Jake did not know how to put this, or explain it to them one bit.

"How are you here?" He asked.

"We were about to ask you the same thing," replied Jane, "You were the last suspicious person I saw before waking up in this time, and here you are."

Jake took a deep breath, "How do I put this," he mumble, looking up at them waiting irritably for an explanation, "Your children are safe in the school," he thought it best to try calm them down first.

Mary chuckled in disbelief, "Safe?"

He nodded.

"What's so safe about them having wanted posters all over the city!"

Jake raised both of his eyebrows, he too was caught off guard, "I haven't seen any posters of them, I only arrive about an hour ago," he turned to Galvani, "Do you perhaps know why this is so?"

Everyone looked at him as he brought to them a tray of tea, biscuits and bread. He did not say a word.

"Do you know, yes or no?" Jane raised her voice.

Galvani glanced over at Jake with a concerned look and wiped his hands on his robes. He saw it was time, he gave them a faint nod.

Jane gestured for him to continue, "Explain then, everything."

Mary seated herself comfortably, "This had better be good."

Galvani seated himself, his expression already telling them that this was not going to be good, "Some days after you dropped them off at the school," he looked at Jake, "many of the Dead Crow agents showed up in this part of the city," he started, "A lot of them also went into the school searching for them... they knew about the diamonds, claimed they had stolen them, I thought then for sure they would be found, but that didn't happen, it turned out Mia was able to hex them and change their appearances with her magic-,"

"Mia?" Denice interrupted, "She also has a poster, but hers is 20 000 gold coins."

Galvani nodded, "She is a witch."

"She is another one from your present time," added Jake. Probably not the best time to mention it.

Jane shook her head violently, "What!?"

"Are you saying she's from the year 2018?" Mary asked.

He nodded, picking up a cup of tea.

"Geez, how many lives have you ruined?" Asked Jane.

Jake frowned, "Ruined? I brought back a few, not ruined."

"You call this 'not ruined'!" She couldn't help but chuckle.

"You three were not supposed to be here, I don't know how u came back to this time," he explained.

"That makes us feel way better," said Jane sarcastically, "Please continue Galavan."

She said his name wrong. Galvani then realized he was not in the position to be correcting these angry moms right now, so he just kept quiet about that and continued with his explanation, "A few weeks since the Dead Crows arrival at the school, a rule was passed that no one was to enter or leave the school until further notice, not on weekends or holidays, I guess one could say they were in the safest and most dangerous place, hiding right under their noses," he pick up a cup, "The problem began when they secretly escaped the school a few weeks ago, through the sewers. They came to me asking about the girl Levina-."

"Wait, Levina," Denice repeated, "That's the name we saw on the list, ranked number one, she also holds the highest bounty, what would they be wanting with her?"

Galvani cleared his throat, "They became mischievous and also got their hands on the list, and saw her poster... they wanted to find her, so I helped them discover her current whereabouts."

"You helped them?" Jane asked calmly, "Why the hell would you help them find someone that dangerous."

Galvani did not like all this pressure being put on him, he felt compelled to push the blame onto Jake, who instructed him to help them should they need anything... to figure out their task. That scenario played in his head and the way he saw it, pushing the blame was going to cause way too much commotion and more anger so he decided it was best not to be completely transparent with them.

"They told me it was purely academic, maybe help out the Dead Crow, I don't know, but I decided to hurry up and help them so they could return to the school before they were caught."

This fib seem to calm them just a tad bit.

Galvani decided he should also cut out the part where he actually helped them figure the location by giving them an idea, "So, a few weeks later, this is now the day before, they came knocking on my door, before midnight, I see it's them with some things packed... they had decided to go searching for Levina."

They were all speechless.

Jane tried to say something but no words came out.

Galvani broke the death defying silence by continuing, "I had told them to return to the school, but at the time it was impossible, it would mean that they would be caught, and this also meant that they could not stay in the city because the Dead Crow would notice that they were missing," He took a deep breath, "I had no choice but to sneak them out of the city, so they were out by yesterday, long before the sun rose," he saw their expressions were blank, but he continued to speak anyway, afraid to give them a chance to, "About midday yesterday, I see the Dead Crow questioning people and showing them their wanted posters."

Jane nodded slowly, staring at her cup of tea, "So you're saying they are out there right now, in the wilds, being hunted by those Dead Crow savages?" she asked, speaking very calmly, in disbelief, with a lot of emotions buried just below the surface.

"It's much safer for them out their than in any place with people right now," Galvani replied.

Mary looked at Jake, shaking her head, "This is your fault... why is this even happening, why are we in this time?"

Jake hesitated, "That much I don't know."

"You don't know?" Denice repeated, staring into the abyss, "You don't know," she was in a loop, "You don't know."

"I'm sorry," Jake replied, "If I knew, you would know."

Mary tried to comfort Denice.

"How can you not know?" Jane asked rhetorically, "You're the one that showed up at my door!" she raised her voice, "You're the one that gave them those Diamonds and then all this happens!"

"I only did what I was supposed to."

Jane leaned forward and whispered, "What were you supposed do, please illuminate, maybe this will all go away."

Galvani just sat there and listened, sipping away at his tea, glad the heat was not on him anymore.

"That I cannot say, right now, I can only ask that you help me."

"That's not going to happen," Jane shot back, "What's going to happen now is you are going to help us find them and you're going to send us back so that we can continue with our lives!"

"That's not possible," replied Jake.

"You brought us back, you can take us back."

Jake saw he was not going to get through to them, "Are you familiar with Emara?" He asked

All there expressions turned surprised, even Galvani did not know this bit of information.

"Now," Jake spoke calmly, "We must not speak about this again, only trust in what I say, because I too am in the dark."

"I don't understand," said Mary.

All the anger that they had in them had poured away and refilled with confusion.

"Me too," Jake replied.

Jane wanted to continue with the questions, but now she had to just deal with it, she was not understanding at all, "What help does she need?"

A while later they were ready, as if going on some kind of hunt for something. They were to leave their bags behind on this short venture, their swords sheathed and new weaponry ready for use.

"So what's the plan?" Mary asked.

"We are going beneath the city," he replied, "In that maze of sewers down there, a door stands that we must find, most probably under the castle in the palace district."

Denice sighed, "Sewers... what's behind this door actually?"

"Something ancient and sacred... hopefully."

"Down in a sewer?"

Jake nodded, "Yes, an odd place to place something, but a place people would least expect something to be hidden in."

Jane was a little hesitant, she was not feeling at all too well about this change of course, "Um, Jake," she called.

"Yes," he replied still tightening his belt.

"This door that we're looking for," she started, "Is it the only thing we are going to help you with... will we be looking for the children after this?"

Mary agreed with the question, "Yes, we want to know that much."

Jake sighed, thinking of a way to put this without another eruption, "That's not a good idea... you three need to remain under the radar, you'll be putting yourselves and them in danger if you go looking for them."

One thing Jake did not know yet was that they were not a secret anymore.

"You're asking us to abandon them?" Denice asked.

It was inevitable, Jake had to now calm them down again, "They have wanted posters, I think it's best that you three stay on the safe side, the Dead Crow is not to be played with... if they find out you're the parents, there is no telling what they are going to do."

Jane took a deep breath and calmed herself, "Jake... I was fine with them at the school, now you expect us to leave them completely, with those savages?" keeping calm was impossible, "They murdered a little girl and laughed about it, you can't possibly expect us to leave them to that!" she pulled out a piece of paper from her pocket and showed it to him, "And no, we are not under the radar, we already have our own posters."

"So you weren't able to stay out of trouble after all," Jake looked at the poster, "This makes things a lot harder."

"It was not our fault," Denice came to their defense, "They were looking for us since the day we woke up here… somehow they knew already."

Jake shook his head, "Nevertheless, you still can't go after them, they are very safe as it is right now."

Jane frowned at him, "How are so sure?"

"The diamonds," he replied, "They won't allow them to die."

Jane looked at him like he was going crazy.

Luckily, Galvani came to his defense, "He's right, they spoke about it to me… when they were in grave danger, by description, those artifacts saved them."

Jane nodded slowly, this was slowly starting to give her some bit of closure, she knew nothing about any kind of magic, but if it was going to keep them safe from any danger, it was enough to reduce the sum of stress. She turned back to Jake, "We need to work on our communication skills from now on, you keep way too much from us."

Jake just nodded, at least now they were calm.

On to the more serious matter, "Where did you get those posters from?" He asked.

"Oh," Jane shoved it back into her pocket, "A courier had stacks of them heading to this town, we stopped him."

"What kind of courier… and how did you stop him," Jake asked, giving her the worried, fearful look.

"Hmm," she hummed, "I don't think you want to know that."

Mary was not afraid to say it, "It was a Dead Crow and I killed him."

Jake looked at her with a fearfully surprised expression. Even the way she replied to the question was as if this was no big deal, "That will be the only Dead Crow you kill… I cannot believe you did that."

"Jake, we've killed…," she counted in her head, "Seven since we got here, the eighth killed himself for some odd reason."

Jake was speechless, he glanced at each of them, checking if this was actually true, there faces said it all, "You three need to be put under a hell of a lot of supervision… killing one Dead Crow is no laughing matter, you've killed seven… you just don't kill them, it's against everything to kill them," he was the one getting upset now.

"What, is their leader that scary?" Mary asked, "Who is he?"

"I imagine that he is."

"Imagine…?" Mary was not taking him seriously anymore, "If we have to defend ourselves, it is what we will do."

Jake saw this as really unbelievable, he looked at their gadgets again, "Please tell me you got that money legally?"

Jane did not want to answer that, but she just shook her head slowly, she did not really understand what she had gotten herself into.

Jake was now the one plagued by stress, rubbing his forehead.

Mary told the story, "This one was a courier too, he told us to surrender because he was on some important errand with a lot of money," she started, "Off course we didn't surrender and then he gave us the money, right before he killed himself."

"For whom was the money meant for exactly?"

"Some family going by the name Maithindor and Ghordiitry," she replied.

Jake chuckled, he had given up, these three had gone beyond the fire, "Let's just go find this door before your posters get here," he suggested.

Jake did not know whether to blame them fully or cut them some slack, since they were very new to this time with no knowledge of anything whatsoever. Though what's done was now done, there is no going back, they just had to move forward, very carefully now, any step off the path and this will not end well at all for them. This was now worse for him, now that he had to be their babysitter and keep them from doing anymore childish things.

"Okay, now that we got that out of the way," Mary broke the silence, "Do we enter the sewers now or when we're at the palace district?"

"I think it would be wise to enter now," Galvani replied, "The palace district is very strict in terms of security."

"You still remember the way to the palace district right?" Jake asked.

Galvani nodded, "Just let me grab a lantern."

Outside, Galvani had led them to an alley by the library. They stood around the trapdoor to the sewers.

The night was not lit by the light of the stars and bright moon today, it was all clouded.

This alley was the best means of going down into the sewers, it was empty.

Jane saw the posters on the wall, "How can one get such a high bounty?" she pointed at Levina's poster, "What must you do to earn that?"

Mary agreed, "I mean, we only have two thousand five hundred gold coins on us, but she has one hundred thousand," she read the faded numbers, "The Dead Crow must be very rich."

Denice crouched down and lifted the trapdoor open, she was disgustingly surprised by the hot, humid stench that came out.

"That smell…" Jane blocked her nose.

"Yes, get used to it," Galvani said, "as you can see I have no weapons, so don't be expecting me to fight any Leechers."

He was the first to head down the ladder with the lantern.

Jane looked at Jake, "Leechers?"

"Don't worry about it, we may not run into them, we must not be loud either."

Everyone followed after Galvani.

"Well… this is definitely a sewer," Jane covered her nose walking over to the edge and stared down at the water in disgust.

Mary noticed the small glowing red light that hovered above them in the center of the tunnel, "Magic light not working too well anymore," she looked around, "Do people come down here often?"

"They did, quite a while back," Galvani replied, "Before the Leech disease scared them off."

Galvani led the way with his lantern.

Jane noticed something quite odd with Jake, "Don't you have a staff?" She asked.

"Oh, no not anymore," he replied, "I need to get a new one very soon."

Denice couldn't take her hand off her nose, "I hate this smell."

Galvani took a deep breath as if he were taking in fresh air, "Well, best you familiarize yourself with it because this is going to be a long walk."

"So this is how they escaped, James and the others?" Jane asked.

Galvani took a turn, "Yes, they were very resourceful as well, mapping out a single route so they wouldn't get lost, the school rules did not keep them from leaving… really determined to find this girl."

"Do you know their motives for finding this girl?" Mary asked.

Galvani shrugged, "She was their age perhaps."

"Where did you send them exactly?" Jake enquired.

"North from here, Adornfell."

"And you certain she's there?"

Galvani sighed, "I'm not certain she's anywhere Jake, but they seemed very sure about it so they had to leave as soon as possible, you know, before she disappears again."

"I hope they find her before she disappears."

"Do you know why they looking for her, what does she know?" Jane asked.

Jake shrugged in return.

"Is this bad communication or you really don't know?"

"I don't know."

Galvani made another turn.

"This is just crazy," Mary threw her hands in the air, "Can you at least explain this door?"

"I guess we could do something to pass the time," Jake replied.

"Yes, enlighten us, maybe we'll get there in no time."

The tunnels and corridors were beginning to look exactly the same, every turn they made just led to another tunnel, the only things that changed were the doors that they passed by once in a while or the staircases.

"Where to begin," Jake put some thought to it, "Ah, yes, Do you know anything about the Lord of Power?"

"I don't think I've heard of such," Jane replied.

Both Mary and Denice also declined.

"Okay, it seems that they tell you nothing in your time, what kind of history do you learn?"

"By the looks of it so far…most of what we were told is a lie," Jane replied, "Something we believed."

"Well, off course you had to believe it, it was what you were fed," Jake said, "It was not like you were able to witness any of the events yourself, so you had to believe something."

"So are you going to tell us about anything?" Mary became a bit impatient.

"I'm trying to figure out what will be relevant now, there's a whole history that you must learn to understand anything."

"I think, the door is most important right now," Jane said.

"The door yes," he began, "One thing you must know is that there isn't just one, there are three, and each of them contain a very powerful and ancient artifact, dating back millennia, thousands of years ago. Each of these artifacts, a fragment of a whole piece said to be initially created by the original gods," he paused for a moment, "Now... this world was the most diverse in the very beginning, a world of many different people, all kinds of races, man, witch, dwarf and elf among them, all living in peace, worshipping them as their gods to gain strength, but then off course, these races began to advance, over time they began to forget about their creators or whom they created and wanted to rule themselves, this began the era of kings and rulers that built nations in their own names... this off course separated them into their races and naturally, because of this separation, wars began, wars that turned to determine the greatest of rulers. These kings wanted to be praised and worshipped and so this happened. These kings being the peoples providers, brought upon weakness to the gods who created them or whom they created, because they needed to be known and worshipped to thrive."

"So what happened to these gods?' Mary asked, "If they needed to be worshipped, what happened when the worshipping stopped?"

"They slowly faded from existence, it's what happens when something is forgotten," he replied, "This was way before the first Lord of Power. What happened was, before these gods were completely lost and forgotten, they decided to use what was left of their power to create this object, powerful enough to bestow upon the purest, the power of an actual god, very few believed this and saw it as some kind of ruse to start praying to them again."

This brief little history lesson was getting them interested, the walk was not so bad anymore.

Jake continued, "Now, the story goes that, a few believed that this tale was true and began to seek out this object."

"They found it?" Jane asked.

Jake nodded, "Yes, they did, but it is still unclear to me what happened, but very soon every other nation in the world found out about this place and then came the war over it, a lot happened and from all that, the first Lord of Power came to be, there was some ritual, I don't remember or know, but this person became the new ruler of this world," he explained, "This brought peace to the world, every nation had to learn to co-exist," Jake took a deep breath, "And that's it in a nutshell."

"That's it?" Jane was surprised, "That can't be… what happened to all the other races, why are these objects sealed, why does Emara or the others exist?"

"I'm sorry, but that bit I do not know yet," Jake replied.

"Galvani?" Jane called.

Galvani shook his head, "I have never come across any text explaining anything, I'm hearing all this for the first time as well, I don't know how Jake knows such ancient history."

They were all disappointed to hear that it was the end of their brief history lesson.

A while had passed since they had come down here and the smell had now become a lot more bearable.

Nothing much lived down here, the only thing that they had seen were rats, not enough to be a threat, but there were a few that roamed the areas. The silence that was now brought after the little talk was now starting to unsettle them quite a bit.

Most of all, their weary legs were starting to ache, remembering that they had no rest since before they arrived to this city earlier today, now travelling through a maze of tunnels that went on forever, rest seemed to evade them whenever they needed it.

"We've entered the tunnels of the lower district, It may get a little dirtier and worse for the nose," Galvani announced.

"Hmm… at least we're getting closer to our destination," Mary looked at the brighter side of things.

"Galvani, why not pass through the rich district?" Jake enquired.

"I don't know the way around there," he replied, "Why, can't you take the stench?"

"It's not that… I fear this side may be a little distracting in terms of getting there as soon as possible."

Jake's words were not pleasing to the ear, and he was right.

It was not long since the announcement declaring the entry into this side of the city, that they began to hear a moan, echo in the silent distance.

Denice was the first to jump, "What was that!" she spoke quite loudly as well, she grabbed a hold of her sword.

"Shh!" Galvani silenced her, lowering his voice, "Don't say a word," he slowed down his movement.

"What is it?" Mary asked, disregarding Galvani's rules.

The moans were followed by some violent coughing and gagging sounds.

"It's a leecher," he slowed to a stop and looked down the tunnel, he did not get any closer to any of the turns that lay just ahead, "There must be a group nearby," he said, too scared to move.

Everyone stopped behind Galvani.

"What do we do?" Mary asked, "Is there a way around?"

"We would have to go far back because there is no platform here to cross the water," he replied.

It was a little too late for going back right now, Denice's voice must have reached over to them because a human figure appeared from a turn at the far end of the tunnel. Jane, Mary and Denice crouched down behind Galvani and examined this new encounter with a lot of fearful disgust and a little curiosity, their eyes were glued to this man known to everyone as a leecher.

Galvani just stared back at it, but he was not interested in examination so he turned around, only to see the others, besides Jake hiding behind him, "What are you doing hiding behind me!" he argued making his way around them all with his lantern, only to hide behind Jake, "I don't have a weapon," he whispered to him.

Denice was now the one in front of everyone, feeling bear and vulnerable, she just stared.

The leecher looked up and noticed them, he just stared at them as well.

This continued on for some moments, both sides still as statues.

Galvani's head popped out from behind Jake, which triggered the leecher, making it cry out loud and start walking towards them, turning into a jog and then a sprint.

Jane unclipped he gauntlet crossbow and loaded a bolt into it. She stood up from behind Mary and aimed it at the leecher.

She released the bolt with her other hand, hitting the leecher on the left side of the chest, turning it and collapsing it to the ground on its back, dead.

Denice looked away, she was disgusted by the fidgeting of the leeches on the man.

Jane made her way to the dead body.

"What are you doing!" Galvani whispered to her aloud, "If one of those leeches bites you, it's over."

Jane just nodded, she did not want to waste the bolt so she pulled it out of the man's chest and wiped it one his shirt, finding it hard to look at the body but as well hard to look away. She returned to the group, "You said there's a group right?" She asked reloading the crossbow.

Galvani nodded.

Mary and Denice had their bows loaded as well.

"Hey!" Jane shouted, "Hey!"

Everyone received a heart attack from Jane's reckless shouting.

"What are you doing?" Galvani stepped forward, "They going to come here!"

"Yeah, that's exactly what I want," she replied, "I'm not heading down there for any surprises."

A pair of leechers appeared from the same turn.

Galvani retreated again.

"I'm afraid swords are too risky in this scenario," said Jake, "Ladies, please."

Denice turned to them, "You're not going to help?"

Galvani was the first to reply to that, "I made it clear, I was not going to be dealing with any of those leechers, I am the guide."

Jake pulled out his longsword, "I'll be ready as a last resort."

Mary and Jane took out the pair that was coming at them.

"Come on Denice, we got this so far, just make your arrows count," Mary said.

Denice turned back to the problem.

They stood side by side, waiting for the next bit to show up. The moans had not stopped.

This time they came in larger numbers, making the defenders a little panicky. It was now a group of five that had appear, running at them.

Three of them defending, were able to shoot down three, the other two came a little to close and their reload speed was not experienced.

Behind the two heading toward them, a horde came from the end, a group of about ten.

Mary was a little hesitant, unable to get the bolt in, she decided it was best to pulled out her sword. As the leecher passed the last few metres, she heel kicked her in the abdomen and used her sword to push it into the river, making a big splash which she jumped away from, too afraid of the water.

The second was bolted down by Jane.

"They're like zombies," Denice declared aiming at the horde and releasing her bolt.

To their little bit of luck, one or two of the these leechers were pushed over the edge and into the water. The space was quite narrow.

Mary made her way back to her position and fired another bolt.

These leechers easily lost their balance, every shot created a stump on the ground that managed to trip them over which provided opportunity for them to use their swords and put them down before the would be able to get back up.

It was silent after the horde, it had seemed that this group was done, all the leechers in this area had be taken care of.

Now the way ahead of them was filled with dead bodies which they carefully pushed over into the water without getting bitten by the leeches. They were so disgusted by this sight, taking the bolts back were not the option anymore.

This had awoken them up from their boredom a bit, right now they were on high alert, their crossbows loaded and swords drawn.

Once it was all clear an ready, Galvani took to the lead again and this time with a lot more haste, with the intent of getting out of this place as soon as possible.

After the silent walk through the remainder of the lower district sewers, they had finally made it to the palace district, a much, much cleaner sewer and a lot less murky and creepy.

"Okay, we have entered into the Palace district sewers," Galvani declared, "Right now we are beneath the castle, as requested by Jake."

"Thank you," He said.

"Now, how do we find this door?"

"Just follow me," Jake replied, taking the lead.

They headed up for a while and came to a stop, in a tunnel that had nothing but walls that stood straight, built from large stone, rectangular blocks.

Jake looked around.

Everyone else looked at him with some measure of confusion.

"There's no door here," Mary stated.

Jake ignored her and looked across the river, looked at the wall as if it held some importance to it. He then looked at the river, conveniently, there was a metal platform placed there for easy crossing.

He made his way across the river and stood on the other side, facing the wall.

The others just did what he did.

"The wall?" Galvani asked.

Jake nodded, "Yes, the wall," he started feeling around, pushing his hand against the stone blocks.

"Jake?" Mary asked a little concerned.

He did not reply, but at that moment he came across a loose block of stone and pushed it in. It fell on the other side into a dark room. Jake nodded, "That was the one," he took a step back.

Jane and her curiosity brought her to the wall and peeked through it. She saw nothing, it was pitch black. She turned back to the others, "I can't see anything."

Just then, a small portion of the wall moved out towards them, which frightened Jane.

The wall stopped and then began to open like an automatic door till it was large enough for people to pass through.

"Found it," Jake said turning to Galvani with a smile.

Galvani, being the light bearer, entered into the dark first.

Denice was a little scared, "Don't places this old and forgotten normally have those dangerous booby-traps?"

"Maybe," Mary replied following the others in, "Let's go."

As they headed down the passage, they started to come across strange masks that were hanging down from the ceiling, it did give them a bit of a scare at first. These masks mostly consisted of two variations, bearing even stranger symbols on them.

"Now there's a lot of creepy masks," Denice said pushing one aside.

Mary was unhappy that they frightened her, so she was pushing them away with force. Having them sway from side to side for Denice to dodge or put to a stop.

They continued passed them and found something different, they had entered into a room taking the shape of a hut, with a lot more different masks hanging from the ceiling. On the other side of the room was a door that everyone walked over to.

"So this is it?"

"Yes," replied Jake.

The door was built from some kind of metallic component, with many different kind of symbols carved in and out of it, and in the centre, a large carving of an hourglass with little stars in it, representing the sand.

One thing that they noticed from this beauty was the fact that this door had no hinges, locks, door knobs or handles.

"Door with the hourglass," Jake whispered, giving it a feel with his fingers.

"Well...," Mary sighed, "That was easy, now what?"

"Yes, getting here is easy," Jake said, "We were just checking if it's open."

"How do you open something with nothing to open it with?" Mary enquired.

"That's a good question," He replied.

Mary's jaw dropped in disbelief.

Galvani brought the lantern closer to the door, "So inside lies this fragment you spoke about?"

Jake nodded.

"By the looks of it, this one has something to do with time," Jane looked at the hourglass.

The only person who quickly lost interest in the door was Denice, her eyes jumped from mask to mask, some seemed to be staring right back at her, "Guys, the door is closed right, let's leave this creepy place before someone else finds it, I mean if that thing in there can create a god, we shouldn't linger."

Jake agreed, "That would be wise."

With haste, they exited through the passageway.

Jake picked up the heavy stone block and placed it in the wall where it was missing which allowed for it to seal itself again.

"What now?" Asked Galvani.

"We find the next door," He replied, "But first... I need a cup of tea and a new staff," he started heading back.

"I need sleep," Denice said, "It's been more than a day since I had any."

Both Mary and Jane agreed with her.

Galvani again took the lead.

The very next day, Jane, Mary and Denice awoken at around midday, having slept on the couches and mattress on the floor.

Galvani and Jake had made food that was placed on the dining table.

"Morning ladies," Galvani greeted, "Made a little late breakfast."

Jane sat up on the couch and stretched her arms, her hair all over the place, "Smells good."

Jake was already seated, reading the newspaper, "You had better enjoy this one," he said, "These will become a very rare treat in your days to come since your bounties will be here very soon."

Everyone sat at the table and enjoyed their breakfast.

After that, they all got themselves cleaned up and ready to leave.

Jake had arranged that they left in the evening to minimize facial recognition. He also gave Galvani some money for his troubles and to get them some food for the road.

That afternoon, Jane had sat at the table with Jake for some bit of questioning.

Mary and Denice were busy passing the time by exploring the house, mainly Galvani's little work station.

"Jake, might you have any idea how the Dead Crow might have known about us?" she asked, "they were searching for us since we had awoken here."

Jake shook his head, "I don't know much about that group," he turned the page, "But even if you were innocent in the actions you committed in killing them, you will never be able to prove your innocence."

"Also, the ones that we came across acted very strange, they had this crazy nature about them, anything you may know about that?"

Jake again shook his head, "I have never come across an agent that acted crazy, they are always formal and respectful."

Jane gave him a weird look. *How can he say that after what she had witnessed.*

"We need to fetch the horses before we leave," Jake mentioned, "The city we are heading to now is far to the east."

They nodded in reply.

The sun had set and Galvani had made his return to the house with all the goods that they needed for the road ahead and Jake's new staff, nothing too fancy, just looked like a wooden stick.

As the night fell, they said their goodbyes to Galvani and left.

CHAPTER 19

The Mountain Pass

The sky was still masked by the large cloak of clouds the next day at which they travelled. The wind was a little strong so James, Mark and Daniel had put on their robes again, just to keep out most of the cold.

The grass had become a lot more lively since the river, but turned lemon by the swift change in seasons.

Still a little paranoid about the night before, they had not dared to slow down for any kind of rest, forever thinking that they could be on their trail again, hiding behind some mage's illusion magic. Fearing that maybe this time, they would not gain the pleasures of an introduction.

Still far from the road and any patrols, it was much safer to say the least, many strangers seldom occupied the plains, sticking to the safety of the main roads, forever patrolled, and the position they were in had a higher chance of being emptier since nobody ever attempted to cross the river.

Mia had her head buried in the map, as usual, staring at their next stop.

James and the others were just busy messing around since there was nothing interesting to see for miles.

"Man, yesterday was messed up," Mark said, "Did you see what I did with my shield?"

James agreed, "Dude, yeah that was cool, that shield you created was like two stories, sending those agents flying."

"I swatted them to the river," his cheerful face disappeared, "I threw them into that river... I can still hear their screams man, but I did not know we could do that," he turned cheerful again.

James pulled out his sword, "We didn't, I lost control over my body, I could only watch what I was doing, disappearing and appearing all over the place," he looked at his sword closely, "But the strange thing was that I was able to keep up with my body, I could see everything at that speed... compared to the time when I tried to test it out myself, I became all tired and my vision was blurry," he explained, "But no lie, I was afraid of what I was doing there... I actually killed someone..." he couldn't stop staring at his sword, looking for any dirt or bloodstains, wondering why his feelings were not as bad as he would have expected when taking the life of someone. He had predicted some kind of trauma, "Do you think that these things we wear... do you think they also change how we feel?"

Daniel tried to justify what James was asking, "Hey, we're not in control, those actions were ours, but we did not sign up for any of this anyway... I mean, killing people was not a part of our contracts, if we had a contract," he explained, "I think being stuck in this place has its downsides, some being doing whatever to survive. These times were quite bad, a lot of killing and even children being force into wars, I think it's also the reason why Marridor taught us all this combat stuff, for situations similar to yesterdays... in the present, it's all just books, books, books and a little fitness, and the camping which only has relevance for us stuck in a time where those skills are actually needed."

"Yeah, I guess so," James replied sheathing his sword again, "Still can't deny the horrible feeling though."

Mark had not listened to everything, "Thanks for the speech Daniel, but all I heard was 'We need to grow a back bone and suck it up to survive'."

Daniel shrugged, "If you put it that way, it sounds as if my speech was bad."

"Oh it was, I just removed all that disgusting sugarcoating," Mark replied.

James looked at his diamond, just dangling from around his neck, "We need to question Jake about these things, I mean I'm grateful that they save us from imminent death, but this controlling thing is kind of scary, do you think it's some kind of enchantment?"

"Don't ask questions that you cannot answer James, that will just be more problematic," Mark said squinting into the distance. He saw nothing but a mountain, he sighed, "That mountain looks pretty far, but I swear it might be growing."

Daniel chuckled, "I think it's your imagination, that mountain is not growing."

Mark mumbled back, "I'm trying to be a little positive here so…"

Daniel just nodded in return and looked to the sky, "We lucky, no rain since we left," he pointed out.

James looked at Mia, who was just a few metres ahead from where they were, he wondered again why she was burying herself in that map. He decided to go up to her and ask, "Is everything fine, seem awfully attached to that map, are we lost, looking for a new route or something?"

She nodded without detaching her eyes from it, "I'm fine and we're not lost,."

James looked ahead, "Hmm, if I'm not wrong, you said we have to reach a mountain, I'm guess it's that one just ahead?"

Mia nodded.

"Then what are you-,"

"Okay, fine," she rolled up the map and got a little angry, "Happy now?" she did not give James the time to respond, "It seems to be bothering you that I'm looking at this map."

James slowed down a bit raising his hands, "Okay, I was just asking if you're fine."

"Okay… I'm not fine," she calmed herself a little.

Daniel and Mark also grew concerned.

"What's wrong Mia?" Daniel asked.

Mia stopped and looked at them, right now she did not feel like receiving any or answering any questions. It was clear to them she was annoyed.

"Yeah, what's bothering you?" Mark asked.

Mia could see some level of worry in their faces, she did not want to be the one to make this all the more upsetting as it already is. She took a deep breath and continued walking, "I'm sorry," she replied, "I'm just angry and confused."

"About?" James asked.

"Look around you," she replied raising her hands in the air, "this is what's making me angry, the fact that we're here and don't know why and now we're expected to do things that we shouldn't, why... we don't know that either," she raised her voice.

"We can't blame ourselves for that," Daniel added.

"Yes, but we can't do anything about it either," the frustration grew in her voice, "Yesterday is not the last time this is going to happen right?"

"I'm afraid so," Daniel replied, "The longer we remain here, the worse it will get, I mean, now we've killed, we will be murderers to the world soon."

Mark did not enjoy this depressing subject, so he tried his best to change it, "I wish I had a spyglass," he acted as if he were actually looking through one.

Daniel pulled the map from Mia's bag and looked for what lay ahead, "There's a village coming up," he announced.

"What, shouldn't we be avoiding such a place," James said, "You know, bounties and all."

Mia shook her head, "Not in this case, we have to pass through the village."

"And why is that?"

Mia pointed on the map, "Look here," she said, "As you can see, this is Mount Terratoar and there's Adornfell right above it, the quickest way to the city is by means of the mountain pass here," she pointed at it, "Going around would take a lot more days and risk being seen, as you can see by the roads."

"I vote mountain pass," Mark said, "I don't care if we have to hike, I'm not spending even more days walking."

"And we would stand a better chance of finding Levina," Mia added.

"Yes, yes, finding the girl who has never been caught for ten years," Mark said, "Ten years... it should only take a few days for us." He said.

"Mark, please," Daniel turned to him, "Just go back to wishing you had a spyglass, your negativity is going to kill us."

James giggled quietly. He then felt a small tug against his robe from behind.

"James," a little girl's voice spoke.

James gasped, with a big smile on his face, but paused just as he was about to speak, he looked around, finally remembering before he made a fool of himself again. He decided to slow his pace a little, allow for some distance between him and the others.

"Hi Levina," he greeted.

"I'm just checking if you're alright."

"Alright?" James repeated surprised, given the fact that it was her who had the cuffs and sores on her body, "Yes... Are you alright?"

She nodded in return, "No stranger has ever helped me before, it feels nice."

"No problem," he replied, "Did you see what happened yesterday with the diamonds and our powers?" He started to make conversation.

"Yes, you were disappearing and he was flying... or jumping really high," she was not too sure, "Can I see it, your diamond."

"Sure," he replied taking it off and handing it over to her.

She held it up by the chain above her head and stared closely into it, "It's so pretty."

"It is, and did you know that it's the strongest rock."

She shook her head, "Really."

"Yup."

"I heard there was nothing prettier than the hourglass of Emara."

James had never heard of such, "Huh, what's that?"

Levina shrugged, "I heard someone say it, but they were also saying that they heard it was pretty."

"James!" Daniel shout from up ahead, "Why you falling behind."

"Don't worry, I'll catch up!" He shouted back.

Levina handed the diamond over to him, "You are nearly at the next village," she declared pointing ahead.

"Sweet, we're one village closer to Adornfell."

"The last one," Levina said, "I'll be leaving for now, be careful," she said fading away.

James waved and picked his pace as soon as she was gone. He rejoined with the others, "So how do we do this?"

"Same as always," Mia replied.

They stood at the edge of this little town. They had just recently arrived and it was late in the afternoon, tired as ever. The sun was still nowhere to be seen, but the day was definitely a shade darker than before.

"Woah," said James as he gazed slowly from one side of the town to the next, "This is not what I was expecting to see at all, I was thinking it would be more like the last town we visited."

This village was much smaller than the town of Lonestar and for worse, did not even have a small border around it, not even a picket fence.

From where they stood, this little village looked a lot worse than the poor district of the magic city.

A lot of the wooden structures, mostly the houses, that lay on the outskirts of the place had been completely demolished, as if there were some kind of war that had occurred a while ago.

"What happened here?" Mia asked.

James headed on forward first, "Come on, let's go find an inn or something."

Everybody else followed behind.

The people, who seemed to be the residents of this town were eyeballing them as if it were their very first time encountering people. The lot of them did not look to have a lot, probably because some of their homes might have been destroyed. Some seemed to have had nothing to eat in days. Even the children that they saw were not lively.

Burnt wood and straw decorated the ground, most homes now stood lacking their primary needs, rooftops completely burnt away, walls and doors missing, and the comforts that made a house a home. One would assume that they were stolen right after the repercussion, which could have been the case. These people have been in this situation for a while now.

This walk on the main road was going to be the most uncomfortable for them, the silence was thick.

At least there was some interaction that occurred.

A small boy, of about eight years came out of nowhere, running toward them, he stopped at Mia. He was covered in ragged clothing and had no shoes to cover his feet.

He walked beside her.

Mia did not know what to do, or expression to pull. She just smiled at him faintly.

"Are you a traveler?" The boy asked.

Mia nodded in return.

The others continued forward.

"Can you please spare a coin?"

Mia pulled out a gold coin from her bag and handed it over to him.

"Thank you miss," He smiled, before running off into one of the demolished buildings not too far away.

Mia stood and watched where he was heading off to.

The boy went into the house, and through the wall, with a missing plank, she saw him kneel down before someone.

Mia did not feel too well leaving these people in this state. She caught up to the others.

The city became somewhat more lively as they entered the part of the town that was not destroyed.

"We've got to help these people," Mia whispered to them.

"I agree," Mark replied, "But we can't, we barely have our own things and we're racing against the clock."

For just a moment there, Mia was actually happy with what Mark had to say, until he continued to talk, "What! How could you say that?" She whispered aloud.

Mark shrugged, "I opened my mouth, besides, I'm just being a bit realistic here," he replied, "you even said yourself, we must hurry."

"I agree with Mark," said Daniel.

"Same," James agreed, "We rest here for the night and leave at first light," he looked ahead, "Because tomorrow we are going for a long hike."

This was democratic, and she lost.

"I don't see any Dead Crow agents around here, just a few of the town guards," Mia said searching the area.

"We should count ourselves a little lucky then," Mark replied.

It was not too long before they came across this towns inn. At least it was fully operational and was kept clean. The sign read : The Midnight Den, and outside, on one of the benches of the porch sat a guard. He looked a little off, it was clear he had quite a bit to drink. It was late in the afternoon so maybe he could pass for a few.

The inn was about the same size as the one in Lonestar from the outside. This one had the difference of bearing two floors instead of one.

James opened the door and stepped in.

The inside greeted them with a lot of warmth, a large temperature difference from the outside. The whole upper level of the inn was visible with a balcony.

On the farthest end of the inn was a man standing behind a counter and a woman walking around serving the people and like all other inns, a notice board was placed for everyone to see.

"Well... the mood did certainly change," Mark pointed out, "Let's get some rooms first, before they get taken by someone else."

This inns room service was a little different and more convenient to the buyer. It was not a big room with a lot of beds, this one had very small single rooms, they were able to get a room for each of them at a fairly cheap price.

After a while, they were all seated at the table, enjoying some food that was properly cooked and seasoned well, with some bread. Mia was the only one who seemed to feel a little guilty for eating whilst thinking about the little boy that had come up to her earlier, spending another night out there with nothing to eat.

"I should've known it was too good to be true," Daniel said, "Dead Crows."

"Where?" Asked James, becoming all jumpy, scanning the area like some hawk.

Daniel pointed him the right way with his head, "There."

There was a group of four agents sitting around at a table near the corner across the room from them, having themselves a good time.

"Hmm, let's not worry about them," James said, "Though... it seems our bounties are here too," he said looking at the notice board.

After eating, they headed upstairs, to where their rooms were. All of them right next to the other. Each one having a small, round table with a lit candle and a small wooden chair.

Before anyone could say their 'goodnights' and go sleep, Mia had something to bring to their attention.

"Guys," she spoke

They all turned to her.

"Hmmhmm," Mark hummed.

"Remember you told me that your diamond was nearly stolen while you were asleep in that other inn?"

"Yeah, but that was when they saw us," Daniel explained, "We are wearing different faces this time, they won't suspect a think."

"Umm... yes, I guess you're right there," she giggled, "almost got a little worried there."

"Yup, no need to worry about anybody stealing anything this time," James added.

Mark sighed, "Okay, Okay, we have some very crazy hiking to do tomorrow, I suggest we get as much rest as we can," he walked over to his room, "Goodnight peoples."

They all entered their separate rooms and closed their doors.

Mia sat on her bed and felt its softness, she moved her hands over the sheets, remembering the last time she had slept on such a comfortable bed.

She took a deep breath, feeling the symptoms of her sleep sinking in real fast the more she sat in the warm, dimly lit room, "Not today," she murmured, standing up and taking her bag with her.

She slowly opened the door and stepped outside, hoping not to disturb the others.

The view from up here was quite nice, she leaned onto the balcony. Her reason for not going to sleep was primarily because she knew it would put the others in grave danger.

Tired to death no doubt, she saw fit to keep herself a little busy. Staring down at the ground floor she noticed the inn keeper and the barstools that were placed on the other side of the counter. Paying him a little visit would be the first thing that she did.

She headed down and seated herself on one of the barstools.

"Hello there young lass," he greeted, "Aren't ye going to be sleeping with your fellow friends?"

She shook her head, "Not today."

"Well then...," he bent over and searched for something behind the counter, "You ought to take your money back then," he placed a few silver coins onto the table.

"Thank you," she took the money.

The inn keeper noticed something on her hip, "What's that you got there, some kind of drumstick?"

Mia saw what he was talking about and giggled, "No, it's a staff, I went to Marridor."

"Ah, you were a student there?"

She nodded.

"Interesting," he nodded slowly, "You know, I don't really see many young mages such as yourself travelling," he leaned forward, "I here most of them stay in the city or go on and join up with the Dead Crow... what are you doing?"

"Just traveling," she replied, "See the world I guess."

"Clever, best enjoy it while you are at your age," he took a deep breath, "Me personally, I never understood the concept of magic, I would have preferred it to stay with the witches if you asked me."

Mia just nodded in return, "I've been meaning to ask, is it safe to take the mountain pass?"

The inn keeper cleared his throat, "Not many speak about that place, No one ever ventures up there and the few whom ever do so, never return," he explained, "Many who go there speak of finding some kind of temple created by the ancient gods, seeking the treasures that lie within... would I pass through there? Only if not in search for such things."

Mia looked at the money in her hand and thought about what he had said, "Thanks for the information."

"Anytime," he replied, "We've got to help out as many lives as we can."

"How many loaves can I get for this?"

He counted the coins, "three, and a bit of cheese."

"I'll take it," she handed over the money.

"Let me give you a bag with that," he said fetching one and putting all the goods inside.

She stood up from her stool.

"Nice meeting you."

Mia smiled, "You too."

Her next destination was outside.

The chilly breeze outside was quite strong and was just the right medicine she needed to keep her up, more so than the warm and cozy inn.

She took in the fresh air and let it out. To her left, she saw the guard was still sitting there, only he was now fast asleep.

She made her way down the steps and began her evening walk down the streets. There was moonlight this time, most of the clouds had drifted off to the ends of the horizon, now it was not completely dark with the beautiful constellations visible.

The streets were not entirely empty, there were a few who roamed at this late hour, with a few guards posted, not looking lively at all or up to some other things, like your typical city guard. They were not to blame though, this place was a little isolated.

Mia walked in the same direction in which they arrived, looking for the child that had asked her for money.

When she finally came across the house, she made a quick turn and continued to it in her slow relaxing pace.

For a while, she stood in front of the house, just examining its state, almost everything was gone, only a small section of the roof had remained, a small hearth still stood against the wall across from her, the door was nowhere to be found and a lot of the wall planks were missing.

She made her way up the steps and in through the doorway.

Inside was an older lady that lay on her back on a sleeping roll with blankets over her. Next to the old lady was the little boy, rolled up in a ball, also asleep with a small blanket over him.

The sight was truly heartbreaking and since rest was not on her to-do list today, she decided to wake them up. She knocked on the wall.

No one responded.

She then placed her bags down against the wall before kneeling down next the boy, "Hey," she shook him.

The boy slowly opened his eyes, still unaware of what was happening. His gaze turned up and when he caught sight of a human figure right above him, he jumped, frightened and moved away.

Mia immediately tried to calm him down as he sat back panting, "It's okay, it's okay," she whispered, "it's only me... do you remember me?"

The boy slowed his breathing and calmed himself down before nodding to the question.

"Is this your mother?"

"Yes," he replied with a shaky voice.

"Do you know what's wrong with her?"

The little boy shook his head rubbing his one eye, "She says she has a really sore headache, she has had it for the past few day now."

Mia's major was not healing but she had known quite a little about it since she favoured all magic. She felt the need to help with the pain so she moved closer to his mother, "Don't tell anyone," she smiled at him.

"Are you going to cure her?" His face lit up with excitement.

"Um, not really, but I can make the pain a lot better, if she has a sickness, we will need medicine for it."

Mia placed her hand over his mother's forehead. Moments later her palm lit up, a bright yellow light.

"Wow," the boys jaw dropped, his eyes wide open.

Her little deed was no doubt draining away a lot of her energy, but she continued to heal the lady till she woke up. She hid her powers after that.

The boy's mother slowly opened her eyes and turned to Mia, "What happened," she managed to utter placing her hand against her forehead.

"Mommy, are you better," the boy spoke excitedly.

She struggled to a sitting position and leaned against the wall, "Who are you?" She asked.

The boy was the first to answer the question, "She is the lady that made you feel better," he was so excited.

Mia sat back against the wall as well, she nodded in response to the boy's description, "I helped you with the pain, but its medicine that will make you better permanently."

The lady bowed down her head, "Thank you, I'm in your debt."

Mia shook her head, "No need, thank you is enough, just happy to help," she took the bag of loaves and handed it over to them, "Here."

The lady accepted it, "I thank you again, I'm Grace," she introduced herself.

Mia could not think of a name so she used something familiar, "I'm Anna."

"Nice to meet you Anna," she said, "You studied at the school of magic?"

She nodded, looking around, "For a short while... what happened here?"

Grace took a deep breath, "Levina happened... according to the Dead Crow."

Once again her symptoms of sleep faded away, her interest grew beyond measure, "They found her?"

She nodded, "About a month ago, she just suddenly appeared and the Dead Crow came swarming after her, many of the magic types."

"So... she destroyed the place?" Mia asked hoping that she would not give an answer she did not want.

"No, she didn't touch a single person... though everyone that saw her was afraid of her still, I suppose that bounty and rumours that we all hear have an effect on people," she explained, "The only people she opposed were the ones she was trying to get away from, the Dead Crow, which were the ones responsible for this place being in this state."

"Oh," that at least was some good news, for a second there she did not want to find out that she was chasing after an actual murderer that would take away the homes of other people and leave them in this state to survive. Hearing it was the Dead Crow's fault, on the other hand, somehow did not really surprise her at all.

"Even after all that destruction, caused by those mages, they did not accomplish anything because she just disappeared again, the way she arrived, in the blink of an eye."

Well, that bit of information was only interesting while it lasted, Mia's eyelids were forcing themselves shut.

"They have been sending people to rebuild this place, but it's a bit slow."

"I'm sorry," she managed to speak.

"Well... at least something's happen."

Mia could not carry the weight of her eyelids anymore, she closed them and drifted away into a deep sleep.

"She's asleep," the boy said.

"Let her rest," she replied giving him some of the bread.

Before the little boy could take his first bite, he received a surprise, "Mom look," she pointed at Mia.

"What's this?"

From the top of her head, a dark blue kind of smoke started to rise and fade away. The smoke then started to come off of her face.

Her hair and face had started to change, all features, even her hair colour went back to normal.

Once the smoke had disappeared, her face had morphed completely.

"Her face changed," the boy said.

Grace took a closer look at Mia's face, "Wait... I've seen her before."

The boy turned to her mother, "It's the pretty lady from the posters."

Grace began to remember, "Yes, she's the witch, her bounty is worth a lot."

"But why do they want to find her, she is a nice person, she even helped you get better."

Grace shrugged, "I think it's a racial matter," she mumbled, "We have to make sure she stays safe while she rests, we can't turn her in either," she rubbed her sons back, "Come on, eat up," she gave him a kiss on the forehead.

Upstairs in one of the inn bedrooms, James had just recently awoken from his great and peaceful sleep, awakened by the light that fell through the window.

This time he was ready to wake up, and pumped for the continuation of their little venture, he sat up immediately and stretched his arms.

The room was very warm, way too hot for his liking so he did not put on the robe this time when he got out of bed, instead he stuffed it in between his sleeping roll before putting the bag on his back.

After leaving the room, he knocked at Mark's door first and opened it. He was fast asleep. None of the light was coming through this curtains so he saw fit to let the sun have the pleasure of waking him up.

He opened the curtains which immediately woke up Mark as he attempted to protect himself from the light.

"Wake up, time for the early morning hike," James said walking out of the room.

He did the same with Daniel.

The last person to wake up was Mia, he knocked on her door, "Hello."

There was no response from inside the room.

He knocked again a little louder, "Hello."

No response again.

After the third time trying he opened the door and stepped in.

Mia was not there. The bed was made and her bag gone.

"Hmm, early bird," he closed the door again and went over to the railing.

Scanning the bottom floor, he did not see Mia anywhere. Only a few tables were occupied with some people having themselves breakfast, two Dead Crows among them. The next thought was that she could be right beneath him, seated by one of the tables so he went around to the other side of the room for a quick check and still he did not find her.

James stood there for a few seconds, waiting for Daniel and Mark to leave their rooms. When that was up, he decided to keep himself a little busy by making his bed.

They were all ready, finally and James had to break the news of missing Mia, "Mia is not here," he spoke quietly.

Mark looked over the balcony, "Have you checked down there?"

James nodded.

"Maybe she is beneath us," Mark added, "Come on, she might be there," he headed for the steps.

James was not even allowed to check Mark's thought box, he just followed after him.

"Mark... it's not cold?" Daniel said to him.

Mark stopped and turned to him, "One, you cannot be too sure and two, stop saying my name."

Downstairs they scanned the area for her but nothing.

"I wonder where she is," Mark mumbled.

James waved his hand at the inn keeper.

He hesitated and slowly raised his, giving James a very weird look.

Mark turned to the Dead Crow agents, and for some odd reason this turned into some kind of stare down.

"Maybe we go outside?" James suggested, he did not fancy asking the inn keeper anymore after that awkward little greeting.

Daniel noticed Mark's game and snapped him out of it, "What are you doing."

"He made eye contact first," he whispered back.

"Let's ask," Daniel went up to the counter, "Morning sir," he greeted, "Have you seen a young girl walk by recently?"

The inn keeper shook his head slowly, his eyes literally popping out of his head, "No, I'm afraid not," he then turned right to the notice board.

Daniel noticed his little gesture and saw the notice board as well. His heart began to race, "Um, well, thank you sir," he stepped away immediately, joining up with the others.

"What did he say?" James asked.

Daniel ignored his question and went straight to the point, "I think they know who we are."

"Guys," Mark whispered, "That Dead Crow is standing up, he is looking right at me."

All three of them headed for the door as soon as the Dead Crow went for something under his cloak.

"Hey, boys!" He shouted making his way to them.

They made their way around the hearth and straight for the exit.

The other agent also got up, leaving his food unattended.

Daniel ran up to the door and threw it open. He jumped out, followed by James who was close behind. Mark had an obstacle in his way, there was a lady busy sweeping the floor he apologized beforehand, before he pushed her aside into the one agents. He was able to get to the door and follow the others out.

James made his way down the stairs, "What do you think happened?" He asked.

Daniel shrugged, "We need to go."

He did not have time to think so he called out her name, "Mia!"

Mark made it down the steps, "What are you doing, they're attacking us with pretty daggers, we have to get out of here,"

James continued to call out her name.

One of the civilians walking by recognized their faces, "Criminals!" He shouted, stepping off of the road, "Guards. Wanted criminals," he pointed at them.

The first agent stepped out and came after them. The second agent made the guard sitting on the bench aware of the situation.

All civilians in the area went into a panic state, calling every single guard in the area before hiding away from view.

Mia was still asleep where she was, at Grace's house. She never heard James's call. To her luck, the little boy was awake and heard the one, he shook her till she came too.

She opened her eyes and looked at the boy, trying to assess the situation.

"Your friends are calling you," he shouted, "Wake up!"

Mia came too quite quickly, only realizing now that she had fallen asleep and allowed for her hex to dispel, "I fell asleep," she stood up.

"Your friend just called you," the boy repeated.

Mia put on her bag and pulled out her staff, "Thank you, bye Grace, sorry but I have to go."

"Bye."

Mia jumped out of the house skipping all the steps and made her way to the main road. She looked up in the direction of the inn and saw two of them standing in the middle of the road, "Idiots!" She started sprinting towards them.

"There she is," Daniel pointed.

This was just before Mark came down after them, "What are you doing, they're attacking us with pretty daggers."

The first agent made it through the door while James still called out Mia's name.

"Head for the Pass!" she shouted.

"Head for the pass, got it," he turned and headed up the road.

Daniel followed him.

Mark had to dodge the incoming attack made by the first agent, before being able to make a run for it.

The agent that just attempted at Mark turned away from him and saw the easier target coming right at him, "The witch," he said with a smile.

A lot of the guards had started to appear from their posts, only having the time to surround Mia while the others were let go.

James turned to see that they were not being chased anymore, "She's surrounded, we have to help."

From Mia, this was not what she wanted, she noticed their sudden stop, "Just go!" She shouted.

"She doesn't want us to help," said James.

"Well... she is the only one there with magic," Mark pointed out, "I think we should just trust her," he started walking away.

James and Daniel were not so sure, but they knew she had some kind of idea up her sleeve, so they chose to follow what Mark had said and trusted her.

"Don't you think we should go after the others as well," One of the guards asked, looking at them make their way to the village's outskirts.

The agent shook his head, "No, those three are nothing without her magic, their faces will be seen and they will be caught... we just prolonging it," he smiled at Mia pulling out his sword.

Mia did not show any fear. She morphed her staff to its original size and created a small sphere of flames in her left palm.

The guards were quite surprised and a little intimidated by the magic, but mostly the lack of fear that she showed. They tightened their grips on the weapons that they held.

"Please step aside," Mia asked.

The agent giggled.

None of the Agents seemed to show any kind of fear, it was only the city guards that were unsure about what they were doing.

"Kill her," the agent ordered.

It was by that order when Mia decided to implement the plan. With her left hand, wielding the flames she swung it, creating a large wave that spread out to the them, and in their blinded state, she used her staff to create a dust cloud by hitting it against the ground. The dust diminished the flames which she had created, keeping those caught in them from burning.

It was a few moments later when the dust had cleared up and the guards were able to see again.

Most of them jumped at the sight of Mia, who was still standing in the centre. They did not hesitate to point their swords and pikes back at her, only this time, most of them were shaking, afraid to make a move.

The agent noticed her as well and was confused, he frowned at her, "I would have thought that you were going to make a run for it... but you're still here?" he coughed from the dust, "It seems you don't understand the concept of a smoke screen."

Mia did not reply, she just looked at him.

The agent then turned to the rest, wearing a really puzzled face, "Well... kill her!"

Without second thought, the pike men went for the kill, stabbing her from all directions.

Nothing happened.

No reaction from Mia.

No blood on the blades.

Confusion filled the crowd.

One of the pike men moved his blade around.

She was not there, just a mirage.

The Dead Crow agent took a deep breath and nodded, "Clever," he smiled, turning around. He saw her far ahead, "I give her that one... creating a double."

"Let's go after her!" A guard shouted.

"No!" The agent stopped them, "Don't."

The guards obeyed.

The agent nodded, still carrying that smile on his face.

A few minutes later she caught up with the others. All surprised that she had escaped.

"How did you do that?" James asked staring into the distance, at the group of soldiers.

Mia was tired and out of breath, "Easily outsmarted," she replied, "Come on let's go."

They headed up the road and came across a large sign board that read : Terratoar Mountain Pass.

"Hmm, the mountain pass," Daniel read.

Beneath the sign was a warning : Do not venture.

"Okay, Okay," Mark took a deep breath, "This sign is doing a really good job scaring me."

"The inn keeper did say that many people do not return," Mia pointed out.

Mark chuckled, "That's it, we're going around, better late than dead."

"No, we taking the pass," Mia insisted, "If we do not linger too longer we will be fine."

"We're like horror movie idiots at this point."

Daniel gave him a brief explanation, "Okay, it's either we take the mountain pass which may be dangerous-,"

"May be," Mark pointed at the sign.

"Or, we travel around and be caught by the Dead Crow or bounty hunters."

Mark thought about it.

"Don't tell me you thinking about it," Mia said.

"I wish I could," he look at the sign, "Let's just go."

"Great."

They started up the road and followed it to the mountain.

CHAPTER 20

The Ancient Temple

Between two high cliffs pressed up close to one another, leaving a space only small enough to create a foot path is where you will find them now still traveling up the ever elevating road, progressively become more and more steep as they made their way up.

The two cliffs beside them were of razor sharp rocks that pointed towards the sky. A lot of plant life grew from the small cracks and areas carrying a bit of soil.

Only a fraction of the blue clear sky was visible to them, forever remaining in the shade, and on a day that the sun had decided to reveal itself.

The path had been going straight ahead for a while, so there was no problem in fearing what was onward. James and Daniel had lead the way, walking side by side, eyes peeled for any kind of abominated creatures that may dwell in these areas. Their fear was of having one of these things creep onto them without their notion, or even poison them with one of their bites. It was quite clear, judging by the everlasting shade and semi-closed up space, that insect life had taking a liking for this place, grown really comfortable. Everything was provided here, vegetation and a lack of much larger predators.

Mark was not as afraid of this place anymore, at least not as much as when he read the sign. He enjoyed it actually, trying hard to pinpoint why the sign was actually made, looking for something to scare him. The hike itself was not bad either, the road not being at all steep enough to start killing his legs.

"I wonder," he thought to himself, "Is that scary sign just for show, because instead of being scared, I actually feel safe here, all nice plants and flowers everywhere and blocked away from any Dead Crow eyes, it's impossible to take that sign seriously now."

Mia shrugged, she was walking beside him paging through one of her note books, "See, you were scared for nothing."

Mark rolled his eyes, "If not the map, some random book," he pointed out, "Well, I guess you can't really navigate around these parts... why not enjoy the scenery for once."

Mia did not turn away from the book but she raised one hand and pointed, "Rock, rock, path, nothing more to see... I'm looking for something here."

Mark took a closer look at the book, "Is that a text book?" he asked, "You stole a text book from school... you really do miss school don't you?"

Mia closed the book, holding her current page with her forefinger, "Yes, actually I do, learning about magic for once is actually fun and I did not steal a text book, I just copied random essential pages into a smaller diary."

"Plants are essential?" He gave her a concerned look.

"Yes they are," she replied, "Did you not attend alchemy class?"

He nodded, "Yup, but what would we need the plants for... food and weapons is all I need."

Mia sighed in defeat, there was no way of getting Mark on the same page as her in understanding, and she was not about to waste her breath trying. She just continued from the page she had left off and kept silent.

"Hmm," Mark hummed, he was really expecting some kind of response from her, "So-"

"Shh," she interrupted him, "I'm busy here, this place has special plant life, so please."

Mark had decided to take this mountain pass expecting to be occupied by fear and the nerves of having to look over his shoulder every second. Since he had been robbed of that, he had fallen terribly bored with nothing to make it go away.

He looked up ahead and saw the path, he looked behind and saw the path, nothing was at all interesting to him.

It was not too long before things started to change for the worse. The path that they have been traveling up for the past couple of hours had now decided to become a lot more steep which made this walk now turn into an exercise which none of them endorsed. The walk was now taking its toll on their legs.

Mia had pulled out her staff and morphed it to its original size, she was now using it as a walking stick to assist her with the climb.

The sharp walls of the cliffs beside them had become their source of rest, by hanging onto them while their legs took some time off. The rocks had also become their aid in helping them take each step, using them to help pull up.

This was also the worst time of day that this could possibly be happing to them. The warmth of the sun that they had longed for was now directly above them absorbing whatever energy that they had left.

There was one thing that seemed to work in their favour whilst climbing this path and it was the very ground that they walked on. Dry and hard with many rocks sticking out of it to use as stepping stones, so slipping back and falling was reduced to a minimum.

Mark was panting and slowly falling behind the rest, being the most unfit in the group, but that did not stop him from talking, "I think I know why that warning was put up there now," he said looking down behind him.

James started laughing, "Shut up Mark, you going to make me lose my balance."

He could not stop panting, "I'm serious man," he pulled himself up, "I'm dying here."

"I think I'm going to have to agree with Mark here," Daniel said.

"We're just unfit, last time we hiked was last year, on our camping trip," James added.

"Yes, but it was not this steep."

"I just hope it doesn't get any steeper than it is, I don't want to be climbing on all fours," Mia said.

Mark looked up at Daniel and wondered why the hell he was climbing, "Daniel, why you climbing, you can fly or levitate or whatever."

"I'm tired," he replied, "and it will make it worse if I try."

James looked ahead and saw some kind of ending, a flat piece of ground, it still continued on being steep afterward though, "I see something guys, we're nearly there."

They struggle their way up to the small piece of flat ground that James had spotted earlier. The greatest bit of relief that they had ever felt was dropping to the ground and allowing their legs to rest.

James threw one fist into the air, "Yes… checkpoint," he uttered taking deep breaths.

Daniel, whom was on the far left of everybody else, noticed something next to him. He saw that this piece of heavenly ground continued on into a cave which was coloured black, he could see nothing beyond the entrance. He sat up and saw the same thing to the right.

After some time resting, they then decided to care about their surroundings.

A lot of unusual plant life grew close to the cliffs around them which made Mia, for one, very excited. She pulled out her book and started to examine.

James and Mark did not want to flinch from their positions, very happy to be sitting there doing nothing.

Mark looked up behind him, seeing the steep hill continue on was not motivational at all, "I don't want to continue."

Daniel stood up and went closer to the entrance of the cave, trying hard to see what was going on inside, nothing but darkness stared back, "What do you suppose is in there?" He asked.

Mia took interest in the other entrance, "No idea."

"And I'd like to keep it that way thank you," Mark said sitting up.

"I'm up for checking it out," Daniel replied, "I would just need a light."

"Curiosity is going to be the death of you."

"Me too," Mia agreed with Daniel, "I have a solution for your light problem."

She pulled out her staff and created a light with her other hand. She allowed the light to hover above the staff, "There, your very own torch," she handed the staff over to him. Then she created a light of her own.

"Sweet thanks," he took the staff, "We'll be a few minutes."

James gave them a thumbs-up.

"I'm not moving, so you will find me in this exact spot," Mark replied.

Both disappeared into the darkness of their own paths, leaving James and Mark to stare on into the sky.

Down one of the dark tunnels, Daniel had already started to feel some regret in his decision to jump forward and start exploring this place. Swaying his torch from side to side, making sure to get everything, searching for something in this hole, hoping to find nothing.

He would continuously look over his shoulder, checking for anything that could be trying to sneak up on him, if such a thing existed in this cave. His mind filled with an endless list of horrors that he was hoping not to receive a heart stopping scare from, being on edge like this, anything could scare him.

As he delved deeper into the darkness, he started to hear squeaking in certain places around him, unsure if it was just his head or if there was something there watching him, "Why am I doing this," he murmured to himself.

The light of his torch was now reflecting off the eyes of creatures that were awake, in there with him, keeping watch. He figure that they were bats and nothing to really fear as long as he did not make any sudden movements that would allow them to go crazy.

He continue on down his way for a while, silent as the darkness itself, till he came across another way to his left.

Standing by the entrance, he stared into the nothingness, listening quietly, for any sound that may come from within. Hearing nothing, he stepped through the entry and held the torch up in front of him.

He gasped as his heart skipped a beat, almost dropping Mia's staff.

Frightened, he could not stop staring at this object that stood in front of him, still as a statue. Some relief came to pull the weight off his shoulders when he discovered that it was an actual statue.

The fear drifted to the side and a lot of disgust stood in its place as he took another step forward. The first thing his senses rejected was the smell of this room, which he gave some bit of comfort by covering up his nose.

The statue gave him the idea of a shrine. He moved close for better examination, kicking something at his feet which he then took priority over.

It was just a bone, among many.

He had seen quite enough for his liking so he stepped out of the room and made his way back with a little more pace in his steps.

Mia on the other side, was not too afraid of the cave. She had it reduced by making the light on her palm brighter, so she was able to see quite far and make greater progress than Daniel. That bats did surprise her but she did well not to disturb them since that would ultimately make things even worse for her.

Her path led to a cave entrance on the right, it was not a dark abyss, it had a source of light from above creating rays that shone upon the most beautiful thing she had ever seen.

She stepped into the cave, lost for words. Walking into a room, surrounding herself by the most majestic garden she had ever seen, filled with an endless variety of plants, a rainbow of colours around her.

In the centre of the cave she looked up, and saw that there was a large opening far above her that let in a lot of light.

With all this around her she became possessed with an idea. Out she walked, all excited and ready to start collecting, almost forgetting about the bats that rested above her.

James stood by the entrance of the cave Mia took, "Do you think they will be back?"

"Yes, it's been a few minutes."

James stared into the abyss and was relieved to finally see a faint light in the distance, "There she is."

"Huh?" Mark looked into the entrance Daniel took, "Back at the same time hey, I see Daniels light as well."

Once they had both revealed themselves from the darkness, each of them bore the most opposite of expressions on their faces.

Mia was more excited and happy, Daniel's was filled with some bit of shock and fear.

Mark compared both of their expressions, "Judging by what I see on you face, I want to know what Mia saw."

Mia removed the light from her palm and dispelled the one that Daniel held, "You won't believe what I saw."

Daniel shook his head with some bit of disgust on his face, "You don't want to see what I saw."

"Hmm, I was right," Mark got to his feet, leaving his bag behind.

"What did you see Mia?" James asked with some bit of enthusiasm.

Before she could answer, however, her excitement dimmed for a moment and grew more interested in whatever horror Daniel had come across, "What did you see?" She stepped closer to the opposite entrance.

"No," Mark shook his head, "Daniel just said, 'we don't want to know what he saw', why does that mean we have to see it?"

"Mark shh," Mia ordered, "What did you see Daniel?"

Daniel took a deep breath, "It's already been describe to you," he handed the staff back.

"Hmm, interesting...," James went up to the cave entrance, "Is it bad that I want to see?"

"Yes," Mark replied immediately, "What about your cave Mia?" He tried to divert the attention.

"You won't like it, just a bunch of alchemy stuff."

"Oh," he felt disappointed.

"Let's go see what you saw," James suggested.

Mia put away her staff and walked in, lighting the way. Mark being the only one who stayed behind, "I'll look after the bags!"

"Come, on Mark," James called, "You will regret not seeing it, besides, we the only ones climbing the mountain."

Mark could not deny the regret part, deep within, he too wanted to know what it was and since whatever it was did not hurt or kill Daniel... *how bad could it be?* He followed after them.

They all walked down the passageway, with only Mark and James who were on edge, till they made it to the entrance.

They stood in front of the statue. Mia made the light bright for better visibility. They all just gawked at the statue, faces of repulsion.

James covered his mouth, "That smell though."

"What do you expect, we got a bowl of blood and bones everywhere," Mark said.

Mia crouched down and picked up one of the broken skulls. She noticed there was a symbol carved onto the forehead, a symbol she only recognized by description, she looked at the statue again and saw the same symbol on the man's forehead, "Wait, this matches the same description Anna's friend made."

Daniel nodded.

"Only… he found the exact same one in that forest," she looked at the blood.

"Didn't he say it was some kind of shrine?" James remembered.

"Yeah, but for what?"

"Evil," Mark replied, "I don't think we should hang around this thing."

"Good idea, let's go," Mia agreed dropping the skull and stepping out of the cave, leading them out.

Outside, they were happy to be back in the light and to see that their bags were still there.

"Well… that's going to make lunch a little hard to eat," said Mark.

Mia proceeded to take out her little alchemy book and a few empty, transparent pouches.

"What are you doing?" James asked.

"She's going to tend to her plants, nothing to worry about," Mark replied for her.

Mia became very unhappy with Mark's disrespectful remark, and the tone it was used in, "I have my own interest okay, so just leave me alone."

James stopped it before it became a little heated again, "Let's not start this now, whilst we are climbing this impossible mountain," he said, "Let's not get under each other's skin."

"I'm not doing anything," Mark defended himself.

"Mark, just eat," Daniel suggested picking his bag and leaning it against the wall.

"No need to tell me twice."

"Okay, see you guys in a while, off to salvage some alchemy ingredients."

"Potions and poisons?"

She nodded with a smile, she turned to Mark with a cold stared, "And for the record, this stuff is going to be useful... for everyone," she stormed into the cave.

"You do enjoy starting fights don't you?"

Mark paused as he was about to take a bite from his bread, he paused for only a moment and continued on as if no one had said anything.

With no response from Mark, James just decided to eat some food as well.

Some minutes later, James had decided to go see the cave Mia had walked into, for a while, he walked in complete darkness, keeping one hand on the wall to his right, just to ensure he was going straight, slowly and careful not to trip over anything. He continued on till he saw the light in the cave at which he decided to start picking up the pace.

There he saw Mia busy collecting some plants with her book placed down beside her, opened on some random page.

"Wow," he was surprised.

Mia receive a fright which she quickly recovered from as soon as she saw him.

James stepped in, "Hmm, this is nice," he looked up for the source of light.

"Told ya," she replied.

"Growing in a cave even," he continued to look up into the light, "If only we could just climb this cave, then we would be fine the rest of the way... maybe," he started doubting when he realized it did not go too high, "Nah, the path is our best bet."

Mia used a small pair of scissors to cut the stems of the plants that she wanted.

James looked around and noticed the cave was pretty large and crowded, "Any help?"

"Did you, for one second listen in alchemy?"

James gave it a bit of thought, "If literally, yes," he replied, "But I don't think I need to, just show me the picture and I'll find it."

"Fair enough," she picked up the book and showed it to him, "Just look for any of the plants in the next few pages."

He was fine with this job at first, but then it came to the searching, a lot of the plants looked exactly the same, only seeing the difference in the ones that carried different colours. He had to look real close in order to see some of the minor differences.

About half an hour later, all were done and ready to begin the dreadful hike again, a hike which took much quicker than the first one, since they had the time to rest for a while.

It was not long before they had reached another platform, another checkpoint for them to take in some air, and this time, they were not met by two dark and creepy caves, with only another death defying hike ahead. This time there was some bit of relief, the road was now just a zig-zag path all the way to the top. Sure it was going to be a very long walk, but this one was going to be a little less scary. Even the fear of falling over was removed since the road was quite wide.

"Okay, a zig-zag path," Mark smiled, staring up into the sky.

"Better isn't it?" Daniel said.

He nodded, "Yeah I guess, but how many zig-zags?"

"The sooner we start, the lesser we will have."

"We must make it before nightfall," Mia said, "Let's get going."

The way up to the top was not at all bad, they did not even need to take the rest, arriving there just as the sun was settling over the far horizon. A horizon that they all took the time to witness and allow to steal away all their problems for just a few moments.

The top was not some flat piece of land that they all predicted would be, it was riddled with small hills for some of its part. It was as well, accompanied by a lot of vegetation and trees.

There was no set path that people had made for those who ventured up here so the map and compass was needed once again, to ensure that they made it to the path down on the other side.

Mia got the others to start picking up dead branches and stones while she looked for a suitable place for them to set up camp.

Today's weather was I bit cold despite the clear skies. A crescent moon stood watch over them this night, along with an ocean of constellations.

They sat themselves around the flickering light of the fire, really close, to gain as much warmth from it.

"I forgot its usually colder up top mountains," Mark said rubbing his hands over the fire.

"Do you think it's safe up here?" Daniel asked, forever skimming out the area.

"Yeah, I highly doubt we will encounter people up here," He replied, "Let's just hope people are our only threat."

Mark stretched his arms and yawned, "I'm so glad we beat this mountain, just a few more days and we will be at Adornfell."

Mia then remembered the conversation that she had with Grace the night before, "I know what happened to that town we visited yesterday."

Everyone wondered why she was bringing up such a subject out of nowhere.

"Mmkay…," James broke the silence.

"It was Levina."

That sparked another fuse from everyone.

"Wait what?" Daniel was surprised.

"Heartless!" Attacked Mark.

James then noticed someone sitting next to him. It was Levina again. She slowly appeared and decided to listen in to what they were talking about.

She greeted James, who just gave a small wave back.

"No need for name-calling," James said.

"Excuse me, she is the reason a lot of people there are homeless," he justified it.

Mia stepped in, "It was not her exactly."

They all silenced themselves, waiting for her to give out an explanation.

"While you guys were asleep, I went to this other women who explained it to me," she began, "She said that as soon as Levina appeared in that town, a massive group of Dead Crow mages did as well, it was them who destroy the town in an attempt to try get her, she also said that Levina never hurt any of the civilians, only those that tried to kill her, which was the Dead Crow."

"And off course they never caught her," said James.

Mia nodded, "She said that Levina just vanished."

"How long ago was this?"

"About a month."

Mark was the only one without much sympathy, "So she was the root of the problem, but not exactly the problem?"

"I guess," Mia replied.

Mark held a twig in the flames, "What is her nickname again?" he asked, "The living curse or something, where ever she shows up, destructions follows… yup perfect nickname."

Levina swayed her hand in the flames, "I don't think she meant it," she said, "I hope so."

"I don't think she meant it," James repeated.

"We don't even know this person James, making assumptions is pretty normal," Mark replied.

James reached forward and grabbed one of the chains hanging from Levina's wrists, he examined it for a moment.

Everyone noticed this little gesture.

"James, are you okay?" Asked Mia.

He let go of the chain immediately, "Just thought I saw something on my hand," he stuttered, the only thing he could think of right off the bat.

Levina laughed at his attempt at lying.

Their night today was very young. The long, weary and probably the most tiring day yet was finally over.

The next day came as a bit of a surprise to all of them, a mask of clouds had returned and so did the chilly breeze.

This was an early morning start for them, really excited about the last few days left.

Mia really took an interest in the plant life that grew up here, she explored it to pass a lot of the time.

The rest were busy trying to better themselves even more with their abilities.

It was round about midday when their time killing activities had come to an end. It had started to drizzle.

They rejoined and made haste, in search for a place that they could take shelter under before it got any worse.

The tree did provide some bit of cover but it was the wind that was getting to them now.

They had almost given up when Mia came up with an idea, "Hey, Mark."

"Yes?"

"Can you create a shield around us, keep the rain out at least?" She suggested.

"Hey, that could work," he replied wasting no time creating the shield.

This was a really impressive idea… in thought, really good until Mark had created the shield but still felt the rain.

He removed it, "Great."

"I guess it doesn't affect rain," Mia said.

"I guess so."

"Don't mountain tops have caves?" James asked.

"They do!" Levina shouted with excitement, walking beside him.

James jumped again. Levina's random arrivals were not getting old.

"If there were caves," Daniel said, "Don't you think vicious monsters would be living there?"

"This one doesn't," Levina announced, "Follow me, it's nearby."

"We should at least try searching for one," he suggested, Levina was walking off, "One more try."

"Ugh fine," Mark uttered.

"It's better than getting all drenched."

They decided to go at it one more time and split up.

This was going to be easy, on James's part, being led to one by his little friend, Levina.

"How much further?" He asked.

She was leading him to some hidden place, "Just around here," she pointed at a giant rock, "Just climb over it, but call your friends first."

James bought them back.

They looked over the rock with some bit of concern.

Levina was sitting on the rock, "I can lead you down there," she stood up, "There's nothing scary, I promise."

"It looks scary," Mark said.

Levina sighed at Mark, "Tell them it's not," she turned to James.

James shrugged, he did not know how to say 'I can't' without drawing any attention to himself again. He, however, did use the weather to his advantage, "It's raining and I don't want to get soaked so I'm going in," he climbed onto the rock and stood next to Levina. He signaled for her to lead the way and so she did.

Levina jumped to the other side and headed down into the cave, James following behind.

"You have a point there," Mark said climbing over after them.

The entrance did not have any steps so it was a little hard to keep from falling from all the soft soil. The passageway down became a little more geometric as they continued, taking a rectangular shape.

"Wow, definitely warmer than outside," Mark said.

The passageway down soon after started to bear some steps and the walls started to show carvings. They were a little hard to see as the light from the entrance faded away, but one could feel them as well with their hands.

Levina came to the end of the passage way and took a right turn.

Mia summoned some light again, "What is this place?" She slowed down to examine the contents of the wall.

"Some ancient civilization cave I guess," replied Daniel.

Levina went down some more steps and took a turn left at the bottom, leading to an open balcony, "We're here!" She announced.

"Civilization... cave?" Mark asked, "I've never heard of such."

"It's some kind of temple," Levina said, "A very old one."

"I guess," James replied.

"Guess what," Mark asked.

"That it's a temple of some kind."

Mia made her light very bright.

This was a massive hall, sizing up to an agora, held up by large pillars. The ground level of the temple was almost completely demolished, some pillars had collapsed leaving rubble in their wake. On the other end of the room was some kind of sinkhole, with a diameter of about twenty metres.

The pillars that remained intact had red banners hanging off them, they also supported most of the second level which carried the balcony that they were on and two separate rooms on either side of the temple, open spaces with a lot more, smaller pillars all around.

There were many wooden torches placed on the walls. Another thing that they came to notice was the ceiling, having statues of men and woman looking down, some wielding weapons and some holding staves and scrolls. Most of them were half naked with robes around them and mimicked that they were in the sky. The statues were really pleasing to look at, reflective and smooth. It was the only part of the temple that look untouched.

Many, if not all of the walls had paintings on them, gold and yellow being the majority of the colours used.

"It's a nice place," Mark complimented, "Time to look for ancient treasure," he turned and took a torch from the wall, "Can you light it up please, I'll do others that I may come across."

Mia used her magic to light the torch.

"Thank you," he headed to the separate room on their current level.

James and Daniel did the same, picking torches and getting them lit up by Mia before heading off to explore. Daniel went to the opposite room on the upper level. James was a little more interested in the giant sinkhole on the ground level of this temple, he took the stairs down with Levina at his side.

Mia followed him down lighting the torches on the wall because James had forgotten already. She was looking at the banners that were hung from the pillars, they all had the exact same set of two symbols.

James riddled his way passed all the obstacles to get to this sinkhole. He stood at the edge and looked down, it was just darkness, not even the torch he held was much help in this situation.

"It's scary looking," Levina said stepping away from it.

James nodded, also stepping away from the edge. He grew a little curious, he wanted to find out how far down it went by chucking something into it. He looked around for a big enough rock that would make a loud thud when it reached the bottom, in doing so he stood his torch against a collapsed pillar and picked up a rock the size of a football with both hands.

"What are you doing?" Levina asked climbing on and taking a seat on the collapsed pillar.

"I want to see how far down it goes," he replied, chucking it down the hole.

He waited for a sound.

He waited a few more seconds of it to reach the bottom.

He continued his wait which made him quiet impatient.

There was nothing.

He crossed his arms, really disappointed, "Hmm, nothing," he looked for another rock.

Mia saw what he was doing but did not want to go near the sinkhole, she was now positioned behind the pillars, examining the wall's paintings. She did not know how to read them or in which order so she just looked to compliment.

These paintings had people on them for the most part, one that did intrigued her a lot was one with a group of people surrounding something that was lighting up and in the centre of that light was one of the symbols that marked the banners. Around most of these artworks were many small rune markings that she did not understand.

James tossed another rock into the sinkhole and heard no impact.

"Maybe it goes on forever" Levina suggested, chucking a small rock in.

"Maybe," he spoke silently and sat next to her, "Thanks for helping us find the cave," he whispered.

She smiled, "Happy to help."

James looked up and noticed, on a large wall that stood at a 45° degree angle facing them, a very large symbol carved out of it. Somehow it looked very familiar to him, he was sure he had seen it before, it was the same as one of the symbols on the banners, but he remembered it from way before this place.

Mia moved away from the paintings on the walls and headed back to the opposite end of the hall, something of interest had caught her attention, it was a pile of wood and branches next to a circle of burnt ashes, "I think someone was here some time ago," she spoke loudly.

James broke out of the trance he was in, "What do you mean?" He turned to her.

"There's a fire place and wood here."

James and Levina both came to investigate as well, "Hmm, our lucky day."

"Yup, no need to go back outside today."

Then it hit him, "Do you still have that amulet with the blue ribbon on you?"

"Oh, yeah," she searched her bag, "Here," she handed it over to him.

James hurried back to the sinkhole and held the amulet up in front of him, comparing both symbols.

They matched.

"Have you seen this symbol before?" He asked Levina.

"No, I don't recognize it," she replied.

"Mia!" He shouted.

"What?" she replied, still busy placing wood of the ashes.

"Did you ever figure out the symbol on this amulet?"

She walked up the his side of the temple, dusting her hands, "No, why?"

James pointed up at the wall, "It's the same symbol."

"What," she took the amulet and did her own examination, "Hey, it's also on the banners and paintings... strange, I wonder why I did not find anything about it, it must be important. The person who had this before you must have found it here as well."

James nodded, "So... Diadora was here too, a long time ago?"

Mia shrugged, "Maybe," she gave him the amulet and headed back to the wood pile.

Mark was still up in his section of the room, he had already lit up all the torches there, on the walls and pillars. He felt like he had hit the jackpot, he had found many trinkets laying around on the floor and chests filled with ancient treasures.

This room was filled with many masks that hung down from the ceiling and a wall painted with paintings, but all that fell away from his interest as soon as he saw the shiny stuff.

He put down his bag and immediately started searching for things he could take.

"Jackpot," he said to himself.

His main focus was on the brightly coloured gems over the gold which plagued the place rendering it less valuable to him.

Daniel had found himself in the armory side of the temple, many chests and weapon racks, mannequins of very valuable amours. Everything was expensive, weapons made of gold and silver with handles fitted with large gems and crystals. Before he took interest in these items, he found himself analyzing the many masks that hanged off the ceiling, followed by the fascination in the many paintings on the walls surrounding him. They made him feel as if he were some kind of expert archeologist, just a feeling, nothing more because he did not know how to decipher any of the symbols or paintings that were done, at this point, he was just making up his own story about them.

He started from one side of the wall, the first image he saw was of a group of people standing around what seemed to be some kind of shining object or symbol. He moved on to the next major image which was a really large drawing of the symbol. Above and below these paintings were the symbols of some ancient language.

Daniel did not understand a single thing he was seeing but he continued to look at the paintings, for admiring purposes.

When he had passed through all the painting on the wall, he gave his head a little shake to get rid of some the confusion that filled his mind, "Were they worshiping something?' He asked himself.

He turned away from the paintings and headed for the steps, "Guys, I found some weapons up here," he took the stairs down and headed to James who was still seated on the pillar by the sinkhole, throwing small gravels into it with Levina.

Daniel stared down the hole, "Is this some kind of sinkhole or something?"

"I guess," James replied.

"I wonder what made it."

"Same," he threw another stone.

Daniel stepped away from it, "Come on, let's go pick some weapons."

James threw the rest of the stones into the sinkhole, "Yeah that's a good idea," he got up and took his bag with him.

Their bags were placed next to the wood.

"Mark!" Daniel called.

"Yes!" He shouted back.

"We found an armory!"

"Give me a sec."

They waited a few seconds for him to show up.

He came into view by the stairs wearing some jewelry around his neck, carrying more things in both his hands. Climbing down, his friends just stared at him as his jewelry swayed and jangled.

Standing in front of them acting normal, as if there was nothing odd about him. He smiled, "Let's go."

"Hmm."

He realized they were looking at all the jewelry around his neck and in his hands, "Oh, I found treasure, ancient treasure on that floor, there's a lot of it," he went over to the campsite and put down his bag along with the trinkets and jewelry he found.

"Okay," Daniel broke the silence.

Most of their time in the armory was spent examining the weapons and testing them out, looking for the lightest and ones that had their own belts and sheaths.

Mia was only there to examine mostly, having the staff, Vicissitude, but she did take a few daggers with gems on them.

Fitting on the armors was also another activity they did, none were taken because of their immense weight, they could not walk for more than ten metres without feeling the weight, it was a real exercise. Some they could not even pick up.

After some time they came to their choices in weaponry and they much preferred the silver made, thin broadswords with gems on the handles. They were the lightest and had their own sheaths. Another thing they added to their arsenal was a couple of daggers. This room also provided them with some smith equipment like a grindstone which they used to ensure their blades were ready for the job.

Although they were unable to tell the time in this closed up area, they figured it was evening when they started to feel hungry.

Mia had turned out the torches that lit the two separate rooms bearing the treasures and weapons.

She had started the fire and spent her time categorizing her plants according to the recipes in her almanac.

Mark and the others just spent most of their time examining their swords and daggers, also the jewelry Mark found.

This is where they spent the rest of the night.

CHAPTER 21

A Short Conversation

The next morning came quick, with no notion of time, the first one to open their eyes would have had to assume it was. They left as soon as possible, so close to their destination, it was becoming a little exciting and they did not want to prolong it, even for a second.

Their new custom, valuable, ancient weapons were now their most prized possessions, each one unique in design and foreign to the rest of the world.

Mia had placed her grinded ingredients into the empty flasks, some were in powder form at the moment, not ready to be used, not ready to be trusted. She did not see herself as an expert in alchemy since she had only been exposed to it for only two terms, hence the distrust in her mixtures, but she followed the instructions as they were, only combining the ones that did not need to be brewed in a certain order.

She had taken recipes from many different types of books in the school's library, also hoping to have gained the chance to browse the city's library since it had a large and more interesting variety.

Nevertheless, these mixtures were useless to her right now in their current state, she needed something to help her properly combine them into a solution.

It was only morning and Mark had wanted to check and see if he could get some more trinkets from the little treasure trove on the second floor, using the excuse of money they may need in the future.

Up the stairs and through the passageways and tunnels to the outside world again. This time again, they were not met by the light of the sun, just more cloud cover, which made it hard to tell the time, it might have been midday and they would not know.

"More clouds, everywhere," said Mark crossing his arms.

"Another gloomy day I guess," Mia sighed.

Daniel was the only one who saw it positively, "Let's just be glad it isn't raining."

It was still evident that the rain had just recently poured over the land, small puddles of water still land mined the area and the grass was still wet, some parts of the ground had turned all muddy and slippery, the trees still dripping as the cold bitter breeze passed by.

Today was not as lively, they did not travel with much haste, as if tired and out of energy. Everyday had been a struggle since they decided to sneak out of the school and go on this 'merry' hunt. They had just realized that they had not taking a single day off, because of their chase to reach Adornfell. Though they had been exposed to quite a few places at which they explored, it all just brushed passed way too quickly, only seeing it because it was in the way of their mission.

"How much longer till we reach the other side of the mountain Mia?" asked Mark.

"No one knows Mark," sighed James.

"You haven't check the map in a while, are you sure we're going the right way?"

Mia was kicking away at some small stones that crossed her path, "I just need the compass and we're good," she replied holding it up to him, "we should be heading down the mountain today and reach the city either tomorrow or the day after."

It was only after their midday break when they started to regain their old selves again. Their tired and gloomy selves were probably the result of sleeping in these very warm places.

Mark's complaining had decreased drastically, he was now busy testing out his new weapons with James and Daniel.

Mia was examining the dagger that she took from the temple. She also practiced with her staff, testing how fast she was able to change from one weapon to another.

The second half of the day was much quicker and they had covered a lot of ground. Everything, however, came to a stop when Mia came across a body of water, she hurried over to the small pond and pulled out a small pot, she filled it with water.

"Mia," James called, "Are you going to start cooking those potions of yours?"

"That's not a good idea," Mark pointed out, "We got a clock to follow."

Mia stopped to think about it a bit. Her initial idea was to boil the water with some of her magic and follow the instructions to the book but then Mark reminded her of the time it would take to do such a thing and how much of her energy it would consume. She sighed, there was no time to do anything right now, she would have to build a fire and brew it slowly, she really wanted to make a potion by herself but this was not going to work.

With some disappointment and thought she retracted her alchemy activity and packed everything back. For now, she would have to settle with finding as much ingredients as she could, since they were quite expensive to get in the shops, and wait for a time to better herself in the subject.

"Come on, let's get off this boring mountain," said Mark.

"Well then, let me be your today's entertainment."

Everybody froze at the sound of this unknown voice.

It was silent for a few moments, nothing but their heads turned and eyes search for the source.

"Who was that," Mia whispered.

Daniel shrugged, "No idea."

Everyone was alerted and afraid to move, afraid to ask.

A few more seconds passed and out of nowhere, a round black object appeared from the distance, someone had thrown it in their direction.

Unable to identify the unknown object, everyone moved some distance away from its landing area, just to remain on the safe side.

James tried to pinpoint the host of this object but was unable to detect anyone in the direction it came from. He then turned to the object and saw a small fuse attached to it, "Bomb!" he shouted turning away and running to the closest tree, hiding behind it. Mia followed after him.

Daniel and Mark went to another tree nearby.

Closing their eyes and blocking their ears, they waited for said bomb to detonate.

They waited.

A little too long.

Mark unblocked his ears and opened his eyes. He decided to peek from behind the tree and investigate the object. He squinted, "What kind of bomb takes forever to blow up?" He whispered.

It finally exploded, having Mark hide his face again. All of them with eyes closed, thinking it might blind them, hiding behind the trees thinking that it may shoot out deadly shards at them, ears blocked thinking it might be too loud and render them deaf for a few moments.

All of their thoughts wrong.

When it was over, they all decided to investigate, still keeping behind the trees for safety.

What they saw instead was just confusing to them.

The explosive left only colourful ribbons and paper strips in its wake. Nothing dangerous, it was the same as some clown's trick at a little kids birthday party.

"Huh?" Daniel blurted out, peeking over Mark.

"Oh," James realized, "I guess he really did mean to be our entertainment."

Mia rolled her eyes and stepped out from behind the tree.

The others came out as well.

Mark went over to the ribbons looking for the explosive's shell, it was still there. He picked it up, it was damaged and had a rough and bumpy texture to it. He turned it and notice there was a picture. A picture that was also a little damaged but not unidentifiable, it was a big smiley face with sharp teeth and red X's for eyes.

"Guys," he held it up to them, "Look familiar?"

They came for a closer look at the image.

Daniel took it from him, "Is this not that crazy guys symbol?"

"Diadora," James answered.

"Oh, that's the guy who spoke to you?"

James nodded.

"I wonder what his motive was," he looked into the distance.

"I wanted to introduce myself," the voice came again.

Everyone turned to its direction and this time saw him, sitting on a giant rock with his legs cross not too far from where they were.

"That time was a little one to one," he smiled.

They could not tell if he was being sinister or just welcoming. A lot of emotion was lost due to the cloth covering his eyes.

He jumped off the rock and took a few steps in their direction.

Everyone went for their swords, Mia morphed her staff to its original size.

Diadora stopped in his tracks and put his hands in the air, "Why you being so hostile?" he gasped, "I've done nothing to any of you," he lowered his hands, "No need for fighting," he shook his hands, "See... no weapons."

None of them let go of their swords.

"Just trust me, we all know not to judge a book by its cover... don't we?"

James shook his head, "We not going to trust you."

"But-," he pointed at Daniel, "The-the gift I sent, don't you like it? I'd be a little heartbroken if you didn't." He sounded really sad saying that.

Mia ignored him, "What do you want?"

He turned to her, "My, my the hate... please do tell why," he put his hands together.

"What you did to James," replied Mia.

He chuckled, "Oh, that," he took a deep breath, "All I did was put him to sleep, I was afraid he would tell the Dead Crow, and I'm sure you know how they feel about breaking rules," he shrugged, "I just did not want to get onto their naughty list," he smiled, "I figured if he had slept for a week, they would think he was crazy... I'm just a guy who wanted to remain on the good side of the Dead Crow, can't have them questioning me, is that a good enough explanation?"

Mia thought about it for a moment.

"What do you want from us then?" James asked.

He raised his finger, "Now, now, I'm not going to answer that one just yet, it will cut the conversation too short," he turned away from them and climbed onto the giant rock again, which he sat upon, "I want to hang on the topic of theft right now, stealing from a sacred place," he took a deep breath, "How do I put this... disrespectful?"

They did not feel too good about his mention of theft, they did do it, technically and it was from some sacred temple that they knew nothing about.

He turned to Mia, "But what's really interesting to me, is that staff of yours Mia, Vicissitude is it?" he smiled, "Now how does one come to bear the staff of change?"

Mia did not know where the staff came from so she did not know what to say, mentioning Jake might be some bit of a problem as well, the thoughts she was having made her forget about time, she was silent for a few seconds.

Diadora broke it, "You see, this is how you come to earn bounties, everything you have has no believable lie to hide the fact that it is stolen, no?"

"So you are here for our bounties then?" James asked.

He chuckled again, "No," his face turned straight, then back to the smile again, "I am a bounty hunter, but I kind of believe that you three are innocent in the crimes of theft that the Dead Crow claim you have committed... you see, I asked them what it was you stole, but they did not tell me, so I thought, you guys may be innocent and that I can help you with that little problem you have," he swayed his headed from side to side, "Maybe."

This man was starting to be a little understanding, someone actually thinking that they were innocent without any kind of explanation. James started to think that maybe, judging him at first sight was not the right thing to do. Now he was speaking of a way to help them.

"How would you be able to help us?" James asked. He really wanted to hear this, from someone like him, a bounty hunter, someone who practically praises the Dead Crow for the good pay they offer in exchange for services.

Diadora giggled, "I guess I'm going to have to reintroduce myself then," he jumped off the rock.

"We know who you are" said Daniel.

He turned to Daniel, "Will you allow me?"

Daniel kept silent.

He started to pace slowly, "I last recall only giving you my first name James, am I right?"

James nodded, "Yes."

"Let's see if you will recognize my last name," he stopped and placed his right hand on his chest, "Fellow travelers, my name is Diadora Maithindor," he gave a small bow.

Silence filled the air as shock surged through their bodies. The man they were talking to right now was a Maithindor. One of the two families that own the great castle in Marridor, the owners of the school. A very important family that everybody knows about.

Diadora looked at them and started laughing, "Why the faces? I'm guessing you are really surprised to hear that."

Mia was able to speak, "You're part of the richest family in Maramel?"

"Ah, the witch knows something," he gave Mia a big smile.

She was not sure if he was intentionally trying to anger her or not, he knew her name, why not just use it.

He raised his hands as if surprised, "Oh I'm sorry, do you prefer Mia?"

"Yes please," she replied.

"I'm still sensing a little hostility from you, so I'm just going to sit here on my rock," he went back.

Mia decided to get some answers from him, "Earlier you said you were a bounty hunter?"

"Yes, I did."

"Why?"

He smiled, "Hmmmmmm, why am I a bounty hunter," he repeated in a thinking stance.

Daniel could see he was just acting, "She means to ask why, you have a lot of money."

"It's called doing the world a public service Miss Milmoure," he replied, "And the money I get is used to help the less fortunate, you know rebuilding their homes... providing them with basic needs," he explained.

At this point, they were not sure if this man was at all bad, just crazy. A noble that is actually helping the world instead of remaining in his home, turning a blind eye to every problem in the world. He was helping people and keeping the world a safer place at the same time.

"Besides, it's my older brother, Darion, that takes care of the family business and stuff, since our parents and eldest brother died."

The only thing that they could think of doing right now is sympathize with him, even though they knew nothing about him.

"You had a second brother?" Mark asked.

Diadora nodded, looking sad now, "Yes, Mario," he sighed, "The brother I looked up to the most."

"I'm sorry about that," James said.

He smiled again, "No need for any of that right now," he took a deep breath, "Now back to you all... I can help you out with those bounties if you come with me," he turned to Mia, "But she will have to die, I can't help her with her case," he clapped once, "What do you say?"

He was being reasonable, in his perspective, but in their perspective, Mia was their friend and going to where ever he would be taking them would lead them off course. The answer was pretty easy.

"Off course... if you choose to defend her, you forfeit your chance at redemption," he explained, "Your choice."

They had a mission and they were not going to kill their friend.

James remembered that he had said he brought no weapons.

"None of that's happening," James replied.

Diadora took a long deep breath, "You choose not to choose... nice, there always more than just two choices," he nodded continuously, he raised his finger, "One thing... something has been bothering me for a while," he cleared his throat, "Why haven't you killed them yet James?" He gave what seemed to be a sinister smile.

"What!" He was surprised, "What are you talking about?"

Mark turned to him, "What is he talking about?"

"I'm asking him the same question," he replied, "What are you talking about?" he asked again.

Diadora shrugged, "I don't know, just a thought that crossed my mind, I may be talking about someone else though," he tapped his forehead, "It happens."

Confused, they concluded his insanity again, he was not making any sense at all now, from giving them a choice which he allowed for the neutral option to speaking about some random person who has not killed some. They did not know what to say anymore, so the best thing for them to do is wait for him to start blurting out more random stuff and hope it ends very soon so that they can continue on their way.

He jumped off the rock again, "Okay, now to be a little more serious," he smiled, "As much as I want to help you clear your names," he hummed, "I kind of need your bounties, all of you," he took a few steps forward, "It's for a good cause... you know that village you just passed by a few days ago? Yeah, it needs rebuilding after the mess the Dead Crow made trying to catch little Levina.

Not something they wanted to think about, since there was nothing they could do about it.

"Oh come on, don't you have hearts," he shook his head.

Mia of all people wanted to help them, especially after getting to know some, but she could not give herself in. *Is this what hard choices were like?* Everything this man has offered, none of them have been able to pick. Though, they all did have 'dying' in them so she could not blame herself if she did not want to.

"Am I just talking to myself here?" He realized.

No one replied.

"Now," he started pacing again, "I am unable to kill you at this moment, but I would love to be your escort, to the prison in the north... the one built for witches," he smiled at Mia.

Mia gave him a disgustingly angry look. Even though this man helped people, something about his presence was bothering her, more than before. She had come to many conclusions about him. He had the mind of clown, the great ambition of a magician, the unpredictable attitude of a lunatic and the look of a serial killer, *was he?* She could not decide if this was him originally or if he was just acting. What drove him to this state of madness, was it wealth or the high class customs, his parent's and brother's death?

"Please perform us a magic trick Mia, you may need magic for this one," he turned to the others, "You three with the swords, just don't pull them out," he suggested.

Mark went on and pulled it out, "You don't have a staff, you can't use magic."

"Shhh, young one," he said with his finger on his lip.

He then held his right hand out in front of him, and just a few moments later something airy started to show up above his palm, like he was absorbing it, and from a point in the centre material started to gather, slowly, molding into something out of nothing.

This man was full of surprises. Mia wanted to label him as a witch but as she watched him materialize something, none of the five categories of magic seemed to match with what he was doing. At first she thought he was conjuring, maybe it was an illusion, playing with their minds or some kind of dark or unknown magic.

"You're also a witch," James pointed out.

He shook his head, "Now now, I am not a witch, don't insult me!" he raised his voice, then he lowered it to a laugh, "What makes you think that I am a part of that treacherous race?"

"For one, how are you looking at us with your eyes covered and two, you doing magic without a staff," he pointed out.

"Who said I was doing magic?"

"Then what is it!" Mia shouted, so eager to know.

He chuckled, "How are we supposed to enjoy this show with so many questions."

The object in his hand was complete, it was another bomb. It dropped into his hand.

The fuse lit.

It was a little larger than the first.

"Guys," Mia's voice started to shake, "I don't think that one will be as welcoming as the first one."

Mark sheathed his sword but he was surprised he was doing it. It was not his intention at all, then he realized what it was, "I want to run but-,"

Mia did not understand what he was talking about.

"I can't move," he announced. His hands were shaking, but that was it, he was paralyzed.

James and Daniel also attempted, but their efforts fell short. They too were paralyzed.

"What! He's going to blow us to bits."

Diadora threw the bomb up and down in his hand, "Why aren't you running, I am giving you time to run before this goes boom."

He just looked at the children, waiting for them to make a run for it, but they just stood there like cattle, unaware of their incoming deaths, "Okay, you can stand there, it's entirely your choice," He said tossing it over to them.

It rolled and stopped right in front of Mark, with the smiley face gawking up at him.

The fuse neared its end.

Mia tried to kick it away, but it did not flinch, instead she felt a sharp pain on her foot. She then tried to pick it up, but it weighed a ton.

She started to panic, "Guys! There's a bomb right in front of you, I hope your powers are working."

Being the only person that could move around, she made her way behind them and crouched, covering her ears and closing her eyes, hoping that this was not her last few moments of life.

The fuse disappeared into the bomb.

Just a moment before it's detonation, Mark's uncontrollable body moved, he created a shield around all of them, all blue with the little tiny stars floating around it.

The bomb went off.

At first, all they could see was a really bright flash, more blinding than the morning sun.

There after a powerful force and sound followed.

Mark remained in his stance, while James and Daniel regained control of their bodies. They fell back in fear of the explosion.

It was over really quickly.

A cloud of smoke filled the area around them, but did not enter into the shield Mark had put up.

Mia uncovered her ears and opened her eyes, so very glad that she was alive and well, she saw the shield Mark create and sighed. Looking around at the smoke cloud that did not want to disappear, she stood up wondering how big this explosion was.

The shield disappeared at an instant and allowed for the large gust of air to attack them, bringing the cloud of dust with it. This was followed by a lot of coughing and covering of the eyes.

The wind blew, helping clear the dust much faster.

"You're a life saver man," James gave him a pat on the back.

The dust had finally cleared up, and in its absence, revealed to them, a lot of shock.

Before they eyes was a massive crater, the size of a small lake. It was about one hundred metres in diameter but only about a metre deep. They were in the centre on this hole, standing on a platform of undamaged ground that spread out behind them, thanks to the shield. Everything else within the diameter was gone, all he trees and plant life, even the pond. Nothing but dirt remained.

To their even greater shock, in the near distance, they heard a cough.

It was Diadora, swatting away at the dust from around his face. He just stood there in the crater without a single scratch on him.

"I hate dust," he continued to cough.

No one could comprehend with what they were witnessing at the moment, all their words stolen away and their jaws unable to keep their mouths shut.

This man just withstood the blast from a bomb powerful enough to wipeout everything in such a large radius and all he did was complain about how annoying the dust was.

"Aah!" he said with his arms wide open, "You survived... you really are protected aren't you?"

Mark's face turned into a disgusted frown, confused as he watched Diadora just stand there and act as though nothing happened.

"Now," he dusted himself, "It's quite clear you guys are not from around here, otherwise you would have known who I was and probably surrendered as soon as you saw me," he pointed out, "But now that you know who I am, I'll gladly answer a question that you may have in mind," he offered.

Now he was ready for a Q and A?

They were all still too clueless and astonished.

"Fine, I'll answer one for you," he offered, "That amulet you still carry... I'm sure you want to know what that symbol means, now that you have seen it all over that temple, yes?" he asked, "I'll tell you anyway... it's not just a symbol," he smiled.

James had something to ask, "What are you if not a witch?"

"I am just your average human, nothing else," he closed his hand into a fist, "It's all I'm willing to share," he opened his hand again, there was a tiny version of the explosives he had made, this one the size of a large marble, "People need me, I've got to go."

Mia said something stupid, "Wait!"

"Huh?"

"Didn't you say you were going to take us to the prison?"

James was shock by the question, along with the others, "What are you doing?" He whispered.

"Oh," Diadora replied.

They all waited for him to attack again, breathing unevenly, wondering why Mia was putting them in this situation again, just as he was about to leave.

"That part comes later," he smiled giving them a small casual salute before dropping the marble sized bomb at his feet.

It blew up into a cloud of black smoke that enveloped him.

As it cleared away, he was gone.

Mark sighed, "Thanks for freaking me out Mia."

"He's gone," Daniel said.

They stood there frozen in shock, waiting for something to happen. But nothing... there was just silence. The conversation with the crazy man was finally over, maybe now they could move on.

Mia stepped forward and jumped down into the crater.

CHAPTER 22

Door of Separation

To the farthest east of Maramel, close to the edge of the Eastern Mountains that divided the rest of the world from this country.

Atop three horses on a hill overlooking the green grass plains that stretched out to the roots of the mountains were our other friends, the party of Jake, Jane, Mary and Denice. Having discovered the first door under Marridor, sealed, they were happy to continue on to the next door with Jake leading the way through this world unknown to them, hoping to find this second door sealed as well.

Far across the fields stood a great city, built from the edge of the mountain. A city with many buildings and farm lands like Marridor.

They all took a moment to breathe in the fresh morning air.

The mountain peaks were pearl white from the settled snow, reflecting light as well as the crystal droplets of the morning dew that settled on the grass.

Jake took a deep breath, "The great witch kingdom of Badalin."

"Wow, looks impressive from here," Denice complimented.

Jane frowned, "Wait, did you say 'witch', I heard they all died."

"Yes, you're quite right, but it is still a witch kingdom, only with the absence of witches," he replied, "Now it is occupied by man."

Jake held his staff in his right hand, "Something tells me that your faces are all over the city."

Mary agreed, "Yeah, they've probably started aging now," she giggled, "How do we go about doing this?"

Jake cleared his throat, "That part you will have to leave to me, I have some practice in illusion magic, all I ask is that you act yourselves and hopefully the luck we have so far continues," he got his horse to start trotting down the hill, "Come on, we only got today for this!"

They started down the hill after him.

They neared the main gate of the city, still keeping off the main road that often had the company of Dead Crows patrolling. The defensive walls of this city became much higher, the closer they got to them, reaching about 12 metres with platforms and watch towers for the soldiers stationed up there. All built from stone.

Above the main gate, which had been recently opened up by the guards, hanged two purple banners, identical to each other with an emblem of a mountain with what looked to be a crown on it with cross swords in the background and small stars circling around everything.

The same emblem was worn on the chest plates on all the city guards.

As they approached the entrance, they found themselves waiting in a short line. There were four carriages in front of them, all carrying goods into the city. The guards at the entrances were carefully inspecting all cargo being brought into the city as well as the courier sheets stating exactly what it was they were bringing into the city. This procedure was carried out for each deliverer or trader before they were allowed to pass the gates.

Jane did not know what Jake had planned, but now she was feeling a little nervous as they drew nearer and nearer to the front. They did not have anything for inspection but the thought of having their faces out in the open was nerve wrecking. The only bit of comfort she could see was the fact that there weren't any agents doing inspection.

The rules of the city had already given themselves away as being strict.

There turn had finally arrived, with nothing for the guards to inspect, maybe it would be much quicker.

First, to Jane, Mary and Denice's surprise, the guards did not recognize them at all. This was shown with very little compromising expressions that may in any way plant some suspicion. Whatever Jake did was working in their favour so they did as he had told them and just remained calm and smiled at them.

On top of all this luck, the guard doing the inspection recognized Jake and gave him a cheerful greeting which he returned.

"Back already, it's only been a month," the guard spoke, "Why you been travelling so much?"

"Ah well, business is business," he replied, "But today, I came here as a tour guide, showing these ladies here the city of Badalin, they a from the Forest Plains far down south."

The guard took a quick look at them and seemed impressed. He nodded at them with a greeting.

They just smiled and waved in return.

"Okay, as long as you're touring and staying in this city, all will be just fine," he stepped out of the way, "Enjoy your stay ladies."

This seemed way easier than expected.

They made their way through the gates and behind the walls of Badalin.

They entered into the farmlands of the city, filled with barns and farmhouses, surrounded by fruit trees and crops with cattle grazing away. It was not as isolated as Marridor.

Jane looked to the right and could see a wooden house, close to the wall, she figured it was where the guards would take their short rests and ate. Next to the house was a row people standing close to the wall, cuffed in chains with one guard, holding a pike keeping watch. It must have been people who tried to smuggle themselves into the city.

In the far distance ahead, you could start to see the buildings crowd each other and get taller.

"Okay, this city looks much bigger than Marridor," she looked ahead, "Or is it because there are no walls?"

Jake shrugged, "I'm not too sure, the walls of Marridor really do prevent you from seeing the whole city at once."

Jake led the way on the main road for a while before separating from it.

They made their way to one of the farmhouses just a little ways from the main road. There stood a tall mango tree and under it, an old man of about fifty sat on a stool with a cowboy hat over his forehead. He seemed to be sleeping or bored, it was the way he was sitting on the chair, with his arms crossed enjoying the sun.

Jake stopped his horse near the tree and hopped off it.

The others did the same.

The old man on the chair fixed his hat and looked up at them, "Jake!" he stood up from his chair and greeted him with a hug, "I did not expect to see you so soon."

"Me too," he replied.

The others were still surprised. So many people seemed to know him, and as a friend by the looks of it.

"What can I do for you today?"

"Not much," he said, "Can I just leave the horses in your barn?"

"Off course, off course, "He turned to his house, "Sera!" He called, "Please open up the barn."

From inside the house, they heard a faint voice reply, "Ok!"

"I see you've brought people with you," he greeted them as well, "My name is Harbert."

"Yes, we have some business to attend to."

"Always attending to business, even at your old age," he laughed.

From the front door of the farmhouse, out came a teenage girl with long blonde hair, wearing casual clothing with a ring of keys in her hand.

She came to notice the arrivals, "Jake?" she smiled.

Jake waved at her, "How is she doing?"

"She's well, and quite happier," He replied.

"That's good," Jake nodded, "Well, we won't be long, we're in kind of a hurry," he said taking the horse's strap.

"No problem," he returned to his chair.

They followed Sera to the barn, not far from Harbert's house.

Sera was already busy testing the different keys on the lock. It took a few moments, Jake and the others had already caught up to her, but when the deed was done she pulled the doors and pushed them wide open, "There."

Sera was tall and fit with light blue eyes.

"Thank you," Jane said leading her horse into the barn.

Jake stood by the entrance, thinking about something that had just occurred to him. He handed his horse to Mary, "I'll be a minute."

He headed to an old used wooden carriage that stood out in the open and called Sera.

She went over to him, "Who are they?" she asked.

"Oh, they're just...," he paused for a second, "Not important, I came here to ask how you're doing?"

She swayed her head, "Hmmm, it's a nice city."

Back at the barn, while the horses enjoyed their breakfast, Jane, Mary and Denice waited for Jake.

Jane took a seat on one of the haystacks, Denice stood by the entrance to the barn, against the wall watching as carriages in the distance passed by, "Jake is really taking his time with that Sera girl."

Jane yawned, "Yup."

"You already sleepy?" She giggled.

"No, just tired," She replied, "It's been a while since we took a weekend off."

"Yeah, I guess you're right, and now that we're wanted murderers, we may never."

Outside, Jake was still sitting on the carriage speaking to Sera.

"Wait a second," Sera realized, "Those women in the barn, I've seen them before."

Jake frowned, "Where?"

"A few days ago, in the newspaper and on notice boards all around the city."

Jake raised his eyebrows, "Hmm, I thought I put a spell on them," he look at his staff.

She laughed, "You know magic doesn't affect me, I'm better at it," she explained, "Why are you with them?"

Jake sighed, "They are here to help me, don't speak about them to anyone."

"Lips are sealed," she said zipping her lips and locking them with an imaginary key, which she then threw away.

Jake got to his feet, "I got to go to the city now, I'll see you when I see you," he explained, "And work on it till no magic can affect you at all."

"Bye," she waved at him, remaining on the old carriage playing with the keys.

Jake appeared in the doorway of the barn and stepped in.

"Finally," Mary said, "Now we can get to business."

Denice found a place where she could sit next to Jane.

"Okay," Jake started, "We are here to find another door, I'm not sure which one it is but I know it's in the most secure part of the city."

"So... no sewer this time?" Mary asked.

Jake nodded, "Correct."

Denice clapped once, "If not leech people, what is it, I'm sure we can take it?"

Jake's expression turned worried, "The city guard."

Mary shrugged, "We bypass guards all the time."

"You said it's in a very secure place?" Jane repeated, "Where exactly?"

"We have to enter the mountain, follow the steps right up to the stewards keep, I heard that he has already found it so we just need to pay him a visit," he explained.

Mary shook her head, "I can already tell that this is a bad idea, 'pay him a visit', do you know this guy?"

"Yes, we're very good friends."

"Okay then, this is a good idea," she changed her mind, "You just do your magic identity thing and we'll be on our way."

"Um... that's where it gets a tad bit complicated," Jake spoke with uncertainty.

Everyone waited for an explanation.

"What do you mean?"

"We cannot use magic for this one," he said, "At least not when we are near the keep."

"Why?" Jane asked, "Will they confiscate your staff or something."

Jake shook his head, "The keep is not only playing host to the city guard, but the Dead Crow as well, and not your standard agent, there will be mages who will be able to detect the magic, so unless there is a witch amongst us, there is no way we are going to use magic without being caught."

"Witch?"

"Yes, a witch is the only being that can use magic and still go undetected."

Mary thought of an even greater idea, "Wait a second, you are this man's friend right?"

Jake nodded, somehow feeling that he was going to regret this nod, even though he had already mentioned it.

"And you are pretty famous, why don't you just head up into the keep yourself and we'll wait here, nobody gets in trouble and no trouble needed to get there, problem solved."

Everyone seemed to love the idea except for Jake.

"I knew you were going to suggest that," he shook his head slowly.

"Then why are we sitting planning when there's a flawless plan already on the table?" asked Mary.

"Because you can't just remain here," he said.

"Why not?" Jane was surprised, "It's safe."

"Because you need friends."

Everyone remained silent for a moment, trying to see the relevance of the answer he just blurted out.

Jake took a deep breath and began to explain, "You have already made an enemy of the Dead Crow yes, but you can't be enemies of the innocent, those who don't know anything. In this day and age, having friends to help you is a priority, I'll start you off with the high, I'll vouch for you when we get there."

They did not, at all get what he was saying but they did understand that he was from this time, judging by the amount of friends that he has and sadly, the only person they could think about that would help them out is Galvani, the only friend that they have managed to make since they got here, if you count Bertha as well, that makes two.

"Okay," Jane stood up, "You're our guide in this time, we'll trust and follow your lead."

Jake nodded, happy to know that everyone was in on this plan, "First we go into town.

There horses were left in the barn under the care of Harbert and Sera, as well as their bags whilst they took off into town.

As they left the farm and rejoined the main road, they followed the carriages until the streets started to get a little more crowded and the ground now covered by bricks. The outskirts of the city was filled with more labour than luxury.

The good thing about this city was perhaps the fact that there were no walls that stood, not one was put into a section of the city that equaled their wealth.

Many of the buildings were constructed from clay bricks which did give more of a luxury feel, more than your standard wooden house found in most towns and villages, but this area was a little more spread out with more work force than customer citizens.

Around most of the public areas stood small stands with notice boards, with a person on it addressing the crowds on many different topics and news that would concern or interest them from outside the city and locally, be it event dates or to outline the newspaper stories to get people to purchase them.

The one they were passing by right now was quite crowded, with a middle aged man on the stage upfront screaming about the most recent news.

"The outside villages have been defiled by the boldest of murderers!" he shouted at the top of his lungs over the chattering crowd.

Jane slowed her pace and listened in.

"Murderers capable of defying the Dead Crow and killing three of them in cold blood while they rested in Lonestar inn!"

"What!" Jane blurted out.

Mary and Denice noticed Jane's interest in the rabbling noise.

"What does this mean!?" the man continued, "Is it a rebellion against the symbol of justice or has the Dead Crow gone lenient!?"

"Oh, a rebellion," Jane chuckled in disbelief.

Mary pulled her by the arm, "Come on Jane, he is just trying to raise the crowd."

Just as they were about to move on and enjoy more of the city, a word brought them right back to the man's attention. His crowd drawing skills were good. Even Jake took interest.

"And now our worst fears have crawled out of the gutters to haunt us once again, a witch!"

The whole crowd became fearful and shocked. Jane and the others moved closer to the gathering, along with a few other citizens who began to take interest as well.

"A young girl by the name of Mia and her friends are dangerous," He held up a poster of Mia, "They, without mercy killed more than fifteen Dead Crow agents and a mage who were trying to keep us safe from this scum!"

"James," Jane murmured, "They've killed?"

"This world is not good to a lot of people," Jake explained, "They must know what it means to survive."

Jane looked at Jake with much discontent, shaking her head, putting the blame on him for all these outcomes.

"Are these murders connected to the ones done at Reelaside Stead, committed by Levina herself?" he continued, "It's been a year since such an incident, and now suddenly, people are taking the lives of our brave Dead Crows."

"Let's go," Jake suggested, "We've still got some distance to cover."

They pushed their way out of the crowd and back into the open where they could breathe again and followed the main road down towards the mountain.

"It's weird." Jane said.

"What?" Mary asked.

"I don't remember any of this ever being taught to us in history, I didn't even know that a witch existed, we were just told magic was banned, because war, not even this famous girl Levina popped up," she replied.

Jake was the one to reply to that answered, "I am guessing it was all erased, all history was altered and changed to suit the leader's needs, they hid all that was too sour and replaced it with heroism and good stories," he explained, "What I noticed is that, everyone born during the last years of the hundred year shift was fed a new history, and thus the reason for the subject being compulsory in your present, to ensure proper order and obedience to the system."

"Hmm," Jane nodded.

"Okay, so this is political, great," said Mary, sarcastically.

"Everything is political," replied Denice.

Down the streets of Badalin they continued, slowly but surely nearing the mountain where the steward resided.

They had now made it to a more decorated part of the city, where most of the shops and motels stood. The city was also equipped with an agora occupied with many stalls, people selling small foods including fruits and vegetables, packed to the brim with many customers and a few of the carriages that traded mobile.

There were children playing with pet animals on the streets and engaging in other activities which led to all kinds of conflicts between them.

All the while, to their fortunes, no Dead Crow mages or agents were around, the city seemed to have a solid guard unit.

Denice began to fiddle with her gauntlet, "Why don't we get ourselves some fruit from that shopping centre?"

"Good idea," Jane agreed.

There seemed to be a lot of things drawing them away.

Later that day, just as it hit noon, the mountain palace had become very close, there was nothing much to see of the actual palace being built into the mountain beside some of the smaller towers and balconies, everything else was invisible. The lower grounds before the flight of stairs was an open space of decorated floors and gardens. There were a few agents and mages posted on the lower grounds and on platforms beside the steps on the way to the top.

After seeing how impossible it was to get to the stewards keep without being seen, they had decided to enter a local inn nearby and order a few drinks.

They went to a table in the corner and with those drinks, ordered some food as well, just to chase away the midday hunger. The place was not so packed, probably at peek when the sun goes down.

"Okay, Jake!" Mary started, "How do you propose we climb that horrible amount of steps without being seen?"

Jake cleared his throat and took a sip from his tankard.

"I'm really starting to like the idea of staying out of this while you speak nicely to him," Denice said, "We could explore the city.

"You're right, it is a good idea," he replied.

Jane gave him a weird frown, she did not believe what he was saying one bit, "Please just let us in on you plan."

Jake took another sip from his drink, "This is good," he looked at the contents of his cup.

"Ugh," she shook her head.

Jake placed his tankard down carefully and brought his hands together, "Okay, for the plan."

"What? Now you catch on?"

"Shh, lower your voice," he instructed, "This is how it will go," he started, "You three will go out and purchase yourself something matching and ceremonial... dancing robes, to be precise, with eye masks, after that you will order a room here where you will change into the clothes."

"Dancing robes?" Jane asked.

"Yes, I know him well, he won't turn down three female dancers."

"Hmm..."

"Don't worry, you won't be entertaining him," Jake assured them, "He's a good man... anyway, I will head up to the top meanwhile and get him to allow you to pass."

Mary nodded, "Sounds solid... and fun."

"Just don't take the masks off once you have them on, my hex will have been dispelled," Jake warned them.

"Well then, let's go shopping," announced Denice.

The sun was setting and everyone ready. Jake had left his staff with the inn keeper and made his way straight to the decorated gardens, being as casual as ever. The first line of guards stopped him. They too recognized him as Jake and allowed him to pass through and make his way to the steps, which he did not want to start to climbing. Standing at the bottom, he stared up into the distance, the entrance looking so small from where he was, but time was a waste, he had to get to the top as soon as possible so he immediately started his climb up the smooth stone steps.

Every once in a while he would be able to take a small rest. After a certain amount of steps there would be a platform, with decorated golden brown vases on each side filled with thistle and fire lilies amongst others, and next to these vases was the royal city guard, wearing heavy armor and renaissance closed helmets with long purple capes also bearing the city's emblem. Each guard carrying a halberd pike in the one hand, all standing still. These pike men were not the only ones occupying these platforms, quite a few of them were playing host to the Dead Crow mages, carrying staves instead, these ones did not prefer the statue position, making eye contact with Jake since they did not wear any helmets.

His climb had reached an end after some time. The first thing he took in was the view of the whole city from up here, all the rooftops and streets still filled with people scurrying about, and to the far distance, a sunset that stared right back at him in orange light.

Turning away from the world he faced the main entrance to the keep, the massive wooden doors open wide, large banners hanging just above. Excellent stonework, put into the pillars and walls designed with carvings and statues of guards. Whatever was not manmade was the mountain itself, which was kept in many places, only adding more beauty with its many different shades of stone.

Guards were posted near the entrance as well. One of them walked up to him, "What is your business?" he asked.

"I wish to make an audience with the steward," Jake replied formally.

"Please wait here," he ordered making his way into the hallway, which seemed quite occupied.

Inside, he could see long tables, all placed before the throne on the other end of the hall. Tables, covered in red silk cloths and lace doilies, filled with empty goblets and plates. A host of people also filled the room, dressing in the most expensive of attires, just socializing.

Jake stood there with his hands behind his back taking in the fresh air that was only exclusive to these heights. The audience was a surprise to him, he did not expect there to be other people here on this day.

A few short minutes passed and the guard came back with whom Jake had requested an audience with.

It was a chubby old man in his late fifties with long blonde hair and a short beard, wearing red and white ceremonial robes over his clothing with jewelry around his neck. Wearing brown leather caiman belly boots.

He was happy to see Jake, greeting him with a hug, "It's good to see you old friend."

"Why so soon?" he asked, "Last I remember you were headed north?"

Jake shrugged, "I seem to be needed everywhere."

The man laughed, "Your consistent visits are going to make you lose all your wait"

Jake turned to the steps and nodded, "It is quite a climb," he then looked over his shoulder, "I was not expecting more than just you here today."

"Oh, it's a little get together, a few members from both the Maithindor and Ghordiitry house are here," he glanced behind him, "They have made it a tradition to come here once in a while."

Jake nodded, "I hope I'm not intruding on anything?"

"No no no, off course not," he replied, "We not going to feast until later in the evening. I'm actually glad you came, only two of the older members showed, most of them never leave their households so I'm tending to the younger ones, What can I help you with?"

Jake put some though into what he was about to say, "I arrived with some women I want you to meet."

The old man looked around, "And are these women invisible?"

Jake shook his head, surprised by the question, "No, they haven't made the climb yet, I wanted your approval first."

The old man took a deep breath, "Jake, come on, we've been friends for long years, I don't think you need my approval, it's not like you're going to bring wanted criminals or assassins hey?" he gave him a pat on the shoulder, "Bring them, always good to meet new people."

"I guess that's my way back down then."

The old man frowned at him, "Why do you keep torturing yourself Jake?"

Jake shrugged.

"I'll be waiting in the hall for your return," he went back inside.

Down, back in the city, in one of the rooms that Jane had ordered from the inn keeper, they had changed into their dancing robes that they had bought from one of the shops. Their outfits included a top, a fixed hip belt, and a full length skirt, you could say it was a belly dance outfit. Each of theirs having many reflective beads fixed onto them for decoration, also wearing shiny bangles around their wrists and ankles, they also wore dancing shoes.

Each of their outfits were a different color. Jane wore violet, Mary was red and Denice was a dark blue.

Aware of the hex being removed, they put on their eye masks, which matched the color of their outfits, beaded with feathers sticking out of them.

Their clothes were left in their rooms.

Denice looked at herself and nodded, "This is different."

"Yeah, we will be met with many surprises here," Jane giggled.

Mary sat on one of the beds, "I just hope they do not take off our masks."

Jane disagreed, "I don't think they will... we are just ordinary dancers to them, we blend in as normal."

Moments later they heard a loud knock on the door.

None of them replied to it.

"It's Jake," the voice spoke from the other side.

"It's open," Mary replied.

Jake stepped in and examined their attire.

"What do you think?" asked Jane.

"That'll do," he replied, "He has agreed to meet with you so we must make haste."

Mary stood up and shrugged, "Ok, we're ready."

"Okay, you definitely look the type, just don't draw any kind of suspicion," he thought for a second, "Just smile at every guard you pass by."

Jake's little bit of advice was a little harder to follow in real life, at least only while they were in the inn. People eyeballing them, wondering what it was they were doing. Outside, it was the opposite of their thoughts, not many took any note of them, it was a lot easier to make their way through the crowds but as soon as Jake led them into the untouched area of beauty protected by the guards, all their nerves started to kick in, suddenly, they stood out again.

The first encounter was with one of the guards, questioning Jake about the dancers. That bit was easy to get through, all he had to mention was the steward and that he requested for them to perform, in addition, the unknown events of the visits from the royal families came in handy as well.

Jake did the talking and the others just smiled when it was necessary.

The climb to the top was not so hard for our three dancers, though it had been cut slow by Jake who had already made the trip. Each platform they had reached was an opportunity for him to take a small breather and for Jane and the others to act as natural as ever, especially in front of the Dead Crow mages.

To the top they finally reached, and the same guard that questioned Jake before entered the hall again.

Jane turned to the city and admired it, but not as much as the far horizon, covered in green and an orange sky, shading the few clouds that drifted ever so slowly.

Mary first noticed the tables and people that occupied the hall, "There's people," she blurted out, standing next to Jake, "There's people," she repeated, "Why are there people?"

"The steward is having a little get together with the Maithindor and Ghordiitry family," Jake replied, "By the looks of it, none of the higher ups are here."

"And you didn't think to tell us this?"

"I did not want you to worry."

Mary shook his head, "Why do I get the feeling we are going to do something we have never done before?"

Jake shrugged.

Denice was another one that started to worry about this situation.

Jane turned to the entrance, "So these are the famous people we've been hearing about?"

Jake nodded.

The guard returned with the steward, who wore a really surprised face when he came to see them, examining there attire, "You didn't tell me they were dancers," he gave them a small nod, "My name is Frederick Haldin, steward of this city."

They remained silent and gave a curtsey.

"Okay," Frederick turned to Jake, "Why did you want me to meet with them?"

Jake leaned forward, "Might we discuss this in private... your quarters?"

"But I have guests."

"We'll only be a moment, it's quite important." He added.

Frederick gave it some thought, he turned to the ladies then back to Jake, "Okay, but sundown we must be done."

Jake agreed to the terms.

"Follow me," he stepped into the hall.

Everyone stepped into the warm, fire lit hall. Floors covered in white marble with a row of grey pillars on each side of the room, made of the same material. Purple banners with the kingdom's emblem hanging from them with wrought iron wall torches beneath. The wide ceiling above them filled with statues and sculptures, with the largest being of four ladies in robes reaching for the centre of the ceiling where the great chandelier hung from.

The other end of the hall was a throne, atop some steps and above it, a wall filled with weapons and shields placed in an neat order with two more banners.

The one missed was the section behind the row of pillars, a corridor of large paintings with even more well designed golden frames. Art of many histories that we do not know of yet. Each painting was separated by the wall torches.

The people inside were all dressed in their best clothing by the looks of it. The women dressed in low back and sheath gowns among others with crystal hair pins and vines in their hair, some with bohemians and other kinds of headpieces, with gemmed earrings, necklaces and bracelets. The men dressed in doublets and other royal clothing including robes, some in shining knights armor. A lot of the other women wore similar clothing but had it more traditional, possessing patterns and bright colours like red and yellow, incorporated with gold and silver pieces of jewelry. Having long braided hair in different styles and some with short afros, others with long curly hair, also bearing head pieces. The same went for the men but as well bearing more traditional colours and attire.

Upon their entry, most of the audience fell silent and glared, frowned at the unexpected visitors, examining their clothing with some kind of terrifying interest.

For the dancers, this attention was scary, each hoping that they would have just passed by this group unnoticed. Their looks were lasers piercing into their souls, a very unsettling feeling, unable to look away, unable to smile.

Jake also felt a little out of place in this royalty gathering, wearing only his ragged robes.

Frederick was there at least, to save them all from the curiosity plaguing their minds, "My apologies everyone," he raised his hands, "I have to show these ladies around, they'll be my daughter's mentors," he smiled.

The others seemed to buy what he was selling.

"Hmm," a lady spoke from nearby, "And I thought there would be some kind of performance."

Frederick started to panic a little, feeling a little unsure of himself, "Well…"

Mary's eyes widened, staring at him, hoping that he does not say anything that would mean what she was currently thinking right now.

"… I will organize something like that if you wish, they are not prepared, I'm just here to show them the place, won't be long," he turned to them, "Come this way."

Mary sighed in relief, he saved them from a really traumatic experience.

"Jake… isn't it?" A man stepped forward bearing a smile, he held a cup of wine, "What brings you here?"

"Uh… well," he was not expecting to be asked anything, he had to kill his hesitation immediately if he was going to sell a lie to them, "I was tasked to find the teachers."

The man gave him a weird look, "Okay… nice to see you again," he raised his cup.

"Same to you," he smiled and gave him a nod.

Frederick broke the awkwardness, "Ok, let me get this done, I'll see you in while," he also gave a slight nod before leading the way again.

Frederick lead them through a door under the pillared corridor.

They could hear the chatters start to creep back as soon as they were out of sight.

He led them up some steps till they reached another section of this keep, a hallway filled with more large paintings and some doorways leading to unknown places. The empty spaces had very tall bronze colored, swirly and flower shaped vases that did not seem to have anything in them.

A few statues were also place against the walls, statues of the city's royal guard.

This particular hall had tall arched windows on the right side letting in what was left of the setting sun.

"You said my quarters right?" Frederick asked.

Jake nodded, "Yes, that would be preferred," he look at one of the paintings as he passed by, "Where are your children?"

"They like going down into the city, sometimes returning late, especial today, since this is a very formal gathering," he replied walking through an arched double door.

Jane couldn't take her eyes off the artworks, some of landscapes, people, others of fruit or flowers and some of exotic weapons.

Frederick led them to another hallway, a very small one with many doors on each side. On the other end was a wide open doorway with a thin, transparent red curtain that lead to a balcony. All the floors seemed to be covered in white marble. This room, however, had a rose red carpet down the centre, and between each of the doors a display case stood bearing some really interesting artifacts. Masks and amulets, smooth rocks and large rusted old keys were among the many objects on display.

He led them to a door on the right, closest to the balcony, "This is where I sleep most of the time," he opened the doors and stepped into the left side of the room.

The bedroom was quite large, leading to another large balcony and like the hall to this room, the main colours here were red and white, from the duvet and drapes of his Four pillars king sized bed, to the patterned carpets and flowers, which did have other variations of color, including oranges and purples.

To the left side of the room was a black grand piano placed in an angle and brown cushion chairs place in a curved order on the other side.

There were shields and weapons displayed on the walls and one painting above the piano.

A large iron chest was place at the feet of his bed with a lock on it.

Frederick allowed them to sit on the chairs. There were only three and all taken so Jane seated herself on the piano bench facing away from it.

Frederick sat on the large iron chest and rubbed his hands, "Now, who are you really?" he smiled.

Everyone else found it strange that he asked such a question, considering the fact that Jake had not revealed anything yet that would give anything away. Nobody was able to reply to that question.

"Okay, Okay, let me explain," he laughed, "You people really need to work on your whispering, and your choice of where you do these little talks is very poor."

Did someone hear and report to him? Did this mean that they were caught and they just did not know it yet?

The silence continued from Frederick's audience, "While you were scheming, my daughter who was also there, overheard your little conversation and decided to tell me," he explained, "But luckily it was her and not someone who would report this scheming to one of the mages of the Dead Crow."

Jane wanted a little more support, since she had nothing to lean on and decided to place her elbow on the piano.

She jumped at the sound of loud notes she had pressed and immediately lowered the lid to prevent any further disturbances.

Jake sighed from both the sudden noise and Frederick's explanation, "That makes things a little simpler."

"Now," he started playing with his beard, "Whom don't you want anyone to see?"

"Now, please do not panic, "Jake warned him in advance, he turned to Denice, "You can remove the masks."

All together they unhooded their masks and exposed their identities.

Frederick's eyes almost popped out of their sockets, he gasped and leaned backwards. His gaze slid from one face to the next.

Denice tried to be a little more welcoming by putting on a faint smile on her face.

When Frederick had finally remember to breath out, he put on a fearful frown, "Wh-What's this?" he stuttered.

"Calm yourself," Jake instructed.

Frederick turned to the door.

It was closed.

He turned back to them and started breathing unevenly, "Do know these people Jake?"

"Off course," he replied.

"Did they force you to do this, are we going to die!" he started to panic.

"Shh," Mary silenced him.

Those orders he followed without question.

"We're not here to do anything to you," Jane said shaking her head.

"They're right," Jake vouched.

He calmed himself a little, "They must be reported," he uttered, "I don't want to be caught harboring them."

Mary shook her head.

Jake took a deep breath, "Look at me... I know you may be confused right now but this is much bigger the both of us, bigger than them and this world," he explained, "We don't have much time, will you hear me out?"

"I don't understand," he replied.

Jake sighed, "It's got to do with the Lord of Power."

Frederick gave a surprised frown, "What are you talking about?"

"First promise me, whatever is said in this room, stays in this room."

"Yes, off course," he was quick to reply, "And them?'

"That will be in a moment."

Frederick sat up and prepared himself, "Now, please let me understand this madness."

Jake leaned forward, "I assume you know the story about the disappearance of all the gods thousands of years ago?"

He nodded in return.

"And the object they created?

"Yes, object of the Lord of Power."

"I have recently discovered some information that will fill the blank space between the first Lord and now."

Every one listened in, especially Jane, Mary and Denice because they were never told to whole story, Jake had cut it off suddenly for some apparent reason.

Jake cleared his throat before beginning, "The thing is, after the first Lord was chosen, don't get me wrong here, peace followed and equality between the races was established... but though the object made the bearer invincible, it did not make him immortal, which led to his death by age," he paused for a moment, "The object, however, placed itself on the shrine again, which lead to thousands of people dying and the rise of conflict again, wars over the possession of the shrine and the next bearer. A new one was eventually chosen to bear all the power... this repeated itself for quite some time, revealing that this was only a temporary solution or maybe the gods just wanted their betrayers to suffer in their absence... so later on, one of the Lords had to make a sacrifice, something that would put these wars over the object to a stop, she came up with a solution."

"What was this solution?" Frederick asked.

"To detach from the material world and all its possessions... to become in some words, an actual god," he explained, "She chose to watch over the world like the old gods did... though to complete this she had to leave the object here, afraid to leave it in one specific place she split it into three parts and by doing so was joined by two others whom were to share the power, join her and help keep them hidden from the world for as long as they were able to watch over it... and so began the cycle of the gods."

Jane shook her head, "Which is...?"

Jake shrugged, "Every millennia or so, there are three who must take their places, and I think we're currently in the third cycle."

Jane shook her head, "I'm more confused."

"Same here," Denice raised her hand.

"I hate history," Mary murmured.

Frederick nodded slowly, "You speak of all these races, but all I remember from any book is the existence of man and witches.... where are the others?"

"I do not know."

"Now it sounds like this little history lesson is a bit faulty," Mary added.

"I am very sure that what I am telling you right now is very accurate," Jake said, "I have a really good source."

Mary chuckled, "Which history book did you swallow?"

Jane stepped in, "Do you think the others were killed off by man as well, like they did the witches?

Jake shrugged, "I don't know that part yet."

"You said that the last time you told us the story," Mary pointed out, "You know the rest don't you."

Jake shook his head, "At the time I only knew that much."

Mary started to get annoyed, "What do you mean... I for one was with you the whole time since that day, never saw you read any books or learn anything new."

Frederick just sat there in silence, watching as they all spoke to each other as good acquaintances, really confused about their actual involvement in this situation. He allowed them to speak for a while before interrupting them, "Sorry, but nothing you have said explains why they're here, in the keep, with me... in my bedroom."

"Oh," Mary pulled a fake smile, "I would gladly like to explain that."

Frederick nodded.

"Jake over here has sent us back in time."

"How many times do I have to tell you, I have no idea why you are here," he replied.

"But you know why our children are right?" Jane shot at him.

Frederick did not understand, shaking his head trying to clear his mind, he interrupted the erupting argument, "Wait, sent back... in time?"

Denice nodded silently.

"That's not possible," he concluded raising his hands, "This has turned into some kind of joke, I have a gathering to host."

"They not lying," Jake said.

Frederick giggled, "No, no such power exists, not in this world," he paused for a moment, "Only the gods can do that."

"And it was the gods that did it."

He frowned at Jake, "Now, why would they do that?" he glanced at the others, "Why would she do that?"

"I'm not too sure of their motives."

Frederick remained silent for a moment, "Why are you telling me this?"

"They needed someone to trust, in this time... as you may know, they have made enemies with everyone."

"You want me to be their friend and ally?" he grabbed his beard in thought, "I... think can do that," he sounded unsure of himself.

Jake had successfully completed one of the tasks he set out to do, now for the next part, "And we came here for something."

Frederick just kept silent and waited for him to speak.

"I believe there is a door in this mountain, it will be in a hidden place, a room filled with masks," he describe.

"Why do you want to see that secret door?"

Jake took a deep breath, "What if I told you that behind it lies one of the three objects."

"Oh," he blurted out rather loudly, "That's what it is."

"You know where it is?" Mary asked.

"Yes."

"Great, that was easy."

"There aren't any monsters or anything that will attack us there right?" Denice asked, referring to the horrible incident whilst finding the first door.

Frederick shook his head slightly, "No."

"Please show it to us," Jake requested.

"Off course," he replied, "You may need to put the masks back on."

They did as he said.

Frederick led them to another large room, filled with display cases and tables complete with many antiques and trinkets. Many banners also hung up against the walls and more statues for decorations, this time of ladies in robes.

He stood in front of an iron wall torch, carrying another in his right hand, "It's behind this wall," he said pulling down the wall torch like a lever.

The lining of the door appear in a rectangular shape a few moments after. Frederick then gave the wall a hard push and it opened up like a regular door.

He stepped in, followed by the others closely behind.

Jake had scanned the area first for any prowling eyes before stepping into the dark passageway.

It was similar to the one in the Marridor sewers, masks hanging from the ceiling.

They made it to the room and found disbelief in what they saw.

The door was opened.

Jake hurried over to it, and opened it up wide.

"It's open," Denice whispered.

"I'm afraid so," Frederick replied.

Jake examined the inside, there was nothing but a small circular display stand, merged with the floor, with nothing on it. He was shocked, "Who did this?"

Frederick shrugged, "A few months ago, I received a visit from an Anonymous," he started to explain.

"An Anonymous?" Jake replied, "Are you talking about…"

Frederick nodded.

Jane stepped in, "What do you mean 'Anonymous', I thought the guards checked everything."

Frederick sighed, "The Anonymous is a very small group of people that exist with all authority, higher than Kings and Dead Crows. Nobody knows who they are, hence the name. They wear a strange white mask and black clothing."

"All authority?"

"Yes," replied Jake, "No one can disobey a single order they give, they can do whatever they want."

Frederick continued with his story, "This one in particular came with a bold, young, black boy and lead him to this place…I was not allowed to enter whilst they were busy, but my curiosity brewed afterwards and I found this."

Jake stepped out of the room and looked for the main symbol on the front. It was a circle that had been split into a few piece, "Door of Separation," he said, "This is not good."

"So someone was able to open it?" Mary asked Frederick.

He nodded.

Jake crossed his arms, thinking, while he stared at the symbol, "We need to find the other one right now, as soon as possible," he said, "With this one missing, something is bound to happen very soon."

"Father?" a female voice spoke.

Everyone jumped at the sound of her voice.

"Oh," Frederick sighed I relief, "It's you Ariella, don't scare me like that."

In the light of the torch held by Frederick, you could see most of her features, a young lady with long blonde hair, wearing a red garment and hair piece.

"What is this room?" she grew curious of it. She then noticed the others, "Why are they here, heard them scheming with Jake."

"They are friendly don't worry," he said, "Ariella, this is Jane, Mary and Denice… Jane, Mary, Denice, this is my daughter Ariella."

Ariella was surprised to hear those names, but she exchanged greetings with them. She then stepped closer to her dad, keeping an eye on them, "Have you seen the wanted posters?" she whispered to him. Loud enough for the others to hear, "The masks are not helping much."

He nodded, "Don't worry, they're friends… off course, something I would wish you would not mention to anyone else."

Ariella understood and moved away from that matter quickly, she went over to the door, "Interesting," she examined the symbols, "What is this?"

"No time for that now dear, we need to leave now," said Frederick, "I have guests to attend to, and our friends here are on their way as well."

She turned to Jake, "Leaving already?"

"I'm afraid so, I have bus-,"

"Have business to attend to, yes yes, always the same, goodbye" she interrupted him making her way to the passage.

Everyone followed her back into the light.

Frederick examined Ariella's clothing, he did not find it appealing, "Please put on something presentable, tonight you will be dining with the Maithindor and Ghordiitry families."

She groaned, "Fine," she said goodbye to the others and headed her own way.

Frederick lead them out to the front and said his farewells to Jake and his new friends before they headed down the steps.

The sun had disappeared at this time, the sky turned very dim and some of the stars started to reveal themselves. Down in the city, it was still quite crowded, as it was not complete darkness yet. Most of the lights had been lit now to increase visibility.

First thing first, Jake went to get his staff from the inn keeper to reinstate the hex whilst Jane, Mary and Denice went up to their room and changed back into their normal clothing.

They ate and got some food for the road.

They exited after everything was done and started heading back.

"So what's our next heading?" Jane asked.

"The Kingdom of Mitheral," he replied, "Far to the west."

Just at that moment, while Jake was looking on ahead, he spotted a young man running towards him, with a satchel bag. He pretended not to see him and carried on walking.

The young man stopped right in front of him "Are you Jake?" he asked, out of breath.

He nodded, "Yes."

The young man then pulled out a scroll, tied by a small blue ribbon, from his bag and handed it over to him.

"Thank you," he took it.

"A pleasure," he replied leaving with haste.

"A letter from someone," Mary said, "You have friends everywhere."

Jake untied the ribbon and opened the letter. It was hard reading the contents in the dark so he stepped closer to a torch for some light. He read it in his head and rolled it back up.

His expression was blank and worried at the same time.

"What does it say?" Denice asked.

Jake did not reply, instead he placed it above the flames and set it alight, "Strange."

"What is it?"

"A message from the Lord of Ethril," he replied starting to walk again, as soon as most of the letter had burnt away, "He has requested my immediate presence."

"What about Mitheral and the third door?" Mary asked.

Jake seemed really concerned about the contents of the letter. He even picked up his pace, "We'll talk later."

Back at Harbert's house, Sera had come out to unlock the barn again, "Already leaving."

"Yes," he replied stepping into the barn.

"Are you going to tell us about the letter now?" Jane insisted.

Jake put on hold what he was doing and sighed, "I have to go down south to Ethril."

"And Mitheral?"

"He sighed again, "I am sorry, but this is where we have to part ways… you must find the other door… I wouldn't leave if it wasn't this important."

"Oh," Denice sounded let down, walking over to her horse.

"You are just going to leave us?" Jane shook her head.

Mary did not say anything, you could see she was not happy at all.

Jane just accepted the fact, "Do you have any idea where the door might be?"

"It should be near the palace, like the ones we've discovered," he replied, "You do have a compass and map right?"

"Yes."

They all exited the barn so that Sera could to lock it again.

Jake placed his hand on Sera's shoulder, "Be sure to better yourself."

She smiled and nodded, "Bye."

"Good luck."

She wave the others goodbye before they left.

They stopped just outside the city, under the stars, in the clear fields of grass and blowing wind.

"So this is farewell?" Jane asked.

"For now," he replied, "You are very resourceful," he complimented, "Being able to find your own way since you awoke leaves me with no doubt you will succeed in finding the other door."

They thanked him.

"Don't get caught," he smiled, "The only advice I can give now."

And from there, they said their farewells and began to head on in their separate directions.

CHAPTER 23

Chasing Ghosts

Across the plains, to the north side of the Mountain. The Party of James had rested near the very bottom of the pass, away from the wide open. Their morning was quite early, to cover a lot of ground in hopes to reach the city of Adornfell while there was still a lot of daylight, in order to prevent the incident that occur in Reelaside Stead from happening again.

This side of the mountain was much easier to go through, not only because it was downhill but because there was no amount of crazy steepness that they had to pass.

The skies were clear today, accompanied by a cool breeze.

What now stood in front of them was more spread out plains of lemon shaded grass, empty lands, and in the farthest distance, some matter of trees and a giant lake downhill.

Amongst all this beauty that they were now witnessing, for some odd reason, Mia had a really confused frown on her face, as if something was missing from this natural landscape. Unsure of herself, she pulled out her compass and looked up ahead in the direction she was facing, everything seemed to be fine. Still unsure of herself, she shook the compass to see if it was working, and spun around once for extra insurance.

Mark was the most happy, glad that this dreadful mountain hike had come to an end. Happy at first, but then he too started wonder about the vast emptiness that lay before them.

James turned to Mia, who was still busy with the compass, "Which direction do we go from here?"

Mia looked at the compass, then up ahead and back down at the compass again, "Straight," she replied, really unsure of herself.

"Wait, wait a second," Mark remembered, "Didn't you say we would make it today?"

"Yes," she replied pulling out the map.

Mark coughed, "There's nothing for another horizon!"

She opened the map, "That lake is where the city should be," she showed them the mark.

"Yeah, it says Adornfell right under the lake, with drawings of buildings as well," James pointed out.

"Hmm," Mark rubbed his chin, "There can only one explanation for this."

Everyone looked at him.

"We've been scammed," he announced, "The map is fake!"

No one took what he said seriously, but he continued.

"For all we know, we could be heading in the wrong direction."

"Mark please," Mia said rolling the map up again, "I say we just go to the lake."

"I think so too," agreed Daniel.

"And what, go for a swim?" he asked, "I'm not prepared to walk for another horizon guys, You said we'd be there Mia."

James took a deep breath, and readied himself for the next walk.

Mark's happiness had diminished rather quickly, it was back to complaining for him, "We're about to get burnt by the sun on a fool's errand."

"Let's just follow the map," said James.

And so they did, they followed the map and continued their little voyage across the tall grass, forever thinking about the existence of their destination, and if Mark was actually right, that the map was a scam, or maybe outdated and that now they were way off course.

The lake drew nearer and so their hope slowly contracted, the large body of water was all they could see and according to the map, this city was fairly large. Mark's little announcement had a very high probability of being true at the moment.

The only thing that now kept them walking on into the emptiness was the thought of having come so far and not, for one second wanting to believe or consider the option that this was all for nothing.

Some things you kind of have to see through to the end, no matter how much doubt is in you. You tell yourself it is not so and that everything is the way it should be.

The sun continued to rise as time passed by. No one said a word. The lake still far away, but now taking a very wide shape.

It was starting to get hot and without a visual of their final destination, they suddenly grew tired, they did not want to go on anymore.

"How does one contact somebody far away in this time?" Mark asked turning back to the mountain, seeing it start to shrink.

"I don't know... a letter?" replied Mia.

Mark sighed, "I meant, is there any magic way, that's faster?"

Mia shrugged and hummed the words 'I don't know', "Why, who do you want to contact?"

"Galvani," he replied, "Tell him there's nothing here."

She ignored him.

James was ahead with Daniel just a few metres behind him.

His eyes were glued to the ground and himself, watching as he stepped on the tall grass that stood in his way. He did occasionally look up at the sun as it burnt his face, "Levina, are you around, we need your help," he murmured to himself, "The lake, must we go to the lake?"

Daniel heard his voice but couldn't make out what he was saying, he did know though that he was not talking to anyone but himself.

James began to murmur to himself again, "The map is a scam, the map is a scam," he repeated to himself, thinking how ridiculous that idea was, "the map is a scam," he chuckled.

A moment later he came across a rock hidden in the tall grass. He picked it up and examined it, it was the about the size of his palm. There was nothing special about it at all, but in that moment of boredom it was something somewhat intriguing. As he held it in his right hand, as he stared at it, he began to feel a little angry. He then closed his hand and tightened his grip as if trying to crush the rock. His eyes raised and looked ahead, then down at the rock again.

Daniel caught up to him and noticed the rock in his hand, "What are you doing?"

"I just want to start this search for Levina already, but we cannot apparently," he replied fidgeting with the rock, "First we meet a magician that can blow up mountains, and now our destination seems to have disappeared."

He flung the rock as hard as he could straight up ahead, it travelled for a short distance, before the strangest of things happened. The rock redirected itself back, as if it hit some kind of surface. James chuckled, "And now rocks can bounce back to you."

The strange phenomenon did not take James by surprise at first, it was still processing in his mind, really trying to figure out if it really just happened. He came to a conclusion, "Woah."

Daniel was also brought back to life by the unexpected event, "Wait what?" he blurted out loudly running over to the position he last saw the rock before it disappeared into the grass.

Mia and Mark saw them acting all strange and decided to investigate as well.

Everyone stood behind Daniel.

"What's happening!?" Mia shouted, hoping for some kind of good news.

The answer James gave out did not sell the phenomenon at all, "This rock bounced back, in midair."

Mia's eyelids dropped.

"He's right," Daniel supported his answer.

"Guys please," Mark stopped them, "Let's not go crazy now."

Daniel did not listen to what he was saying and proceeded to test it out himself. He threw the rock at full strength.

His experiment was a success, but at another cost. The rock met with whatever surface it bounced off before, but it was literally right in front of him so the force of its redirection was much stronger, meeting with Mark's face right on the forehead.

"Ow!" he screamed as the rock bounce off his head, feeling a sharp pain.

Both his hands went for the pain and covered it as he fell backwards into the grass, stomping his feet as is head throbbed in stinging pain.

Daniel and Mia rushed over to help him.

They sat him up. His eyes were watering.

The first thing Daniel did after helping him sit up was apologize.

He did not except it, "What were you thinking!?" he looked up at him.

Mia took of her bag and placed it beside him, "Mark, please calm down," she instructed.

"What!?" he shouted back.

"Please move your hands, let me heal you."

James stood there, looking down at them, he could not help but burst out laughing, silently. He turned away from them to hide the evidence. His interest immediately turned back to the mysterious invisible force that threw the rock back.

Mark slowly and carefully lifted his hands from his forehead. He looked at his hands, which were now covered in blood.

"Ooo," Daniel said as the wound on his forehead came to view, "I'm really sorry bro."

Mark gave him a disgusting look, "Shut up."

His forehead had already swollen and turned purple in colour. Some blood rushed down his cheek.

"Ok," Mia prepared herself, "I'm no expert healer but I can stop the pain and reduce the swelling," she pointed out, placing both her hands just above the sore, "Daniel please get a roll of bandages and a patch in my bag, should be by the small pouch inside."

"Sure thing," he got to it immediately.

James, on the other hand was busy taking careful steps towards this invisible force with one arm stretched out in front of him to feel the first impact.

He came into contact with this object, it felt smooth against his fingertips. He placed his other hand on it and began to caress it, "This is some kind of wall," he reported.

"Come again," Mia turned to him.

"It's a wall," he repeated, "an invisible wall."

Mia frowned in confusion, "Invisible wall," she murmured to herself, nothing of such was known to her, "Use your ability to check how far it goes," She suggested.

"Shot, good idea," he agreed taking of his bag.

Daniel handed the patch to Mia first, "I'm surprised you did not pass out from that hit," he said trying to be funny.

"I'm surprised the same rock hasn't found its way to your face yet." He replied.

"Hold still," Mia instructed, slowly placing the patch over the wound.

He flinched as it made contact, "That stings."

"Yeah, I put a solution, like alcohol, to help kill bacteria," she held it in place with one hand and turned to Daniel, "Bandage please."

He handed the roll over to her.

Mia then start to wrap the bandage around his head a few times, "Scissors please," she requested.

Daniel started his search for the scissors as it was not requested before.

James came running past them in a blur, checking in the other direction.

Mia cut the bandage and tucked it in from the top at the back of his head, "Done," she got to her feet.

"Thanks," he said struggling up, "Now I look like an idiot."

"Nah, not really, same as a head band," Daniel tried again to make things better.

Mark began to search around, "Now we'd that rock get to?"

Mia went on to investigate the wall just as James came back, panting, he leaned against it, "I didn't go all the way but it seems to be curved, it may be some circular wall."

"Thanks for the analysis James," Mia said looking up into the sky, "I wonder how high it goes, Daniel?"

"No need, no need," Mark interrupted, "I have a better idea," he came up to them and threw the rock up into the sky.

Everyone moved out of the area, keeping a close eye on the rock as it hit the wall some metres into the air and made its way back down.

"What are you doing, trying to hurt someone else?" Mia frowned at him.

He shrugged in return, "It's pretty high, not like we're going to climb over it."

"So this might be some kind of dome?" Mia asked.

"Maybe," Daniel replied.

"And I bet this wall is the reason why we are not seeing anything," James tapped it.

"It might be some kind of shield, the biggest one I've ever... seen?" Mia frowned. She took a few steps back.

"And how are we going to get passed this annoying wall?" Mark asked.

Mia pulled out her staff and pointed it at the wall, "Maybe a little magic will do the trick... please steer clear."

James picked up his bag and moved out of the way with the others.

At first, Mia used the basics of Destruction magic, firing your usual ball of fire at it. This worked, but only for a moment, the fireball opened up a small hole in its wake, too small for even their bags to squeeze in. But this was not the actual problem that they faced, the wall regenerated immediately after.

She tried again, using a large fire spell, but it was not enough, the hole was bigger yes, but it just regenerated again.

"Wow, we finally arrive at our destination and an invisible wall is what's stopping us from going any further," Mark threw his arms in the air, "Why would this be placed here anyway?"

James shrugged, "Probably a way to keep Levina in... perhaps."

Mia nodded, "You could be right, they may have her trapped in there to keep her from leaving."

"That's fantastic, but now it's keeping us out."

"Wait, I may have an idea," Mia interrupted, morphing her staff into a crossbow.

Daniel could not see the sense in that, "How's an arrow going to top fire?"

Mia put on her bag, "You know enchantment cubes?"

He nodded.

"Well, as a witch, I don't really need them," she explained, "I'm going to enchant it with an explosion."

The bolt loaded on Mia's crossbow began to glow a slight tint of orange, "Ready ourselves," she instructed.

Everyone kept quite close to the shot area, but also, hopefully at a safe enough distance from any harm that the explosion might bring toward them.

Mark was afraid of getting hurt again, "What is the blast radius of that thing?"

"No idea," she replied.

Mark immediately went for the safer and took a few more steps back.

The bolt loaded on the crossbow started to glow more brightly and an aura that began to circle around it. She waited until the bolt started to hiss from the heat before she released it.

On impact, the bolt created a great, fiery explosion that sent a shock wave of air in all directions.

"Now!" she shouted running for it.

There was a layer of smoke which block their view, leaving it only to chance that the explosion worked and that none of them would be running into any walls.

To their luck, nobody broke a nose or lumped there forehead, they had made it to the other side of it and watched as it rapidly regenerated itself again.

"Yes! We made it," Mark rejoiced.

"It worked," Mia said cheerfully.

"Ah… guys," James stole their bit of celebration. Daniel standing next to him, wearing the same fearful expression.

"The city is on fire," He said.

Mark and Mia both came to the realization as well, and made their way to the edge of the hill.

They stood in a row and looked into the distance as smoke rose from different parts of the city, buildings demolished and rubble soiling the grounds.

Mark put some positivity on the table, "At least we're at the end, and still in one piece," he couldn't reframe from the sight.

James wanted to get down to business immediately, "And now we can start searching," he started down the hill.

As soon as they had made it down the hill, to the outskirts of the city, all was not just smoke and some rubble, it was worse, unlike anything they had ever seen before. As they entered into the city, among all the destruction was an amount of dead people, those innocent.

The city was not filled with high buildings, most things here had one or two extra floors at most, but there were watch towers in different area that overlooked the city, standing many metres tall.

A lot of the shops and houses they were passing right now were brought to the ground, demolished and/or burnt down, something that can only be accomplished by magic, there weren't any types of siege weapons that would explain otherwise.

The section at which they entered through was silent, with only the presence of death. To the distance, some bit of explosions could be heard. As they walked down the one street, climbing over rocks and piles of rubble, they could only witness this aftermath, terrified beyond measure, seeing people who had been crushed by the rocks, some bolted by arrows and others with dagger and sword wounds.

For people from a time where politics and threats were the worst things to happen, this was something that did not do well with them, something now burnt into their memory. This was only seen in movies and games that they played and watched, seeing it in real life gave off a feeling they did not know or understand.

Signs lay burnt and windows shattered all over the place.

"This is madness," Mia uttered in disbelief, "No evacuation, no restrictions against harming civilians, no regard for humanity at all."

"Looks like the Dead Crow is using Lethal force, the reason... I don't know," said James, "Do you think we should hide our faces?"

Daniel shook his head, "I don't think that would help in the slightest, they killing civilians as well," he pointed out.

Mark climbed up a pile of rubble and looked ahead, "If people still worship the Dead Crow after this, I won't know who to blame."

"The thing is, the Dead Crow can pin the blame on anyone and the world will trust them," she said, "Where do you think we should begin our search?"

"I'm guessing where the explosions were happening," Daniel suggested.

"Psst, Hey!" A loud whisper came from nearby.

They all stopped and scanned the area.

"Hey!" they heard it again.

They turned to its direction. There they saw a man peering through a dusted, broken display window from behind a corner of some shop.

The man soon realized that it was a big mistake calling them, he came to recognize their faces and hid away immediately.

Mia went to investigate, "Hello?" she greeted walking up to the display window, "We're not a threat," she stepped through the display window, careful not to cut herself from the glass.

The shop she stepped into was unrecognizable, everything was a mess, shelves had fallen over, counters swept clean of their possessions, broken glass and ceramic materials all over the place with chairs and tables laying everywhere. Most of the stuff was missing, most probably looted by some people during the chaos.

With her staff in one hand in its smaller size, she spotted the man sitting in the corner, rolled up in a ball, filled with the terror one gets when a ghost appears out of nowhere. The man was injured, his right shoulder suffering from a cut that came from something sharp. He had managed to soil it with dust and dry up the blood that was now staining him.

Daniel and James were next to appear. Daniel being the logical one, using the door to gain entry into the shop. Mark remained on the pile of rocks and found a comfortable place where he could seat himself while keeping watch of the area.

"You're the witch," the man stuttered, "Please don't hurt me."

"We're not here to hurt anyone," she replied crouching down beside him.

"You people are wanted criminals, murderers," he continued to stutter, "And you're a witch."

Mia was ticked off a little, "Yes, I'm a witch, doesn't mean I'm going to hurt you," she frowned at him, not giving off the friendly welcoming face, but she was unhappy about this notion that being a certain race meant that she was a bad person.

She began to inspect the wound once the man had calmed himself a little, "Let me help you," she placed her hand over the wound and started the healing process.

Daniel and James began exploring the shop, there was nothing much to see upfront so they went into the back, this place was just like any general store.

It was a short while, but after the man was all bandaged up by Mia, he began to grow some bit of trust in them. He got up from his little corner, "Thank you," he said walking over to a fallen chair. He stood it up and dusted it with his hand before sitting on it, "I'm Earl... So what are you kids doing here?"

Mark had grown utterly bored, being out their alone, nothing out of the ordinary happening so he decided that things were all safe and made his way to the shop as well.

"We're here looking for someone," Mia replied.

"Coast is clear," Mark reported, "No Dead Crows around here."

Earl asked the same question again, "What are you kids doing here, this place is infested with Dead Crow agents and mages."

"Like I said," Mia repeated herself, "We're looking for someone," then she started to take notice of her surroundings, "What happened here?"

"Oh," he shook his head, "bad things happened here, really bad."

"Can you tell us?" she asked.

Earl nodded, "About three weeks ago, nothing was happening, all of us going about our normal lives," he started, "When suddenly out of nowhere, Levina shows up, and at that very moment, the Dead Crow saw her, this was immediately followed by a wide city blockade, as you may have seen, the thing the mages created to keep everybody in and everyone else out," he took a deep breath, "Everyone was alerted about the girl and naturally, everyone started to panic."

James and Daniel both came out from the back with some random items and began to listen in on what the man was saying.

"No one was allowed the leave, no one allowed to enter under any kind of circumstance... the first few days of the blockade was fine, people continued with their lives as normal and inspections were held on a daily basis, unfortunately the girl was not found."

"Then what?" asked Mark.

"The citizens started to complain about the blockade, no deliveries were being made, stocks were running low, everything was put to a pause. Most of the people had stopped believing that this girl was even still around, because everyone knew her face, but was not among them, and that's when the riots started and the demands to end the blockade began... this was when the real problem began. Some of the mages that lived in the city had decided to try break the shield, they were killed which put to a stop, a lot of the commotion. One thing the agents then remembered was that Levina could wear the face of anyone and walk amongst them as an innocent, after the realization, an order came from one of the Dead Crow leaders saying that as long as someone was still breathing, that person could be her which brings us to this current moment," he concluded.

Mia remembered the article that she had read from Galvani, "But the newspaper said it was her that was killing all he innocent people."

Earl frowned, "What, no that can't be true, it was the Dead Crow that started these killings and made this mess... Levina has not been seen since the blockade," he looked down at his palms, "I never knew the Dead Crow was capable of such."

"Thank you!" Mark announced, "Someone with some sense around here."

"It's not your fault," said Mia, "They are liars."

"So this means they haven't found her yet?" asked James.

Earl nodded in response.

Mia started searching around for any kind of supplies.

"I suggest you leave the way you came, if they find you, they will show no mercy."

"I'm sorry, but we came here looking for someone and we're not leaving until we find them," Mark said.

Earl shrugged, "I can't convince you to do anything but I hope you find this person you are looking for, and hope they are still alive."

Mia found some medical supplies, only a few more patches and bandages. After packing a few of the things, she asked the man to look after their bags whilst they go on their little search.

He agreed and gave them thanks for their hospitality.

Out the door they went and into the streets again, heading deeper into the city, closer to the commotion.

As they drew nearer and nearer to the commotion, they started to slow their paces a bit and become a lot more stealthy. The rubble and buildings made it easier to hide away from any persons, their strict caution gave them very little opportunity to search the areas as they had begun to see some people doing as they did, hiding away from the enemy. The Dead Crow agents started to become more frequent as well, chasing down whomever they came to see.

This hiding and being bundled up in one place was not helping them in the slightest, so they decided to enter a nearby building at which they could start scheming, find an easier way to approach this matter.

This area was a lot more serious, Dead Crows patrolled the streets in groups, some led by a mage, leaving no stone unturned, some fighting those who were able to defend themselves, showing not a single grain of mercy.

The building they were in had some cover, sure it was emptied and burnt, but it was a place they could remain in for a few moments, hiding behind a white sheet curtain.

"The extermination of a whole city just to find one girl," Mia peeked from behind the curtain, "This is crazy, what has this girl done?"

"That we can only figure out when we find her," replied Daniel.

"Do you think she is heartless for allowing all these people to just suffer like this?" asked Mark.

James sighed, "Put yourself in her position Mark, you would've done the same."

Mia stepped away from the curtains and joined up with the others, "How do we do this?"

"Hmm, the classic way," Daniel suggested, "If we want to find her, we going to have to split up and cover more ground... now, I'm not sure if she will believe us but we must now asked every single person we meet up with and hope she is one of them," he explained, "This way we cover more ground, just don't get yourself caught, these people are dangerous, especially the mages."

The terms were given and everyone had agreed upon them, this was to be their plan till someone captured the flag. The building was the last place they all saw each other, heading down their own alley ways, prepared for anything that could come their way.

James had made sure to blur himself every time he made a move out in the open, to reduce the risk of being caught.

Daniel's ability was a little more risky, not as evasive as speed. He would have himself levitate to higher ground, to places that could not be reached to search for his target.

Mark was the most afraid in this mission, always looking over his shoulder. I suppose fear, is one of the greatest contributions in a situation like this, keeping you on edge at a constant and always on high alert. He, however, played it even more safe, creating a small shield around himself just to be sure an arrow or jolt of lightning does not sneak up on him.

Mia did not possess any ability from the diamonds so she replied solely on her magic and staff which she had currently morphed into a crossbow, loaded and ready to fire, enchanted with an aura that gave off a blue colour. Her plan here was to silence any Dead Crow that would find her, to put on halt any further actions that could lead to the whole city being aware of their presence.

She also equipped herself with the same spell she used to see the auras of other people, Perceive Life, which made her eyes a shade of light green. Not being as experienced, this hex was only for a short distance. She stopped using it after some time since it was also consuming its own amount of energy from her.

Thanks to the speed James had, he was quite far from everybody else, lurking down an alley, keeping watch, in front, behind and above himself. His heart racing, with beads of sweat running down his forehead from all the running he had been doing. Tip-toeing, he made his way to the edge of the passageway, and just before he could take a peek, a voice came up from behind him.

"Hey!"

In this moment of fear and exhilaration, he received the fright of his life. He turned back and tripped over a rock falling backwards with a thud, landing in plain sight, visible to anyone that could be passing by.

He slowly opened his eyes, unaware of where he was, and was met with Levina, starring down at him with a smile, "Levina?" he said as he turned his head to the one side, then to the other. After realizing that he was out in the open, he sat up quickly and crawled his way back into hiding.

"Levina!" he whispered out loud, "Don't scare me like that, I've been sneaking around."

She laughed, "I know."

"Shhh," he silenced her looking around the corner, "They'll hear you."

"They'll hear you," she replied.

James had forgotten again, but this time he was not going to correct himself, "Please, I'm trying to concentrate here, I need to find this girl."

She frowned at him and crossed her arms, "And I'm trying to help you find her."

James was still too busy scouting the area, but he did get the just of what she was saying, "Wait, you can help!"

She nodded with a smile, "I know where she is."

James was so happy to hear those words, "That's great, can you show me?"

"Yes."

An explosion went of just around the corner, it scared the heart out of James. He took a peek and saw it was a Dead Crow mage, blowing up someone's house. Behind him was an archer that seemed to be looking for a target, ready to release the arrow.

He turned back to Levina, "Okay, how are we going to do this?"

Levina gave it a bit of thought, "I'll tell you where to run and I'll appear by you and point you to the next direction."

James nodded, "Ready when you are."

Levina pointed across the street, "Count three buildings and I'll meet you there," she disappeared.

James readied himself for the next run and went for it, running past the first building, making his way around obstacles and past the next street into the alley of the second build. Before reaching the third, he ran by, without being able to check the streets, a Dead Crow agent, that jumped at the sight of what he saw. He was left there wondering about what just occurred to him.

James almost lost his balance seeing the agent at such short notice, but was able to make it through to the third build where he could see Levina waiting for him.

She pointed down the road, "Go to that haystack," she disappeared again.

"Who are you?" a faint female voice came from behind him.

His heart skipped a beat, wasting no time checking what was behind him, he ran over to the next destination. He requested immediately for the next destination, "Where to now Levina?"

"That fallen building over there."

After that, they went to at least three other stops before reaching the end of the road.

At this moment they were hiding behind a small two-story house that still seemed to be intact.

Levina fell silent and signaled for James to be quiet as well.

"Where to know?" he whispered.

"We're here," she replied, "See the broken-down back door, go inside, she's there."

This was the moment of truth, the very reason why he was here, why he decided to leave the school in the first place. The girl he was looking for since he found out she and the ghost had the same name, all this was on the table, all these problems he has faced and now that he was in front... well, just outside hiding against the wall following Levina's instructions, he was nervous, his heart beating fast. Standing there unable to move, he looked down at Levina again, "Are you sure?"

Levina nodded repeatedly.

James took a deep breath and stretched his neck, as if he were preparing for a fight and stood away from the wall. He tip-toed to the door, with Levina doing the same closely behind him.

The edge of the door frame was all that stood between him and her now, it was all so silent, all the noises from all around the city seemed to fade away into an even farther distance. As he stood there, thinking of how he should approach her, how he was going to get her to believe him.

His thoughts were cut short when Levina gave him a push from behind, throwing him into the doorway.

He froze.

He stared into a kitchen, all in a looted mess, and there she was. A girl stood in the centre of the room, next to the kitchen counter with her right hand on it facing the other way.

The one thing that stumped James was her appearance, only the hair, it was a ginger curly colour. It was a little confusing until he remembered the little story Earl told them.

"Go in," Levina said persistently.

James nodded in return and took a step into the kitchen, remaining ever silent, watching his step. There was no time for any thoughts right now, he just went for it, "Levina?" he said.

The girl turned around swiftly, and for the split second James was able to see her face. She vanished.

"Woah!" James uttered, shocked by this unreal event, "She disappeared."

James was then not sure if he had actually seen someone standing there, and for a moment he stood there until Levina brought him back.

"Yes, she disappeared," she tapped him on the arm, "Like the stories."

"She's a ghost," James concluded.

"No she isn't," Levina argued.

It was like James had already given up, he shook his head, "She just disappeared, to who knows where."

Levina pointed at the staircase, "She's upstairs."

"Oh," he nodded, "Thanks,"

His silent and stealthy skills were thrown out the window as soon as he took the first step on the wooden staircase, creaked louder than a lousy puppy. No doubt she heard it.

Trying to make the second step sound a little less alarming, by moving at a much slower pace, he failed. They just sung louder. With nothing working in his favour, he decided to make it to the top as casually as he could.

Upstairs, he found himself in a bedroom, turned completely upside-down, "Neat," he murmured to himself sarcastically, "Levina, where is she?" he whispered.

Levina pointed to the closed wardrobe up against the wall beside him.

James waste no time getting there, throwing open the doors, disappointed to having found nothing but a few clothes hanging, "I'm guessing she disappeared again," he sighed.

Attempting to close shut the wardrobe. He found himself paralyzed.

A moment passed and he found himself on the other side of the room, next to the window facing the wardrobe.

There she was again. The ginger girl, standing by the wardrobe with a knife in her right hand. Confused by the little stunt James pulled, she turned around, with an astonished look on her face, which turned into a frown when she spotted him, "How did you do that!?"

James looked at the knife, "Did you just try to kill me?"

"Yes I just tried to kill you," she replied, "How did you do that?" she repeated the question, lowering her hand.

James looked at her and realized that he was talking to a middle-aged woman, "Wait... you're not a teenager," he turned to Levina, who was standing right next to him, "Are you sure this is her?"

Levina looked up at him with concern, "Yes, I'm sure."

The ginger lady was as concerned as Levina was right now, "What are you talking to?"

James turned back to the lady, "Someone."

She shook her head.

"You are Levina right?" he asked with a bit of stutter in his voice, "I'm looking for her."

"Isn't everyone?" she replied, "And why would you, you've got a price on your head."

"Yes I have a price on my head," he did not deny, "Please answer the question so that I can get back to my friends, this place is dangerous, we want to leave before the Dead Crow finds us."

"Wait... you can leave?"

James nodded, "Ye, we entered about an hour ago."

"I'll go with you then."

"Are you Levina?" he asked again.

She looked back at him with uncertainty, deciding something in that mind of hers. She smiled at him and nodded.

James squinted at her, "I don't believe you."

"James, it is her!" Levina shouted beside him.

"Please shh," he replied.

The lady was thrown into another void, "Who are you telling to keep quiet?"

"Never mind about that, just prove to me you're who you say you are."

The lady took a deep breath, "Okay, here's your proof," she closed her eyes and a dark blue, thin smoke started to come off her, shedding away her current appearance from head to toe.

As the smoke drifted away, a smaller tall figure stood in its place. A teenage girl, wearing some kind of black thieves attire. Black leather high boots, black pants with a sheath belt, a black leather vest which left her arms bear and black gauntlets on her forearms. She had straight, long, black hair and green eyes.

James was lost in a trance, not only hypnotized by her little magic trick, but her beauty as well. He could not detach, eyes wide open.

She looked at him, "What?" she smiled faintly, "Here's my proof."

The smile killed him.

Realizing that he was taking a little too long to answer the question, he cleared his throat, "You're her," he nodded.

Little Levina next the him spoke, "I told you it was her... I'll see you later," she faded away.

"Yes, I'm her," she raised her arms, "Happy now?"

"James nodded, "Very... Let's go."

They headed for the door.

CHAPTER 24

The Living Curse

Through the backdoor of the house they exited. They both remained there for a few moments while commotion was live just around the corner.

Levina peered from the one side and saw the coast was clear. She made her way down the passage between the houses, James following from behind, wondering, why he was following her and where it is she was heading.

He had to ask, "Uhm… sorry to disturb, but where are you going?"

"Looting a few places before we leave," she replied scouting the area, "I need supplies."

"Hmm," he said feeling this was way too easy, beyond anything that he could have imagined, every scenario that took place in his head before the actual meet with this girl was filled with a lot of disbelief and an insane level convincing in order to gain even a shred of trust. It was like no resistance came from her… okay, there was the attempt at murder a few minutes ago, but the thought still remained, "I'm surprised really," he spoke again, "You trusted me right off the bat."

She stopped with her observation of the area and turned to him, looking pretty annoyed, "Look, you're the first person that I've met that did not try to kill or run away from me," she spoke quickly, "And you too have quite the price on your head, which means you're enemy of the Dead Crow," she turned back to the matter at hand, "Besides, you have a way out of this place apparently, I have no idea whether you're going to double-cross me and turn me in to save yourselves," She turned back to him again, "So trust, no... in this scenario, we a just partners, where you are helping me more than I am you," she smiled, "And you have some ability that may come in handy, so I trust you don't need me to babysit you?"

James felt a little insulted, "No," he replied.

"Good, now, are we going to find your friends are you still conducting your useless interview?"

"Let's go," he replied.

They left their current position and headed out with Levina leading the way.

In another part of the city, quite far from James, Mia found herself hiding behind a building from some Dead Crow agents that had spotted her unfortunately. She stood crouched behind a wall close to the corner, loading one of her crossbow bolts. She had already used a few on some agents she had come across. One stood in the middle of the street, frozen with a light shade of blue all over his skin as if he had frostbite, his clothing and hair had small amounts of frosts and overall, a small amount of mist drifted around him. She saw no other way to deal with them non-lethally.

The other agents had found this man and were now giving out orders to search for her. They had also called in some magic reinforcements into the area.

The bolt she had loaded was starting to glow blue, whilst she listened in on their little conversation.

"Finally, you have arrived," she heard them say.

"What is it?" another voice asked.

Listening was not enough for her so she decided to take a peek and see what was actually transpiring. Surrounding the frozen body was a number of agents and among them, four which held staves.

They explained to them the incident, and also dispersed in all directions.

She hid herself again, and watched as her loaded bolt begin to gain its aura. She took a deep breath, trying to calm herself, preparing for the next move. Her gaze turned to the other end of the alley, for another inspection.

Her heart skipped a beat.

On the other end of the path was a bow man that had just come into appearance, also shock by the sudden encounter, but no hesitation to act, "She's here!" he shouted at the top of his lungs, as he swiftly drew an arrow and loaded it.

Mia wasted no time aiming her bow at him.

Both shot at each other at the same time.

Everything happened so fast, with no time to move.

The Dead Crow archer was hit in the chest by the arrow. The bolts enchanted magic immediately started its work, swiftly enveloping the man's body, freezing him in a matter of seconds.

Mia got hit in the right shoulder, the arrow passed over the outer edge, cutting through her shirt, leaving a deep wound in its place.

The pain she felt was excruciating.

Trying very hard not to scream, she held her crossbow in her right hand and used her left to press down the wound as the blood poured out. She wanted to sit down and heal, but since the man shouted, voices were coming from all around her.

"Over there!" another screamed from the near distance.

Mia had to act immediately, with no notion of the distance between her and the nearest Dead Crow, it was heart stopping, knowing they were closing that gap with every second.

She morphed her crossbow into a staff and used it to get to her feet, using her left arm, since the other had failed to respond properly to her commands. The blood was running down her arm, ready to start dripping from her elbow so she just let it hang completely to prolong that from happening.

Luckily for her, this section of the city had been destroyed quite a bit because there was an opening through a wall. She hurried over to it before the first drop of blood could give away her tracks and climbed over the rubble to hide behind the wall.

The agents took sight of the frozen body first and began to investigate, murmuring in shock.

Mia stood, literally just on the other side of the wall, in searing pain, with some tears forming in her eyes. She took a look at her arm and saw the blood was making its way down her fingers, about to start dripping.

She realized that her current position was highly unsafe, with only a wall between her and them. Looking around the room, she spotted some stairs across from her. It was the only way to a safer place right now so she had to do it before they got too close to hear anything. Her climb to the top was not easy, but she was able to do it quietly and find her way to a bedroom.

It was completely demolished, with most of the wall missing to the left and a lot of the roof gone. It was a place anyone could spot you, if they were far enough, so she made her way to the wall on the other end of the room and sat against it, near the edge which was now to her right. she morphed her staff back to a cross bow and reloaded it before placing it right beside her. Next it was time to tend to the open wound. She pulled up her sleeve and began the healing process.

Quite some distance away, we head on back to Levina, who was currently busy in some abandoned supply shop, taking her time in getting some of the things she needed, a rucksack, a sleeping roll and other minor things while James kept watch of the area for any agents.

She headed into the backroom and took whatever it she needed for survival just threw it into her bag, "It'll have to do," she put it on her back.

James turned to her, "Are you done?"

Levina did not reply. She just stood still and stared into space, right passed James. Her jaw dropped slowly and eyes opened wide, keeping a confused frown with a pinch of shock.

James was not getting what she was doing. It seemed as though she was looking at him for a moment, which made him feel really awkward, wondering why the face.

Levina then started squinting, taking steps towards him.

At this point, James felt he should say something, or ask what the problem was.

"He-he's flying," she uttered, she pointed at him, "He's flying," she repeated.

James realized that it was not him she was looking at, but what was behind him. He turned to see what was happening, "Oh," he saw.

Quite a lot houses from where they stood, was Daniel, levitating to higher floors. It was really putting him out in the open and he did not seem to notice.

"I guess you've found one of my friends, that's Daniel," he said, "Come on, let's get to him before he moves on."

Levina was speechless, but also very curious.

James stepped out into the open, keeping an eye on his levitating friend, forgetting about his surroundings, which led him to being caught.

"Hey!" an agent shouted from the distance.

He immediately stepped back into the shop, out of sight, "And now we've been caught."

"Ugh," she shook her head, "How many?"

James raised one finger.

She took off her bag and handed it over to him, "Hold here," she said pulling out a small black pocket knife.

"What are going to do with that?" asked James, with some level of concern.

"Shh," she silenced him before disappearing into thin air.

She appeared again immediately after, entering the shop.

James had no time to react.

"Let's go to your flying friend," she said.

James was unable to move, his reaction delayed, unable to ask how she had done that.

She came into the room and pulled him by the arm, "Come on, before he leaves."

They both stepped outside.

The first thing James looked for was the agent that had spotted him.

He was gone.

This was followed by another delayed reaction, James shook his head, "Whe-where is he?"

Levina did not reply, she just pulled him by the arm till they had made it across the street. She came up with a suggestion, "Okay, let's fasten the pace a little, use whatever ability you pulled in that house to get to him, you'll meet me there."

"I'll meet you there?" he sounded a bit confused. He was the fastest according to him, "Okay, got it."

James activated his ability and was the first to leave. He ran as quickly as he could to the building and made it there in just a few seconds.

To his even greater surprise, Levina was already there, waiting for him. He was confused, clearly remembering that he had left her behind.

She stood next to him with her arms crossed and stared up at the second floor, which was missing a wall, "Go on, call him."

James was still confused, and now a tad bit unhappy, "Daniel!" he shouted.

It was a few seconds before his head appeared from the top, "James?"

"I found her."

She waved up at him.

Daniel waved back before jumping off the edge. He levitated down to their level and greeted properly, "Hi."

"Hi."

Levina was more intrigued by his ability, seeing it up close.

Mia had reduced a lot of the pain in her arm, but without a patch or any bandages, she was unable to cover up the wound, which was still open. She figured it was going to be difficult anyway.

She shifted to the edge of the wall and took a sneak peek of what was going on.

Nothing was dangerous, only strange, she saw a group of agents bring together a wooden ladder which had been placed up against a three story build, almost exceeding its height.

They were looking for higher ground, some good vantage points. Since there weren't any towers nearby, this building was the next best thing.

Three mages started their way up the ladder and climbed to the top of this building, a building that could barely stand on its own. The bottom floor was missing a lot of its walls, with only a pillar on one corner barely holding everything up like a broken table leg.

Up top they started to scout, each mage standing at a corner.

Mia hid herself again and picked up her crossbow, placed it on her lap and began the process of another enchantment, taking an orange colour.

"Search Everywhere!" an agent ordered.

All the other agents scattered in all directions like disturbed ants.

It was a few moments before Mia's bolt was fully enchanted and ready to be used. She took deep breaths, preparing for her shot. Looking down at her arm, she could see it was now a little shaky, she sucked it up and used it to hold the crossbow properly, closed her eyes for a moment and visualized her target.

She was unable to bring her uneven breathing to calmer levels so she decided at that moment to hold her breath.

She could feel her heart beating.

A second later she moved into view and went straight for the target. Before a reaction could be given from her enemies, she released the bolt and hit the table leg.

On impact, an explosion was created, forcing her to hide herself again as the building began to collapse.

She closed her eyes and waited, hearing only the fearful screams of the agents and mages in the buildings collapse radius.

An instant passed, after the rubble had settled, it was all silent.

Mia sighed in relief, knowing she was now safe... but only for that moment.

The noise created by the building's collapse brought the Dead Crow rushing to the scene.

The agents were surprised that mages were among the dead.

This made it much more dangerous for her, since this was now the place of commotion, it will most definitely be searched carefully. Her next plan was going to have a fifty-fifty effect on the Dead Crows gathered here, she loaded another bow and allowed it to enchant. While it did, she took a little peek again and saw that they were grouped in one area, and a few scattered in others. Her plan was to use fear to try drive them off.

The bolt was ready to be fired so she moved into view again and aimed it at the biggest crowd, releasing it and hiding before anyone could see her.

The explosion went off, no doubt taking out a lot of the agents. This explosion worked in her favour and created fear in the minds of those who survived. They cleared out the area, probably in fear of being next.

Mia was tired now, having depleted most of her energy, she sat there panting with only one thing left to do, something dangerous, but had to be carried out.

She reloaded her crossbow and enchanted it with a dark red aura which was ready in a few seconds. After doing so she aimed it up into the sky and fired it.

As it reached a certain height, it lit up like a flare and exploded into fire crackers.

This was a really terrible idea on her part, now hoping that her friends find her before the Dead Crow does.

Back at James, the party had grown by one. Daniel had just joined, being the easiest one to find. He was, however, curious about our new follower, Levina, wanting to ask some questions right off the bat, but unable since they were in a wee bit of a hurry to find Mia and Mark, who won't be as easy to locate, being stuck to the ground and all.

Levina had suggest that they head up to one of the city's watchtowers and scout the whole area in that way. All the enemies encountered there were easily taken care of by Levina.

From up top, the lake of this town was visible and with the city in the picture now, you could see there was a dock there with many small fishing boats and wooden platforms leading out into the water. The whole city seemed to surround the lake as well, with buildings on the other side as well, suffering the same consequences.

The Dead Crow count seemed endless in this town, like they were sending in reinforcements every once in a while.

Levina leaned over the edge ever so carelessly, "Okay, how will I recognized your other friends, powers?"

"No not really," he replied, "One of them is wearing a black shirt, she is carrying a silver and black weapon," he described.

"If I remember... Mia right?" she asked.

"Yes, and the other has a bandage around his head," he described Mark.

"That's kind of shallow."

James shrugged in return, "It stands out."

Each of them faced their own direction and scanned out the area, but Daniel's curiosity needed immediate medication, so he shifted closer and closer to James, till he was right beside him, "So... how'd you find her?" he whispered.

The first thing that came to James was Levina, the little ghost, "Uhm... Luck I guess," he whispered back, "And I'm pretty fast," he secured his lie.

Daniel nodded in return, he was quit disappointed in his reply, kind of hoping that he was going to tell the story, have it contain all the sweet bits.

"It's weird," James continued, "When I found her at first, she disappeared."

"What like a ghost?" he became intrigued.

James looked into the distance, far beyond the city in some thought and nodded, "I guess you could say that... oh yeah, and she tried to kill me, but I couldn't control my body again and found myself on the other side of the room."

Now this is what Daniel was hoping to hear, he was glad it came out without any requests, "So she just trusted you?" he asked.

"No, she's only helping us cause she wants to leave this city as well," he replied, "That's why I am carrying this bag."

"Ah, I was wondering about that."

"It's just... whatever she did, it was strange, she just disappears and appears again."

"Teleporter!"

James snapped his finger, "You may be right."

It was the only thing he was able to except, it is only teleportation that could allow her to be much faster than him. Jumping from one location to another seemed an appropriate description to what she was doing.

"Hey!" she interrupted, "Quit your gossiping and come see this."

James and Daniel walked over to her side.

"What's that?" she pointed into the near distance at some red mark lifting higher into the sky.

"Hmm, some kind of flare," Daniel deducted as it exploded like fire crackers.

"What?" Levina sounded confused, "What are you saying, that's clearly a firecracker."

THE LORD OF POWER

Daniel shrugged, knowing she might not know what a flare is, "Yeah, signal fire."

"It could be Mia," said James.

"Wow, your friend is not very clever," said Levina, staring at the smoke that remained behind, "calling every Dead Crow over to her... we need to get there quick," She turned to James, "Use your abilities, I'll meet you there," she instructed before disappearing.

"Woah," Daniel stepped back.

James nodded, "Yup, let's go," he left in a blur.

Mia watched as the bright red colours turn to smoke and her bolt slow to a stop and change course because of gravity. She allowed it to reappear in its slot by reloading a new one. She took a deep breath, "I hope the right people show up," she murmured to herself.

Right before her eyes, something appeared. She almost screamed.

It was Levina, she stood there for a moment, "Black shirt, silver weapon," she murmured crouching down in front of her, "Mia?"

She nodded in return, not too sure about the trusting part, "Who are you?" she asked, already aware of whom she is, just wondering if she would say it.

"Levina," she replied taking a look at her shoulder, "You're hurt... wish I had my bag."

Mia was unable to assess the situation. Levina had just appeared in front of her and already ready to help her out. She could not take her eyes of her.

Levina stood up again and looked around for anything that could help but found nothing. Then she stood in the middle of the room thinking, tapping her one foot as if waiting for someone., "You know, your fast friend is pretty slow."

She could only mean James, which meant, to her, that he had already found her and settled things.

"Mia!" a voice shouted from nearby. It was James.

"Up here!" Levina replied, "Bring my bag quickly."

Daniel was standing on the last bits of what used to be a roof. He jumped of and landed next to Levina, "Couldn't find the door," he smiled.

"Even came before him."

He noticed Mia sitting against the wall, "Oh my, you're hurt!" he became alert, "Where's James and the bag?" he turned to Levina.

"Lost," she shrugged shaking her head slowly.

James ran into room in a rush and handed the bag over to Levina, "Couldn't find the hole in the wall," she turned to Mia, "You're hurt," he went over to her, to see the cut, "What happened?"

Levina pulled out a box of medical supplies and walked over to Mia, "Move out of the way," she ordered, "What cut you?"

"An arrow."

She placed the things beside her and examined it. She turned to the others, "I've got this, you two go look for your other friend, we don't have time!" she raised her voice.

Levina turned back to Mia and started by pulling out a corked bottle of some transparent substance. She pulled the cork out with her teeth and spat it out, "This is going to hurt."

Mia nodded, closing her eyes and looking away.

Levina held up her wounded arm with one hand and with the other, poured a bit of the solution over it.

Mia felt the pain immediately, trying hard not to cry out, jerking her cut arm whilst the other grabbed ahold of her leg and squeezed.

"It's almost over," she said picking up a small patch from the box, sprinkling a little more of the solution onto it and placing it carefully over the cut. The pain rose again for a few moment but seeped again, just a little under the unbearable point.

"Please hold it in place," she instructed.

Mia did as she said.

The next and final step was wrapping it around with a bandage to hold it in place.

"You're a medic?" she asked holding her arm up for the bandage.

"Nah," she shook her head, "But I know quite a bit, patching myself has been my lessons," she smiled, "And... done," she said tucking the bandage in.

"Thanks," she said picking up her crossbow and morphing it into a staff.

"Wow, that's a nice... weapon you've got," she did not know what to call it.

Mia used it to get to her feet, "Yeah, it changes to whatever weapon I wish it to be."

They both made it downstairs and out the hole from whence they came. Mia lead her to the area which she had destroyed.

Levina was surprised by the body count, "Did you-," she pointed at them over the rubble.

Mia nodded in return, "Had no choice, they were going to kill me," she replied, feeling a little unhappy that she admitted, but it was better than a lie, since all the proof lay there right in front of her.

"Not complaining or anything, just glad that there is less of them to worry about," she climbed onto the rubble and closed her eyes whilst letting the breeze brush passed her hair.

The moment of silence was peaceful, but all thrown away as soon as she opened them again.

Far down the street, she noticed a rather large group of Dead Crow agents, they all seemed to be surrounding something and just outside that circle of theirs, a few metres before, James and Daniel hid, behind some rocks, "What's happening down there?"

Mia turned to the same direction and saw the group of Dead Crows as well as James and Daniel, "What the hell?," she squinted, "Let's go check it out."

They both snuck their way up to the little hiding spot James and Daniel had picked and crouched beside them. The group was awfully close, numbering about twenty-five Dead Crows. A surprise to Mia and Levina, they did not even turn to check surroundings, something was stealing away too much of their attention.

"What's happening?" Mia whispered to James.

"Good news and very bad news," he replied, "We found Mark, but he is in the centre of that crowd."

"What!" she whispered aloud.

"He has a shield activated though, the only problem now it trying to get him out," Daniel explained.

"So your last friend is over there in that crowd?" asked Levina. Daniel nodded.

"So you are just going to sit here?" she raised her brows.

"We don't have a plan."

"I do… it involves you standing up and drawing away their attention," she took a deep breath and stood up.

The rest followed her lead and showed themselves, very unsure with what they were doing.

"And now to divert their attention," she said climbing the large pile of rubble.

When she was set, she pulled out her pocket knife, "Hey Dead Crows!" she raised both her arms up beside her, "Looking for me!?"

Every agent and mage turned away from Mark. Their reactions were filled with some fear, most witnessing her in the flesh for the first time. Most only living with the rumours that so often get spread like wild fire. They stood there, not knowing what to do as she stood there in plain sight.

Levina was baffled, she expected them to start attacking or charging at her or something, allowing Mark to make an escape. She dropped her arms.

"Get her!" One of them mages shouted stomping his staff.

The agents began to charge in their direction whilst the archers loaded their arrows and the mages prepared their spells.

"Finally," said Levina.

Mark let out a sigh of relief. He had become invisible to the agents since Levina's little intro.

James, Daniel and Mia were now afraid, standing right behind the primary target. They began to take a few steps back.

Levina noticed the fear in them and sought to comfort it, "Don't worry," she smiled, "Just don't blink," she turned back to the horde and raise her left hand into the air just before disappearing again.

That very second she disappear, she reappeared again next to Mia. No one had caught on to what was happening.

"Let's go," she said tapping Mia on the shoulder.

They all turned to her bearing faces that had just experienced a paranormal activity.

Then came the gags and moans, the sounds of death.

They turned to the noises, coming from the horde of Dead Crows and watched in fear as they witnessed every single one of them drop whatever weapon they had and grab a hold of their necks, struggling to breathe, gasping and coughing out blood. And from the tiny holes between their fingers, blood, the red water seeping through, traveling down their hands and palms, dripping onto the ground.

They were dying, all of them at the same time, falling to their knees, trying so very hard to cling onto their slipping lives.

Mark, on the other side of the crowd, was frightened and confused, his shield had disappeared leaving him defenseless. He waited for it to be over, as it branded itself into his mind.

"Hey, Mark!" Levina shouted, "Let's go."

Out of fear, Mark obey her orders and had begun to walk towards them, passing by the suffering of these men and women around him, witnessing their pain as some took in their last breath.

"Ah, bandage around his head," Levina said, "And that's everyone."

When it was all just a little calmer, they led Levina back to the shop, where they had left all their belongings before the search. The last thing playing in their minds being the deaths of all those people, all unexplainable.

They walked in through the front door and found Earl there, still sitting on the chair waiting for their return. His face lit up as soon as they stepped in, "You made it back, did you perhaps find the person you were looking for?"

Mark nodded, carrying a straight face, as if the mission was a fail.

Levina stepped into the shop last and eyeballed Earl.

His eyes nearly escaped their sockets as he began to breath unevenly.

Levina seemed to recognize his expression, she shook her head and rolled her eyes at him, "Ugh, I'm not going to hurt you."

He nodded slowly in return, "How are you?" he asked.

"Fine," she replied taking her bag from James.

"So what happened here is perfectly 'fine' to you," Earl's mood changed.

"No, and I did not kill a single civilian while I was here, you can thank your Dead Crow friends for that," she said making her way to the back room, a little off her happy mood.

Earl saw the point in what she was saying, but most importantly happy that he did not die by her hand like all rumours seem to say. He leaned closer to Mark, "Why were you looking for her?" he whispered.

"No idea," he shrugged.

Earl frowned and sat back again.

Mia joined Levina at the back, but she did not pack anymore extra material. She stood against the wall, watching as she packed in some things, "What you did back there, was it magic?"

She continued to pack, "No, why?"

"Just a question."

She shrugged, "Okay."

"What is it then?"

"Not going to disclose that."

"Fair enough," she replied, "It's just I've seen someone else do things they did not consider as magic."

"You mean your friends?"

She never thought of that, "I guess… but this guy could create bombs out of nothing."

Levina froze for a moment, "Sounds… neat," she continued with her search.

Out front Earl was still talking quietly to the others, "You youngsters are looking for serious trouble aren't you?"

"Tell me about," Mark replied, changing the subject, "Is this your shop?"

Earl nodded, "My hard work, all just taken away, and I don't think Diadora might have the money to help us rebuild this place, it is much too big, we may be on our own, if there is anyone left to rebuild that is."

That name again, Diadora, he seems to be helping a lot of people. James was not seeing anything bad in this man anymore. The only reason he was an enemy to them was because they were on the wanted list, but even then he wanted to help clear their names, except for Mia. He wondered what he would think if Diadora were here to see this mess the Dead Crow created.

After a short while, Levina came out from the back with Mia ready to leave this city. Mia gave the man some of the gold pieces from the money Galvani gave them as payment for what they took.

Earl was resistant but took it in the end. They said their farewells and headed out his shop.

The amount of time that they spent there was not short at all, the running and hiding seemed to allow it to pass by rather quickly. The sun was already lowering down in the west.

The little walk to the outskirts of this city was meet with a lot of silence, everyone taking a stroll with their thoughts. Most of them wondering... *what now?*. This whole chase has come to an end, what were they going to do?

James was the one with the little ghost following him around.

One thing that was present in all their minds, the minds of our time travelers, was all the death and suffering they had just witnessed in this city. All of it was not familiar to them and something they feared would have to sink in as long as they were here.

As they exited the outskirts, they all started to feel a little safe again, only having to worry about the location of this invisible wall. Up on top of the hill, Mia morphed her staff into a crossbow and began the enchantment process

"What are you going to do with that crossbow?" Levina asked.

"It's how we got in," she replied, "I'm going to create an explosion and allow for everyone to exit before the shield regenerates."

James picked up a rock.

Mark moved out of the way as soon as he realized.

He threw the rock and saw it bounce off the shield not too far from their current position.

The bolt in Mia's crossbow was ready to be fired, "Ok, everyone get ready, you must be quick," she said aiming it at the wall.

Levina went to go join up with the others and waited.

Mia released the bolt, creating an explosion that broke a hole into the barrier.

Everyone hurried passed it and made it to the other side safely

Levina turned to the wall and only saw the lake to the far distance, "So this wall was keeping the city hidden from the outside world," she shrugged, "Oh well, I'm free at last, thanks to you."

"No problem," James replied.

Levina stood in front of all of them, "I really appreciate it, I'll see you when I see you," she bowed her head, "It's nice to meet people who don't want to kill me, farewell," she turned towards the sunset.

James took a few steps forward in her direction, he could not let it just end like that, after all this, it couldn't be, "Wait, we need to know who you are?"

Levina stopped in her tracks and sighed, "I'm guess now is the time I get to ask you, why were you looking for me?" she turned back to them.

James was ready to disclose everything, "Weren't you the one that sent us after you?"

Everyone, including Levina was thrown into confusion.

"What?" she asked, "I don't know who you are... I've never seen you."

James took a deep breath, "Quite a while ago, in the basement of an old women's shop, I met a girl, with your name, only... she was more like a ghost," he explained, "a little girl of about seven years in age in broken chains around her wrists and ankles wearing a black dress... she asked me to help you."

Levina looked at him with concern, she shook her head, "I don't know what you are talking about."

Daniel interfered, "Yes James, what are you talking about?"

"You won't know," He replied.

Levina seemed frozen.

"Does the description not seem familiar?"

She gave him a slight nod, "That was me, about ten years ago."

James felt he was getting somewhere, "Yes, that same girl came to me and lead us straight to you, helping me find you."

Levina turned to the tall grass, then back to him, "I can summon things but what you are saying is complete madness, a ghost of me, ten years ago, that is not possible, whatever it is you saw was just in your head, I really have to leave now," she turned away.

"He's telling the truth," a little girl's voice spoke.

Levina appeared right next to him.

Levina turned back to the voice. Her face filled up with shock and began to feel a little shaky at the sight of her younger self. Her jaw shook as she tried to let out a sound. Nothing wanted to escape.

James was surprised by the expression on her face. He turned to the ghost, "Wait, can she see you?"

Little Levina nodded.

Mia, Daniel and Mark were still in the blank, unaware for what was actually transpiring. Levina did not seem to be showing herself to them. Since James had clearly said they would not understand, they opted to be the third party and just listen.

Levina started to stutter, "How did-," she could not stop staring at the little ghost.

"Levina calm down," little Levina said, "I found some friends that can help you, you can trust them."

"Yes, let us help you," said James.

"Help?"

"Yes," little Levina replied, "You're going to need it."

Levina turned to the rest of the group, "Who are you people?"

"That we'll explain later," Mia replied walking up to James, "We can't stay here."

Mark and Daniel followed in their own realm of confusion, saying nothing.

Levina looked at her younger self again, feeling a little hesitant.

Little Levina nodded and smiled at her before she disappeared.

She was left there to commune with her own thoughts for a while.

Back in the city, inside the invisible walls to the western side, atop the highest watchtower bearing a flat roof. On the edge of this rooftop sat a familiar face, one you have only met a few times in the this duration, and now we shall be with him for the last time. He sat on the edge with his legs crossed, resting his head on his left hand. The man we have come to know as Diadora Maithindor.

He sat there, head facing in the direction of Levina, bearing no expression on his face.

Just behind him, an anonymous man appeared out of thin air, "What is happening?" the man asked in a calm tone.

Diadora did not turn around, he just gave his reply, "She is making new friends, It's kind of sweet," he smiled.

"With the ones who came back to this place, I wonder what it is they are planning."

Diadora shrugged, "No idea, they were always unpredictable, being above us all."

The man sighed, "Explain to me their uses."

"Okay, let me explain it all," Diadora said, "When they first arrived, I decided to pay them a little visit, it turned out that they were with Jake, but that's not important right now, that jewelry they wear, I wanted to see if it would allow me to get near to them, speak to them, and it did," he started, "Then came the second visit, when I saw one of them in particular, I wanted to see if I would be allowed to curse him, I was successful but the curse remains dormant, and for the third and final time, I decided to be lethal, and that's when I figured. Those diamond only protect them when faced with death, this shows how weak the ones protecting them may be, which brings us to your question," he paused for a moment, "James, he has speed, which is useless, then there is Mark, he protects, no need to explain any further, but then we have Daniel... his ability of flight, he is a real gifted one."

"Okay then, you know what to do."

Diadora nodded in return and created a small explosive the size of a large marble, "Oh, and something strange happened as well."

"Yes?"

"There parents are here, I don't see any significance in them though."

"Oh, I think I might know why they are, just leave that part to me."

"Will do," he said turning to the town, "What about this city?"

"When have no need for them anymore"

Diadora's smile grew, "Will do."

"But not Armageddon, just give them something to breath in," he said, just before he disappeared.

Outside the wall, James and the others waited for her answer, to say something.

She had just come to a decision, "Okay, I'll allow you to help me, since you got me out of this situation."

"Great," James said, filling up with a little joy, "What's our heading?"

She took a deep breath, "Where we're going is very dangerous," she explained, "It is far to the west, the oceans... two worlds are about to meet."

James frowned, "What do you mean?"

"Come on, I'll explain that stuff later," she said turning away to the sunset.

Mia took in the fresh air as they all started to follow the sun, "I'm glad we added another girl into the group," Mia declared.

"And a girl who is very similar to you," said Levina.

"What do you mean by that?" she asked, a little baffled.

Levina turned to her and smiled, "I am also a witch," she replied, just before she frowned, looking at them... counting, "Umm... I think someone is missing."

Everyone turned around and grew shocked. Levina was right, there was someone missing in the group.

Daniel.

CPSIA information can be obtained
at www.ICGtesting.com
Printed in the USA
BVHW031013020419
544363BV00001B/11/P

9 781543 492453